Also by Philip Caputo

Acts of Faith

Ten Thousand Days of Thunder

13 Seconds: A Look Back at the Kent State Shootings

Ghosts of Tsavo

In the Shadows of the Morning

The Voyage

Exiles

Equation for Evil

Means of Escape

Indian Country

DelCorso's Gallery

Horn of Africa

A Rumor of War

CROSSERS

CROSSERS

Philip Caputo

Alfred A. Knopf   New York 2009

THIS IS A BORZOI BOOK
PUBLISHED BY ALFRED A. KNOPF

www.aaknopf.com

Grateful acknowledgment is made to Roger Clyne for permission to reprint an excerpt from "Switchblade" by Roger Clyne. Reprinted by permission of Roger Clyne.

Library of Congress Cataloging-in-Publication Data
Caputo, Philip.
Crossers : a novel / by Philip Caputo. — 1st ed.
p. cm.
"This is a Borzoi book"—T.p. verso.
ISBN 978-0-375-41167-0
1. Widows—Fiction. 2. Drug traffic—Fiction. 3. Family secrets—Fiction. 4. Mexican-American Border Region—Fiction. 5. Arizona—Fiction. I. Title.
PS3553.A625C76 2009
813'.54—dc22 2009019096

Manufactured in the United States of America
First Edition

This is another one for Leslie

Acknowledgments

MY DEEPEST GRATITUDE to my editor, Ash Green; my agent, Aaron Priest; and to Frances Jalet-Miller for their encouragement and invaluable advice. And a thousand thanks to Chuck Bowden, J.P.S. Brown, Bob and Gayle Bergier, Julian Cardona, Daniel Cantu, Rubén Ceballos, Laura Chester, Meade "Doc" Clyne, Don Henry Ford, Glen Goodwin, Bryan Gutiérrez, Axel Holm, Ross and Susan Humphreys, Karen Wessel Marcus, Jim and Tina McManus, John Mencer, Bevan Olyphant, and Grace Wystrach.

Source materials included the following: the archives of the *Arizona Daily Star*, the Patagonia-Sonoita *Weekly Bulletin*, and the Pimeria Alta Historical Society; and *Drug Lord: The Life and Death of a Mexican Kingpin*, by Terrence E. Poppa; *Hidden Treasures of Santa Cruz County*, by Betty Barr; *The Man Who Tasted Shapes*, by Richard E. Cytowic, M.D.; *On the Border*, by Tom Miller; *The Reaper's Line*, by Lee Morgan; and *Voice of the Borderlands*, by Drummond Hadley.

CROSSERS

Ben Erskine

We fly from our time and place to the settlement of Lochiel, the present-day ghost town then home to four hundred souls: adobe houses and miners' shacks, a post office, a school, a few stores, and three saloons islanded on the mile-high grasslands of the San Rafael Valley and tethered to the outside world by a single road that writhes westward through the Patagonia Mountains to its end in Nogales, the road deeply rutted by the giant wagons trundling silver and copper ore out of the mountains to Lochiel's smelter, its stack leaking smoke into an otherwise unblemished desert sky.

The black tendril leans in a light breeze, and a faint, sooty mist sifts down on the tin roof of a nearby bungalow—the house-cum-courtroom of Joshua Pittman, the justice of the peace. A clean-shaven man of forty, wearing a collarless shirt and a vest he can no longer button over his portly torso, he is seated on a spindle-backed chair on his front porch, booted feet crossed atop the porch rail as he reads the *Border Vidette.* The issue is dated August 6, 1903; it's two days old, delivered from Nogales, some twenty miles away, by a mailman on horseback. The Justice, as he's often called, reads almost every word; as a leading citizen in a town most of whose inhabitants are illiterate in English and Spanish, he considers it his duty to keep abreast of events in the world beyond Lochiel.

In his dusty yard stands his nephew, Ben Erskine, a boy just past the threshold of adolescence, tall for his age, as lean as one of the ocotillo wands that fence the yard. He wears a loose-fitting cotton shirt, dungarees tucked into a pair of scruffy boots, and a high-peaked, dirty hat, its brim rolled up tightly at the sides. A boy on an idle Saturday, playing a solitary game of mumblety-peg in the shade of a cottonwood. The hunting knife in his hand is a prize possession, its four-inch blade mirror-bright and sharp enough to cleanly slice a page of his uncle's newspaper. What makes this knife special are the engravings on each side of the blade. At first glance they resemble scrollwork; but with a closer look, the pattern reveals itself to be a dancing girl in three different intertwined poses. Holding the knife up to the light at the correct angle and turning it slowly side to side creates an illusion of movement. The three figures merge into one; the dancing girl comes to life, her ample hips swaying. Ownership of the knife has made Ben the envy of the other boys at Lochiel's one-room school. Many was the afternoon after class when they gathered around him for a demonstration and a chance to gawk at the forbidden. These entertainments have continued into the summer vacation, but they will end soon. Next month, after a year in his uncle's care, Ben will rejoin his mother, stepfather, and older brother, Jeffrey, in Tucson, where he is to begin high school. This isn't something he's looking forward to, not because he dislikes school—he is in fact an eager student—but because he doesn't get along with his stepfather, a Southern Pacific supervisor named Rudy Hollister.

Skinny legs spread, Ben flips the knife into the ground a few inches from his right foot, then stretches his legs farther and plants his foot next to the knife, buried up to the dancing girl's neck. He is almost doing the splits. He can't move another inch, so he pulls his legs together, withdraws the knife, and begins again.

The Justice folds the newspaper, swings his feet off the rail, and looks at his nephew. "One of these days you are going to stick that thing clear through your foot," he says slowly and deliberately, as if he's passing sentence in his courtroom.

"Yes, sir."

"What do you mean? Yes, you are going to stick yourself in the foot?"

Ben pauses a moment, tips his hat back with two fingers as he's seen the cowhands do, and grins his peculiar grin. It slashes across his face like a soldier's hash mark and is often misinterpreted by those who don't know him well. To them, it looks like a sneer, cocky, even a little cruel.

"I did not mean that at all," he says. "I'm too accurate with it to stick myself."

"Right glad you are so confident," Joshua says, arching his sandy brown eyebrows. He squints at the sun, which is swinging from east to southeast over the far blue ranges of Sonora. "Your uncle's favorite refreshment needs replenishment. Seeing as how you have got so much free time, take a ride over to Esteban's for me."

Esteban's is a cantina in Santa Cruz, a small pueblo some six or seven miles over the border. In Joshua's estimation, the tequila sold there is superior to the brands peddled in Lochiel's saloons—raw smuggled hooch suitable for the uneducated palates of cowboys and miners, but not for a discriminating man such as himself.

"I'll saddle Maggie right away," Ben replies. Any chance to ride his pinto mare is welcome.

He collects the money from his uncle and starts toward the livery stables. Joshua watches him walk away, the shirt billowing as if it were hanging from a coat hanger, empty of flesh and bone. He's grown close to Ben in the past year, closer than he wanted to, and tries not to think about the boy's departure. He'd become accustomed to loneliness. When Ben came to live with him, nine years had passed since he buried Gabriela and the infant son who'd died with her, strangled by the umbilical cord, *hanged* by the organ that had sustained him in the womb.

That was in Nogales, where Joshua had been serving as postmaster. After the funeral he returned home and opened the door, and the silence inside seemed to lunge at him as if alive. He walked out, abandoning everything he and Gabriela had owned, and never went back. No, the silence in this house will not be half so dreadful when Ben leaves for Tucson, but it will take some getting used to.

Hattie had written him last summer: "There's nothing we can do with him, and this is the last straw." For some petty slight, Ben had declared that he was going to whip his stepfather, who greeted the threat with a laugh. So she said, and Joshua had no reason to doubt his sister. Rudy Hollister was good-natured and was besides six feet two inches tall, with the arms and shoulders of the section hand he'd been before the railroad promoted him to supervisor. When Ben rushed him, he placed a hand on the boy's forehead and allowed him to flail the air until he could no longer keep his arms up. As reported by Hattie, Hollister said, "Don't look like you're ready to lick me just yet," and that should have been the end of it. But the humiliation had been too much for Ben. He seized a poker from the fireplace and threw it at his stepfather—"like a red Indian would throw a lance."

Ben's missile struck wide of its mark, but it raised Rudy's ire. "Tanned his hide but good," Hattie's letter went on. "First and only time Rudy laid a hand on either one of the boys. The only reason I can figure Ben hates him like he does is for not being his father, like he thinks Tom's death was Rudy's fault."

That did not surprise the Justice. Ben had worshiped his father, though he was often away from home, as a U.S. Customs officer patrolling the border, then as a territorial ranger, chasing outlaws and rustlers. Maybe Ben worshiped him *because* he was gone so much. The irony was that Tom Erskine, who'd survived gunfire from Mexican smugglers and white desperadoes, died as the result of a kick from a rank horse. Ruptured his liver.

Six months later Hattie married Rudy and moved to Tucson. Said she needed a man in the house to help her raise two rambunctious boys. Still, her swift remarriage caused a scandal in Lochiel. Might have had the decency to at least wait a year, the town gossips whispered. The rumor was that good-looking, fun-loving Hattie needed a man for other purposes. There was something, well, *carnal* about her; during Tom's absences, a hunger plain to every man in town would come into her eyes. She often went on solitary rides—the woman could ride like an Apache brave—spurring her horse into reckless gallops to blow off sexual steam.

Having described "the last straw," she listed Ben's previous offenses. Got into a gang fight and knocked a Mexican kid cold with a chunk of railroad spike hurled from his slingshot, and then, fearing he'd killed the kid, saddled his horse and fled into the mountains for three days, worrying her sick. With her case built (and pretty skillfully, thought the man of the law), she came to the point: would Joshua take Ben in for the next year? A big thing to ask of him, but she was at her wit's end, and Ben looked up to his uncle, the former cavalryman who had fought Geronimo.

Joshua smiled at the flattery. It wasn't as if he and Geronimo had met in a single combat. He had been in only a couple of brief skirmishes during the final campaign against the Apaches in '86. His memories consisted mostly of heat, dust, and burning eyes on endless, monotonous rides, pursuing a phantom across the desert and through the Dragoons and the Chiricahuas, until, with his people starved and exhausted, the phantom called it quits in a place called Skeleton Canyon. No, it wasn't flattery that convinced him to agree to Hattie's request. Rudy Hollister was only half of Ben's argument; the other half, he suspected, was Hattie herself. No great shakes as a mother, Joshua had reluctantly concluded. When Ben and Jeff were toddlers, she often left them alone in the house for hours, strapping them into high chairs so they wouldn't get into mischief while she visited with her friends or went shopping or took one of her rides. In matters of discipline she was inconsistent, indulgent one day, and the next . . . Well, there was that time when Ben was eight and engaged in some sort of obstreperous behavior. Hattie punished him by forcing him to walk barefoot over a trail cobbled with shale and junk rock chipped like half-finished spear points. He stubbed his toes, his feet bled, and he cried to her to pick him up, but she continued the torture until, in her reckoning, he'd learned his lesson.

Joshua figured he could do better, and the past year has proved him right. Not a lick of trouble, unless you count the time the schoolteacher caught Ben putting on a show with his unusual knife at recess. She wouldn't allow Ben to bring it to school from then on, and reprimanded Joshua for allowing his nephew to keep such an immoral object—and him the justice of the peace!

Ben is wearing the knife when he rides out of Lochiel, crossing into Mexico as easily as one might cross a street in Tucson or Phoenix. There is no barbed wire to impede him, no signpost except for a tall stone boundary marker to tell him that he is leaving the Arizona Territory. He's made this trip before but feels a small buzz nonetheless—it's an adventure for a thirteen-year-old to ride alone into another country on a fine horse like Maggie, small, lithe, and fast, a possession he prizes more than the knife hanging from his belt in a plain leather sheath.

He holds her to a lively walk, though he's tempted to strike a lope to cool his face. A tropical humidity burdens the air, for it is the monsoon season on the vast Sonoran Desert, the time of year that stockmen anticipate with hope and fear: if the rains succeed, their herds will prosper and so will they; if the rains fail, as they did in the nineties, the grass will wither, the calves birthed in spring will grow weak and fall prey to coyotes and cougars, and the cows gathered in the fall will go to market underweight. The owners of big spreads will survive; the small operators will be droughted out.

The rains have been abundant this year. The grasslands have gone from pale yellow to bright green, "green as Ireland," Ben heard an immigrant miner say. Fat cattle graze everywhere, and golden poppies speckle the roadside. Far to the southeast a compact storm sweeps the horizon, a moving black island in the sea of sky, the rain an opaque curtain hung from cloud to earth. To the southwest, more clouds, towering over the San Antonios, spread out in a black anvil that sparks lightning.

Ben rides alongside the Santa Cruz River for well over an hour, passing a campesino on a burro, then a range of low hills crowned with old mine tailings. Near the start of the river's westward bend, he enters the pueblo—small houses and stores flanking a fissured dirt street that leads into the plaza. It is siesta time. A couple of women in brilliant Indian garb are drawing water from the communal well; a man sits smoking on the bandstand steps; otherwise no one is out in the fierce midday heat. Esteban's, a flat-roofed adobe with the ends of its roof beams protruding from the front wall and CANTINA painted above its door, is a few houses down from the church, the grandest building in town, grander than the nearby courthouse.

Ben knots Maggie's reins to the hitching rail beside three other horses, one a big sorrel that must go seventeen hands. It is dim inside—a couple of windows admit patches of light in which dust motes swirl and sparkle. Three vaqueros sit drinking at crude tables against a wall, two together, the other by himself, tipping a beer bottle to his lips. All three look at Ben. He nods. The two seated together return the nod, but the third makes no movement, just squints at Ben as he crosses the dirt floor, worn as smooth as marble, gleaming in the places where the window light strikes it.

Esteban is in the back room. Ben hears clinks and clatters and surmises that he is stocking shelves. He stands at the bar. On the wall behind it planks supported by stout pegs hold dusty glasses, unlabeled bottles, and squat earthenware jugs. Ben waits a minute or two, feeling the solitary man's eyes on his back. The sensation makes him nervous, and he raps the bar loudly with his knuckles to gain Esteban's attention.

A voice behind him slurs, "Está ocupado. Tenga paciencia."

Ben turns and looks at the lone vaquero, heavyset, with a mestizo's complexion and the standard Mexican mustache, hooked over his mouth like a black bracket. A felt sombrero hangs from his thick neck by its stampede strap, stained chaps sheath his outstretched legs, and big cruel-looking spurs—the kind sometimes called Spanish, sometimes Chihuahuan—are clamped to his boots.

"¿Tú comprendes, gringuito?"

He practically spits the contemptuous word "littlegringo."

"Sí, comprendo," Ben answers, offering his crooked grin to mask his unease. The Mexican makes it obvious, with a hard glare, that he doesn't like that smile—to him, it looks insolent.

"¿Ese pinto es tuyo?" he asks, gesturing out a window that frames Maggie and one of the other horses.

Ben replies that the pinto is his.

"Parece fino."

"Pues."

"Me gusta tu caballo." He pauses, squints, smiles without mirth, then stands up. Accustomed to Mexicans not much taller than himself, Ben is surprised by his height. Spurs clanking, he lurches to the bar and leans on it, inches away. The vaquero isn't armed, but that isn't much comfort. He's as tall and powerfully built as Rudy Hollister.

"Sí, me gusta tu caballo," he repeats, the vapors of his beer breath almost visible. "Pero no me gustan los gringos, y mucho menos los gringuitos."

I like your horse, but I don't like gringos, and little gringos even less. A prickling rises up Ben's arms, a tightness in his throat. He wants to bolt but doesn't, sensing that any sudden move will only incite this ugly borracho. Just then Esteban emerges from the back room. He's short, muscular, dressed in the white cotton shirt and trousers of a peon. But he's no peon, he's a barkeep in a border cantina, and he sizes up the situation in two seconds flat.

"¿Qué quiere, amigo?" he amiably asks the big man. "¿Otra cerveza o"—he places his hands on a drawer under the bar—"algo más?"

The drunk is not so drunk that he doesn't understand the message of Esteban's hidden hands: the "something else" he's been offered isn't drinkable. He snorts and replies, sure, he'll have another beer. Esteban pulls one from a shelf. The vaquero grabs it, slams a few pesos on the bar, and weaves back to his table.

"Hola, Ben," Esteban says. "¿Qué pasa? Cómo está tu tío?"

"Bien, pero con sed."

"Oye." Esteban leans forward and lowers his voice. "Me llegó lo bueno . . . Lo que le gusta a tu tío."

The drunk nonetheless overhears. "¡Lo bueno! ¿Qué estoy tomando yo? ¿Del drenaje? Y al cabroncito le das lo bueno. Y tan joven para pistear."

Esteban ignores him, then motions Ben to come with him. *Cabroncito*—little bastard. Ben again feels like running out. Instead he obeys the summons, ducks under the bar, and follows Esteban into the cramped, windowless storeroom that is as dark as a closet save for a single plane of light, slipping through a crack in the back door. Esteban burns a candle and removes from a shelf a glazed ceramic jug with its cork sealed in wax.

"Esta es. Mira." Pointing at a word printed under the name of the distiller: REPOSADO. It means, as Ben has learned from his previous trips, that the tequila has been aged a long time and is of the highest quality.

"¿Cuánto es?"

"Dos."

Before leaving, Uncle Joshua instructed him to bargain, but Ben is more than anxious to be on his way and dips into his pocket without argument.

"Bueno," Esteban says, palming the two silver dollars. "Oye. Sálgate por aquí." He gestures at the back door, then adds with a twitch of his head, "El borracho."

"Hasta luego."

Walking around to the front, Ben stuffs the jug into a saddlebag, mounts up, and starts down the street at a trot. *Gringuito. Cabroncito.* What was he picking on me for? he asks himself. What did I do to him? The sheer unreasonableness of the Mexican's hostility agitates and frightens him as much as the hostility itself.

A wind has sprung up in advance of the thunderstorm building to the south. A dust devil twirls crazily ahead, seeming to lead Ben out of Santa Cruz before it spins itself out. At a wash a herd of thirsty corrientes blocks his way. He urges Maggie on and whoops to clear a path through the jostling mass of pale hides and high, curved horns. Maggie plods up the opposite bank, and Ben rides on toward the border, once more at a brisk walk. He hasn't gone far when he hears rapid hoofbeats behind him. He knows who it is even before he turns to see him, mounted on the sorrel at a full gallop. Ben's thought is, He wants to steal my horse! Maggie, as startled as he by the oncoming rider, lunges forward. Ben kicks her hard and slacks the reins, and she takes off, neck outstretched, mane flying. He doesn't dare turn to see if the vaquero is gaining, and doesn't need to. He can tell by the sound that he is. In a few seconds the sorrel is alongside, its nose half a length behind Maggie's, the Mexican brandishing a ramal braided to his reins. An observer watching from afar would think the two riders were high-spirited cowhands, running a race.

"¡A ver qué tan hombrecito eres!" the Mexican yells, leaning over as he cracks Maggie's haunch with the ramal.

Thinking that some predator is attacking her from behind, which is in fact the case, the mare whirls off the road, kicking with both back legs at the same time, the violent movement nearly pitching Ben over her neck and jerking his feet from the stirrups. He manages to hold his seat but cannot get his stirrups back as Maggie twists and bucks. He cannot believe he's still on, but because he's been riding since age four, he knows he won't be for long, knows further that he had better bail before he's thrown. He lands hard, his legs crumple from the impact, and he rolls two or three times through the grass and over the rocks the grass conceals.

The wind knocked out of him, his ribs bruised, he lies there for several moments, staring at a harrier circling high above. When he realizes that he hasn't broken any bones, he sits up and sees Maggie some ten or twenty yards away, ground-tied by the reins hanging from her neck. She seems to be looking at him apologetically. Ben wants to say, "Got nothin to feel bad about, wasn't your fault," but he can't speak. His tongue and throat feel as if they're coated with sand.

He gets to his feet and then notices the sorrel standing under an empty saddle some distance away, near the old mine tailings. The gringo-hater lies sprawled in the middle of the road, motionless. His horse must have reared when Maggie kicked, Ben thinks, and being so drunk, he couldn't hold his seat. Hope his neck is broke.

What he should do now is ride home as fast as the mare can carry him, but that is not what he does. Leading Maggie by the reins, he approaches the prone figure as a hunter would a fallen bear or mountain lion, uncertain if it's dead or merely wounded. The wind blows harder, lightning rives a plum-colored cloud advancing northward.

The Mexican appears to be dead, an arm flung over his chest, eyes half open, mustache matted with the blood trickling from his nostrils; but then he makes a sound—it's something between a sigh and a snore—and Ben notices the big chest rising, falling, rising. What if this crazy horse thief revives and comes after him as he rides homeward?

Fear rises again in Ben's throat, and he hates this drunken vaquero for making him afraid. He kneels behind his tormentor's head and bends low, draws his knife, and with one swift stroke he opens in the Mexican's throat a second mouth that vomits blood over his hand and shirt.

The man's legs thrash, digging the Spanish spurs into the ground; he wheezes and gurgles, and when the arm on his chest flops to the ground with a spastic movement, Ben jumps aside. Trembling, he stares at the body, now still, and at the scarlet grin arcing almost ear to ear in the brown throat. A thrill of conquest shudders through him—he feels like a David standing over the slain Goliath. And yet he can't believe he's done what he's done. It now seems as though the knife drew itself and of its own will slashed into living flesh.

He wipes the blade in the grass, then scours his hand and shirt with dirt from the road. The dead man's horse still stands near the mine tailings. Nearby Maggie grazes on succulent tufts of blue grama. The harrier glides low, seeking prey. The thunderstorm rolls on, passing to the west, while the sky directly overhead is clear. Nothing much has changed except Ben Erskine.

A calm descends upon this Ben who is no longer the Ben he'd been and can never be again. The trembling stops. His mind is cold and clear and thinks ahead. Some traveler is bound to come upon the body and fly into Santa Cruz with the news that a man with his throat cut lies in the middle of the road. The report will reach the ears of the local law. Possibly Esteban and the two customers will tell them about what happened in the cantina. Of course, by the time the rurales ride out to look for him, he will be back in Lochiel, beyond their reach. But can he take that chance? His instincts tell him to hide the body now, while there is no one around. The problem is, where can he hide it out here in all this open country? He can't drag it very far—the Mexican must weigh more than two hundred pounds. Then he looks toward the dead man's horse and the mine tailings, cascading down the slopes of the low hills.

He approaches the sorrel carefully, removes the riata from the saddle, and returns to the road. He cinches the loop over the Mexican's ankles, giving the rope a few extra turns for good measure, then wraps the opposite end around his saddle horn and remounts Maggie. The smell of blood makes the pinto nervous. Ben settles her down, and she has no trouble pulling the corpse over the open ground and up one of the hills. Ben halts there, unties the riata from the saddle horn and, after some tugging and shoving that soaks him in sweat, rolls the body into a mine shaft. Trailing the rope still bound to its ankles, it tumbles straight down fifteen or twenty feet to land on its side, the legs bent against the side of the hole, which isn't much wider than the Mexican is tall. *Was* tall. Ben scrambles down to unsaddle the sorrel and take off its reins and headstall. That done, he sends the horse away with a loud yell and a slap on the rump. Lugging the tack uphill works up more sweat. He tosses it into the pit with its former owner. *A ver qué tan hombrecito eres.* The Mexican's last words. *Let's see what you have, little man.* Reckon you found out, you horse-thievin' son of a bitch.

Ben mounts up and starts for the border and Lochiel, spurring the pinto into a racehorse's run. It's as though he's in flight, though no one pursues him.

Joshua Pittman is in his office, studying a case he is to hear tomorrow: a dispute between two stockmen over water rights. He's had trouble concentrating. Ben should have returned an hour ago. His anxiety eases when he hears, through the open window, hoof clops out back and the squeal of the gate swinging open. He goes out to the porch, and there is Ben, leading his horse into the yard. Maggie is lathered, blown out.

"What took you so long? You're too young to have been dancing with the señoritas."

Ben makes no reply, takes the jug out of a saddlebag and, with a skittering, sidelong glance of his pale gray eyes, hands it to his uncle.

"I'd better cool Maggie down before I put her up," Ben declares, still with that evasive look, his voice subdued.

Joshua sets the jug down and leans against a post. "Don't want to put yourself up wet either," he remarks, gesturing at his nephew's sweat-stained, dirt-spattered shirt. "Whatever held you up, you sure did come home in a hurry it looks like."

"Knew we was late."

"Were late. You've had eight years of schooling."

"Yes, sir."

Ben goes to his horse, tugs the latigo to loosen the girth, and walks the mare around the yard, passing into and out of the cottonwood's lengthening shadow, mottled by the late-afternoon light shooting through the branches. His head is bent contemplatively; the fingers of his free hand open and close, as if he's molding an invisible lump of clay.

The Justice steps off the porch. "Run into trouble?"

Ben halts and makes a vague movement with his head.

"That a yes?"

Ben nods.

"Well, what kind of trouble?"

"Somebody tried to steal my horse."

Joshua flinches. He'd expected to hear that it was mild trouble, boy trouble, like a run-in with some rough kids. "Who was it?"

"A Messikin."

"Stands to reason it was a Mexican, you being in Mexico at the time."

This droll comment is intended to ease Ben's agitation, but it has the opposite effect. Looking at his uncle squarely for the first time since his return, he snaps in response, "What do you reckon? That he come up to me and said, 'Howdeedo, my name is Pablo and I'm here to steal your horse?' "

"Don't get sassy."

"I'm sorry, sir. It's just that . . . You know that hunting trip I went on last fall with my friends? When we saw the mountain lion a-sneakin' up on our packhorse and shot it? This Messikin scared me more'n that lion did. Never been so scared. I still am—some."

Ben's lips quiver as he speaks, and Joshua draws closer to him, raising a hand to give his shoulder a reassuring squeeze; but the movement is immediately checked by the peculiar expression in the boy's eyes. There is no fright in them, and not much boy either. They seem somehow older and harder.

"There's nothing to be scared of now. Doubt that Mexican is going to come here after your horse."

"Ain't no doubt about it," Ben affirms, the harshness of his tone matching his look. "He was chasin' me and tried to make Maggie throw me so he could take her. But he was the one got throwed. Busted his neck, I think. He's dead, Uncle Josh."

Startled, Joshua does not say anything. He then notices something that startles him more: he'd mistaken the nature of the reddish brown blemishes spattered across the front of Ben's shirt and on the right sleeve.

"What's this?" he asks, rubbing a large blot on the cuff.

"That?" Ben says with a quick look. "I reckon it's dirt."

Cupping the boy's elbow in his hand, Joshua guides him to the porch, sits down on the stoop, and motions Ben to sit beside him. "Maggie can wait. You've got a lot to tell me, and I had better hear it. I had better hear it all."

. . .

That night Ben sleeps fitfully, troubled by strange dreams. There is a mystical streak in the family, which he has inherited. He wakes, sits up, and sees his father standing at the foot of his bed, the beloved father wearing a wide-brimmed hat and a leather vest with his ranger's badge pinned to it, a Winchester Model 94 at his side. Tom Erskine tells him he is a good boy, there is nothing to worry about, nothing to fear. "Go to sleep, son," he whispers, and Ben does, undisturbed by any more bad dreams.

While he sleeps, the Justice records the confession in his diary, a clothbound ledger with a leather spine. (He is a faithful diarist, and after his death in 1928, his journals will find their way into the Arizona Historical Society's Tucson archives, where they will be read by a descendant many decades later.) Most of the entries, written in the clear hand of one trained in old-fashioned penmanship, take up a page at most and concern events in town, or observations on the weather, or the particulars of an interesting court case. A few reveal Joshua's deepest thoughts and feelings—his loneliness, his desire to meet a woman who will evict his longing for Gabriela.

The entry for August 8, 1903, covers five full pages and is less legible, with words crossed out and rewritten in the spaces between the lines. Joshua maintains a dispassionate tone in the first three pages, which describe the incident. While the hurried scrawl communicates emotional turmoil, the straitjacketed language reads like a police report or a dictated deposition. The sole exception is this sentence: "When his assailant showed signs of life, Ben, thinking he would come to and resume pursuit, unsheathed his knife and cut the man's throat." The last four words are underscored: *cut the man's throat.*

What follows are Joshua's reactions to what he's heard. He begins with a bit of self-recrimination, mentioning how dangerous the border was in those days, with bandits and renegades ranging freely on both sides. To send a thirteen-year-old across the line, alone and for such a frivolous purpose, was a dereliction of his duties as the boy's guardian. The fact that Ben had not met with trouble on previous trips had made

Joshua complacent. "It could have been Ben lying out there with a broken neck or worse," he continues. "The thought makes my soul tremble."

But as his commentary goes on, it becomes evident that what might have happened did not disturb him nearly so much as what did. He describes the Mexican as "a common thug who doubtless needed killing"; but he regrets with all his being that his nephew had to be the one to do it. He judges, moreover, that Ben did not need to kill him. The man of the law cannot escape drawing that conclusion, though he does not state it plainly. He writes that at Ben's age he would have fled as soon as he saw that his attacker had been knocked unconscious; that he would have lacked the cold-blooded nerve to slash the man's throat and the presence of mind, like a seasoned criminal's, to dispose of the corpse.

Joshua Pittman is a man of the western frontier, raised in west Texas during the Comanche wars. He's seen something of greed and violence and the miscreant passions to which all men are heir; but the diary makes it plain that his nephew has presented him with something he's not encountered before, something he cannot quite grasp but that nonetheless expands his notions of what is possible. A boy goes off on a mundane errand and returns a blood-splattered killer. How can that be? Where is Providence to allow such a thing to happen? He is like a man who has been changed by a new and powerful perception. Scribbling by the light of a kerosene lantern, he pauses, pressing the tip of the pen's wooden shaft to his cheek as he ponders how to express this new perception and incorporate it into the realm of his experience. Unable to find the language, he reads over what he's written, and that is when he strikes a bold line under the words "cut the man's throat."

He then digresses into a brief reminiscence of his father, Caleb Pittman, a twice-wounded Confederate veteran who, bearing a wagonload of bitterness and belligerence, left Georgia to ranger in Texas and kill Comanches with as much zest as he had Yankees. Indeed, Pittman family lore is filled with tales of hard-shell ancestors fighting Indians and whites and, when they ran out of natural enemies, each other. Could there have been something in young Ben's blood that had lain dormant until its awaited hour came, the pupa cracked, and the creature was born, there on that dusty road to Santa Cruz?

The Justice stops himself from further indulgence in such pointless speculations and concludes: "It is a terrible thing to kill a man, even when it is justified. A few hours ago, I would not have believed someone Ben's age would have it in him to do what he did in the way he did it. Ben himself could not have known until the deed was accomplished. I do not know how this discovery will affect him."

That question will be answered in later years.

Transcript 1 of an oral history compiled for the Arizona Historical Society. The subject, T.J. Babcock, 78, was interviewed at his home in Springdale, Arizona, on April 6–8, 1966.

I have lived longer than I deserve. Been shot at and missed and shit on and hit, if you'll pardon the language, but am still on the right side of the ground and looking age eighty square in the eye.

I have seen a great many changes too, and I cannot keep up with them anymore. I was born in Bisbee, Arizona, just two years after they captured Geronimo, and as a boy, I knew fellas, Mexicans and Americans, who had been in scrapes with the A-patch, but only last year I was down to Phoenix and saw a jet airliner taking off.

There is no name to go with the J that is my middle initial. My ma and pa, in what must have been a fit of insanity, named me Thaddeus but didn't give me a middle name. I got made fun of a lot, so I started to call myself T, but that didn't sound quite right, so I added the J, and all who have known me since know me as T.J.

My pa, who had a normal name, Mike, worked in the copper mine in Bisbee. When I was about three or four, he moved us down to Mexico, to Cananea, because he got a foreman's job there with the Consolidated Copper Company, then owned by the famous Colonel Greene, who I don't think ever was a colonel. I grew up in Mexico, went to school there, and by the time I was twelve or thereabouts, I was more Mexican than American, could speak and read and write Spanish better than I could English. If it wasn't for this fella my ma hired to school me in my native lingo, I probably couldn't speak it right to this day.

The book part of my education ended when I was fourteen, much to my parents' disappointment, and I too became an employee of Colonel Greene, but not in the mine. I wanted nothing to do with mine work. The colonel owned a big ranch—it was called the RO. Worked it for some time, then I signed on as a hand with its San Rafael division, just across the border in Arizona. It was the vaquero's life for me.

Now, as it is Ben Erskine you want to hear about, I will skip over a few years and tell you how I come to meet him and how him and me rode off together to fight in the Revolution in Mexico. It went like this:

the San Rafael raised registered Herefords for the purposes of breeding. Running registered cattle is a whole lot different than running ordinary range cattle, especially the way it I learned how to do it down in Mexico. Hell, them cows was half wild. Along about 1910, I up and quit. The foreman didn't like me, and I liked him even less. Said he was interested in scientific cattle breeding, and I reckon he reckoned my way of doing things wasn't scientific enough for his tastes, so I saddled up and rode off, which is a cowboy's right. Cowboys don't ask permission from no one, including scientists.

I was in Nogales—on the Sonoran side—spending the last of my money on the señoritas—when I met Jeffrey Erskine. He was having a beer in the bar of the hotel I was staying at. We got to talking, and Jeff mentioned that he was buying some steers in Mexico. Him and his brother, Ben, were running a rawhide steer operation across the line. You might not be acquainted with that term, *rawhiding*. It's not used anymore because nobody rawhides anymore. It means raising cattle on as low overhead as you can get away with. No buildings or barns, no machinery or windmills, just a corral or two, a few horses, and your stock. Most rawhiders were fellas getting started in the cattle business, they ran their cattle on leased land, and usually it was steers instead of cow-calf. Raising steers was speculative, a little like playing the stock market, I guess. You could make good money fast by buying steers cheap, then fattening them up, keeping your eye on prices, and when you figured they'd fetch top dollar, you would sell, and then buy another bunch for as low as you could find, usually in Mexico, where things was cheaper.

And that pretty much describes Jeff's operation. He had ten sections under lease up in the San Rafael Valley, east of the ranch that had the same name. I was impressed with him right off. He was just past six foot, and pretty well put together, but that wasn't what impressed me. He was the same age as me, but you know how there's some people who seem like they were born forty years old? That was Jeff—a serious fella. He wore this mustache, reddish gold, that added to his—well, I reckon you would call it his maturity. Now, humility never has been one of my strong suits, so I asked him if he could use a top hand because I was one.

Jeff didn't say nothing for a spell; don't think he could take a leak without pondering aforehand. Then he said he already had a top hand in his brother. The only trouble was, his brother had a habit of going off on what Jeff called "adventures" without a word of warning. So, sure he could use a top hand, but all he could promise was a cot in a tent and chuck, and this top hand would have to do some cooking and cleaning up.

So I threw in. Had nothing better to do. We lived right hard, I will tell you that. This tent they had was a canvas wall tent Jeff had got from the soldiers over to Fort Huachuca. It had a little stove for heat, and it was pitched at the head of a draw a little ways west of the Huachuca Mountains. We had us a fly where we did the cooking, and it was beans and hash and tortillas and coffee seven days a week. Never forget the first meal I ate there. Ben had put a pot of beans on the fire in the morning, but he forgot to put the lid on it. When we come back after riding all day, I was so hungry I could have eaten the back end out of a wooden horse and dug right in. Crunchiest damn beans I'd ever put my mouth to, and when I got the hollow filled up, I wondered what was making those beans so crunchy like, and investigated the pot and saw it was grasshoppers, big ones—this was summertime. Them hoppers flew into the pot while we were gone and baked themselves. I about threw up, and Ben laughed, and Jeff, who was a book-reading man, said that over to Europe folks considered grasshoppers a delicacy and dipped them in chocolate and ate them like they was candy.

I was impressed with Ben right off the bat, but in a different way than with his brother. He was skinnier and light on his feet, but he was one helluva man with a horse or with a rope. And there was something watchful about him, like he was expecting someone to jump him any second, but it wasn't a scared kind of watchfulness. He was relaxed and coiled up at the same time. You got the impression that if somebody did jump him, the one who did the jumping was gone to come out second best. Ben had a funny way of smiling, too. One end of his mouth would go way up and the other end way down, and I saw later on that if he smiled at you like that, well, you had better talk fast or shoot fast.

I told you Jeff was a book reader. Most of the books were about cattle breeding. He was taking a correspondence course from some agricultural college somewhere, and every now and then he would ride over to the post office in Lochiel and pick up these books they sent him, and he even took the tests and mailed them back. Like I said, a serious man.

That year of 1910 was the year of the big comet, Halley's. It was pinned up there in the sky like a carnation made of fire. On full moon nights, with that comet shining up there, you almost thought it was daylight. Truth to tell, I didn't know what a comet was till Jeff explained it. Said that one come from way out in the universe somewhere and was traveling, oh, hell, I can't remember how fast he said, maybe a million miles an hour. I remember asking him, What do you mean, a million miles an hour? I been looking at that thing for a week and it ain't moved an inch. But I took his word for it.

The reason I'm talking about that comet is the trip we took into Mexico in the fall to buy more steers. We'd got a herd together in the corrals over to Naco and were fixing to drive them to our range the next day. We overheard some vaqueros talking about the comet, that the big extra light in the sky got the cattle fidgety, and they said that it was un mal agüero, a bad omen, that it meant war and death were a-coming. It was real spooky talk. They were saying that they'd heard about pillars of fire in the middle of the country. I come to find out a long time later that it was a volcano that blew up, but to them vaqueros, who was about as unscientific as anybody can get, it was another omen. The days of Díaz were over, there was a fella named Madero who was gone to take power and give the land to the people, but there would be a lot of war and death and famine and disease first. Lord they was talking like folks out of Bible days. It had been up to me, we would have cleared out right then.

So the Revolution got started, and I thought the revolucionarios were right. The rich folks in Mexico and the big-shot foreigners like Colonel Greene had pretty much treated ordinary folks like dogs, and now the dogs was biting back. Jeff and me had some right lively conversations about that. He said the revolucionarios weren't like ours, George Washington and all, but were socialists, and that made them dangerous. He explained to me what a socialist was, and the way he explained it, I agreed that a socialist wasn't anybody I would care to associate with. But I didn't think the Mexicans fighting Díaz were like that. They wanted a fair shake was all, and I sure couldn't fault any man for that. Ben didn't have much to say on this subject. He never was one for talking, but I got the idea that he saw things like I did. He would not tolerate nobody trying to push him around, and didn't think any man had a right to push another man around.

I know one thing—the Revolution made it tough for Jeff to buy Mexican steers. Pancho Villa and his like had run the hacendados off their ranches or hung 'em or shot 'em, and there wasn't nobody to do business with. Jeff was having a helluva time finding steers at the right price on the American side of the line, and that was putting a crimp in his plans, which were to start to making himself a cattle baron.

It was me who come up with the solution. If it was true that the hacendados had been run off or shot or hung, then their cattle must be a-wandering around with no one to look after them, meaning we didn't have to go through the formality of buying them. We'd just take them. Couldn't get 'em no cheaper than that, could you? Jeff and Ben thought it was a fine idea, Ben on account of he was getting bored punching cattle and was looking for some action. Jeff saw the sense of it from a business angle.

Back in those days it was common for Mexicans to cross the line and steal cattle from us gringos—and it was common for gringos to return the favor. It was a kind of game. We didn't think of it as rustling, and the Mexicans didn't neither. Of course, if you was the one getting rustled, then you saw it different.

Two of the ten sections Jeff had leased was right on the border, and that's where we crossed. The rancho grande on the other side was called the Santa Barbara, and it must've run halfway down to Mexico City. It was owned by a Spaniard name of Álvarez, and owing to the fact that the revolucionarios hated Spaniards more than anybody else, we reckoned he'd been one of the first run off, shot, or hung. The big comet was gone from the sky by this time, but we had us a full moon. We rounded up, I think it was fifty-odd head without a hitch and drove them across and built a fire for our running irons and put our brand to 'em.

It was so damn easy, we tried it again the next night, while we still had a moon. We'd gathered up maybe twenty of these corriente steers when the Spaniard showed up with a few of his vaqueros and caught us red-handed. So there was one hacendado who hadn't been run off, shot, or hung, and wasn't we surprised! Asked us, polite like, what we thought we was a-doing, and Jeff said that some of our cattle had got away and we were sorting out ours from his. I had to translate that to the Spanish fella. Álvarez pulled a pistol and about stuck it in Jeff's face and told Jeff that if we didn't clear out muy pronto, we'd leave our bones there in Old Mexico. Before I could translate that, Ben drew his six-gun and stuck it in Álvarez's ear and said that his bones was gone to be laying right next to ours if he didn't put that pistol away. It was a peculiar-looking pistol, a kind I'd never seen before.

There I was on my horse, figuring the vaqueros was gone to open up any second, but Álvarez was between them and Ben, and I thought they didn't shoot because they were afraid of hitting their boss. Turned out that wasn't the case. They were afraid of hitting Ben! Right in the middle of that good old-fashioned Mexican standoff, one of the vaqueros called out, "¡Hola Ben! ¡Soy yo, Francisco!" Found out later on that Ben and this Francisco had become compadres on one of Ben's trips into Sonora a while before—one of them "adventures" Jeff said he went on. Well, Francisco said to go ahead and take the cattle from that hijo de puta of a Spaniard. That kind of distracted Álvarez. He turned in the saddle to see which one of his vaqueros had called him a son of a bitch, and Ben took advantage and cracked him up the side of the head with the barrel of his six-gun, but he didn't hit him hard enough to knock him out, and Álvarez pulled the trigger of that peculiar pistol. Must have shot four, five rounds quicker than I can say it. He'd shot in the direction of his own men, but I can't say if it was on purpose or accidental. He didn't hit a one of them, and then that Francisco fella shot him off his horse, and the other vaqueros plugged him while he was on the ground, and that was the end of the trail for Don Álvarez.

All of it happened in maybe five seconds, and I was right scared and confused. That was the first man I'd ever seen killed before my eyes. Now the cattle had scattered from all the gunfire, and damn if the vaqueros didn't help us gather them back up. Jeff was kind of troubled how we came to be in possession of them, and I said to him that I reckoned now we was socialists, too. He didn't think that was too funny. Francisco was telling us what a son of a bitch Álvarez was, treated his vaqueros and their families like they was scum, and that they'd been looking for a chance to get rid of him and we gave it to them. Ben had helped himself to the Spaniard's pistol, as he no longer had use for it, and told me it was a German Luger, an automatic. Francisco said that now that him and his boys had killed a hacendado, they had better join up with the revolucionarios, and he thought that we ought to join up with them. We didn't say nothing, but as we was riding back, the wind blew this piece of paper front of my horse, and the horse shied and dumped me right out the saddle. Wasn't hurt, just kind of embarrassed, and I picked up that paper when we got back to the U.S. of A. side of the line, and by the light of the branding fire, I saw that it said in English, "Attention Gringos! Come south of the border to fight with Pancho Villa for gold and glory! Railroaders, dynamiters, machine gunners wanted." It was a damn recruiting poster for the Revolution.

Me and Ben got to doing some heavy talking. It went something like this: in all that big country, what were the chances that a piece of paper should blow right in front of my horse? It could not have been a coincidence. There must've been a purpose to it. We found out what that was a few days later, when we heard that the revolucionarios had taken over Álvarez's hacienda. Ben and me decided that we had been given a sign and that we oughta ride down there and see what was going on and join up. What we knew about machine guns and dynamite and railroading wouldn't have filled a shot glass, but we figured, what the hell. Jeff wasn't mad. Guess he was used to Ben taking off on adventures, and I think he was glad to be shed of me on account of my socialistic ideas.

1

On a raw November afternoon, when low-lying clouds made Lower Manhattan seem more claustral than usual, Gil Castle left his office early to make a five o'clock appointment with his counselor at the House of Hope. In the lobby of his building, he buttoned the collar of his trench coat, took a twist out of the belt before buckling it, aligned the buckle with the flap, then stepped out into the noise and jostle of the capital of capitalism, walking briskly down Exchange Street to catch the subway for Grand Central and the 3:17 express to Stamford. Half an inch under six feet, with graying black hair combed back in a style reminiscent of a 1940s movie actor, a trim build, and mahogany brown eyes flanking a thin raptor's nose that lent to his face the patrician severity of a Florentine prince, he made a pleasing impression on most people but his looks lacked the voltage to draw second glances from women. And in fact Castle didn't draw any as he weaved through the pedestrian crowds; he would not have been aware of them even if he had. Since Amanda's death, he had become sexually inert, dead to desire and, beyond that, to the desire for desire.

Shoulders hunched against the damp wind's bite, one hand jammed in his coat pocket, briefcase swinging from the other, he marched on toward the Exchange Street station. The faint rumble of subway trains rising through sidewalk vents, the rush of heating plants blowing exhaust on rooftops, the sounds of traffic and countless feet treading pavement fused into one sound: the hum of the New York financial district, whose frantic busyness had once energized him, now stirred up a surly resentment. He recalled the commentaries he'd heard and read after 9/11. The day when everything changed forever. *We will never be the same again.* People seemed to really believe that bullshit, to want it to be so, as if they'd been yearning for some great and terrible event to tear them from their empty pursuit of stuff and the money to buy it, from their trivial amusements, their shallow celebrity worship, their love of titillating scandals, Monica Lewinsky blowing the president in the Oval Office. But the bustle through which he passed, young men and women scurrying by with iPod buds pinned to their ears, babbling into cell phones, signified that the cataclysm that was supposed to have changed everything had changed nothing, except for the families of those slaughtered on that exquisite morning. And for the soldiers fighting and dying in Afghanistan. Otherwise New York and America had moved on. It was important in America to move on, to avoid living in the past. That, Castle supposed, made him somewhat un-American. He could not help but live in the past; it clung to him like a second skin.

His sour discontent extended to his forthcoming appointment with Ms. Hartley, his counselor or therapist or whatever she was. Her platitudes and banalities, which her mellow Lauren Bacall voice wrapped in a cloak of profundity, grated on him. Nevertheless he was going to see her, partly out of habit—he'd been attending two sessions a week for some eight or nine months, one alone with her, one with a group—and partly to keep his two daughters at bay. After the disaster Jay Strauss, head of his firm's retail division, had told him to take some time off to "get yourself back together." Morgan and Justine had become alarmed by his behavior during his leave. This sociable father of theirs, this neatnik who always tied a perfect Windsor knot and never wore the same suit twice in a row, had turned into a minor-league Howard Hughes, secluding himself in his house, going without shaving or showering for days on end, letting his hair grow long. To their minds, his unhygienic reclusiveness was evidence that far from getting himself together, he was coming further apart. Clearly an intervention was warranted.

It was Morgan, the elder and a devout believer in the nostrums of the therapeutic culture, who had found the House of Hope on the Internet. This clinic that offered counseling to the bereaved was just what he needed, she said. He *had* to realize that he wasn't alone; by sharing his suffering, he would relieve it. He'd resisted her urgings to sign up. He could not think Amanda's name without breaking into tears; to utter it aloud to a stranger was unimaginable. Even the name of the place sounded ridiculous—the House of Hope, like you went there for hope as you might go to IHOP for pancakes. Morgan, however, was used to having her way; she'd always been like that, and her job as a literary publicist—importuning reluctant newspaper editors to interview her authors, bookstore managers to set up readings and signings—had honed the trait. She roped her sister into her campaign. Jussie was in her second year at Columbia Law and employed reasoned arguments to reinforce Morgan's strident nagging. The sibling tag-team at last pummeled him into submission. How odd. His girls had become the parents, he the child.

The thirtyish Ms. Hartley was kind and earnest and much given to the cant of her profession: healing and closure and the grieving process, as if grief were something like digestion. Castle was sure she had never known grief from the inside, never felt its iron grip. Most of her advice was useless, like her suggestion that he cut his leave of absence short and return to work. She assured him that reestablishing familiar routines would do him a world of good. It did not. Nor did the presence of others in his group who had lost spouses make him feel less alone, any more than his own presence made them feel less alone. He'd discovered that deep sorrow, like bone pain, is profoundly isolating. It won't allow itself to be shared. For that matter, he did not want to share it in the hope of achieving what Ms. Hartley said was his ultimate goal—acceptance. Why should he *accept* the senseless murder of his wife by a gang of homicidal zealots?

Maybe some wounds weren't meant to heal. America seemed to have become a society dedicated to the proposition that no one should suffer, at least not for long. A Xanax in my tummy, and all's right with the world. Castle had taken to reading the Roman stoics like Seneca and certain Greek tragedians like Aeschylus, whose voices spoke to him, across an ocean of time, with a thoughtfulness and a gravity utterly absent from Ms. Hartley's psychobabble. And as in the November gloom he approached the Exchange Street station, a chorus from the *Oresteia* sang somberly in his mind's ear. *He who learns must suffer. And even now in our sleep pain that cannot forget falls drop by drop upon the heart, and in our own despair, against our will, comes wisdom to us by the awful grace of God.* Suddenly, at the station's mouth, the clammy subterranean air lofting up into his nostrils, he stopped and, without making a conscious decision, turned around and headed for Ground Zero. This was peculiar. Although HarrimanCutler's offices were only a short distance from it, he always walked blocks out of his way to avoid setting eyes on it. Two months ago, during the observances of 9/11's first anniversary, he made sure not to turn on the news. But now, for what reason he didn't know, a compulsion like a magnetic force drew him to see and smell and touch the place where Amanda had been blown to atoms, also for a reason he didn't know.

He climbed up to a platform and joined a crowd watching giant shovels take bites of debris and spew it, giant mouthful by giant mouthful, into dump trucks. Workers in hard hats and hazmat suits descended into an excavation deep as a stone quarry. Cutting torches flashed amid the wreckage, which by this time had taken on an orderly appearance. Gone were the smoking, jumbled mountains of melted steel and pulverized concrete he'd seen in photographs; gone as well the tall, jagged fragment of a tower's facade that had thrust out of the ruins like a broken idol from some vanished civilization. How strange to see so much light pouring into these streets. It wasn't a cheering light; it heightened the impression of a vast desolation, like the sun on an empty plain. What awful power had directed those nineteen men to wreak this calamity? His pastel Episcopalianism rejected the existence of the devil except as metaphor, yet the scene before him testified that real evil roamed the earth. Castle had studied the photographs of the hijackers in newspapers and newsmagazines, paying special attention to Muhammad Atta, the ringleader, the Egyptian engineer with the unsmiling mouth and hooded eyes. A sinister face, but no more sinister than the mug shot of an ordinary criminal, its lineaments offering no clue to the madness within. No, not madness. The attacks had been too well planned and executed to have been the work of lunatics. That was a new thing in Castle's experience, and it was beyond grasp—an insane act perpetrated by sane minds.

He watched the workmen, he watched a team of dogs sniffing for remains in the mass grave of three thousand human beings. Mandy's grave. Having been left without a body to bury had deepened the cruelty. Amanda hadn't been killed, she'd been *annihilated* in that supernova of exploding jet fuel.

He left the platform, ducked under a sawhorse barricade, and strode over hoses and past pumps and grinding machinery toward a mound of rubble, an incongruous figure in his pinstripes and trench coat. Spotting a hard hat on the ground, he put it on, figuring to masquerade as a city official who had business there. With the furtive movements of a shoplifter, he plunged a hand into the mound and filled a coat pocket with dirt and ash, imagining, or pretending, that it contained some remnant of Amanda. Before someone saw through his paltry disguise, he walked away quickly, dropping the hard hat. He would place the contents of his pocket in an urn, like funeral ashes. Or maybe he would scatter them over Long Island Sound, where she'd loved to sail on summer weekends. It would provide a catharsis of sorts. Closure, in Ms. Hartley's annoying argot.

The atmosphere from Ground Zero lingered as he walked back toward the subway. The air felt charged with menace, as before a thunderstorm. He'd made predictions throughout his career. The market was going to be bullish or bearish, this stock or mutual fund or commodity should be bought, sold, held. But nothing was predictable, was it? And if nothing was predictable, how was one to make sense of anything—or anyone? It was as if the fireballs of the exploding airliners had revealed a terrible truth previously hidden from him—his whole benign life and the faith it was founded on, that reason triumphs in the end, had been beautiful illusions.

As he rode the uptown train to Grand Central, paranoia overtook him. That dark-complected man in the doorway could be an Arab with a bomb or a gun concealed under his padded jacket. Why not? Anything at any moment. The policemen and National Guardsmen patrolling Grand Central did not reassure him. If some suicide bomber decided to blow himself up, right now at rush hour, they could not stop him. Beneath the zodiac on the terminal's dome, painted stars on a painted sky, Castle dodged through the hurrying crowds toward the track for the Stamford train. He'd missed the 3:17 but was on time for the next express. An unshaven derelict approaching from the side—"Hey, got some spare change?"—so startled him that he almost broke into a run.

He walked down the platform, found a nearly empty car, and sat next to the window, alert and watchful, his back stiff, his knees locked, his briefcase on the seat beside him to deter unwanted company. Afraid of what? he wondered as more passengers entered the car. Of being blown up by some fanatic from the Arabian deserts? The terrorist who killed him would be doing him a favor. Of the unknown, the unpredictable? Yes, that. Of another strike that would take someone else dear to him? That, too. Morgan, sporty, competitive Morgan, slender Justine, her willowy frame belying her tough, lawyerly mind. To lose his daughters would be unendurable. Maybe he should talk to his girls, urge them to move someplace safer, insist on it. As the soldier who loses faith in his commander trembles before the enemy, so did Castle's loss of faith in an understandable world bring on this queasy dread of the armies gathering even now in desert huts and city apartments and mountain villages to plot new outrages; the fevered armies delirious with visions of the paradise they would gain by killing themselves and hundreds or thousands of innocents who weren't innocents in their eyes but infidels deserving of death.

Soon enough the car was packed. A stylishly dressed young woman stood in the aisle, glancing at the briefcase that occupied the empty seat, then at him. She looked safe enough. He put the case on his lap, and she sat down and pulled a book from her shoulder bag. It could just as easily have been a grenade or a canister of poison gas. What was wrong with the Metro-North railroad? Airline passengers were being screened and searched and wanded as never before, but rail commuters weren't given even the most cursory once-over. Imagine releasing poison gas in a crowded car. It had happened once, in Japan he thought it was. Sarin gas, if he remembered right.

The train rolled through the underground darkness, then into the fading daylight and past the Westchester suburbs into Connecticut. As it approached Stamford, another frightening thought came to him: the stuff in his pocket was as likely to contain remains of the hijackers as anything of Amanda. He knocked his knees together, drummed the briefcase with his fingers, and even as he said to himself, *For chrissake, get a grip*, he stood up, crouching under the luggage rack, and muttered, "Excuse me," to the young woman. She swung her legs aside, and he wriggled past her into the doorway. The train stopped, the doors snapped open. He got out. In the late-autumn dusk, several commuters on the platform threw quick, puzzled looks at the well-dressed fiftyish man dipping into his coat pocket and flinging dirt over the tracks, like someone scattering grass seed over a lawn. He felt embarrassed but relieved. He called the House of Hope and canceled his appointment with Ms. Hartley, then caught the train for New Canaan.

Half an hour later he pulled into his drive on Oenoke Ridge. For ten years, he and Amanda had shared the white frame colonial with black shutters and the plaque beside the front door declaring the name of its original owner, one Seth Raymond, and the year it was built, 1801. Its windows were darkened. He unlocked the door. As always, Amanda's absence was a presence in itself. Samantha slightly deflected the blow, bolting inside through the dog door in back to prance around him, giddy, as if he'd been gone for a month. He petted her, thinking,

They live outside of time; a few hours can seem like a month to a dog. The English setter trailed him to the hall closet, where he hung his coat, then to the bar in the den, where he knocked back a scotch to calm his nerves, then upstairs to the master bedroom, where he changed into jeans and a sweatshirt. He took a piss. "I went to . . . ," he said aloud as he came out of the bathroom. He was going to tell Mandy about his visit to Ground Zero. It wasn't the first time he'd begun to speak to her before catching himself. There were times when he half-expected to see her.

To the kitchen, where he warmed two slices of leftover pizza and washed them down with several glasses of wine. To the den, where he tried to read the *Times* and the *Wall Street Journal* but couldn't get past the first paragraph of any story. He caught *Headline News* on CNN . . . Much talk about getting UN inspectors back into Iraq . . . Was there a connection between Saddam Hussein and 9/11 . . . WMD . . . A new addition to the lexicon, WMD . . . At nine-thirty he returned to the bedroom and undressed and went into the bathroom and took an Ambien. He held the bottle for a moment before putting it back in the medicine cabinet and counted the remaining pills. Six. Aware of his state of mind, his doctor allowed him only ten per prescription.

Castle fell onto the unmade bed, hands crossed over his waist. The interregnum of fear that had gripped him on the train had passed; grief, the true monarch of his heart, resumed its oppression. It was a physical sensation, like a weight on his chest, while from within came a sharp, cold prickling, as if he were breathing ground glass. Would it be this bad, he wondered, if she had died in an accidental plane crash? If she'd been murdered by a mugger? One image that kept coming back to him was of Mandy at the moment she knew she was going to die. She would not have been hysterical, she would not have been begging for mercy, she would have been crying quietly, resigned to her fate, for a phlegmatic, even a tragic temperament dwelled beneath her jaunty exterior. The picture knifed Castle right through his marrow, she imprisoned in that hurtling missile among strangers, facing her death without him, while in the cockpit Muhammad Atta, hands on the yoke and throttles, prayers to Allah on his lips, aimed for the north tower with no feeling for the lives he was about to extinguish. Amanda had been the victim of a huge atrocity calculated down to the last small detail, and that stark fact made all the difference in the world.

Samantha stood beside the bed, her long snout resting on the mattress, and whimpered a plea to have her ears tickled or her head rubbed, but he couldn't move his arms against the weight pressing down on him. Morgan had told him to sell the place and move into a condominium before he drove himself crazy. Sensible advice, but he couldn't bring himself to do it. Nor to sell Amanda's car, still in the garage, or her little sloop, still in the boatyard. He hadn't got rid of her clothes and shoes and jewelry, her hairbrushes and cosmetics and the hundred and one other things that belonged to her. Everything was as she'd left it, right down to the Tampax in the bathroom closet. Castle wasn't sure why he clung to her possessions. Ms. Hartley assured him his was a normal reaction to a traumatic loss. To remove her belongings would be to acknowledge that she really was gone, and he wasn't ready for the acceptance stage. He, or some part of him, was still in the denial stage. Another tidy explanation from the young woman whose job was to cage unruly emotions in airtight categories. Denial. Acceptance. Crap. Let the wild beasts pounce and devour, Castle thought. They will anyway.

Sam's demands for affection grew more insistent. He managed to reach over and ruffle her floppy ears. Her claws clicking on the hardwood floor, she moved to the other side of the bed. She was seven years old now, and he could not break her of the habit she'd had since she was a pup of going first to his side of the bed for a good-morning and a good-night petting, then to Mandy's. Nearly every night and every morning she would stand there for a minute or longer, as she was now, and it broke Castle's heart to see her, waiting and wagging her tail in expectation of the touch that could never come.

He remembered the last time he and Mandy made love on this same bed—the balmy night before he left for Atlanta on business, she for Boston to visit her family before she was to fly on to L.A. She had been a large woman with large, healthy appetites. She liked to eat and pummeled her body with cycling and sit-ups and swimming at the Y to keep her weight under what she called "the George Foreman range." That strong, ample body, so much life in it. Anthropologists found bones of protohumans who'd walked the earth with mastodons and saber-toothed tigers. How could there be not a fragment left of her?

There is no pain so great as the memory of joy in present sorrow. His second marriage, in contrast to the first, had been happy, happier than he thought possible. He supposed that was why his pain could find no relief—he could not forget the joys. The heaviness increased, crushing him into the mattress; it had a color—black, of course—a taste, a metallic taste, it was almost tangible. He began to weep. It had been like this for more than a year; he could see no end to it. Too many reminders, prompts to a memory that needed none: this house no longer theirs but his; the friends no longer theirs but his; the neighbors no longer theirs but his.

Go to sleep in mourning and wake up in dread of each new day, like a man with terminal cancer. The hell of this cancer was that it wasn't terminal.

He went downstairs with the movements of someone in a trance, Sam following him. In the den, surrounded by his books, by his prints of leaping trout and flushing grouse, by the trophies attesting to his triumphs in skeet-shooting matches and country-club tennis tournaments, observed from above by the heads of a whitetail buck, a bull elk, and the big glass eye of a mounted tarpon, from below by Samantha, lying on the worn, antique Bukhara, and from his desk by his mother and father, his daughters, and Amanda, with her direct, green-eyed gaze and faint smile, her upper lip thin and straight, the lower lip full, suggesting a tension between the New England rigor and the southern sensuality in her blood—her father's ancestors were Massachusetts Puritans, her mother's French Huguenots from Charleston—Castle opened a door behind which stood a tall black safe. He twirled the combination lock, and from the firearms standing upright in felt-lined racks, he selected an old Fox Sterlingworth side-by-side with a double trigger. His favorite shotgun. It had been his father's. He opened a drawer below the gun racks and took a twelve-gauge shell from out of its box and loaded the right barrel and thumbed the safety off. Turning the photographs facedown, as if to spare everyone the sight, he sat at his desk, placed the gun stock on the floor and, leaning a little forward, put the muzzle in his mouth, his thumb on the front trigger.

There he sat, looking a bit like a Turk smoking a hookah, his face wearing a relaxed, thoughtful expression. He was actually in a semblance of a cheerful mood and restrained his thumb to give himself a moment to savor it. Then his brow creased as a picture of what he would look like afterward flashed in the brain he intended to blow apart. If his daughters were to discover his body, they would be horrified. Could he do that to them? *Yes.* And what of Sam? Who would take care of her? She was more than a pet, she was his hunting buddy, a partner. Could he leave her alone? *Yes.* Yes, if by applying a little more pressure on the trigger, he would hurl himself to Amanda's side. But he wasn't convinced that that was where he would go. He envied those who believed in the immortality of the soul, but he considered himself a realist—anyone who managed half a billion in assets had to be or he would soon be out of a job—and Amanda, declared the realist, wasn't anywhere. Annihilated body *and soul.* She lived on only in his memory, and if he pressed a little harder, he would obliterate all that remained of her. There would be surcease from pain, yes, but nothing more. The end of everything. Eternal darkness. His resolve drained away as another piece of wisdom came to him: his terror of oblivion exceeded his longing for it. He took the gun out of his mouth, unloaded it, and returned it to the safe. He could almost hear the monarch cackling, *You can't get away from me that easily.*

Climbing the stairs to the bathroom, he gulped three Ambiens, not in expectation that thirty milligrams would be enough to kill him but in the certainty that they would give him an installment of death. The installment lasted nearly fourteen hours, from darkness to noon of the next day. He woke to the sound of Samantha slurping water from the toilet bowl. Dry-mouthed and groggy, his knees rubbery from the aftereffects of the drug, he sat up, cleared his head, and then shuffled downstairs to fill Sam's water dish and food bowl. In the den the red light on his answering machine was flickering—eight messages. The caller ID informed him that four were from his office, two from Morgan, and two from anonymous callers, probably telemarketers. He would deal with the office later. He played back Morgan's messages, the first just a call to find out how he was doing, the second a follow-up. "*Dad? Where are you? Are you all right? Please call me.*" A great worrier, Morgan was. A shiver passed through him when he thought of what he would have done to her had last night's attempt, or rather attempted attempt, succeeded.

He sat for a while, gazing at the tarpon hung above the doorway, the 120-pounder he'd caught years ago in the Florida Keys, and attempted to bend his normally analytical mind to his predicament. He had proven that death, the boundary beyond which all his ills could not pass, was also a boundary he could not cross until his natural time was up. He was condemned to live. But how was he to live with this pain that was like a chronic migraine of the heart? He was going to go mad if he didn't find some way out. Out. Yes, *out.* Morgan was right. Out of this memory-haunted house, and more—out of the East altogether, far away from all these reminders. It was the only solution he could think of.

From a cabinet beneath a bookcase, he removed a box containing the condolence letters and sympathy cards he had saved. Among them was a letter from Monica Erskine, his cousin Blaine's wife.

SAN IGNACIO CATTLE COMPANY
POB 651
Patagonia, Arizona 85624
Tel: 520-394-2118 E-mail: sanignacio@dakota.net

September 13, 2001

Dear Gil,

Your sister has called us with the terrible news. I have been sitting here for an hour trying to think of something to say. Everything seems so inadequate. This is an outrage beyond words. Blaine, Aunt Sally, and I cannot imagine what you must be thinking and feeling. Our sympathy (Sympathy? What a pathetic word) gets all mixed up with anger. Rage, really. There is no pit in hell deep enough or fire hot enough for the monsters who did this. We are so, so sorry we never got to meet Amanda.

We have been thinking if there is anything we can do for you. Sally suggested that you might feel a need at some point to get away for a while. If you do, we have a place for you. It's the original homestead your great-uncle Jeff built. Maybe you remember it from the last time you were out here. It isn't much, but we have fixed it up some. When we hire extra hands for branding or gathering, we put them up there. You would be most welcome to it. Just call or write or e-mail, and we'll have it ready for you.

I will write you a better letter once my mind has wrapped itself around this awful thing. All I can do for now is express my deepest condolences. Blaine and Sally do, too.

Sincerely yours,
Monica

It was a generous offer, considering that he wasn't close to anyone on his mother's side of the family. He hadn't met them until he was in his late thirties and had seen them only three or four times since. So he felt like an intruder when he phoned Monica to ask if the offer still stood. It did, she replied, surprised to hear from him after all this time.

Her recently divorced brother had been living in the place, but found it too lonesome and had moved back to Tucson. Castle said his stay might be for longer than a while. Was that all right? He would, of course, pay rent, whatever they thought was fair. Yes, she answered after a few moments' hesitation. Yes, he was welcome, and forget about rent. When could they expect him? In a few weeks.

CASTLE SPENT THOSE WEEKS methodically cutting ties. At his office he gave notice to Jay Strauss and his partners in the Castle Group, Melissa Josephson and Joyce Redding, that he was taking early retirement. They all three asked him to reconsider, but their entreaties were largely ceremonial; in the past year it had become as obvious to them as it was to Castle himself that he'd been merely going through the motions, a crippled lion who had to rely on his females to do the hunting on the veldts of the capital markets.

He informed his daughters and his younger sister, Anne, that he was leaving for good. All approved except Morgan, who in characteristic fashion argued that he was doing what the terrorists wanted, fleeing, and that it would be much better if he resumed his therapy. He crushed an impulse to tell her that the only thing babbling to the banal Ms. Hartley had accomplished was to bring him to the edge of suicide.

But for several days it looked like Castle wasn't going anywhere. He'd drawn up a long to-do list and proceeded to do nothing. The closer he came to the date he'd set for his departure, the more he felt the gravity of the familiar pulling at him. It was as though he'd grown so accustomed to his misery that he was reluctant to do anything that might alleviate it. Extraordinary measures were called for.

He purged the house of everything Amanda had owned. Strangling at birth all temptations to linger over some object or picture in bitter reverie, he cleaned out her closets and drawers, emptied her desk, tore the dresses and coats from the mothballed hanger bags in the attic, and ruthlessly added to the pile their wedding album and every photo he could of her or of them together. He stuffed the lot into plastic lawn bags and hauled them to Goodwill. He sold her sloop and her car and wished there were an agency to which he could consign the comical hum Amanda made when she couldn't or wouldn't answer some question of his, or the mock pout she put on when she suffered a minor disappointment—all the little tics that he remembered about her.

The house was on the market only a week before it sold, for twice what he'd paid for it. After he peddled his furniture at an estate sale, Anne insisted he stay with her and her husband in Redding. He then consulted with his lawyer on how best to dispose of his financial assets, which with the proceeds from the house now totaled in the low eight figures. He was surprised, and somewhat embarrassed, by how hard it was to get rid of even a minor fortune, portioning his out to various charities and conservation groups, to a scholarship fund for minority students at his prep school, Hotchkiss, and to a trust for his daughters and any future grandchildren. Combined with his generous retirement package, what remained was considerably more than enough to sustain him in style if he lived to be a hundred, which he fervently hoped he would not.

His sister held a valedictory Christmas dinner for the whole family. Morgan and Justine came in from the city and stayed the night. They cried when he left the next morning. With all his belongings fitting easily into the cargo compartment of his Suburban and with his dog for company, he saw himself as a refugee of the strange new war that had begun on a temperate September morning. Were it not for his girls, he would have felt deracinated, jobless, wifeless, parentless (his father had died of esophageal cancer at sixty-seven; his mother had fallen to a stroke three years ago).

There was no rush, and he made the trip in easy stages, watching the landscapes change from hills to plains to desert to mountains and back to desert. He caught the New Year's Eve celebrations in Times Square on a motel-room TV in New Mexico, spent New Year's Day driving through eastern Arizona, and at last, a week after starting out, arrived at the San Ignacio.

His house in New Canaan had had twelve rooms, his new dwelling two, heated by a wood-burning stove. It was off the grid, electricity supplied by a generator, and was sheltered in a grove of Emory oaks backed by a ridge and sided by two low hills. The front porch, supported by varnished pine posts, looked out upon the grasslands and tree-speckled canyons of the San Rafael Valley, rolling away to the Patagonia Mountains and the San Antonios in Mexico, a view most people would have described as "breathtaking" or "inspirational." Castle did not find it so. Although he wasn't blind to the beauty of his surroundings and was grateful that there was nothing in them to prompt the wrong memories, he hadn't come out for inspiration and breathtaking vistas, nor with any illusions that living close to nature in the great American West would release him from his despotic grief and the fear it sometimes permitted to share its reign. An easing of his bondage, not an ending, was all he expected of his solitary life in the sequestered adobe. It was a kind of halfway house between the iron lockdown he'd known and the liberation he'd sought with a twelve-gauge shotgun.

2

SOMETHING WAS OUTSIDE. Something she'd heard or smelled on the cold drafts sneaking through the cracks in the window frames roused Samantha from her sleep and drew her to the door. Castle caught her movement out of the corner of his eye as he sat reading—the movement not of the dog herself but of her shadow, passing along the wall on the opposite side of the room. He laid the book on his lap and looked at her as she faced the door, so alert and motionless that she and her silhouette resembled two dogs on point. A low growl deep within her chest made her sound more menacing than she was.

"Just a coyote, maybe javelina," Castle said. "Lie down, Sam."

The dog responded neither to the reassurance nor to the command, rumbling at whatever had disturbed her, coyote or javelina, maybe something more dangerous, like a bear or mountain lion. Then she started barking, which she did only when a two-legged stranger approached the house. Castle went to the door and called, "Who's there? Anyone there?" He hadn't heard a car drive up. Someone on foot, and out here on a frigid January night could only be a *mojado*—a wetback, a gross misnomer in a land where the rivers ran dry ten months of the year—or a *burrero*, as the drug runners were called. Blaine and Monica had warned him that the valley was a highway for contraband people and narcotics. He waited for whoever or whatever was out there to pass on, but as Sam kept barking, he threw on his coat, got a spotlight, and to stop the dog from bolting outside, opened the door just enough to allow himself through. No wind and no moon, and the brighter stars—Sirius, Rigel, Aldebaran—looked close enough to touch. His breath plumed in the cold. It surprised him, how cold winter nights could be on the high desert, as cold as the New England he'd left barely more than two weeks ago. He swept the light over his car and the rock-walled shed that housed the well-pump and generator, pointed it into the pool of solid blackness made by the clustering oaks. Seeing nothing, he circled around and shined the lantern at the ridge behind the house. The beam caught a fleeting patch of white, and a moment later he heard branches cracking as a large animal moved through the trees. It must have been a deer flagging its tail in flight. He stood listening for a few seconds. The silence was total, the sort of silence he imagined prevailed on some dead planet.

Inside, her alarm over, Sam had returned to her fleece bed beside the stove. She raised her eyes to him as he hung his coat on a wall peg near the door.

"Since when? Since when did you start barking at deer?"

Castle pulled another log from the firewood tub and tossed it into the stove, then settled back into his chair to resume reading. Seneca's *Ad Marciam de consolatione.* The Loeb Classical Library edition, in the red covers, with the Latin text facing the English translation. He'd sent away for these books so he could read Seneca in the original in an attempt to reacquaint himself with the Latin he'd studied at Hotchkiss but had long since forgotten. The mental discipline of translating was good for him, stopped him from thinking on his bad nights. Tonight was that kind of night.

No, there was nothing out here to bid memories, but they came anyway, striking without warning. Earlier he'd been grilling the quail he'd shot that day on an old stone barbecue pit he'd repaired with the help of Gerardo Murrieta, the ranch's full-time cowboy. He'd hunted with Sam two hours in the morning, another two in the afternoon, and came home with five birds in his game vest. He got a mesquite fire going, and while the wood burned down to coals, he cleaned and plucked the quail and stuffed sage into their cavities and brushed the skin with a mixture of garlic and olive oil before placing them on the grill. As he drew in the scent of sizzling meat, his eye reached out to the tin roofs and the windmill of ranch headquarters, on a flat below him, and beyond to the bare cottonwoods fringing the Santa Cruz River, and then across the breadth of the San Rafael, the pale winter grass almost white in the dusk and speckled by the red and black hides of grazing cattle.

As he was turning the birds, Amanda stepped out of the shower and embraced him from behind and nibbled the back of his head and neck and both shoulders. There, by the smoking grill in the desert twilight, Castle could hear her husky voice and feel her wet lips on his skin. Of all his memories, this was the most frequent and the most vivid, too vivid to be called a memory; a reexperiencing, rather, and it brought on the same cold grating in his lungs, like breathing ground glass, that he'd felt so often before. "Oh, Christ, Mandy, Mandy," he cried aloud, his eyes flooding. He turned away from his task, unable to go on with it, and did not shed tears so much as heave them in violent spasms. By the time he recovered, the quail were charred to a crisp. He fed them to his dog.

Quam in omni vita servasti morum prohibitatem ver cundiam . . . Quam in omni vita servasti morum prohibitatem ver cundiam, in hac quoque at praestabis; est enim in quaedam at dolandi modestia. Trying to unravel that sentence practically tore the ligaments in his brain. He reached into the magazine rack for his Latin textbook, an artifact from his prep school days, but it was of no help. In defeat, he turned to the English translation on the opposite page. *That correctness of character which you have maintained all your life, you will exhibit in this matter also; for there is such a thing as moderation even in grieving.*

Marcia, the recipient of Seneca's essay, had lost a beloved son in his youth, and Castle wondered how she'd reacted to such bleak consolation. There is such a thing as moderation even in grieving? (Much as he admired Seneca, he often argued with him across the gulf of two thousand years.) I don't think so, except when the loss isn't much—your old aunt Tillie, say. But when the loss is grave, and the pain scalds your nerves until they're numb, leaving only an emptiness as if all your organs have been sucked out and your skin and bones become a vessel for a vacuum, well, how do you moderate that, Lucius Annaeus Seneca?

He read on, following the translation. *So many funerals pass our doors, yet we never think of death . . . Who of us ever ventured to think upon exile, upon want, upon grief?* He underlined those phrases, and then these: *That man lost his children; you also may lose yours . . . Such is the delusion that deceives and weakens us while we suffer misfortunes which we never foresaw that we ourselves could possibly suffer. He robs present ills of their power who has perceived their coming beforehand.* Starting another argument, Castle scribbled in the margin, "True, but so many things can't be foreseen." Like fanatics hijacking airliners and turning them into guided missiles, he thought. But with Seneca's larger point he agreed, at least insofar as it applied to himself. He hadn't foreseen any evil befalling him for the simple reason that none ever had.

A fortunate son all right, raised in Tokeneke, where shaded private roads wound past the mansions of board chairmen and Wall Street lawyers and investment bankers. It was the toniest neighborhood in Darien, tony enough in its own right, a Wasp preserve when he was growing up, not a synagogue within the town limits, just one Catholic church—a mere chapel compared with St. Luke's Episcopalian—and the only blacks to be seen were those who cleaned the houses or bused tables at the Tokeneke Club. His father was a cardiologist whose patients included many of those same chairmen, lawyers, and investment bankers, along with a few prominent New York and Connecticut politicians. The doctor had also inherited a respectable portfolio from Castle's grandfather, a social-climbing contractor who'd Americanized his surname (his father, one Giuliano Castelli, had emigrated from Italy in the 1880s), married a New England Brahmin, and had the moxie to say yes when a friend named Thomas Watson asked if he would invest in Watson's new company, International Business Machines.

Castle's mother, Grace, who liked to joke that she was "an Arizona cowgirl what done right good for herself" in marrying a doctor from a moneyed eastern family, finished her education after the war, and began teaching English at a private school in Stamford. She was active in the kinds of charities that drew women of her status, but she always made time for Gil and his sister, helping them with their homework, taking them to tennis lessons, riding lessons, sailing lessons. She tended to dote on him, creating in Anne a resentment that persisted into adulthood. Other than that, theirs was a happy family, and since, as Tolstoy famously remarked, all happy families are alike, there was nothing more to be said about it.

Castle's future was assured from birth. All he had to do was walk into it, and he did, proceeding from Darien Country Day to Hotchkiss to Princeton to the Wharton School, spared from Vietnam by student deferments and from the excesses of the sixties by a moderateness inherent in his nature. After Wharton he learned his craft at a small brokerage house, then was hired by HarrimanCutler, fourth-largest investment firm on the planet. He became a star in the retail division, rising to senior vice president and senior consultant, then was elected to the Executive Club, reserved for the firm's top producers. At fifty, he knew he'd gone as high as he could go. Whatever it took to summit in the ranges of pure capitalism—an overweening greed, a driving ambition born of some deep insecurity—was missing in Gillespie Castle. And that was all right. He was very well off, insulated from all financial shocks short of a nine-plus on the economic Richter scale.

Misfortune has a way of choosing some unprecedented means or other of impressing its power on those who might be said to have forgotten it. Forgotten it? he asked himself with some bitterness. He'd scarcely known it. His father's death at a relatively early age and his mother's a decade later had been blows but didn't qualify as tragedies. Otherwise he could think of only one misfortune that had clouded his clement existence before September 11, 2001: his divorce from his first wife. It was not the garden-variety suburban breakup—Eileen had left him for another woman—and there had been some savage arguments over child custody early in the proceedings. Castle, as conventional as he was temperate, objected to their daughters growing up in a Sapphic household and petitioned for primary custody. Eileen argued that her sexual orientation had no bearing on her rights as a mother. They battled for months through their lawyers but reached a settlement eventually, with as little bloodshed as could be hoped for. The judge, Solomon-like, split the difference, formulating a complicated arrangement by which Morgan and Justine would spend exactly 182 days a year with their father and 183 with their mother and same-sex stepparent.

Some two years later, through mutual friends, he met Amanda Farmington. In one more year they were married in Boston, the reception held at her parents' yacht club in Hingham.

In his drafty cloister on the Arizona desert, he heard once again the dance music drifting over the harbor, the clang of bell buoys, the quarrelsome cries of seagulls coming to him from across a continent, from out of the unrecoverable past. *No pain so great as the memory of joy in present sorrow.* He was crying again, though not as he had earlier in the day—a kind of seepage from his eyes. He pondered the only original idea he'd heard Ms. Hartley express: that his remembered joys tormented him because he was exaggerating them, transforming his marriage into a perfect idyll, much as a refugee transforms his lost homeland into an Eden that never existed. He considered that proposition in the hopes of finding in it some truth to dull the hurt; but he concluded that he was not the victim of a delusion. Yes, he and Amanda had quarreled over one thing or another—she had a short fuse, her eruptions of temper startling by their contrast with her usual composure. But he could not recall a moment when he'd regretted marrying her, nor a moment when he'd felt even a passing attraction to someone else. On the mornings when he woke before she did, he would turn over and look at her serene face and think how lucky he was. His one mistake had been to believe his luck would last.

He went to the kitchen and poured himself a scotch, measuring its depth with three fingers laid against the glass. Then he returned to his chair and his Seneca, and fell asleep, the book open on his lap. Sam, licking his arm, woke him at two A.M. He got into his long underwear and went to bed.

Rising at seven, he put on fur-lined slippers and a wool robe and hopped down the path to the shed and turned on the generator. A heavy frost lay on the grass, and the whole valley glittered in the morning sunlight. The outside thermometer read twenty-two degrees. It was no more than fifty inside, the fire having died during the night. He built a new one, then stood rubbing his hands over the cast-iron stove. His father, a passionate outdoorsman and an admirer of Teddy Roosevelt, would have approved of these rigors. Like TR, Dr. Castle feared that privilege bred pansies and took his son on hunting, fishing, and camping expeditions in the Adirondacks from an early age. He'd also signed him up, in the summer of Gil's fourteenth year, for boxing lessons at an inner-city gym in Bridgeport. From June to August, Castle banged the heavy bag and the speed bag and sparred with black and Hispanic boys, who taught him what it was like to get hit and to bleed. He was an athletic kid with quick reflexes, but he proved to be an indifferent fighter, mostly because he was reluctant to hit back. He was more adept with a rod and gun. By the time he finished Hotchkiss, he could cast a fly sixty feet to a rising trout and was outshooting his father and his cronies on the skeet range at the venerable Campfire Club in Chappaqua. On a Christmas vacation, at a hunting camp in upstate New York, he bagged his first deer, a six-point buck. One shot at a hundred yards.

His hands warmed, Castle put coffee on the propane range. While it brewed, he fetched his boots and brush pants from the bedroom and got dressed in front of the stove, now throwing off waves of heat. The coffeepot, a vintage percolator with fire-blackened enameled sides, filled the room with its aroma. He poured a mug full and sat at the table, reflecting on the peculiarity of his ending up here, in the cabin his great-uncle built when Arizona was still a territory. Had he come to dwell in a place like this involuntarily, he would have been seen as a man who'd fallen from a pinnacle of success, the victim of a financial collapse, of alcoholism or drug addiction. But he'd chosen to live here, and he liked the bare-bones simplicity of it. The main room was maybe twelve by eighteen feet, the kitchen at one end, the sitting area at the other, furnished with a couple of old armchairs over which ratty cowhides had been draped. The bedroom was just large enough to accommodate a double bed, a small dresser, and an ancient Mexican armoire, the several colors it had worn over the years showing through the chips in its present coat of aquamarine. The bathroom, added on when indoor plumbing came to the ranch, was no bigger than a closet and equipped with fixtures—a rust-streaked pedestal sink, a metal shower stall, a toilet with a wooden seat and flush tank—that belonged in a museum.

Finished with his coffee, he took last night's dinner dishes from the drying rack and stacked them in the cupboard, then made his bed in a fashion that would have passed a boot-camp inspection. Order was critical; if he let this place become a mess, he himself might begin to delaminate. He buckled a beeper collar to Sam's neck, uncased his twenty-gauge Beretta, and went outside. As he was about to open the cargo door of his dust-filmed Suburban, he caught his imperfect reflection in the rear window and was startled to see that the face staring back at him was a replica of his father's in his sixties, the stubble on his jaw sparkling with silver. Recalling the time he had let himself go, alarming his daughters, he reminded himself to shave when he got back.

He opened the cargo door, and as he retrieved his stained hunting vest from the interior, Sam jumped in, immediately settling herself on her sheepskin bed.

"Out," he said, tugging her collar. The dog looked at him, confused. "C'mon, out. We're sticking close to home today."

She leaped to the ground. He turned on the beeper and set off, climbing the ridge behind the house. Sam was over it well ahead of him, the two-tone ranging beep growing fainter as she ran down the far side. At the top he paused to catch his breath and take in the intimidating vastness of the country. A narrow arroyo ditched the canyon below, while in the distance, beyond cinnamon-brown foothills dotted with dark green oaks and junipers, the Huachucas rose to nearly ten thousand feet, their upper slopes darkened by dense pine forests and their peaks covered in snow, as if some fragment of the Colorado Rockies had broken off and drifted into the southwest. His eye followed the mountains in their fall toward Mexico, where a desert plateau reached to a horizon as ruler-straight as the horizon on a tranquil sea, except for a cone-shaped mountain, rising far away in Sonora.

The collar's point-beep went off, steady and insistent. Sam had found birds. He couldn't see her, but she sounded fairly close. He sidestepped down the ridge toward the arroyo, stumbling on the rocks and shale camouflaged by the knee-high grass. Last night's sadness had faded, and yet this thought—If there is a God in heaven, and if He sheds his awful grace, He will cause me to trip and fall this moment and the gun to go off and make an end—streaked into Castle's mind. It streaked out when he spotted Sam, on a hard point under an oak tree, her white coat shining in the broken light, her neck outstretched and nose low to the ground, her tail extended like a feathered lance. It was a sight he'd beheld countless times, and it never ceased to thrill him. In the quivering tension between her instinct to pounce and her breeding to hold fast, there was a beauty that made him feel he could go on after all. This was why he hunted with her—she got him through the day.

The birds Sam was pointing were Mearns' quail, a species that held so tight, a hunter practically had to step on them to put them in the air. Castle approached slowly, the gun in his crooked elbow. He'd decided not to shoot these quail. Shooting them would somehow spoil the magic. He was two feet behind Sam when a male and female broke cover, flying away in a V. Sam flinched but stayed put.

"Good girl," he said softly. "More in there, eh?"

He took a few steps and stood alongside the dog. The covey exploded almost from underfoot, a land mine of feathers and beating wings. One bird slapped his hat brim as it took off, the others flushed in every direction, the sudden change from silent arrest to swift and noisy motion simply breathtaking. Castle fired twice into the air, to give Sam the impression that he'd shot and missed. He didn't want her to think that all her effort had been wasted.

Immediately she bounded off, circling to find the singles and doubles from the broken covey. Partway up the ridge, where a couple of birds had flown, she stopped as if she'd hit a wall. She did not strike a point but merely stood still, staring into a manzanita thicket.

"What've you got?" he said, walking toward her.

Something moved in the thicket, a dark shape. Thinking it might be a javelina, he put the gun in his shoulder and thumbed the safety. A boar javelina could disembowel a dog with its tusks.

"Get away from there, Sam. Sam! Come!"

She didn't move. When he was five or ten yards away, Castle heard a low groan, almost human. He crept closer—and made a quick jump backward when he saw a man lying amid the tangled, reddish branches of the manzanita, a young, brown-faced man with matted black hair wearing sneakers, dirt-smeared khaki jeans, and a dark blue padded jacket. As Castle parted the branches with his gun barrel, he raised his head and let out a hoarse cry: "¡No! ¡Por Dios! ¡No!" The Mexican was shivering. His filthy clothes and the burrs and grass stuck in his hair indicated that he'd spent the night out here. A wonder he hadn't frozen to death.

Always trust your dog, Castle thought. This must have been the intruder Sam had barked at last night. He broke the gun and unloaded it and showed the man the two shells before putting them in his pocket. "It's okay. Don't be afraid."

Though he'd seen border crossers before at a distance, huddled wretchedly at roadsides, waiting under the watchful gazes of the Border Patrol agents for the big buses marked DEPARTMENT OF HOMELAND SECURITY to take them to the station for processing and deportation, this was the first one he'd encountered face-to-face. He wasn't sure what to do.

"Agua," the man whispered. "¿Tiene agua? Por favor."

Castle pulled a water bottle from out of the game pocket in the back of his vest and, kneeling down, put the bottle to the man's mouth. He seized it with both hands and gulped, water dribbling down his chin.

"Gracias, señor."

"Can you walk?" How the hell did you say it in Spanish? "Like this." He spread two fingers and moved them back and forth. "Comprende?"

The Mexican looked at him quizzically. "¿Usted . . . americano?"

That was easy enough. Castle nodded.

"¿Estoy en los Estados Unidos?"

"I don't understand. No comprendo."

"Esto . . ." The man patted the ground with his hand, then waved it in a semicircle. "¿Estados Unidos? Yewnayta Stays?"

"Okay. Yes. Sí. This is the United States. Sí."

"Gracias a Dios." He locked his hands and raised them toward the sky. "Gracias a Dios," he repeated, then clutched Castle's arms in tears. "Y usted también, señor. Gracias, mil gracias."

The display of gratitude moved Castle and somehow embarrassed him. "Can you walk?" Again, he mimicked walking with his fingers.

The man tried to stand but couldn't until Castle clasped him under his arms and pulled him to his feet. He took a couple of steps, then dropped to his knees. "No lo puedo. No más caminar."

That must be it. Caminar. Walk. The Mexican was no more than five feet four or five but was heavyset.

"What's your name?" Castle pointed at him. "You. Name. Uh . . . Cómo . . . Cómo . . ."

"Miguel. Me llamo Miguel."

"Okay, Miguel. We have to get you to some help. Uh . . . necesario . . . caminar, necesario. I can't carry you over this—" he gestured at the steep ridge. "¿Comprende?"

"Sí."

Castle got him up again, and draping Miguel's arm over his shoulders, his own arm around Miguel's waist, started to climb.

Ben Erskine

Transcript 2—T.J. Babcock

We left at sunup on a warm, windy day in the spring of the year 1911. The grass was still winter yellow, but the cottonwoods along the Santa Cruz were budding out. Ben was wearing that German pistol, even though Álvarez had shot off most of the bullets in it and Ben didn't have any to replace them. He had his six-gun in his saddlebag and a Winchester Model 94 in his saddle scabbard. His pa's old rifle, he said. I was armed in a like way, and the both of us were pretty excited. It was a fine day, and we was a-goin to war for gold and glory and the little-shots of Old Mexico!

Álvarez's hacienda was only about ten miles south of the line, and we got there before noon. We rode up to a low rise and could see it below us and a little ways off, in some cottonwoods beside a dry wash. The place looked like one of those old Spanish missions—there was the main house and a chapel and some outbuildings, with an adobe wall all around. A lot of horses were picketed outside the wall, and smoke from campfires was curling up through the trees and bending back and stretching out in the wind like horsetails. In a minute, a band of revolucionarios come loping out of the trees, maybe a dozen. They were dressed in every which way, and all of them were armed to the teeth with every kind of pistol and Mauser and Winchester, with the bullets in their bandoliers like rows of brass teeth. The one thing that was the same was this red sash each one had around his waist. They was a right colorful group, I will tell you that. And you could see by the way they rode, easy and relaxed, like each man and his horse wasn't a horse and man but one thing, that they'd been vaqueros before they were revolucionarios, or maybe banditos, or maybe both.

They pulled up a few yards in front of us, and I can't say they looked welcoming. Their jefe, a light-skinned fella with a nose like an eagle's beak and eyes like an eagle, you know, real alert but with nothing behind them, eased on up to us. He said in this soft voice—you almost couldn't hear him but it gave you a chill, that softness—"¿Quiénes son ustedes? ¿Por qué ustedes están aquí?"

Ben took out that recruiting paper and held it out to him, but he didn't move a finger, just stared, so then Ben said, "Somos americanos, y estamos aquí para luchar por Pancho Villa y la revolución."

The jefe didn't say nothing for maybe five seconds, and then he started to laugh. Thought he was gone to split a seam, and them others laughing right along, and when they got done having a good time, he asked for our guns and said, "Vengan conmigo," in that quiet voice that made it feel like the temperature had gone down thirty degrees.

We was brought into a big room where we found out that the fella we thought was the jefe wasn't. The real chief was standing behind a big desk with two other men, looking at a map that covered the desk like a tablecloth. He was tall for a Mexican, pretty close to mine and Ben's height, and he had a big black mustache that swooped out like he had crow's wings pasted under his nose, and he was wearing a regular sort of uniform with brass buttons and all and a Sam Brown belt and holster with one of them Luger pistols. We stood there for a long time, while he talked with his compadres and looked at that map, and then he dismissed the two men and looked us up and down and introduced himself as Colonel Candelario Bracamonte, comandante of El Batallón de la Banda Roja, meaning the Red Sash Battalion.

Next thing, he said, in passable English—he was an educated man—that he wasn't sure if he should enlist us or have us shot as gringo spies. He said that President Taft had ordered twenty thousand American troops to the border because the Americans wanted Díaz to stay in power to make Mexico safe for them to do business in. So maybe Ben and me was scouts for this army President Taft was sending.

Then he changed his tune. Said he'd heard that we'd taken part in the liberation of Rancho Santa Barbara and Hacienda Álvarez. We nodded like we was bobbing for apples, didn't say a word that all we'd come down to do was rustle cattle. Long and the short of it was, the colonel believed us and told the fella we'd thought was the jefe to give us back our rifles and pistols and to enroll us in the company of Capitán Ybarra. He grinned a little and told us we'd find Capitán Ybarra an interesting commanding officer.

We found out what he meant when we went out into the courtyard to get signed up. Capitán Ybarra was Capitán Ynez Ybarra, what the revolucionarios called a soldadera, a lady soldier. There was a lot of them in the Revolution, but Ben and me didn't know that then, and we couldn't think what to make of her, with her long Indian skirt and cavalry boots and a pistola and a gunbelt that looked like it was made out of bullets. She couldn't have been more than twenty years old and two inches over five foot. Her hair was coal black and tumbled down to her waist under a stiff, wide-brimmed hat—it reminded me of the hats the mission padres wore. The thing you noticed right off was her face, not because she was beautiful because she wasn't. I don't mean she was ugly, just not beautiful, with this dark mestizo skin and a Yaqui's hawklike nose. The saddest face I'd ever seen, her mouth turned down so you thought she was gone to start crying and this sorrowfulness in her black eyes, but a special kind of sorrowfulness—there was a fire behind it you could see if you looked close, kind of like a candle flame burning behind a window shade. What that face did to you if you were a man was to make you want to touch it real soft like and to be afraid of touching it at the same time, like maybe she'd bite your finger off.

For old T.J. Babcock it was love at first sight.

I will tell you, it is right distracting to find yourself in love with your new commanding officer, but I won't get into that, at least not for now.

Ynez gave us the once-over and asked if we was surprised that their capitán was a woman, and Ben answered that we were, and she said she could ride, shoot, and fight as good as any man, and Ben said we did not doubt she could, and she said she would not allow no man to be in her outfit who couldn't ride and shoot as good as her. Francisco, who was standing nearby, vouched that we was muy hombres, and Ynez said she wanted to see for herself and told us to follow her. She went out the courtyard, and watching that gal walk, her shoulders throwed back, her skirt swishing around her boots with their spurs, and her hips swinging under the skirt, I fell deeper in love, and deeper yet after she'd saddled this little bay mare and jumped onto its back like she was spring-loaded.

Ben and me mounted up, and we rode out of the cottonwoods easy like, Ynez with a quirt between her teeth, and when we was out in the open she put quirt and spurs to that mare and took off across the desert fast as a jockey in the stretch. Ben and me had one helluva time keeping up with her. She was making straight for a clump of mesquite, with us galloping alongside her. For a second it looked like she was gone to ride right through them thorny trees, but when she was maybe a yard short, she turned that mare on a dime and spun around them and then ran for another clump a ways away and did the same thing. It was like the barrel races you see in rodeos.

She pulled up and drew her pistol and pointed at a rock on top of a low hill maybe fifty yards off and said, "I want you to hit that rock like this." She shot, and the dust flew off that rock, which wasn't no bigger than a basket. It is right hard to hit a target that size from that distance with a pistol when you are standing up, much less from the saddle, like Ynez done. Ben drew the Luger, and I aimed my revolver, and just as we were about to fire, what should come loping up over the hill but a coyote. Ynez yelled, "Shoot him!" I let go and hit a good yard short, and the coyote took off a-running. Ben got off the two rounds left in the Luger, and the coyote tumbled ass over teakettle and laid down dead. Ynez looked at him in this admiring way that made me jealous.

"Bueno," she said. "Tomorrow night we will find out how well you fight. There is a detachment of Díaz's soldiers in Santa Cruz. We are going to attack them."

Ben said he knew Santa Cruz, had been there many times. Ynez asked him how well he knew it, and Ben said he was familiar with every street—it wasn't much of a town.

"Good," said Ynez. "You will be at my side and help me direct the company. Our mission will be to seize the plaza."

I got a little bit more jealous, and as we was riding back to the hacienda, I thought I'd talk to her some, in the way of getting her interested in me. You wouldn't know it to look at me now, but when I was young, I never had no problem acquiring female companionship. I asked her where she'd learned to ride and shoot, and she told me that her husband had taught her. Well, it kind of dampened my hopes to hear that she was married, until she said that her husband was dead, killed a couple of months before in a battle, and she'd taken over the company he commanded and so become a soldadera. Well, my hopes went up again but got the wet-blanket treatment in the next minute when she said, "I loved Luis more than my own life, and now I love his memory." So now I was jealous of a dead man. I wanted to say that a memory can't love you back and that I could, but I kept my mouth shut.

Losing her husband had put that tragical look on her face, and the way he died lit the fire behind it. He'd been captured by federal troops, and they strangled him with barbed wire and left his body for the buzzards and the varmints. Ynez hardly recognized him when she found him. "I hate them," she said. "I hate them all," and then she let out a string of cuss words I would not repeat to you in English or Spanish.

Back at the hacienda she gave us our red sashes from out of a chest that was full of them. We put 'em on and kind of strutted around, like we'd just taken Mexico City. Along about late afternoon Ynez and the other company commander, fella nicknamed El Agave, shouted orders for the battalion to muster in formation.

Colonel Bracamonte come out of the house with his uniform all buttoned up and wearing a sword with two fellas beside him. One of them called out, "¡Batallón! ¡Atención!" Six fellas from our company fell out of ranks and lined up a few yards in front of the wall that surrounded the courtyard, holding their rifles alongside their legs. And there's my Ynez standing next to them. Lord, it was to be an execution, and that's when I felt this excitement, except it wasn't excitement exactly, there was something else mixed up with it that I don't have the word for . . . Dread, I reckon. Excitement mixed up with dread, so I couldn't tell the one from the other.

The colonel, stiff and soldierlike, walked over to the firing squad and said to bring the prisoners out. I hadn't noticed before that there was a fella standing guard by the door to this tiny chapel. The guard went inside, and him and a couple of others dragged out two young men with their hands tied behind their backs and a priest and a woman of fifty-odd, real tall and wearing a frilly dress and high-button shoes like she was going to a dance. I will never forget that woman. She had this dignified way about her. Dignified and haughty, too. You could have thought she was the queen of Spain herself. Well, turns out it was Doña Álvarez and her sons.

The priest was reading from his prayer book and made the sign of the cross over Álvarez's sons as the guards stood them against the wall and put blindfolds on them. Some more guards was holding on to Doña Álvarez and the padre, I guess to make sure they didn't interfere with the execution. That woman was staring at the firing squad like she could have killed them with her look. One thing I remember was the light. It was late in the afternoon, and the light hit the pale yellow wall and made it look like it was made of buttermilk. I don't know why that sticks in my mind.

Colonel Bracamonte read something about Álvarez's sons being guilty of crimes against the Revolution, and then he raised his sword and ordered the firing squad to take aim. Doña Álvarez shouted out, "¡Valentía, mis hijos!" One of them was having trouble being brave, shaking like he had the palsy.

I am not ashamed to tell you that I shut my eyes when the guns went off. I just couldn't look at them two fellas, no older than me and Ben, shot down like that, no matter what crimes they'd committed. When I opened my eyes again, I saw blood spattered on the wall and the chips the bullets made and the two bodies laying in the dust and the woman I was in love with stand over them and give each one a finishing shot in the head. Doña Álvarez screamed that she was a murderous bitch and that all of us was murderers and criminals and butchers. She got free of the fella that was holding on to her and knelt down by her dead sons and kept yelling, "¡Puta homicida! ¡Asesinos! ¡Criminales!" Ynez laid a hand on her shoulder and stroked her hair and bent down to say something to her—I couldn't hear what but figured she was trying to give her some words of comfort, if there was any comfort you could give a woman who'd just seen what she had—and then Ynez stepped back and shot Doña Álvarez in the back of the head. It happened so quick I didn't have time to shut my eyes, so I saw this spray fly out from the front of her head, and her thrown forward onto whatever was left of her face, which couldn't have been much.

Now it was the padre's turn to start carrying on. He hollered out that every last one of us was gone to burn in the fires of hell—the last thing he ever got to say. Colonel Bracamonte shot him down. Come to find out later that the colonel hated priests more than anything. A donkey cart was brought up and the bodies loaded into it, and as it was being driven out the courtyard to wherever the graves was to be dug, Bracamonte turned to us and said, "¡Mueran todos los Diazistas! ¡Viva la revolución! ¡Viva Madero!" The battalion shouted the same words back at him, and while all that shouting was a-going on, Ben turned to me and said, "T.J., we have thrown in with a mighty rough bunch," and I started to laughing. Couldn't stop myself, couldn't figure out what the hell I was laughing at.

Around sundown the revolucionarios had them a big fiesta. They started in to playing these revolutionary songs, corridos de la revolución. "La Adelita" is the one I remember best—it was about a woman a soldier falls in love with.

I wasn't in much of a fiesta mood, owing to what I'd seen that day, but when I heard the second verse, I got all achy inside. Si Adelita quisiera ser mi esposa. That's what I wanted—to make Ynez my wife and dress her in satin. I'd watched her kill a woman in cold blood, and I was still in love with her. I couldn't make no sense of it.

Well, I had plenty of rivals for her affections. I'd say half the battalion was looking at her all moon-eyed while they sang that song. She was their Adelita. I asked her to dance, and she said yes, but she wouldn't let me hold her close. I asked her how come she shot Doña Álvarez. She looked up at me with that mournful face and said it was because she felt sorry for her, that she wanted to spare her the pain of living out her life with the memory of her sons and her husband. The priest had forgiven the boys their sins, so they was in heaven now, and Doña Álvarez was with them. You know, if I hadn't been raised up in Mexico, I would have thought that a right strange reason to kill somebody.

Some fella tried to cut in on me, and I told him más tarde, muchacho. I had something to say to Ynez and I said it. I was in love with her. She laughed. I think that was the only time I ever saw her laugh. I've got to ask you to pardon my language again. Ynez had a foul mouth and said that I wasn't in love with her, that all I wanted was, you know, *chingar,* fuck, because that was all gringos wanted from Mexican women. She let go of me and walked off, but damn if I didn't see just a little bit of interest in them black eyes of hers.

The fiesta went on till Bracamonte ordered everyone to hit the hay. Me and Ben got our bedrolls and stretched out next to our horses. He laid his head on his saddle and was snoring inside of thirty seconds, but I had too many mixed-up thoughts buzzing through my head. I poked him in the ribs and told him I couldn't get no shut-eye. He cussed me and said that I might have the decency to let him get some. I said that the executions didn't seem right somehow. Ben reckoned they wasn't, but this here was a war. He was a hard man, Ben was, harder than me, he'd got himself accustomed to bloodshed somehow. Then he sat up and got out his makings and rolled one for himself and one for me and we smoked and he thought for a spell and said that these Messican revolutionaries—I never could get him to say "Mexican" the right way—appeared to be folks long on justice and short on mercy, and that we had best keep that in mind. I told him that Ynez had killed Doña Álvarez out of mercy so she could be in heaven with her boys and her husband.

Ben thought that was the most damn fool thing he'd ever heard, and finally I got it off my chest, that I was in love with Ynez. Now *that,* said Ben, was even more of a damn fool thing. Ben was funny when it come to women. One time when we was in Mexico on a cattle-buying trip, I'd drug him over to a cantina in Nogales where we could line us up a couple of señoritas, and he wanted nothing to do with the ladies of the night, nor the day neither. Said he wasn't gone to do that with no gal till he was married. I argued with him that a wife would expect her husband to know what the hell he was doing and how could he if he hadn't some practice. And he said he'd learned to walk without practice. I reminded him that he'd crawled first, but he didn't see my logic. Anyway, he snubbed out his cigarette and told me to stop thinking with what was between my legs and to get some sleep. We were a-going into battle inside of twenty-four hours, and if I didn't have a clear head I might get myself killed.

I damn near did.

We got rousted out at dawn. First order of business was looting the hacienda's storerooms for flour and beans and coffee and whatever else might come in handy. While all that was going on, a crowd of peons come marching down the ranch road and gathered outside the walls and asked to see the jefe. These peons raised corn and alfalfa and other crops on the Santa Barbara, and they wanted to know what was to become of them now that the rancho was under new ownership.

Colonel Bracamonte stood up on a box and told them that the rancho sure enough did have new owners and they were it. Bracamonte threw them a big white grin under that big black mustache, but them peons just stared at him without a word. It took him a while to get the idea across, but finally some of them got it, so when Bracamonte called out Viva la revolución, they shouted it back at him.

The battalion left for Santa Cruz middle of the afternoon. The plan was to make a night attack on the federal garrison. That country down there didn't look no different than in Arizona, grasslands and arroyos and mesquite and prickly pear and so damn many rocks you thought that God didn't rest on the seventh day but made rocks and dumped 'em all right there. We rode cross-country, to make sure nobody could alert Díaz's troops that we were a-coming. Our company was in the lead, with the colonel and his aides leading us and the Yaquis maybe half a mile ahead as scouts. Sometimes, coming over a rise, we could see them, loping along on foot with their bows and arrows, them Indians could have kept up that pace all day and had enough left over to have them a dance at night. Behind us was the donkey carts and burros, and the camp follower gals walking alongside. I calculate that altogether there was about a hundred fifty, sixty of us. Ben and me were in high spirits, this was what we'd joined up for, not to watch executions. And Ben was tickled pink because he'd found some ammunition at the hacienda for that fancy Luger.

The next part of my story is hard to tell, but I will tell it.

When we came to the Santa Cruz River, Colonel Bracamonte called a halt to rest his soldiers and water the horses. We were gone to wait there till sundown and make the rest of the march under cover of darkness. Me and Ben rolled us some smokes and were taking it easy. I remember looking downriver and seeing the Colonel huddled with Ynez and his other officers and some Yaqui scouts.

Then Ynez come up and said the colonel wanted to see us. That ain't exactly right. She was looking at Ben when she said it, but Ben being my compadre, I decided I should go along too. When we got there, we saw a rough kind of map of Santa Cruz drawed in the dirt, and the colonel said to Ben that he'd heard from Ynez that Ben knew the town and asked if it was accurate. Ben told him it wasn't and drawed a correct map. The colonel looked at it and then he switched from Spanish to English. "I order you to shoot that man" was what he said, and made a kind of movement with his head at a scout the name of Apache Juan. Ben and me looked at him like we hadn't heard right, so he repeated his order, and Ben said, "What the hell for?"

Bracamonte's face turned to stone. "Because I have ordered you to."

Ben said that he wouldn't shoot nobody without a good reason, and being told to do it, colonel or no colonel, wasn't a good reason, it was no reason at all.

I could tell no one had ever talked to Bracamonte like that, but he held his temper and told Ben something like that he'd been suspicious of Apache Juan from the minute he'd joined up and now his suspicions were confirmed because he'd asked Apache Juan a lot of questions and wasn't satisfied with his answers.

I have got to hand it to Ben. It was plain to him and me that we was being put to the test, that if he didn't do as ordered, it was gone to go hard for both of us. But Ben said he still hadn't heard a good reason—if the colonel didn't like the answers that fella gave, then he should shoot him himself.

Bracamonte stared at him for what felt like an hour, and Ben stared right back, one hard man to another. For a second there I thought the colonel was gone to do what Ben said, then turn his pistol on us. But he grinned cold like and more or less said that us gringos were a pain in the ass and . . . Well, I can't remember his exact words, but they went something like this: "I have determined that this man is a traitor and a spy. He gave us wrong information about the town. He is going to desert us tonight and warn the federals of our approach. You have your reason, señor, now follow my orders."

Ben hesitated just the littlest bit—it was right unusual for him to hesitate—and looked over at Apache Juan like he was trying to judge for his own self if the fella was a spy and a traitor. I shot first. I was pretty handy with a pistol, but I'd never shot a man in my life, and my hand was shaking so bad when I drew my Colt that it threw my aim off. I winged him in the leg. He spun around and grabbed his leg, and right then Pow! Ben fired the Luger, and Apache Juan dropped like a bale from a hayloft. He was still twitching when some other soldiers took his boots.

So now Ben and me was executioners, too. We'd come for gold and glory and so far hadn't seen none of either. The past fifty-some years, I have asked myself a hundred times over, Why did you shoot that man? And near as I can figure, it was because I knew Apache Juan was a doomed man no matter what and I just wanted to get it over with. And Ben? He never did say what was a-going on in his mind, and I never asked. He wasn't one to explain himself anyway. Once he done a thing, it was done, and there was no looking back.

Bracamonte said "Bueno," that was all, but you could tell his opinion of us, and Ynez's too, had changed. They trusted us now. Helluva way to earn their trust. So the sun went down, and we left Apache Juan for the coyotes and the buzzards.

The battalion rode out single file through the cottonwoods alongside the river. There wasn't a moon, and riding under those big trees was like riding through a tunnel with a blindfold on. Must have been close to midnight when the word come back in whispers to dismount. A few men were left behind to picket and guard the horses. The rest of us moved out afoot. The river made a bend between us and Santa Cruz, and we waded across it. Coming out from under the cottonwoods was like going from night to day, on account of our eyes had got so used to the pitch black. The town was dark, not a light burning anywhere, but we could make out some houses and the bell towers of the church. The colonel with El Agave's company split off to circle around to the west side of the town. They were supposed to take the federal troops' barracks. With Ben as a guide, Ynez led our company up the main street toward the plaza. Truth to tell, I thought I was gone to wet my pants from being scared and keyed up at the same time.

Somebody a couple of streets over, where the first company was, shouted. Couldn't hear what exactly, but we heard the gunshot clear enough. Found out later it was a federal sentry who'd spotted El Agave's men. They shot back, then there was more yelling, then more shooting, a whole lot of it, and stray rounds cracked over our heads like little whips. Ynez yelled, "Line of skirmishers, left!" Being ignorant of soldiering, Ben and me didn't know what the hell that meant, but we saw our company shaking itself out from single file into a firing line, so we got the idea. What folks these days would call on-the-job training. "¡Adelante!" Ynez ordered, and we started to advance on the plaza. The church was off to our left, a courthouse directly across, and a bandstand in the middle. All of a sudden I heard a noise the likes of which I'd never heard before. The federals had them a machine gun on the bandstand! Would have wiped us out if it hadn't been for two things—the gunners couldn't see us too clear, and they was seven, eight feet off the ground on the bandstand, so the rounds flew high. Some of our boys shot back. A few of them, like Francisco, could handle a gun, but most, even though Ynez said she wouldn't have no man who didn't shoot like her, could not have hit a fat bull's ass with a canoe paddle. They seemed to be shooting every which way but straight up in the air. Ben yelled to them to aim at the muzzle flashes of the machine gun. The machine gunners got the same idea and shot at our muzzle flashes. A couple of men got hit. Then I saw Ynez go down, flat on her face, under a tree at the edge of the plaza. Without thinking, I ran over to her to carry her out of the line of fire. The machine gunners must have seen me. Anyway, they fired in my direction and chopped chunks out of the tree trunk maybe a foot over my head. Told you I'd damn near got myself killed on account of that woman. She screamed at me, "Get down, you fool!" She hadn't been shot! That sure was one time I didn't mind getting called a fool, and I flung myself down right next to her.

The machine gun stopped firing for a few seconds, I reckon it had jammed, and Ben called out for me, so I ran over to him. He said, "Come with us!" Then him and Francisco and a few of Francisco's compadres made a dash for the church, and I followed. Ben and Francisco sure did know that town like the backs of their hands. They led us—there wasn't but six of us all told—down a little street back of the church, then turned up another street, then another one, and the next thing I knew, we were jammed up tight against the wall of the courthouse, facing the back of the bandstand. Meantime that infernal gun had got to firing again, and there was so much shooting over to the federal barracks, I thought the bullets was gone to knock the building down. Ben told us to open up on the bandstand with everything we had, and we did. We couldn't see nothing but the outline of it, but you would have thought we'd hit them gunners just by accident. We didn't, and they turned their gun around and let loose at us, which is just what Ben had in mind. He wanted them to think the whole outfit had circled around to their rear. Ynez figured out what was going on, and as soon as that gun had been swung around, we could hear that high voice of hers crying out, "¡Adelante compañeros!" And the men with her stormed the bandstand and killed the gunners point-blank and captured the machine gun.

That was not the end of the battle, no, sir. It went on till first light. We held about half the pueblo, and Díaz's soldiers held the other half, a stalemate kind of. Ben kept yelling to our men to fire at the enemy's muzzle flashes and then move and fire again. Come dawn, his eyes were like a crazy man's. We were all like crazy people, and little by little we got the upper hand. The shooting stopped for good, and there was dead men just about everywhere, the barracks walls was all chewed up, and in one place where about ten federals lay in a heap, blood was running down the street like it had rained blood. El Agave's company had got hit hard—about half of them was dead or wounded. Ynez's company lost maybe ten. The townsfolk was all hunkered down in their casitas.

The colonel climbed up to the church bell tower to get a better look at things with his field glasses, and called down that some of the federals was getting away, heading north. He come running down and told Ynez that he would hold the town with what was left of the first company and that her company was to pursue the retreating troops and cut 'em down. We hotfooted it back to the horses, mounted up, and started after 'em. By that time they were out of sight. It took us a while to pick up their trail, but once we did, they was easy to follow, on account of most was a-horseback and left a lot of sign. Ben and a few Yaqui scouts done the tracking, and Ben was as good at it as those Indians. The federal troops were making for the border. Some of 'em was already across it, most likely—Santa Cruz was just about an hour's ride south of it. The way Ynez figured it, they knew the U.S. of A. was backing Díaz and was sending soldiers to the border, so they calculated they'd be safe once they got over the line. She said we'd chase them right into the United States if we had to. And I said, "Whoa! Hold on there! What if the American troops had got there and we run into 'em?" And Ynez said that we'd fight them, too, like a band of tatter-ass Mexican insurrectos taking on the United States Army wasn't no big deal.

This woman, I thought to myself, is as crazy as a rat trapped in an outhouse, and you know, the crazier she got, the more in love with her I got. But I looked at Ben and said, "We can't go shooting at American soldiers. If they catch us, they'll hang us for sure." Ben said back, "T.J., we have thrown in with these people. They're our people now." Ben was like that. He had his own personal code, and he was set to follow it even if it meant getting into a fight with the soldiers of his own country.

We caught up with the federals who were afoot one or two or three at a time. They'd thrown their rifles away, and they'd put their hands up, and the revolucionarios shot them down, no questions asked. Me and Ben took no part in that, but we didn't do nothing to stop it neither.

We rode on. The border these days isn't much to look at, and there was even less of it then. Most times a fella couldn't tell what country he was in, but pretty soon Ben and me knew we were in the U.S. of A. on account of we recognized the lay of the land. We was in the foothills of the Huachuca Mountains and not too far from Fort Huachuca, where there'd been soldiers since in the days of the Apache Wars. Ben told that to Ynez, and I guess she had second thoughts about tangling with the gringo army because she passed the word that if we ran into any more of the retreating federals, there was to be no shooting guns. She told the Yaquis to finish them with their bows and arrows. Which is what they done. We come across a horse been rid to death, and the rider was running half a mile ahead, and the Yaquis made a pincushion out of him. And the next one and the one after that. They were gone to run out of arrows that way, so what they did was to pull them out by the arrowhead if the arrow went straight through, and most of the arrows shot from them long bows did just that.

I reckon the Yaquis killed a good half dozen, and I was sickened by it and told Ynez, Goddammit, this ain't war, this here is cold-blooded murder. She said that I was now in my own country and was free to ride away if I was so bothered by it. Well, you know what? I could not leave her side, and another thing—I wasn't entirely sure that that rattlesnake of a Mexican witch-woman would not have shot me in the back for a deserter.

I hadn't seen the worst. We caught up with two soldiers still ahorseback. The Yaquis ran after them, shooting their arrows on the run, and managed to stick the horses, and you know, being a cowhand, that bothered me more than seeing men shot the same way. The Indians was fixing to shoot the two soldiers, but Ynez stopped them. We rode them down and surrounded them, and Ynez told a couple of our men to tie them up. One was an officer, a lieutenant I think, and the other one was a sergeant. I figured that my telling Ynez that it was all cold-blooded murder had got to her conscience, if she had one, and she was gone to take them prisoner and at least give them a fair trial before shooting them. The both of them were right surprised and confused to hear a gal giving the orders. The lieutenant, a young fella, looked like he had mostly Spanish blood—he had light hair and blue eyes and fair skin. And he was scared to about dirtying his britches when Ynez looked down at him and the sergeant and said, "You bastards murdered my husband." Of course she meant that bastards like them had done the murdering. Anyway, that was her idea of a fair trial.

Next thing, a couple of our men knocked them cold with rifle butts. Then the Yaquis piled dry bear grass on top of them and dead branches on top of the grass and lit a fire. That woke them up, and they started to screaming—I still have bad dreams about that, me, looking eighty in the eye, and I can still hear those screams in my sleep sometimes. They rolled out from under the brush piles, both on fire, and the smell—well, I will spare you that. In a second there was no screams, just the black bodies twitching funnylike. Oh, my Lord, the little-shots of Mexico had been treated like dogs, and now they were biting back, and then some. "Basta," said Ynez, and turned her horse, and with the smoke rising up behind us, we rode on back into Old Mexico.

By the time we got back to Santa Cruz, we were just about asleep in our saddles. Colonel Bracamonte had rousted the scared townspeople out of their houses and told them they was now liberated, and then put them to work to burying the dead, which I reckon did not make them feel all that liberated. Ynez gave him a full report of our doings, and he was happy to beat the band about capturing the machine gun. He come walking over to where Ben and me and Francisco were flopped down in the plaza and promoted the three of us on the spot. He made Ben a lieutenant and said he was second in command of the company, and he made sergeants out of me and Francisco. So there we were, Teniente Erskine and Sargento Babcock, but if Bracamonte had made me a full-blown general, I could not have cared less—all I wanted was something to eat and a good ten hours' sleep.

We rode with the Red Sash Battalion for another three months I think it was, anyhow until the Revolution was over. I ought to say, till we *thought* it was over. There was fighting and trouble in Mexico for another twenty years before things got settled down. My memory is not as good about those three months like it is about those first three days—everything is kind of jumbled up—but I know we was plumb wore out from riding and fighting and killing. We took railway junctions and garrisons and towns all through Sonora. We liberated a few more haciendas from the hacendados, and after each fight we got bigger than we was before, what with federal troops deserting and joining up. We didn't have to worry about what generals call supply lines because we'd take whatever we needed—guns from the garrisons, food and liquor from the haciendas or from the stores in a town—the stores that was owned by Spaniards or folks loyal to Díaz. In the end, the battalion could muster around three hundred men—and a few women, too, soldaderas like Ynez, gals with big gold earrings and bandoliers crissy-crossed on their hefty bosoms.

Oh Lord, the things we done, the things we seen! Every now and then we'd come across hanged men swinging from cottonwoods, the bodies dried up and blackened, like scarecrows, but they didn't all scare the crows. One time we saw three fellas a-swinging from a tree in the distance, and as we got closer, Ben said, "They're still alive," on account of they was moving around. When we got closer still, we seen that it was ravens doing the moving, covered the bodies head to boot, looked like they was dressed in black feathers with all those ravens hanging on to 'em and pecking out bits and pieces. And I never will forget seeing a coyote cross our path with what looked like a broken tree branch in its jaws and it turned out to be a human arm. These are gruesome things to tell, but that's the way it was. Not much glory in it, and as far as the gold went, Ben and me still had the same Yankee dollars we rode in with, and not a lot of those neither. Soldiers of fortune with no fortune, that was us.

You know, seeing and doing the things we done made me harder, and I reckon Ben got even harder than when he started off. But Ynez got softer, strange to say. She fought like hell when there was fighting to be done, but there wasn't no more of that other stuff. She'd come to be longer on mercy than on justice. After one of those battles, the mad went out of her sad-mad look. Ynez come up to me and said, "Babcock, I have done terrible things." And I said that all of us had, but it was like she didn't hear me. "For the love of my husband, I have condemned my soul to hell." This was real Mexican kind of talk. But she went to a padre in one pueblo while he was burying dead folks and confessed her sins. That rattlesnake woman had done defanged herself, all that vengeance poison was gone out of her. By her lights, her soul done been cleansed of murder and she aimed to keep it that way.

Thinking back on those times, there's two stories about Ben that stick in my mind. First off, he got promoted to captain. This is how it happened. One night after we'd routed federals from a railroad depot, he woke me up with the toe of his boot. "T.J., something's wrong," he said in a real low voice. I looked around and saw our men asleep, and all I heard was a little crackling from the dying campfires and snoring and the sound of a rock or two getting kicked by the picketed horses as they moved about. "Ain't nothing wrong," I told Ben, but he insisted there was, said he could feel there was some danger out there.

Now, there is something I didn't tell you about Ben. He claimed to have supernatural powers. Said it ran in the family. Some grandmother or auntie of his could talk to the spirits of dead people, and when he was a kid in school, he wrote down a date in his copybook for no reason—a date that was a couple of months in the future. Well, when that date come around, the grandmother or auntie who had conversations with the departed died herself. Even though I wasn't a scientific fella, I did not believe in that spooky stuff. Anyway, I told Ben that if he was so all-fired sure something was wrong, he'd best wake up Ynez and tell her, which is what he done. Ynez had pretty much the same reaction as me, but once an idea got into Ben's head you could not pry it out with a crowbar, and he saddled up his horse and rode out.

Wasn't five minutes later I heard a gunshot and jumped out of my bedroll. The whole company was awake now. There came a regular fusillade and Ben galloping back shouting like that Paul Revere fella that the federals were right behind him. The enemy charged right into us, a-yelling and a-shooting like hell wouldn't have it. Horses broke their ties and went running right into that confused mess of men fighting each other hand to hand. You almost couldn't tell who was who, and I think some of our men shot each other. Worst fight I'd been in, but we outnumbered the counterattacking federals two to one and got the upper hand. I'd say we killed more than half of them and captured the rest.

The old Ynez would have executed the prisoners right then and there, but this was the new Ynez and she gave them a choice—she could leave them to the mercies of the desert or they could join us. They didn't have no trouble making up their minds. Fact was, one of the prisoners told us, the whole reason they'd tried a sneak attack was because they'd found themselves out in the wasteland with no food and water and figured to surprise us and take our supplies and our horses.

Ynez told Ben that he was a hero of the Revolution and that the next time he got a feeling something was wrong, she sure would pay attention to him. When Bracamonte learned what Ben had done, he promoted him to capitán and put him in command of the other company. The fella he replaced, El Agave—he was called that because he'd as soon stick you as look at you and had a big thirst for mescal—was damn mad.

The way I heard it, he still had some of the mescal he'd looted from a cantina, got drunk, and said they would be having snowball fights in hell before he took orders from a gringo, that he was more of a man than any gringo, and was gone to prove it. Ben was setting on a stoop with Francisco, cleaning his Luger, when El Agave walked up the street calling him a cabrón and some other such things and that he was there to settle who was the better man. Ben was real calm and, with that cockeyed grin on his face, said that he'd be glad to oblige El Agave, just give him a minute to put his pistol back together. El Agave told him to go to hell or some such and drew down on him. Drunk as he was, he would have had a hard time hitting the ground with his hat, but one bullet threw dust into Ben's face, and he rolled away, a-hollering. Then there was another shot, and when Ben looked up, El Agave was laying dead in the street and Bracamonte standing over him with his pistol out. Ben collected his wits and said muchas gracias to the colonel and that he was in debt to him for saving his life. Bracamonte said back that maybe Ben could repay him someday, but for now to think no more about it.

Well, the day did come, a long time later, for Ben to return the favor, but that is a story for another time.

This incident I have just told you about happened in June of 1911. A few days later the colonel went into Hermosillo for a powwow with some other revolutionary leaders. When he come back, he announced that President Díaz had done quit and gone into exile and Francisco Madero had entered Mexico City to take over the country. We had won the damn war! The boys shot their guns into the air and whooped and hollered. The jefe of the town threw a fiesta, and it went on half the night.

That night I throwed caution to the winds and told Ynez that I didn't give a damn if she was my commanding officer, I was gone to kiss her like a man who meant it, and I picked her up and did just that. Wasn't I surprised when she kissed me back! And then said she wasn't my commanding officer anymore. "Are you gone to marry me or what?" I asked. Damn if she didn't say, "Sí, Babcock." I let out a real loud cowboy yip and kissed her again and kind of let my hands wander into forbidden territory. She stopped me and said there was to be no fooling around till we was married, and there was another condition: I would have to agree to live with her in Mexico; she intended to stay and help build a new country. What with the waste and destruction that war had brought down—like it had been omened by the comet—building a new Mexico was gone to be a tall order. But that was okay with me. Truth to tell, if Ynez wanted to live on the moon, I would have gone there.

A couple days later we got official word by telegraph that we was to be demobilized. It was kind of a sad day saying adiós to our compadres. Ben looked down at the mouth. He said, "T.J., I'm not sure what I'm gone to do now." I said that maybe he could throw back in with his brother. He didn't say nothing, just shook his head real slow like, but I knew what he meant. After fighting in the Revolution, punching cows would be pretty tame, and him, only twenty-one and a capitán, it would be hard to play second fiddle to Jeff. So then I suggested that he stay in Mexico and give me and Ynez a hand in the building of the new Mexico. Now, I didn't have a shade of a notion what that meant, or how to go about it, I just liked the way it sounded. Anyway, Ben shook his head again. Next day he rode off back across the line, and I was sorry to see him go, thinking we'd never see each other again. That did not turn out to be the case.

3

THESE PEOPLE CAN DRIVE you nuts," Monica said in an undertone. It was a Saturday, and she was off from her teaching job at the Patagonia grammar school. She, Aunt Sally, and Castle were sitting in the cluttered kitchen of the main house while Miguel slept under a blanket on the living room sofa. "They break down your fences and break your heart, and you don't know what the hell to do about them."

A lifetime on cattle ranches—she'd been raised on one before marrying into another—had made her look both older and younger than her age, fifty-one. Desert sun and wind had dug furrows into her strong, square face, accented by a straight nose and electric blue eyes, while her body, molded by years on horseback, years of pitching feed bales from pickup trucks and wrestling calves at branding time, belonged to a woman of thirty. She wasn't shy about showing it off, as she was now, wearing Levi's tight as leotards and a snug blouse unbuttoned at the top to disclose a glimpse of freckled cleavage.

"How do you mean, drive you nuts?" Castle asked.

"One minute they make you want to build the Great Wall of China on the border. The next minute you feel sorry for them and want to help them get to wherever they're going," Monica replied. "Some of these crossers have stories that make *The Grapes of Wrath* read like a comic book."

"What did he tell you?"

Monica, who spoke Spanish fairly well, had engaged Miguel in a brief conversation before, still shivering, he collapsed on the kitchen floor. The hike over the ridge and the brief but bumpy ride in Castle's car to ranch headquarters had sapped his last strength. He didn't awaken even when they dragged him into the living room and lifted him onto the sofa. He lay so still that Castle, as Sally got a wool blanket from the closet, put an ear to his chest to make sure he had a heartbeat.

"Not much," Monica answered. "Said that we saved his life and that he's from Oaxaca."

"That's way south, 'bout a thousand miles," Sally said. Long gray hair yanked back in a ponytail, garbed in a ratty terrycloth bathrobe over a cotton nightgown, she nonetheless managed to convey a regal impression, still the boss of the outfit at seventy-nine. "Who knows what this Miguel went through to get this far."

"When I found him, he thought I was going to shoot him," Castle said. "Next thing, he asked if he was in the U.S. The poor guy had no idea. When I told him, yeah, he was in the United States, he thanked God all over the place and cried."

"That's what I mean. Breaks your heart." Like Castle's mother, like a lot of ranch girls, Monica had been sent to boarding school when she was in her teens. It had leached the country from her accent, but some still seeped through, as in the way she'd said "Breaks your heart." *Brikes yore haart.* "Tell him that story, Sally."

"Which one?"

"About the wet Gerardo found last year."

Sally leaned forward, as if she were about to let him in on a secret. "Gerardo was out checking cattle on our lease. He come across a Mexican sitting all by himself under a tree next to a Forest Service road. Gerardo asked him what he was doing. Said he was waiting for someone to pick him up and drive him to Chicago. Said if his ride didn't show up soon, he'd walk it, if Gerardo would give him directions. Well, Gerardo had to tell him that Chicago was about two thousand miles away. The Mexican just stared at him, then said that his coyote told him Chicago was two days' walk north. More like two months, Gerardo said, and the Mexican started bawling like a baby. Gerardo set him on his horse, and they rode double back to here. We called the Border Patrol and told the Mexican not to worry. All the Border Patrol would do is drop him off on the other side, where he could hook up with another coyote and try again. Hope he made it. That's a story with a happy ending, Gil. The other ones, well, you must've read about them."

"I try not to read the newspapers," he said.

"They freeze to death in the mountains, die of thirst in the desert. And all for what? A damn job on an asparagus farm or a landscaping crew." Sally rested her chin on her wrinkled hands. "Wasn't so bad ten years ago, but it's a big business now, thousands pouring through."

"And that's when you start wanting to build the Great Wall of China," said Monica. "Have you had breakfast?"

"I like to hunt on an empty stomach."

"Well, you ain't hunting now," Sally observed.

Monica got out of her chair, her cowboy boots and long legs giving the impression that she was six feet tall. Like Amanda when she wore heels—Castle could not help make the comparison.

"Huevos rancheros and frijoles okay?"

"Don't go through any trouble."

"No trouble." She pulled a skillet from a rack hanging over the sink. "You might as well wait out here till Blaine and Gerardo get back. They should be along directly."

The two men had been buying feed in Sonoita when Monica called Blaine's cell phone to tell him about Castle's discovery. Monica brought him the eggs smothered in salsa, with the frijoles and a warm tortilla folded into a square. He began to eat.

"More coffee?"

"Sure."

She refilled his cup, poured two more for herself and Sally, and sat down. "The wets I guess I can put up with. But the coyotes and the drug mules—hideous people."

Sally said, "Banging at your door at three in the morning, demanding food and water. Ain't polite about it, neither. Demanding, like we're some all-night diner." She gave a brittle, ironic laugh to indicate that these nocturnal calls had become so routine they could now only amuse her. "Reminds me of another story, the peanut butter sandwiches. Tell Gil about that one, Monica."

"One time I made peanut butter sandwiches for a gang of burreros, and Blaine went outside with the sandwiches stacked up in one hand and his gun in the other. Just in case. Not that you would want to shoot them. There's maybe twenty, thirty people in this whole damn valley. You can bet the drug bosses know where each one of us lives. Make trouble for them, they'll give it back to you in spades. How are the eggs?"

"Fine. Thanks."

"The ranch west of us? Last year, drug runners opened up on the Border Patrol with assault rifles. We could hear it. Poor Blaine, he almost had a flashback to Vietnam."

Castle was shocked to hear that this peaceful-looking valley could be the scene of such an incident. "Christ," he said. "It sounds like inner-city L.A."

"More like the days of Pancho Villa, except now the bad guys ride in Dodge Rams instead of on horses and bang away with AK-47s instead of Winchesters. I've got a gun right at my bedside," Monica went on. "Blaine and Gerardo carry whenever they're gathering or checking fences near the border. Cell phone on one hip, pistol on the other. The Wild West meets the twenty-first century. And now we've got vigilantes coming in, the Minutemen. All we need is for the Apaches to get riled up, and we'll be right back where we started."

"So what happened with the peanut butter sandwiches?"

She snickered. "A couple of weeks later we were out of town. When we got home, we found the house had been broken into and a bunch of steaks, from a beef we'd butchered, had been stolen from the freezer. We were pretty sure it was the same guys. Letting us know they didn't much care for peanut butter and could break in and take whatever they wanted."

"Might have been you give 'em crunchy and they liked creamy," Sally interjected.

"Last night Sam started barking," Castle said. "She always barks when people come near the house. It must have been Miguel. He must have seen the light in my window and was coming for help, but the barking scared him off." He looked through the archway between the kitchen and the living room at the unconscious man. If a lost, hapless, half-dead migrant could come so close at night, then surely drug smugglers could barge right in, and they weren't likely to be scared by a dog, not if they were carrying assault rifles. "Do you think I should get a gun?"

"What do you hunt with? Rocks?" Sally asked with a smile.

"A bird gun isn't much of a gun."

He put his dish in the dishwasher and, while Monica straightened up the kitchen, went into the living room and sat down across from Miguel to wait for Blaine and Gerardo. A copy of *Western Horseman* did not hold his attention. Beside it *Tucson* magazine was open to a short back-page article about Blaine and Monica's son, Rick Erskine, a country rock singer of regional fame. He was currently on an extended tour of the Southwest. Castle, who hadn't seen him since he was a boy and still thought of him that way, was startled to look at a picture of a strikingly handsome twenty-four-year-old and to read that he was now a married man.

He set the magazine down, allowing his eyes to roam the room with its thick adobe walls and oak-beamed ceiling, its pueblo-style fireplace flanked by photographs of Jeffrey and Benjamin Erskine. Jeff's was a standard head shot that showed him wearing a brushy mustache and a suit and tie knotted to a celluloid collar. Ben's picture dated back to the 1930s and could have been a movie poster for a cornball western. He was mounted on a rearing black horse adorned with a silver-studded breast collar and headstall, its white-stockinged forelegs pawing the air as Ben held the reins in one hand and raised his Stetson high with the other in a flamboyant salute, his mouth skewed into a cocky, crooked grin. Castle had a vague memory of attending his grandfather's funeral when he was nine. Ben had been a man barnacled in legend, but beyond a few fragmentary stories, Castle knew little about him. For that matter, owing to his mother's reticence about her family, he and his sister had grown up knowing almost as little about their western forebears as they did about their father's ancestors in Italy. Grace had once described Castle's grandmother, Ida, as a woman who was "either a saint or a doormat or maybe a little of both." If she'd said more, he could not remember it. Her brother, Frank, who had come out of the war a decorated hero only to be killed several years later in a mine accident, had been "a brave and wonderful boy who was always trying to prove he was as much of a man as our father considered himself to be." And of that father she'd scarcely uttered a word. Fifteen years ago, when Castle made his first trip to the San Ignacio, on the pretext of going bird hunting but in reality to make contact with his relatives, he'd heard a muddled story from Blaine that their grandfather had been tried for killing a man in a dispute, the origins of which were obscure. Upon his return to Connecticut, Castle asked his mother if any of it was true and why she'd kept it from him. "Your grandfather was a man who had outlived his time, only he didn't know it," Grace replied. He pressed her to explain that enigmatic comment, but all she said was, "Let's say that I have conflicting feelings about him," her tone making it clear that further inquiries would not be welcome.

He was half lost in this reverie when, through a front window, he saw Blaine's Ford 350, with the ranch's name and brand, an *S* bisected by an *I*, painted on its doors and feed bales stacked in the bed, rattle into the side yard, which was a combined parking lot and junkyard for gooseneck stock trailers and several other trucks in varying states of usefulness. Gerardo drove on toward the horse corrals as Blaine crossed the yard with the slow, stiff walk that resulted from old rodeo injuries and numerous throws from the backs of spooked horses. Six feet two and about ten pounds on the bright side of emaciated, wearing a dirty brown cowboy hat and a tattered striped shirt, gloves stuffed into the back pocket of his jeans and a jackknife in a leather case on his belt, he was the picture of the working cattleman.

He came in and took off his hat, uncovering a shock of wiry, reddish blond hair flecked with gray and rising straight up on top, like a rooster's comb. He and Castle were the same age, but that was all they had in common besides their DNA. Even that wasn't much in evidence as far as their appearances went. Castle favored his father's side, Blaine the Erskines: a fine, sharp-ridged nose, faded gray eyes, and thin lips that, when he smiled, duplicated their grandfather's odd grin.

"That him?" Blaine asked, gesturing at Miguel.

"No," Monica answered. "That's a Pizza Hut delivery boy taking a nap."

"It is my cross to bear to be married to a smart-mouth woman." He turned to his cousin. "Congratulations. You caught your first illegal alien."

"I didn't catch him. I found him. Actually, Sam found him."

"Some dog. She points Mexicans."

"He's from Oaxaca," Monica informed her husband.

"There's a boy come a long way," he said with a lift of his pale eyebrows. "He's been fed?"

Monica shook her head. "He dropped almost the minute he came in."

"We'd best feed him somethin'. Somethin' hot. He ain't only starved, he's probably got hypothermia, and you can die of that in the snap of a finger."

"I've got the split pea and ham from yesterday in the fridge."

"That'll do. We don't want an illegal dyin' in our house. That happens, next thing we'll have an ACLU lawyer accusin' us of murderin' the poor son of a bitch."

"Otherwise we'd let him die?" Monica glanced ironically at Castle. "Blaine would hate for anyone to think he has feelings for his fellow man."

"Oh hell, you know what I meant," he said, and took the soup from the refrigerator and popped it into the microwave.

Blaine had taken charge in his usual fashion. Castle—despite his accomplishments as an outdoorsman, his success on Wall Street, and a personal fortune that, before he'd given three-fourths of it away, could have bought the whole San Ignacio in cash—often felt, well, less manly in his cousin's presence. Aside from the abilities to ride and rope one would expect in a rancher, Blaine was a fairly skilled carpenter, plumber, auto mechanic, and veterinarian because he had to be. When things broke down out here, phoning a repairman wasn't an option. If a cow was having trouble giving birth or a horse went lame, he had to treat the animal himself. Castle's handiness was pretty much limited to changing flats and lightbulbs, but more than his ineptness at manual tasks caused his feelings of inadequacy. In contrast to his own early life, Blaine's had been hard. He was only four when he'd lost his father. Ben had taken him under his wing, but Blaine lost him too a few years later. At eighteen, after a troubled high school career—he would have been expelled if he hadn't been the star pitcher for Patagonia High's baseball team—he enlisted in the army and served two tours with the Special Forces in Vietnam, where he was wounded and won a Bronze Star.

The war—that was the Grand Canyon yawning between him and Castle. In past visits to the ranch—there had been only two—they had argued about it, Castle maintaining that it had been senseless, Blaine that it hadn't been and could have been won "if they didn't make us fight with one hand tied behind our backs"; but their difference of opinion was beside the point. Lately Castle had begun to think that Vietnam had put steel into his cousin's soul as well as into his flesh, had trained him to confront almost any situation and master it. To expect the unexpected, the sudden ambush, the booby trap in the trail. Castle wondered if he'd missed out on something, some excruciating ordeal that might have left him better equipped to cope with the one great disaster of his life.

When Blaine woke him, Miguel sprang up with a startled look on his round face. He threw off the blanket and swung his short legs to the floor and pitched forward, as if he were about to run out the door. Then, seeing the familiar faces of Castle and Monica, he relaxed somewhat, though his glance darted back and forth like a captive animal's before it settled on Blaine.

"Mi esposo," Monica said by way of introduction.

Miguel nodded. Blaine set the soup bowl atop the issue of *Western Horseman* on the coffee table and gestured for him to eat. He drained the bowl in about half a minute.

"Mucho gusto, gracias."

"De nada," Blaine said, and sat in a cracked leather armchair and asked Miguel to describe what had happened to him. Miguel answered with short, choppy phrases that Blaine interrupted with more questions. This went on for some time, Miguel becoming more and more agitated, his lips quivering.

Blaine looked at Monica and said he couldn't follow the rambling, disjointed story. Neither could she, and suggested that Gerardo and Elena might get Miguel to make sense.

Blaine left and returned shortly with the couple. Miguel settled down. It might have been the presence of fellow Hispanics that calmed him, but Castle thought it was the profound serenity that emanated from both people and enveloped everyone near them. Gerardo was about fifty years old, a man economical in speech, five eight at the tallest, narrow-hipped and thick-chested, with spare features that recalled portraits of the conquistadors. His graceful carriage, endowed by a life on horseback and by work demanding agility and balance, was complemented by an inner poise that came from knowing who and what he was, the who and the what wrapped up in a single word, *vaquero.* This composure impressed Castle because it was so unlike the manner of the frantic multitaskers he'd worked with in New York, answering e-mails and talking to clients at the same time, shouting into cell phones as they scuttled herky-jerky through the noisy, crowded, artificial canyons of their vertical world. Gerardo seemed to have absorbed the desert's stillness into his very cells; his silences were a language unto themselves, speaking of the impermanence of all things human and the eternity of the arroyos, the mesas, and distant blue mountains.

Like a lot of long-married couples, he and Elena had grown to resemble each other, though the resemblance wasn't in their looks. She was darker, more Indian in appearance, and her short, stout figure, communicating both comfort and a barrellike durability, had none of her husband's athletic grace. She was also a great talker, but she shared his air of equanimity, hers arising from piety rather than from daily contact with the natural world. She said a rosary every day to the Virgin of Guadalupe, crossed herself whenever she heard bad news, and except in severe weather, drove the twenty rough miles to Patagonia to attend Sunday Mass at St. Theresa's. An old grief showed in her small, black eyes even when she laughed, its marks embedded there like the glyphs the ancient Hohokam had etched into the desert rocks. She'd lost two of her five children—disease claimed a daughter in infancy, an auto accident took a son in his teens—and yet sorrow had not mastered her. She'd achieved an acceptance that was not resignation, and she'd done it without the ministrations of a therapist. Castle yearned to know what Elena's secret was. Like her husband, she seemed to possess a way of knowing and understanding that had vanished from the modern world. It was certainly beyond him, for all his education.

Elena nestled beside Miguel on the sofa, placed a hand on his knee, and murmured to him in a motherly tone. Whatever she said, it drew a faint, tentative smile from him. Gerardo took a tobacco pouch and papers out of his pocket and rolled a cigarette for him, which he inhaled as greedily as he'd drunk Castle's water and devoured Monica's soup. Then, prodded by a few questions from the couple, he began his story again. Castle couldn't tell if this version was more coherent than the previous one. At one point Miguel took out his wallet and showed photographs—of his family, Castle assumed—and then produced a small plastic bag containing a few papers, presumably documents to corroborate some point he was making. A few minutes later his voice rose to a high pitch, cracked, and broke into sobs. Elena whispered, "Pobre hombre," poor man, and put an arm around his shoulders.

Composing himself, Miguel resumed his account. It took quite a while. Castle's attention wandered until he became aware of a silence in the room. Miguel was finished. His listeners looked at one another. Sally, shaking her head, said, "Lordy, lordy," then Blaine declared, "We're gone to have to call the sheriff and Border Patrol." He glanced at Gerardo to second the motion, which Gerardo did with a bob of his head.

Apparently Miguel understood some English; he folded his small hands in supplication and pleaded, "¡No La Migra! No Border Patrol! ¡Por favor!"

Blaine went to the phone in the kitchen. Castle asked Monica, "What's going on?"

"You heard, he's calling the cops." Her tone implied that she wished there were an alternative.

"Can't somebody tell him that the Border Patrol will drop him off on the other side and he can give it another try?" Castle suggested. "That's what you told me they do, right?"

"Not this time around," Sally said. "Looks like we've got us two men murdered on our land and the witness in our house."

That seized Castle's full attention. "*What?* What happened?"

"It would be easier to tell you what didn't," Monica replied.

His full name was Miguel Espinoza, she began, he was thirty years old and had owned a small produce-exporting business that went belly-up because of 9/11: an entire year's crop rotted on the tarmac waiting for U.S. airspace to reopen. (Another casualty, thought Castle. How far the shock waves reached!) Miguel scraped by, peddling in vegetable markets, doing odd jobs, and earning barely enough to feed his wife and four children. A month ago he was approached by a recruiter assembling a group of workers for a meatpacker in Kansas; Miguel could join them if he could come up with the fee—fifteen hundred dollars, to be paid to the coyote when he got to the border. The sum was stunning to a man of Miguel's means, and he hardly knew where Kansas was except that it was in the United States, but the job, the recruiter promised, paid nine dollars an hour, more than he earned in a day in the markets of Oaxaca. He sold his old car, borrowed from friends, and was soon on his way.

With several others he traveled northward in a bus to Hermosillo, befriending two other Oaxaca men who had been hired to work in the same meatpacking factory, Héctor and Reynaldo. Between Hermosillo and Cananea, where they were to meet their coyote, the Moses who would lead them into the promised land, the bus was waylaid by *bajadores*—bandits—who took turns raping the women and relieved the men of their cash and watches and whatever else they had of value. So Miguel, Héctor, and Reynaldo arrived in Cananea with only the clothes on their backs and a few changes of socks and underwear in their *mochilas*, their backpacks.

They were stashed in a hostel on a side street. When their coyote, a fat man wearing a ring on every finger, came for them, they had to tell him that they had been robbed of all their money. What an unfortunate thing! Maybe they knew someone who could wire them more? They did not. Very unfortunate! Of course, he could not take them *al otro lado*—to the other side—for nothing. But he was a man of compassion, he would try to help them. They were to wait for him, and under no circumstances were they to leave the hostel.

Late in the afternoon the coyote returned with a young man as skinny as he himself was fat. They were led outside. God was smiling on them, said the coyote. They were young and strong, so they could be of assistance to his friend, who was experiencing a sudden emergency. If they did as his friend asked, which was to carry some marijuana over the border, their debt would be paid. Héctor and Reynaldo agreed immediately; Miguel was frightened and balked at first, but after coming so far through so many troubles, he decided to take the risk.

That night they found themselves riding in the back of a pickup truck with three marijuana bales wrapped in burlap. The skinny man—Héctor had nicknamed him el Lápiz, The Pencil—was driving. A group of migrants—*pollos*, The Pencil called them—were in a van some distance ahead. At the border a *pollero*—a chicken herder—would walk them into the United States. After they were on their way, The Pencil would lead Miguel, Héctor, and Reynaldo down the trail, keeping a safe distance behind the migrants. If La Migra agents were patrolling the area or waiting up the trail, they would be decoyed by the pollos and their pollero, and the three men and The Pencil would slip through unnoticed. The Pencil would guide them to a road and then summon another man with his cell phone. This man would take delivery of the drugs and drive Miguel and his friends to a safe house in the city of Tucson. From there they would be given transport to the meatpacking factory in Kansas.

El Lápiz concluded his instructions with a warning. They were not to lose the load, or to get any crazy ideas about making off with it. The fat man knew where their families lived . . . No more need be said. All of this thoroughly terrified Miguel, but there was no going back.

He had yet to see the worst, Monica said.

The truck came to a sudden stop. Up ahead they saw that the migrants' van had also stopped. Someone yelled, "*¡Judicial!*" They knew what that meant—the Mexican federal police. They heard more shouts, then many gunshots. The Pencil stomped on the gas and sped away in reverse. In the darkness he misjudged the road and backed into a ditch, nearly rolling the truck over. He jumped out, crying, "Get the hell out! It's not federales! It's bandits! They'll kill us!" Miguel and his companions piled out of the truck as their guide ran off in a panic. Abandoned, the three men didn't know where they were or what to do. "Grab the bales!" Héctor said. "We must run!" But run where? "North, you idiots, and that star points north!" He stabbed a finger at the sky, but Miguel could not see what star he meant.

They shouldered the bales and fled. It was freezing cold, but the walking warmed them. By daybreak they were among low, tree-covered hills beneath high mountains capped in snow. When the day grew warm enough for sleep, they hid in the woods and rested. In the afternoon they resumed their trek, Héctor keeping direction by the sun. Each bale felt like a hundred kilos instead of twenty. They wanted to throw them away but remembered The Pencil's warnings. They drank dirty water pooled in rocky niches of the arroyos and walked until they were stumbling like drunks.

Finally they came to a road—not much of a road, just two tracks beside a broad wash overgrown with high brush. This must be it, Héctor declared, pointing at tire marks. The man in the car must be driving up and down, looking for them. All they had to do now was wait for him to come by. Miguel and Reynaldo weren't so sure—to them, it seemed as if Héctor believed it was so because he hoped it was so.

They piled brush atop the bales in case La Migra showed up, then concealed themselves in the tall weeds in the wash. The bad water he'd drunk had given Miguel diarrhea. Shy about relieving himself in front of his companions, he went to the far side of the wash and squatted. Just as he did, he heard a vehicle approaching. My God, Héctor had been right. When Miguel rose halfway up, he saw a peculiar conveyance—it resembled a small tractor except that it had four wheels instead of three—moving slowly down the road. The driver was looking at the ground rather than ahead. Héctor jumped out of the weeds and flagged it down. The driver climbed off and began to speak to him. Miguel was about to pull his pants up to rejoin his friends when the diarrhea pains shot through his belly again and drove him back into a squat. He believed that God caused those pains to come at that moment because God, for His own reasons—who can truly know the mind of God?—had willed that he should live and his compañeros die. As he emptied his bowels, he heard Héctor call out and saw the stranger pull a gun from under his jacket. There came a sharp crack, and Reynaldo fell. Two more gunshots quickly followed, and Héctor dropped.

Miguel flung himself down and cowered in the underbrush, his pants around his ankles and his heart pounding. After some minutes passed, he dared to raise his head and observed the stranger walking through the wash, the pistol in his hand. Miguel got a good look at him. He was tall and well built and bare-headed, a *güero*—a blond—but Miguel couldn't tell if he was a gringo or a fair-haired Mexican. Miguel ducked back down, curling up to make himself as small as possible. More minutes passed. He heard the vehicle drive off. Still he lay, afraid to move. He lay there until dusk, and then he found the courage to get up and see what had happened. Héctor's and Reynaldo's bodies lay near each other, Reynaldo with a bullet hole in his head, Héctor with blood all over his chest. The brush pile had been torn apart and the marijuana bales were gone.

He ran, ran blindly into the hills until he could run no more, but he kept moving, stumbling and falling in the darkness, weeping for his wife and children, cursing the smuggler who'd promised him a job in Kansas, cursing himself for leaving Oaxaca, then weeping again because the load had been lost and now bad men would come to his house to kill his family . . . It was for this that God allowed him to live?

"And you were right, Gil, " Monica said. Her retelling of the saga almost word for word had taken close to half an hour. Miguel had left some time ago with Gerardo and Elena; they had brought him to their house to bathe and give him a change of clothes. "He saw the light in your place. He was going to ask for help, but the dog scared him off. He ran over the hill, and that was the last thing he remembered till you found him."

Castle, trying to absorb everything he'd heard, said nothing.

"It's like everything that can happen to an illegal happened to him," she added.

Blaine, smoking a cigarette, nodded. "But some of it don't add up."

Monica looked at him, a question in her brilliant blue eyes.

"These dopers use guys they know and trust to mule their stuff over. They don't give sixty kilos of dope to strangers."

"You're not suggesting that he—"

"No, that little guy didn't shoot his buddies and make off with the merca," Blaine said, exhaling smoke through his nostrils. "But it don't add up all the same, and then there's that massacre on the other side. Christ almighty. Who would do a thing like that?"

"Bandits, like he said. Bandits posing as federales."

"There ain't much difference between bandits and federales," said Sally.

"Well, finding out what the hell went on is gone to be their job." Blaine motioned out the front window at a green and white Border Patrol truck towing a horse trailer. It was followed by two Santa Cruz county sheriff's squad cars.

4

Blaine and a Border Patrol tracker studied a topographic map draped over the coffee table while two sheriff's deputies and another cop—an undercover agent in civilian clothes who'd identified himself only as Nacho—questioned Miguel in the Murrietas' house, near the corrals. Nacho said he'd heard about the massacre of the migrants from a Mexican informant and wanted to find out if Miguel could "connect a dot or two." The homicides that had occurred on this side of the line fell under the Sheriff Department's jurisdiction. Of course, it could not be said for sure that Héctor and Reynaldo had been murdered until their bodies were found, and that was the tracker's job.

Earlier the tracker had put his own questions to Miguel. Could he describe the scene of the shootings a little more clearly? He could not. How far was it from here? He didn't know. How about in which direction? He had no idea.

"It could of been any one of half a dozen places on this ranch," Blaine said now, poking a pencil at the map. "My best guess is right here."

The tracker, a Navaho named John Morales, leaned over and squinted. "Why there?"

"This road runs alongside a big wash, Juniper Canyon it's called. And it's inside of five miles of where my cousin found him. The way I figure, that old boy didn't walk far in the dark, him bein' as beat as he was and not knowin' the country."

"Better get a start. I haven't got all week to look for a couple of ten-sevens."

"Ten-seven?" asked Castle, sitting on the other side of the room.

"A corpse," Morales answered. He slapped a tan Stetson on his crew cut and stood. In a dark green uniform with a semiautomatic pistol and lawman's accoutrements—handcuffs, magazine case, flashlight, and VHF radio—belted to his waist, he was an impressive-looking figure of six feet, with a steer wrestler's shoulders and the profile of a

Roman general. "You show me where you found him and I'll backtrack from there," he said to Castle.

"We'll be goin' with you," Blaine said.

The tracker frowned and shook his head. "I can't be responsible for any civilians."

"Number one, this is *my* ranch. Number two, there's not a square yard of it me and Gerardo don't know. And Gerardo—now, don't take offense, John—can cut sign better'n any man alive. Track a lost cow over bare rock. Seen him do it."

"Okay," Morales said after pondering a moment. "But I'm the cow boss. Nobody rides out ahead of me and fucks up the trail."

Blaine got up with a slow, deliberate movement. "Let's go, cousin."

Castle hesitated. He considered himself a spectator in the theater of life, removed from the march of events great and small, and that included this particular event. "You go over the ridge behind my place," he said. "Two-thirds of the way down, a little to the left, you'll see a big manzanita thicket. Can't miss it. You start from there."

"For chrissake, Gil, it was you who found him," Blaine said impatiently. "Least you can do is show us where. Then you can go back to readin your books or shootin' quail or whatever the hell it is you do with yourself all day."

The remark stung and struck Castle as unfair, but he didn't want to argue. Besides, maybe Blaine was right. He'd stepped into this drama, if unintentionally, and he could not now step out of it in good conscience. "All right."

"You can ride along with us after. Another pair of eyes. I'll put you on Rojo. He's so calm, you'll think we're feedin' him tranquilizers."

Morales unloaded his horse from the trailer and led it to the corral that held the ranch's herd of cow ponies, where Blaine and Gerardo caught and saddled their mounts and Castle's. Castle clutched Rojo's mane and swung on board, feeling very much like the tenderfoot he was. As, following the others, he nudged the roan gelding out onto the road, Nacho and the deputies, with Miguel in tow, emerged from the Murrietas' house, directly across from the corral. Miguel was shaved and washed and in clean clothes, but he looked pathetic nonetheless. Sally, changed out of her robe and nightgown, stood nearby with Monica and Elena.

"Get anything out of him?" Morales asked

Nacho twitched a shoulder. Of medium height, potbellied and

bespectacled, he looked more like a supermarket clerk than an undercover agent. On the other hand, a good undercover agent would not look like one. "Not much more than I got from my snitch," he said. "Miguel didn't see the massacre, just heard the gunshots. There's something weird going on over there."

Morales rested his hands on his saddle horn. "What's weird about bandits?"

"Whoever killed them didn't take a thing, that's what my snitch told me. Wallets, money, watches, rings—everything was still on them. And the women's clothes weren't messed up, like they would have been if they'd been raped. It's like some psychos wasted those people just for the helluva it. Or like something terrorists would do."

"*Terrorists?*" Castle blurted out.

"I'm talking narco-terrorists, not Osama bin Laden," said Nacho.

To Castle, this was hardly reassuring. One of the deputies meanwhile led Miguel to the patrol car, in which a third cop waited behind the wheel. As he climbed in, Miguel threw a fleeting, bewildered glance at Castle and his saviors.

"So what happens to him now?" Monica asked Nacho.

"Mr. Espinoza is what we call an I-two-forty-seven detainee, ma'am. Meaning a special case."

"He's a suspect?"

"It'll be up to the sheriff to decide that, but I kind of doubt it. If Héctor's and Reynaldo's bodies are found and it looks like what happened is what he says happened, they'll hold him as a material witness. Protective custody in the county jail till the investigation's over."

"We're not going to find anything by yakking here," Morales said, and they rode at a slow trot in single file, the Navaho in the lead. The deputies, one a rookie, the other a sergeant, followed them in the second patrol car as far as Castle's cabin. They parked there and, slinging assault rifles over their shoulders, proceeded on foot alongside the mounted party to provide security.

Earlier, preoccupied with horsemanship, Castle had failed to notice that Gerardo and his cousin were also armed, Blaine wearing a refurbished Luger in a military-style flap holster, Gerardo a revolver. Turning in the saddle, he asked Blaine, "Why the guns?" They had three cops to guard them.

"We got us a real badass out here somewheres," Blaine answered. "If my old A-team was with us, I'd still carry this piece. I don't rely on nobody to take care of me. I take care of me."

If they hadn't been on a search for dead bodies, Castle could have believed they were riding for pleasure on a fine winter afternoon, the high desert air so pure it seemed as if there were no atmosphere at all. The snow-rimmed Huachucas were bright in the sun, a light breeze was blowing, and white clouds drifted like a fleet of blimps over the mountains and past a real tethered blimp floating above the Fort Huachuca army base. It was, he'd heard, loaded with surveillance cameras and all manner of high-tech electronics, its purpose to detect planes flying drugs into the United States.

They rode over the ridge. Castle directed them to the manzanita thicket. Morales and Gerardo dismounted, studied the ground, and set off across the arroyo, leading their horses. They walked along at a normal pace, barely pausing. Whatever sign they were reading, it was all Sanskrit to Castle. It was in fact invisible. He could see nothing but grass and rock and scrub.

"As another pair of eyes, I'm not much good," he murmured to Blaine, riding beside him.

"Look there." Blaine pointed ahead. "That line of bent grass? It's bent in the opposite direction to the grass around it. That's where he was walkin'. It's his breadcrumbs."

Castle strained to see the breadcrumbs, but they remained hidden. Morales and Gerardo followed them north for a distance, then west, then east, then north again. Alone and terrified in the moonless dark, Miguel had gone in circles. The meandering route led to another arroyo, paved with red and brown boulders. Morales squatted, examined the rocks, then walked up and down the arroyo. He'd lost the track. Gerardo, making his own survey, stopped by a huge boulder and called out, "Oye, John. Ven aquí." He gestured at the boulder's surface and at a smaller rock lying beside it. He and the Navaho conversed for a while in Spanish, motioning downstream, or what would have been downstream if water had been running.

"That little rock got knocked off the big one, that's what Gerardo's sayin'," Blaine explained before Castle asked. "The small one is red, got a lot of iron oxide in it. If it had been kicked off a while back, the stain it left on the big one would have been faded by now, but it ain't. So whatever knocked it off, two legs or four, did it in the last couple of days."

Morales and Gerardo made their way slowly down the arroyo, eyes lowered. When they stopped some thirty yards away, Gerardo summoned Blaine and Castle with a wave of his arm. They rode to where the two other men stood on a slab of slanting rock, its base powdered with sand. In the sand, clear as a plaster cast, was the print of a tennis shoe with a diamond tread.

"Did I tell you Gerardo can track a lost cow over bare rock or what?" Blaine crowed. "Now ain't you glad we came along?"

"Blaine, your company alone makes it all worthwhile," Morales quipped.

He and Gerardo remounted. Because the lower arroyo was mostly pulverized gravel, it was easy to track from horseback, almost as easy as tracking in snow. At a point where the arroyo plunged some twenty feet down a sheer rock wall, the footprints turned off onto a stock trail that wandered through a dense oak and juniper forest. Mexican jays flitted through the trees, making harsh cries. Knotty branches scraped the riders' faces, and on the ground prickly pear spread oval stems bristling with barbed spines. Finally the stock trail came out onto a road with a broad wash beyond it and low hills beyond the wash.

"Juniper Canyon." Blaine flashed a satisfied grin that his guess had proved right. "Straight-line distance, we ain't three miles from where we started."

Miguel's footprints led up the road. Morales could tell, by their depth and the length of the stride, that he'd been running. There were several old tire tracks in the reddish beige dust. One pair, deep corrugated treads spaced more narrowly than a car's or truck's, was new. It had been made by an ATV.

As they rode around a bend, the horses threw their noses into the air, snorted, and danced nervous little jigs.

"Must be right close," Morales said. "Nothing like the smell of a corpse to give a horse the fits."

They dismounted and led the horses into the woods and hitched them to the stout branch of an old black oak, then went up the road on foot, following Miguel's prints and the four-wheeler's ruts. Morales held up when he came to a break in the ATV's track.

"The driver stopped the vehicle here, and those must be his. He was wearing hiking boots." Morales pointed at footprints with a zigzag pattern to the soles that led a few feet into the sandy wash, choked with willows and the gray-green whisks of Apache broom. Then, walking a little farther, Morales declared, "Well, we've got us a homicide, sure enough." Ten yards away was the first body—Reynaldo's, Castle assumed, because Miguel said he'd been shot in the head, and there was a dime-size hole above one eye. A great amount of blood, all his body had held, had pumped out the much larger hole in the back of his skull, leaving a rust-colored stain in the ground. Héctor's corpse lay behind Reynaldo's and a few yards off to its right. He was on his side, and with his head pillowed on one hand, he could have been mistaken for a man taking a nap were it not for the two ragged exit wounds, one in the back of his shoulder, the other in the chest. The bodies had been in a deep freeze overnight, but now, as they thawed, the men picked up the smell that had spooked the horses, an odor something like rotting garbage.

Castle stood, staring at the corpses with morbid fascination, reminded once again of his sheltered life. Soon to be fifty-six years old, he never had seen dead men before, much less men who had died violently. He had even been spared from the sight of his father's body; he hadn't been at the hospital when Dr. Castle expired at two o'clock in the morning, and because that once-handsome, vigorous man had been ravaged by his cancer, his mother had insisted on a closed coffin at the visitation.

"You boys stay put," the older deputy, the sergeant, commanded. "Too many people walking around will contaminate the crime scene."

Taking care where they stepped to avoid erasing any part of whatever story was written in the earth, he and the rookie searched for shell casings from the killer's gun but did not find any.

"Probably used a revolver," the sergeant said. "If it was a semiauto, the dude policed up his brass, left as little evidence as possible."

A short distance from Héctor's body, hidden by a clump of broom, the two policemen found the brush pile in which Miguel said he and his friends had cached the marijuana. It appeared to have been kicked apart, and a few fragments of burlap hung from the tangled branches.

Morales in the meantime moved deeper into the wash, scaring up a jackrabbit as he vanished into the willow thickets. He returned about fifteen minutes later.

"Everything I've seen so far pretty much confirms Miguel's story. He took a dump over on the other side, like he said. He laid down over there for quite a while—the grass is flattened, like a deer bed. And then he came back to see what happened to his compañeros." Morales paused, gazing thoughtfully. "That's what I love about tracking. Sign doesn't commit perjury. You know how to read it, it's a truth-teller every time."

"So what truth is it tellin'?" asked Blaine.

Morales dropped to one knee and drew a diagram in the dirt with a forefinger. "The one guy, the guy shot twice . . ."

"That would be Héctor," Blaine said. "Other one is Reynaldo."

"Héctor is laying down over here," Morales continued. "He hears the ATV, goes to the edge of the road and flags it down. The driver gets off. Him and Héctor are standing almost face-to-face by the vehicle. Then Héctor walks a ways back into the wash to where the dope is stashed. The driver follows him a couple of yards but stops right here"—he makes another mark with his finger—"maybe ten or twelve feet from Héctor. Reynaldo is over here, off to Héctor's left. Okay, Miguel says he saw Reynaldo drop first. A well-aimed shot to the head. Reynaldo's dead before he hits the ground. Then the killer pivots to cap Héctor—you can see where he did, there's a kind of arc-shaped mark where he turned his feet. Héctor's turned and started to run. The first round hits him square in the back, comes out his chest. I'm no ballistics expert, but I'd guess the impact spun him around, and the next round catches him in the upper chest and comes out his shoulder. That's page one of the story."

"Page two bein' what?"

"Then the killer goes looking for Miguel."

"The sign tells you that?"

"I found prints matching his out in the wash. He was moving back and forth like he was looking for something or someone, and my money would be on someone. See what I'm saying?"

"He knew there was three of them."

"Right. So he doesn't find Miguel. He can't keep up the search. He's just killed a couple of people. So he pulls the brush apart and snatches the merca. Drags the bales to the ATV—the drag marks are plain as day—loads up, and takes off—fast. You look at the tire treads, you see where the wheels spun and the vehicle swerved when he punched the gas. There it is, there's the story."

Blaine squinted at him, chicken claws forming at the corners of his eyes. "But there's a whole lot don't make sense. You're sayin' some guy just happens to be drivin' by on his four-wheeler, just happens to be carryin' a gun, just happens to run into those old boys, just happens to know they've got a load of dope hidden in them rocks, then holes them both and rips the stuff off? That's about three too many coincidences for me to swallow."

Morales stood and ran his fingers around the brim of his hat.

"Blaine! The perp didn't just *happen* to run into them. He had to be the guy who was supposed to take delivery. He probably didn't know about what went down on the other side, so when his mules didn't show, he must've figured they were ripping him off and went looking for them. Maybe it was just blind luck that he did find them, or maybe he had some tracking skills and picked up their trail. How did he know where they'd stashed the dope? He asked them, and Héctor and Reynaldo, figuring this was their guy, told him. *Sí, señor, tenemos la merca*, and there it is, under that brush."

"So why kill them if they was bein' so cooperative?"

"I'm a tracker. I know what the ground tells me happened or probably happened. Why it happened and motive and all that shit, that's for the sheriff. I don't investigate crimes."

"But hell, you got to have a good guess to make it add up."

"Maybe the plan was to kill them all along."

Blaine scuffed the ground with a boot. "John, the drug boss what sent those three sad sacks over the line with all that merchandise got to have an IQ not much bigger than my hat size."

"Been done before, turning migrants into mules to pay their way. Those three, they were just backs to put the stuff on."

The sergeant and his partner used their VHF radio to summon a team of investigators.

"Could be a while before they get here," the sergeant added. "But you boys stick around. They might have a few questions for you. You in particular, sir," he said, looking at Castle. "You found the only eyewitness, and that's what got this pretty little ball rolling."

They returned to where the horses were tied and sat in the shade. Castle wanted nothing more than to go back to his cabin, to his dog and his Seneca. It gladdened his heart to know that he had rescued Miguel, but that simple act of mercy had somehow enmeshed him in something he wanted no part of. He pondered the chain of accidents that had led him to this point, beginning with his decision, made for no special reason, to hunt close to home this morning. A chain of accidents, yes, but when he looked at it in its totality, it did not seem accidental; it had the quality of fate, as if the course of his life and Miguel's were destined to meet. Break one link, and he would not be here with his cowboy cousin and a Navaho tracker and a Mexican vaquero and two dead strangers lying amid the willows and broom across a road in the desert.

Blaine tapped a cigarette out of his pack and offered one to

Morales, who shook his head. "Those things will kill you sure as a bullet."

"Not these." Blaine held up the blue package with the face of an Indian in full headdress. "This here brand has got none of those additives and preservatives. It's a healthy cigarette."

Morales snorted. "I like that. A healthy cigarette. Like healthy strychnine."

Blaine took a deep drag, tilted his head back, and exhaled a long plume of smoke. "There. I feel better already." Gerardo rolled one of his own. He understood almost as little English as Castle did Spanish, but he seemed content to sit there smoking in silent detachment.

"I was just thinkin', John," said Blaine abruptly, "that our granddad, mine and Gil's, wouldn't of put up with none of this shit. He was at one time a deputy sheriff of Santa Cruz County. Back in the twenties and thirties."

"Are you leading up to something or just passing time?"

Blaine said, "He'd found out some son of a bitch killed two men on his land, he wouldn't of called the law—"

"Of course not," Morales interrupted. "He *was* the law."

"Even when he wasn't, is what I'm sayin'. He would of made it his business to find the son of a bitch, and when he did . . . I'll tell you a story. This was back before he was a lawman, nineteen eighteen or around then. He was out checkin' the range and caught this guy with a runnin' iron and a San Ignacio calf with a piggin' rope round its back legs. Ben got the old drop on him and got off his horse and cold-cocked him with a butt stroke of his saddle gun. He didn't want to waste good rope tyin' him up, so he got his cutters and snipped off some barbed wire from a fence nearby and wrapped it around the rustler's wrists and ankles. Ben flung him over the horse and rode with him all the way to Patagonia, to the town marshal's office, and dumped the guy right there. Marshal comes out, Ben says, 'Caught this fella a-tryin' to steal one of our calves. You don't take care of him, I will.' " Blaine snubbed the cigarette in the dirt, then field-stripped it—an old habit from Vietnam. "Did your mama ever tell you that story, Gil?"

"She hardly ever talked about him," Castle said, a split-screen image in his mind: the Darien matron tending her garden on Scott's Cove; her father cracking a rustler's jaw with a rifle butt and tying him up with barbed wire. That such a woman had sprung from such a man seemed almost unnatural, as if parent and offspring belonged to two distinct species.

"That's the kind of man he was," said Blaine, with reverence. " 'You don't take care of him, I will.' "

"Different times," said Morales. "Nowadays the rustler would probably sue."

"They wasn't much for lawsuits back then. But if Ben was alive today, count on it, the son of a bitch what shot those two sad sacks wouldn't enjoy his newfound wealth for long."

"The dude with the IQ your hat size. Maybe he's not so dumb after all."

"I don't care if he's Albert goddamn Einstein. I don't want him and those other greaseballs usin' my ranch as a highway for the poison they're peddlin', grass, coke, or heroin." Blaine scooped up a handful of dirt and sifted it through his fingers. "Sung to the land," he said in a quieter voice. "An Aussie commando I knew in Vietnam told me that's what the aboriginal folks say about a place that's a part of you so much, you'd die of bein' away from it. Sung to the land. That's how I feel about this ranch. I've always taken good care of it, and I intend to continue doin' just that."

Morales clapped him on the shoulder. "Know the feeling. But we both know that this valley has been a drug corridor for twenty years."

"Yeah. But this here shootin' puts things on a different level." Blaine paused and watched a harrier soar over the wash. "I've got a near-eighty-year-old mother to think about. Feisty as all hell and probably in better shape than me, but she is lookin' at eighty."

The sound of approaching cars intruded. In a moment a small convoy came jouncing down the road—two SUVs from the sheriff's department and an ambulance with its roof lights flashing but its siren off. One of the cars swung off sideways to block the road. A patrolman climbed out and immediately began to rope off the area with yellow tape stamped with black lettering, KEEP OUT—CRIME SCENE, though it was unlikely anyone would come tramping through this remote area. Two plainclothesmen emerged from the second car, and while one—a homicide detective who gave his name as Lieutenant Soto—questioned Castle, Blaine, and Gerardo. Morales led the other, carrying a camera and a black briefcase, to the bodies. He photographed them from different angles, then took pictures of the four-wheeler's tire marks and the footprints. When he was finished, he signaled the EMTs, who pulled out a stretcher and body bags from the ambulance and went up the wash to collect Héctor and Reynaldo. All this investigative activity had a degree of unreality—it looked like a scene from a cop show—but those were real corpses being placed into the body bags. How would their families be located? Castle asked himself. Who would notify them, new citizens in the nation of grief? He could almost hear the lamentations that would rise from obscure villages in Mexico, and those but a few voices in the vast chorus of mourning singing even now in homes in America, in Afghanistan, in a thousand other places. If you could broadcast the groans and shrieks and howls of a single day, the sound would deafen the world.

Morales returned. "We're done. The rest is up to them," he said, jerking his head at the detectives as they poked through the brush.

"What do you think?" asked Blaine. "I mean the chances they'll catch the guy?"

Morales glanced at the EMTs, shoving one of the bodies into the ambulance. "Two more dead drug mules? Don't think this will be on the sheriff's A-list."

CASTLE'S ACT of human decency had opened a breach in his sanctuary's walls, and the world he thought he'd renounced came marching in. All next day reporters phoned the ranch, asking to interview him. Monica took the calls—there was no phone in the cabin—and relayed them to Castle on his cell. He did not answer one, prompting the reporters to call again. Monica got annoyed. "I feel like your press secretary," she said. "Can I give them your cell number?" No, she could not. "Just tell them I'm out of town."

His refusals did not keep his name out of the papers or off the air. Though bodies turned up almost every day on the Arizona desert, Héctor's and Reynaldo's deaths, and Miguel's ordeal, possessed sufficient novelty to make the evening news on TV and the front pages of the *Arizona Daily Star* in Tucson, the *Nogales International*, and Patagonia's local weekly, the *Bulletin*. **TWO BORDER CROSSERS MURDERED—Hunter's Rescue of Lost Migrant Leads to Grisly Find,** its headline cried from the vending machines in front of the post office and the Stage Stop Hotel. All this sensationalism had made Castle the center of a repulsive attention. One day, as he was buying groceries in the Patagonia Market, he was practically accosted by a man he'd never seen before. "Hey! You're the guy who found those dead Mexicans!" He fled without correcting the man's misinformation—he'd found a *live* Mexican—and holed up in his cabin for the next week.

Almost every night he lay awake till past midnight, listening for footsteps outside, waiting for Sam to warn him of intruders. In the penumbra between sleep and waking, he experienced visions, half dream, half hallucination, of Héctor's and Reynaldo's wounds, of dried blood, of the killer's boot prints in the dust. He snapped out of one at four in the morning, convinced that the murderer was sneaking up on his cabin to kill him. There was no reason for the man to come after him, but at such an hour the rational mind is overthrown by the lizard brain. He got up, loaded his shotgun, and propped it against the wall next to his bed, which made him feel only a little less vulnerable. The next day he drove to the Walgreens in Nogales to renew his Ambien prescription. The pharmacist told him he could pick it up in an hour. Castle took the opportunity to go to the sporting goods department at Wal-Mart, where he bought a .357 Magnum revolver, two boxes of ammunition, and a set of paper targets. He practiced behind his house. Although he was less adept with a pistol than with a rifle or shotgun, he put more than half his shots in the black at twenty-five yards. That left the question as to whether he was capable of shooting another human being, even in self-defense. The possibility could not be dismissed that if confronted by someone who meant to take his life, he would let him take it.

5

WHEN THE PROFESSOR FINISHED SHOWERING and stepped into the bedroom, he found Clarice lying on the bed on her stomach, her bare rear end hoisted.

"Woof!" she said, twisting her head to look at him with a maniacal grin. "Woof! Woof!"

She wasn't acting on one of her sudden, mindless impulses. Not fifteen minutes ago, fully dressed in her park ranger's uniform, she'd left his hotel room. She must have deliberately left the door ajar, then sneaked back in and taken off her clothes, which, he noticed, were draped neatly over a chair—more evidence of premeditation. For all he knew, she'd been posturing there on the floor the whole time he was in the shower, doggedly (the adverb seemed apt) waiting for her scrubbed lover to come to her.

He said calmly, "I thought I told you to leave."

"Not before you fuck me, Euclid." She added a syllable to the name she knew him by—E—yew-clid—and wiggled her ass. She was somewhere in her early forties, a few years older than he, but her bottom, like the rest of her body, had been kept fit by the long treks she made up desert canyons and mountainsides, searching for lost hunters and hikers—a woman skilled in effecting rescues of everyone but herself.

Her shamelessness disgusted him, but his cock reacted to her presentation as his knee would to the tap of a physician's mallet. A surprise—he thought last night's festivities had depleted him for at least a week. Well, the easiest way to get rid of her, the *only* way as far as his cock was concerned, was to do what she wanted. Peeling off the towel wrapped around his waist, he climbed onto the bed and knelt behind her, caressing the divided globe of her bottom with both hands, its curves evoking a sound like a trumpet—Ta-ra-ta-ta!—its smoothness causing a luminous green blob to shimmer before his eyes, its creamy color summoning up a scent like flowers. Fucking Clarice was a multimodal experience, a son et lumière show, with shape prompting sound, texture color, color smell—the full sensory package of his peculiar condition. He threw himself into the act with élan, not so much for the pleasure of it as to get himself off and her out of the room as quickly as possible. He accomplished the first goal in less than two minutes.

"Now that wasn't so difficult, was it?" she said, squirming into her panties, her tanned face aglow with triumph.

How he regretted taking up with this lustful lunatic, the randy ranger. The Professor led a precarious life. His work—his calling, as he liked to think of it—required the concentration of a high-wire artist working without a net. Unpredictable Clarice threatened his ability to keep his balance.

"On your way," he said. "I'm running late."

"Such a busy, busy boy." She got into her uniform and passed a comb through her hair, tinted a macadam shade of black and cropped raggedly short, as if by a stylist with delirium tremens. "Late for what? Why is it you won't tell me what you do?"

"Consider the possibility that it's none of your business."

She pressed the tip of his nose as if it were a doorbell. "You wouldn't be a narc, would you, darling?"

He clutched her wrist and fixed upon her the unnerving stare of his deep-set, preternaturally blue eyes, a stare that seemed to look through its object rather than at it, with the emotionless concentration of a predator studying its prey before a pounce.

"Hey, okay, asshole, I get your point," she said, and he relaxed his grip.

"Now it really is time for you to go," he said almost tenderly.

With relief, he watched the door close behind her. For good measure, he locked it. Patience, he counseled himself. Wait for her to end it. She was bound to sooner rather than later. Clarice openly boasted of her many conquests of younger men, and although she was faithful to whomever she was screwing at the time (she'd once described herself as a "serial slut"), she got bored fairly quickly and moved on.

The Professor had inherited some of his Mexican mother's theatrical, quasi-pagan Catholicism. Even though his rendezvous with Nacho was going to be routine, he considered it prudent to go forth in a state of grace. Returning to the bathroom, he soaked a washcloth in water as hot as he could stand and cleansed Clarice from his privates while silently reciting an Act of Contrition, followed by a prayer to Jesús Malverde, patron saint of border traffickers. The Professor did not directly traffic in drugs or people—his main commodity was information—but he figured Malverde's protection covered that as well.

After dressing (pressed blue jeans, ostrich-skin cowboy boots, a brown leather jacket), he rode the antique elevator—it had a folding cage door, a brass dial and floor arrow, even an elevator operator—down to the lobby. He always stayed at the Gadsden on his sorties into Douglas because, being a history buff and something of a romantic, he liked its exceedingly retro atmosphere, its Italian marble columns and swooping staircase, up which Pancho Villa was said to have ridden his horse in a fit of revolutionary enthusiasm, evoking images of Douglas's glory days as a rich copper-mining town. He handed his key—a metal key, not some flimsy plastic card—to the desk clerk and paid his bill. Although the Gadsden wasn't so retro that it didn't take credit cards, he paid in cash. It was his habit to leave a light paper trail. "See you next trip, Mr. Carrington," the clerk said. This was the identity he assumed on the U.S. side of the line, Euclid J. Carrington. Managing the activities of his various incarnations, all united in the person of The Professor, was his high-wire act. A careless step, a distraction at the wrong moment, an incautious word uttered to the wrong person could have terrible consequences, of which a bullet in the brain would be the least terrible.

Outside, on this nippy Sunday morning, G Avenue was empty, the quiet hinting at the deserted town Douglas might have become if, after Phelps Dodge shut down the copper smelters in the 1980s, a brisk trade in narcotics, passing through the port of entry from Agua Prieta, had not provided new employment opportunities for some of its citizens and restored its prosperity. The Professor walked around to the parking lot in back of the Gadsden and got into his rented Ford Explorer. His own car—or rather, the car belonging to his other avatar, Gregorio Bonham, a captain in the Mexican Federal Judicial Police—was stashed at MFJP headquarters in Agua Prieta, where he had spent Friday and Saturday snooping into the recent activities of Yvonne Menéndez, the city's narco-queen. As he always did when a meeting with Nacho had been arranged, he'd crossed the line on foot, informing the U.S. Customs cop that he was an American tourist returning from a day trip, a masquerade to which his appearance lent authenticity. He looked more gringo than most gringos, his English father's genes having won supremacy over his mother's, except for the tinge of olive in his complexion, which was barely noticeable.

Very little about him was noticeable, as befitted a man who preferred the shadows to the light. He was of unimpressive stature, exactly five feet nine and a half inches tall and 160 pounds. His maple-brown hair was cut short (he eschewed the shaggy look affected by most clandestine operatives), and his features were so well proportioned and symmetrical as to be unmemorable. Indeed, a large mole on his left cheek having been surgically removed some time ago, his face looked like one of those generic faces that used to appear in back-page magazine ads for mail-order artists' schools. DRAW ME AND WIN TWO FREE LESSONS! The one striking aspect of his appearance were those pale eyes that looked as if a pair of thumbs had pressed them halfway back into his skull and that seemed to be lit from within, the fixity of their gaze unsettling to everyone who met them. This stare wasn't something he affected to frighten people, though he occasionally found its intimidation useful. He was simply focused, noticing details, on the lookout for threats, for the tics of expression or gesture that betrayed a liar. He was a hunter whose quarry was reliable information—"actionable intelligence," in military jargon—and like all hunters, he was acutely aware of his environment at all times.

Before starting off, he called Nacho on his—that is, Carrington's—cell phone.

"U.S. Border Patrol. Agent Gomez speaking," Nacho answered.

"Ignacio. I'm running late."

"I'll be waiting."

Less than an hour later he parked beside Nacho's unmarked Jeep Cherokee at the junction of two ranch roads in the San Bernardino Valley. Under a blank winter sky the vehicles were lost in the vastness of the desert uplands rising westward to the Chiricahuas, eastward to the embrowned crags of the Peloncillos, where Geronimo had surrendered. The Professor loved it out here—the emptiness, the silence, the Sonoran Desert's wholeness that mocked the lines little men had drawn on their maps.

He climbed into the Cherokee and with a cursory handshake said, "Awfully good to see you again, Ignacio." Despite his American schooling and U.S. Army service, his English still bore traces of his father's Briticisms.

"*Nacho* is okay. We've known each other long enough."

"You're not a tortilla chip," The Professor joked. Concerned that the Border Patrol agent would think he was a screwball, he couldn't tell him that he preferred calling him Ignacio because he didn't like the way calling him Nacho *felt.* It was hard to describe—something like grabbing a handful of tacks; whereas *Ignacio* evoked a smooth, pleasant sensation, like closing his fist over a glob of shaving cream.

"So what held you up?"

"A meaningless relationship."

"That nympho park ranger?"

The Professor nodded. There was very little Nacho didn't know about him, including his sexual liaisons. Conversely, there was very little about Nacho that he didn't know. Although some might consider him a snitch, he did not view himself as such. If he was, then Nacho was *his* snitch, which made their relationship more collegial or at least symbiotic.

"You've seen these?" Nacho asked, brusquely coming to the point. He handed The Professor a file folder of newspaper clippings. **Mexi-**

can Authorities Baffled by Mass Slaying of Immigrants, read a headline in the *Arizona Daily Star*. "I'm baffled, too. No robbery, no rape, no attempt to kidnap them for the ransom. More like an act of terrorism than anything else."

"Why does this concern you?"

"We're wondering if something's going on we ought to know about," said Nacho.

"Terrorism about covers it. We're pretty sure Yvonne was behind it."

"I guess that doesn't surprise me. La Roja is quite the little lady," Nacho remarked, in reference to the reputation for viciousness Yvonne had established for herself since she'd taken over the Menéndez organization from her husband, Fermín, murdered last year. She had put out the contract on him. Later, when the Border Patrol and U.S. Customs clamped down on her operations, seizing half her loads on tips from informants, she conducted a snitch hunt with a ferocity that impressed her male counterparts in the trade—and they were not easily impressed when it came to acts of violence. In about six weeks fourteen people were tortured and murdered. That only two were informants was of no concern to her. "Better that a dozen innocents die than two guilty ones get away with it," she'd said. The discovery of the mutilated bodies, lined up beside a desert cattle tank, made headlines all over Mexico. Fingers, hands, and feet had been chopped off and scattered around the well to feed the coyotes and vultures. **CHARCA DE MUERTE!!!—The Pond of Death—**screamed the tabloids over gruesome photographs.

"So who is she trying to terrorize?" Nacho inquired.

"There are rumors. We do know she can't stand wetbacks or wetback smugglers. They burn the routes. They attract too many of your boys. So one theory is that she was sending a message to the polleros to run their chickens somewhere else."

"Carrasco doesn't like pollos and polleros for the same reason."

"C'mon, Ignacio," The Professor said in a scoffing tone. Joaquín Carrasco, mero mero of the Hermosillo Cartel, was the most businesslike of Mexico's narcotraficantes. Murdering webacks wasn't his style.

Nacho peered at him over his John Lennon glasses, but like everyone else's, his gaze couldn't hold The Professor's and caromed like a billiard ball off the cushion. For a moment or two, he looked away toward a treeless summit of the Chiricahuas, where the snow lay like a slab of whitewashed concrete. Then he said, "But I'm thinking, there's a problem with your theory. The San Pedro Valley and Douglas are Yvonne's territory. The massacre took place in the San Rafael, and that's Carrasco's."

"You've got the geography right."

"There's no reason why Yvonne should give a good goddamn if wets are burning the San Rafael routes. They're not hers."

"Right again."

"This is starting to feel like a tooth extraction," said Nacho. "Don't make my life difficult. You're on our side of the line at the moment."

"I am still a citizen of El Norte," The Professor said in mock indignation.

"Yeah, with a federal warrant outstanding for your arrest and some people in the CIA who would love to settle accounts."

"They've got better things to do now. Busy hunting terrorists, real and imagined. Besides, I'm too valuable to the Department of Homeland Security right where I am."

"Don't get smug," Nacho scolded. "So these rumors . . ."

"Let's say we're not sure what Yvonne is up to. Let's say we're keeping an eye on her. She's a woman in a man's world. Also ambitious."

"I know that. I'm asking about these rumors."

"Ever see that old movie *Key Largo*?"

"What the hell are you talking about?"

"There's a moment in it when the Humphrey Bogart character asks the Edward G. Robinson character, Johnny Rocco, what he wants. And Rocco says, 'More. That's right! I want more.' There's Yvonne for you. She couldn't spell *enough* in English or Spanish."

"Look, the Agua Prieta Cartel is too small to go head-to-head with Carrasco," Nacho said. "She wouldn't think of muscling in on him if she didn't have somebody behind her."

"A valid supposition."

Nacho sighed, exasperated with the evasive answers.

An evasiveness The Professor considered appropriate. He was a captain of federales, yes, but he was also Joaquín Carrasco's eyes and ears on both sides of the line, keeping tabs on gringo law enforcement agencies while at the same time monitoring the loyalties and honesty of the multitudes Carrasco employed, from the managers of his marijuana plantations to the dealers who marketed his products in the

United States. The Professor much admired Carrasco, in whom an astute mind—he would have been a CEO in any other culture—was camouflaged by coarse peasant features. Yvonne's flamboyant violence drew the sort of publicity he abhorred for the negative effect it had on business. The "Pond of Death" incident had been bad enough; the slaughter of the migrants was worse, and not only because of the attention it attracted; it was a kind of declaration on her part.

The Professor's role in Carrasco's organization required discretion. How much information should he give about Carrasco's conflict with the mercurial La Roja, so named for her brittle red hair? Information was the currency of undercover work—you had to give some to get some—but it was never wise to blow the whole wad. Speaking in a low, monotonous voice, he dribbled out another rumor he'd gathered in Agua Prieta: Yvonne had entered into alliance with the Gulf Cartel, the largest and most powerful of the Mexican drug rings.

Nacho, hands folded on his paunch, listened attentively. "And with them on her side, she'd be strong enough to challenge Carrasco."

"Another valid supposition," said The Professor. "You know, if she doesn't behave herself, it could cause you guys as much trouble as it could us."

"Who's 'us'? The federales or Carrasco?" Nacho questioned, a wink in his voice.

The Professor answered with a fugitive smile.

Nacho leaned over and squeezed his knee. "I love these get-togethers. I've never run into anybody like you. I can't figure out if you're in this for yourself, if you're a double agent, a triple agent, a quadruple agent, or what."

"I'm an agent of history."

Nacho gave him a baffled scowl.

"What's happening right here, right now, is history in the making," said The Professor. "Forget the drugs for the moment. All these wets crossing the border—half a million, a million every year—is the biggest migration in the world today. Did you know that?"

"Guess I do now."

"We can't escape history, but we're not helpless. We can guide it, we can manage it."

Nacho threw him a little bow. "Gracias, Profesor. Gracias por la lección."

"You're not listening. We have a common interest. So let's bring in the drugs. Carrasco doesn't like conflict. He doesn't want a war on this part of the border. Look at what's going on in Nuevo Laredo. Half a dozen gangs fighting each other. Machine-gun fire every night, cars blowing up on the street, rocket-propelled grenades. The last police chief was in office for exactly one day before he got capped. Baghdad on the Rio Grande. Do we want that in Agua Prieta? In Naco? In Nogales? We damn well fucking don't."

"¡Oye, amigo! I get it. Organized crime is preferable to disorganized crime. What do you expect us to do?"

"To give us a hand, in case we have to ask for it. Cooperation between the law enforcement agencies of our two friendly countries—a beautiful thing, no? All right, you convened the meeting. What else is on your agenda?"

Pausing, Nacho pulled a document from his file folder and handed it to The Professor. It was a photocopy of a homicide report from the Santa Cruz County sheriff's office.

"You're familiar with this little incident?" asked Nacho.

"Heard about it. What do you want to talk about it for? Who gives a shit?"

"No one," said Nacho. "I wouldn't give a shit, except that over there"—hooking a thumb out the back window, which faced south—"we've got seven dead migrants, and over here, we've got two dead burreros. Two out of three, who happened to be following the wets, who were supposed to act as decoys—"

"You and me, we exchange strategic information," The Professor interrupted, irritated. "Three mules would have been carrying sixty or seventy kilos max. What's that worth? A little north of a hundred grand? This is small-unit stuff."

"Still, I'm thinking, you tell me Yvonne ordered the massacre. You tell me she's maybe muscling in on Carrasco's routes. I'm thinking, Are there dots here that need connecting? If there are, does it mean anything?"

"You're thinking that a load of dope was mixed up in it all. Whose dope? Did it belong to Joaquín, and did Yvonne rip him off and cap the mules just to show she can?"

"You were the one talking about a war, so sure, I'm wondering if this might've been the first shot," Nacho said. "Whose dope was it?"

"No idea. Joaquín would never hire pollos to haul a load, not even a small one. Chickens don't make good mules. My guess would be that they were working for some freelancer and that they bumped into some bajadores. Two dots is all you've got, and nada in between."

"Well, if you hear anything more about this, let me know."

"When did the Border Patrol get into investigating homicide?"

"Information I could pass on to the sheriff. Cooperation between law enforcement agencies—a beautiful thing, no? I need to stretch my legs."

They got out and slouched against the front of the Cherokee. It was getting on to midday, but a pronounced chill remained in the air.

"I'm thinking," The Professor said in mimic of Nacho's idiom, "that in the quid pro quo, today it's been more quid than quo."

Nacho looked down at his shoes with a small private smile. He was an honest agent, as honest as someone in undercover work could be. Like The Professor, he also had to make compromises, giving in order to get; but there were certain lines he could not cross. That was fine with The Professor. He would rather deal with an honest agent than with a crooked one. The latter inevitably got greedy, got sloppy, and got caught, and there would go another source, off to jail.

"For example, we've heard whispers that you boys, having reduced the traffic in the San Pedro, are now going to shift resources to the west," The Professor prompted. "But that covers a lot of territory."

Nacho, still gazing at his shoes, weighed his options. He had to consider not only what to say but how to say it.

"The road that runs up from Altar to Sásabe?" he answered. "It's become a wetback interstate. Thirty vehicles per hour, twenty-four-seven. Trucks, vans, schoolbuses. Four to five thousand people a day."

That told The Professor some of what he needed to know—Border Patrol would be moving men and equipment like ground sensors and surveillance cameras to curtail immigrant trafficking in the Altar Valley. Drug loads moving through would be at greater risk of capture; Carrasco would be well advised to avoid the area for the time being. It would help to know how many men were to be deployed, which roads and trails they would concentrate on, where they were going to plant the sensors; but there was no point in trying to wheedle those sorts of specifics out of Nacho, assuming he even knew them. That was one of the lines he could not cross.

"So the scales are a bit more balanced," The Professor said, holding his two hands out, one slightly above the other. "Anything to make them like this?" He raised the lower hand alongside the upper.

Nacho nodded. "I saved the best for last. Vicente Cruz is on this side. Nogales. He showed up there about two weeks ago."

"Ah," said The Professor, making sure not to betray his excitement. "Bold move. Reckless, I'd say."

"Not so bold. He figured he's safer here than there. Knew we had nothing on him. No evidence, no witnesses that haven't suffered severe memory loss."

"Nobody hauled him in for a conversation?"

"Oh, sure. Soon as we got a fix on him, we asked ICE to pop him on immigration charges. The idea was we'd send him to Florence as an illegal and then sweat a confession out of him That didn't work, because it turns out the son of a bitch is a U.S. citizen. ICE had to let him go."

"Didn't know he was an American."

"Neither did we. He's laying low," Nacho continued. "His profile got any lower, he could walk under an ant without knocking his hat off. Could be he's retired."

"He's the right age, and he's got the money now."

"He's living with his older brother out on the south River Road. The brother's straight, but you know, he had to take his brother in. Can't turn your back on blood. A nephew is living out there, too."

"Who is?"

"Billy Cruz. He runs one of those shuttle services in Nogales, you know, for legal border crossers going to Tucson or Phoenix. Don't have much else on him."

"Dogs?"

"Two Rottweilers that belong to Vicente. Also a pistolero to go with the dogs."

Four men, a pair of attack dogs, The Professor thought. The house would be problematic. "Does he ever leave the place?"

"He likes to eat at a seafood restaurant in Nogales. He kind of holds court there a couple, three nights a week, with the pistolero along. Tehuantepec, it's called. It's in that shopping mall on Grand, just past Mariposa."

"Food any good?"

"They do shrimp in a brandy and cream sauce that's terrific. Shrimp is flown in fresh every day from Guaymas."

"I'll have to try it. Muchas gracias."

"De nada," replied Nacho. "So now I've done you a good deed."

"And I'll be doing you one. A wash, I'd say."

"Besa mi culo. I'm doing the bigger favor. I've gone out way out on a limb, giving you this. Time comes to return the favor, I'll expect you to be there." Nacho pushed himself away from the Cherokee's grill. "No mess, okay?"

"You didn't need to ask that," The Professor said.

6

IT WAS THE LAST DAY of the season, and Castle was to go quail hunting with Blaine and a neighboring rancher. On the road to the main house, the Suburban's tires spewed chunks of mud—a winter storm had passed through last night, dropping snow that had melted with first light. He parked and saw his aunt lugging feed bags into the "senior citizens' center," as Blaine had dubbed the corral where she kept two geriatric Hereford cows, one aged Texas longhorn, and a bay horse that was nearly a hundred in human years. Spotting him, Sally shuffled to the fence in her high rubber boots and called, "You shoot a mess of 'em, Gil! I just love them little things!" With her pewter-colored ponytail drooping back from under a greasy cowboy hat, wearing a sheepskin coat over her bathrobe, she looked like a cross between a bag lady and a septuagenarian hippie.

"I'll try," Castle said, walking toward her. "But seven each is the limit."

"Makes twenny-one with the three of you." Blaine had got his height from his father. Sally was about five four, and her small face, an oval of crow's feet and fissures, looked up at him from between the two top rails. "Blaine's a good deer hunter, but when it comes to birds, he couldn't hit his scrawny ass with both hands, so you shoot his limit for him, y'hear? A mess of 'em is what we want."

"Yes, ma'am."

"Elena's got a Messikin way of cookin' 'em," she said, dragging feed bags into the center of the corral. "Breakfast, Nick!" Castle heard her yell to the horse as he went to the door. "I ain't a-bringin' it to you, you come and get it or forget it!"

Inside, Blaine, with his Luger belted on, was drinking coffee at the kitchen table with Monica and another woman, whom Monica introduced as Tessa McBride.

"Hi, there," she said. She looked fortyish, and when she reached up to shake Castle's hand, he felt calluses and a strong grip.

"I've just been filling Tessa in on what happened here," Monica said. She must have color-rinsed her hair this morning; Castle had never seen it quite so blond.

"I've been away," Tessa explained in a low voice that, on the phone, could be mistaken for a man's. "Missed out on the excitement."

"Tessa's been showing her work all over, Scottsdale, Santa Fe, Las Cruces," Monica exclaimed. "She's a painter. Western landscapes."

"The most sentimental genre there is," said Tessa. "You know, cactus in the sunset, mounted Indians with bowed heads. I try to avoid that. I like to paint subdivisions, crappy subdivisions, and strip malls against beautiful mountains. To show what an ugly mess we're making of the landscape."

This struck Castle as more information than was warranted upon first meeting someone. She sounded as if she were promoting her style to a potential buyer.

"Anyway, art is only my sideline," she added.

"What's the line?" asked Castle.

"Cattle. I own the Crown A up the road."

He turned to Blaine. "Is the other guy coming here, or are we picking him up?"

Tessa smiled. Incomplete or incompetent orthodontics had left her with prominent eyeteeth that gave her a vaguely lupine look. "I'm the other guy."

It was only then that Castle noticed a hunting vest with blaze orange recoil pads draped over her chair.

"Forgot to mention that our hunting partner is female," Blaine said. "I don't think of Tess that way, as a woman I mean . . . Well, I guess that don't sound exactly right—"

"Oh, *no.*" Monica, fingers to her temples, squeezed her eyes shut. "It's just the right thing, as usual."

"One of the boys is what I meant to say."

"Dig that hole any deeper, and you'll hit oil," Tessa chided amiably. "Ready if you are."

When she stood to put on the hunting vest draped over her chair,

Castle saw a moderately tall woman with breasts disproportionately large for the rest of her—they formed a sloping shelf over a flat stomach, slim hips, and stalky legs. It was as if the bosom of a German soprano had been grafted onto the waist and limbs of a ballerina.

"And since I'm one of the boys, I'll drive," she said.

Outside, he let Sam out of the Suburban and put her in the back of Tessa's mud-spackled pickup, occupied by a German shorthair that growled at Sam's intrusion on his space.

"Knock it off, Klaus," Tessa commanded, then, like a mother excusing a surly child, explained to Castle that her dog was used to working alone.

Klaus, after giving Sam a few sniffs, which she reciprocated, flopped down onto the straw scattered over the truck bed. Blaine had meanwhile gone to the corral to talk to his mother. Or rather, to argue with her.

He had a complicated relationship with Sally. Although he ran the Ignacio's day-to-day operations, she remained president of the family corporation that owned the ranch and tended to treat her son like a hired hand.

"Now you stay put, Mama, while we're gone," Castle and Tessa overheard him say. "I don't want to come back and find you've gone out again. Don't make me worry about you."

"Worrying is your problem, not mine. I've been running this place since Uncle Jeff died, and that's getting to be on to forty years. How the hell do you think I got to be this old? By not knowing what I was doing?"

Blaine flung his long arms out wide. "Dammit! It's gotten to be dangerous around here."

"I've got that pistol you bought me, " she said, her voice rising to a near shriek. There she stood, nearly a foot shorter, and she seemed in her defiance bigger than he, her presence filling the space all around her.

"You couldn't hit nothin' if it was standin' right in front of you. You stick around here. That's all I'm gonna say."

"You got that right. That's all you're gonna say. I give the orders around here. Don't you go giving me any, Blaine Erskine."

"That Sally," Tessa remarked, shaking her head. She was leaning against the side of the truck, arms folded under her breasts. Castle couldn't keep his eyes off them, an attraction more curious than lecherous. He wondered if he was looking at a silicone job, though he couldn't imagine a ranch woman indulging herself in such cosmetic surgery. "Hope the hell I'm not like that twenty, thirty years down the road. A cantankerous old lady running cows."

"How many have you got?" he asked, to make conversation.

An awkward silence followed, then Tessa said: "You're not supposed to ask that, Gil. How big someone's ranch is, or how many head they run. It's like asking how much somebody earns."

It was a civil admonishment given to someone ignorant of western etiquette. He apologized, and she replied, "No problem."

Blaine strode toward them, his head down, and wrenched the pickup's door open as if he meant to tear it off its hinges. "Goddamn old woman, I'd smack her over the head with a fence post, but all that'd do is bust a perfectly good post."

They got in the truck, Castle in the middle, drawing his legs together to avoid touching Tessa's. She switched on the ignition, pulled out of the yard, and asked Blaine, "What exactly was all that about?"

He scowled. "Yesterday she drove on out to our allotment with a load of supplement. Does that all the time, drives way out there all by herself. She's got them beefs trained to come to the horn. Blows it, and they come trottin' over. I've told her to stop doin' that. We got us a killer runnin' around loose. And even if that wasn't the case, what if some drug mules see an old lady with a truck? They're gone to get some idea in their heads that maybe would not of been there otherwise. Besides, she's blind as a bat, can hardly see past the hood. But she don't listen. You heard her. 'I give the orders around here. Don't you be givin' me any, Blaine Erskine.' Like I'm eighteen goddamn years old."

"But you love her all the same, right?" Tessa said.

"She sure don't make it easy."

They rode in silence until they came to a T junction marked by carved wooden road signs tacked to a post. Beside it, a metal sign erected by the U.S. Border Patrol warned: CAUTION. SMUGGLING AND ILLEGAL IMMIGRATION MAY BE ENCOUNTERED IN THIS AREA. BE AWARE OF YOUR SURROUNDINGS. Castle wondered aloud what difference awareness of one's surroundings would make.

"It means that if you see some marijuanistas, you either pretend you don't see them, or you tip your hat and say 'Bienvenidos a los Estados

Unidos and have a nice day," Tessa said, offering further instructions in the ways of the West, the modern West.

They drove north down the main road through the San Rafael Valley. The rangelands loped away toward the mountains in the east and west, the grass the color of champagne in the afternoon light and the cottonwoods marking the course of Santa Cruz River bare of leaves. A coyote trotted across the road ahead, pausing briefly to glance at the oncoming truck before vanishing into the tall grass. Nearing the spot where the road hooked westward, Tessa pointed at a rose-colored adobe ranch house tucked away in a hollow amid a grove of cottonwoods.

"That's the Crown A. And since you asked, it's twenty-five hundred acres deeded, three thousand more under Forest Service grazing allotment, and a hundred and ten head of purebred Angus, grass-fed cradle to grave. Small potatoes compared to the cattle baron sitting on your right."

Blaine snorted. "You think the San Ignacio is a big outfit, you ain't never seen one. I worked for one out past the Santa Catalinas before I went into the army. A lot of it's housing developments now, but back then? Four hundred seventy-five thousand acres and maybe three, four thousand head. We'd spend half the year gatherin' from one end of the ranch, and then start all over at the other end."

The road took them past the shipping corrals for the Vaca Ranch, largest in the valley after the San Ignacio. In the distance, in a trough between two wavelike hills, horses grazed.

"And after I got out of the army, I rode for the San Bernardino down in Sonora." Blaine wasn't finished with his paean to big outfits. "You didn't think acres there, you thought square miles, a thousand of 'em, big as Rhode Island. Some of the last old-timey vaqueros worked there. It's where me and Gerardo first got to be amigos. He was the remudero back then. We'd be three, four months in the saddle. There was nothin' like it, ridin' the far wing on the big drives in the fall and them vaqueros singin' Norteño songs at night round the fire. *That* was cowboyin'. What we do here, it ain't much more'n farmin'."

"Got your point," Tessa said.

"I wasn't makin' a point. Just conversation."

"Conversation implies that other people get to say something."

Blaine clasped his big, raw hands behind his neck and leaned back. "Well, say somethin' then. Tell my cuzzy here about the health benefits of that *or*-ganic beef you raise."

"Improves your sex life," she said breezily. "Organic beef is low in cholesterol, therefore less plaque in your arteries, therefore increased blood flow to vital areas. You can throw your Viagra out the window."

"And if you butcher them grass-fed beefs in the spring, before they've got summer grass in their bellies and fat on 'em, it's like bitin' into your belt."

"See, Gil, your cousin doesn't think what I do is real ranching. It's a New Age hobby. Right, Blaine?"

Blaine said nothing. Castle got the impression that he and Tessa had argued these points before. They went on, banging through ice-crusted potholes, the land now closing around them in embraces of low hills, now opening up to present vistas of wind-ruffled meadows lunging into Mexico.

"Some country, one of the last short-grass prairies left in the whole Southwest," Blaine commented. "I never get tired of it. No matter how bad things are goin', you feel good just lookin' at it."

"It looks a lot like East Africa," Castle said. "The yellow grass, those low trees."

"Some of that grass *is* African." Tessa shifted to low to ease the truck down a steep, rocky incline, the rear end slewing sideways on the slick film of surface mud. "Why they imported it here, I have no idea. It's not as good as native grama—"

"Them brilliant minds with degrees in range management are who done it," Blaine interjected. "Blue or black grama, you can graze up to thirty-two head a section. Love grass, twenty-five. That's what comes of tryin' to improve on God."

"You've been to Africa?" Tessa asked, shooting a sideways glance at Castle.

"Yes. Kenya."

"Photography or hunting?"

"Birds, not big game. Guinea fowl, francolin, sand grouse."

In the early African morning, after a gargantuan breakfast in camp, Castle, his hunting partner, Mandy, and a guide were moving through a dense scrub thicket when a loud snort close by sent the guide into a crouch. He signaled for quiet and raised the .470 double he carried in case they encountered a lion or Cape buffalo. "Heard a buff," he whispered, and Mandy clamped a hand to her mouth to smother laughter. "What's so bloody funny?" the guide snapped. "That was me," she answered with embarrassed hilarity and pointed at her backside. And everyone, in a release of tension, broke out laughing. Castle was so much there that he started to laugh now, which instantly provoked an urge to sob. He managed to stifle it.

"I've wanted to go to Africa ever since I was a girl," Tessa said. "Maybe one of these years . . ." She broke off and motioned at a bird that had just launched itself from off a fence post. "Look, a prairie falcon."

It was a merlin, not a prairie falcon, but Castle did not correct her, fearing that his voice would break if he spoke. The memory, coming with such clarity and without forewarning, depressed him.

"I'm new to birding," Tessa was saying, apparently aware that she might have made a misidentification. "I suppose it's a contradiction, bird watching and bird shooting. But consistency is the hobgoblin of little minds, whoever said that."

"Emerson." Castle said. " 'A foolish consistency is the hobgoblin of little minds, philosophers and divines. With consistency a great soul has nothing to do.' "

"Well now. And Monica told me you're a stockbroker."

This remark rankled Castle. "Was. And brokers have been known to read more than quarterly reports."

His defensiveness drew a flinch from her. "Hey, I wasn't implying that."

Yeah, you were, Castle thought, but kept it to himself.

They were on lightly grazed government land now, and the grass bordering the road rose almost to the truck's door handles. Tessa stopped at a Texas gate. Blaine climbed out and went to it with his stiff-kneed walk, bent slightly at the waist.

"An old stove-up cowboy," she remarked. "He's like something out of another century, and I don't mean the twentieth."

Blaine swung the gate open, Tessa drove through, then waited for Blaine to close the gate. She followed a faint two-track alongside a wash and parked next to a windmill, its blades turning, stopping, turning again in the spasmodic wind. They got out of the truck. When Tessa reached behind her neck to gather her chestnut brown hair and pile it atop her head, Castle caught himself staring at the back of her slender neck. She placed a baseball cap over her hairdo and pointed toward a range of oak-studded hills cut up by grassy canyons.

"What we'll do is follow one of those canyons more or less east till we come to a tank. We can water the dogs there. Then we swing north and back west down the next canyon."

She spoke like an infantry officer planning an attack. The dogs were pacing in the truck bed, letting out eager whines. Castle turned on Sam's collar, Tessa did likewise with Klaus's—it mimicked a hawk's screech—and then opened the tailgate and released them. Both animals leaped out and tore off at a dead run, mad to do the one thing they'd been born to do. Castle and Tessa blew whistles to call them back in. The temperature had climbed considerably in the past hour—it was warm enough for shirtsleeves. The hunters crossed the wash in single file, then spread out and set off up the first canyon. The dogs had settled down and were quartering ahead, their collars giving off a cacophony of low beeps and shrieks. The canyon narrowed, and the arroyo that cut through it fell in a series of rocky ledges, the pools below the ledges covered by membranes of ice. A short time later Sam's collar fell into the quick, steady pulse that meant she'd stopped. Klaus's signal joined in. *Beep-beep-beep, scree-scree-scree.* The dogs were out of sight, somewhere in the oaks covering the ridge on the right side of the canyon.

With his arthritic joints Blaine had fallen behind. Castle and Tessa waited for him to catch up. They found Sam on a hard point on the slope of the ridge, Klaus honoring alongside her. It would be nearly impossible to shoot the quail amid the dense trees, so Castle volunteered to kick them out while Blaine and Tessa positioned themselves on the meadow above. If the birds broke in their direction, they would have clear shots. He came up behind Sam, locked up so tight she looked like a statue of herself. Nothing happened as he walked slowly past her—the quail had moved recently, leaving enough scent to convince the dogs they were still there. There were egg-shaped scrapes in the dirt, where the birds had been scratching for seeds.

Sam and Klaus broke point and stalked uphill to the meadow. Klaus, a young dog, seemed a little unsure of himself. Sam was all business, utterly focused on her task, transformed from the sweet, slightly goofy pet she was around the house into a predator. Castle's belly tightened as she locked up once more, her long snout aimed at a clump of catclaw. Klaus honored again. A splendid sight—the orange-ticked white setter and the mottled-brown shorthair in total arrest.

A cock broke cover, streaking straight away for the trees on the far side of the meadow. Knowing the rest of the covey would flush at any second, Castle and Tessa held their fire; but Blaine couldn't resist and shot twice, downing the bird with his second barrel. Four more burst from the catclaw, a wild, thunderous beating of wings. Three curved sharply behind Castle, but the fourth, another male, quartered in front of him, a dark blur against the pale winter sky. He swung out ahead and fired and felt all the old, confused feelings of regret and elation as the bird tumbled, feathers drifting in the path of its fall. The dogs remained staunch—the entire covey hadn't yet flown. With the quickness that came from long practice, Castle ejected the spent shell and reloaded the bottom barrel.

"Got one of the hens," Tessa said, breaking her gun to insert two fresh shells. The remaining birds exploded at that moment, flying right at the three people and only a couple of yards overhead. They had to pivot 180 degrees to shoot. The reports of their six shots were almost simultaneous. Four quail dropped as if they'd flown into an invisible wall. Castle accounted for one, Blaine for another, Tessa for a pair.

"Nice double!" he said to her, a little out of breath. "Nice shooting!"

She acknowledged the praise with a nod. "I'm forced to admit that it was."

They spent the next fifteen minutes trailing the dogs in erratic circles to retrieve the dead birds. Blaine's first was the biggest, round as a ball, and they stood around admiring its black breast and belly speckled with white, the clownish whorls of the facial markings that gave the Mearns' its other name—harlequin quail.

"Beautiful things, ain't they?" he said. "Weren't so damn good to eat, I couldn't hunt 'em."

"And I wouldn't hunt with you if you felt any different," Tessa said.

Castle complimented his shooting—he was better than Sally said he was.

"Yeah, you listen to her, I never done anything right in my life except to marry Monica."

Half an hour later they came to the dirt tank. The dogs leaped in to drink and cool themselves, scaring a killdeer that rose with a cry of alarm. Soaking wet and looking sleek as an otter, Klaus bounded away and got his first point of the day: three birds, two of which flew into cover before anyone could get a bead on them. Castle killed the third. They worked westward down another canyon, found no more coveys, and returned to the truck, where they rested the dogs and field-dressed the quail and placed them in freezer bags.

"Eight," said Castle. "Sally told me she wanted a mess of 'em."

"Good old Mama, givin' orders to everybody."

From the cooler in the backseat Tessa got the sandwiches and soft drinks Monica had packed. Sitting against the truck, looking out toward a butte called Saddle Mountain and the snowy peak of Mount Wrightson in the far-off Santa Ritas, they ate lunch. Sam, curled up beside Castle, lifted her head, perked her ears, and barked. Rising to see what had aroused her, Castle saw four young Mexicans dressed in black—black baseball caps, black jackets, black trousers, black tennis shoes—approaching the truck. They halted when Castle showed himself.

"¡Señor!" one shouted. "¡Quisiéramos agua! ¿Tiene agua?"

At the sound of the voice, Blaine and Tessa stood up.

"¡Tenemos mucho sed! ¡Quisiéramos agua!"

"Drug runners, Gil. You can tell by the way they're dressed," Blaine muttered. "Dropped their loads, and now they're hoofin back to old Meh-hee-co."

"¡Por favor! ¡Necesitamos agua! ¡Agua y nada más!"

As the Mexicans advanced, Blaine's face blushed with anger. "¡No tenemos agua! ¡Vamos!" he yelled, and shocked everyone by drawing his pistol, which he held in both hands and aimed squarely at the man who had spoken. "Go on, get the fuck out of here!"

"Okay. Está bien," the man called, raising his hand. "No problema." He turned and disappeared into the wash with his companions. Dissolved was more like it. They were there and then not there.

"Christ, Blaine," Castle said. "Did you have to do that?"

Blaine holstered the Luger. "Yeah, I did. Maybe when those boys get back to Mexico, they'll pass the word that there's one gringo ain't gone to put up with their crap." He stood looking at where the drug runners had been. "Quisiéramos agua. Fuckin' horseshit. It wasn't water they wanted, it was the truck. They didn't see us sittin' behind it and figured they'd hot-wire it and give themselves a ride home."

Tessa looked at him as if she'd never seen him in her life. He sat down again and in a moment recovered himself. "You two want to hunt some more, go ahead. I'll hang back and give my legs a break and guard the wagon train."

Castle, a little shaken by the encounter—the drug runners' black garb and the suddenness with which they'd appeared and disappeared, his cousin's swift rage, his transformation into someone else—was ready to call it a day; but he didn't want to disappoint Sally's hopes for a quail feast.

"Well, that was a surprise," he said to Tessa as they pushed up a new canyon. "Think Blaine was right? They were going to steal the truck?"

She shrugged in the most charming way, a quick, awkward, schoolgirlish lift and fall of her shoulders. "Probably not. Guess I can't blame him for being a little edgy, after what happened. But pulling that pistol—"

Sam, lunging over a narrow arroyo, interrupted her. In a glorious display of skill and athleticism, the setter caught bird scent in midleap, spun halfway around while still in the air, and hit the ground on point, her body bent like a bow.

Mearns' quail sometimes double-covey, and the one Sam had scented was such a covey—two dozen birds blasted skyward. Castle and Tessa each shot a double, then, flushing half a dozen singles on the follow-up, killed four more.

"That's about enough," he said. "Any more, and it'll just be butchery."

Taking a breather before the hike back, they sat under the umbrella of a tall Emory oak. Castle asked where she'd learned to shoot so well. Her father had taught her. Not just an avid wing shooter, an obsessive one, she said, volunteering that he'd been a film industry lawyer in L.A., where she'd been raised with two older brothers who shared their dad's enthusiasms.

"If I didn't learn, he wouldn't have paid any attention to me at all. This was Dad's favorite gun."

"May I?"

She handed the over-and-under to him. He snapped it into his shoulder, felt its balance, and admired the scrollwork on its receiver, the finish of its walnut stock. A Parazzi. New, its price tag would roughly equal the cost of a low-mileage used car.

"Dad did pretty well for himself," she said, noticing that he'd appraised the shotgun's value "For us, too. I guess you could say I'm a trust fund brat."

"So what brought you here from L.A.?" he asked. "Or is that prying?"

Brown eyes, each above a spray of cheekbone freckles, looked at him with an expression that was earnest and forthright but not innocent. "Dad hunted this valley every year and loved it. He bought the

Crown A years ago. Planned to retire on it, but lawyering for Columbia, Paramount, and so forth—that wasn't the fast lane in the legal business, that was Daytona. Mucho stress, mucho three-martini lunches. Heart attack at sixty-one. That doesn't answer your question, does it?"

Castle handed the gun back to her. "Uh . . . No, but if—"

"I'm a hermit," she said. "I don't like people all that much."

"You don't strike me as a misanthrope."

"I'm not, but that's my ambition. I lived in Scottsdale when I was younger. Worked as a graphic designer, lived way out in the desert with two dogs and two horses. I woke up one day and found that the desert had disappeared. I was surrounded by houses and golf courses and said the hell with this and moved out here. So what brought—" She stopped herself.

"What brought me out here?"

Tessa was silent for a moment. "A slip of the tongue. Monica told me, and to not mention it. I'm sorry. For mentioning it."

"That's okay." He intended to leave it at that but was somehow compelled to go further. "She was a freelance photographer. Travel magazines mostly. She had an assignment to take pictures of some posh new resort in Hawaii. She'd decided to spend the weekend with her family in Boston because I was going to be away in Atlanta that same weekend. Monday morning she flew out of Boston for her connection in L.A. The plane she was on was the one they crashed into the north tower."

"She was on one of the planes? Monica didn't tell me that."

"American Airlines eleven," he said. The flight number had a fateful ring, like the *Titanic.* "Know where I was when it happened? Shooting skeet with a customer I was wooing in Atlanta. A big-shot sports agent. I was hoping to convince him that his stable of quarterbacks and home-run hitters should invest with our firm. He wasn't shooting well, he was frustrated and pissed off with himself. I gave him some instructions and he improved and that relieved me. See, I wanted him to be in a good mood when I pitched him. That's what I thought was important. We finished up and went into the clubhouse for lunch. The TV was on, and that's when I first heard of it."

Tessa reached out to touch him sympathetically but quickly withdrew her hand, as if he were a man who'd been struck by lightning and still carried the charge. "I can't imagine what that must have been like."

"I couldn't either, before it happened. There were a lot of things I couldn't imagine."

"You think you're immune," she said, with a knowing movement of her head, an indication that perhaps something terrible and unexpected had happened to her.

"Now I can imagine just about anything," Castle carried on. "Like the way those drug runners popped up out of nowhere. I said it was a surprise. Really, it wasn't. Spooky, but not a surprise. I think if a meteor crashed right in front of us right this second, it wouldn't surprise me. One minute the person you love most in the world is here, and then, quick as you can flip a light switch, she's . . . she's . . . ashes, she's air. Like she'd never been . . . And what drives you crazy is that somebody did that to her . . ."

What did surprise Castle was that he had spoken his heart to a woman he scarcely knew. He regretted it; it created an awkwardness, erected a barrier between them.

"I don't know that I could bear a loss like that," she said. "I admire you for . . . for going on."

"Well, don't. There's nothing to admire. If I had a choice, I'd take it."

He stopped himself before confessing that he'd attempted suicide, or rather had attempted an attempt.

"Some times we're living through," she said. "I've got a daughter in Kuwait. In the army. If we go into Iraq, and it damn well looks like we will, she'll be one of the first. Having a daughter go to war was something I couldn't imagine."

"A daughter," he murmured, his thoughts springing to Morgan and Justine. "An army nurse?"

"Nurse? I wish. Beth is with the Third Infantry Division, drives a truck in a supply battalion." And Beth, she offered, had always been restless, had been doing poorly at Southern Cal, and in the middle of her sophomore year, dropped out, and enlisted. "At this stage of my life, I figured I'd be thinking about boyfriends and planning a wedding."

Castle said nothing. There didn't seem to be anything to say. He watched the wind rippling the grass, listened to it shaking the leaves above them.

"She's all I've got. She's *it.* I remember my grandmother telling me that when my dad was in North Africa, her heart would stop every time she heard a car pull into the drive. She would think that she was going to open the door and see an army chaplain standing there with a telegram. Well, I hope it won't be my turn now. Waiting for an army chaplain to show up and tell me my baby girl has been killed."

Here, he thought, was someone who could anticipate disaster. That didn't necessarily mean the blow would be softened, should it come. Now it was he who reached out to her, the movement awkward and tentative. He allowed his hand to fall lightly on her upraised knee. The contact felt strange and somehow wrong; and yet he did not remove his hand.

"It'll be all right," he said, though he had no reason to make this optimistic prophecy.

"I pray she does. No, I don't. Haven't got much in the way of religion. Elena said she would do my praying for me. Say a rosary for Beth every day."

They didn't speak for a while, locked in their private thoughts. Then, to get off the somber line of conversation, he said: "Elena will be cooking the quail tonight. You'll be there?"

"Didn't get an invitation."

He stood and reached behind his back to pat the birds in his game pocket. "We've got sixteen. Two apiece with two left over. Enough with a side dish. "

She looked up at him with a slightly amused expression. "Is that an invitation?"

"I guess it is," he answered. "Yes."

THEY ATE AT A PICNIC TABLE on the porch of the main house by the light of a Coleman lantern hung from a beam, warmed by the coals in the outdoor fireplace over which Elena had grilled the birds, slathered in garlic butter and stuffed with roasted serrano peppers. Monica arranged the seating so Castle was beside Tessa, who had changed out of her field clothes into an buckskin jacket over a embroidered black shirt and a pair of western-cut trousers that flattered her taut hips and slim legs. Her hair, cascading over her shoulders from under a black Stetson, shone in the lantern light. She threw off an intense sexuality, as some women do in their late forties, early fifties—a kind of vivid autumnal bloom before winter sets in. He complimented her on the outfit, and she smiled, raising a hand to her lips to mask her protruding eyeteeth.

"It's my rodeo-queen getup," she said. "A tourist's idea of what a cowgirl should look like."

He wasn't sure if that meant he was a tourist, but he considered it prudent not to ask. For most of the meal the conversation flew around subjects he wasn't familiar with, horses and cattle prices and ranch work in general. When those were exhausted, Monica asked Tessa if she'd heard from her daughter. Lines formed on Tessa's tanned forehead. Beth had sent an e-mail the other day, and while there were things she was censored from saying, it looked like her supply outfit would soon be rolling into Iraq.

Sally mentioned the headlines she'd seen in the papers—the signals brigade based at Fort Huachuca had also received orders for the Persian Gulf. "Let's hope they get it over with quick, and all of them and your girl get home safe," she said.

With a nod, Tessa acknowledged these sentiments and looked to Blaine, apparently expecting to hear a similar expression of neighborly concern from him.

Instead, he issued a declaration: "It's about damn time. About damn time we took it to 'em. After Pearl Harbor, we didn't sit on our thumbs before we did something about it."

Castle observed that something had been done, that *it* had been taken to *them* in Afghanistan.

"That was more like a warm-up," Blaine said.

"A warm-up?" asked Tessa. And then in response to Blaine's quizzical squint: "If Beth has to risk her life, I want it to be for a good reason."

"Takin' out Saddam seems a good reason to me."

"I'm not sure it is. I wish I could be, but I'm not."

"Well, you've *got* to be. If the balloon goes up, you're gone to have to be behind your girl, one hundred percent."

"Do you suppose I won't be?" Tessa asked angrily. "I'll support *her*, but I don't have to be a cheerleader for a war."

"Makes no sense to support her and not support what she's bein' sent to do."

"Well, I guess that's another example of consistency being the hobgoblin of little minds."

"You're not sayin' I've got a small mind, are you, Tess?" Blaine's semijocular tone was undermined by the belligerent look on his lank, sunburned face.

"No. I am saying that I don't have one."

Monica cast a reproachful look at her husband. "You might think differently if Rick was there."

"The hell I would," Blaine said. "We've got to take it to 'em, and it can't be like it was in Vietnam, the troops riskin' their lives over there and a mob of fuckin' dopeheads protestin' over here."

"Don't you use that F-word that I can hear it," Sally said. "I hate that word."

"You don't exactly talk like you sing in a church choir, y'know. And besides, it's ain't a word you never heard before."

"And that's why I hate it."

"Blaine, you don't really mean that someone who's got questions about this is a dope-smoking hippie, do you?" Tessa interjected, with mock incredulity.

"We can't afford the bullshit that went on back in Vietnam days, that's my meaning."

Castle heard in this dispute loud echoes of the sour arguments he and Blaine had waged years ago. His instincts told him that Tessa's doubts about this war, should it come, made more sense than Blaine's certainties.

"All Tessa is saying is that we ought to think twice before jumping into this thing with both feet," he ventured cautiously.

Blaine slapped the table with his palm, and in the Coleman's glare, his expression turned malignant, much as it had earlier in the day, when he'd confronted the drug mules. "I'll be goddamned. I will be *goddamned.* What in the hell is wrong with you, cuzzy?"

"Wrong with me?" asked Castle, stunned that his comment, which he had thought was as reasonable and inoffensive as a soft-boiled egg, had provoked such a violent reaction.

"I'd of thought that if anybody would want to take it to 'em, it would be you," Blaine snarled with a thrust of his jaw. "If it had been my wife, I would have—"

"Blaine, *please . . . ,*" Monica said, nudging his ribs with her elbow. She looked at Castle, pleading with him to overlook her husband's obtuse remark.

But he could not overlook it. To bring Mandy into this was inexcusable. "If you're so hot for this war, why don't you reenlist?" he said, resentment heating his face. "If I wanted to take it to 'em, I'd do it myself. I wouldn't expect a bunch of nineteen- and twenty-year-old kids to settle scores for me. I never wanted revenge anyway. Might as well try to get revenge on an earthquake or a hurricane, that's the way I feel about it. If you think that means there's something wrong with me, I guess that's your privilege."

At another, withering look from Monica, Blaine turned sheepish. "Well, all right, I should of watched my words. I didn't mean nothin' personal by it."

Except that it had been personal. Because, Castle suspected, his cousin had a personal, emotional stake in the forthcoming martial enterprise. Something seemed to be gnawing at Blaine, maybe a bitterness lingering from his own lost war, maybe the frustrations of running a border ranch—all the problems he could do nothing about, like drug smugglers. Maybe Saddam Hussein had become, to his mind, a substitute for everything that was wrong in his world but would somehow be set to rights by a mighty American host blitzing up the Euphrates. A vicarious triumph would be his, the way a football fan stands straighter and puffs out his chest and feels better all around when his team wins.

An uncomfortable quiet had fallen over the table. The mossy axiom, never discuss politics or religion at social gatherings, had proven true. Everybody was searching for a way back to the conviviality that had prevailed not ten minutes ago. Monica found one at last. Their son's southwestern tour would wind up in Tucson this Friday night—a gig at the Rialto Theater, which, Castle gathered by the emphasis she placed on the name, was a prestigious venue. Blaine and Monica then began a tag-team disquisition on Rick's musical career. She was keen to affirm that his group, the Double Sixes—named after the now-vanished highway Route 66, was a true *indie* band. Independent, Blaine elaborated, from the Nashville mafia. And from sleazy booking agents and record company hustlers, Monica added with an emphatic nod that sent ripples through her hair. By touring a lot—Rick was almost constantly on the road—the band had won a certain regional fame, a kind of cult following, college kids, mostly. Their debut CD, just out, could be their big breakthrough, Blaine crowed. However it went, the Double Sixes were going places, just a question of time; hell, these boys were musical outlaws, like Willie Nelson and Waylon Jennings in the old days, and it took time for outlaws to get accepted . . .

"They'll be playing tracks from the CD," Monica said. "We've got complimentary tickets. Why don't you two join us?" She looked at

Castle and Tessa, as if they were a couple. This was disconcerting. Was she matchmaking? Tessa stammered that she wasn't sure . . . a young crowd . . . She would feel out of place, like a chaperone . . . She turned to Castle with an inquisitive expression, but he couldn't read what her question was. Sure, he would be happy to go, he said to Monica. He hadn't seen Rick since he was in, what? Eighth grade?

Tessa said, "Well, in that case, I'll go, too. I could use a night out, I suppose."

When the evening was over, he walked her to her car. Orion glittered in the south, the Dog Star at its heel as brilliant as an airplane's landing light. Still accustomed to the sparsely starred skies of the urbanized East, he momentarily mistook the Milky Way, arcing horizon to horizon, for a wispy cloud. Tessa got behind the wheel and said, before closing the door, "I hope you didn't mind."

An emotion he couldn't name was moving through him, filtering into the tips of his fingers. "Mind?"

"Me accepting the invitation."

"No. Why should I?"

"The way Monica put it . . . I thought maybe you felt like you are being pushed into something . . . What I mean is . . . I want you to know that I'm not . . . Oh, shit—" She shook her head at her verbal fumbling. "See you Friday night."

She drove off. Castle stood alone and watched the taillights recede into the darkness with a feeling absent so long he hadn't recognized it at first—anticipation.

7

WITHIN SIGHT of the high steel fence dividing Nogales, Sonora, from Nogales, Arizona, its Mexican side decorated with graffiti—"Borders are scars on the face of the earth"—and with white crosses commemorating migrants who now gazed upon the face of the Virgin, some murdered by bandits, most by the desert, roughly a block from the port of entry where cars backed up for half a mile waited to cross into El Norte while day-tripping tourists and documented Mexicans went through pedestrian turnstiles in both directions past Indian women begging with their ragged children, the returning Mexicans lugging plastic bags from Wal-Mart and Safeway and discount stores, the departing tourists bargain-rate treasures from the emporiums on Avenida Obregón—Zapotec rugs, copper chairs, ceramic washbasins, wood carvings, belts, jackets, straw hats, religious icons—in the middle of Calle Juárez near the enterprises that flourished in every border town from Matamoros to Tijuana—cheap hotels, currency exchanges, farmacias mostly patronized by aging gringos seeking half-price medications for their many ailments—The Professor sat in the St. Regis bar, nursing a Dos Equis as waiters in white shirts and black aprons served customers seated at round tables on straight-backed chairs, a stereo played Norteño ballads, and five muted TVs broadcast various sporting events—a soccer match, a Lakers game, highlights from last week's Super Bowl, in which The Professor had won a thousand dollars from his comandante.

Five TVs, four tuned to U.S. channels, the old love-hate, thought El Profesor, waiting for Gloria to show up. We (he was mindful that the pronoun was somewhat ambiguous in his case) love all things American—the sports, the jobs, the Yankee dollars, the cars, the Big Macs and Supersize Coca-Colas; and we hate all things American—the arrogance, the crazed energy of the place—but we are slowly taking back with demographics what was stolen from us with the gun a century and a half ago. California, Arizona, New Mexico, and Texas belonged to us before the Battle of Chapultepec and the Gadsden Purchase, and Santa Fe was founded years before those bung-in-the-butt Pilgrims ever saw Plymouth Rock, so it is only fitting and just that Mexico, pitiable Mexico, so far from God and so close to the United States, as Díaz famously said, should return in a bloodless invasion. No guns, no cannons, just numbers. And we are winning! All over the U.S.A., in hotels, airports, supermarkets, train stations, and hospitals you saw signs in English and Spanish; you dialed toll-free numbers and heard recorded voices say, "For English, press one or stay on the line. Para español, marque el número dos." Did you hear such instructions in Korean? Chinese? Vietnamese? Swahili? Not that Jesús and María staggering behind their coyote with hopes of making beds in a Holiday Inn or cutting lawns in Pennsylvania are thinking, Well, here we are, reconquistadores erasing with our feet the artificial line the gringos drew on maps. They were unconscious agents of history, pushed northward by poverty, by the desire for stuff, or if they already had stuff, by the desire for more of it. Yet there were conscious agents like himself who saw this irresistible human flood for what it was, *la reconquista*.

Years ago, when he was with the DEA, he'd confiscated bricks of cocaine in Texas with these words stamped on their wrappers: THIS IS OUR WAR ON THE NORTH AMERICANS. Were drugs a legitimate weapon in la reconquista? Of course they were. If gringo society was so fucked up that it produced multitudes of crackheads, heroin junkies, coke snorters, and dope smokers, why shouldn't Mexicans give the Americans what they wanted and profit handsomely in the process? In pueblos all over Sonora new streetlights burned on newly paved streets; water flowed from faucets in houses that had previously relied on bucket wells or backyard standpipes. The electricity and the water and the asphalt came from Carrasco. He'd bought irrigation equipment and new tractors and fertilizer for the campesinos, and the beneficiaries of his largesse repaid him with their allegiance, serving as his informants and supplying him with madrinas to do menial tasks, with mules to drive or carry his products. He was their padrino, Don Joaquín. The Professor considered himself a man with a social conscience, and it pleased him, when he made his rounds of the countryside, to see the improvements in the people's lives and to know he'd had a hand in it. Yes, with every needle poked into an arm in L.A. or Phoenix or Chicago, with every joint smoked and crack pipe lit, the people in Carrasco's field of operations lived a little better. And this, too, was fitting and just.

But more than material benefits excused the narco-trafficking. He recalled a conversation that took place in Hermosillo, in the office of a certain Sonoran legislator. Present were his comandante, Victor Zaragoza, Carrasco, and himself, Capitán Bonham. It seemed that the politician, to whose reelection campaign Carrasco had contributed large sums, was having second thoughts about holding up his end of the bargain, which was to keep state and federal prosecutors from hindering Carrasco's activities. People were talking, complained the legislator, people were gossiping that he was in bed with a drug lord. "Well, you are!" Carrasco said, laughing. He was seated on a sofa, his big chest straining the snap buttons of his cowboy shirt and his belly bulging over a hand-tooled belt with a silver buckle the size of a coffee saucer. "These people speak the truth, and you know, a famous Roman emperor named Marcus Aurelius once said that no man need fear the truth."

Hearing a man who hadn't finished high school quote Marcus Aurelius appeared to fluster the politician; he saw then, if he hadn't before, that he wasn't dealing with a babo. He protested that he wasn't afraid, merely concerned. For Joaquín! Not for himself! Pressures might be put on him by people he could not ignore. Not that he and Joaquín should sever ties, but perhaps a little distancing would be in order. Carrasco listened politely and said nothing. True, the legislator went on, this business was a very good business, and true, so long as the Americans had an insatiable appetite for drugs, there was no way to stop it, but . . . "Just this past Sunday, the bishop said Mass, and his sermon was about narcotics trafficking, and he said there could be no moral justification for it, and he was looking right at me when he said it!"

Joaquín, leaning his broad head a little to the side, regarded the legislator with a straightforward expression. "Whatever the moral question, it is justified historically. To smuggle drugs to the Americans is a tool of historical revenge, and you know what I mean. Who needs any more justification than that? It is an act of patriotism. Do you consider yourself a patriot, my friend?" "¡Por supuesto!" replied the politician. "¡Absolutamente!" Carrasco stood and donned his cowboy hat. "Then let me hear no more talk about second thoughts and distancing."

The Professor's respect for him had increased twofold that afternoon. Here was a man who could think! A vanquished country's revenge on its oppressor. It was so right!

His beer was getting warm, but he refrained from guzzling it and ordering a cold one. Drinking in daylight always dulled him, and he needed to stay sharp for this evening's work. Gloria, living up to the El Norte stereotype of the mañana mexicana, was nearly half an hour late. He glanced idly at the TV directly across from his barstool, suspended above the mirrored backbar with its gold-leafed cornices. A college basketball game on ESPN. Cigarette smoke formed a pale haze around the paddle fans, twirling slowly beneath the pressed-tin ceiling. A waiter brought a bowl of limes to three young British tourists drinking tequila shooters, their accents evoking memories of The Professor's father. Went back to England years ago, split up from Mom, whose madness was serious enough to make her impossible to live with but not serious enough to warrant being institutionalized. He seldom gave a thought to either of them. He was his own parent, he was The Professor, father as well as mother to Gregorio Bonham and Euclid J. Carrington.

Where the fuck was Gloria?

"¿Capitán, otra cerveza?" asked the bartender.

And just as the bartender gave him a fresh bottle, a tall young woman walked in and spoke to the Nogales city cop who worked off hours as a doorman-slash-bouncer. The cop pointed at El Profesor, and she, cracking vertebrae in every male neck in the place, paraded across the floor in stiletto heels and stood next to him.

"Buenas tardes, Capitán."

A body that could have been molded only by the hand of a loving God, every bit of six feet in those heels; tight turquoise pants and a white blouse; long black hair, opal eyes, smooth, fawn-colored skin—Gloria was, well, glorious.

"Mucho gusto," he said, a thickness in his throat. "Encantado."

She apologized for her tardiness—an unavoidable delay—and asked if she could sit down. ¡Por supuesto! She ordered a Coca-Cola with lime. When he went for his wallet, she tapped his wrist.

"I pay for my own drinks. I'm not a bar girl."

Her speech was educated, none of that rough Sonoran slur.

"You're certainly not. You're everything Victor said you were, and more. Preciosa, you are a national treasure."

Gloria smiled and ever so slightly raised and lowered her plucked eyebrows to say that ornate flattery could not interest her less. "We have business to conduct, Capitán."

"Gregorio, please."

She took a cigarette out of her purse. He lit it for her and said, "An associate of mine is going to do some work for me. He is very skilled at what he does, a craftsman, an artist. He will be paid well for his services, but I would like to give him a bonus, and you will be the bonus. His name is Félix."

"Who pays? You or this Félix?"

"I do."

She sipped her Coke and looked at him directly and without warmth. "One hundred fifty U.S. for one hour, five hundred for the night. Also, I expect to be taken out for dinner first. Also, I don't take it up the ass for any amount. Be sure Félix the artist understands that before he calls."

The Professor hesitated. The sound of her voice as she uttered certain words, like *culo*, stimulated his other senses. A kind of cool, tingling sensation in his fingertips, a taste of salt, white rhomboids sparkling before his eyes.

"The five hundred, then. Félix will take one look at you and wish for more than an hour."

"In advance, please. And don't be conspicuous."

He reached into his inside jacket pocket for his money clip and, as inconspicuously as possible, counted out five hundred dollars and slipped the bills into Gloria's purse, hanging from the barstool. "For another fifty, would you agree to a . . . a . . . shall we call it a screen test?" he asked.

Gloria passed him an embossed business card that read, in Spanish on one side, English on the other: "Border Rose Escort Service—For Discriminating Gentlemen. Discretion Guaranteed." Below were her landline and mobile phone numbers. "This screen test, as you call it, what did you have in mind?"

"Nothing that will take too much time. I am to meet Félix soon."

"The artist. And now"—warming up at last, stroking the back of his hand with her coral-lacquered fingernails—"I will teach you the meaning of artistry."

Which she did, stripped down to her purple satin underwear as she knelt and took him into her mouth in a room on the second floor of the St. Regis. When she was finished, he was ready to give her fifty more to reward her for truth in advertising.

"That's a beautiful color," he said, gesturing at her bra and panties.

"Purple for Lent."

"Lent doesn't start for another two weeks."

"I'm getting in the mood."

"What are you giving up?"

She freshened her lipstick. "Wearing blue and red. Yourself, what do you give up?"

"Certainly not you," he said, his mind flashing on Clarice. How could he waste his time on that nut when there was one such as Gloria so near? "I will see you again, I hope."

"You have my card."

Sexual acts always intensified his condition; Gloria's performance had brought it to a new level. Usually, when one sensory experience stirred another, the effect vanished with the stimulus, but now, as he walked up Avenida López Mateo toward the Church of the Immaculate Conception, the color of her underwear lingered in his mind's eye, rousing a powerful, persistent scent. He couldn't quite find the words for it—indeed, he was seldom able to describe these sensations with any precision. Approximations had to serve. Musky was the best he could do at the moment. A damp muskiness, pleasant but almost unpleasant, something like the odor of decaying leaves after a rain.

In his youth in Mexico City he'd confessed to his closest friend, Emilio, that he could hear surfaces and shapes and smell colors. Emilio thought he was crazy. Because his religious-fanatic mother was also a manic depressive, he himself thought he was nuts, or at the very least the victim of an addled imagination. After Emilio he confessed his secret to no one until, while he was attending Georgetown, he volunteered to become a subject in a research study. It was conducted by a prominent neurologist, who interviewed him at length and put him through tests with sophisticated equipment that measured electrical impulses in his brain and recorded the effects that various drugs had on his cortex. The scientist told him his condition was called synesthesia and that it arose in something called the limbic brain. Merely to know that it had a name was a relief. Synesthesia affected very few people but was not, the neurologist assured him, a mental illness or a flight of the imagination. In the synesthete, the boundaries between the senses are not clearly drawn, and in some cases are nonexistent, allowing two or more senses to combine without losing their distinct identities. That was why he could hear shapes without losing his hearing, smell colors without losing his sense of smell. For The Professor that was a moment of enlightenment and still greater relief—he wasn't mad, he was a rarity, a marvel.

For years afterward he thought of his gift as little more than a fascinating curiosity that made life more interesting and enriching. Only when he was discharged from the U.S. Army and, as a newly naturalized American citizen, joined the DEA did he find a practical use for it. With his Mexican heritage and bilingual skills and combat experience in Panama to recommend him, the DEA assigned him to its El Paso Division, first as liaison to the antidrug commandos he'd helped train at the School of the Americas at Fort Benning, later to the Intelligence Center as an undercover agent. At this he excelled. He made deals and infiltrated the Juárez Cartel up to its highest levels. Undercover work caused many clandestine operatives to lose touch with the real world, but he suffered little mental distress playing outlaw and lawman at the same time, gliding between two different worlds with ease because he'd lived in two different worlds all his life.

A young girl was selling flatbreads in front of the church. He bought a slice, earning a stare of disbelief and gratitude when he gave her five dollars and told her to keep the change. One must keep the muscles of generosity toned. He went inside, dipped his fingers into the holy-water font, crossed himself, and sat down in the rear pew of the nave, next to a shrine to the Virgin, upon which vigil candles flickered in little glass jars. Except for three or four pious women at prayer, the church was empty. He was ten minutes early and settled back to wait for Félix Cabrera, who had been among his trainees at Benning, one of the best. Without question the right man for tonight's job, a professional's professional who'd done missions before in the United States, one in Phoenix, another in El Paso, a third in Dallas. El Verdugo, the Executioner, he was called for his meticulousness, for his preternatural calm—the man probably had a pulse rate of around fifty—and his accuracy with a pistol. Once, out on Carrasco's ranch near Caborca, The Professor—no mean marksman himself—had challenged him to a contest shooting Gambel's quail with .45 semiautomatics. Stationary birds were prohibited—they had to be hit on the run at a range of fifteen or twenty yards. When the match was over, Félix had accounted for nine, The Professor for five. He was not abashed to have been outshot by such a margin, for if the pupil is not greater than the teacher, then the teacher has failed.

The careers of teacher and pupil had followed similar paths. After graduating from the School of the Americas, Félix served with the Special Air Mobile Forces Group of the Mexican army, dueling with the Gulf Cartel in Tamaulipas and Matamoros until he and some thirty members of his battalion experienced a collective epiphany: they were earning roughly five hundred dollars a month fighting the cartel; they could do much better by joining it. They went to work as enforcers and assassins, as escorts for drug shipments, tasks for which their martial skills and martial virtues of discipline and valor made them far superior to the cholos previously employed in those capacities. Los Zetas, they called themselves, after the radio call sign of their old battalion commander, Zeta.

Then, as narco-barons often did, the cartel's boss overreached. He attempted to kidnap and kill an American DEA agent and an FBI agent, which brought pressure from Washington on Mexico City to do something about him. He was busted and sent to Las Palmas prison. Though he continued to operate from his jail cell, some Zetas felt they owed no more loyalty to him and struck out on their own, scattering across northern Mexico. Félix fetched up in his native Sonora with several comrades and hired themselves out to Joaquín Carrasco.

That was when teacher and pupil were reunited, The Professor having deserted the DEA a couple of years before Félix had deserted the army. The cause of his flight could be traced to the kidnapping, torture, and murder of his friend, another undercover agent, named Carlos Aguilar. Carlos was an explorer who'd made an astonishing discovery—the Juárez Cartel operated a vast marijuana plantation in southern Chihuahua that employed several hundred field hands and was guarded by soldiers and state police. There was no way an operation that big could be clandestine; it had to have the full consent of the Mexican government. Though no cartel operated without some sort of official sanction, the partnership between the Juárez gang and the government was especially blatant. Exposing it became Carlos's personal crusade.

One day he disappeared. His decomposed body was found in the Chihuahuan desert a month later. He'd been shot through the back of the head. Forensic experts determined that both shoulders and his ribs and jaw had been broken. In time informants came forth with details about what had been done to him, and it was truly unspeakable. He'd been tortured by experts for days before the Angels of Mercy sang to them, and they executed him. The El Paso office sent every available agent into Mexico to find out who had murdered its man and who had ordered his killing. The Professor was among them. For weeks, at enormous risk to himself—if he was caught, he would have suffered even worse treatment than Aguilar—he tracked down leads, met with snitches, compiled lists of names, and made a discovery of his own: Carlos's torturers had been trained by the CIA, back when the Agency was involved in the drug trade to finance the Contras in Nicaragua. One of his colleagues uncovered a still more interesting fact—the word to abduct Aguilar had come not from the Juárez boss but from the commanding general of the Fifth Military District in Chihuahua City, whose soldiers protected the plantation, and who, it was said, received mordida amounting to a hundred thousand dollars a month.

Sometime after this information came to light, the special agent in charge summoned The Professor and the other agents back to El Paso. They were at first bewildered and then enraged when they learned why: the general was married to the sister of the minister of defense, who had gotten wind of the investigation. In this instance, the pressure flowed from Mexico City to Washington. To implicate El General in the drug trade and in the torture and murder of an American law enforcement agent would greatly embarrass the Mexican government. Phone calls were made to El Paso. The agent in charge had heard from no less a figure than the head of the Latin American desk in the U.S. State Department. To avoid an international scandal and to maintain amicable relations between the United States and its southern neighbor, the investigation was to proceed no further.

The Professor didn't turn in his gun and badge in righteous indignation, like Dirty Harry in the movies. Being a good soldier, he obeyed orders. He stopped investigating and took a month's vacation. It was a working holiday. He knew the identities of the three men who'd tortured Aguilar. He capped one in Mexico and trailed the second across the border to a house in Eagle Pass, Texas, shooting him through the window as he watched TV. There was law, and then there was justice. A week after disposing of him, The Professor picked up the trail of the third man. It led back into Mexico. He was on the road, south of Juárez, when his mobile phone jingled. The caller didn't identify himself. He knew it was someone in the El Paso office by what was said. "This is to say thanks for doing what we all wanted to do. The dude you capped last week was still on the CIA's payroll, a top informant. The spooks are pissed. They know you were the shooter, and we can't help you. Don't know where you are, but I know you're in deep shit." The anonymous caller went on to say that the mierda was rolling downhill—the CIA had prevailed upon the attorney general's office to prevail upon the DEA to apprehend its rogue agent. In fact, a warrant had been issued for his arrest. "And that's the least of your problems, know what I'm saying?"

He did. The Agency probably had an open contract out on him as well. So the question was, where were his chances of survival better? Mexico or the United States? He opted for Mexico, in effect repatriating himself. He traveled to Mexico City, where he set about counterfeiting a whole new identity. It was his own version of a witness protection program. He knew the right people; obtaining forgeries of the necessary documents—passport, driver's license, birth certificate—

was not difficult. He made certain cosmetic changes—dying his dirty blond hair to dark brown, removing the mole from his left cheek—but otherwise he didn't get fancy. Thus was Gregorio Bonham born.

Señor Bonham journeyed to Hermosillo, checked in to a cheap hotel, then sought an interview with Victor Zaragoza, the federal police comandante in Sonora. The Professor wasn't as familiar with the Hermosillo Cartel as he was with Juárez, but he did know that the way to Carrasco led through the comandante. In the lingua franca of the trade, he had given Carrasco *la plaza*, meaning that he had licensed Carrasco to traffic in the state, for which he received a certain amount in protection money. At police headquarters, The Professor was told that the comandante wasn't in and to come back the following day. He did and got the same story. On his third try he was allowed into the comandante's office. Except for the automatic rifles racked along a wall, it was as nondescript as a budget motel room. Zaragoza, a tall man with severe Castilian features and the build of a slightly underfed wolf, motioned for him to sit in the chair in front of his desk. "Who are you, and what are you doing here?"

The Professor was perfectly candid—he wished to meet Joaquín Carrasco; he believed he could be of great service to Don Joaquín, for he knew that the Hermosillo Cartel was at war with the Juárez organization over control of smuggling routes. The comandante glared at him, then said, affecting incredulity: "Joaquín Carrasco is a criminal, and you are telling *me* you wish to go to work for him? Are you crazy?" The Professor assured him of his sanity. "This is amusing," said the comandante. "Tell me everything about yourself. I need to determine if I should arrest you or have you committed to an asylum." He presented his curriculum vitae, his entire history; he enumerated his assets, which he thought would be as advantageous to Don Joaquín as they had been to the DEA. Zaragoza concluded the meeting, went to the door, and summoned two men, one of whom wore an Oakland Raiders T-shirt and looked as if he might have played middle linebacker. "This man is out of his mind," Zaragoza said. "See if you can help him recover his senses."

The goons took him out to a car and drove to a small unoccupied house near the bus terminal. There they tied him to a chair, put a hood over his head, and began to punch him in the liver, in the kidneys, in the ribs. He'd expected something like this—indeed, he would have been suspicious if it didn't happen. The beating continued off and on for a couple of hours. He tried to distract himself from the pain by focusing on the smells aroused by the blackness under the hood. Then he heard Zaragoza's voice: "Basta!" The blows ceased, the hood was removed, and the comandante stood over him with the passport and birth certificate he'd obtained in Mexico City. "We found these in your hotel room," he said. "They're forgeries." Of course they were. Who are you? I told you, Gregorio Bonham. Is that your real name? No, I told you so in your office. What is your real name? I told you that, too. Tell me again. He did. And you say you were an agent of the DEA? Yes. But you still are, aren't you? No. I am being completely honest with you. We will see about that. Zaragoza turned to his thugs. "He's still crazy," he said, and left.

After more pummeling, he was forced to lie tied up on the bare concrete floor, where he spent the night. The next day his tormentors, who may well have been trained by the same people who'd tutored Carlos Aguilar's torturers, shoved his head into a tub of water until he was at the point of drowning. This was repeated three more times before the comandante reappeared to put the same questions to him. He gave the same answers. "How I wish I could believe you!" exclaimed Zaragoza, and once again left. More punches, more bobbing for apples in the tub, and then a new method—he was poked in the thighs with an electric cattle prod, with the promise that his testicles would be next. On his third visit, Zaragoza informed him that he had done some checking with certain friends in the United States. It seemed he was being truthful about his work with the DEA, but he wasn't convinced that Señor Bonham, as he now called himself, was no longer in their employ. The Oakland Raider jerked him to his feet, pulled his pants down, and flung him onto the floor. His smaller teammate poked him between the legs with the cattle prod, but didn't switch it on. "Listen, pendejo, I don't enjoy this, I am not a sadist," said Zaragoza. "If you don't tell me the truth, those huevos of yours are going to get fried." "Go ahead," The Professor gasped. "I won't tell you anything different." At a gesture from Zaragoza, Oakland stood him on his feet and pulled his pants back up. "Muchacho, you've got cojones, I'll say that for you," declared the comandante. He gathered from that comment that he'd passed his employment test.

The thugs returned him to his hotel and told him to stay there. He staggered to his room and collapsed onto the bed, aching all over. Sometime later in the afternoon a knock awakened him. He opened the door. His visitor was a short, heavyset man in the costume of the prosperous ranchero—a straw cowboy hat, a snug waist-length jacket, snakeskin boots. Four men were with him, dressed like vaqueros, though herding cattle was not what they did for a living. Joaquín Carrasco motioned to his bodyguards to wait in the corridor, entered the room, doffed his hat, and sat down in the only chair. "Do you know who I am?" he asked. Yes. And how did he know? "I recognize you from photographs in our files." "The files of the DEA?" That was correct. "But you no longer are in their service?" That too was correct. Carrasco folded his knotty peasant's hands over his mouth and flossed his front teeth with a thumbnail. "You know," he said, "that thing those Juárez boys did to your friend was very bad for business. Bad for everyone, not just them. It was very stupid! It drew so much attention! I don't wish to make the same mistake. If you were sent here to spy for the DEA, tell me. Nothing will happen to you. I will even pay for your transportation back to the United States, I swear it." The Professor replied that he had no desire to go back to the United States. The government of the United States had allowed the death of his friend to go unavenged, it had betrayed him; now he would betray it in turn. His wish was to enlist his services with Don Joaquín. "So how shall I call you? By your real name or this Gregorio Bonham?" inquired Carrasco. He preferred El Profesor. When he was instructing for the American army, that was what his students called him, out of respect. "Then El Profesor it will be. Get yourself cleaned up, and pack your things. You will come with me to my ranch and we can discuss what you can do for me."

With Carrasco's blessings, The Professor resumed his pursuit of the third and final torturer of Carlos Aguilar and nailed him a week later. In the meantime a new president representing a new political party, the first one to take power since the Revolution, had been elected. The former minister of defense, the brother-in-law of the general commanding the military forces in Chihuahua, had been replaced. Carrasco felt the time was right; he could eliminate the Juárez Cartel's chief patron without fear of government retaliation. The Professor was given the mission, and nothing could have pleased him more. No micromanager, Don Joaquín had only one instruction: "This new government won't shed any tears for our general, but we don't want to alarm them." The implication was clear—it should look like an accident. To assist him in his work, Carrasco, through Comandante Zaragoza, secured him a badge and a card identifying him as Capitán Gregorio Bonham. He was also issued a nine-millimeter pistol, a radio, handcuffs, and for appearances' sake if for no other reason, a black field uniform and bulletproof vest. He was, however, to perform this task in plainclothes.

Capitán Bonham established contact with the federales in Chihuahua City, with whom the general had unwisely not shared any but the crumbs of the mordida pie. He kept his quarry under surveillance for several weeks and developed snitches within the officer's retinue, who likewise had not benefited to a degree they thought they deserved. One informed him about the general's vacation plans—he would be flying in his private plane to Costa Rica on a certain date. The Professor, bringing all his skills and experience to bear, worked quickly to take advantage of this wonderful opportunity. The Cessna went down somewhere in the Sierra Madre Occidental. The collateral damage—the pilot and the general's wife—was regrettable, but with its protector's demise, the Juárez Cartel lost all its armor. Its warehouses and plantations were raided, the boss and his underlings were imprisoned.

The succeeding months brought The Professor no cause for regrets. He formed a singular loyalty to Joaquín Carrasco, in whose empire he had found a refuge and a home. And in him Carrasco found an extraordinarily able lieutenant. When two snitches whose informing had led to the confiscation of fifty kilos of coke fled to Phoenix, Don Joaquín dispatched The Professor and Félix, newly on the payroll and eager to show what he could do, to find them. The search took more than a week. They located the chingados shooting pool in a central Phoenix garage. A stifling summer night. The garage door was open. Félix, backed up by his ex-teacher, walked through it and said, "Sabe por qué estoy aquí," and capped them with fine precision. Four bullets, two bodies, no one else hurt.

The success of that and subsequent missions persuaded Carrasco to expand The Professor's duties beyond enforcement. He was summoned to another tête-à-tête at the Santa Clara ranch. "You have not had any big troubles being two people," Don Joaquín began. "Do you think you could be three?" He supposed so. Why? "Because you would be perfect for this. You speak English like a gringo, you look like a gringo—shit, muchacho, you *are* a gringo! All that is needed is for you to establish a new American identity for yourself. You would be able to do that?" He would, though doing so might take more time in the

United States than it had in Mexico. Joaquín shook his head. "I know people in Tucson and Phoenix who do that every day for fucking mojados. They can get you whatever you need. Social Security card. Driver's license. Passport." And what, exactly, was he going to do with this new identity? Carrasco gave him a sly look. "Escúchame, compa! You will be my ears, my eyes al otro lado, understand? You will find out what the gringo chotas are up to and let me know." The Professor said, "You know what that means, I hope." Joaquín knew—now and then, to keep La Migra and the chotas contented, a load and its mules would have to be sacrificed. No big deal. A cost of doing business. "My eyes, my ears on the other side, and on this side, too. I have confidence you can do both. Está bien?"

The Professor prospered. He bought a ranchito for himself outside Magdalena, that lovely old mission town where the bones of Father Kino rested. He later purchased a seaside condo in San Carlos, where Don Joaquín, a passionate fisherman, maintained a villa. By the standards of the country, The Professor was fabulously rich; by the standards of the trade, of modest means. That didn't bother him. Narco-trafficking, after all, was market capitalism with the muzzle off. Like the stock exchange, it ran on greed and fear, with revenge thrown into the mix. But of the three, greed was the most dangerous. It led to fatal mistakes in judgment. Keeping it in check had allowed him to survive and thrive in a world where average life expectancy was about where it had been in the eleventh century. As for fear, it had been his companion for so long, he thought he would miss it, the taste and smell of it, if ever he had to live without it. As for revenge, he had satisfied it when he took out the general; and in the slaking of that thirst, he had acquired a clearer vision of himself and his place in the scheme of things.

Now, waiting for Félix in the Church of the Immaculate Conception, he was inclined to view the circumstances leading to his switch in allegiance, to his crossings and recrossings of borders both geographical and figurative, as destined. It was as if history had guided him into becoming its agent.

His fellow renegade appeared, right on time. Félix Cabrera glided down the aisle garbed in pressed slacks, a black leather sport jacket, and polished loafers. He knelt at the shrine to the Virgin without acknowledging The Professor's presence, made the sign of the cross, and lit a vigil candle—probably for his father, dying of cancer in a Mexico City hospital. He crossed himself again, rose, and slid into the pew beside The Professor, who pulled an envelope out of his inside pocket and handed it to Félix. Inside were surveillance photographs taken in the last week

Félix studied them, squinting in the dim light.

"Ahora hablaremos inglés," The Professor whispered. English as a precaution. Although there was no one who could possibly overhear, you couldn't be too careful. "Vicente is hiding out on the other side. Almost every night he eats, drinks at a restaurant, Tehuantepec it's called. Sits at the same table, in a back corner with friends. He has a pistolero with him. You will have to take him out, too."

Félix cocked his chin to say that this would be no difficulty and looked at him, a question in his yellowish green eyes.

"Ten thousand. ¿Bien?"

"Está bien."

"A bonus in addition," The Professor said, passing Gloria's card. "Bought and paid for. She wants to be taken to dinner first and told me to tell you she doesn't take it up the ass."

Félix smiled. "A little extra cash would be better. The hospital bills for my father . . ."

"She is muy mota. When you see her, you'll forget cash, you may even forget your father." He dipped into a side pocket and placed a set of car keys in Félix's hand. "It's in the parking lot behind the McDonald's. A dark blue Chevrolet Blazer. California plates. The piece is inside the door panel. Passenger side. You have gloves?" he asked. Félix had been fingerprinted when he was at Fort Benning.

"Of course," Félix replied, a little insulted that The Professor would think he'd overlook that detail.

A middle-aged woman dressed in mourning interrupted the conversation. She knelt, lit a candle, and prayed for a minute or two.

"Follow me to the restaurant," The Professor said when she left. "This Tehuantepec is in a shopping plaza. At one end there is a farmacia, a Walgreens. Park there and wait. I'll go into the restaurant first to make sure he's there and no problems. I'll call you on your mobile. If I say *listos*, it's on. If I say *espera*, that's what you do. If I say *muy malo*, it means a big problem and you are to get out immediately. Questions?"

Félix shook his head and left. Outside the lights were coming on, and cirrus clouds colored by the sunset striped the sky directly overhead. The Professor trailed Félix down López Mateo to Calle Juárez, past the border wall with its slogans and crosses and bill posters advertising festivals and concerts, Félix sliding through the crowds as if they weren't there, light-footed and relaxed, like a jaguar with bigger game in mind moving through a clutch of rabbits. Inside the pedestrian port of entry, he calmly showed a forged border-crossing card to the U.S. Customs officer behind the counter, and was waved on. Following him, The Professor produced his U.S. passport, and when the customs agent asked if he had any fruits or vegetables in his possession, he quite honestly answered no.

Maintaining their distance from each other, he and Félix climbed the stairs by the handsome old U.S. Customs House, cut through a gas station at the corner of Crawford and Terrace, climbed another set of stairs to the McDonald's, and entered the twenty-four-hour lot where tourists visiting Nogales for the day usually left their cars.

From his car The Professor watched Félix get into the Blazer, stolen in Arizona by a ring that supplied Carrasco with vehicles. The California plates had been stamped out in an auto-body shop that specialized in such arts. He waited for Félix to uncover the Colt concealed behind the door panel, then pulled out through the McDonald's, the golden arches throwing off an odor resembling burnt toast. One of the interesting things about his condition: it was idiosyncratic. There was no correlation between the perception of one sense and the sense it called up. If there was, the arches' bright yellow would have smelled like what it resembled, cheap, squeeze-bottle mustard, say. Instead, burnt toast.

A cavernous and somewhat run-down fitness center took up one side of the Mariposa Plaza on Grand Avenue. Tehuantepec, its name painted across the front of the building over the words ¡MARISCOS FRESCOS! and renderings of a fish and a prawn, was at the end of a row of downscale shops, next to a Shakey's Pizza with one letter of its neon sign burned out. SHAK-Y'S. The Professor had visited Tehuantepec three times in the past couple of weeks to observe Vicente Cruz. Its interior was as unpromising as the exterior, but the worn tile floor, the cheesy travel posters on the walls, the shabby tables, and the rickety chairs were deceptive: the cuisine was excellent, especially the shrimp in cream and brandy sauce that Nacho had recommended. The restaurant drew very few Anglos; virtually all the customers, like the staff, were Mexican, and he assumed not all were legal residents of los Estados Unidos. A plus. Illegals were less likely to come forth as cooperative witnesses, should something go wrong.

He parked and strolled through the lot, looking for Cruz's silver

Lexus, doubtlessly purchased with the proceeds from the twelve kilos of coke he'd ripped off from Carrasco last summer. The shipment, packed into the frame of a pickup truck, had been destined for Phoenix, but somewhere between Phoenix and the border, the truck and the coke and Cruz vanished. Carrasco's instructions to The Professor had been simple: "Twenty thousand to roast the pig." The Professor had never met Cruz but knew him by reputation: a drunk and a loudmouth, with a taste for nightclubs, expensive cars, and ostentatious women. He should have been easy to track down, but he'd proved elusive. Informants reported him in various places, but the information was usually wrong or outdated. About two months ago a Border Patrol agent was gunned down when he came across some mules cutting through the border fence. Within a day The Professor learned from snitches that Cruz had killed the agent—reliable ears had heard the gritón bragging about it in a pueblo near Cananea, Imuris. The Professor got there that night and was astonished to find that Cruz had dissolved again.

Even now, as he located the Lexus, it rankled El Profesor that he'd had to rely on Nacho's tip to discover Cruz's whereabouts. Cruz's carelessness rankled further, even though it turned to his advantage. The babo had violated a fundamental rule—never establish a pattern—by eating at the same table in the same restaurant at the same time almost every night. How could he have failed to catch up with such an idiot for so long? He made it a point never to allow emotions to interfere with business, but he took Cruz's slipshod ways personally, as if the man knew he was being pursued by one of the best and didn't give a damn.

He went inside. The Tehuantepec had a dining room and a barroom, connected by an archway. To escape, Félix would have to pass through the bar into the dining room, through the dining room to the front door. He trusted that his ex-pupil's resourcefulness and the shock of the assault would create a clear avenue of retreat; but if some fool decided to play hero, there could be civilian casualties—that is, a mess—and he'd promised Nacho not to make one.

He sat at the bar and ordered a Dos Equis. Glancing over his shoulder, he saw Cruz, a chubby man with thick gray hair, presiding at his usual table alongside his pistolero, both with their backs to the wall. Cruz, The Professor had learned from sources on both sides of the line, was not lying quite as low as Nacho believed; he was now moving merca for Yvonne. (If he remained true to form, he was ripping her off whenever an opportunity presented itself.) Three more men sat with him and his bodyguard, talking loudly over a clutter of beer bottles. One was the nephew Nacho had mentioned, Billy Cruz, about whom The Professor had picked up a few scraps. Billy, it seemed, was a coyote and maintained his shuttle service as a legitimate front. He was believed to dabble in the drug trade, possibly in association with Tío Vicente, but it was mostly a small-scale sideline. The Professor had passed that morsel on to Nacho; otherwise, Billy and the other two were of no concern to him.

A TV on a platform directly over the elder Cruz's head was tuned to a sports channel. If he followed his normal pattern, Cruz would order dinner in another fifteen, twenty minutes, but he wasn't going to eat it tonight. A feeling of almost divine power surged through The Professor, a hot, metallic flow, as if his blood had turned to mercury. You thieving cabrón, I know your life expectancy is now shorter than a mosquito's, and you don't. He went to the men's room, locked the door, and dialed Félix's mobile.

"Listos," he said in an undertone, then returned to the bar.

Félix padded in a few minutes later, jacket buttoned in the middle. He took a stool at the end of the bar, ordered a drink that he was careful not to touch, then swung sideways and pretended to watch the TV while he studied his quarry—a nice touch. He was planning it out, figuring where to place himself, rehearsing the action in his mind. That was essential, to see it happening before it happened. Then Félix went to the bathroom to put the latex surgical glove on his shooting hand. His jacket was unbuttoned when he came out, and now it would have to be all speed and training and experience before anyone noticed the gun butt protruding from his waistband. He covered the room in four or five smooth strides, eyes fixed on his targets with what The Professor knew would be extreme tunnel vision. Félix could not allow himself to see anything but those two men, could not allow himself to be aware of anything else.

He was about six feet from the table when he called out in a friendly voice, "Oye! Vicente!" and as Cruz looked up to squint at this stranger greeting him: "¡Sabe por qué estoy aquí!— You know why I am here!" In the same moment, with a flowing, almost balletic movement of his arm, he drew the Colt and fired twice into Cruz, then turned the gun left to right, firing twice more into the pistolero. A .45-caliber semiautomatic makes a terrific noise in an enclosed space, and the sound and the swiftness of the action had had the shock effect The Professor had counted on—nobody had time to react. The customers were fastened to their seats, as still as figures in a freeze frame, as Félix backed away from the table, then pirouetted through the arch into the dining room.

The freeze frame twitched back into motion. Billy and the other survivors from Vicente's table tipped it over as they went to his aid, the bottles shattering on the floor. Several customers fled, probably because they wanted no dealings with the police, whom the bartender, over a waitress's screams, was phoning in panicky Spanglish. "¡Hola! Hello! Nine eleven! Shooting aquí! Restaurante Tehuantepec! Tehuantepec restaurant! ¡Sí! Yes! Grand Avenue! A shooting!" The Professor pushed through a knot of stunned onlookers to make sure Cruz was dead. He was—slumped in the corner, head to one side, the wall behind and above him smeared with blood, bone chips, parts of his brain. The pistolero had taken both shots through the chest.

On the sidewalk outside three or four people stood around the Colt that Félix had dropped when he had no more use for it. They looked at the weapon in a kind of awestruck state, as if it were some holy object. Félix was not in sight, on the road by now. He would abandon the car downtown—in the unlikely event that somebody had made the plates—cross back into Mexico on foot, and give Gloria a call. He'd certainly earned his bonus. Two shots to the head. The Professor would not have risked it, would have aimed for the body, a surer thing—but if the pupil is not greater than the teacher, then the teacher has failed.

He heard the mad gulping of police and ambulance sirens as he drove out onto Mariposa and headed south. A green sign over the highway read: MEXICO 2KM. When he passed through the gate, flipping his federal police ID to the Mexican customs guard, he dialed the Santa Clara on his mobile. Carrasco answered.

"Hola," The Professor said. "This is your cook. The pig has been roasted."

8

CASTLE LOATHED all country-western music except the old-time stuff that he'd listened to while pulling all-nighters in college, signals from stations in Gatlinburg and Jackson and Fayetteville ricocheting off the ionosphere into his room at Princeton—Hank Williams, Johnny Cash, or Waylon Jennings lamenting faithless hearts, bad roads, hard times, and sinners longing for salvation. Raucous and rowdy or mournful and plaintive, those songs had the authenticity of lived experience. But the modern tunes, rooted in the suburbs and shopping mall instead of the cotton fields and the prison yard, all sounded alike to him, full of fabricated emotions and as predictable and standardized as a room in a Days Inn or the front page of *USA Today.* Hard to sing about hard times when you're living in a cul-de-sac and a McDonald's Happy Meal is a five-minute drive away; and now that the backwoods revival tents had been replaced by megachurches whose media-savvy ministers preached Redemption Lite to their consumers, no sinner need feel the longing to be saved, or for that matter, feel like a sinner at all.

So he was encouraged when the Double Sixes—Rick Erskine on vocals and lead guitar, backed up by an electric bass, a drummer, a keyboardist, and a horn player—jumped out onto the stage garbed in white shirts and rumpled black linen suits, without a cowboy hat on a single head. The opening number began with the horn riffing a Mexican theme that was suddenly silenced by harsh, dissonant chords from Rick's guitar, the keyboardist and the drummer leaping in over a bluesy baseline. "High Speed Chase," it was called, a kind of epic in the vein of "Pancho and Lefty," about doper desperadoes in flight from the Border Patrol. It set the tone for the songs that followed. Not a whiff of sentimentality in any of them, with thoughtful lyrics, *too* thoughtful for the major labels, which probably accounted for the band's confinement to provincial popularity. They sang of modern-day outlaws, not in a Wild West that had never died but in a West that had been tamed and then reverted to a new and more toxic wildness—narcs and narcosnitches, shady gringos looking to score in Mexico, blood and money and blood money, the crackle of drug-war bullets, crooked cops with straight teeth as white as migrants' skulls grinning under the saguaros—the *feral* West straight out of this morning's editions of the

ARIZONA DAILY STAR

Serving Tucson since 1877 • WEDNESDAY, FEBRUARY 10, 2003

Two Killed in Gangland-Style Shooting in Nogales

By Ramon Alvarez and Melinda Norris

NOGALES—A modest restaurant in this border city was the scene Thursday night of a shooting that left two men dead and that one Nogales police officer described as "something right out of 'The Godfather.' " The victims were identified as . . .

The paper had been lying on the backseat when Blaine and Monica picked him up, and Castle, even with his news-phobia, was drawn to it with the same lurid fascination that compels motorists to gawk at an ugly accident. The Mariposa Mall was behind the Walgreens where he'd filled his Ambien prescription the other week. That a locale so commonplace had been the setting for a "gangland-style" assassination jarred his sense of the expected. Such events were supposed to occur in moody Italian joints on side streets in Brooklyn or New Jersey, not in a Mexican seafood restaurant in a down-at-the-heels shopping mall in a middling-size Arizona town. Maybe he needed to revise his mantra to: anything at any moment *anywhere*. He'd begun to ask himself if he'd chosen the wrong place for a refuge. Maybe he should have gone all the way, to a Tibetan lamasery, a cabin in the Alaskan bush.

The shooting was all they'd talked about on the ride into Tucson. Castle had looked out the window at the theatrical sunset reddening the clouds over the Santa Ritas and thought of Miguel, cringing in his own waste as he watched his two friends shot down in cold blood. In these borderlands beauty cohabited with violence—Blaine and Gerardo's world of cattle and horses and operatic landscapes, the parallel world of drug lords and coyotes and murder.

In the dark ages before cineplexes, the Rialto had been a movie theater, its interior ornamented to resemble the opera houses of a still-earlier epoch in entertainment. As part of a campaign, not entirely successful, to revivify Tucson's tired downtown, it had been converted into a concert hall, one that catered to the young and the fit, for the seats on the lobby floor had been removed, requiring the audience to stand throughout the performance. The more sedentary had to go to the balcony. This was where Castle sat with Tessa, Blaine, and Monica, far enough from the stage not to be totally deafened by the refrigerator-size speakers. Below, the audience, mostly undergraduates judging from the names of colleges emblazoned on their sweatshirts and jackets, stood in a kind of rapture, swaying to the music, singing along on the choruses, whooping, hollering, holding overhead cigarette lighters or cell phone cameras, whose bright screens made electronic fires amid the lighters' flames.

The music was disturbing, but not in the unpleasant way the news story had been disturbing. As listening to the blues cured the blues, listening to Rick's music—Monica called the genre "desert rock"—somehow eased Castle's disquiet. Despite himself, he was having a good time. The massed youth beneath him made him feel younger and their high spirits raised his; yet he was aware that he would not be enjoying himself half as much if Tessa were not beside him. She had exchanged her rodeo-queen outfit of the other night for something more urban—a satiny, cream-colored blouse, loose-fitting trousers with an autumn leaf pattern, and a pair of low-heeled beige pumps. Conversation was impossible, sound waves from the giant speakers penetrated skin, vibrated internal organs. Tessa tilted her head toward Castle's ear to say, "They're very good!" He nodded and rubbed his sleeve, the nearness of her lips bringing on a sudden, pleasurable chill.

At the break they went backstage to meet the band. A scrawny kid the last time Castle had seen him, Rick Erskine was now a towering young man, an inch taller than his father and, fortunately, heir to Monica's looks. He embraced her and shook hands with Blaine, then with Castle.

"Dad told me you were staying at the place. Good to see you again." There was an uncomfortable pause. Shy, like many musicians when off stage, Rick brushed his long, light hair with his fingers. He knew about Amanda's death, of course, but he seemed unsure of what to say, or if he should say anything. Castle rescued him by asking where the band had been touring.

"Everywhere from El Paso to San Diego," he answered. "Next month it'll be Puerto Peñasco."

That fishing village, on the Sea of Cortez, had become the spring-break destination for southwestern colleges.

"He packs 'em in down there," said Blaine enthusiastically. Castle would not have thought his hard-bitten cousin would be so pleased to have a singer and songwriter for a son—he would have wanted Rick to carry on with ranching, or to go into some practical line of work, say mine engineering, like his grandfather.

The performance concluded with an antiwar song. It wasn't as overt as the pacifist anthems of the sixties, and the overamplified lyrics were hard to make out, but the message was clear enough and wrenched cheers from the throats of the audience. Blaine cheered right along with them, seemingly oblivious to the tune's sentiments, which, if they'd been expressed in plain conversation, would have provoked one of his truculent speeches.

At the end of the set Tessa remained in her seat while Blaine, Monica, and Castle rose to applaud; then, realizing that this might be mistaken for displeasure, she stood and joined in, albeit without much spirit. No exceptional degree of perception was needed to know that the last song had carried her far away, to another desert, where the engines of war cast their long shadows. She scarcely spoke during the drive home. Castle and she sat an arm's length apart, but as the pickup jounced down the dirt road to her place, he, as timorous as a high school kid on a first date, reached across the space between them and clasped her hand. He told himself that this gesture was meant to reassure her that he understood why she was so removed, that she could count on him if she needed someone to talk to. There was more to it, of course, but he wasn't ready to face the truth of his desire. He was happy to feel her return the pressure, a brief squeeze that communicated thanks, and perhaps something else.

When Blaine stopped at her front gate, she snatched her hand away and climbed out before Castle could ask to see her in.

"Good night, everyone," she said brusquely. "And thanks. I had a good time."

With her jacket tossed over her shoulders, Tessa strode up the path to her door, a silhouette in the darkness until a motion-sensitive spotlight above the door flashed on, and in its glare the orange and russet leaves printed on her billowy trousers seemed to swirl about her legs, to swirl and tumble, like real leaves stirred by a breeze.

Ben Erskine

Transcript 1 of interview conducted for the Arizona Historical Society with Jeffrey Erskine. The interview took place at Mr. Erskine's ranch, the San Ignacio, on May 6, 1966.

My brother was loved and admired by a lot of folks on both sides of the border, for good reason. He was also feared and hated, likewise for good reason. Most of the ones who feared and hated him were riffraff, but some were decent people, like Mae Wilcox. Her and her husband owned a small ranch near to ours, and Mae had forbidden her kids to play with Ben's because her boy, when he wasn't but fifteen, sassed Ben and Ben would not accept his apology when he offered it later on, and in fact never spoke a word to that boy for the rest of his life. The whole notion of Christian forgiveness was as foreign to him as eating carrots is to a wolf. The man could carry a grudge like a pack mule. Generally speaking, it didn't take much to get on Ben's wrong side, and once you were there, you stayed there—unless you threatened him or his. In that case, you wound up on the wrong side of the ground. He killed his first man when he was only thirteen. This happened when our mother kicked him out of the house and sent him to live for a spell with her older brother in Lochiel. A Mexican had pulled a knife on him and tried to steal his horse, but somehow or other Ben wrestled the knife out of his hands and stabbed him to death. That's the story I heard from our uncle Josh. Ben himself wouldn't talk about it.

Another story: in '05 Ben and me had found work in the Pride of the West mine in the Patagonia Mountains, near to the towns of Washington Camp and Duquesne. There was a whole lot of mines operating in that area in those days, and the two towns must have had at least a thousand people in each one of them. Nothing much left to them now. The Pride of the West was one of the big operations, copper and silver mostly, a shaft mine, and it was damn hard work busting hard rock four hundred feet underground ten hours a day, six days a week, in a tunnel you could barely stand up straight in.

We had fetched up there because our mother, Hattie, had pulled up stakes from Tucson and moved out to California with our stepfather, and the both of them had made it clear without saying so that we would not be welcome to travel with them. Our mother was a peculiar woman, not what most folks would think of when you say the word *mother.* But the main problem was Ben and our stepdad—Rudy Hollister was his name. They were always at each other's throats. Rudy was a nice enough fella, but Ben hated him for stepping into our dad's boots, or trying to. Our dad had been a territorial ranger and died from a horse kick back in '01. Like I was saying, Ben hated Rudy, and no matter how nice you might be, you can be hated just so long before you start to hate back.

So when the Southern Pacific railroad—that was Rudy's employer—gave him a promotion and a transfer to San Diego, he saw his chance to get shed of Ben. Our mother, well, she was not overflowing with affection for me, but she come to be at Ben's throat, too, and was just as happy as Rudy to get away from him. And Ben was glad to be rid of her. So when Hattie and Rudy stepped on the train for California, the two of us stayed behind in Arizona. We got jobs in the mine and moved into a boardinghouse the mine company had built in Washington Camp. The way I felt about things, and still do, all these sixty years later, was that Hattie was like a she-wolf, leaving her young behind to slink off with her new mate. She had turned Ben and me into orphans, which I state as fact without feeling sorry for myself, nor for Ben neither.

Even when I was seventeen, I had my sights set on becoming a cattleman. My brother and I had worked cattle on school vacations on ranches outside Tucson, and we were the both us damn good with a rope and could ride as well as the next man. The mine paid decent wages, and I saved every dime I could to one day buy me a few head and make a start.

Well, I have wandered off the point. I was fixing to tell you how Ben never could tolerate an insult or any man ever getting the better of him. I have told you that hard-rock mining as it was practiced a long time ago was damn hard work. One day Ben, who was skinny like our dad, considerably skinnier than me, hell, he was skinny enough that some folks said he could take a shower in a shotgun barrel without his elbows touching the sides, hurt his back shoveling waste rock into an ore car. Now, in the days before the socialists come along with their labor unions, a miner who hurt himself was out of work and out of luck. But the supervisor had taken a liking to Ben and, when he found out Ben had gone to two years of high school and could read, write, and do sums, gave him a job in the payroll office.

It came to pass that on a day in '06 one miner, a big fella called Brophy got drunk and, in the paymaster's office, accused Ben of crediting him less hours than he'd put in, which made him come up two bucks short in his pay envelope. The paymaster checked the figures and told Brophy to pipe down, that his hours was calculated by the timekeeper, not by Ben, and that if Brophy had an argument, he should take it up with the timekeeper. Way I heard it, Brophy said something like, "Like hell, that scrawny snot-nose is what done it!" My brother, not being one to let a challenge go unanswered or to allow someone else to fight his battles for him, said that Brophy could not count two plus two when sober, much less in his present condition, and for that wisecrack he got knocked cold by a punch to the jaw.

If you consider that Ben was sixteen and maybe a hundred forty pounds with his boots on and the miner was a grown man a good sixty pounds heavier, it was no disgrace, but that night in our bunks in the boardinghouse, he told me that he'd been called a cheat and been sucker-punched and could not permit it to pass unavenged. There was a blacksmith in camp, name of McNamara. He'd been a professional prizefighter in Ireland, and when he came to America, he'd hoboed from one western mining town to another and earned lunch money by walking into saloons and declaring that he could whip any man in the place. Take into account that his opponents were not scienced and almost always intoxicated, the man never did go hungry.

Ben talked this McNamara into teaching him to box. The lessons took place at night after work in the blacksmith's shop. To build himself up, Ben lifted weights with barbells McNamara forged out of scrap iron. I went along to watch my ribby brother and this hefty Irishman stripped to the waist, all greased up in sweat and the sweat shining in the lantern while they sparred. The training went on for a long spell, more than a month, and that proved that Ben, who had a habit of skipping from one endeavor to another, could sure be of one mind when it came to getting even.

He was crafty, too. When he figured he was ready, he did not walk up to Brophy and challenge him to a fight; he waited until everything could be in his favor. It was on a Saturday afternoon, after the day shift, and Ben borrowed a horse from the blacksmith and rode over to the saloon where Brophy was tying one on. This saloon wasn't like the ones in the westerns. It did have swinging doors, but it was otherwise a kind of giant tent, like a circus tent thrown over a wood platform. I went along to make sure my brother didn't get himself killed.

Well, I need not have had any worries about that. All of a sudden Ben let out a wild yell, like an Apache war whoop, and jumped his horse up the steps and through the door and crashed smack-dab into Brophy. He was pretty drunk and you probably could have knocked him over by blowing on him, so you can imagine what happened when he had a head-on collision with a horse. Hit the floor like he'd been poleaxed. Ben jumped from the saddle on top of him and commenced to whale on him with everything he had. Managed to bust both hands and make Brophy so his mother would not have recognized him.

I don't have a lot in the way of formal education. I, too, never graduated high school, quit in my last year, when my mother took off for California. But I put great stock in education and have tried to teach myself lessons I missed in school. I read a lot, and I recall reading an essay by a historian name of Frederick Jackson Turner. It was written in 1893 or around then, and it was Mr. Turner's idea that the figures from the United States census of 1890 showed that no clear line could be drawn between the settled and the unsettled parts of the West. That was also the year of the Battle of Wounded Knee up in the Dakotas—the last of the Indian wars. In so many words, the frontier that had existed for more than three centuries was gone, and the old Wild West a thing of the past.

The reason I bring this up is, first of all, Ben was born in 1890, and second of all, the Wild West might have disappeared from Kansas and Colorado and such places, but it lived on down here in this border country for a good long time. Sure, the Apaches were whipped and penned up on reservations, but we had outlaws and rustlers and gunfighters raising hell in Arizona and New Mexico damn near into the 1920s. Pancho Villa got his start in life as a cattle rustler. The whole reason the Territorial Rangers were formed was to clean up Arizona so it would be respectable and fit for statehood, which as you know it didn't get until 1912.

I am not off on a side trail, like you might think. You are not the first person to ask me about Ben, him being the legend he was, and so I have spent some time trying to figure his life out. I come back to the words a newspaper friend of Ben's, Tim Forbes, spoke at Ben's funeral ten years ago. He said something like "Benjamin Erskine was the last ember of the true Old West," and that he was like the Old Testament Hebrews in his fierce, unbending beliefs because he grew up in a desert and lived among his herds and the harshness of nature, just like those Old Testament folks.

Of course, I grew up the same way in the same times, but Ben and I were completely different, like we weren't born of the same man and woman. Ben was an adventurer, a soldier of fortune, and a lawman, and he put about twelve men in the ground—the ones he didn't put in jail. I consider myself a businessman, and except for a couple schoolboy scuffles, I have never been in a fistfight. What made the difference was . . . well, I guess you'd have to call it fate. Ben was a lightning rod for trouble; sometimes he looked for it and sometimes it found him.

It was in '07 that we got laid off from the mine. We didn't know it then, but there had been financial panic way off in New York, and the prices of silver and copper had gone down the drain, so the mines cut back on production or shut down altogether. For about a year Ben and I were saddle bums, working ranches in Arizona and in Mexico. Then we teamed up with a vaquero name of Martín Mendoza capturing unbranded bulls. They were wild animals and were hard to find, hiding out in the brushiest, most remote country they could get into. The three of us spent days tracking 'em down in the mountains, and when we finally got one cornered, we'd ride in and rope him, taking turns heading and heeling. That Martín could throw a loop like I'd never seen a man throw one—his riata would shoot out from his hand like a rawhide snake. He hardly ever missed, which was a good thing, because if you did miss, you stood a fair chance of being charged and knocked off your horse by one of those bulls, and then he was likely to gore or stomp you to death.

It was dangerous, exciting work, but it wasn't exciting enough for my brother, so for a spell he apprenticed himself out to a professional hunter that ranchers had hired to get rid of cattle-killing mountain lions. The hunter ran them down with a pack of dogs, big, rangy redbones and like breeds, and Ben often said there was no sound to quicken your blood like their cries when in pursuit, unless it was the baying they made when they'd treed or cornered the lion. The hunter and Ben would ride hell for leather to catch up with the pack, and if the cougar decided to fight, they would come upon a scene of bloody mayhem, three or four dogs mauled or gutted, the others lunging in to snap at the cat's hindquarters and the lion hissing and snarling and lashing out with its forepaws. That's when Ben and his boss would dismount and wade in through those bloodied-up, howling dogs and finish the cougar with their revolvers.

It was said of Ben that he could have given an Apache lessons in tracking. He learned how from his days hunting wild bulls and mountain lions.

Along about 1910 I had saved enough money to buy a few head of corriente steers down in Mexico. Ben's wildness did not extend to whiskey and women, the two things that empty a cowboy's pockets the quickest, so he had saved up some himself and chipped in. I filed for a quarter section of rangeland up here in the San Rafael under the Homestead Act and leased another ten sections, and that was the start of the San Ignacio. We were old-time rawhiders and lived like rawhiders in a tent with a wood-burning stove and were in the saddle most every day. Fall of that year, we drove our first herd to market, pushing them to the railhead at Sonoita.

Ben and I had some differences—he had this habit of disappearing on me for days on end, riding down into Sonora for I don't know what reasons. Spring of the next year he and a hand we had working for us, a T.J. Babcock, up and left me to go fight in the Mexican Revolution. To my mind, it was the screwiest thing any two gringos could do, but this Babcock had been raised mostly in Mexico, in Cananea, where they had that big miners' strike in '05. I think he picked up a lot of foreign ideas there, the man was practically a damn Red, and I believe he talked my brother into joining him and those revolutionary thugs like Pancho Villa. Ben was a man of few words, so I don't know much about what he and Babcock did in the Revolution. If Babcock is still alive and you can track him down, you can ask him. I did gather, from the little my brother told me when he got back that summer, that he saw some right terrible things and was party to them besides.

I thought, or maybe it was hoped, that seeing and doing those things had got something out of his system, but if anything, he was more restless and thirsting for action than before. That man craved it like a drunk does his whiskey. He wasn't of much help to me, running the ranch.

I don't recall what year this was—sometime after I got married to Lilly in 1912 and built a little house for us—it's just up the road from this one, still standing—that Ben got himself in a little trouble with the law. He captured a mustang, a blue roan stallion that had been running loose in the Huachucas and that had become like a famous outlaw because he gave the slip to every cowhand who tried to catch him. Ben and Martín spotted him one day and went after him. Martín's throw missed—must have been the only time in his life he did miss. Ben's did not. He brought the roan to the ranch, branded him, named him Spirit for his ghostly color and for his temperament, and broke him to the saddle.

There was a law on the books prohibiting the appropriation of maverick horses. They were considered public property and were to be turned over to the county court for auction. Word of Ben's capture spread, and when the county attorney in Nogales heard of it, he issued a court order for Ben to surrender that horse.

No way was he going to. The prosecutor sent a mounted posse to take the animal. Ben got forewarned, I don't know from who or how. He got Spirit out of the corral and waited for the posse up on an oak ridge. When he saw them, he rode out from hiding and waved his hat and let out a vaquero's yell. The chase was on. He led the posse into the mountains where he and Spirit knew every canyon and trail. It was no contest, so he decided to make it one by taunting the posse. He'd ride to the crest of a hill and wait there in full view. When the posse got to within fifty yards or so, he'd spur Spirit into a run. The game went on for an entire morning, until the posse quit. Ben rode on for another thirty miles, to a ranch in the low desert country near Tucson, where he left Spirit in the care of a rancher we'd worked for years before. Then he hopped the next train heading south. About a month later, he retrieved the stallion and rode him back down here, proud as could be.

I mention these hijinks because they and other wild things he did went a long way into making his legend. Not that he was a legend like Wyatt Earp was, but he'd become a kind of hero to certain folks in Santa Cruz and Cochise and Pima counties. You see, Arizona had finally got admitted to the union—the curtain had come down on the hell-roaring territorial days. That was okay with most people, including myself—about time Arizona caught up with the twentieth century. But down here on the border, there were other people who weren't so happy with progress and civilization. They felt life was getting to be a little too regulated, you know, like they were being fenced in, and somebody like Ben reminded them of the old days of the open range and doing what you damn well pleased and poking your thumb in the eye of the law. It's passing strange when I think about it. Ben wasn't yet twenty-five, he ought to have belonged to the future, not to a time gone by. It seemed to suit him, though, and he did his best to live up to the picture folks had of him.

Capturing wild horses and leading posses on breakneck chases, even that got to be too tame for him. In 1915 he up and disappeared on me again. Found out later that he and Mendoza and his old sidekick Babcock had joined up with Yaqui Indians running guns into Old Mexico. Mexico was a damn mess back then. One general would take power, then another general would overthrow him and be el presidente till another general threw him out. To go running guns into that madhouse seemed just crazy to me. I was getting worried that my kid brother was going to turn into one more border renegade and end up behind bars or dead. I recollect—it must have been in 1916—sitting him down and saying to him, "Ben, either you're my partner in this ranch or you're not. If you don't want to be, say so, and I'll buy you out. But if you are, then dammit, you've got to stick around and do the work and not go running off on these harebrained adventures." Ben promised he'd be more steady, like a business partner should.

I had a talk with Lilly about him, and we decided to be matchmakers, calculating that if Ben met the right gal and took on the responsibilities of married life, he might be more reliable and live longer besides. I reckon we were sticking our noses where they didn't belong. Still and all, we felt that it was our duty to nudge him, kind of, into a more regular life. It so happened that Lilly knew of a single young lady, Ida Barnes. She was seventeen, the only child of Merle and Ellen Barnes. They were middling-prosperous folks who ran a lumberyard and sawmill near to the town of Canelo. One day I drove the wagon over to their place to buy some boards I needed for a new corral, but really I wanted to see their daughter for myself and more or less to find out how things stood with her, you know, if she had her a boyfriend or fiancé.

When I drove up and hitched my team, I heard this female voice call to me from the yard, "Good day, sir. If you have business with my father, he is up in the mountains sawing timber with his crew, but my mother should be able to take care of you." The voice was coming from above me, and there was Ida, sitting on a tree branch in a spotless white muslin dress and a straw hat. Her feet in high-button shoes were crossed at the ankles, and she was smiling to beat the band and looked relaxed, like she was sitting on a porch swing instead of a tree branch six, seven feet off the ground. I thanked her for her information and then asked her what she was doing up there, and she said she liked the view.

A while later, as I was loading up my wagon, the mailman rode in. Ida jumped right out of that tree and without so much as a stumble ran over to the mailman, asking if he had a letter for her. He did not. She was right disappointed. "You never bring any mail for me," she said, like it was his fault. I thought that a gal who would climb a tree dressed like it was a Sunday and then jump to the ground light as a cat was just the gal for Ben. When I got home, I told him about Miss Barnes and said that she was hoping someone would write her a letter. I left it at that, hoping he would take the hint, and he did.

She wrote him back, and pretty soon he got an invitation to Sunday dinner. I'll never forget how my brother looked when he drove off in our carriage, bathed and shaved and dressed to make an impression. Beaver-hide Stetson, corduroy jacket, starched white shirt, bandanna with a silver clasp, handmade Mexican boots. You add to his appearance his reputation as a dashing fella, which had gone before him, and you can see why he just bowled that impressionable young gal right over.

They courted all that summer and in September Ben proposed. Ida said yes but told him he would have to ask for her father's approval. As the story has come down to me, Ben stopped by the following day and sat out on the front porch jawing about horses and cattle prices with Merle Barnes. Ida stood inside with her ear pressed to the door. There was a break in the conversation, and Ben asked, "What would you say if Ida and me got married?" in a way so offhanded the old man didn't hear the question. Ben repeated it in the same casual way. "Reckon that would be all right," Merle answered, and then him and my brother went back to talking about livestock.

So they got married a couple of weeks later, by a justice of the peace in Tucson. I'll say this for Ben—he tried real hard to follow my advice to settle down and break himself to the saddle of marriage and family responsibilities. He got a job managing the store at the Yaqui reservation at Xavier del Bac, south of Tucson, and earned side money turning out bits, spurs, and horseshoes for sale. He even took a correspondence course to earn a high school degree.

But he wasn't cut out for a life like that. Ida wrote Lilly a letter one time and mentioned that Ben had become subject to what she called "spells of cloudy weather." Lilly and I knew what she meant—we'd seen those spells ourselves. Ben would sull up all of a sudden, and for no reason we could figure out, act like he was mad about something but wouldn't say what, and then just as quick, he'd snap out of it. But we got the feeling from Ida's letter that these storms were becoming more frequent. I'm no philosopher, sure as hell no psychologist, but I reckoned that Ben was trying to be somebody he wasn't and it was getting to him. He looked up to me—I say that without bragging. He admired men who were even-tempered and thought things through and were steady of purpose, and he wanted to be that way himself. Hell's bells, I wanted him to be that way. But he couldn't be.

In 1917, after the U.S. got itself into the First World War, Ben declared that he was going to enlist. Said that with his battle experience in Mexico, he could be of valuable service to the army. Maybe so. But I wonder now if he was looking to jump the fence, I mean get away from a dull job and a way of life that fit him like a shirt two sizes too small. In the end Ida talked him out of joining up. She was pregnant—she would miscarry that child—and Ben, rightly so, I think, decided his place was at her side. I believe he always regretted not going to the war. In years to come I would hear him say that he felt he missed out on something terrible and grand.

What he did do was to become a cattleman in his own right. He quit the store job and filed a claim for a section of undeveloped land under the Homestead Act. If he proved up, the land would be his in five years. He named his place after Ida's initials—the IB-Bar. It was at the foot of the Huachuca Mountains, which wasn't ideal cattle country, full of tight canyons and steep hillsides, but it had a spring, which was a thing of value in our dry country. A tumbledown log cabin built by an early settler stood below the spring. Ben fixed it up, and Ida and he lived in it for a year or so. Then, on the slope of a south-facing ridge, low enough to be out of the wind but high enough to be safe from flooding in the summer monsoons, he built an adobe-brick house with my help and the help of his old partner, Martín Mendoza. Martín hired on and moved into the cabin with his wife, Lourdes. Ben dug a well, fenced the property, put up a corral and a barn. Ida planted a vegetable garden and ordered a new cast-iron stove with a warming oven and water-heating compartment from the Sears Roebuck catalog. It came by ox-drawn wagon from the train station in Nogales, along with a bed to replace the one Ben and Martín had built out of oak trees they'd cut down themselves. There they were, almost twenty years into this century, living like pioneers. Ida was happy. Just eighteen years old, and she had a place she could call her own.

And my brother? He wasn't cut out to be a cattleman either, even though he was good at it. He worked that ranch off and on till '38, when he sold out and incorporated the IB-Bar into the San Ignacio and once more became my partner. When I say "off and on," I mean more off than on. He was a deputy sheriff for about ten of those years, and he continued to go soldier-of-fortuning down in Mexico. It was that craving of his for action, for danger. Just like he used to disappear on me for days and sometimes weeks, he did the same to Ida and their two kids, Frank and Grace. Because of the way he lived his life, there were all kinds of men who came after him, looking for revenge. One time he and Martín fought a gun battle with a pair of desperadoes right in the backyard, in full view of Ida and the children. Ida died early, you know, she was just shy of fifty-two years old, and there were some people, his own daughter was one and my Lilly another, who thought that the strain of living with a man like Ben was what killed her. Personally I think that's nonsense, but I do know he put his family through an awful lot, and that if I'd been a woman, I would not have wanted to be married to my brother.

9

TWO DAYS after the concert Tessa invited Castle to ride with her and a day hand; they were going to move a bull to a new pasture. As he knew nothing about herding cattle and could be of no help whatsoever, might even be a hindrance, he assumed she'd extended the invitation because she wanted his company, which pleased and scared him at the same time. Actually, what scared him was the undeniable fact that he enjoyed her company, an enjoyment that struck him as inappropriate and possibly dangerous, threatening the stability of his solitude.

When he arrived at Tessa's corral, he found that the hand, whose name was Tim McIntyre, had already saddled and bridled a horse for him. Though he was grateful to be spared the embarrassment of demonstrating his incompetence at tacking up, it was a greater embarrassment to have someone else do the job. McIntyre, a young, central-casting cowboy wearing spurs and thorn-scarred butterfly chaps, didn't help matters, greeting him with the slightly disdainful look a wrangler would bestow on a dude ranch guest. Some of his masculine pride was restored when Tessa, who'd wrenched a knee yesterday, asked him to help her mount up. She wedged her left boot in the stirrup, he grasped her waist with both hands, and as he boosted her into the saddle, her thighs and hips brushed his chest, sending a thrill through him. He hadn't felt anything like it for a very long time.

They rode out three abreast. It was a brilliant morning. A warm breeze out of Mexico whispered that spring was on the way, and in it the tall yellow grass on a nearby hill rippled like the fur of some great blond beast.

"I was more mad than sad," Tessa said abruptly, as if she were picking up the thread of an earlier conversation. "Night before last," she added into his perplexed silence, and he realized she was talking about the swift change in her mood at the end of the concert. "I couldn't say anything to Blaine and Monica, so I just . . . withdrew."

"No explanation required."

Her baseball cap—more practical headgear on a windy day than a cowboy hat—was tilted back, and the sun fell full on her face as she turned to speak to him, igniting a sparkle of tiny gold flecks in her brown eyes. "If I thought it was *required*, I wouldn't give it."

"Okay, what were you mad at?"

"All those kids having such a great time. Rick having such a great time getting adored by his fans. *Me* having a good time."

"And Beth over there," Castle said.

"It didn't feel right. And Blaine . . . the way he clapped at that protest song, after all that chest-thumping he did at dinner, all that bumper-sticker bullshit patriotism. Because it was his celebrity son singing it. It just pissed me off."

She would have gone on, but just then McIntyre interrupted her. "He'll be in there, saw him there yesterday," he said, pointing at a canyon ahead, where a windmill's blades fanned above a parklike stand of low oaks.

They rode single file into the canyon. The shadows of the trees so camouflaged the Angus that Castle didn't see them until they stirred at the riders' approach. The young bull, amid a herd of cows and calves, eyed them balefully.

"Hold up here," Tessa said to Castle. "Tim and I will cut him out." She paused for a beat and said, "If he runs in your direction, head him off." This was a gesture on her part, and a kind one—she wanted him to feel he had a role to play.

She and McIntyre nudged their horses into the herd. The scene was bewitching—the black cattle milling in the dappled sunlight, the ballet of the two riders, weaving through the trees, the lightsome swing of Tessa's chestnut hair as she turned her horse this way and that, deftly maneuvering the bull until he stood all alone. She kept an eye on him while McIntyre separated a cow from its calf, then pushed it toward the bull.

"Ready to go," Tessa called.

Castle trotted up to her. The calf was bleating piteously for its mother.

"Why the cow?" he asked.

"A traveling companion. Cattle are herd animals. If he"—indicating the bull with a twitch of her head—"was alone, he'd be harder to move. One of these days I'll join the modern age and buy some bull in a bottle."

"Which is what?"

"Sperm. Artificial insemination. But for now my girls will have to get pregnant the old-fashioned way."

Despite the cow's presence, the bull proved difficult, lumbering off into clumps of trees, where he would stand stubbornly until McIntyre, ducking under low branches, got him moving again. A couple of times the cow tried to run back to her calf. On one of these occasions, Castle was closest to her, and he rode after her and turned her, earning approving nods from Tessa and McIntyre. Finally both animals settled down, and they proceeded at a slow walk along a fenceline atop a long ridge crowded with juniper and manzanita. The ridge sloped off gradually into open grasslands. The snows on the Huachucas, several miles eastward, had retreated with the warmer, drier weather; all that remained was a thin, broken white line at the very top.

"This is what we want, an easy pace," Tessa said. "Don't want the bull to get overheated. Hot bulls are hard to handle."

"So it is said," drawled McIntyre with a grin. Tessa laughed at her unintentional double entendre, and Castle laughed with her. It had been so long since he'd heard himself laugh that he almost didn't recognize the sound of it.

They pushed down the ridge and into the open country, following another trail toward a fenced trough and windmill. A drug runners' trail, McIntyre pointed out. "You can tell by the footprints and how straight it is," he said. "Those mules don't wander like cattle, make a beeline to their drop point. Reckon I would, too, humpin' fifty pounds on my back." Having imparted this bit of modern western fieldcraft, he motioned at a small herd of Angus that made dark spots on a hillside about a quarter of a mile away. "Cows're yonder," he said.

"All right, you gather them," Tessa said. "Gil and I will pen the groom-to-be."

As McIntyre struck off, Castle and Tessa drove the bull and his traveling companion toward the fence enclosing the windmill. To spare her stiff knee, he swung out of the saddle to open the gate, a typical Texas gate, with three strands of barbed wire stretched taut between the fence posts and locked by two wire loops, one around the top of the gatepost, one at the bottom. The tension was such that he could not pull the top loop free one-handed, so he dropped the reins to unfasten it with both hands. Just as he did, his horse turned and bolted. When Tessa shouted, "You son of a bitch!" he wasn't sure if she was referring to him or his horse.

With a jab of her spurs, she took off after the runaway, which vanished for a second as it fled into a draw, then reappeared, lunging up the other side. Feeling more than ever the bungling tenderfoot, Castle watched the chase, his breath held. Pitched slightly forward in the saddle, her hair flying back from under her cap, Tessa raced alongside Castle's horse until, winded from its gallop, it fell into a fast walk. Tessa slowed down, to avoid panicking him into another sprint for freedom, then leaned over, grabbed the loose reins, and jerked him to a halt. She led him back at an easy jog.

"Well, that was stimulating," she said, looking at Castle reproachfully. "Next time . . ."

"I know. Hand the reins to you." He gazed up at her. Her bosom heaved under her denim jacket, and there was a high color in her cheeks. "You were . . ." He hesitated. This was some woman. "You were a sight to see."

He opened the gate while she held his horse; then they moved the bull into the pen with the cow.

"Keep an eye on them," Tessa said, passing the reins back to him. "I'm going to give Tim a hand."

She loped away through the wind-teased grass. Castle watched her for a moment or two, then made himself turn away, as if he'd stolen a glimpse of her while she undressed. Something like that. It wasn't desire he felt, but the memory of desire, no, the *possibility* of desire. And that was what shamed him—Mandy hadn't been dead two years.

After the bull was introduced to his new harem, they drove the cow back to her calf and returned to the house. Castle and Tessa unsaddled their horses and turned them out to graze. McIntyre loaded his into his trailer, declining an invitation to lunch—he had more work to do that afternoon at another ranch.

"I hope you're not going to turn me down," Tessa said to Castle.

He did not. The morning's work had given him an appetite, and the fact was, the prospect of eating alone in his cabin depressed him. He followed her into a screened-in porch, where Klaus rose from his bed to greet his mistress. Inside the house, living room, dining room, and kitchen were combined under a gently peaked ceiling with log beams. Three high plank doors, bleached with age, led off a corridor, presumably to the bedrooms. Like Blaine and Monica's, Tessa's place was a mess, which she begged him to excuse. She hadn't had a chance to straighten up and made a show of it, picking a sofa pillow from off the floor, tidying a Navaho blanket balled up on a chair. He suspected that she would not have straightened up even if she'd had the chance. When he'd come out to live on the San Ignacio, Blaine had noticed him looking askance at the general sloppiness of the place, and to set him straight, informed him that "you can tell a good rancher from a bad one by the condition of his fences and cattle, not by how pretty his house is." Still, he hadn't quite gotten used to the rural dweller's carelessness about appearances, the cluttered living spaces, the junked automobiles and trailers and appliances littering the yards of even prosperous ranchers. He could not help but compare Tessa's domestic disarray with Mandy's fastidious housekeeping. Curiously, though, the comparison was not unfavorable. Now that he thought of it, there had been something a little sterile about the tidiness of the white-frame colonial on Oenoke Ridge, each room possessing the unlived-in look of a photograph in an interior decoration magazine. Thinking further, he recalled that Mandy's rigid orderliness—a result of her spending so much of her life on sailboats, where every line had to be coiled just so—at times got on his nerves.

He gazed around while Tessa brewed coffee and reheated a chili she'd made the day before. Over the fireplace hung a large oil painting, done in photo-realist style. Brown tract houses as identical as army barracks crowded beneath a vast, flat, barren mound resembling a mesa. What appeared to be buzzards specked a dirty sky above the mound; a yellow bulldozer crawled up its face. Mountains shimmered in the background, barely visible. Looking more closely at the foreground, he made out a banner draped over a wall running the whole length of the painting. On the banner were the words "Vista Montaña—2&3 BR homes—Starting at 150K."

"This is one of yours?"

Tessa came away from the stove and leaned her elbows on the counter dividing the kitchen from the rest of the room. "Yup. My masterpiece. Ugly as hell, isn't it?"

"First time I ever heard an artist ask if her masterpiece is ugly."

"That's what makes it beautiful. That's a real place, on the freeway going into Tucson. As you can see, there's not much of a vista of the montañas. That hill in the middle distance is the Tucson landfill. But you couldn't very well call a housing development *Vista Landfill*, could you?"

"One of your unsentimental landscapes."

"I like to think I've invented a whole new subgenre. Subdivision-scape."

She turned to the stove, ladled the chili into bowls, and set them with a plate of warm tortillas on a long table made of massive oak planks bound with cast iron bands. They sat across from each other and began to eat.

"How's the chili?" she asked.

"You can ride, you can shoot, you can cook," Castle replied.

Her cheeks flushed at the enumeration of her virtues; then, noticing him studying the family photos that stood on a bookshelf in easel frames, she volunteered that the older couple in one were her parents, the two towering young men who flanked her in another were her brothers—taken years ago, she said—and the smiling blond girl in cap and gown was Beth at her high school graduation.

"That other one is her after she finished basic training," Tessa said. "Doesn't look like the same girl, does it?"

No, it didn't, and he supposed she wasn't the same girl, staring sternly from under a black beret.

"You're looking at the outcome of a mistake in judgment," Tessa said. "The lovely outcome of an unlovely story."

He paused and asked awkwardly, "Out of wedlock, you mean? That's not so unlovely these days."

"It is if you never wanted to have sex with the guy."

He couldn't think how to respond to that declaration and mumbled that it was none of his business.

But she chose to make it his business. It had happened in Scottsdale. She'd had too much to drink at a party after the Arabian horse show. The owner of the winning horse drove her back to her apartment. An older man, around forty, an eastern European immigrant with a string of expensive horses, a trophy wife, and three sports cars. Some Romanian or Ukrainian . . . rumored to be mixed up with the Russian mob in L.A.

"He was a big guy, but didn't look or behave like a gangster," Tessa went on, her jaw tightening. "Courtly, in a European way, you know? Walked me to the door, and then I did a dumb thing. Invited him inside. Don't know what the hell I was thinking—the guy's *wife* was at the party. I realized my mistake and asked him to leave, and he said, 'You are going to offer me a drink and then you will say you are going to change into something more comfortable.' Exactly like that. Like dialogue out of some old movie he'd seen. I told him I was going to do nothing of the kind and that he'd better get out, and that's when he stopped being courtly." She looked at Castle defiantly, as if challenging him to believe her. The golden flecks in her irises flashed. "I wanted to kill that son of a bitch," she said, mercifully omitting a graphic description but with a ferocity accentuated by her wolfish eyeteeth. "My dad was a lawyer, and I knew how it would go if I went to the cops. When I found out I was pregnant, I made my own arrangements. If I'd been less well brought up, I probably would have blackmailed the bastard into paying for the abortion. Well, the time came, I went to the clinic, and I found out that I couldn't go through with it. Could not do it. Quit my job, went home to California. My brothers wanted to shoot him, my dad was incensed, wanted me to file a complaint and take the bastard to court, but I begged him to drop it. All I wanted to do was forget it had happened. Not that I ever have. So I had Beth and got another job. Truth is, if it hadn't been for Dad's money, I probably would have wound up in a trailer park."

Castle was stunned. "So you didn't come out here because you were crowded in Scottsdale."

"No," she said, still with her defiant look. "I lied. The part I told the truth about is that I don't like people, in large numbers anyway."

"And Beth . . . ?" he started to ask.

Tessa grimaced. "For a while I was sorry I didn't get the abortion. She reminded me of him and that night. I got past that, but . . . the lies I told her when she was little! I gave her the truth when she was old enough, but you can imagine how it hit her. She didn't know what to think, how to fit the whole thing into her way of understanding. And you know, it's weird, how something like what happened to me can make you feel guilty. Maybe I even blamed myself. If hadn't asked him in . . ."

"Oh, Tess, that's just—"

"Sure. Crazy to think that way. It's not something a man can grasp, how utterly, utterly filthy something like that can make you feel."

"I can grasp it well enough," he said, a little offended by the suggestion that his sex rendered him incapable of empathy.

"Gil, nobody around here has heard this. You will keep it to yourself, won't you?"

He had no idea why she'd chosen to share this confidence with him. It tied them into a kind of conspiratorial bond, one he hadn't sought, but he assured her he would tell no one.

"Well, there you have my soap opera," Tessa said.

The way she accented *my* invited him to tell her something about himself, and eager to get off the subject of her rape, he took her up on it. His first marriage, the half-comic, half-horrifying night Eileen admitted to her lesbian affair, the dreadful child custody hearings. Tessa listened to his tale with an attentiveness that was not mere courtesy. It seemed absurdly tame, somewhat Cheeveresque, compared with her saga. While he spoke, he kept picturing the brute slamming the door behind him, throwing her to the floor, and tearing at her clothes. He steered the conversation off the reefs of their respective disasters into quieter waters. They spoke of their children, Castle boasting of Morgan's achievements in the publishing world, of Justine's three-point-four average at Columbia Law, Tessa admitting that she'd been glad when Beth joined the army, thought the discipline and training would be good for her, give her some focus—she'd enlisted a couple of months *before* 9/11, so the furthest thought from Tessa's mind, and Beth's, was the chance that she would go to war.

"I keep hoping this war won't happen, but I know it will. It's a rotten feeling, waiting for the inevitable. Enough? Enough soul baring?"

"Enough," Castle said.

She stood and began to clear the dishes. He insisted that he clean up.

"It's a deal," she said. "I'd rather muck out a horse stall than do dishes—as you can see." She motioned at the dirty plates stacked by the sink.

While he rinsed them before placing them in the dishwasher, and scrubbed the chili sauce ringing the pot, she went into the living room and put a CD in the player. He heard Ella Fitzgerald singing "Shall We Dance," the tune and Ella's voice sounding anomalously urban in an Arizona ranch house, each of whose windows framed a Charles Russell landscape; tune and voice also evoked a sharp nostalgic pang, a wholly unexpected longing to be out of here and back east, in a noisy Manhattan bar with a martini in front of him and Mandy beside him.

"Shall we?"

He put the scrub brush down and turned to see Tessa with her hand held out to him.

"Dance?" he asked.

"You know how, don't you?"

"Sure. I'm actually pretty good."

"Well, then . . ."

"What about your knee?"

"All loosened up. C'mon."

Four hours of playing cowboy had stiffened his middle-age back and legs; he felt unsure of himself for other reasons. What was he to make of her invitation? Was she flirting? Overcoming his inhibitions, he took her left hand, placed his right arm around her back, and led her around in a foxtrot.

"Well, by God, you are good," she said.

"Miss Covington's dance class in eighth grade."

And when Ella segued into the bittersweet "But Not for Me," he held Tessa as he had his partners at Miss Covington's—at a chaste distance. This wasn't easy—avoiding the touch of those Ride of the Valkyries breasts of hers almost required a full extension of his arm. They continued to "Nice Work If You Can Get It," the two of them smelling of horse sweat and saddle leather, dancing to Gershwin in the San Rafael Valley.

"So did your experience with your first wife sour you on women?"

"It never soured me. Made me a little cautious was all."

"I was damn sour on men for a good ten years."

"I can imagine."

"Not that I was celibate. Anything but. I became a good old-fashioned vamp. Beat the hell out of men in the only way I knew how. Drive 'em crazy and then drop 'em. It's no wonder Beth got a little screwed up."

They were back to soul baring, and hers was getting a little too bare for him. Her candor puzzled him. Maybe she'd succumbed to the modern American tendency, which he deplored, to be Up Front About Everything, a confessionalism fostered by those awful daytime talk shows, people blabbing their innermost secrets into living rooms all over the country. The other possibility was that Tessa was lonely and needed someone to talk to.

"So when I started to sweeten up again," she continued, "I discovered that seventy-five percent of the men were spoken for, and the twenty-five percent who weren't, weren't for a good reason."

He asked, "And that's what drove you out here?"

"I'd been wanting to make the change for a while, but I had to wait till Beth started college," she answered. "She would have hated living here. We'd kept this place in the family after Dad died. Hired a guy to manage it. He was running it into the ground, and Mom and my brothers wanted to sell it. But I convinced them to let me run it, and if I couldn't make it profitable, at least I'd stop it from losing money. So here I am, a hermit."

"Makes two of us, I guess."

The next tune was "Let's Call the Whole Thing Off." With his hand pressed to the small of her back, feeling the warmth of her through her shirt, they two-stepped across the floor between the fireplace and the sofa. "Does it ever get it to you, the isolation?"

"Sometimes. Nights, mostly. But I'm up at five and in bed by nine, so I don't have that much night to get through. A couple of my friends in Patagonia think I'm a little cuckoo, living out here by myself. The smuggling, the drug running."

"It doesn't worry you?"

"The drug runners will leave you alone if you leave them alone, ninety-nine times out of a hundred. It's the one time that's the problem—that's all it would take. One bad guy."

"Like the guy who shot Miguel's friends."

"Miguel? Oh yeah, Miguel. The one you rescued. A lot of these drug mules, you know, snort coke or spray epinephrine into their noses. A boost to help them hump their loads. So you get some eighteen-year-old punk who's buzzed, scared of running into Border Patrol. He's hungry, he's thirsty, he sees this lonely ranch house . . . I keep a twelve-gauge riot gun in my bedroom, just in case."

"Well, I don't think you're cuckoo. I think you're a brave woman."

Letting go of his left hand, she snapped her fingers and tossed her head one side to the other, so that her hair flew wildly, teasingly past her face. "That's me all right! ¡Muy valiente!"

After they'd danced five numbers in a row, her knee began to bother her, and they stopped. She poured two mugs of coffee, and they sat down, facing the kiva fireplace that gave off a breath of charred oak and mesquite.

"And does the isolation ever get to you?" she asked.

"Sure. But there's my aunt, Blaine and Monica, Gerardo and Elena. Call me a semihermit."

"You must miss your girls."

"I do. But it's better than . . ."

Better than being back there, he thought.

Tessa, sitting with her sore leg propped on the coffee table, raised the mug to her lips and held it there briefly, looking at him intensely.

"Are you able to keep your mind off . . . What I mean is, are you able to keep yourself occupied? You can't possibly hunt all day, and now the season is over anyway."

"I go on long hikes, long enough to tire me out so I can sleep. Do a bit of bird watching. Sometimes I'll run Sam just to watch her point—she doesn't know the season's over." He shrugged. How aimless and idle this all must seem to her. "And I read a lot."

"What do you read?"

"Philosophy."

"You're kidding! Are we talking Plato and Aristotle or Deepak Chopra?"

"The Greek and Roman stoics. Seneca mostly."

"Seneca. I'm afraid you've got me there."

"He wrote back in the time of Nero. Reading him helps me live with it," he said, aware that he was lowering his guard. "That's all I want—to learn how to live with it. I don't expect to get over it."

From the pained look Tessa bestowed on him, he worried that he might have sounded as if he were pleading for her pity. That hadn't been his intention—a good thing, because she didn't give him any.

"Don't go slamming the door on yourself like that. You do get over things, even the worst."

"Seneca thought of suicide," he said, not listening to her. "He was so sickly when he was young that he thought of doing away with himself. The only thing that stopped him was worry that his father couldn't bear the loss. That rings so true. So true. It was like he was talking to me." He was silent for a beat, then added in an undertone, "Like he was talking *about* me."

Tessa frowned, mystified as to where he was going with this digression. Then he disclosed the secret occulted in his heart for months. He told her everything, from his pilgrimage to Ground Zero to the moment he realized he could not pull the trigger and why he could not: fear of extinction, the greater fear of what his suicide would have done to his daughters.

Tessa said nothing, her forehead creased. He couldn't tell if she was as astonished to hear his confession as he'd been to make it, or if she was mortified for him, as if, on a reckless impulse, he had stripped himself to bare some ugly surgical scar. He searched her face, and her expression softening, he knew instinctively that if she had not tried to kill herself, she had at one time given it serious consideration; knew further that here was someone he could speak to about anything, without regret, without fear of censure.

"You're the only one who knows anything about this," he said.

She nodded in silent consent to keep his secret as he'd consented to keep hers, and with that gesture, she cemented their bond.

"Gil, doesn't it tell you something?" she asked. "Doesn't it tell you something that you couldn't go through with it?"

He shook his head. The only lesson his failure had taught was that, despairing of despair itself, he had merely commuted his self-execution to a life sentence.

"You couldn't pull that trigger because you *cared* about your girls. You cared about yourself. You're not as dead inside as you think you are. You have people to live for, you have something to live for."

In this commentary he heard an unfortunate echo of Ms. Hartley, but at least it had come, this time, from someone who had suffered a loss. Whatever loss it is that rape inflicts—of faith, of trust, of self-respect.

10

THEY SAW each other off and on for the next month. They went riding or walking on her ranch and danced again in her living room to Ella and Ellington. They met once by accident at the post office in Patagonia and had lunch at Santos's café, then did some bird watching at the preserve outside of town, where Castle, playing Henry Higgins to her Eliza Doolittle, schooled her in identification of the songbirds that had begun their northward journeys from Mexico. She called them "border crossers with wings," and he liked that image of free creatures soaring above man's boundaries.

One morning as the cottonwoods were greening up, he sat with her at the north end of the valley and watched her paint the ruins of a homestead—a romantic subject, she said, that she hoped to render unromantically. Whatever that meant. She set up her portable easel and began to sketch the broken walls, the collapsed roof, the chunks of adobe brick scattered in the grass. Samantha and Klaus were with them, running off in ever wider circles. She'd begun to apply paint to the sketch when the dogs disappeared and did not respond to his calls. He went to look for them, and found them a quarter of an hour later, pointing a covey of quail. After flushing the birds, he leashed the dogs and walked them back. Tessa, frowning at her canvas, did not seem to notice his return. He looked at the painting and marveled at how well she was capturing her subject without slavishly reproducing it.

"You've got it," he said.

"Got what?"

"The lonesomeness, the desolation . . ."

"Yeah, I did. That's exactly what I *don't* want to get. The abandoned homestead out on the lone prairie." She clamped the tip of the brush between her teeth. "Somebody told me once that there are no unpoetic subjects, only unpoetic poets. Ditto, I suppose, for painters, but dammit, some things you just can't do anything with. They're inherently sentimental."

"Not ugly enough for you?"

She laughed.

"Sentimental or not, I like it," he said. "It's damn good."

"Sold," she said.

When he returned to his cabin later that afternoon, Castle found its seclusion less than congenial. He sat down to read Seneca but couldn't concentrate, remembering the pleasure he'd found in watching Tessa as she sat under the small umbrella attached to the easel, her hands making swift, sure strokes. He thought about the secrets they'd entrusted to each other. How incredible. He hadn't been looking for a friend and confidante, but he'd found one.

Restless, he put the book down and paced the room. Sam, claws clicking on the worn wooden floor, followed as if she were leashed to him. The dog stopped and seemed to gaze at him bewildered when, Ella Fitzgerald singing in his head, Castle took Tessa's hand, put his arm around her waist, and fell into a slow, gliding two-step. In this make-believe he did not hold her at a discreet distance but drew her close. Although he did not have a strong imagination, the melody playing in his mind swung him into a fantasy vivid enough to stir physical sensations—Tessa's cheek pressed to his, her lush breasts crushed against him. He grew light-headed, and this lightness, this buoyancy, flowed throughout his body. He felt that he was almost floating, dancing on the legs of a man half his age. He was like someone under the spell of a powerful narcotic, for as he twirled from corner to corner, he was aware of the absence of the anguish that had tormented him for the past year and a half. Was it possible that he, whose emotional range had been restricted to sorrow and fear, was experiencing not the mere cessation of pain but happiness? Was it possible he was falling in love?

Suddenly Ella's voice fell silent, and he stopped dancing. Falling in love? he asked himself as he stood by the stove, looking at the ash powdering its apron. He couldn't be. If his mourning could be eased this soon after Amanda's death, it could not have been as deep as he'd thought; and if that was so, his love for her could not have been as profound as he believed. That violated his view of himself as a man who'd suffered a near-mortal wound, from which recovery lay far in the future, if there was to be any recovery at all; a serious man who had so loved his wife that her death had foreclosed, for years to come, any chance of knowing love again. This happiness he felt, or thought he felt, must be illusory, like his imaginary dance partner, the opposite of phantom pain—phantom relief. Real or not, he didn't trust it. He hadn't earned it. Every martyr treasures his torment to some degree, and Castle, in his own eyes a martyr to the world's madness and to love, treasured his. He almost missed it.

Mandy returned it to him very early the next morning; he saw her clearly, standing at his bedside in the black pantsuit she'd worn the day she'd taken the shuttle to Boston. Her hair was pinned up, with two wisps dangling past her ears, exactly as it had been then, the last time he'd seen her alive. The last time he'd seen her, period. A flame of wild joy shot up in him like a gas jet. "Take care, darling, take care," she said, and then vanished, leaving him kneeling on the bed, his arms outstretched, as if he'd been reaching out to embrace her. The joyous flame guttered out.

He woke with a start, stumbled into the bathroom, flipped on the light switch, turned on the tap, and splashed cold water on his face. The dream had been so real, limning Amanda in every detail, that he almost believed he'd actually seen her, or her ghost. Long ago Grace had told him and his sister that a mystical streak ran in her family. A great-aunt of hers had been a medium. Grace herself claimed that her mother visited her often after her death. Had the vision of Mandy been a hallucination? Some trick that misfiring neurons performed in the shadows of semislumber? All neat and scientific. Still, he wasn't convinced. She had, for chrissake, *spoken* to him. But whether he'd experienced a dream, a hallucination, or an actual haunting, he wanted only to see her again.

Grief is a chronic malaria of the heart, periods of remission alternating with spasms of relapse. For the next three days he saw no one and did almost nothing, lying in bed till late morning. He could well have remained there all day if it hadn't been for Sam, whose whines and whimpers to be let out or fed roused him from his immobility. He neglected himself, reverting to the disheveled recluse who had so alarmed Morgan and Justine.

On the fourth day Monica dropped Elena off at his cabin. She cleaned it every Saturday. Both women looked in mild shock at the figure who answered the door—grizzled, unkempt, still in his bathrobe at ten in the morning.

"I've got shopping to do in Nogales," Monica said as Elena waddled to the shed for the mop, broom, and vacuum cleaner. "I won't be done before she is. Could you drive her back?"

Castle didn't see why the woman couldn't walk—it was only a mile—but agreed to drive her.

"And a delivery from your electronic postal service." Monica handed him an e-mail from Morgan. He'd asked his girls to write him letters, but they regarded that means of communication as primitive as smoke signals and continued to e-mail him in care of the San Ignacio's address.

Monica squinted at him, and he thought he saw her wrinkle her nose; after three days without so much as a sponge bath, he must be pretty ripe. "Are you okay, Gil? Nobody's seen you for days."

"A little under the weather."

"Tessa said she's phoned you a few times, but no luck."

"I left my cell in the car," he said dully. "It's a dead zone out here."

"Then use our landline. Give her a ring. She's something of a nervous wreck."

There was a momentary silence before he asked if anything was the matter.

"She hasn't heard from Beth. That's to be expected. Still, it's tough on her." Monica saw the puzzlement on his face. "You haven't heard?"

"Heard?"

"We've bombed Baghdad and invaded Iraq."

"What? When?"

"Bush announced it last night. Blaine is about ready to reenlist," she added, sprinkling the remark with a dash of sarcasm. "Says we're going to win this one, and he'd like to be there when we do. Call Tessa. I've got to run."

He brewed coffee and then sat at the kitchen table to read Morgan's message, which she must have written before the president's declaration; otherwise, it would have contained an antiwar tirade. She began by offering news about herself—she'd been put in charge of a marketing campaign for a hot new commercial novel, a "genre buster" combining the occult with a detective story. And about the family—last week, Anne and Peter had treated her and Justine to brunch at their country club in Redding. His absence was felt by all. This led her to repeat the comments she'd made before his departure from Connecticut—that he was doing what the terrorists wanted. Some families of the victims had formed a group to advise a committee that was choosing a design for a 9/11 memorial. He should come back and join them. What a wonderful way to honor Amanda's memory! That piece of unsolicited counsel shot a ray of irritation through the dense overcast of Castle's mood.

While Elena, a ball of sanitizing energy, swept and dusted, he got a writing pad and pen from a drawer and sat down to reply. He thanked Morgan for taking the time to write, congratulated her on her new responsibility, remarked that she'd made a few observations he needed to respond to, and then paused, considering how he ought to respond.

You say that I've done exactly what the terrorists want, he began. *Do you know what they want? Does anybody? Do they? I've read that they hate our freedoms and our way of life, but I wonder if they love our way of life and hate themselves for loving it and us for having it. So they kill themselves and us . . .*

He paused again and saw, through the kitchen window, an Anna's hummingbird dipping its beak into the feeder hung from a back porch rafter. It flew off, so swiftly it seemed to have dissolved. He took out a second sheet and scribbled a paragraph defending his move west, then addressed her unasked-for advice.

I admire those people you wrote me about, the ones who keep soldiering on, who are involved in this memorial business and so on. But I don't think one ought to be built. Memorials are always pretty, tidy walkways and monuments and flowers, and they kind of create an amnesia. You forget how horrible and disgusting it was. There were people jumping out of 80th-story windows to escape the flames. Think about that. It was so awful up there that jumping a thousand feet was the better way to go. You know what happens to a body when it hits the pavement from 80 floors up? It explodes. Like a water-filled balloon, except it isn't filled with water. If New York is going to build a memorial, then they should have photographs of that on the walls, so then we'll all remember that this is what happens when faith becomes fanaticism and fanaticism becomes nihilism, this is what human beings can do to each other.

After reading over what he'd written, he stared out the window. With no idea what to say next, he signed off, *Love, Dad.* He stamped and addressed the envelope and sank into another morbid remembrance.

Morgan had been close to Amanda, regarding her more as an older sister than as a stepmother, and it was she who'd insisted they put up a missing-person flier, not because she thought there was any hope that Mandy had survived but because it would be an act of solidarity with all those who'd lost someone that day. She scanned Amanda's photograph into her computer and ran off copies and persuaded Castle to join her. He saw no sense in it, but he was then in an almost hypnotic state, without a will of his own, liable to do just about anything anybody told him to do, and so he rode the train into the city with Morgan and pinned the fliers to the bulletin board in Grand Central. They took the subway downtown, where a noxious stench lingered from the still-smoldering wound blocks away and the scent of wreaths laid beside a fire station mingled with it, and to this day he could not smell flowers without recalling that other odor, resembling the stink of a burning landfill. Pale dust and ash lay thick on some streets, and their feet left prints in the dust as they traipsed along, posting Mandy's picture on lampposts and on trees in Thompson Park and on the walls of firehouses and hospitals. The same photograph that stood framed on his desk at home was staring back at him from among the thousands of other fliers, that mournful wallpaper of New York City in the days following the attack, faces and names and pleas . . . HAVE YOU SEEN THIS MAN . . . IF YOU KNOW THE WHEREABOUTS OF THIS WOMAN . . . Prayers, really, each one representing some family clinging to an illusion that mom, dad, sister, brother, lover, husband, wife had not been cremated or buried under a mountain of concrete and powdered glass and melted steel but was lying in a trauma ward somewhere, or wandering about not knowing his or her name. Castle was overwhelmed by the enormity of it all. MISSING 9/11/01. AMANDA F. CASTLE. SHE IS 5'10"

TALL AND 155 POUNDS, AUBURN HAIR, GREEN EYES. ANYONE WHO KNOWS OF HER WHEREABOUTS, PLEASE CONTACT . . . Christ, it read like a poster for a lost cat.

"Terminado," Elena said, startling him. "Feenish." He turned to her, and she asked, motioning at Morgan's e-mail, "¿Son malas noticias?"

It took him a moment to translate the question, and then he realized that his eyes were glistening.

"No. No bad news . . . No malas noticias . . . It's . . . *es* . . ."

She clasped his hand and held it firmly, sympathetically, telling him, through the language of her touch, that she understood what "it" was. Of course she did. This woman who'd lost two of her five children was no stranger to sorrow. Castle looked into the copper disk of her face, at the black hair veined with gray. Her kindness moved him. She let him go. As he rose to dress before driving her back, she motioned at the coffeepot. He nodded. She poured herself a cup and settled into a chair. Her way of letting him know that she was in no hurry; she would wait while he cleaned himself up.

When he emerged from the bathroom, showered and shaved, she said, "Mucho mejor," much better, and then spoke to him in an earnest voice, but her meaning eluded him. He asked her to repeat what she'd said, más despacio—more slowly. This she did, enunciating each word as if speaking to a small child.

"Lo siento," he said, still unable to understand her. "No entiendo."

Elena threw her stout arms up in frustration. They went outside to his car just as Monica drove in.

"Got back early," she called. "I can take her." She gave Castle an approving glance. "Big improvement. The grizzled-prospector look didn't become you."

Elena spoke to her.

"There was something she was trying to tell you?" Monica asked him.

"I think so."

"She wants me to translate."

Castle heard the Mexican woman utter to Monica the same words she had to him: *Cuando perdí mis hijos, cuidé mi sentimiento en vez de ellos.*

"I'm not sure if I've got it right. Something like this: 'When I lost my children, I took care of my sadness instead of them.' " Monica shrugged. "I'm not quite sure what she means."

Nor was Castle—the phrase was almost as opaque in English as it had been in Spanish.

The riddle teased him as he drove into Patagonia to mail his letter. After he'd checked his post office box, crammed with bills and junk mail, he leashed Sam and walked her past the clinic, then the marshal's office and the town jail, a windowless concrete box built by the WPA during the Depression, then across Third Avenue to the broad parkway that had been a roadbed for the Southern Pacific back in the days when Patagonia had been a mining town and cow town. The last big mine had shut down more than forty years ago. Since then Patagonia had reinvented itself, though it hadn't settled on a clear identity. It was a little bit of an artists' colony, a little bit of a tourist town, and a little bit of a redoubt for aging hippies and other eccentrics who preferred backwaters to the mainstream; a little bit of a cow town still, rusty horse trailers parked on side streets, worn saddles draped over the porch rails of moored double-wides; and more than a little bit of a Mexican pueblo, home to Mendozas and Sánchezes and Garcías, from whose tin-roofed houses radios blared brassy Norteño ballads over the yips of mongrel dogs scuffling in dusty yards. He walked to the edge of town, where he saw two Coues whitetails browsing and a javelina rooting in a mesquite forest, then turned and headed back toward the post office and his car. A couple of dirt-caked pickups were parked in front of the Wagon Wheel Saloon, and a crowd of bird watchers had assembled around a van near the Stage Stop Hotel. The newspaper vending machines in front of the hotel had been emptied, all but one, its display window framing an *Arizona Daily Star*. He bought the paper. The front page cried war news. BOMBS OVER BAGHDAD. A hundred thousand American troops were storming up the Euphrates Valley from Kuwait, with no need for documentation, their guns and tanks sufficing as visas. The notion of the United States Army as a horde of illegal aliens grimly amused Castle.

His grumbling stomach—he hadn't eaten all day, had in fact eaten very little during his prolonged funk—drew him across Naugle Avenue to Santos's café. He sat down under the awning outside, tethered Sam to a table leg, and ordered menudo and tortillas and tried to read the paper. It reminded him of why he avoided the news. Shock and awe. Cruise missiles. A tank battle with Hussein's Republican Guard. The delirium of war, all the blind violence of the world. The vast and bloody spectacle unfolding in Iraq reduced his own troubles to the microscopic; but the Olympian perspective did not release him from them, any more than a crippled ant's awareness of its insignificance, were an ant a conscious being, would relieve it of its suffering. *When I lost my children, I took care of my sadness instead of them.* He had the feeling that he'd heard that phrase, or one like it, before. The waitress brought his steaming menudo, the warm tortillas wrapped in cloth, and then he remembered. He hadn't heard it—he'd read it in Seneca's letter to Marcia. *You hug and embrace the sorrow you have kept alive in place of your son.* The language was more elegant, but the idea was the same, proving that you did not have to be a brilliant philosopher to know a thing or two about life, about the maimed heart and its perverse inclination to aggravate its wounds.

There, eating menudo in a border-town café, Castle experienced a sudden illumination. He had always regarded his sorrow as a force outside himself, not subject to his will; indeed, his will often seemed subject to it. And that was true in its earlier stages. Only now, because of a few words spoken by a simple Mexican woman, did it occur to him that he had since nurtured and strengthened his misery by taking a morbid pleasure in it. The dream, the apparition, whatever it was, had been the fabrication of his own unhappy mind; and when presented with the possibility of relief, that mind had fiendishly concocted the means to sustain its agonies. His grief had fed on itself; it had become a habit.

The question was, how to break it? He'd proven he was no candidate for formal therapy. He would have to be his own counselor. He paid the check, and taking up Sam's leash, he walked back to his car. As he climbed in, his glance fell on his cell phone, in a tray beside the floor shift. He didn't decide to check his voice mail; he was compelled to do it. There were two messages, the first a hang-up, the second from Tessa: *"Hello, Gil. Just wanted to talk. I've been welded to the TV since Bush's announcement, and I . . . Give me a call if you get the chance."* She spoke with a casualness that was so artificial, it called attention to the distress it was meant to conceal. He could hear in her voice her dread of a future visit from a man in an army uniform. She didn't want to talk to someone, she needed to. She needed *him.*

Her phone rang seven or eight times before she answered.

"Tess, it's Gil. I just got—"

"Oh, hi! Hi!" she interrupted.

"You sound out of breath."

"Ran in from outside. I was cleaning out the tackroom. Trying to stay busy."

"I got your message."

"Oh. I'm sorry I'd called so late. It was after midnight."

"I mean I just picked it up. Didn't check my messages till now. Still feel like talking?"

"Sure. Sure."

Here was a reason to live—to be at her side, to ease her fears if he could, to be a friend.

"I'm in town," he said. "I could stop by on my way back, if that's okay."

"I'd like that, Gil. I'd like that very much."

11

Yvonne's driver, also foreman of the Tres Encinos ranch, stopped the Land Cruiser where the road ended, on a ridge overlooking a canyon shaded by sycamores. Like ghosts, she thought. The white-barked trees looked like ghosts. Ghosts were very much on her mind, spirits from the past. She could feel their presence.

"This is as far it goes on the north," Jiménez said, and with a brown, gnarled finger pointed at a barbed-wire fence about a kilometer away. "Allí está la frontera. Beyond it is the United States."

Hours of banging down ranch roads more suited to horses or burros than to motor vehicles had given Yvonne a sore back and made her a little irritable. "What else would be beyond it? Europe?"

"Señora?"

"A joke. Let us go on."

"Go on where?"

"To the border. I want to go right up to it," she said in a voice that closed off all possibility of discussion.

Unacquainted with her imperious ways, Jiménez argued that La Señora Menéndez couldn't see any more from there than she could from here, and besides, there was no more road.

"We will walk." She turned to the passengers in the backseat: her bodyguards, Marco and Heraclio, and sitting between them, her son, Julián. Skinny, wearing a rose-colored shirt, he looked like a flamingo flanked by two well-fed vultures. "Is everybody up for a little walk?"

Of course they were. They would be up for anything she wanted to do.

She removed a plastic freezer bag from her purse, stuffed it into her pants pocket, and got out of the car. It was a temperate morning, perfect for a stroll, but the cattle trail leading down into the canyon was rocky, and Julián had trouble negotiating it in his cowboy boots, the red and white boots with knifepoint toes she had told him not to wear. "Only a maricón would dare to be seen in such boots," she'd taunted, but he ignored her. Yvonne was shod in sturdy walking shoes and clad in Levi's, a denim shirt, and a wide-brimmed straw hat. Not a fashionable outfit, but it was practical and created the image she wished to project: the ranchera, out inspecting her new property. On paper rancho Los Tres Encinos did not belong to her. The sale had been completed weeks ago between its former owner and her cousin, a real estate broker in Douglas. Later he sold half of it to La Morita Enterprises, S.A., and later still, the other half to San Pedro Properties, S.A. The officers of the two front companies were her two elder sisters and their husbands. The complicated transactions were necessary to hide from nosy investigators the identity of the true owner—Yvonne herself. She had put up the money for the back-to-back purchases, thus giving it a double scrubbing.

With Jiménez in front, the group tramped through the canyon. Marco and Heraclio, each armed with a .40-caliber automatic pistol, prowled beside Yvonne, watchful and assured, like the predators they were. Julián cursed the rocks scuffing his pretty boots.

"Is there some purpose to this, Mother?" he asked, petulantly.

"I never do anything for the hell of it, you know that."

They came to the border fence, which was in disrepair. A bullet-sieved metal sign hung from the top wire: U.S. GOVERNMENT PROPERTY. DO NOT MOLEST UNDER PENALTY OF LAW. Nearby an old concrete monument rose into the branches of an Emory oak. The plaque at its base was weather-worn, but its words were still legible: BOUNDARY OF THE UNITED STATES. TREATY OF 1853. REESTABLISHED BY TREATIES OF 1882–89.

"Ridiculous," Yvonne said.

"What is?" Jiménez asked.

"Do you see any difference between that over there and this over here? There is nothing in the land to tell you, here is Mexico, here is the United States. The whole idea of a border seems to me ridiculous."

"Perhaps that is so," Jiménez remarked. "All the same, it is there."

She regarded the foreman, a typical Sonoran vaquero—muscles like twisted hemp, a simple mind, which wasn't the same thing as being simpleminded, a good, strong, honest face. She liked the face. She liked him. She hoped it never would be necessary to have him killed.

"That ranch on the other side is called the San Ignacio, is it not?" she asked, though she knew its name. She'd heard it most of her life. The ghosts lived there.

Jiménez nodded. "We share the fence line. Almost twenty kilometers."

"What can you tell me about your American neighbors?"

"Their name is Erskine," he answered, pronouncing it *Airskeen.*

Yvonne knew that. "What can you tell me about them besides that?"

"Not much. I do not know them. The boss does. He talks to them."

"About what?"

"Sometimes their cattle wander onto our land. They call the boss and ask him to gather the strays and drive them back to the line. Sometimes our cattle wander onto their land. The boss telephones them and asks them to return the favor, and they do. It is easy to tell which belongs to who. Their cattle are black, ours white." He gestured toward a far hillside, where Charolais cows stood out in the yellow grass like plaster statues. "The boss says it is important to be good neighbors."

"Let us develop good habits," Yvonne said. "He is no longer the boss."

"Claro, señora."

"Listen. I'm going to give you my first instructions as la nueva jefa. From now on there will be no more doing favors for those people over there. If we find their cattle on this rancho, we keep them. Understood?"

Jiménez hooked his thumbs into his belt and cleared his throat. "Sí, señora."

"The party starts soon. It would be good if the hostess showed up," said Julián.

She looked at him, slouched against a sycamore, arms folded across his narrow chest, an insolent smile on his face.

"You come with me," she commanded. Then to Marco and Heraclio: "Pull these apart so I can pass through."

While Marco pressed his foot on a low wire, Heraclio tugged the strand above it, creating a gap that Yvonne, bending low and turning sideways, stepped through onto the soil of the United States. It wasn't as daring an act as it appeared. She'd been born in the U.S. and had lived there till she was twelve, when her mother remarried and moved back to Mexico.

Julián hesitated on the other side of the fence. "What do you think you are doing?"

"Get some balls, mi hijo, and come over here with me."

There was enough Latino macho in him to accept the challenge. "This is stupid. What if La Migra shows up?" He pointed at the tread-marks in the rough drag road that ran along the American side of the boundary. "They patrol here all the time."

"I show them this," said Yvonne, plucking her U.S. passport from a back pocket of her jeans.

"And me? What do I show them?"

"Turn around and show them your ass."

She crossed the drag road, went on a few yards more, and ground her heels into the dirt, ground them hard, making deep impressions. "There. I have planted my flag."

Julián responded to this declaration with a bewildered squint.

"This ranch is going to be mine," Yvonne said. "I am going to buy it."

"I didn't know it was for sale."

"It isn't, but it will be. You and I are going to talk about the future."

"No, we are not. Not here. We are not going to talk about anything, the two of us standing here like a couple of mojados waiting for a ride."

It pleased her when he stood up to her; pleased her that when she got out of the business, as she intended to someday, she could turn it over to him, assured that he would have the strength of mind not to screw it up. She reached out and stroked the hair on his temple, red hair like hers, the color inherited from her father, the father who would have loved her, given her presents on her birthday, and been kind and gentle to her always. Had he lived, she would have been spared the things her stepfather had done to her because there would have been no stepfather.

"You are right," she said to Julián. "This is not the appropriate place. But one thing before we go."

With a hard kick, she gouged a hole in the ground, in the ground stained with sin and blood, the blood of her lost father. She kicked and kicked till she'd dug up a small mound of loose soil, then pulled out the freezer bag and handed it to her son. "Fill this with that. We are going to scatter the dirt on Abuela's grave the next time we visit. It will make her happy in heaven."

"I had a feeling this was about her," Julián muttered. "If she is in heaven, she cannot be happier than she is now. That is what a priest would tell you."

"We are far from any priests, mi hijo. Now do as I ask."

Julián, grumbling that she never *asked*, she only gave orders, squatted down and scooped the dirt into the bag.

THE RANCH HOUSE, corrals, and outbuildings were clustered in a grove of álamos watered by a ciénaga. A rock dam slabbed across the ciénaga formed a duck pond behind the house, overlooked by a low hill atop which three ancient oaks—hence the ranch's name—grew in a straight line, like trees in an orchard. A pretty spot, thought Yvonne, returning from her tour. More important, it was secure. Anyone who tried to get to her here would have a hard time of it; and once she'd cultivated the allegiance of the local inhabitants, a campaign she was beginning with today's fiesta, she would have plenty of informants to alert her to intruders well ahead of time. Human radar stations, an early warning system. Boredom would be the only problem. Rural life never had suited her temperament; she'd had a bellyful of it when she was a girl. She liked a good time. She liked to dance. She liked to hold court in the crowded bars and discos that the Menéndez organization owned in Agua Prieta, Naco, and Cananea. Sure, when things got too dull, she could always escape to her Agua Prieta town house or to her villa in Zihuatanejo, with its spectacular ocean view; but the fact was, she would be spending most of her time on the ranch, at least until she'd consolidated her hold on the routes through the San Rafael Valley. Its maze of hidden canyons and side canyons had been pathways for one kind of contraband or another for as long as anyone could remember—liquor during Prohibition; tires, gasoline, and other rationed commodities during the Second World War; today marijuana, cocaine, and methamphetamines. Joaquín Carrasco, that fat little shit, regarded these pathways as his exclusively. Soon she would disabuse him of that illusion. She now owned ten thousand hectares of his territory, a wedge she was going to drive into the very heart of his operations. "Grabbing market share" was how Julián had put it, in the lingo he'd picked up in business school in the United States. Whatever you called it, it was going to be a difficult and dangerous undertaking, but now that she'd formed an alliance with the Gulf Cartel, she would have the power to pull it off: the manpower, the financial power, and the firepower, to which she could add the power of her own ruthless reputation. Inspire terror in ally and adversary alike; that was the key to maintaining loyalty within and to overcoming enemies from without.

Preparations for the fiesta were well under way. The Norteño band she'd hired—Víctor Castillo and the Golden Roosters—were tuning their instruments. Burly men in straw cowboy hats were setting up picnic tables in the front yard or hauling coolers of beer from a pickup truck. A half dozen of Yvonne's pistoleros, gathered around a firepit with a few local-boy vaqueros, were guzzling cans of Tecate and going to bed with rosamaría, the pungent smell of their joints mingling with the savory scent of carnitas bubbling over the fire in a copper vat.

"Getting a head start?" Yvonne called, striding toward the house, Julián beside her.

"¡Sí!" answered one of her boys. "And nobody will be able to catch us!"

Through the laughter, she overheard one young vaquero ask another, "¿Es esa vieja la nueva jefa?" She hesitated, tempted to tell the cowboy, "Yes, I am the new boss, and who the hell are you to call me an old woman?" She thought better of it and went inside.

The house dated back to the 1920s, built of thick adobe walls, its casement windows cutting the sunlight into squares that lay atop the tiles of glazed clay. The click of Julián's boot heels echoed in the parlor; like the other rooms, it was almost empty. Except for a few pieces, the previous owner had taken his furniture with him—family heirlooms, he'd said.

"Wait for me in the study," she told Julián, then entered her bedroom, where a huge canopy bed stood under a beamed ceiling four meters high. The thought crossed her mind that she would like to fuck somebody on its starched white sheets, shrouded by its filmy white curtains, but she couldn't think of any attractive candidates. Considering the ravishments she'd endured from her stepfather and the perversities her husband had subjected her to, it astonished her that she was still capable of sexual desire.

Dámaso García and Fermín Menéndez—two sick pendejos. Of all the deaths she was responsible for, those were the only ones that had given her any pleasure. She had arranged for others to rid her of Fermín—it was as much a business affair as it was personal—but she had killed her stepfather with her own hands when she was sixteen. They were living on a wretched ejido then, where Dámaso grew squash and melons, working occasional shifts at the big copper mine in Cananea to supplement his income, much of which went to beer and bacanora. Just the three of them—he, Rosario, and Yvonne. Her sisters had left home two years before, running off with the first men who were halfway nice to them to get away from Dámaso. Thereafter Yvonne became the sole object of his unholy attentions. He was a fairly normal man when sober, a monster when drunk. He drank quite a lot, so Yvonne and her mother were more acquainted with the monster. One winter afternoon, after he'd visited her bed the previous night, she was helping him split mesquite for firewood. Strong and tall, taller than most girls her age (it was said she got her height from her part-Irish father), she was doing all the work because Dámaso had sunk into the remorse that almost always descended on him after he'd beaten Rosario or gratified himself with her daughter. He sat on the ground near the woodpile, swearing he was sorry for what he'd done, pledging never to do it again, to quit drinking, to go to confession and beg God's forgiveness.

Yvonne found his meaningless repentances more contemptible than the acts that had provoked them. If a man was to behave like a monster, better that he be a monster all the time and not feel bad about it afterward. On that afternoon he put on a greater show of contrition than usual, breaking into sobs and lowering his head to his uplifted knees after she said, "God may forgive you, but I never will." Years later she would think that if he had not dropped his head in that manner, as if offering himself for sacrifice, she might not have struck. But he did and she did, swinging the ax into the back of his neck with the force and accuracy of an executioner, nearly decapitating him. Then with great calm (even now she remembered how calm she'd been) she went into the house and announced to her mother, "Dámaso is dead. I killed him."

Rosario ran into the yard and stared at the corpse and the blood, an immense amount of it, for a long time without speaking a word. Finally she clasped Yvonne's hand and said, "God did not bless me with a son, but He gave me one daughter with a man's heart." Yvonne was feeling the first twinges of panic. "I am going to have to run away or go to prison," she cried. "You will do neither one," said Rosario. "We have got to get rid of the body. The ax, too. Come on, we have a lot to do."

They wrapped Dámaso's body in a tarp, managed to load him into the bed of the rattletrap truck that carried his squash and melons to market, and drove far out into the desert, where Yvonne hacked out a shallow grave with the ax. His head had come off on the bumpy ride. They buried it with the body, threw in the ax, and covered the grave. "We will leave the truck out here," Rosario said. "We are going to say that Dámaso got very drunk and drove away, never to be seen again."

On the long walk back to the ejido, Yvonne sobbed, still fearing that her only choice was flight or prison. Why, she asked Rosario, why in the name of God had she married such a horrible man? "All those years I raised you and your sisters alone. I was tired of it. Then Dámaso came along. How was I to know he would be the way he was?" They walked on, following the tire tracks when they could. "You know, it is those gringos who are to blame. They killed your father and left me alone. They are the guilty ones." It wasn't the first time Yvonne had heard about the gringos who'd murdered her father. Actually, only one gringo, but Rosario always spoke as if the killer's whole family had been in on it.

They got home at twilight, parched and exhausted. "Remember, mi hija, the story is, Dámaso abandoned us. We are going to have to move to town and find work, it is going to be tough, but now . . ." She embraced her daughter; there was a solidarity between them, the solidarity of conspirators, and she did not have to finish the sentence because Yvonne knew—now they were free.

How strong, how clearheaded her mother had been then, Yvonne reflected, shedding her dusty clothes. And how small and frail at the end. The cancer had reduced Rosario, never a big woman, to the size of a child; and she seemed to grow smaller each time Yvonne visited her, there in St. Joseph's Hospital in Tucson. Sometimes she expected to walk into that room and find nothing left of her mother but an empty hospital gown and a dent in the pillow.

She ejected the memory from her mind and stepped into the bathroom to shower. A sidelong glance in the full-length mirror on the door moved her to face herself straight on. A vieja, was she? Not a bad figure for a woman of fifty-two. Some sag in the tits, some thickening in the waist, and—turning to look over her shoulder—some flabbiness in the ass and thighs, but not bad all in all. Her height was an advantage, equitably distributing the few excess kilos she carried. She focused on her face and decided that it wasn't bad, either. Its worst flaw were the tiny pits, remnants of adolescent acne, cratering her cheeks; but a light brush of powder and rouge took care of those.

The fiesta had started by the time she finished dressing and putting on her makeup. Loud voices, the bray of horns, and the high, warbling cries of the Golden Roosters came from outside. Through the bedroom window she saw the cabs of pickup trucks poking above the low wall enclosing the backyard. Also two army Humvees, with machine guns mounted on their roofs. Most of her guests were neighboring rancheros and ranch hands, or townspeople from Santa Cruz and San Lazaro; but she'd also invited the comandante of the local military zone. He had been recommended by a general, a personal friend. Carrasco had federal and state cops in his hip pocket; she had a general and a whole squad of colonels, as well the commander of the Agua Prieta garrison. Maintaining good relations with the army was critical to her operations: rural defense forces guarded her marijuana plantations; soldiers provided security for her shipments. The mordida amounted to many thousands a month but was worth every peso.

When she entered the study, she found Julián sitting at the desk, a virtual mesa of walnut that easily accommodated a desktop computer, a laptop, a printer, two telephones, and a fax machine. He was drinking a can of soda. Julián did not touch alcohol, and he never used product. That was what had fucked up his father, among other things. Fermín had been addicted to Marlboros laced with crack.

"¡Muy mota!" he said, admiring his mother's outfit—a two-tone western shirt, cream across the shoulders, the rest emerald green; cream-colored pants with a silver concho belt; a pair of lizard-skin boots; and a silver and obsidian necklace with matching earrings. The shirt complemented her green eyes and the jewelry made a nice contrast with her hair.

"It is hardly elegant," she sniffed. "A black cocktail dress would be elegant."

"In a rustic way, it is. You are the rustically elegant ranchera."

She winced as he swiveled the high-backed leather chair to one side and crossed his legs in an effeminate way, one pointy boot tapping the air. "Don't sit like that, " she said.

He uncrossed his legs and spread them apart and grabbed his crotch. "Manly enough for you?"

She overlooked his impudence. They were, after all, a team. The union of her ruthlessness and cunning with his organizational talents had transformed the Menéndez organization—or the Agua Prieta Cartel, as the chotas called it—from a joke into a disciplined and efficient enterprise. If he was a maricón, at least he was a smart one, upon whom an expensive education had not been wasted. "This is a business, and it's time we started running it like one," Julián had declared not long after his father's death, an event as liberating for him as it had been for her. Fermín was a peasant and a tyrant who had imposed on the cartel a despotism of outmoded methods better suited to running a corner grocery than a multimillion-dollar industry. Among his many other idiocies, he'd kept all the family profits in just two banks, both in Douglas. One seizure warrant from the FBI or U.S. Customs, and the Menéndezes would have been broke.

With the help of American and Mexican lawyers, Julián had distributed the accounts to twenty banks and investment firms throughout the United States and Mexico. He established the straw companies through which profits were washed in land deals and legitimate businesses from car washes to discos to restaurants. He'd computerized records—where the mota had been grown, the weight of each load and who it had been assigned to, and the amount of mordida and to whom it was paid (a roster that included U.S. Customs agents at the Douglas port of entry). Fermín had kept such information on scraps of paper or in his head, and since his crack habit had further shrunk his head's naturally limited capacity, it was easy for disloyal people to rip him off or snitch out a shipment and get away with it. Yvonne often thought that she could have put up with his sexual perversions if he hadn't been so stupid, or with his stupidities if he hadn't been so perverse. The two together were intolerable. When Fermín turned down an offer from the Gulf Cartel to partner up in shipping Colombian coke through Agua Prieta—he wanted nothing to do with Colombians—Yvonne saw her opportunity. She got word to the Gulf boss, who was running his affairs from his cell in Palomas prison, that if he would rid her of Fermín, he would have a deal.

After she took over, the thieves and snitches thought they could get away with even more from her than they had from her late husband. Because of her sex, of course. She ended that misconception forever with the now-famous "Pond of Death" incident. Housecleaning, after all, was woman's work. Yvonne herself had phoned the police with the "anonymous" tip that led them to the water hole. She wanted the bodies to be discovered and all the tabloid headlines the discovery could grab. It was important to set an example right away.

"You wanted to talk about the future," Julián said. "No time like the present."

Yvonne stood looking out the window, her back to him. Ghosts. "You know, I was thinking about the past when I was getting ready. About Abuela. How small she looked. Small. Small. Small. She could not have weighed more than thirty kilos."

Julián sighed. His mother spoke in subdued tones, as she always did when the subject was Rosario. Though he welcomed these gentle contours of voice, a pleasing contrast to her normal sharps and flats, he was sick of hearing about his sanctified grandmother, dead for six months. "Let us not indulge in nostalgia," he said. "The past is gone."

"The hell it is!" she shot back, sounding more like herself, each word as piercing as a thorn. Looking at her tall figure from behind, crowned by red hair, he thought of an ocotillo wand in the spring, with its scarlet blossoms, its setaceous stalk. He said nothing.

Nor did Yvonne, gazing at the pond. Ducks swam on the polished surface mirroring the álamos trees, the tussocks of golden sacoton girdling its shores. Superimposed on this scene, like her reflection in the window, was an image of Rosario the day before she died, caged by the guardrails on the bed, skull as hairless as a stone, skin almost translucent, like wax paper except for the bruising. One skeletal hand was almost blue, and that hand had risen slowly toward Yvonne, risen slowly, as if the IV tube stuck in her wrist were heavy as a fire hose. Yet it gripped her hand with amazing strength.

"It will not be long now," Rosario rasped. "You are going to do something, mi hija?"

"Yes, Mamá."

"Tell me what you are going to do."

"I will when it is done," Yvonne answered, though she had no idea what action she was going to take. She did now, but not then.

"I pray to live to see it. Those people did very well for themselves while we suffered."

All those love songs, Yvonne thought. All those love poems. All that drivel about love the priests preached at Sunday Mass. Why didn't someone compose a song, a poem, or a sermon about hate? Hate was stronger than love. Hate had kept her mother alive longer than the doctors had predicted. It had coursed through her veins for half a century. Like mercury, it had poisoned the milk in her breasts, and on that hot and bitter drink Yvonne had suckled. Sometimes it seemed as though she, the daughter with a man's heart, had known from infancy that she was destined to be the instrument of her mother's revenge.

Rosario relaxed her fingers. The bloodless hand fell to the bed, causing the drip bottle to jiggle on its metal stand. "You have the power to act now," she said in a hollow whisper. "It took you a long time to get it, but now you have it. Make use of it. Cuanto antes mejor—the sooner the better."

"I will, Mamá. I vow it."

"Alive or dead, do not fail me."

"I won't."

The past is gone? Yvonne asked silently, continuing to look out the window. The past is never gone. The arrow of time was all one thing, the notch and feathers of what was, the shaft of what is, the tip of what is to come.

She motioned to Julián to shut the door, both for privacy and to dampen the racket outside, then took the chair he had just vacated. He sat in the only other one in the room, a worn armchair jammed against the wall opposite the desk, between two bookcases that reached almost to the ceiling. The shelves were empty, the books having been shipped out with the furniture.

"All right, the future," Yvonne said. "As I said, I am going to buy the San Ignacio ranch."

"And I had mentioned the slight problem that it isn't for sale."

"This place wasn't for sale a few months ago, but I persuaded Señor Amador that it would be in his best interests to sell."

"Your methods of persuasion will not work on the other side like they do on this side."

"There are other methods. Listen. I am going to make those gringos suffer. I am going to make their lives miserable. When I get through with them, they will be begging for someone, anyone to take it off their hands."

Again, the voice like a thorn, pricking, stabbing. "So this *is* all about Abuela, isn't it? Abuela and her old nonsense."

"It is about justice."

Folding his hands on his lap, Julián looked up at the bookcases. "We should buy a library, fill up those empty shelves. It would warm up the room."

"Stop being cute. Did you hear me?"

"Impossible not to," he said, and bent toward her, hands on his knees, as if he were about to lunge at her. She could think straighter than his father ever did, except when it came to this. In this, she was as crazy as Abuela had been. "There is no room in business for sentiment. No room for waging some old woman's vendetta with no profit in it. You did everything you could for Abuela. She died a rich woman. What need is there to do anymore? She is in her grave. Let her grievances lie there with her."

"What a fine speech! Grievances—is that what you call them? Pues, they are *my* grievances, too. It was my father those people murdered and got away with it."

"You never even knew him!" Julián said, raising his voice.

"I made a promise to her on her deathbed. A promise like that is sacred."

"That word does not sound quite right on your lips. If you insist on settling old scores, why not send Marco and Heraclio over there and shoot the gringos? Blow their fucking heads off. Make an end of it."

"You know, I had considered doing that very thing. I decided it would be too risky."

Julián relaxed and slumped back into the chair. "That represents some evolution in your thinking."

" 'That represents some evolution in your thinking,' " Yvonne mimicked. "This isn't purely a personal matter. Getting my hands on that ranch will be a very good move from a business standpoint. I am sure you see the advantages."

"I am not sure you do."

"With that place and this one in our hands, we will *own* both sides of the border for a distance of twenty kilometers," she said, to show how well she knew. "When the airstrip is finished, we will fly the merca in—our mota, the Gulf's perico—load it onto backs or into trucks, and send it across. We will have our own people on the other side to guide it through and to keep an eye on what La Migra is up to. No problems with some cowboy calling the cops because he sees suspicious people, a suspicious vehicle. And we won't have so many expenses paying mordida to customs inspectors at ports of entry because—"

"We will have our own port of entry," Julián finished for her.

"Precisamente. For us, there will be no border."

"I like this kind of talk much better. Now you are talking sense."

"What? Did you think I had not taken all of this into consideration? I have thought of every detail that can be thought of."

"It is your motives that trouble me. This—this passion of yours to get even for something that happened so long ago could cloud your judgment."

"Nothing clouds my judgment," she said with indignation. "I am a practical woman."

"Then tell me, mi mujer pragmática, how you are going to persuade our American neighbors to sell out?"

She paused for a moment. "I won't tell you. I will show you. Vicente's nephew, Billy Cruz . . . I sent word to him to come today. For this very reason."

"Billy Cruz? That pollero?" asked Julián, incredulously. His mother despised migrant smugglers.

"Him," she replied. "Go outside and see if he's arrived. Tell him we would like a word with him in private."

She studied Cruz as he came in with Julián, a black Stetson pulled low over his forehead. She had met him only once before, and then briefly. Vicente told her that his nephew had been a prizefighter in his youth, and she saw that now, in his middle thirties, he retained a boxer's physique, its pleasing lines accentuated by his snug striped shirt and tight Levi's.

"Buenas tardes, Billy," she cooed, rising and extending her hand.

"Buenas tardes," he responded in a high, boyish voice that didn't match the macho man's body.

"I am a traditionalist about certain courtesies," she said. "Please remove your hat."

He snickered and bared his head. A good-looking guy—why hadn't she seen that on their first meeting? Dense, flaxen hair, dark brown eyes, a square chin. His nose had been broken—in the ring, she supposed—and scar tissue marred his blond eyebrows; but these imperfections added to his appeal. Un buena cogida, she would bet.

"Have a seat," she said, motioning at the chair. "I figure you would prefer we speak in English."

"I'm okay in Spanish."

She propped herself against the desk, palms on its edge, and flirted a little with her eyes. "But I think my English is better than your Spanish, and I wouldn't want there to be any misunderstandings between us."

He slouched into the chair with a studied nonchalance, placed his hat on his lap, and clasped his hands behind his head. Julián stood leaning against the door.

"First of all," said Yvonne, "let me say that I'm sorry about Tío Vicente."

"You're a little late. He died nearly two months ago."

"I've been busy," Yvonne said. "But I was sorry to lose him. He was very clever at devising ways to conceal merchandise in trucks. One time he cut out the gas tank and installed a false tank inside, and you couldn't see the welds with a magnifying glass, and dogs couldn't smell the merca."

"Yeah. He ran an auto body shop for years. In Nogales."

"But maybe he wasn't so clever in other ways," she said.

Julián pushed off the door. "We heard that he stole a load of perico from Joaquín Carrasco. He ordered your uncle's assassination."

"Don't know a thing about it," Cruz said.

"I wouldn't expect you to," said Yvonne. "But you know, after he came to work for me, I sometimes asked myself the same question the girlfriend of a married man asks herself—if he is cheating on his wife with me, will he cheat on me with someone else?"

Cruz sat up straighter and fingered the brim of his Stetson. "Is that what you wanted to talk about?"

"No. You seem a little . . . tense. Like a drink? A beer? A shot of bacanora? Tengo lo bueno."

"I've got all afternoon to drink."

"I want you to know something, Billy," she said. "If I had been in Carrasco's shoes, I would have put out a contract on your tío. But I'm in my shoes, and Vicente was working for me when they killed him. There will be a settling of accounts."

"I stay clear of that shit," Cruz said. "So I'll pretend I didn't hear that."

"Yes, it's good to be deaf sometimes. Your uncle told me you're a businessman. You have a little business in Nogales."

"A shuttle service. We take people to Tucson and Phoenix. Mexicans, mostly."

"Documented Mexicans," she said.

"That's right."

"But your main business is with the other kind. So tell me about that business. I don't know much about it. It's a good business?"

"Thinking of getting into it?" Cruz asked, smirking.

He seemed to be feeling more sure of himself. She was surprised that his cocky manner didn't irk her. In fact, she liked it. At that moment, unbidden, a fantasy flickered through her mind, like scenes from a triple-X movie: Billy lay flat on his strong young back on her canopy bed, she on top of him; the vaquero who had called her an old woman was manacled to the bedpost, watching through the gauzy curtains as Billy pumped her full of the sweet marmalade of his little limb. La mermelada de membrillo. Look at this, cowboy, look at me ride this one, and then tell me I am an old woman. The picture shook her composure. Several seconds passed before she recovered it.

"I've got enough to keep me occupied," she said, once more in command of herself, though her voice had grown husky. "I'm curious, that's all."

"Rip the seats out of a nine-passenger van, and you can fit eighteen, twenty pollos inside. Mexicans, you gross fifteen hundred a head. Central Americans, it's five grand. Chinese, Arabs, ten thousand."

"You've smuggled Chinese and Arabs? At ten thousand a head? Better money than I thought."

"Not many. Ninety percent of my customers are Mexican."

"What happens if a load gets busted? Lose a load of mota and you're out of luck."

"We charge up front. And I don't lose too many loads."

Es un poco presuntuoso, Yvonne thought. He is a little smug. "That's right, your tío told me you're very proficient. You know the trails, the back roads in the San Rafael and the Huachuca mountains like the back of your hand. A human map is what he called you."

"I know the country pretty good. I have to."

She paced around the desk and sat behind it, facing him directly. "And do you know a ranch over there, the San Ignacio?"

"It's right across the line from you, ten miles from here, I'd guess. An old lady and her son own it."

"And have you been herding your chickens through that ranch?"

"No."

"Why not?"

Cruz hesitated and began to fidget with his hat again. "There's two brothers in Santa Cruz who own the routes into the San Rafael. I rent my routes from them. It's a kind of toll, and right now the ones that go through that ranch aren't for rent."

"That toll must add a lot to your overhead."

"A cost of doing business," Cruz said in his high tenor. He sounded like a sixteen-year-old.

"These Santa Cruz cowboys, these brothers, work for Joaquín Carrasco."

"I—I don't know who they work for. I stay out of that."

"Take it from me, Carrasco is their mero mero. So this toll you pay them goes into the pockets of the man who ordered your uncle's murder. Doesn't that trouble you, Billy? Where is your family loyalty?"

Julián, she could see, was growing impatient, but she was having fun with this.

"Like I told you, I stay out of that shit," Cruz said. "I don't know and I don't care who works for who."

"And who do you work for?"

"I'm self-employed. I work for myself."

Yvonne shook her head. "Trabajas para mí. You work for me."

Cruz widened his eyes in mock astonishment, or maybe it wasn't so mock. "Since when?"

"Since right now. For your Santa Cruz cowboys to move their merca into the San Ignacio, they would have to move it through here first. Do you see any? No. I own this rancho. That means that I own the routes through here. Anybody who moves anything across the line from here—I don't care if it's mojados or mota or coke or a load of fucking onions—doesn't do it without my permission. And I'm not giving it, except to you. Do you have anything to say, Billy?"

"Not much. I guess you do."

"I do talk a lot," Yvonne said, falling back into an amiable tone. "I'm a sociable person. No matter what you may have heard about me, I'm actually easy to get along with."

"As long as you do what she wants," Julián interjected.

"How's that for a respectful son?" She rose and moved round to the front of the desk again, perching atop it, her ankles crossed. "And what I want you to do is the opposite of what you're doing now. From now on, until I tell you otherwise, you'll herd your chickens through here to the San Ignacio and *nowhere else*. Every other route in the San Rafael Valley is off limits. You'll be doing me a service and yourself one—

I won't charge you any tolls. All I ask is that you see to it that your strawberry pickers and toilet scrubbers don't fuck this place up. What they do on the other side is another matter. The more they fuck it up, the better I'll like it. Now do you have anything to say?"

Evidently he did not. He scowled, his scarred eyebrows crawling together like yellow caterpillars with segments of their bodies missing.

"You're worried about what your Santa Cruz cowboys will say about this arrangement?"

"It's something to think about."

"But not for long, because what they'll have to say is exactly, precisely nothing."

Cruz jerked his shoulders up to touch his ears. A shrug? A twitch? She couldn't tell. "What's this all about? You want me to create a diversion, is that it? If the Border Patrol is busy chasing my people, there'll be less of them to chase yours?"

"That's part of it, Billy. The rest isn't your concern." Giving in to an urge to touch him, she hopped off the desk, crossed the room in two quick steps, and took hold of his hands, rubbing his calloused palms with her fingertips. "Strong hands. You know, a strong man out here in all this big, open country might think to himself, 'Shit, I can do as I please out here. Who is there to see me?' He might be tempted to herd his dirty chickens in the wrong places. That would be a bad idea."

He said nothing. Yvonne, never content to make a point without underlining it, went on. "There was a terrible incident this past January. Not too far from here. Some bajadores ambushed a carload of mojados and killed all of them. Do you remember that incident? It was in all the newspapers."

"Sure do remember. Those were my people."

"Really? I didn't know that," she said truthfully. All the better, a fortunate coincidence. The dead chickens continued to serve a purpose. "So that's one load you did lose."

"Yeah. And it wasn't bandits. Nothing was taken. Not a watch, not a wallet. They were killed for no reason."

"Yes, that's what the newspapers said. You know, the man who used to own this ranch was so frightened by those murders that he put it up for sale. I talked to him about it. He said that anyone who could commit such a horrible act was likely to do anything. It was just too dangerous for him to stay here. But then, he was very old and alone."

Cruz dropped his gaze, raised it again. Holding on to his hands, she sensed the tension in him, the fear. She owned him. Bought and paid for. "Anything on your mind, Billy? Anything you'd like to tell me?"

"Not a thing."

"All right, then." She let him go and stepped back. "What do you say to our new arrangement?"

"Do I have a choice?"

"What do you think?"

"And you, what do you think?" she asked Julián after dismissing Cruz.

"You should try to make yourself less obvious. You were looking at him like you wanted to tear the clothes off his back. You're almost old enough to be his mother."

"Maybe it was you who wanted to tear his clothes off."

"Eres una perra. Siempre tienes la regla."

"I stopped the rag two years ago. The plan, mi hijo. What do you think? Dozens of mojados, maybe hundreds, running through the San Ignacio week after week, like a plague of locusts. A few months of that and—"

"They will be begging for someone to take the place off their hands." Julián, a shoulder to the wall, hands in his pockets, adopted a reflective air. "But you know, these rancheros are tied to their land. Mexicans or gringos, no le hace. They are all tied to it. And those are difficult ties to break."

"It wasn't so difficult to break the ties of the guy who owned this place. Everything is for sale, that's what my real estate cousin says, and he's right. I am going to make our American neighbors so afraid of losing everything they've got, they will be greedy for anything they can get."

"You are becoming a philosopher, mother."

"Philosopher? No, a general. Like Pancho Villa. He invaded the United States, so I am going to invade a little piece of it myself." She felt giddy. She laughed. "Señor Cruz will be my field commander, his chickens my army."

"Don't get carried away with yourself," Julián said. "Pancho Villa lost his battle."

12

SPRING IS NOT THE SEASON of renewal in the Sonoran Desert. It is the dry time of year, an annual drought. From mid-March till late July, the skies really are not cloudy all day, and after a while the clear blue overhead becomes monotonous and oppressive. Trees do leaf out, the cottonwoods first, the mesquites last, and desert flowers blossom, adding splashes of color to the dun landscape; but the grasses soon turn brittle as old newspaper, dirt tanks shrink from ponds to puddles to cracked mudholes, and rattlesnakes stir from their winter dormancy, each one as mean as a man awakening with a bad hangover, likely to strike at anything that draws too near, human, horse, cow, or dog. Spring is the season when migrants die in greater numbers, hundreds every year, their naked corpses (naked because in the derangement of extreme dehydration they rip off their clothes) sprawled in the greasewood and brittle-bush thickets, sometimes within sight of the road or highway they were struggling to reach. Spring is the season when even the lightning is dry, igniting range fires and forest fires on the mountainsides. And spring is the season when farmers and ranchers on both sides of the border talk endlessly and obsessively about rain. They think about it, dream about it, wait anxiously for it. The summer monsoons begin in July, hustled into Sonora and Arizona by the chubascos whirling in off the Gulf of California, and they end two months later; but their arrival and abundance is never guaranteed. Like a precocious child, they might show early promise and then fail; or they might withhold themselves and then pour forth torrents too late; or they might turn capricious—long arid days or weeks punctuated by brief biblical downpours that do little but scour the soil, wash out roads, and produce awesome flash floods, thundering and frothing in the arroyos, plucking giant trees by the roots like so many dandelions; or the rains might not come at all.

The spring of that year was especially trying for Tessa McBride. There were the usual woes of running a ranch—a mountain lion killed two of her calves, a well pump burned out—but it was the war that strained her nerves. About a week after the first bombs fell, Castle went with her to buy a new pump at a hardware store in Sierra Vista, a patulous hodgepodge of malls and subdivisions littering the desert near Fort Huachuca. Traffic was stalled near the junction of Highway 90 and the road to the main gate while a convoy of trucks and Humvees painted desert tan rolled out of the base, bound for an airfield somewhere and deployment to Iraq. The rumbling military vehicles, the unsmiling soldiers behind the wheels in their black berets and camouflage uniforms charged the air with a certain drama; universal history was rattling Arizona hinterlands that had scarcely felt the tremors of 9/11. Waiting for the convoy to pass, Castle noticed a stone monument with a plaque bearing a relief of a mounted cavalryman and the words FORT HUACHUCA—1877. Behind it, constructed of the same river rock, stood a small building that looked as if it dated back to the fort's beginnings as an outpost during the Apache Wars. A sign out front declared that it was now a WIDOWS' SUPPORT CENTER.

"I'll bet that's going to be a busy place pretty soon," Tessa said. She lowered her window and shouted to the two military policemen directing traffic, "What about parents?" When they didn't respond, she blew the horn to get their attention. "Hey! Do you have a support center for parents?"

One of the soldiers, wearing an armband with the letters MP sewn on it, sauntered over like a highway patrolman who has nabbed a speeder. "What's the trouble, ma'am?"

"No trouble. You have a support center for widows. I want to know if you've got one for parents."

The MP scowled. "If you want any information, you can see the base information officer, ma'am. You can get a visitor's pass at the main gate."

"I don't want a visitor's pass!" Tessa said. Her voice had a quavering, fragile sound. "If my daughter gets killed over there, can I count on counseling from the army, or do I just get left with a coffin and a flag?"

"Tess, what the hell are you doing?" said Castle, a little alarmed. He had never seen her behave this way.

"I can't answer that," the MP replied. "I suggest you contact the base information officer."

The tail end of the convoy had meanwhile gone past, and the other soldier was signaling civilian traffic to come ahead. The car behind Tessa's pickup honked its horn; then the driver pulled out into the left lane and shot by.

"You'll have to move your vehicle. You're blocking the road, ma'am," said the MP, putting an edge on the last word to let her know that his reservoir of patience was draining fast.

"I will do that, but only because you're so damn polite. And thanks for being so extremely helpful."

"What the hell were you busting his chops for?" asked Castle as they drove on. "He's only a soldier like Beth. A kid."

"A robot is what he is," Tessa snapped. " 'You will have to move your vehicle, ma'am. Your *vee-hick-el.*' " She seemed to find her unreasonableness gratifying. "Why couldn't he have said 'truck'? What's wrong with 'truck'?"

Castle sat beside her almost every night for the next two weeks. He would drive to the Crown A around five in the afternoon, they would eat dinner—she cooked, he cleaned up—and then they'd begin their vigil in front of the TV. Sitting on the couch with space between them, like an old married couple, they followed the progress of the Third Infantry Division (the unit to which Beth's supply battalion was attached) as it battered its way toward Baghdad. They became familiar with places they'd never heard of before, Najaf and Nasiriyah and Karbala, and they got an education in the sectarian rivalries of Islam.

"Exactly what the hell makes a Shiite a Shiite and a Sunni a Sunni?" Tessa asked one night. "And why do they hate each other?"

Castle didn't know; he supposed it was for the same reason Catholics and Protestants in Northern Ireland hated each other, that is to say, for no good reason at all.

They were watching CNN when the early reports came in that an American supply convoy had been ambushed. Several soldiers killed; several more, including two women, missing in action. She flew into her bedroom and flew out again, clutching one of Beth's letters. The return address bore the name and number of her daughter's battalion. "What unit were they from?" she shouted at the TV. A reporter, against a background of mud-walled huts and date palm trees, was giving further details . . . Eleven confirmed dead, five missing, the two women believed to have been captured by the Iraqi army . . . Names withheld pending notification of next of kin . . . "Then tell us the goddamn unit!" Tessa hollered, then switched to CBS, NBC, ABC, Fox, yelling the same question. She turned to Beth's basic training photograph. "What did you have to join the fucking army for? If you had your shit together, you'd still be in school."

She did not come back to herself until, a day or two later, the female soldiers were identified as Privates First Class Jessica Lynch and Lori Piestewa. Lynch had been rescued from an Iraqi hospital by Special Forces; Piestewa, a Hopi Indian from Arizona, had died of her wounds. Tessa hugged Castle and cried out thanks that Beth was all right, her joy and gratitude immediately producing guilt. That poor girl's family. Christ, what right did she have to be so happy?

One April afternoon they took a break from war-watching to treat a cow with a prolapsed uterus. Castle acted as a kind of surgeon's assistant for Tessa and Tim McIntyre, who held a lidocaine syringe in one hand, a long curved needle and cotton string in the other. McIntyre prodded the cow, trailed by its three-day-old calf, into a steel headstall in one of Tessa's corrals. She called for the syringe, instructing Castle to stand aside when she jabbed the needle into the animal's haunches—there was a danger of getting kicked or sprayed with cowshit. Neither of these mishaps occurred.

"My dad told me that my granddad used to do this out on the range with a Coke bottle," McIntyre said while they waited for the anesthetic to take effect. "He'd carry one of them sixteen-ounce bottles in his saddlebag, along with a carpet needle and kitchen twine. Come across a prolapsed cow, he'd shove the uterus back in with the bottle, then he'd stitch her up."

"What happened to the Coke bottle?" asked Tessa, intrigued by this novel method.

"Oh, he'd leave it in there. It stopped the uterus from poppin' out again."

"I imagine it would stop a bull from getting in," said Tessa.

McIntyre blushed and looked down at his scruffy boots. He was a devout born-again Christian; a bumper sticker on his truck proclaimed his membership in an organization called Cowboys for Christ. "Never thought of it that way," he said, "but I suppose that is true."

The cow's tail had stopped switching, indicating that her backside had been numbed. McIntyre slipped on a long latex glove and, with his fist, pushed the bulging uterus back into place, burying his arm nearly up to the elbow. Castle grimaced when he withdrew it, the glove glistening with slime, flecked with blood. Tessa took the needle and thread—it was as thick as a big-game fishing line—and began to suture the cow's vaginal opening. She'd done two stitches when the extension phone in the stable rang. She jerked her head up and gave the stable a wary look, as if an intruder might be hiding there.

"Finish up," she said, handing the needle to McIntyre.

She was crying when she returned, threw herself at Castle, and embraced him. "It was her! Beth! Calling from Baghdad." She kissed him full on the lips; then, to show she was merely expressing her happiness, she kissed McIntyre in the same way. Castle thought his might have lasted a second longer than the cowboy's. "Her outfit is at the Baghdad airport," Tessa went on. "Can you imagine? Getting a phone call way out here from way over there? Somebody hooked up a sat phone. She couldn't talk for long, less than a minute. But she's okay. Never even had a close call. Oh, how wonderful to hear her voice!"

And to hear Tessa, you would have thought the war was over. For all practical purposes it was—Baghdad had been captured, Saddam had fled, his statue had been toppled. Castle looked into Tessa's eyes, conscious that he'd made a long inner journey in the past month, a journey that was only halfway complete; yet he'd come far enough to share in her joy. He offered to take her to dinner to celebrate. He did not tell her that they would be celebrating more than the news of Beth's deliverance. He didn't know how to put it into words; or rather he did know, but he considered them words better thought than spoken: She needed him, he needed her, and in that mutuality he'd found the key to breaking his habit of seeing himself as the victim of an inexpressible tragedy.

They went to Elvira's on the Sonoran side of Nogales. Dressed in another of her rodeo-queen outfits—snug pants, a fringed vest over a pearl-button shirt, a jaunty flat-brimmed hat—she drew stares from the taxi drivers congregated on International Street. It is the custom at Elvira's to serve free shots of tequila before dinner. Tessa knocked hers back in the accepted fashion, sucking on a slice of lime, licking salt off her hand, then downing the shot in one gulp. Castle felt slightly dizzy, looking at the sheen of the lime juice on her red lips, at the tip of her tongue, flicking over the salt in the web of her hand.

They ordered margaritas with dinner and toasted Beth. Thereafter, over his chicken mole and her shrimp in garlic and butter sauce, they spoke of things other than the war, for the first time in weeks. Light stuff at first. Movies they'd seen or wanted to see. Their favorite albums. Then Tessa said that she was struggling to put her ranch into the black. Castle understood nothing about raising cattle but knew profit and loss, and suggested she build a Web site advertising her grass-fed beef. Combine it with a direct-mail campaign to independent meat markets in Tucson. He had the impression that she was captivated by the ranching way of life and paid little attention to the business end of things. Advising her on such matters gratified him; he thought it showed her that although he could not rope a calf, mend a fence, or heal a prolapsed uterus, he was nevertheless a strong and competent male.

Having drunk two margaritas at dinner on top of the tequila she slugged down before, she swayed when they stood to leave and grasped the back of a chair to steady herself.

"Christ, I'm smashed."

"You don't sound like it."

"Hasn't affected my speech, but motor control is slipping. I'm going to have to hang on to you."

Outside he threw an arm around her shoulders, and she slipped hers around his waist and clutched his belt, leaning into him as they walked back to the pedestrian crossing. The streetlights were on, and neon signs blazed the names of cheap hotels and border bars. The cab drivers stared at her again.

"They won't think I'm drunk," she said with a tease in her voice. "They'll think we're in love. "

They had to let go of each other at the port of entry. Tessa had recovered somewhat and got through the customs line without a stumble. On the other side they resumed walking arm in arm, up the Terrace Street ramp, then up Crawford to the lot where he'd parked.

"Made it," Tessa said, slumping into her seat. "I wish to say that you've been wonderful, putting up with my hysterics."

"If one of my girls was over there, I'd be hysterical myself."

"Do you suppose it would be less scary if it were a son instead of a daughter?"

"That's not supposed to make a difference anymore."

"Yeah, except that it does."

He pulled out of the lot and turned onto South Grand, passing the old city hall. Tessa asked, "So do you think we could be?"

"Could be what?"

"What we looked like on the walk back."

An intoxication that had nothing to do with tequila rushed into his skull. Instantly, she reached over and pressed two fingers to his lips.

"Don't answer. That wasn't fair of me," she said. "It's the tequila talking. Just want you to know that I am. Which puts you under no obligation."

. . .

He walked her to her door, under the numberless stars of a sky unsullied by smog or city glow. She asked, "Would you care for another dance, Mr. Castle?" They went inside. She switched on a light, put the Ella Fitzgerald CD in the player, and then turned the light off. Dancing in the dark to those Gershwin tunes, those incongruous urban melodies rising on Ella's spellbinding voice, ablated his self-consciousness, his usual reserve. He held her close and spun her around without bumping into a thing. He felt masterful. The kiss he gave her, on the second dance, was as timid as a fourteen-year-old's. Her response was fervent, encouraging him to try again. Her body went limp in surrender, though not passive surrender. They fell on the couch, she on top of him, tugging at the buttons on his shirt. He fumbled with the snaps on hers, and then she knelt upright, stripped to the waist, and bowed, her breasts tumbling to his lips. He took one into his mouth, suckling while she held his head. They broke apart and finished undressing. Neither spoke, aware that one word would break the spell; they would see each other as ridiculous, a man of nearly fifty-seven and a woman of forty-five tearing at belt buckles and zippers, kicking off shoes, pulling off socks like frenzied adolescents. When their naked bodies came together again, Castle was lanced by the fear that he would suffer a mortifying failure. He imagined Tessa stroking his arm while she murmured that it was all right, darling, it happens to every man once in a while. He was ecstatic to discover that she would not have to offer any such soothing reassurance. They lay side by side, not talking, feeling serene. Tessa playfully ruffled his thinning hair, tweaked his ear. "Will your dog suffer if you spend the night?" she asked. "I damn sure will if you don't."

The next morning, as he drove home, Castle recalled overhearing an intimate conversation between his female partners at Harriman-Cutler. They were saying, in effect, that a man and woman could not be friends because the wild beast of sexual intercourse inevitably leaped between them, leaving them no choice but to part or become lovers. They'd spoken as if desire were the enemy of friendship. Nonsense, he thought now. There could be no real communion between men and women without it. In the moment of orgasm, they became one flesh, one soul, all distinctions between the carnal and the spiritual as meaningless as gravity is to a bird.

The road from her ranch to the San Ignacio ran level most of the way, except for one point where it climbed a gentle rise. He parked there and looked across the valley, reaching as an inland sea reaches to the shores of its bounding mountain ranges. Far away, over Mexico, a dying range fire made the only blot on the morning sky. A hawk gyred above the heaves and falls of the land, stitched by the frail, green thread of the cottonwoods bordering the Santa Cruz River. He caught movement in that direction and saw a herd of Sonoran pronghorns, prancing toward the river and its pledge of water. Despite the road, the fences, and the glint of a ranch house's tin roof here and there, he imagined that the Spanish missionaries who had crossed into the San Rafael four hundred years ago would find much that was familiar. The West. She had been plundered and abused and disfigured for centuries. It seemed wondrous that places like this still existed, that any of the West's old enchantment remained, that hers could still be the geography of promise, the landscape of hope. Mirages, perhaps, exerting the charm of the vague, the illusory; and yet Castle saw in the vista before him the chance that he would soon break his shackles to the past and overthrow the tyrant that had oppressed him nearly every waking hour. Tessa had awakened him to this possibility, Tessa and the land. Was it a chimera? It almost made no difference. The chance, glimmering on the horizon, the chance was enough.

BEN ERSKINE

Transcript 3—T.J. Babcock

Ynez and me had settled in Cananea, in a little casita next door to her mother's place. Pretty quick I become the father of a baby boy, Roberto. Like I said before, Ynez was just a hair over five foot tall, but she was strong for her size and . . . vigorous, if you know what I mean. Flat wore me out. Roberto was still suckling on her tit when she got pregnant again and we had another boy. We named him Candelario, after our old comandante. By this time, it was 1915, and things in Mexico had gone all to hell. First off Madero got overthrown and then assassinated by a counterrevolutionary, General Huerta. A whole passel of generals rose up against him—Villa, Zapata, Carranza, Obregón—and sent him off into exile. Then they fell to fighting among each other, with Carranza and Obregón joining together in the north against Villa and Zapata in the south. Full-bore, flat-out civil war. Armed bands running all over the countryside, some of them nothing more than bandit gangs.

In between having babies, Ynez worked on some committee that looked out for the miners in Cananea, kind of like a labor union. She made a few pesos at that and I made a few, cowboying on the ranchos near town. But as the war got worse and worse, work got harder and harder to find. Ynez was finding out that building a new Mexico was damn near impossible; might as well try to build a house in the middle of an earthquake. Long and the short of it was, about the only way you could make a living was to join one of the armies. You know, each one of them traveled with its own printing presses and issued its own money—there was Zapatista pesos and Carranzista pesos and so forth and so on. Obregón was el supremo in Sonora, so I figured to enlist with him. Found out through our old compañero, Francisco Montoya, that Colonel Bracamonte was now a brigadier general under Obregón. I wrote to him and said I was all set to join up, and where do I sign?

Damn if a week or so later, the colonel—I still called him that even though he was a general now—didn't show up at our casita in person. He offered me employment, but not the kind I was expecting.

It was like this: Obregón was fixing to do battle with Villa, who everybody thought was damn near unbeatable, and had put the colonel in charge of raising and training a battalion of Yaqui Indians. You know, them Yaquis was the hardest-fighting Indians in Mexico and maybe anywhere, only ones who had whipped the Spaniards way back in the olden times, and even the A-patch could not lay claim to that. Now some of 'em was still running around with bows and arrows, and Villa had him machine guns and German cannons.

So Bracamonte sat me down in our little house close by the copper mine. He still had that big crow's-wing mustache and them eyes like diamond drill bits. He told me he'd made contact with a fella he called a "munitions supplier" in Arizona, fella with some sort of Dutch-like name I can't remember. This Dutchman had told the colonel he'd laid hands on surplus U.S. Army rifles and ammo that he'd be glad to sell, payment in gold or Yankee dollars. Bracamonte had the gold and two problems—how to get it to the Dutchman and how to get the rifles into Mexico. In times gone by the second problem wouldn't have been one—the Yaqui had been smuggling one thing or another across the border ever since there was a border, but now U.S. Cavalry patrols was all along it, trying to put a stop to gunrunning into Old Mexico.

The colonel told me he needed a gringo to be his agent in the U.S. of A., a gringo he could trust. This here agent was to deliver the gold to the Dutchman, make sure Bracamonte was getting what he paid for, and then give the Yaqui a hand in moving the goods past the cavalry patrols. He wanted me to be the agent, and if I could pull it off, I'd get paid in gold too, 10 percent of the five thousand dollars he was going to pay the Dutchman. Five hundred bucks was a considerable lot in 1915, a damn fortune in Mexico. But I had no idea how I was going to go about the job, knew I would need help, and reckoned Ben would be the one to give it. Him and me had been in touch off and on, so I asked the colonel if he remembered Capitán Erskine and would he trust him like he did me? And he said, "Por supuesto." And I said that I wanted to cut him in because I couldn't handle a job like this all by my lonesome. He thought a minute and then said that was a good idea and, just in case Ben balked, to remind him of the debt he owed, and that if he threw in and everything went okay, he could consider it paid in full. Then he bored into me with the diamond bits and told me not to forget that I had a pregnant wife in Cananea. I got his drift. Reckon Bracamonte's trust had its limits.

I took the train to Nogales. Had me two six-shooters under my coat and a change of underwear and socks and fifteen pounds of gold ingots in an old-time carpet bag. Didn't even think of crossing the line in the regular way. Waited till dark and sneaked over on foot. Took another train to Patagonia, where I inquired about Ben's whereabouts and found out he was living up on his brother's ranch. Next day I got a ride there from a friend of Jeff's in a Model A Ford—first time I'd ever rid in an automobile.

Old Jeff had prospered and had built up the San Ignacio ranch and had got married to a gal name of Lilly and built him a little house and was fixing to build a bigger one. The three of us had us a reunion, and later on I took Ben outside and told him what was up and asked if he could lend a hand. Told him what I was getting paid for it, but I could offer him only ten percent of my ten percent on account of I was now pa to two children and there was no work to be had south of the line. Ben didn't care about the money, he never did. Jumped right on it, said he owed one to the colonel, so I didn't even have to mention that. Best part was, it turned out him and a Mexican was partnered rounding up wild cattle and that for a spell they'd worked the country west of Nogales, where the Old Yaqui Trail, the main smuggling route, run through. This Mexican was part Yaqui and knew that country like the back of his hand, Ben said. I was kind of shy about letting a third party in, but Ben was insistent, and it turned out he was right to be.

I borrowed a horse from Jeff. Ben naturally didn't tell him what we was up to. Said we'd got a job to gather some loose stock and that we'd be back in a couple of weeks. So we delivered the gold to the Dutchman. He ran a general store near to the Indian mission at Xavier del

Bac, and had the merchandise stored in a root cellar under his barn—a hundred Springfields, a Colt machine gun, and a damn wagonload of ammunition. The Mexican—Mendoza was his name—had some family at the mission, and they pitched in to put a pack train together. Took a couple days to round enough mules to carry all that hardware. There was about twenty-odd Yaqui to guard it, all of 'em afoot, on account of the Yaqui not being horse Indians.

The three of us were a-horseback. Our job was to ride out ahead and scout for cavalry patrols and camps and to warn the Indians in case we saw any. Didn't have much distance to cover, fifty, sixty miles, but moving at night and with them slow-walking mules, it took us a while. Three nights, if I remember right. Dawn of the third day, me and Ben and Mendoza crossed trails with a patrol, them colored troopers called Buffalo Soldiers. Their officer, a white fella looked like he'd got out of West Point the day before, asked us what we were doing there, and Ben told him, "Looking for wild cattle, and did you see any?" The shavetail shook his head and asked us if we had seen anything of a suspicious nature, like Yaqui smugglers. Well, that patrol was heading up a canyon toward where the pack train was laid up for the day, so Ben told him that we'd seen a whole bunch of contrabandistas over to Ruby, which was a good ten, twelve miles west of where our boys was. That lieutenant thanked us and trotted off on a wild-goose chase. We had a good laugh at the boy's expense. Truth to tell, it was kind of exciting, damn near romantic. We was genuine renegades, helping Indians get away from the U.S. Cavalry!

Crossed the border that night and was in Bracamonte's camp by noon the next day. Yaqui all over the place, learning how to drill. Come to find out later that their battalion turned the tide at the great battle of Celaya, where Obregón gave that old bandito Villa his first real defeat. Anyhow, the colonel was right pleased with our work. Gave us each un gran abrazo and handed me a sack full of gold in little ingots. I gave fifty dollars' worth to Ben, and he gave half of his to Mendoza. We stuck around for another week, giving the colonel a hand at showing the Indians how to shoot Springfields and machine guns. So that was how we come to lay hands on the gold we was promised in the recruitment poster four years before and Ben come to paying his debt.

Him and me and the colonel was to cross trails again a whole lot later on, when Ben come to be in Bracamonte's debt a second time and had to pay him back. I can't talk about that right now. I am hoarse from all the yakking I've done so far and have got to see a doctor tomorrow about my many infirmities.

13

A WEEK HAD PASSED since Castle and Tessa ended their lives of celibacy—hers had been longer than his. They found the renewed pleasures of physical love so delightful that they repeated their first night's performance twice more, making a ritual of it. They danced—dancing was sex with your clothes on, she said—before racing to the bedroom, a disaster area because it was also her studio, and they made love washed in the fumes of oil paints, varnish, and turpentine. He detected those odors clinging to him faintly as, whistling to himself, he washed the breakfast dishes in his cabin's stained sink.

He heard his aunt's 1973 Chevy pickup pull into his drive, its clicking valve tappets and rattling fenders as identifiable as a bird call. Before he could get to the front door, Sally bustled through it without knocking. Her appearance jolted him. Her hair coiffed into a tidy bun, her makeup on, she wore in place of her standard bag-lady outfit a white blouse, a tan skirt with slash pockets tipped by embroidered triangles, and low-heeled pumps.

"I need you to drive me to Florence," she announced, dispensing with the formality of a polite greeting. "If I was to drive myself up there in that junker of mine, Blaine would pitch such a fit, I'd have to take a belt to him to shut him up."

"Florence is . . . ?"

"About eighty miles north of Tucson. They're holding Miguel up there in some kind of detention place for illegal aliens. I aim to visit him. See how he's getting on."

"What brought this on?" Castle asked. Miguel Espinoza had receded far back into his mind.

"It'll take us three hours to get there. Let's go. I'll explain on the way."

There was no denying her when she was in command mode. He

got his wallet and keys, supplied Sam with food and water, and they started off.

Sally said that her old friend Danny Rodriguez, the Santa Cruz County sheriff, had been out to the ranch a few days ago, asking if she might be willing to sell a couple of good horses for his back-country search-and-rescue squad. She had a bay and a dun that she could part with for the right price. While he was looking them over, she asked how the murder investigation was coming along. No new leads, Rodriguez told her. Meanwhile the sole eyewitness had been transferred to protective custody in Florence, because of overcrowding in the county jail.

"After Danny left—we couldn't come to terms on the horses, by the by—I got to thinking about Miguel, locked up in a foreign country a thousand miles from his wife and kids. I own that I've got a soft spot for him, did from the day he showed up here. So I called the sheriff to find out how I could pay Miguel a call. Seemed to me the Good Lord was telling me that I should visit him and find out if there's anything I can do for him."

It was odd to hear her assert that she was responding to a summons from heaven. She wasn't a churchgoer and was more likely than not to invoke the Lord's name in vain, as she did when Castle reminded her to fasten her seat belt and she reached up for the buckle, wincing and muttering, "Goddamn arthritis in this shoulder."

She then pulled a sheet of paper out of her purse. "This place they're holding him is called the Department of Homeland Security Special Processing Center. A fancy name for a jail. It says here that visiting hours are from nine till three and that female visitors can't wear provocative clothes. Ha! I could walk in there naked as a newborn and I wouldn't provoke the horniest fella they got in the place."

They descended from the valley down the sinuous road to Patagonia. Two Border Patrol trucks rolled by, the dust hovering like a thin pink-tinged mist. Within half an hour they were on the state highway, heading toward the Sonoita crossroads.

"Blaine thinks I'm crazy for doing this," Sally said. "That boy is changing in his old age."

"Oh? He seems the same to me."

"You haven't known him good enough to see the difference. He ain't lighthearted like he used to be. Always cracking jokes. That part of him reminds me of his dad. Oh, how Frank could make me laugh.

He had a way of seeing the humorous side of things. It's what got him through the war. Blaine has a goodly touch of that in him, but the last little while, he's started to sull up a lot, and that part reminds me of his granddad."

"You mean Ben or your father?"

"Ben. He'd get like that. Quiet in a way that made you feel that if somebody did something he didn't like or said the wrong thing, something bad was gone to happen, and there were times when something did. Ben Erskine was not a man you wanted to fool with."

"Blaine told me once that Ben was tried for shooting a man," Castle said, hoping to encourage her to open up about his mysterious grandfather. "I can't say I know much more than that. My mother never breathed a word about it."

"Probably because she was ashamed of it," Sally began. "Fella he shot, Rafael Quinn, everybody called him Rafe for short. It come out at the trial that Rafe shot first, and he found out that if you was to shoot at Ben Erskine, you had better not miss, and he missed. Ben shot him dead as Julius Caesar. The jury acquitted him, on grounds it was self-defense." She paused. "But some folks did not see it that way. Mexicans mostly, but some white folks, too. They said Ben didn't need to kill him."

"Why, if it was self-defense?"

"Rafe was Irish and Mexican, which ain't the best combination for a peaceable nature, and he did not have one. But if you let him spout off, he'd cool down. Ben didn't let him. Rafe and him had words, what about I do not recall, and the next thing anyone knew, they was blazing at each other."

Sally then fell silent and did not speak again until they were approaching the crossroads.

"That's where it happened, nineteen fifty-one," she said, pointing out the window toward the right side of the road, in the general direction of a convenience store, a gas station, and a restaurant called the Steak Out. "The Sonoita shipping pens used to be there. Long gone now. The newspapers said it was the last Old West gunfight in Arizona."

This sketchy account left Castle yearning for more. The phrase *last Old West gunfight* threw a cloak of the remote, mythic past over the episode; yet it had happened in his lifetime. At the crossroads he turned onto Highway 83, an asphalt cord dangling off the interstate, twenty-five miles to the north. Poppies sprouted here and there, daubs of mellow gold in the vast khaki Sonoita grasslands, rolling away toward the stark Whetstone Mountains.

"So was my mother one of the people who thought Ben didn't have to do it?" he asked.

"Can't say. Do know she was mortified, seeing her dad on trial for second-degree murder. Things between them hadn't been right for some time."

"Why?"

Sally bent forward and massaged her knees. "More'n an hour in a car, and my joints need a lube job. Uncle Jeff used to say your granddad could carry a grudge like a pack mule, and that was true."

"He had a *grudge* against my mother?"

"She'd run off with your pa during the war. I hope she told you about that. That she eloped."

"She did, but I—"

"The thing about Ben," Sally rolled on, "is that you never knew what would put you on the wrong side of him and what wouldn't. He was unpredictable. I recollect an incident between him and another rancher, this would have been a year or so after Frank and me got married, when some of Ben's cattle drifted onto the other rancher's land. This fella was a quarrelsome man. He phoned Ben and told him to come get his cows, but when Ben didn't show up fast enough to suit him, he roped a calf and dragged it back onto San Ignacio land. Killed the poor little thing. Ben got him to pay for the calf, but it took some doing. Now you would think a man like Ben would come down like God's own wrath on a fella who done him a serious wrong. But later on, when the rancher fella got hurt in an auto accident just before spring branding, Ben visited him in the hospital, and then got some hands together and gathered the fella's calves and branded 'em for him. That man could forgive when he was of a mind to, but what put him in a forgiving mind and what didn't, nobody could puzzle out, Ben least of all, I'll bet."

"So I take it he didn't forgive my mother for eloping?"

"Didn't speak to her nor your pa neither from the day they run off to the day Grace showed up for his trial. Seven years."

Castle whistled. Given his own mild temperament, maintaining an antagonism for that long toward one's own daughter struck him as an incredible emotional feat.

"The funny thing was, up until she eloped, Ben treated her like she was Queen of the May," his aunt said. "Wasn't hard on her like he was on my Frank."

"Because he expected more of his son?"

"Couldn't say. I do know that no matter what Frank done, he always come up short in Ben's eyes. Frank was a top hand by the time he was sixteen, won prizes in junior rodeos, got good grades in school, and was a helluva fine ballplayer. Never was enough for old Ben. Like if Frank pitched a winning game, Ben would want to know how come he didn't pitch a no-hitter. That sorta thing. The war changed all that. Frank volunteered for the paratroops, probably to prove something to his pa, and come home from France with his medals, and Ben was so proud of him he gave him the saber and uniform the Mexicans had given to him."

Castle blinked. "Saber? Uniform?"

"Ben fought in the Mexican Revolution. He was a captain or colonel or some such."

His grandfather, a soldier of fortune. He'd learned more about the man in the last half hour than he had in his entire life. "What can you tell me about that?"

"Don't know anything about it except that he had this uniform with fancy gold braid and the saber. My Frank was excited as a little kid at Christmas to get them because of what they meant—him and Ben was now on equal footing. That's how things were after the war. Frank had come way up in his pa's estimation, and Grace had come down."

Castle caught a note in this commentary: her description of Frank's excitement carried a hint of disapproval—of Ben for being such a demanding father, of Frank for being so avid to win his esteem.

He cruised off Highway 83 and joined the traffic streaming down the I-10 freeway toward downtown Tucson, its office towers rising in the distance through a faint brownish reef of smog. Off to the right, silhouetted against the Santa Catalina Mountains, a jet fighter swooped in to land at Davis Monthan, the air force base sprawling out into the deserts east of the city.

"That's where Grace met your pa," Sally said, indicating the base with a movement of her head.

"I know that much at least."

"She was a Red Cross girl, passing out coffee and doughnuts to the flyboys, and one day Tony stopped by her wagon, and bingo! That was it for the both of 'em. She was a fine-looking gal, and he was a good-looking man. And a talker! Lord, how that man could talk."

"Yeah," Castle said, smiling at the memory of his father's volubility. "Name the subject, and he'd go on about it for half an hour."

"That was Tony, all right. Him and Ben never did hit it off right. Ben wasn't much of a conversationalist. Said whatever needed to be said in as few words as he could get away with."

"Well, I thank you, Sally. My mother never told me a tenth of all this." He felt a flicker of resentment for her withholding so much family lore and history from him. "I don't know why she had to keep it all such a big secret."

Sally rubbed her knees once again, then pushed the seat back, sighing as she stretched her legs to their full length. "Could be Grace never told you anything because it was just too hurtful. Her ma died not long after the trial, a year more and her brother, my Frank, got killed in that mine accident. Five years on, it was her pa. She'd lost everybody."

All her memories of this place were bad ones, Castle thought. A plausible explanation, yet it seemed incomplete.

"Take the next exit," Sally said. "It'll lead you to the Florence highway."

Castle swung into the right lane. He'd almost forgotten the purpose of this trip.

14

FLORENCE WAS AN OLD MINING TOWN settled beneath the flinty, saguaro-picketed hills between Phoenix and Tucson. The veins of silver and copper had been bled out long ago, and now its major industry, the industry that saved it from becoming one more western ghost town, was incarceration. It had got its start in the corrections business early in the last century with the building of the Arizona Territorial prison. From that modest beginning, Florence had evolved into a kind of desert gulag.

When Castle and Sally arrived, about noon, they saw one kind of cop car or another everywhere they looked: patrol cars, vans, and trucks emblazoned with the emblems of the Florence city police, the Pinal County sheriff's police, the Arizona state police, the U.S. Border Patrol, the Department of Homeland Security. The town had to have the lowest crime rate in the world. Muscle-bound prison guards, employees of a private firm called the Corrections Corporation of America, crowded Gibby's cantina downtown, where he and his aunt ate a quick lunch. After getting directions, they drove past the state penitentiary, a vast reservation of battleship-gray Quonset huts, cell blocks, and guard towers surrounded by high chain-link fences crowned with razor wire, and then the Pinal County jail, before crossing the Gila River, which was not a river but a wide, brushy swath of gravel and dust, to arrive at their destination, the Department of Homeland Security Special Processing Center.

Like a church built atop the ruins of a pagan temple, this state-of-the-art lockup for illegal aliens awaiting deportation had been erected (by the same private corporation that operated the penitentiary) upon the remnants of a POW camp for Axis troops captured in the North Africa campaign. Prefab barracks and buildings with blue roofs and geometric patterns on the walls—Castle guessed they were supposed to project a southwestern look—huddled behind yet more chain link twenty feet high and yet more razor wire, glittering in the sunlight like deadly tinsel. If not quite as depressing as the state pen, it was depressing enough.

He parked on the street. Sally freshened her makeup and patted her hair to be sure her bun was in place. They checked in at the guard station, gave the name of the inmate they wished to see, then were escorted into an administration building, where they presented their driver's licenses to verify their identities and underwent a body search, to which Sally objected—"Do I look like somebody who intends to stage a jailbreak?" she said to the female guard who wanded her. Her purse was inspected, and to her further annoyance, the cigarettes and Power Bars she'd bought in town for Miguel were confiscated and placed in a locker. The woman assured her they would eventually be given to Miguel—after they were inspected, of course.

A male guard ushered them to a visitation room. One long row of cubicles divided by plastic partitions faced another through a wall of bulletproof glass. Inmates garbed in red jumpsuits sat on one side, their visitors on the other, and conversed through telephones. It was the first time Castle had seen the inside of a jail, and though this one did not call itself a jail, he felt its stifling embrace. Led by another guard, Miguel came in, walking with short, shuffling steps, as if he were in leg irons. He sat in the cubicle opposite Castle and Sally's, while the guards stood nearby, hands crossed over their crotches, their postures suggesting that they could spring from complete immobility into violent movement in an instant.

Picking up the phone, Miguel said he was so happy to see his visitors, a statement belied by his slumped shoulders and the mixture of fear and confusion in his eyes. He had put on weight—evidently he was fed well. Sally, speaking in Spanish and then translating for her nephew's benefit, told him about the cigarettes and candy bars and asked if there was anything else he needed. Miguel snorted. Yes, to get out of here! We can't do that for you, said Sally. Miguel stared through the glass. I know you cannot. There is nothing nobody can do. Some people who said they protected the rights of migrants had come to the jail to interview certain prisoners. They told him the government could not hold him for such a long time and promised to take up his case and get him released, but so far nothing. More of his bad luck. All his life luck has been bad, but never so bad as now. God had abandoned him. Castle asked his aunt to convey his assurances that God had not abandoned Miguel, though he suspected that the Deity was indifferent to the matter of Miguel's fate. No, I am abandoned by God, Miguel insisted. Twice he saved me, first from the killer, then from dying of the cold and hunger. But why, if I am to spend my days in this terrible place, like I am a criminal? I am kept behind bars, like it was me who killed my friends. He lit a cigarette. For what reason does this happen to me?

You are a witness to a crime, Castle explained, avoiding the larger metaphysical question. If the police capture the murderer, they will ask you to identify him if you can, and to testify in court. After Sally translated, Miguel's nose twitched, as before a sneeze; it was a big, jutting nose, shaped like a toucan's beak. Identify him? All he saw was a young blond man, tall and broad-shouldered, rough-looking, you know, like un boxeador. There must be a million men who look like that in the United States. If he were standing in this very room, Miguel could not say with certainty, Yes, that was the man he'd seen shoot Héctor and Reynaldo. He had told that to the police when they sat him down in the police station in Nogales and showed him many photographs, asking if any of the faces looked familiar. None did.

Miguel glanced sidelong at the other inmates, speaking to their visitors. Then, leaning toward his, he whispered that after he'd looked at the photographs, he'd been allowed to phone his wife, Esperanza was her name. He'd told her how he'd been robbed of the money he was to pay the coyote, how he'd agreed to work off the fee by carrying drugs, how his companions had been murdered. She also had bad news. That very day, before she'd heard from her husband, a man had come to the house to demand the money for transporting him over the border. This man, Miguel surmised, must have been sent by the coyote, the fat man of the ringed fingers. Esperanza had been very frightened and confused. Where was her husband? Hadn't he paid the money? Miguel was in the United States, the emissary assured her, but the fee had not been paid. He would give her a week. If she didn't have it when he next came by, there would be much trouble. What should she do? she asked Miguel. Borrow the money, he said. Get it any way you can. These people are very dangerous.

Some days later, following his transfer to Florence, Miguel was permitted to make another call to inform his wife of his whereabouts. Had she paid the debt? She had, borrowing some from friends, some from relatives. But now there was new cause for worry. When the man returned, he'd asked Esperanza if she had heard from her esposo. Yes. What did he say? She informed him of all Miguel had told her in his first phone conversation. Then the man said, When you speak to your esposo again, we have a message for him. He is not to say nothing more to the police of what he saw. If he does, it will go very bad for him and for you. He did not see nothing, do you understand?

"So you see, it would be bad for me to say anything more to the police," Miguel said, his eyes welling up. "I would be in fear of my life! Of Esperanza's life! The lives of my children! Is there no way to get me out of here?"

Castle exchanged glances with his aunt. He felt a helpless pity, and a connection to the man—after all, both their lives, each in its own way, had been wrecked by 9/11.

The visit came to an abrupt end when one of the guards tapped Miguel on the shoulder and said, "Time's up." Castle and Sally barely had a chance to say adiós before he was led away.

"Well, there must be a way to get him out," Sally said when they were back in the car. "I'm gone to have a talk with Rodriguez."

"Maybe I'll go with you. I've got something I'd like to mention," Castle said.

"What's that?"

"You remember that Border Patrol tracker, Morales? When we were out at the crime scene, he speculated that the killer knew who and what he was after."

"So . . . ," said Sally, creasing her brow.

"So the threat that was made to Miguel's wife sort of confirms that. The killer and the coyote, the fat guy, were partners in using illegals to mule dope."

She poked his arm. "You ought to leave the detective work to the detectives."

SHE PHONED the sheriff the next day, Monday, and he agreed to make time for her. That afternoon she and Castle drove to his Nogales office, behind the county jail in a drab warehouse district across from the Southern Pacific tracks. A blocky, square-faced man with dense black hair graying at the sides, Rodriguez sat behind his desk, his chin cradled in a palm, and listened patiently as Castle, despite Sally's advice, reported the threat to Miguel's wife and presented his theory. "It does sort of suggest," he said hesitantly, "that whoever did the shooting didn't just stumble into those guys, that he was working with the coyotes."

With a smile and a nod, the sheriff humored his amateur sleuthing. "We figured that out all by ourselves," he said. "Soto's questioned a slew of snitches. So far, nothing."

"Soto?"

"The officer in charge of the investigation."

Castle remembered the detective who'd questioned him at the crime scene. "Miguel is afraid there'll be retaliation against his family," he said.

Rodriguez pointed out that he couldn't do anything about a threat made a thousand miles away in a foreign country.

"I realize that. But I thought maybe you could contact the police in Oaxaca to provide protection for his wife and kids?"

A look of impatience flitted over the sheriff's face. "You're not too familiar with Mexico, are you, Mr. Castle?"

No, he supposed he wasn't. Well then, declared Rodriguez, he should know that in the murky world of Mexican trafficking, whether the commodity was narcotics or people, it wasn't merely difficult to distinguish the cops from the criminals, it was impossible. "In other words," he continued, "I wouldn't let the police down there know that I know about the threat. Get it? We don't want to make things worse for Mr. and Mrs. Espinoza."

Castle nodded to say that he did get it and also the implication bundled into the sheriff's educational comment—that good intentions can have bad effects.

"Thanks anyway," Rodriguez said. "You've done your citizen's duty."

"That isn't all we come here for." Sally cocked her chin. "We're not quite done with this Miguel business."

The sheriff pushed his chair back, locked his fingers behind his head, and gave her an easy grin. "Had any second thoughts on my offer for those two horses, the dun and the bay?"

"I have not," she replied sharply. "And don't change the subject. It don't seem right. Or fair, locking him up there in Florence like a common criminal . . ."

"He *is* a criminal. An illegal alien who was muling dope over the border."

"You haven't charged him with a crime, have you? He's been in there going on three months it must be. He ought to be let go."

"You sure are taking a personal interest in this mojado. How come?"

"I reckon because he fetched up on our ranch," Sally said. "Kind of makes us feel responsible for him some way or the other."

"But you're not. He's my responsibility."

"Well then, isn't there something you can do?"

"You'll be happy to know there is. Miguel will be a free man within a week."

Sally flung her arms out wide. "Why in hell didn't you say so right off the bat?"

"Because I didn't know that's what you two wanted to talked about. The county attorney got a letter from some immigrant rights do-gooders, to the effect that their lawyer was going to file a motion for Miguel's release. So our lawyer advised me that to save a lot of hassle, he was going to depose Mr. Espinoza. Then we inform DHS that we're releasing him from material witness hold."

"What's that mean—depose him?" asked Sally.

"Take a deposition. A sworn statement about what he did, what he saw. It will be videotaped. Then we'll turn him over to Immigration, and he'll put be put on a bus and deported." Rodriguez raised his palms as Castle started to speak. "And your next question would be, What happens if we catch a suspect? A whole bunch of ifs. If the guy confesses, no problem. If he doesn't and if the attorney thinks there's enough evidence to go to trial, we request the Mexican authorities to get Miguel back here to testify, taxpayers' expense. That's assuming our star witness stays in Mexico. Odds are, the second he's on the other side, some enganchador will fix him up with another coyote and he'll try again, and—"

"What the hell is an enganchador?" Castle interrupted.

"A broker who connects wetbacks with coyotes. Odds are he'll find one and if—there's another *if*—he doesn't get caught or shot or kidnapped or die of thirst, he'll disappear into the U.S. And in that case, all we could do is have the deposition placed in the record, and the defendant's lawyer will move for dismissal because his client was denied his constitutional right to cross-examine the witness. Is there anything else you'd like to know?"

The question was accompanied by a glance at the clock on the wall, indicating that the past twenty minutes had been about fifteen minutes longer than he cared to spend on this subject.

So Miguel Espinoza, thought Castle, this migrant who had endured Odyssean perils and hardships for a meatpacking job paying nine dollars an hour, this droplet in the human tide flooding northward, would soon be traveling in the opposite direction, back to the poverty he'd sought to escape in the first place. Either that, or face the hazards of one more run at the border.

"And there's no other recourse?"

Rodriguez considered the question. "I suppose I could ask DHS to issue him a temporary stay permit, to keep him around to identify anybody we pick up. They're usually good for about ninety days. But with one of those in his fat little hands, Miguel will do what he'd do if he got smuggled across again—disappear. He'll find a job somewhere and disappear."

A sparkle enlivened Sally's eyes as she looked at Castle. An almost telepathic communication passed between them—a sentiment rather than a thought that they were being called to effect a second rescue, that they could no more abandon Miguel now than when Castle first found him.

"What if he didn't disappear?" she asked, turning to the sheriff.

"What if he got a job right here in Santa Cruz County and you knew where to find him if you had to?"

"What are you getting at?"

"There's a whole lot that needs doing around the ranch that's not getting done. Enough odd jobs to keep a man busy for a good while."

Rodriguez waited to absorb her comment before speaking again. "You'd hire Espinoza as your handyman?"

"Sure. If it was okay with him, and if you got this permit for him. Like you said, that little fella is only gonna try again if gets pitched back over the line, so what's the sense in it?"

A pained expression soured Rodriguez's genial face. Joining his thumb to his index and middle fingers, he rubbed a spot above the bridge of his nose. "It would be up to the feds whether to issue the permit. I'd have to convince them that we're getting somewhere on the investigation, that the interests of justice wouldn't be served if Miguel was deported. Meaning I'd have to do some heavy shading on the truth."

She dismissed the procedural problems with flaps of her wrinkled hands. "Now you listen to me, Danny boy, I know you know how to cut corners. Comes to illegals, you've got two, three of your Mexican relations living right here in Nogales who scraped their backs on barbed wire, but they're legal now, and they didn't get to be that way because they pledged allegiance to the flag."

"Careful, you don't know half of what you think you know," the sheriff said. "The bottom line is, my department isn't a day-labor agency for illegal aliens." He stood and adjusted the clip holding his black tie to his tan uniform shirt. "Now I've got a meeting with the county manager in ten minutes."

"If you just give this a little consideration, I'll consider cutting you a deal on the dun and the bay."

To Castle, the blandishment almost smacked of a transaction in a slave market—trading horses for a human being—but he could not raise finicky objections now.

Rodriguez put on a look of indignation that was not entirely convincing. "Sally, right now I almost could charge you with attempted bribery."

"Oh hell, bribery," she sniffed as he opened the door for her. "I was just offering to do a favor for a friend."

"See what I can do," the sheriff said under his breath.

. . .

Miguel was delivered to the San Ignacio like a UPS package the next weekend. On the day he arrived Blaine and Monica were in Douglas for a meeting of the Border Ranchers Association, and Castle was with Sally in the kitchen of the main house. A knock at the door interrupted them. Sally answered. A dark-complected young man who had the look of a cop but wore civilian clothes stood outside, Miguel beside him, carrying a flight bag. "Here he is," the young man said, and drove away without another word.

The story Miguel gave was this: after giving his videotaped testimony, he was taken to a courtroom in the jail for a hearing, issued a temporary visa, and to his joy, set free. Or almost free. He was driven in a caged wagon to the county jail in Nogales, where a policeman, a jefe (this must have been Rodriguez himself) informed him that a job was waiting at the rancho San Ignacio, reminded him that his permit was valid for only three months, and warned him to stay put or he would find himself locked up again. Miguel had nothing but the clothes on his back, his visa, a change of socks and underwear, and a toothbrush in the flight bag, but he considered himself a fortunate man, for once. He was five feet four inches and 150 pounds of gratitude, and he embraced his benefactors.

Rodriguez appeared the following day, pulling a stock trailer behind his pickup. He said he would like another look at the horses, and after he'd taken one, he made an offer. Sally accepted it without further discussion. The dun and the bay were loaded into the trailer. Only then did the sheriff acknowledge Miguel's presence—she had already put him to work pruning her mulberry trees.

"I'll lay odds that that wet takes off on you first chance he gets," Rodriguez said.

"You're on, Danny." As he drove away, she turned to Castle with a triumphant look. "Didn't I say he knew how to cut corners?"

And that was how Miguel Espinoza became an employee of the San Ignacio Cattle Company. Sally started him at a salary of eight hundred a month and put him up, rent free, in a small Airstream trailer parked behind Gerardo and Elena's house. It served as bunkhouse for itinerant cowhands during the branding and roundup seasons. Elena was happy with her new neighbor—it would be nice to have someone else to talk to—but her husband was displeased, very much displeased. He insisted that the trailer be moved someplace else, the farther from his house the better. "¿Por qué?" asked Sally. "Está bien donde está." Meaning, Castle gathered, that she thought the trailer was fine where it was. Gerardo would not say why he wanted it moved, but remained adamant. He was perhaps the only person around capable of defying Sally's wishes. With his help, Castle hitched the Airstream to his Suburban and towed it to a shady, level spot a short distance from his cabin. Gerardo shook his head and said, "No. Este lugar no es bueno. Ahora está muy cerca a tu casa." Castle's Spanish having slightly improved, he understood that the trailer's new location also did not meet with his approval, that it was too close to Castle's dwelling. "No comprendo," Castle said. "What's the matter?" Tipping his hat back, Gerardo gave him an earnest look. "Hágame caso, Señor Gil. Este mojado trae la mala suerte." Aside from his name and the Mexican slang for wetback—mojado—Castle understood nothing. In any event, he was not going to haul the Airstream all over looking for a site that met Gerardo's specifications, whatever those were. "It's okay here," he said. "¿Comprende? Está bien aquí." The vaquero shrugged, as if to say, *Whatever you want*, and Castle backed the trailer in.

When he returned to the main house, Sally was interrogating her new hire. Had he ever done house painting before? Oh, yes. After his produce business had gone bankrupt, he'd done many small jobs to make ends meet. She assigned him to begin scraping the blistered window frames and outside woodwork; then she and Castle went to Nogales to buy primer, paint, rollers, and brushes. On the way, he mentioned the words Gerardo had spoken to him—he was pretty sure he recalled them correctly—and asked for a translation.

"He was telling you to heed his words that the wetback brings bad luck," she said.

"What the hell did he mean by that?"

"Ask him. Been around Mexicans all my life, Gil, and one thing I learned is that they don't think the same as us. It's the Catholic Church and all that Indian blood."

"What would the Catholic Church have to do with it?"

"It's a spooky religion. You mix it with lots of Indian blood, and you get folks who think spooky."

At Home Depot, through her thick eyeglasses, Sally peered at color charts for an hour before she settled on the right shade of light brown for the exterior walls, the right tone of blue for the window frames and trim. By the time she and Castle returned, in the late afternoon, Miguel had finished scraping and sanding the front windows down to bare wood and was hard at work on the side.

"Now look at that!" Sally marveled. "It had been a gringo, he'd call it a day and be having a beer. Where did that nonsense about lazy Mexicans ever get started? Never seen a one of 'em didn't work his tail off."

When Blaine and Monica got back from Douglas on Sunday afternoon, Miguel was painting the fascia boards under the front porch and Castle was in the cramped office off the living room, going over the books with his aunt to determine if the ranch could afford even so meager a salary as she'd offered. It could, just barely—Monica had not been exaggerating months ago, when she'd described the San Ignacio's profit margin as being "thin as a credit card." Outside they heard Blaine's truck pull into the yard and him exclaim, "What the hell is this!" Sally sighed and said, "Well, here we go," and went into the living room, Castle following her. They hadn't mentioned their meeting with the sheriff, because they hadn't thought anything would come of it; so Blaine and Monica were completely surprised to find Miguel on the premises.

"Welcome back," Sally said as her son and daughter-in-law came in and set their suitcases down. "How'd things go in Douglas?"

"Fine," Blaine replied, frowning. "Ma, that Mexican outside, that's—"

"It is. Sit down. A lot has gone on the past couple of days."

Blaine clomped across the tile floor and sank into the long leather sofa. Monica sat next to him. Sally remained on her feet, apparently to hold the advantage, as she explained how the ranch's payroll had been increased by one.

"You sold two horses for half their worth and hired that wet without talkin' to me first?" he railed. "Goddammit, Ma, you haven't made one good business decision in the last ten years, but this beats 'em all."

"Don't you lecture me!" she retaliated, wagging a finger in a parody of a scolding schoolmarm.

"All right, you two, don't start," Monica said. "Sally, Blaine is right. You should have consulted us first." She turned to Castle and chastised him for not saying anything. "It's like you two were intriguing behind our backs."

He wished he could vanish. He was little more than a guest here and had no right to meddle in the ranch's business affairs.

"Eight hundred a month for a handyman we don't need, an illegal to boot," Blaine carried on.

"For the time being, he's legal. And I'll remind you that your bosom amigo, Gerardo, wasn't legal when he came here, wasn't till that amnesty back in 'eighty-six. And eight hundred a month is only half what we'd pay a regular ranch hand. Far as my business sense goes, I've seen a dozen families sell out since I've been running this place, and we're still here."

"We wouldn't be if I had left it all up to you."

"Now, you listen to me. I still pay the piper around here, and I call the tune. Me and Gil have had a look at the accounts, and we can afford him."

Blaine turned to, or, rather, *on* his cousin. "Seems to me you've got a lot of time on your hands. You could of done this beautification project free of charge, or is that kinda work beneath you?"

Eight hundred a month, he thought. The part of his portfolio he'd kept for himself earned four hundred *a day* every day from dividends and interest alone. Ignoring his cousin's jibe, he said he would help out with Miguel's wages.

Blaine laughed sarcastically. "Damn generous of you, Mr. Deep Pockets. Know what I'm of a mind to do? Fire that little son of a bitch and drive him to the border myself and toss his wetback ass over the fence back into Mexico."

"Oh, Blaine!" Monica said. "Stop that! You sound like a trailer-park redneck. Look, how about I mix a batch of margaritas, and we can all have a drink and talk this over like civilized people."

"I *am* a goddamn redneck and I don't want a margarita!". He stomped into the kitchen, where he pulled a Tecate from the refrigerator. Returning to the sofa, he ripped the top off the can and guzzled, smacking his lips. "There we go—beer is what us rednecks drink. Too bad it ain't a Bud Light. Tell you what, cuzzy—"

"You can stop that cuzzy stuff," Castle said in a level voice.

"All right, then, *Gil.* Gil, you are gone to do more than help out with our handyman's wages. You'll pay all of 'em."

The next day, taking to heart Blaine's remarks about hard manual labor being beneath him, Castle pitched in, wielding a paintbrush alongside Miguel. It made for a charming picture, one that touched the egalitarian regions of his nature: the migrant and the onetime senior vice president of the fourth-largest investment firm on earth, working side by side in the hot sun. That evening he invited Miguel to dinner in his cabin, where he cooked a can of beans and a few quail left over in the freezer. The two men began instructing each other in their native languages. ¿Cómo se dice frijoles en inglés? *Beans.* ¿Cómo se llama esto en español?—pointing at Sam, lying on her bed in front of the stove—*perro.* En inglés, *dog.* ¿Cómo se llama esto?—holding up a fork—*tenedor.*

The next day, with the aid of a dictionary and a phrase book, Castle learned the names of Miguel's children, that the vegetables he'd exported had come off an uncle's farm, and that until his flight to the United States, he had never been farther than a few miles from Oaxaca. Castle attempted to relate some of his own biography, but his Spanish was too primitive for such a complicated story. All Miguel got out of it was that his American companion had been widowed, and for that he was sorry. It wasn't good for a man to be alone. A friendship grew between them, or as much friendship as there could be between two men who could barely communicate.

Castle had arranged for eight hundred dollars to be automatically transferred from his account to the San Ignacio's bank in Tucson each month. At the end of his first week on the job, Sally paid Miguel two hundred, then Castle drove him to a Western Union in Nogales so he could wire money to his wife.

Afterward he had dinner with Tessa at her place. He'd seen her regularly since his trip to Florence and had kept her abreast of each episode in the ongoing series that was Miguel Espinoza. She remarked that he was going a bit overboard: he'd practically made Miguel his ward. Was it really necessary to chauffeur him all the way to Nogales? He answered that he probably would not have done any of it had it not been for her—she had liberated him, she'd opened the door through which he had stepped back into the world, into *life.* But her remark got him thinking. Am I going to these lengths for my own benefit as much as for his? Well, so what if he was? There was such a thing as selfish altruism.

The painting was finished in two weeks. The pale brown walls shone like wet sand, and the blue on the door and window frames mimicked the color of the Arizona sky. The sight of the house changed Blaine's feelings toward his new employee. "Looks like it was just built," he said with some exaggeration. "Damn good job. Hell, with the outside lookin' like this, can't have the inside lookin' like it does, so he might as well do it."

But Gerardo continued to maintain a distance, hardly exchanging more than a buenos días or a buenas tardes with Miguel. Castle often reflected on Gerardo's comment and once thought he grasped its meaning. It was a moment on another trip to the Western Union. A man hurriedly wheeling a shopping cart laden with groceries and a screaming child—the Western Union was in the Safeway—accidentally crashed into Miguel, almost knocking him down. The howling kid had put the reckless cart-pusher in a bad temper. Instead of apologizing, he snarled, "Watch where you're going!" Castle stepped in and said, "You should watch where you're going," and came close to getting into a fistfight, which he would have lost—the man was twenty years younger and as many pounds heavier than he. With the altercation over, Miguel looked silently at Castle as he rubbed his ribs. It was then that Castle saw him through the hard, unsentimental eyes of the old vaquero. Miguel was a natural-born victim. Hadn't he said as much himself? "*All my life my luck has been bad.*" A peculiar kind of bad luck, though, a contagious bad luck. He had a sweet, sad, hapless quality that elicited tender feelings in people like Castle and Sally at the same time that it provoked, indeed, seemed to *invite*, the blind cruelty in the world to strike him; and because that cruelty was indiscriminate, it was as likely to fall on others—Héctor and Reynaldo came immediately to mind—as on him.

This perception no sooner came to Castle than he dismissed it as nonsense, hoodoo, what his aunt would have called spooky thinking. Later, when Gerardo's presentiment proved accurate, he would wonder if it was a mistake to trust his reason over his instincts. Miguel was not responsible for the events that took place on the San Ignacio that summer, no more than he'd been responsible for the deaths of his friends; yet such an uncanny occurrence of misfortunes followed his arrival that he seemed to be their cause. It was as though his mere presence had summoned a malice—the senseless malice Castle sought to evade—to come in, come in.

Ben Erskine

Transcript of interview with Martín Mendoza, 75, conducted at Mr. Mendoza's residence in Patagonia, Arizona, on August 30, 1966. This transcript has been translated from the Spanish by the AHS.

Ghosts and bones.

That is what I think of when I think of that old ranch, the IB-Bar. Don Benjamín put the bones in the ground, and sometimes their ghosts, you know, walked around. I think soon my bones will be in the ground, too, but they will be next to the bones of my wife and I will be happy there, so my ghost will not walk around. Do you hear how I speak? A lot of people like my voice, they say it sounds like the voice of one who speaks on the radio. A doctor has told me that I have in my throat a cancer, from too many cigars, and it is this cancer that will soon put my bones in the ground. Many of them are broken. I was a vaquero from the time I was a boy. Bad horses have thrown me. Bad cows have smashed me against the boards of corrals.

I was Don Benjamín's good friend. We rode together for many years, more than twenty. We captured wild bulls in the mountains. We captured the gray horse, the one he called Spirit. We took guns into Mexico for the Yaqui. I have Yaqui blood, you know. My mother was Yaqui, and her father, my grandfather, was a very fine deer dancer, a pure Yaqui, what is called Yoeme, a man with magic in his heart. You know, in this world there are people with magic in their hearts and people with disturbances in their hearts.

I do not know what was in Benjamín's heart. He was a gringo, and their hearts are difficult to know. My wife Lourdes was a little afraid of him. Sometimes she told me, "There is a devil in that man." She said she could see it, this demon she could feel it. I thought she was being foolish. Then, one day, maybe I saw this devil with my own eyes.

So now I will tell a secret. I have been the guardian of this secret for a very long time. I had sworn to Benjamín I would never tell it, but he is dead now ten years, so I do not think his soul will be angry with me.

I think it was in the year 1919. It was in the summer, a good summer when a great many squalls blew in from the southwest and brought rain that was badly needed. A good summer, yes, but a bad time. There was war in Mexico, and bandits and rebels crossed the border all the time to make raids on ranches for horses, for cattle, whatever they could steal. Benjamín and me, we never went anywhere without our pistols and rifles. We had loaded Winchesters in our houses and taught our wives to shoot them for when we were not there.

So one day we were looking for some missing cattle, me and Benjamín and two young gringo vaqueros who worked for his hermano, for Señor Jeffrey. Parker and Bond, yes, I remember their names. We discovered that these cattle were stolen and taken into Mexico. We followed their trail into Mexico. A big rain fell and washed out the trail, and after the rain stopped, Benjamín said we must keep looking, so we did. Pretty quick we saw a herd of Herefords, which were like ours. We rode over to inspect the brands, and we discovered that they did not belong to us. Benjamín, he said, "It makes no difference, we will take these cattle." I told him that this was not a good idea, but he did not listen. I had heard stories from him that long before he and Señor Jeffrey had taken Mexican cattle and had got away with it. Maybe he thought he would again.

But he did not. We were rounding up the cows when we were surprised by the owner and two of his vaqueros. We were so busy gathering the cattle that we did not see them ride up with their pistols drawn. They took our guns from us, and the owner—he was called Diego Puerta—asked who was our boss, and Benjamín said that he was. Don Diego said that me and Parker and Bond were free to go, but that Benjamín must come with him to explain himself to the rurales. We said no, we will stay with our boss, to do anything else would be, you know, very cowardly. But Don Benjamín, he was no coward, no, he was very brave. He said to us that there was no need for us to risk ourselves, and that we should do as Don Diego said and ride back to the border and report to Señor Jeffrey that he was arrested. This was, as I have said to you, very brave because the rurales would throw him in jail for a long time and maybe even hang him.

So we rode very fast to the line, but after we got across, we reined our horses and talked about what to do next. We felt very bad, leaving Benjamín like that.

Then we saw riders coming toward us from the south. In one more minute we saw that they were Don Diego's vaqueros and they were leading two horses—Don Diego's and Spirit. Don Diego was walking behind them with Benjamín, who had his special pistol—the Luger automatic—stuck in the back of Don Diego's head. We could not speak. We thought that maybe we were seeing a vision.

Benjamín pushed Don Diego across the border, into the hands of Parker and Bond. He told them to hold on to Don Diego. Then, with his pistol aimed at the vaqueros, he went to the saddlebags on Spirit and took our guns from them and gave them back to us. He had recovered his gun and our guns! We were even more amazed. Then Benjamín grabbed Don Diego and pushed him down to his hands and knees and kicked him in the butt, you know, like he would kick a dog. He kicked him twice. He kicked him over the border, back into Mexico, and said that Don Diego should go back to where he came from. Parker and Bond were laughing. Don Diego stood up, very angry, and he called to his vaqueros, "Shoot him! Kill him!" But the vaqueros' guns were in their holsters, and we had ours pointed at them, and there was nothing they could do. Don Diego mounted his horse and looked at Benjamín and said, "You are going to die for this." Then he rode away with his men.

We rode toward the ranch. Parker and Bond laughed some more. They shook Benjamín's hand, they slapped his back, they asked him how he had worked this magic. How had he, the captive, become the captor? Benjamín did not explain, he wished to keep his magic secret. Me, I was not laughing. I had a bad feeling. Don Diego was more than a ranchero, he was an hacendado, a man of great dignity. I thought Benjamín should have been happy to have won back his liberty. For him to kick Don Diego in the butt, to disgrace him and humiliate him before the very eyes of his men, that was going too far. On the ride home I whispered to Benjamín, "He means what he says. He will try to kill you." Do you know what he said to me? "I know." That was all. "I know."

One day two men on horseback came to the ranch, old friends of Benjamín's. They had fought with him in the Revolution. They came to him with a warning—Don Diego had offered a big reward to anyone who killed him. Two hundred and fifty dollars. In those times Mexico was full of desperate men who would have killed anyone for a few pesos.

The following days were difficult. They were most difficult for our women. La señora Ida was carrying a child, and so was Lourdes. She was angry with Benjamín and with me, too. "You were no better than the thieves who stole our cattle," she said. "You will be lucky if God does not punish you." We ate dinner together almost every night, the four of us, and I remember many nights when the ranch dogs started barking and Benjamín would place his Luger on the dining table, and we blew out the lamps and sat quietly in the dark, listening for footsteps, for the sound of horses' hooves.

Now the thing I swore not to tell. This happened on a very hot day in September, after the squalls were finished. Benjamín and me had to go out and move some cattle from grazing land he rented from the government. We were going to move the cattle closer to a water hole. We rode down a road through country that was very good country for an ambush—a lot of hills and woods and arroyos and canyons. Both of us were on the lookout. It was very still, no wind, and the only sound we could hear were the calls of the Mexican jays. We listened for other sounds, you know, a man's cough, or the snorting of a horse, or rustling in the brush. And we looked side to side into the trees for something that should not be there, like the shining of a rifle barrel in the sun.

We came to the top of a hill. Not too far ahead, on the road, we saw two mounted men approaching us. Benjamín pulled Spirit off the road and dismounted and drew his Winchester from the scabbard on his saddle. He did this very quickly and signaled me to come with him, and I did. We climbed up a big rock that looked over the road. We laid down there. I had my pistol out. We could see the riders, but they could not see us. They came closer—Mexicans, wearing straw hats and sandals and dirty white shirts. A big man and a small one. The big man rode in front, with a shotgun across the pommel of his saddle. The small man was not armed and rode a burro and led another with heavy sacks roped to its packsaddle.

I returned my pistol to the holster and said in a low voice, "Peons. They are not assassins."

Benjamín whispered to me that maybe they were assassins who were trying to look like peons.

Pretty soon the big man on the horse was right below us. Benjamín jumped up and aimed the Winchester and shouted, "Halt! Hands up!" The big man was startled, as who would not be who finds himself on a lonely road and a man pointing a rifle at him from above? I think he thought we were bandits. He jerked his head around and yelled to the smaller one, "My son, watch out!" I do not know if Benjamín heard that. I know I did. When he did that, he turned around in the saddle, his shotgun slipped from the pommel and he went to grab it to keep it from falling to the ground, and that was when Benjamín shot him.

All of this happened, you understand, very fast. The big man fell from the horse, and his foot got caught in the stirrup, and the frightened horse ran very fast into the woods, dragging him. At the same time the small man dropped his lead rope and turned his burro to flee. Quickly, very, very quickly, Benjamín worked the lever of his rifle and shot him in the back, and he fell, and the riding burro and the pack burro both went crazy, bucking and jumping. One ran off in one direction, the pack burro in another direction. It crashed into a tree, it was so crazy, and the sacks came off and spilled the things inside.

"Let us make sure they are finished!" Benjamín said to me, and we climbed off the rock and followed the blood trail of the big man into the woods. We found him lying on the rocks of an arroyo not too far away. His horse had bucked his foot from the stirrup and had run away somewhere. Benjamín threw a rock at the big man to make sure he was dead. He was. There was a bullet hole in his shoulder, but the thing that killed him was his galloping horse dragging him over the rocks. His face and head were all smashed up, like somebody had beat him with a club. It was a terrible thing to see.

We ran back to the road to look at the small man. He, too, was dead. The bullet had gone right through him, made a big hole in his chest coming out. We saw that when we turned him over, and that he was not a small man but only a boy. Maybe thirteen, maybe fourteen. And that was when I knew I had heard correctly when I heard the big man call out, "My son!" I went over to see what had come out of the sacks on the pack burro. I found bags of tobacco and whiskey and beer bottles packed in straw, and I cried out, "Ayyy, Benjamín, they are not assassins, like I told you. They are smugglers. Smugglers and nothing more."

Yes, that was all, and small-timers, too, a father and his son making some extra money smuggling whiskey and tobacco into Mexico. You see, in those times, before alcohol was forbidden in the United States, Mexicans would buy it in the United States and bring it into Mexico because whiskey, and tobacco, too, had big taxes on them.

"If they are smugglers," Benjamín asked me, "why were they riding north with the contraband?" I answered him, "I don't know. How can I know? But they cannot be assassins."

I remember Benjamín going down on one knee, holding his rifle, and looking at the dead boy. He looked at him for a long time without saying nothing. I do not know what he was thinking. I did know what I was thinking, that my friend had murdered these two peons and that I was at his side when he did. I had fear of my own thoughts.

After a time Benjamín stood up and said he was sorry that this must happen. If he had known it was only a boy, he would not have shot him. If the big man had not gone for his shotgun, he would not have shot him. Me, I was not sure the big man had reached for the shotgun, and even if he had, what was Benjamín to expect, jumping up like that aiming a rifle at a man on a lonely road? But what did any of that matter?

Benjamín said we must bury them, and we did. Ghosts and bones! We dragged the boy to where his father lay in the arroyo, and we piled rocks on top of them. It took a long time. We buried the shotgun and the contraband, too, because, I think, Benjamín worried that someone might find them and ask questions. In those days, you know, gringos often got away with killing Mexicans, but because he had shot a little boy in the back, I think Benjamín feared he would not get away with it.

He said he was not going to speak of this to nobody, not even to his wife, Ida. And I was not to say nothing to nobody. He made me swear it. I will always remember how he looked at me—his eyes were gray and hard, like the metal of a gun. I was to take, you know, an oath, and I did, because I could not betray my friend, and for another reason. I was like Lourdes. I was a little afraid of him.

15

THE TRIBULATIONS THAT WERE to afflict the San Ignacio, the bad luck of Gerardo's foreboding (though not all of it, as would be discovered, was blind bad luck) began on a warm, windy day in June. Castle, still eager to show Blaine that he was willing to pitch in with the ranch's dirty work, had volunteered to help rebuild a fence in a remote pasture. It had been torn apart, apparently by illegal aliens, and an irrigation pipe had been cut, draining a storage tank dry. As Blaine planned to graze cattle in that pasture later on, to fatten them on the succulent grass that would sprout with the summer monsoons, the repairs had to be done now.

Right after dawn Castle set off on foot for the main house, walking Sam on lead; on lead because the weather had turned hot enough to wake up the rattlesnakes. Gerardo had recently shot a four-foot-long Mojave near the horse corrals. Impatient to run and hunt, as always, Sam strained at the leash, towing her master along at better than four miles an hour. At that pace, he was the picture of a fit middle-aged male, enjoying a brisk walk; but the frown that cut a vertical ditch in his forehead indicated that something was on his mind. And there was. He and Tessa had had their first quarrel.

Two nights earlier they had gone to dinner and the movies in Tucson. Too tired to make the long drive home, they had checked in to a motel off the freeway. The anodyne anonymity of their room was oddly exciting; it aroused them into the abandoned lovemaking of romantic desperadoes snatching a night together. In the morning, as he checked out, he picked up a newspaper at the front desk. When he noticed the date—June 12—the night's lingering joys and pleasures curdled into shame.

He was withdrawn on the return trip, and he could not shake off his sullen mood. When they arrived at her place, troubled by the change in him, Tessa asked what was the matter.

"Nothing," he'd answered. What else could he say?

"Nothing? One minute you can't get enough of me, the next you hardly say a word for sixty miles."

"Look, I can't explain it to myself," he said, annoyed with her for asking for an explanation, and with himself for his inability to offer one. "Yesterday was her birthday. I didn't even realize it till I picked up the paper in the motel. She would have been forty-four."

Tessa sat with her hand on the door handle and sighed. "And you're not feeling quite right about last night, are you? It felt like a dirty weekend. It felt like adultery."

"A dirty weekend? *Adultery?*" he echoed. "No, no, it wasn't that." He wasn't able to go on; the accuracy of her intuition—not quite a bull's-eye but close enough—left him tongue-tied.

"Know what?" said Tessa, not without anger. "I am not going to be in the ridiculous position of competing with a ghost."

"For chrissake, Tess, that's off base."

"I don't think so." She got out of the car and stood looking at him through the open door. "I thought you had things sorted out. I guess you don't. You need more time, and I'm giving it to you."

"Meaning?"

"Meaning you know what. Call me when you've got it figured out."

He thought that she was being unreasonable, insensitive to his situation. Did she really believe a man who'd lost his wife in such a manner would get over it in less than two years? "I get it," he said, losing his temper. "You've been waiting for an excuse like this. Drive 'em crazy and drop 'em, you said that about yourself. Fuck 'em and forget 'em." Instantly, he regretted his words and apologized; but it was like firing a gun and then trying to recall the bullet.

"I ought to slap your face!"

Then she slammed the door and stomped off toward her front door.

Now, walking along, he pictured her abundant hair and the pinpoints glinting in her irises, like amber chips in brown earth; he heard her contralto voice in its various modes—frank, tender, flip—and knew life would be bleak without her. But he was wary of the happiness Tessa brought him. He'd written to Morgan and Justine last month, telling them about his new relationship. He'd thought then that he was seeking their approval, which he got in a letter from Morgan—no e-mail, but a real letter in her loopy schoolgirl's hand—expressing their delight, their hope to come out to Arizona soon and meet Tessa. But he wondered now if he'd secretly wanted their disapproval, to confirm that the voice in his own head, the voice that objected to love, that rebuked happiness, was the one he should listen to.

Sam jerked him out of these cloudy reflections, lunging toward the oak-shaded arroyo beside the road. She fell into a hard point. A Mearns' pair burst from under a skein of fallen branches, the hen streaking off to the left, the cock quartering away into the trees beyond the arroyo. Sam started to dash in the direction of the hen's flight. Castle checked her when he saw a rattler basking on a rock not five yards away. He tugged the dog back onto the road, his heart pounding.

Road and arroyo wound down to the grassy flat that contained the cheerful clutter of ranch headquarters, considerably less cluttered since he and Miguel had cleaned up the backyard, hauling truckloads of junk to the Patagonia landfill. His mood improved—the scare had been somehow therapeutic—he called out a "Good morning" to Sally, who was tossing supplement from a canvas morral to her geriatric pets.

"Mornin', Gil," she replied from behind the rough-board corral.

"Saw a rattler on my way down, about the size of the one Gerardo killed."

She shrugged; rattlesnakes were so common this time of year, he might as well have told her he'd seen a squirrel.

"Didn't stick around to see if it was a Mojave or a diamondback."

"A Mojave is greenish, a d-back is more brown. Either one would ruin your day." She walked off with her morral, summoning her animals to "come and get it or forget it."

Castle released Sam to run around with Blaine's Australian heelers in the backyard, enclosed by chicken wire fastened to rough oak posts. In the middle of the yard the rusted remains of a Model-T truck sat on its rims like an iron sculpture. It was the one piece of scrap that had not been hauled away, partly because it was too big, mostly because Blaine would not part with it. It had been their grandfather's first truck, which made it a treasured heirloom. Looking at the corroded antique, the tidy yard, the dogs chasing each other, a feeling of pride overtook Castle, though he had no stake in this ranch beyond the little bit of sweat equity he'd put into it. He'd made a discovery at his cabin. A chunk of plaster had flaked off a corner of an outer wall, exposing the adobe brick. A name and date, J. B. ERSKINE—1912, had been inscribed on one, probably with a finger or a stick before the mud had hardened. He'd been told the cabin had been the original homestead, but to see the archaeological proof gave him a quiet thrill. Knowing that the same walls that had sheltered his ancestors now sheltered him gave him a sense of continuity, of belonging. The two-room adobe was no longer a provisional hideout; it was home.

"How'd you get here?" Blaine said, coming out of the house.

"I walked, for the exercise."

Blaine took off his hat, ruffled the rooster's crest atop his head, and snorted. Walking was no way to get anywhere so long as a horse or pickup was handy; walking for exercise was beyond pointless.

"Well, if that's what you want, you'll get your fill today," Blaine said.

Miguel, supervised by a scowling Gerardo, was loading Blaine's Ford with gear: doughnuts of barbed wire resembling steel crowns of thorn, flexible irrigation pipe, bundles of T-posts, and two post drivers. He was struggling with one of the drivers, so Castle helped him lift it into the truck. It consisted of a solid piece of cast iron with short handles attached, tapering down to a tube about a yard long. It must have weighed forty or fifty pounds.

They piled in, Miguel riding outside in the bed, Gerardo in the front seat, Castle in the rear, which closely resembled the interior of a Dumpster—tools, plastic bags, work gloves, a shovel, stained Carhartt coats stiffened from dried sweat.

Blaine lowered the window and called to his mother that they were leaving.

"Figured you'd got in the truck to go somewheres," Sally answered back, shambling out of the corral.

"Count on her to make some smart-mouth remark no matter what the occasion," Blaine grumbled as they started off, the Ford with its worn shocks rocking down a rough road like a small boat in heavy seas. "Look at her, feedin' those damn animals in her PJs and bathrobe. That longhorn is the most pampered bovine ever to walk on four legs. Got the run of the place, not afraid of man nor horse, no sir, no respect at all. The whole reason she paid good money for that son of a bitch was because it reminded her of the old days of the open range. She can be mean as a female rattler with PMS, but she's got her sentimental side. If the longhorn ain't, that Mexican in back is the living proof."

Castle said nothing. Miguel was living proof that he also had his sentimental side.

"Her eightieth birthday is comin up the end of the month," Blaine went on. "I need your advice, Gil. More'n that, I need your help with something."

"I'm listening," Castle said. It was unprecedented for his cousin to ask his advice about anything.

"It's like this. Ma owns half the ranch, and me and Monica the other half. We put the ranch into conservation easements about ten years ago, so it ain't worth what it would be if we'd held on to development rights. Still and all, land values have gone up, and I figure her share would come in north of five million."

"And you'd owe estate taxes on four million of that when she dies," Castle said, guessing at Blaine's line of thought.

"Which we ain't got. We'd either have to borrow the money or sell it. Break up the ranch. And if we sold it, we'd owe capital gains on top of the estate taxes. I had a talk with a lawyer a while back, and he told me that he thought a trust would be a good idea. Ma would put her fifty percent in something he called a LIRT—"

"A living irrevocable trust, right," said Castle, pleased to show his expertise.

"And that's where I need your help. The way he explained it, Ma would turn things over to a trustee, who'd have a say in how they was run. You'd have an easier time convincing an airline pilot to turn his plane over to a passenger. Monica calls the old lady a control freak. I call her mule-stubborn and set in her ways. Hell, it took us more'n a year to talk her into the conservation easements. But I think if you talked to her—"

"Me?"

"She won't listen to me. Thinks I'm an eighteen-year-old, and a dumb one besides." Blaine paused to negotiate a difficult stretch of road, where foot-deep ruts ran like crooked rails alongside a rock-cobbled hump that would break an axle at any speed over three miles an hour. "But she respects you. Brags on you to her old-biddy friends. How she's got this nephew who was a Wall Street big shot."

Castle laughed. "That's because she's never met a real Wall Street big shot. I was pretty much a middle shot."

"Whatever kind of shot you were, she might just listen to you. Takin' care of this ranch is what gets me up in the morning. Don't think I could get up without it."

" 'Sung to the land,' " Castle said. "I think that's how you put it."

"It's how that Aussie I knew in Vietnam put it. This is land with a history, damn straight it is. This road we're on was an old Spanish trace that run from Chihuahua in Mexico all the way to San Diego. I saw it marked on a vellum map that must have been two hundred years old. Spaniards was runnin' cattle here before there was a United States. I think about that and about Ben and Jeff homesteading this place and how they had to fight off rustlers and droughts and hung on in the Depression, and it's like we don't own it, it's like we . . . well, I can't think of the words."

"Like it's been entrusted to you?"

"That would be about right. It would damn near kill me to lose it or any part of it."

And, Castle reflected, looking at the wind-brushed ranges, the oaks, the gyring hawks, he did not want to lose it either. "All right. I'll talk to her, first chance I get."

They drove on, not much faster than had the Spanish traders in their creaking oxcarts, swung off onto a two-track leading across a meadow of grama and red-stemmed hog potato, and stopped near a windmill at the mouth of a canyon. The storage tank stood close by, and the ground all around it had been turned into a small marsh, wet grass sparkling in the sunlight, ponds glimmering in the low spots. They climbed out and sloshed through the muck to the tank, which Blaine tapped twice with a rock, both taps producing a hollow ring.

"Son of a bitch," he said in a low voice. "Gerardo wasn't kiddin'. Bone dry. Five thousand gallons wasted, just wasted." He picked up the black rubber pipe, roughly the thickness of a fire hose, that snaked from the tank to a round trough several yards away. "They wanted a drink, all they had to do was turn on the pump on the tank and then turn it off. Instead they cut the goddamn pipe."

"Hay mucha basura—allí," Gerardo said, motioning toward a wide draw.

They went to it, and looked down into a miniature landfill. Scattered up and down the draw were jackets, socks, trousers, gallon water jugs, men's briefs and women's panties, cosmetic kits, empty cigarette packages, combs, hairbrushes, candles, boots, tennis shoes, religious cards bearing pictures of the Virgin or of the Sacred Heart, dripping blood.

"This fuckin' mess wasn't left by one bunch," Blaine said. "Somebody's been runnin' wetbacks through here, and that's peculiar. Drug mules are what we usually get." He picked up one of the cosmetic kits—it resembled a tiny paint box—and tossed it aside. "Nope, wasn't drug mules who left this. Don't know many who wear lipstick. Let's get to the fence."

It spanned the canyon for a distance of about fifty yards and had been knocked down completely in two places, while in other places wobbly stakes leaned, wires sagged or hung like barbed tendrils. Footprints were everywhere, footprints on footprints, and tire marks as well.

"See what happened, cuzzy? That draw yonder winds down to the border, about three miles away. The coyotes have been walkin' 'em across the line and up the draw to here. The last bunch cut the pipe and changed clothes and washed up—that's so they don't look or smell like illegals when they get to wherever they're goin'. Then they waited for their rides. The drivers made a couple of gates by smashin' their trucks right through the fence. If I gotta choose between coyotes and drug mules, I'll take the mules any day. They've got better manners, they ain't messy. All right, we'll have to string some new wire and replace or reset the T-posts, one end to the other."

He backed the truck up to the fence, and they unloaded the wire, posts, and drivers.

"This is how it's done," he said, grabbing a driver by its handles. Grunting from the strain, he raised it, slipping the hollow end over the top of the stake, then let it drop, giving gravity a boost with a hard downward thrust of his arms. The iron core at the top end of the driver banged into the post, hammering it an inch or so into the ground. "All there is to it. Have at it."

Castle grasped the handles and, bending his knees, heaved the monster upward until his quivering arms were extended almost straight out. He let it fall, giving it a shove at the same time, and steel rang on steel, and the post sank another inch.

"Five, six inches to go." Blaine tapped Castle on the back of the neck. "We call post drivers crybabies, and now you see why. Ten minutes with one of those brings tears to a grown man's eyes."

Miguel and Gerardo started at one end of the canyon, Blaine and Castle at the other. They stayed at it all morning, spelling each other on the post drivers, cutting old wire, stringing new, pausing only to mop their faces or drink warm water from saddle canteens. No tears had come to Castle's eyes, but he did shed blood and sweat, his arms clawed by the barbs, the sun a furnace burning with a directness and intensity unknown at more northerly latitudes. When the job was done, his shoulders were so sore, he felt as if he'd been doing bench presses for the past two or three hours; but the hard labor had banished the last remnants of the gloomy introspection that had plagued him earlier. Maybe I need more of this, he thought, looking with satisfaction at the fence, all set to rights, the new wire taut and glimmering in the fierce midday light.

They wolfed sandwiches, washing them down with cold beers from the cooler. After lunch Blaine fetched two boxes of plastic lawn bags from the truck and told Castle and Miguel to pick up the garbage while he and Gerardo mended the broken water line. The janitorial task wasn't to be undertaken for aesthetic or sanitary purposes. Cattle would eat almost anything; a cow could choke to death trying to swallow a jacket, and the shards of a plastic water jug could tear her intestines.

"This shit pisses me off more'n the fence or the storage tank," Blaine said in a bitter tone. "It's like a mob broke into my house and trashed the place."

Though Castle understood his cousin's resentment—turning this pristine landscape into a garbage dump bespoke a carelessness that pissed him off, too—he found items in the litter that stirred his curiosity, even his compassion. A paperback book, *El diario de Anne Frank*, with a woman's name written on the flyleaf. A well-tailored sport jacket, neatly folded, as if its owner expected to come back for it at any moment. These were not the possessions of poor, semiliterate, itinerant farm workers. What had driven them to turn themselves into human contraband, to be bootlegged across an imaginary line in the desert? Perhaps they saw what the settlers and fortune seekers had seen, crossing the Great Plains, what the Irish and Poles and Jews and Italians (like Castle's own great-grandfather) had seen, shimmering beyond the western ocean: gold and land for the taking, yes, a chance to change one's luck, yes, but more: a promise as wide as the continent, as boundless as the human imagination, that seemed to say, *Here all things are possible*. What things almost didn't matter. To clarify them by naming them would be to vulgarize that sublime expectation, that ineffable dream in the minds of the awake. As that promise had beckoned the migrants of long ago westward, so had it called these northward. Were these thoughts more examples of sentimentality? Castle asked himself. Was he romanticizing? He couldn't dismiss the possibility that the multitudes pouring out of the south were merely going where the dollars were and regarded America as nothing more than a vast employment agency. This much he was sure of—he wasn't filling trash bags with clothes and shoes and backpacks but with the discarded pasts of people intent on remaking their lives. In that sense, he and they were citizens of the same country.

He didn't dare express any of this to Blaine when, the repairs to the water line completed, he and Gerardo joined in the cleanup. Blaine's mood had darkened, he was in no frame of mind to hear any suggestions that the trespassers who had vandalized his ranch might deserve some sympathy. He stomped on a water jug and murmured, more to himself than to Castle, "I'm tryin' real hard not to hate the people who done this." Then he fell into a wordless brooding and stayed there the rest of the afternoon. Castle recalled Sally's description of their grandfather: *"He'd get quiet in a way that made you feel that if somebody did or said the wrong thing, something bad was gone to happen."*

16

WHAT HAPPENED the next day wasn't as bad as it could have been.

Blaine and Gerardo decided to check the fences on the ranch's grazing allotment in the Canelo Hills, rugged country corrugated by deep ravines. Castle tagged along. They drove out of headquarters before dawn, hauling three horses and a pack mule in a gooseneck trailer, and arrived at the allotment's boundary at first light. The animals were taken out, saddled, and bridled, and Gerardo packed the fencing gear—wire, posts, and the dreaded post drivers—onto the mule's back and covered it with a canvas tarp and secured the tarp with rope tied into diamond hitches. They mounted up and began to climb into the hills. Thin clouds glowed like filaments of molten brass over the Huachucas, a great, dark, fissured wall almost two miles high. Blaine rode his favorite mount, the black gelding called Tequila, Castle a gentle pinto with a fierce name—Comanche. Gerardo, bringing up the rear, was on a gray, leading the mule. All three carried pistols,

Blaine his grandfather's Luger, Gerardo his six-shooter, Castle his .357 Magnum. Blaine had insisted on the sidearms as defense against rattlesnakes and smugglers—pretty much one and the same to him. Castle had continued to practice with his revolver and was reasonably confident he could hit a rattler. As for smugglers . . .

The fence line climbed higher, out of the oak and juniper uplands, then cornered and ran north through tall forests of piñon and Chihuahua and Ponderosa pine so old they had been young trees when the Spanish were building missions in North America. A resinous scent perfumed the warm air, the horses' hooves plodded on soft pine-needle loam. Blaine reined up and pointed across a canyon at a bear, ambling up a mountain meadow, its dense black fur rippling and shiny. If Castle hadn't known he was only five miles from the Mexican border, he would have thought he was in Montana. The world was full of awful possibilities, yes, but they seemed remote up here on these high country slopes.

They crossed the canyon, then followed the fence line in its descent back into the uplands. Here and there, mother cows and calves grazed on the sparse hillsides. By noon they had ridden more than half the allotment's boundary fence, found only one damaged section, repaired it, and came to a cattle guard on a narrow, rubble-strewn road, where they broke for lunch. Dismounting, Castle felt every mile of the eight they'd covered, his knees stiff, his thigh muscles sore. Gerardo strung a picket line between two trees, and they tied the horses and the mule to it, loosened the girths, and sat in the shade eating cold machaca wrapped in Elena's tortillas, washed down with tepid water from their canteens. A wind had sprung up, a hot wind out of the south. Flies buzzed. A Gila woodpecker sailed down the road in erratic, bouncing flight, as if jerked by invisible strings. His hat off, Blaine leaned against a juniper and lit a cigarette—one of the natural tobacco cigarettes he thought were good for his health.

"Know I've been thinkin'?" he asked Castle.

"Haven't got a clue."

"The word *lariat* comes from the Spanish, *la reata*, and *buckaroo* was how the old-time Texas cowboys had come to pronounce *vaquero*."

Puzzled by this etymological observation, Castle quizzed him with a look.

"Those Spaniards I was talkin' about yesterday, the first vaqueros? There's not much difference between the way they done things and the way I do 'em now. We're into the twenty-first century, and I go a-horseback, I throw a loop on a stray, I burn a brand into a cow's hide. I'm so far behind our own times, I couldn't catch up if I was wearing rocket-propelled tennis shoes. I'm like those Amish farmers, except I don't drive a buggy."

Castle heard in Blaine's commentary resignation to his fate as an anachronism—and pride in his outmoded craft. "The Spanish vaqueros didn't carry cell phones," he said, gesturing at the one on his cousin's belt. "You're not that far behind."

"Nope, I don't suppose—"

He was interrupted by a woman's cry. "¡Señores! ¡Socorro!"

She was not a woman but a teenage girl, one of three, stumbling down the road in dirty jeans and sweaty T-shirts, windbreakers tied around their waists. Flecks of grass clung to their black hair, and their eyes were glassy and dull from exhaustion. The one who'd cried out, the shortest of the three, held out an empty tequila bottle. "Agua," she pleaded, flopping on the ground. "Un poco de agua, por favor."

Blaine gave her his saddle canteen. She gulped from it and passed it to her friends, and in no time it was empty, all two quarts. Gerardo spread a cloth containing the rest of the tortillas on the ground, as if he were a servant at an elegant picnic. The tortillas vanished almost as quickly as the water. The desperate look in the girls' eyes faded—they were not going to die.

The short one, in hybridized Spanish and English, said her companions were sisters, she their cousin. They were trying to get to Denver, where a relative had found them jobs as motel maids. They had crossed the border two nights ago with twenty other migrants, farm workers accustomed to traveling rough country on foot. They were city girls from Hermosillo and had not been able to keep up. Their coyote deserted them with no food and only a little water in the tequila bottle. After wandering and sleeping in the wilderness for forty-eight hours, they'd come to this road and had been on it since this morning, hoping it led to a house or a town. Was there a house or town on this road?

No, replied Gerardo. None.

Blaine tried to call the Border Patrol on his cell, but this whole region was one vast dead zone.

"Those coyotes sure are wonderful people," he said. "How the hell do you leave three kids out here without food or water, knowin' they'll probably die a slow death? Takes a real special kind of son of a bitch to do that."

Castle said, "Yesterday, you were trying not to hate these people."

"Go to hell, cuzzy."

"So what do we do now?"

"Can't take 'em with us and can't leave 'em here, that's all I know right now."

Under the circumstances, the appearance of a Border Patrol truck, moving slowly up the road, seemed providential. Wearing sunglasses under his tan cowboy hat, the agent was leaning out the window, his eyes on the ground.

Blaine flagged him down. When he got out of the truck, they saw it was Morales, the Navaho tracker.

He looked at the girls. "Hey, Blaine. We've got to stop meeting like this."

"At least these ones are alive. Another day, and they wouldn't of been."

Morales questioned the trio briefly, then took them into custody, locking them in the back of his truck. They did not protest, deportation being the preferable alternative.

"We caught the bunch they were with last night," he said. "They told us these three got left behind. Picked up their tracks this morning."

"Catch the coyote?"

"Yeah. A guy we've caught before, and this time he's going away for a while."

"You oughta charge the son of a bitch with attempted murder."

"Don't I wish." He removed his sunglasses, blew on them, and rubbed the lenses with a handkerchief. "I was going to stop by your place and pass on some info. This guy turned out to be a pretty good conversationalist. Told us that he's chicken herding for a big operation. The mero mero is an American, name of Cruz. Cruz got permission to cross illegals through here."

"Permission from who?" inquired Blaine. "Sure as shit didn't get it from me."

Morales laughed. "From the Menéndez family. The Agua Prieta Cartel. The boss is a woman who broke through the glass ceiling of the drug trade. Yvonne Menéndez. I thought you'd like to know what's going on."

"Obliged, John. I'd be more obliged if you people did something about it."

"That's not up to me."

"So now we know something we didn't know ten minutes ago," said Blaine after Morales left with his prisoners. "Figured it was right peculiar to be crossin' wets through here."

"I'm not getting something," Castle said. "A drug smuggler gave an immigrant smuggler *permission*? What's that all about?"

His cousin removed his hat and wiped the sweatband. "The narcotraffickers own the routes. They say what moves where because they've got the money and the guns."

He turned to Gerardo and passed on Morales's intelligence, to which Gerardo made a long reply.

"Sí, es verdad," Blaine said, then looked at Castle. "Gerardo thinks that the coyote who ditched those kids has got no more soul than the four-legged kind, and he didn't lose it, he sold it. He reminded me of an old saying the Mexicans have got, that God locked up the devil in a cave by the Rio Grande, but that he gets out sometimes on a swing slung between the mountains. Could be he's swung over our way." He looked out over the valley. "This is pretty country where some damn ugly things happen, Gil. Maybe that was always true, but there's somethin' here now that didn't used to be here."

They mounted up and continued to ride the fence, down into a ravine of rose-colored gravel and rock, up over a hill, down into another ravine, and up again. At the top they paused to rest the horses. Below, the San Rafael spread to the hazy lift of the Patagonias. From this height, the valley looked like an undulating plain, all of a piece, distance concealing its countless canyons, gulches, gullies, draws.

Something here that didn't used to be here. The phrase hung in Castle's mind. The borderlands were open and full of light, but their enchanting face concealed a darker, more complicated landscape, as distance eclipsed the valley's shadowed labyrinth, in which ugly things happened. The migrants massacred the night before Miguel's companions were murdered. How did you commit such an act if you hadn't made a bargain with your soul? And how—his thoughts now ranging beyond this part of the world—did you tape a bomb belt to your waist and blow yourself up in a crowded restaurant in Tel Aviv? What power granted you the power to fly airplanes full of people into buildings full of people? Whatever was here that didn't used to be here was everywhere. There was no sanctuary. The devil's swing had carried him very far from his cave on the Rio Grande.

It was late in the afternoon when they found a pasture gate wide open and fresh four-wheeler tracks leading through it.

"Somebody can't read," Blaine said, tapping a metal sign that read PLEASE CLOSE GATE. "Let's see if we can't teach him how."

They followed the tracks for about a quarter of a mile and came upon the quad, parked under a tree. It was painted in hunter's camouflage; a dry cell battery case was in the cargo carrier, fastened with bungee cord.

"Wouldn't be a hunter this time of year," Blaine said.

Then Gerardo sat up straight in the saddle and said, "*Escuche*"—listen.

"Punto uno . . . Punto . . . Read . . . Clear . . . Hold up . . ." A voice, carried to their ears by a downdraft of cooling air, came from up on a steep, brushy ridge in front of them. . . . "One's coming . . . Stay low . . ."

Blaine brought a finger to his lips and signaled to dismount. "Think we've got something more than a bozo out for a spin in the country," he whispered. "I want to find out who that is, what he's up to."

His eyes were suddenly bright as dimes with an eager, predatory glint.

"Think that's a good idea?" Castle said.

"Why wouldn't it be?"

"Remember what Miguel told us way back when? The killer was driving a quad."

"Cuzzy, everyone in this county owns a quad. *I* own a quad. Let's go."

When, sweating and out of breath from the climb, they topped the ridge, they could hear the voice clearly. "Have they crossed yet? Okay, está bien. Tell them to wait." A pause. "I'll tell you when it's clear."

Blaine leading in a stalker's crouch, they filed through a manzanita jungle that ended in a clearing with an aerial photographer's view of the valley, the border, and a not-inconsiderable slice of Mexico. Ten yards away a man in a camouflage shirt sat with his back to them as he scanned with binoculars, tracking the movement of a vehicle on a road far below and a mile away. A white vehicle, Castle saw with his naked eye. Probably a Border Patrol truck. The man lowered the binoculars and brought a handheld radio to his lips.

"¿Punto uno? Punto dos. Another one's coming. Viene otro mapista. Right . . . okay, he's passed. Tell them to cross . . . go hard . . . ¿Comprende? Duro adelante . . ."

Blaine walked out into the clearing and shouted, "And who might you be?"

The man dropped the radio, sprang to his feet, and spun around, blinking at a trio who must have looked like extras in a western—chaps, spurs, and pistols. He was a scrawny six-footer, with tousled brown hair and a pale, blotchy face.

"I asked who you might be. I know you can talk. Just heard you having a conversation."

The man collected himself, and with a grin that displayed several missing teeth, he held out his hand. "Idaho Jim."

Blaine squinted at him. "Think I've seen you around town."

"Which town would that be?"

"Patagonia. You're one of those meth-heads lives over on Roadrunner Lane."

Idaho Jim dropped his hand but held his smile. "Think I've seen you, too. You're Blaine Erskine, aren't you?"

"What're you doing here?"

"Bird watching," answered Idaho Jim, touching the binoculars hung around his stalk of a neck.

"Seen any?"

"A peregrine falcon."

"Did you? My cousin over here"—he motioned at Castle—"is a bird watcher. Why don't you tell him what a peregrine falcon looks like?"

"It's got wings and feathers."

"And you've got a sense of humor, Idaho." Blaine bent down and picked up the radio and a sheet of white cardboard covered in acetate. He read the writing on it aloud. "Santa Cruz County Sheriff . . . U.S. Border Patrol . . . Cochise County Sheriff. Do all bird watchers carry lists of law enforcement radio frequencies?"

"You're sounding like a dude who's carrying a badge himself. Are you?"

"Nope. But I've heard from a friend who does that some narco-bitch name of Menéndez has given the green light to a coyote name of Cruz to cross aliens right through my ranch. Which one are you scouting for?"

Idaho Jim said nothing. Blaine cupped his bony shoulders with sham friendliness. He was toying with the man and, Castle thought, enjoying it a little too much. With a sudden movement, he snatched the binoculars and jerked Idaho Jim's head forward with the strap, popping it loose. "I'll be taking these and that fancy radio. Now get your skinny meth-head ass out of here."

"This is public land," protested Idaho Jim, defending his rights as a citizen. "You can't tell me or anybody to get off."

He had more nerve than Castle, at first look, would have given him credit for.

"You're gone to do three things," Blaine said. "You're gone to go back to your quad and drive on out of here. Then you'll close the gate behind you, like somebody who was brought up right. Then you're never gone to set foot on my ranch again."

"Know something? You ought not to fuck around, because it's not just me you're fucking with."

Blaine smashed him in the face, then hit him twice in the gut, and as Idaho Jim fell forward, he grabbed his collar and flung him facedown to the ground. "Fuckin' around? You think I'm fuckin' around, you mudsuckin' piece of shit?" Stepping back, he kicked the man in the ribs. Idaho Jim yelped and clutched his side. Blaine brought his boot heel down hard on the small of his back, drawing another yelp, then leaped on him. Seizing his hair in his left hand, he yanked his head back, drew the Luger with his right, and pressed the muzzle to Idaho Jim's temple. "I'll show you fuckin' around."

Immobilized till then—Blaine's fury had been as swift and stunning as a blind-side collision—Castle grabbed his cousin around the waist and with all his strength pulled him off. Blaine twisted to get free. Castle tightened his grip, afraid the pistol would accidentally discharge. "That's enough! Put it down!" They swayed back and forth, as if in a weird dance. Gerardo jumped in and wrested the Luger from Blaine's hand.

Blaine quit struggling. "Let go, Gil. I'm all right now."

"You sure?" His heart racing, Castle released him.

"¿Punto dos? Punto uno . . . Hey, you there man?" a voice on the radio squawked in a Mexican accent.

Blaine picked it up and snarled into the mouthpiece, "Hey, cabrón. Punto Dos is off the fuckin' air!"

He threw the radio to the ground, hefted a rock the size of a bowling ball, and smashed the radio to bits, then did the same to the binoculars.

Idaho Jim had raised himself to all fours. "I'm all right, but I ain't gone to stay all right if that mudsucker don't get out of my sight," Blaine said.

He had been doing battle, in his own mind, not with the devil who'd escaped from his far-off cave but with one of the devil's minions, whom Castle now helped get to his feet.

"Can you walk?"

His blemished face smudged with dirt, a palm to his bleeding mouth, Idaho Jim nodded.

"You should do that," Castle said. "Walk out of here right now."

17

When it was all over, he stood there, looking at me and Gerardo, like . . . like he just realized what he'd almost done."

Castle had finished telling Tessa about Blaine's outburst, really more a fit of temporary insanity.

She frowned. "You don't think he really meant to kill the guy?"

"Yeah, I do," Castle admitted. "I think he would have if I hadn't pulled him off." The remark sounded a bit self-serving, so he amended it. "Well, he might have."

They were walking down an old mining road through a canyon in the Patagonia Mountains, looking for a pair of Mexican spotted owls that one of Monica's fellow teachers, an obsessive bird watcher, had located.

As upsetting as the encounter with Idaho Jim had been, it had merely diverted Castle from the emptiness he'd felt in Tessa's absence. He had to make amends for his ignorant remark. Unsure of how best to go about this, he'd consulted Monica, who, now that school had let out for the summer, was around during the day. He'd found her in the office, toting up the ranch accounts with a calculator.

After hearing the details of their quarrel, she professed to be disappointed in him. "You all but called her a tramp," she scolded, shaking her head. "I know what you've been going through, she knows, but frankly, I think you're a jerk for talking trash like that."

In lame self-defense, he said that he had apologized immediately.

"You tell a woman you've been sleeping with, who you've been confiding in, that you think all she wants is to fuck and forget you, and then you say you're sorry? *Please.*" She stopped and gave him an inquiring look. "Are you in love with her?"

The question stymied him.

"Well, are you?"

He swallowed. "Yes."

"Have you told her?"

"No."

"Then try thinking about her instead of your own tortured self. You're making love to her, you're telling her all about yourself, but maybe she's thinking that you're using her. She's a milestone on your road to recovery, and when you get there, it'll be adiós, Tessa."

"I would never—," he started to protest.

Monica raised a sun-cracked hand. "That's it for advice to the lovelorn. I've got work to do. Flowers are traditional, and you're a traditional kind of guy. Try that, and call me in the morning."

He ordered a bouquet of yellow roses from a florist in Nogales and added a few Arizona poppies that he picked himself—he thought they would provide a more personal touch—and wrote a letter of apology that babbled on for three pages, was reduced to one on the first revision, and after several more, to two sentences: "I have never been sorrier for anything I've ever said or done than I am for what I said to you. I must, *must* see you again." He drove past her ranch a few times before he saw her pickup missing from the driveway. Pulling in, he walked quickly to her front door, carrying the flowers wrapped in cellophane and tied with ribbon and with his note attached, and dropped them off, his skin tingling.

He had to wait for what seemed an agonizingly long time for her reply. She gave it in person, driving up to his cabin as he sat on the front porch, brushing knots out of Samantha's fur. The sight of her, climbing out of her truck with a package under her arm, brought on a clamor of excitement, expectation, dread, and curiosity. Her hair was pinned up under a kerchief, and she was wearing a spattered denim shirt outside her jeans, its tails knotted around her waist. She gave him a stiff, tentative wave. He waved back and smelled paint and varnish as she climbed the steps. Without saying anything, she handed him the package. It had a brown paper wrapper and was about the size and weight of a serving tray.

"To say thanks for the flowers and the note," she said finally.

He tore off the wrapper and saw the painting he'd admired, of the ruined homestead, in a rustic oak frame. She had transformed it, creating a dusky, brownish sky in which the sun shone with a bronze Turneresque light.

"I thought that by taking the blue out of the sky I saved it," she said. "I hope you still like it."

"I love it."

Turning it over, he noticed a three-by-five card folded over the wire hanger, its ends taped with Scotch tape. He looked at her inquisitively. She signaled him, with a gesture, to open the card. On the inside she'd written, in the calligraphy of a wedding announcement, "I must, *must* see you, too."

"Ah, Tess, I—" He moved toward her. She bowed her head a little, holding her palms up. "Not just yet, Gil. I only wanted you to know that I forgive you, and I hope you forgive me."

"For what?" he asked.

"For . . ." She hesitated. "That thing I said, about competing with a ghost. That was a little stupid."

Quickly, she turned to leave. He asked where she was going. Home, she answered. She had a lot of things to do, things she'd neglected in order to complete the painting.

"Since both of us must, must see each other," he said, "when do we see each other next?"

"Name it."

He invited her to look for the owls later that afternoon.

He'd stayed off the subjects of their quarrel and the confused state of his heart. Talking about Blaine's explosion seemed the safer topic. After he'd described the incident, she mentioned that a Border Patrol friend had told her the traffickers had lookouts all over the place.

"They have codes and scanners, very sophisticated, almost like a military operation," she added. "For all we know, one of them is watching us right now."

Castle's gaze followed her hand as she pointed to a slab jutting a thousand feet above. The Patagonias were not nearly as high as the Huachucas or the Santa Ritas, but their abrupt slopes, topped by soaring red-rock buttes, lent them a dramatic, formidable look. Here and there the entrance to an abandoned mine gaped in a mountainside, marked by a sign warning travelers to stay out in English and Spanish. DANGER! ¡PELIGROSO! Like the Apaches, miners and prospectors were long gone, the last mine having shut down in the 1950s; but the mountains hadn't reverted to an unpeopled wilderness. In places lay tin cans with Mexican labels, strips of polypropylene cord, a discarded jacket or pair of trousers. The convoluted canyons and defiles were designed for smugglers.

"Sometimes I wonder if I made a mistake, coming out here," he said.

She touched his arm. "I hope it hasn't been *entirely* a mistake."

"All right. Poor choice of words. I'm getting to be like Blaine—always saying the wrong thing."

"Did you have some other place in mind?"

"No. I guess there's more trouble here than I bargained for."

"Sounds like your cousin is making some of that trouble, more than he needs to."

That was his opinion as well, yet he felt compelled to defend Blaine. "He's only protecting what's his. He wants to run his ranch without people knocking holes in fences and draining water tanks and scouting for drug runners. You know, I felt like smacking that character myself. I felt good about it when Blaine did."

"Would you have stuck a gun in his head and threatened to kill him?"

"No."

"That's where Blaine crossed the line. Sometimes I think he thinks it's still eighteen eighty out here. Sometimes I think he wishes it were."

They walked slowly along in a comfortable silence, occasionally stopping to sweep the trees with binoculars. The altitude, the deep shade cast by the pines, and the time of day—it was five in the afternoon—tamed the ferocity of the sun.

"Okay, Mr. Birdologist, what's that?" she asked when a bird flew across their path to light on the trunk of a pine. Castle trained his binoculars on it and, noting the sandy brown head, announced, "Arizona woodpecker."

Tessa consulted her Sibley's. "Says here it's uncommon. How wonderful." Then, as the woodpecker flitted off and she tried to track its flight with her binoculars, she said, "Gil, look at that."

The mouth of a cave yawned some thirty or forty feet above the road. Beside it, carved into the rock, was a relief of the Virgin, her robes painted in blue and white. A shrine of some sort. They climbed a steep path that running water had worn into the rock, streaked with the bluish green of copper deposits, and stepped onto a ledge in front of the entrance to the cave, which was really an alcove some six feet deep and slightly less high. Inside, vigil candles flickered in little glass jars; scapulars, a small wooden rosary, and few other amulets lay on the floor. The folds of the Virgin's clothing and the features on her face had been carved by skilled hands, and the paint on the frieze had been touched up.

"It's still being used," Tessa said in a hushed voice. "Who would be coming way out here to light those candles?"

"Migrants?" Castle guessed.

Tessa sat down, her legs dangling over the ledge. Castle sat next to her.

Sweat on her forehead and upper lip glistened in the sun, setting early over the rimrock to the west. In that light he noticed how the flaws in her looks—her prominent eyeteeth, her nose, which looked like the kind usually associated with English aristocracy—somehow neutralized each other so that the composite was beautiful.

"You wouldn't find something like this in boring old Connecticut, would you?" she asked lightheartedly. "Cocktails and golden retrievers and brie. Brie, for chrissake. I forbid you to even think of leaving here."

"I don't have any immediate travel plans."

"Excellent. Have you been thinking things over?"

"Sorting things out, you mean?"

"Yes."

"Look, I didn't expect to . . . You know, this soon. You'll have to be patient with me."

"God, I hope I don't come off like I'm pushing you. I just wouldn't want to be a—a phase till you've gotten over it." She stopped. "I'm not bad when it comes to putting things badly, either. I don't suppose it's something you do get over."

Her comment about being a phase was so close to Monica's insight that he wondered if they'd spoken. "No," he said, "but you learn to live with it, like you learn to live with a missing limb. You're always aware of the absence, but you go on. I've come that far in the last six months. I've learned it's possible to go on."

"There, you see. Coming out here has been good for you, for all the trouble."

"You've been good for me."

"It hasn't been one-sided. I could go through this alone, but I wouldn't want to."

The news from Iraq had not been good. Looting and rioting in Baghdad, roadside bombs, ambushes—testimony that the president's declaration of victory, delivered last month from the deck of an aircraft carrier, had been premature.

"Heard from Beth?" he asked.

"An e-mail. She said it's quiet where she is, and there are rumors her unit might be deployed back to Kuwait and then home. God, I hope that's true. Everything about this is hard. Beth thinks we're doing the right thing over there—I suppose she has to believe that—and I don't, but I can't tell her so."

"It would come between you."

"Yes. And I couldn't bear anything coming between us." Tessa turned to look at the shrine, where the candlelight flickered off the rough walls. "It's strange, isn't it? You wonder what makes this spot sacred and who carved that statue. It must have taken him a long time. Look at the detail, how beautifully it's painted. It's really quite magical."

"My aunt would say it's spooky. She thinks the Catholic religion, or the way the Mexicans practice it, is spooky."

"A decidedly norteamericana way of looking at things."

On an impulse, she rose and ducked into the alcove, picked up a long, thin stick that was used to light the vigil candles, put it in the flame of one till it caught, then lit three that had gone out.

"Just in case there's something to the spookiness," she said, backing out. "One for Beth, one for you, one for you and me."

He clasped both hands to the small of her back and drew her to him. She looked at him expectantly.

"You're not a phase," he said. "You're . . . I don't know why it is that I can say almost anything to you except how I feel about you."

"Try."

"I need you. I'm in love with you."

She reached behind his head and pulled his face to hers and gave him the kiss of his life, long, ardent, and wanton, her tongue flicking the inside of his lips. He was speechless after she let him go, embraced her again, and kissed her as she had him. Both fell to their knees. She popped the buttons on his shirt, and lightly, softly fingered the hairs on his chest, then caressed the skin on his belly, her touch like feathers brushing his body. He felt her fumbling with his belt as she whispered, "And I need you, Gil. Now."

Suddenly, drawing away a little, she tugged her T-shirt over her head, her glorious breasts bursting out, an explosion of lush flesh. "The hell with owls. How about it, darling?"

"Now? Here?"

She threw a sidelong, mischievous glance at the statue of Virgin. "What? Do you think it would be sacrilegious?"

"No." He laughed, patting his hand on the ledge's surface. "Uncomfortable."

"Don't be dull," she said, and quickly kicked off her tennis shoes and wriggled out of her jeans and panties. She lay back on her elbows, looking at him. "It's wonderful. Smooth as marble."

He knelt between her legs and kissed her once more. "You astonish me."

"I'm going to do more than that."

18

YVONNE'S SHIRT SMELLED as if it had been scorched under an iron, the sun burned through her hat, its brim so wide it looked as if she were wearing a straw umbrella, and the air seemed to be sucking the moisture right out of her body. A good thing she'd slathered her face and hands in lotion before venturing out into this furnace of an afternoon; at her age, a woman could not be too careful about her skin.

She stood watching a bulldozer plow a path through the desert brush on a broad mesa. Workmen trudged behind it, piling up the brush for burning later on, while ahead others cut down mesquite trees with chainsaws and a backhoe ripped the stumps out of the ground. A pleasing sight, all this activity. The only idle ones were the squad of soldiers loaned by the regional comandante to guard the airstrip construction. They lolled around an army water tanker, heat waves shimmering off the metal.

"How much longer?" she asked Julián, who stood beside her, squinting through sunglasses.

"Two or three more days, I am told."

"Good. I talked to our partners on the telephone this morning. They expect to fly in a load next week."

"Come, I'll show you something."

With Marco and Heraclio following, he brought her through the scrub to a long trench filled with plastic fuel drums. "We will store the merca here until it is ready to move."

"With the gasoline?"

"No, Mother," said Julián, patiently. "The fuel will be stored elsewhere. The coke goes here, in the barrels. We will cover this trench with steel matting and build a ramada over that to protect it from the heat."

He was in his executive mode, which also pleased her. "You think of everything."

Julián made a little bow. "Linares and Acevado are here. In the almacén, scared shitless."

"They should be. Let's go and hear their excuses."

The warehouse where she cured and processed marijuana plants, an aluminum-sided structure that resembled a huge Quonset hut, was at the far end of the mesa. Inside, a crew was stripping and grading the leaves, another was compressing them into twenty-kilo bales in a trash compactor, and a third was wrapping the bales in burlap. You could get high from the smell alone. In one corner of the building was a small office where Julián kept his orderly records and accounts in binders. Cigarette smoke fogged the tiny room; butts were piled high in the ashtray. Linares and Acevado, sitting on folding chairs and puffing Marlboros, were scared all right. Yvonne could tolerate losing a load now and then, but the size of the one lost three days ago and La Migra's trumpeting of the seizure in the American press exceeded the limits of her tolerance. The people she'd spoken to earlier had heard about it and brought it up in their conversation. The implication was clear: her Gulf Cartel partners might lose confidence if she couldn't guarantee the security of their merca. Five hundred kilos of mota was one thing, five hundred of coke would be another altogether.

Like naughty schoolboys in the principal's office, the two men jumped up when Yvonne entered with Julián and her bodyguards. There was scarcely room for six people, and Acevado motioned to her to take his chair.

"No, you sit down," she said in her prickliest voice. "Well, which one of you wants to go first?"

They looked at each other. Linares, built like a bull, managed her lookouts on the American side; Acevado, a slender man with a saturnine face, was in charge of her runners. Both were experienced—they had worked for Carrasco before she persuaded them that changing employers was in their interests—and she read in their expressions the hope that their competence would be grounds for leniency.

Acevado spoke first. "We were told it was clear, and it was. I crossed five burreros, and then five more. No problems. There was not no trouble until they got to the drop. La Migra was right there, waiting for them. A fucking ambush. Somebody snitched out the load, you ask me."

"I didn't ask you." She turned to Linares, who lit another cigarette. "Put that thing out! I can hardly breathe in here. How did your boys miss La Migra? They have scanners, they can listen in on the chotas' radio traffic."

Linares shrugged his massive shoulders. "My guy got burned. They destroyed his radio and his binoculars. He was blind and deaf. He couldn't know the fuckers were setting up an ambush."

"What guy is this?"

"One of my gringos. I use them because, you know, they do not have no trouble understanding what the chotas are talking about on the radio."

She gestured to Heraclio to open the door to let the smoke out. "Chico," she said quietly to Linares, "we are not talking small change here. We are talking a street value of eight hundred thousand. Your guy has all this shit—scanners, radios, binoculars, night-vision goggles. How did he not know that La Migra was coming after him?"

Linares, looking confused, shook his head, which was as big as the rest of him, a monument of a head. "La Migra? It was the rancher who burned him. The rancher and two of his cowboys."

"The rancher," Yvonne said under her breath. "Do you mean Erskine?"

"Him."

"What was he doing there? That route is not on his ranch."

"It is land he leases from the government, for the purposes of grazing."

"Tell me more, Linares. Tell me everything you know."

He spread his hands as if making a plea. "All I can tell you is what my guy told me."

When he was finished, a sensation like the hot flashes of menopause pulsed through her brain. She couldn't think. Fighting to contain her rage, she moved to the air conditioner and, bending at the waist, washed her face in the frigid blasts. "And this gringo of yours, he let that asshole get away with it? He must have grapes for balls."

Marco and Heraclio laughed.

"What was he to do?" Linares begged. "There were three of them with guns."

"You live in Patagonia. Do you know this Erskine?"

"Only by sight."

"That's good enough. He must not be allowed to get away with this. I expect you to educate him. I don't care how you do it, so long as it is done."

"Señora, I—"

"What's the matter?" she interrupted. "You're a big guy. Or do you also have grapes for balls?"

"I was going to say I think we should let this pass. You know how it is en el otro lado. Erskine is a big ranchero over there, an important man. If something happens to him, it would bring much trouble. It would be bad for business."

"Bad for business. That sounds like Carrasco. You do not work for Carrasco now. Bad for business." Controlling her temper wasn't natural for Yvonne. It grew in proportion to her efforts to hold it in check, until the pressure became intolerable. She flew at Linares, shrieking, "Was what happened the other day *good* for business?" She slapped his face, hard enough to make her palm sting. "It is good for business to lose a load like that because that hijo de su chingada madre stuck his nose where it does not belong?"

Linares rubbed his cheek. "No, of course not, but—"

"But nothing! Break his arms, break his legs, kill him, but you see to it he never does nothing like that again. If he does, it will be a bad business for you. Do you require further explanation?"

He shook his great head and flinched when she flung her arm, not to strike him again but to indicate the door. "I am finished with you two."

Acevado and Linares left, looking very relieved to have gotten off with no more than a scolding.

JULIÁN DROVE HER back to the house, with Marco and Heraclio trailing close behind in their car. Although it was only five kilometers, the trip took half an hour over the rough ranch road, and the bone-jarring ride did little to lighten Yvonne's humor. She was exhausted, having not slept more than four hours a night for the past month. Setting a frantic pace, she'd cut deals with jumpy American clients in motel rooms from Agua Prieta to Nogales, collected money, distributed mordida to her generals and colonels and American customs agents, lined up a construction crew for the airstrip, and all the while fought a sporadic war with Joaquín Carrasco.

A war she'd begun when she'd ordered the assassinations of Carrasco's minions in Santa Cruz, the two brothers who had been renting routes to Billy Cruz. Carrasco retaliated by hijacking one of her shipments and killing two of her best runners. She struck back, dispatching Marco and Heraclio to ambush four of Carrasco's people in Puerto Peñasco, the resort town on the Sea of Cortez where he owned hotels and nightclubs. Her boys cut off the victims' heads, stuffed them in burlap sacks, and walked into a club and rolled the trophies across the dance floor, an act that inspired terror in the tourists who frequented Puerto Peñasco. Carrasco's hotels, she'd heard, were begging for guests, and the bands in his discos were playing to almost-empty houses. She was hitting the fat little shit in the wallet, where it hurt most. But she was paying a price. The strain, the lack of sleep were affecting her looks. Dark half moons cradled her eyes, her face was drawn, wrinkles were multiplying.

"With your permission," said Julián as they neared the house, "I think I should tell Linares to ignore what you told him to do."

"What? *What?* Are you crazy?"

"He's right. Harming Erskine would cause problems you do not need. Absolutely do not need."

"Those people have been the curse of my life," she said, and smacked the dashboard. "Of my entire life! And now they do this!"

"I know your mind. This gives you an excuse. If you put Erskine in the hospital or the morgue, you think it will even the score and hasten the day when you can take over that place."

"What if I do?"

"Recall what I said some time ago. That this passion of yours could cloud your judgment? Pues, the clouds are rolling in."

They passed through the ranch gate. Three guards with AR-15s waved at them.

"This would not be the same thing as taking care of a snitch," Julián went on, to her annoyance. "Erskine is not in the business. If the chotas find out it was done on your orders, they will devote much attention to you."

"They would not find out a thing if it were done carefully."

"It is not worth the risk." Julián parked the car and got out, and displaying some temper of his own, he slammed the door. "¡Escúchame! ¡No puedes resolver todos tus problemas por medio de la violencia! ¡Debes enfrentar este problema de una manera razonable!"

"Violence has solved most of my problems," she said.

They went up the gravel path to the front door. More guards lazed about on lawn chairs, assault rifles in their laps.

"It will not solve this one," Julián said. "It will only bring new ones. Ten paciencia. You will have your chance to get even."

The house was dim and cool inside, the ferocious heat kept at bay by the shade trees, the thick walls. Yvonne removed her hat and sailed it across the room to a landing on a chair. "Está bien. I am tired enough not to be lectured by my own son. Está bien. Tell Linares to back off. Tell him, one panocha to another."

One cunt to another, thought Julián. What a mother I have been blessed with. "I knew you would see reason," he said pleasantly. "I want you to listen to something. Víctor has composed a corrido about you. It will make you feel better."

In the library, its bookshelves still vacant, she sat at the massive desk while Julián removed a DVD from a drawer, showing her the title on its paper sleeve: "Besos para mis enemigos," por Víctor Castillo y Los Gallos de Oro—*Kisses for My Enemies*, by Víctor Castillo and the Golden Roosters. Leaning over her shoulder, he booted the laptop and inserted the disc.

A photograph flashes on the screen—a policeman standing beside a shot-up truck, a dead man slumped at the wheel. A ragged drumbeat imitates the sound of gunfire as the photo fades into another showing a body sprawled on the street in a slick of blood, then a third of two men shot to death in a car, one lying in the front seat, the other in back, and the Golden Roosters begin to play a thumping, up-tempo Norteño polka, Castillo to sing . . .

I know the barking of dogs,
I know the jackals' howl.
Daughter of the ejido who rose from nothing
To reign, queen of dark waters . . .

A corpse under a scarlet-spattered sheet dissolves into the body of a young woman slouched in a car seat, sluttish pose, legs parted, breasts partly exposed, red tendrils pouring down her face from the hole in her forehead . . .

These kisses I give to my enemies.
They shout like serpents
But I kiss them with all my heart . . .

A police mug shot of a crew-cut young man. His name and nickname printed below, El Cholo, blends into the wide, smiling face of El Toro, into a handsome Indian with slightly slanted eyes, Chino, who becomes the face of El Chapo . . .

I hear the dogs bark on the desert,
The jackals mourn on bones,
And the snakes still shouting
From the ejido of my youth.
I whisper to them with guns
And press my lips to theirs . . .

Two more faces, these of the Santa Cruz brothers, nicknamed Guerrero and El Colchón, overlap to a video of a hefty, mustachioed man seated on a floor, stripped to the waist, wrists handcuffed. A voice in the background speaks unintelligible words, and the man looks up and sideways as a pistol with a silencer thrusts at him from the edge of the frame and is pressed to his temple. Comes then a muffled crack, and his eyes roll back in his head, blood leaking from his nostrils and down one cheek as he slowly sinks, like a drunk who can no longer sit straight, sinks and at last falls backward into a wall. Quick fade to a photo of him at another time, looking straight into the camera, the horns and accordion and rattling drum playing the bouncy tune behind Víctor Castillo's trilling voice . . .

I who rose from nothing to take
What is mine,
From my throne on dark waters
I deliver these kisses for my enemies . . .

Fade to black.

. . .

Yvonne was mesmerized. She recognized most of the names—all Carrasco's men. "I have never seen anything like this."

Julián ejected the DVD and slipped it back into its sleeve. "I like to think of it as a documentary set to music, a record of the damage you have done to Carrasco's organization."

"It is very professionally done."

"A friend of mine made it," said Julián with a self-satisfied smile. "He produces music videos. We got the photographs from the newspapers and police files. The video of the execution was shot by Marco with his own camera. Heraclio was the one who fired the pistol."

"An interesting production from someone who was just lecturing me that violence does not solve problems."

"I said it does not solve *all* problems. Think of this"—he waved the DVD in her face—"as psychological warfare. It is innovative. Everyone who sees it will see that Carrasco has lost control. It will disgrace him. A woman, the queen of dark waters, is stronger than he."

"And how do you plan to do that?"

"We are going to mass-produce it. Distribute it all over. People with computers will download it, send it to their friends. Carrasco himself will see it eventually, I am sure of that. All we need is your approval to go ahead."

"It's brilliant, a brilliant idea, mi hijo." She reached up and brushed his cheekbones with her fingertips. "You have your father's eyes, but what's behind them, that is all mine."

Yvonne rose. She decided to take a much-needed nap.

Ben Erskine

Transcript of an interview with Timothy Forbes. Mr. Forbes, 68, is a retired newspaper reporter and now an adjunct professor of journalism at the University of Arizona. This transcript is the consolidated record of two separate conversations that took place on June 12 and June 23, 1966, at the Arizona Inn.

"Last of Atascosa killers caught! Sonora mob attacks U.S. deputy! Mexican soldiers escort lawman, prisoner across border! Full story of daring arrest!—The third culprit wanted in the savage slaying of a couple in Atascosa was nabbed in Mexico yesterday by a bold lawman who flouted rules and regulations to bring the fiend to justice in the United States." [Interviewer's note: Mr. Forbes was reading the decked headlines and the first paragraph of a story he wrote for the *Nogales Herald* editions of April 7, 1922.]

Ouch! If one of my students turned in a lead like that, I'd tell him to take up plumbing. I might at least have written the *alleged* fiend.

The Atascosa murders were Ben's first big case and my first big story. It made his name as a lawman, mine as a reporter. Not that being a star on a border-town daily meant I was Pulitzer Prize material. I came to Nogales after I dropped out of Harvard. Yes, Harvard. It was the oil to my water. Only thing I liked about the place was writing for the *Crimson* and the boxing team—I was light-heavyweight champ.

The *Herald*'s editorial staff consisted of the editor, Jason Childs, the deputy editor, and three reporters, two part-time, one full-time—me. Mostly I covered the crime beat and the county court. Nogales was a lively town for just five thousand people, so I wasn't bored. Boxing was how I got to know Ben. He respected me because I could throw leather. Fancied himself as a fighter. Said he'd learned to box in the mining camps after he dropped out of high school, that some Irish blacksmith had taught him. One day not long after I'd started with the paper, I was checking the police blotter in the sheriff's office. Ben was sparring with the jailer, who looked like he trained on enchiladas, and doing a pretty good job of batting him around. When they were finished, I mentioned that I'd done some fighting myself. Ben took it as a challenge. He said, "Take off your shirt and put 'em on, and let's see what you've got." I was just twenty-one and knew that he and Sheriff Lassiter—that would be Harold Lassiter—thought of themselves as red-blooded westerners and me as an eastern sissy. So I stripped down, put on the gloves, and corrected that misimpression. Don't know what that Irishman taught Ben, but let's say that as a boxer, he knew the words but didn't hear the music.

That was the beginning of what I'll call our friendship, for lack of a better term. He was a hard man to get to know. Something closed off and self-contained about him. Guarded. He was a man who expressed himself eloquently in action, not in words. He certainly wasn't the introspective type. I remember only one time that he let his guard down and gave me a peek at his inner workings. I had written a hero-worshiping article about one of his exploits—he'd captured an armed robber—and said something like "Deputy Sheriff Benjamin Erskine appears to be a lawman who is afraid of nothing." Ben scoffed at that overblown description. "I've been scared plenty of times, Tim," he said to me. "Sometimes I've scared myself." That was an unusual remark for him to make, and I asked what he'd meant by it. He seemed to realize that he'd stepped into unfamiliar territory and clammed up, so I was left to draw my own conclusion.

There did seem to be a kind of . . . oh, a—a tension in his manner, like he was keeping a tight rein on himself. A lot of the cops I got to know in forty years in the newspaper business were like that. That old saying, "It takes a thief to catch a thief," what does that mean? That a cop who's good at capturing criminals is good at it because he's got some criminal in him. The lawman and the outlaw have more in common with each other than they do with the rest of us. You might say they share the same devil, but with a difference. The true outlaw is somebody who believes he's beyond redemption and embraces his devil. The sociopath denies that he has one, and I suppose your devout, do-good Christian citizen tries to exorcise his.

What I'm saying is this, and it comes from knowing Ben for a good many years: he'd done something in the past—I didn't know what and still don't—that made him scared of himself. He knew that he had a devil. But he was a guy with a moral code that wouldn't allow him to embrace it. He wasn't a sociopath, so he couldn't deny its existence, and he was no Bible-thumper, so expelling it was out of the question. All he could do was leash it—to a badge. I think he became a cop to avoid becoming a criminal. No, I can't say we were friends. I was a reporter, he was my source, and after our boxing match, he made it a point to call the paper with news tips. I was grateful, and so was Childs. Lassiter held the press in contempt, and getting anything out of him was like getting a priest to tell what he'd heard in the confessional.

I remember the date—August 26, 1921. I was at my desk typing a story when Childs told me to get over to the sheriff's office—the Atascosa post office and general store had been robbed, the postmaster and his wife murdered, and another woman injured.

I was running in as Ben was running out with another lawman, a county ranger named Curt Tibbets. County rangers were unpaid auxiliary deputies. Most of them were ex-professionals who'd left police work for one reason or another and then found out that they couldn't stay away from it. I quote Hemingway—"Certainly there is no hunting like the hunting of man and those who have hunted armed men long enough and liked it, never really care for anything else thereafter." Tibbets looked the part. Handlebar mustache, cat's whiskers at the corners of his eyes, two pearl-handled Colt revolvers, and the air of someone who could summon up reserves of unpleasantness if the situation required it. That could describe Ben, too. Quite a team, that pair.

It was Ben who'd phoned Childs about the murders. When he saw me, he said, "We're going out there now. Want to come along?" I could not think of a more unnecessary question to ask a reporter. We got into the sheriff's touring car and picked up an ambulance at the hospital, then, at the train station, a fingerprint expert who'd come down from the Pima County sheriff's office in Tucson. We headed west toward Atascosa, the ambulance trailing. Ben was driving. Tibbets filled me in—the murder victims were Oliver and Margaret Palmer, both twenty-five; the injured woman—she'd been slightly wounded in the arm—was Meg's younger sister, Dorothy Killian. There were two other survivors, Oliver's nineteen-year-old sister, Ellen, and the Palmers' four-year-old daughter, Catherine.

Atascosa was twenty-odd miles from Nogales, a typical Arizona mining town. Boom. Bust. Boom. Bust. In '21 it was bust and looked like it was going to stay that way except for those five people. Five years before it had had a population of a thousand; now not a soul. Weathered frame buildings boarded up, an adobe schoolhouse, also boarded up. The mines up on the hillsides were shut down. An arid wind hissing down deserted streets, a windmill's blades turning and making a sound half squeal, half moan, like some living thing in dull pain. Even if I hadn't known what had happened there, the place would have given me the creeps.

You're probably wondering why the post office and the general store were still in operation. It was for the convenience of local ranch families. Also, the post office had a telephone, the only one in about a hundred square miles. Inside it was a shambles—chairs overturned, drawers rifled, boxes, bottles, canned goods, flour sacks strewn all over, the phone ripped out of the wall. Oliver Palmer lay facedown in front of an open safe, two bullet holes in his back. Meg was the worst sight, still-staring eyes, her mouth open wide. All her front teeth had been bashed out, and her lips were blue-black and swollen and lacerated from heavy blows. There was a bullet hole to one side of her forehead, a neat perforation the size of a thumbnail. The exit wound was anything but neat. Blood spatters on a wall, bloodstains on the floor. God, I didn't believe two bodies could hold so much blood. The Palmers had been lying there dead for twenty-four hours, and we had to cover our noses and mouths with whatever we had.

I wasn't prepared for what I saw, and I don't think the others were either. We weren't looking at a crime—it was an atrocity. For me, it was my introduction into what human beings are capable of when the restraints are off—conscience, the law, fear of punishment, whatever holds the beast at bay. I heard Ben mutter, "That little girl of theirs must've seen all this."

Ben and Tibbets panned the wreckage for clues. The fingerprint expert dusted the wooden phone box lying on the floor. Ben pried a slug out of a wall with his jackknife. Tibbets picked up a cigarette butt outside the front door and noted that the smoker had snuffed it by snapping it in two between his fingers. There were three sets of footprints in the yard, the deep heel marks indicating they'd been made by men wearing cowboy boots. The corral next to the store was empty, the gate thrown open. Ben surmised that the gang had stampeded the Palmers' horses—he turned out to be right about that. He was a helluva sign cutter, the man could decipher marks in the ground like a cryptologist cracking a code, and he soon sorted out the tracks of the killers' mounts. We followed them down a street to the edge of town. As expected, they led south, toward the border. With a day's head start, the gang would now be deep into Sonora. Following them in the car would be impossible. Tibbets said, "We're going to have a daisy of a time catching them," and Ben said, "Oh, we'll catch them. If it takes ten years, we'll see them swing." Tibbets nodded, more to agree with Ben's outrage than out of any certainty of capturing the criminals. He said, "Even if we do, it's going to be next to impossible to get them out of Mexico." Ben said it would be difficult, but not impossible.

What he meant was this—the United States did not recognize the Mexican government, largely because there wasn't much of a government to recognize, and so there was no extradition treaty between the two countries. That's why Old Mexico had become a refuge for every crook and killer who could get there and wasn't prone to homesickness. A Mexican who committed a crime in the United States was guaranteed safety, but if the criminal was an American, what Mexican authorities there were might be persuaded to hand him over. And Ben had a hunch the Palmer killers were American. He pointed at the hoofprints and said, "These horses are American shod. An American horseshoe bends inward at the ends and the ends are rounded off. A Mexican shoe"—'Messikin' is how he pronounced it—"is a straight U and the ends are square. Might not mean a thing. Might be these sons of bitches stole their horses off some gringo's ranch. But it might be they're as red, white, and blue as us standing here."

The ambulance drivers carried the bodies out and brought them to the county morgue. We went to the O'Donnell ranch to talk to Ellen Palmer and Dorothy Killian. Pretty tough cookies, those two. After the bandits fled, they and little Catherine walked eight miles across the desert in summer heat to get help from the O'Donnells—their nearest neighbors. That Dorothy made this trek with a wounded arm made it all the more remarkable. O'Donnell was the one who reported the crime, driving to the sheriff's office down that miserable road in the middle of the night.

Dorothy had a bandage around her arm. She and Ellen were sitting on the couch, Catherine between them. I'll always remember her, a little girl with ash blond hair, motionless as a large doll, a fixed stare, no expression on her face, not a sound from her. I wasn't familiar then with the term "catatonic shock," but that was the state she was in. Pretty soon we found out why.

It happened late in the afternoon on the previous day. Ellen and Dorothy had been in the living quarters in back, helping Meg with her chores and looking after Catherine, when Oliver called to his wife to come to the front. They had customers. Patrons were rare, and the two younger women went to the door to see who they were: three vaqueros, two Mexicans and an American—anyway he had fair hair and skin and looked like an American, though the girls heard him ask Oliver for tobacco and rolling paper in Spanish. One of the Mexicans was bearded, the other wore a mustache. Their curiosity satisfied, Ellen and Dorothy returned to the rooms in the rear of the building.

A few minutes later they heard a pistol shot, followed by a shotgun blast, followed by another pistol, all in about five seconds. Meg screamed. Catherine flew to the door and stood there for a moment, paralyzed by what she saw. Ellen grabbed her, pushed her under the couch, and squeezed in alongside her, cupping a hand over her mouth. Dorothy attempted to escape through a back door, but the mustached bandit spotted her, chased her down, and dragged her across the floor to the front. She cried out, seeing her brother-in-law sprawled in a pool of blood, his shotgun beside him. Meg screamed again, "Oh, please, for God's sake! Stop!" The bandit let go of Dorothy and glanced at Meg and said "¡Oro!" Gold! Meg had gold-crowned front teeth. Mustache shot her in the shoulder. She fell facedown. Dorothy watched him roll her onto her back and force her mouth open with her fingers. Then, with the butt of his pistol, he bashed out Meg's front teeth. She lay there, writhing and moaning, until he put a bullet through her head.

While Fair-Hair rifled through the safe—all they got, by the way, was a hundred dollars in cash and some stamps and a book of blank postal money orders—Mustache ripped the phone from the wall, and Beard tore canned goods off the shelves and stuffed them in a sack. Dorothy—this was one gutsy young lady—crawled to the shotgun and swung it to shoot the one emptying the safe, the guy who looked American. But he caught the movement out of the corner of his eye and shot her. She slumped to the floor and passed out.

After the last shot Ellen and Catherine, hiding under the couch, heard one of the bandits enter the back rooms. He and his accomplices must have thought they'd killed Dorothy and now wanted to make sure they'd left no other witnesses. He opened a closet door and made a quick search, then approached the couch and stood in front of it. Ellen could see the tips of his boots, inches away. I can still recall her exact words: "I thought he could hear my heart beating, so I made it stop. I did. And I will hear for the whole rest of my life the sound his boot heels made on the wooden floor and the jingling of his spurs."

The Atascosa killings were the most sensational in Arizona's history. Of course, Arizona didn't have much of a history in 1921. I was Childs's wonder boy. He gave me a dollar-a-week raise. The thrill we get out of horror and tragedy is what makes us reporters so beloved.

Lassiter sent wanted posters all over the country, and a five-thousand-dollar reward was offered for each of the killers. Ranchers and cowhands in four counties saddled up to look for them—automobiles were useless. Childs sent me to join up with one of the posses. I got little news out of it, only what we call today a color story, but the color was enough. Vigilantes chasing notorious outlaws through the desert. Grim-faced men on horseback. Winchesters in saddle scabbards. Campfires under the Milky Way. I was living one of the Western potboilers I'd read as a kid. Hard to believe, me sitting here now, sipping a martini beside a swimming pool, that all that happened just forty-five years ago.

Back to Ben and Tibbets. They were checking out tips, talking to informants in Mexico. Ben was obsessed. He convinced Lassiter to take him off all other cases. The first big break didn't come till the winter. Ben had a lot of friends in Mexico in high places and low, and one of them was a Major General Bracamonte, commander of all the military forces in Sonora. Back in those days the army and the cops were one and the same in Mexico. Ben had contacted him, telling him that the gang were in Mexico and to be on the lookout. In late November the general wired him. Some of his soldiers had quelled a disturbance in a cantina in a pueblo called Soric. It seemed a light-skinned man who spoke Spanish with an American accent had gotten drunk, bragged about robbing some place across the line, and then threatened a patron with a gun. Another customer ran to fetch soldiers from the army post nearby, but by the time they got to the cantina, the belligerent one was gone.

Ben gave me a full account of what happened next. He and Tibbets got to Soric by car, as fast as those awful roads would allow. They borrowed horses and picked up the outlaw's trail. It led back across the border. They followed it for two days before they spotted their man up in the Parajito Mountains. He was pretty visible from a distance—it was cold, and he was wearing a red mackinaw.

But he had also caught sight of them. A wild chase ensued, right out of the Lone Ranger and every oater Hollywood ever turned out. A couple of miles into it the fugitive's horse stumbled and dumped him out of the saddle. He tried to run, but the two-man posse caught up with him in seconds. His sombrero had come off, and what they saw was a blond-haired, blue-eyed six-footer standing before them. Still, when Ben commanded, "Hands in the air," he feigned confusion, so Ben humored him and said, "¡Las manos arriba, pronto!" and the guy raised his hands.

Covered by Tibbets, Ben removed the prisoner's gunbelt, then put the cuffs on him. A pat-down turned up a booklet of blank postal money orders in his mackinaw pocket and twenty dollars in his wallet. Ben told him he was under arrest for murder and armed robbery and, still in Spanish, asked his name. He answered that it was Jorge Ramos and that he'd done nothing wrong. "Yeah, you did," Ben said, now in English. "You did plenty wrong, you and your two amigos. Who are they? Give us their names." And the prisoner said, "No entiendo inglés." Ben had no patience for this guy's language problems. He looked at Tibbets and said, "It's a long ride back to Nogales, and this son of a bitch has lost his horse. What do you say we hang him right here?" Tibbets nodded. With no further word, Ben looped a lariat over Jorge Ramos's neck, tossed the other end over a cottonwood branch, and tied it to his saddle horn. Then he mounted up and eased his horse forward, taking slack out of the rope.

Samuel Johnson once remarked that being sentenced to hang concentrates the mind wonderfully. It really concentrated Ramos's mind. He acquired a full command of the English language in two seconds. "I didn't kill anybody!" he protested. "It was those loco Mexicans. They did the shooting." By keeping tension on the rope, Ben persuaded him to identify the crazy Mexicans—Manuel Quiroga and Plácido Santos.

"And who the hell are you?"

"George Ramsey."

The lawmen rounded up Ramsey's horse, manacled him to the saddle, and escorted him to the county jail, where he repeated his denial of killing the Palmers and told how he, Quiroga, and Santos rode to a hideout in Mexico, divided the loot, and then split up. He swore he had no idea of their whereabouts. He had returned to the United States, planning to cash in the money orders.

A little aside here—it says something about Ben, although I'm not sure what exactly. When I interviewed him and Tibbets about the arrest, I commented that the bluff about hanging Ramsey worked pretty well. Ben gave me a smile—he had a peculiar crooked smile—and said, "It worked because it wasn't a bluff." That seemed to surprise Tibbets as much as it did me.

My story about the arrest and Ramsey's confession got picked up by the papers in Tucson and Phoenix and produced a flood of hot tips. All but one of them proved to be not so hot. The exception came from a rancher in Bear Valley, who reported that one of his vaqueros knew Plácido Santos and where he was hiding out—at a ranch his brothers owned in the Peña Blanca Mountains.

More Wild West stuff. Ben and Tibbets rode out there and barged into the ranch house and leveled their guns at five people eating dinner by lantern light—Plácido's mother, his three brothers, and Plácido himself, who was easily singled out by his beard.

They brought him to the local justice of the peace, held him there for the night, and had him in the county jail the following morning. Ellen and Dorothy were called in to identify him, and they did. I was there when Ben and Tibbets started questioning him. Plácido, of course, swore he was innocent.

Ben said, "Ramsey told us you and Manuel Quiroga shot Palmer and his wife."

Plácido was just twenty years old and a not-very-savvy outlaw. Instead of keeping his mouth shut, he blurted out that it was Quiroga and Ramsey who'd killed the Palmers. So Ben and his partner paid a visit to Ramsey's cell. They suggested that I step out for lunch, a long one. They put him through a grilling that did not meet even the lax standards of decorum of that day. Ramsey cracked, admitting that he and Quiroga had shot Oliver Palmer, Quiroga firing first, Ramsey after Palmer got off a round with his shotgun. But he swore it was Quiroga alone who'd murdered Meg and smashed out her teeth.

Ben told me he would have traded Ramsey, Plácido, and ten more felons for him. To complicate things, he'd got word that Quiroga was a Mexican citizen. But Ben didn't think so because two sets of fingerprints had been lifted at the crime scene. One set matched Plácido's. The other set, from the phone box, matched those of a guy who'd done two years at Leavenworth for smuggling Chinese over the California line—a Manuel Quiroga, a U.S. citizen, birthplace Yuma, Arizona. So if Ben and Tibbets found him, there wouldn't be any big complications getting him out of Mexico for trial here. Or so they thought.

You know, if I'd had any ambition, I would have turned this story into a book. Or maybe a screenplay—it had its Hollywood twists. In early April of '22 one of Ben's Mexican informants crossed the street and paid him a call. Francisco Montoya. I seem to recall that he and Ben had fought together in the Revolution. He knew what and who Ben was looking for. This Montoya had been drinking a beer that afternoon in a cantina on the Sonoran side of Nogales and noticed the bartender trying to pawn something off on another customer, who wasn't interested. The barkeep went up to Montoya and asked him, "What will you give me for these?" He turned a little buckskin pouch upside down, and three gold teeth clattered onto the bar. Montoya asked where he'd got them. Some hombre who'd been in the bar earlier in the day, he said. Wanted a peso each. The barkeep paid him two. "I'll pay you three," Montoya offered and pocketed the pouch. He turned it over to Ben.

Ben was pretty excited, as you can imagine. The last report he'd received, Quiroga was hiding out somewhere in the northern Sierra Madres. Maybe he'd got tired of the great outdoors and came into Nogales for some fun. Maybe he needed some quick cash. The coroner's autopsy had determined that Meg was missing six teeth—three upper, three lower. Ben was sure Quiroga would try to peddle the remaining three, if he hadn't done so already. His plan was to check the pawnshops on the Mexican side. The problem was, he had no authority to conduct an investigation across the line and, if he did find his man, no authority to arrest him.

He went anyway. He paid a courtesy call on the commander of the Nogales military garrison, a Colonel Suárez, and told him he was in Mexico unofficially and unarmed, just nosing around for information about the slippery Señor Quiroga. Suárez wasn't enthusiastic but said he would cooperate with Ben if Ben cooperated with him. He was to give any evidence he found to the Mexican authorities, and in case he located Quiroga, he was to inform Suárez immediately. "This man may be Mexican," he said. "If he is, I remind you that the president of Mexico himself could not send this Manuel Quiroga out of this country."

Ben made the rounds of the pawnshops. No luck. He was on his way to the cantina where Montoya had bought the teeth when he noticed a man leaning over the counter in a jewelry store, deep in conversation with the owner. A hairline that looked like it started an inch above his eyebrows, a skewed nose above a dense black mustache—the man fit Quiroga's description. Ben walked in for a closer look and got more than that. On the counter were three gold-capped teeth.

Unable to get his price, the seller walked out. The shopkeeper followed him into the street and said, "All right, two pesos." Ben was right behind. The guy was smoking a cigarette, and when he turned to look at the shopkeeper, he snapped it in two. That clinched it for Ben. You remember? Tibbets had found a cigarette broken like that at the post office. Ben called out that he'd pay three. Quiroga said the gringo had a deal. Ben paid him, then pocketed the teeth and uncorked one to Quiroga's jaw and wrestled him to the ground. Just as he reached for the handcuffs in his back pocket, the shopkeeper yelled, "Robbery!" distracting Ben for a second, which was long enough for Quiroga to break free. Instead of running away, he pulled a switchblade and flicked it open. Ben told me that to him the blade looked as long as a sword. Quiroga was grinning as he crouched and said, "Come on, cabrón. My friend wants to kiss you!" Ben circled, his eyes on the knife. Quiroga struck, Ben dodged, and then came another quick thrust, Ben whirled sideways and tripped Quiroga as he lunged forward. leaped on his back, grabbed him by the hair, and bashed his forehead into the pavement. The knife fell from his hand. Ben clapped one bracelet to his wrist and the other to his own and jerked his semiconscious prisoner to his feet.

The shopkeeper was still sounding the alarm about a robbery, and a small crowd had gathered, and to their eyes it looked like a gringo was robbing a Mexican. Someone tossed a bottle that knocked Ben's hat off—his favorite Stetson, he told me. Cost him thirty bucks. He grabbed the knife and held it to Quiroga's neck, yelling that he would cut his throat if anybody tried to free him. Another one of his bluffs that wasn't a bluff? I don't know.

Somebody had alerted the garrison. A squad of soldiers appeared, broke through the crowd, and took Ben and Quiroga into custody. Suárez was incensed with Ben for breaking his word. "Look at the trouble you have caused, and for what? Did I not tell you that not even the president can turn a Mexican over to you people?" When he calmed down, Ben vowed that he could prove Quiroga was an American citizen, if Suárez agreed to hold him for forty-eight hours. And how would he prove that? the colonel wanted to know. Ben wiped the handle of the knife and, with the tip pointed at Quiroga, ordered Quiroga to grab it. He was flummoxed, but Suárez seemed to get the idea. "Do as he says," he told Quiroga.

Ben returned to the sheriff's office with the knife wrapped in his bandanna. Word of his single-handed invasion of Mexico had flown across the line, and Lassiter dressed him down for creating an international incident, then congratulated him. Ben phoned the fingerprint expert in Tucson. He came down on the next day's train, dusted the knife, and lifted Quiroga's prints. They matched the ones from the phone box.

With the print cards and the expert in tow, Ben hurried back to the colonel's headquarters. The evidence did not entirely persuade the colonel, probably because Quiroga had by this time attained folk hero status in Nogales. Suárez was afraid of a riot if he turned him over. Ben had a last card to play. Call General Bracamonte in Hermosillo. Suárez did, and after some back-and-forth, the general commanded the colonel to release Quiroga to Ben's custody as a foreign criminal illegally in Mexico.

From Jesse James to Al Capone, we've done a pretty good job of worshiping outlaws, but we're no match for the Mexicans in that department. Suárez had to muster an entire company of soldiers, led by him with drawn saber, to escort Ben and his prisoner to the border. They made that long walk under flurries of rocks, bottles, and bricks, people calling Suárez a traitor and yelling for Ben's blood. When they got to International Street, a gringo lynch mob was waiting on the other side. Quiroga balked. Suárez poked him in the rear end with his saber, and in the time it took to cross the street, the folk hero became the devil incarnate. The good citizens of Nogales, Arizona, were hollering, "Hang the dirty Mexican! Stretch the greaseball's neck!"

I was there covering it all. If you suffer from too many benign illusions about human nature, a mob will cure you. I looked at Mexicans on one side of the street shouting for Ben's blood and at Anglo-Saxons on the other side shouting for Quiroga's, and what I saw were two troops of baboons. Lassiter showed up in his car with two deputies and shoved Quiroga inside, and I imagine there was one criminal damn happy to see the inside of a jail.

The trials started in July. George Ramsey pleaded guilty to the murder of Oliver Palmer and agreed to testify against Quiroga. The quid for that quo was a life sentence. Plácido Santos pled not guilty to armed robbery and accessory to murder, was convicted, and also got life. Quiroga's trial lasted over two weeks. His lawyer conjured up a couple of alibi witnesses who claimed they'd seen the defendant in Sonora on the day of the crime, but their testimony was blown to pieces by Ramsey's. Dorothy Killian took the stand and described what had been done to Meg, and when the prosecutor asked her to identify the man who'd murdered and mutilated her sister-in-law, she pointed at Quiroga and said, "That's him right there." The jury was out for less than half an hour. Guilty on all counts, without recommendation for mercy. The judge accepted that recommendation when Quiroga came up for sentencing two weeks later. "Manuel Quiroga, I sentence you to be hanged by the neck till dead, this sentence to be carried out on October 30, 1922."

Of all our vain hopes, I guess the vainest is the hope that reason will prevail over emotion. In spite of evidence to the contrary, a lot of Mexicans clung to the belief that Quiroga was innocent, that he was a Mexican citizen abducted by the gringos, the victim of a frame-up, and so on. A corrido was composed to that effect. A swarm of his worshipers gathered around the courthouse and sang the corrido on the day he and Plácido were to be transferred from the county jail to the state penitentiary at Florence. Lassiter had to call for a detachment of soldiers from Camp Little to break up the mob. He also decided it would be safer to make the transfer at night. At about ten o'clock—this would have been in late August, early September—he and a deputy, Bill Wilson, shackled Quiroga and Plácido together and put them in the back of Lassiter's car. Ben was supposed to accompany the sheriff on the drive to Florence, but he begged off. He had a wife and kid, and he'd just found out that his wife was pregnant again. He'd spent so little time with her in the past several months he thought it best to go home, now that the drama was over. So Wilson went in his place. And that saved his life.

This is what happened. Somehow, some way, one of Quiroga's adoring fans had smuggled a pipe wrench into Lassiter's car. About thirty miles up the Nogales-Tucson road, Quiroga picked up the wrench with his free hand and smashed Wilson in the back of the head—Wilson was driving. With the car out of control, Lassiter drew his gun and turned around, and Quiroga struck him in the temple; then he and Plácido, still handcuffed together, leaped out. The car careened into a ditch, crushing Wilson against the steering wheel and throwing Lassiter out. A rancher found the wreck early the next morning, both men dead.

Somebody told me it was the biggest manhunt ever in the whole Southwest. Five hundred deputies, county rangers, and deputized ranchers scoured the desert on horseback for days. Even a few Apache scouts from Fort Huachuca joined in. The Old West revived once again, but with a modern touch—a U.S. Army biplane looked from the air.

Even with an airplane and bloodhounds and an entire army in on the search, I was sure Ben and Tibbets would be the ones to find the fugitives. They led a group of six deputies, and I got the okay to ride along with them. I had never seen Ben so—well, "grim" and "determined" don't describe the half of it. He had a kind of terrible resolve. He'd been fond of Lassiter.

The posse started where Quiroga and Plácido had jumped out of the car—their footprints were clear in the dust. Two sets of tracks, side by side—the fugitives were still handcuffed to each other. The morning of the third day Tibbets spotted blood on a clump of Spanish bayonet, and it was still sticky. A little farther on we came to a shack by an abandoned mine, and there Ben picked up a bloodstained file. With their shackles cut, the outlaws could travel faster. That they had come so far through such harsh country in hundred-degree heat cuffed together was astonishing. "Right tough boys, they just might make it into Mexico," Tibbets said, sounding as if he'd acquired a begrudging respect for them. Not so Ben. He said, "I'll follow them to goddamn Brazil if I have to, and you are welcome to come along, or not."

We trailed them for a while longer to a box canyon, with an almost sheer rock wall rising at its head. "They're in there, laying up for the day," Ben whispered, then ordered us to dismount and tie our horses. Two deputies were sent up the ridge on one side, two more to the opposite ridge. The remaining two were to block the canyon's mouth while Ben and Tibbets went in. You know how quiet it is on the desert at midday? You swear you can hear your blood gurgling through your veins. I sang the Harvard fight song to myself. Couldn't get it out of my head. *Hit the line for Harvard, for Harvard wins today. We will show the sons of Eli that the Crimson still holds sway . . .* At the crack of two quick shots—that was the signal—we rushed in. Near the head of the canyon, in the shadow of the rock wall, Ben and Tibbets stood holding their pistols on Quiroga and Plácido. The bracelets of the filed handcuffs dangled from their wrists. A new pair joined them together once again. Their clothes had been shredded by cactus and thorns, their arms were slashed, their lips were swollen to the size of hot dogs, and they were raving from thirst and exhaustion.

They were given water, which was as much clemency as Ben and Tibbets intended to show them. "You two walked arm in arm for fifty damn miles, you can walk a little further," Ben told them. A while later, under heavy guard, they were whisked off to Florence, Plácido for the rest of his life, Quiroga to keep his appointment with the hangman. He'd confessed to killing Lassiter and Wilson, even bragged about it.

And so I got another big scoop, another raise, and a few days later, a job offer from the *Daily Star* for twice what I was making at the *Herald.* I was reluctant to accept it, out of loyalty to Childs. He was a gentleman in his own crusty way. "If you don't take it," he said, "I'll fire you for being an idiot."

Tibbets and Ben were each awarded seventy-five hundred dollars for the captures of Ramsey, Santos, and Quiroga, and here I must applaud them. They agreed to keep half their share and to put the other half in trust for the Palmers' daughter, Catherine. The bank where they put the money survived the Great Depression, and Catherine used it to pay for her college education. You're damn right I applaud them, and her, too.

Talk about a story having legs—this one was a centipede. On September 30, eight hours before he was to be hanged, Quiroga was granted a stay of execution by the governor. The Mexican consul general in Phoenix had sent him a letter stating that the question of Quiroga's citizenship had not been properly investigated. Until it was resolved, Arizona had no right to execute him. The governor kicked the ball to the state supreme court. This peculiar turn of events was the first story I covered for the *Star.* I phoned Ben for his reaction, and I remember that conversation word for word.

He said, "You want my official reaction or what I really think?"

"What you really think."

"All right, but I'd better not see it in your newspaper."

"In that case, give me both."

"Officially, I am confident that once they look at the evidence, the court will see that Quiroga is an American citizen and do the right thing. Unofficially, when me and Curt cornered those two SOBs in that box, we agreed that if a one of them so much as twitched an eyebrow in a way we didn't like, we'd shoot 'em both. Well, they didn't twitch, so we didn't shoot, and right now, I am damn sorry we didn't."

In the end the supreme court ruled in favor of Quiroga's U.S. citizenship. The superior court set a new execution date—November 18, 1922.

Ben and Tibbets were invited to the hanging, and I got authorization from the warden to cover it. The gallows were at the end of a corridor on death row. Led by two guards, Quiroga walked in, calm and composed. He'd confessed to a priest and received the last rites of the Church, so I guess he was confident that his bloodstained soul was going to get to heaven after all. I watched him comb his hair and mustache with his fingers before a guard dropped a black hood over his head. Then the noose was tightened, the trap was sprung, and Manuel Quiroga was dead.

It's not a pretty thing to see a man hanged, even one like him. As we filed out, all in a somber mood, I asked Ben if he had any comments. He merely shook his head.

The execution made the front pages of every paper in the state. The Republican organization of Santa Cruz County appealed to Ben to run for sheriff. It would be no contest. Hell, he could have run for U.S. Senator, and it would have been no contest. But he declined. He put it to me like this: "I've got no interest in kissing babies' cheeks or grown-ups' behinds."

And I applaud him for that, too.

19

CASTLE SAT on his front porch in the warmth of late morning, reading *De vita beata.*

All that the universe obliges us to suffer must be borne with high courage, Seneca said to him from across the gulf of time. *This is the sacred obligation by which we are bound—to submit to the human lot and not be disquieted by those things we have no power to avoid.*

He laid the book on his lap. The universe obliges us to suffer? What kind of universe is that? he asked himself. Really, it didn't oblige you to do anything. It didn't care if you suffered or not, didn't care a whit for your hopes or dreads, your pains or pleasures. Suffering had no objective meaning, hidden away in the void but perceivable through the telescope of philosophy or faith. Its only meaning was what the sufferer chose to give it, and if he could not find a reason, why then, it had no meaning whatsoever. He wasn't in the right mood for the Roman's stern remedies; maybe he'd gone from being a stoic to a hedonist, dwelling on the sensations of making love to Tessa by the shrine in the mountains.

Afterward they found the owls, perched on an oak branch in the seclusion of the upper canyon. One looked at Castle and Tessa as they stalked toward the tree. Its round dark eyes stared out from a face shaped like an apple cut down the middle, the feathers on its white-barred breast stirred in a breeze eddying down the canyon walls. Tessa smiled and squeezed his arm, whispering, "We're so lucky." Luck—maybe. To be with her and to see the birds in that setting was more like grace.

Sally's truck, banging like a junk wagon, snapped him out of his trance. He could see her through the spattered windshield, her small head with its Coke-bottle glasses pitched forward over the wheel. Hay bales were stacked in the bed. She was going to pick up Castle before heading out to feed more of her pets, a half-dozen corriente steers that

Blaine had described as "so old they'd be in a nursing home if they was people." Castle had promised Blaine he'd talk to her about her estate, and with her eightieth birthday just days away, now was as good a time as any.

The steers were pastured on a leased quarter section beyond the northernmost boundary of the San Ignacio's deeded land. Sally's driving was cause for anxiety. She would brake when it wasn't necessary and fail to when it was, as when she rounded a curve too fast and nearly ran off the road. Castle offered to take the wheel.

"Don't get nervous. I could drive this road blindfolded," she said.

With her eyesight, she practically was.

They passed through a wire gate and into sun-burnt hills and park-like stands of trees. A sign at the roadside bore the silhouette of a cow and the words OPEN RANGE to warn motorists that they might find cattle on the road.

"I do like that," said Sally. "Open range. Was a time when there weren't so damn many fences in this valley. Reminded me of where I grew up in western New Mexico. No fences anywhere. The high lonesome."

And she reminisced about her childhood and her father and neighboring ranchers gathering their stock in the fall, sometimes a thousand head or more, and driving them over the Continental Divide and across the Plains of St. Augustine to the railhead at Magdalena. Her mother would drive the chuck wagon on some trips, and Sally and her brothers—she was the youngest of four children—were pulled out of school to go along, she in the wagon, her brothers riding herd with the men.

"My earliest memory is of when I was five years old, settin beside my ma and all those cattle flowing like a river. Lord, that was a thing to see."

She stopped the truck on a rise and gave the horn three long blasts. "My boys are well trained. They'll be coming along presently. There were wells every ten miles or so on the Magdalena Trail. You couldn't move cattle much further in a day. The whole trip took maybe ten days. When we got to Magdalena, the hands would go into town to do what cowboys always done at the end of a drive." A laugh. "Found out when I was older that on the trips when my ma did not drive the wagon, Pa went in to visit the ladies, too. Seen them steers yet?"

Castle shook his head. She honked the horn again.

"Few years ago me and Blaine and Monica took a trip up there. I wanted to see our old place. Nothing much left but a fallen-down windmill and a few corral boards. Then we got out on the highway and visited the Plains and saw these great big white dishes out there, must have been two dozen of 'em. Radio telescopes, Blaine told me. Said astronomers used 'em to send signals way the hell out into the universe. He had some name for 'em I do not recall."

"The Very Large Array," Castle said.

"That's it. Well now, looking at those things out there on what used to be the Magdalena Trail made me feel like I was a thousand years old. Could not believe I had rode the wagons crost those Plains of Saint Augustine when I was a kid and had lived long enough to see those thingamajigs sending signals to Lord knows where."

This seemed to provide an opening to the topic Castle wanted to bring up, but he could not think of a graceful way to get into it.

The corrientes appeared, ambling, almost hobbling over a hill, stringy-muscled steers with spotted hides and curved, widespread horns, direct descendants of the first cattle brought to the New World, living relics, a bit like Sally herself.

"Used to be roping steers in the rodeo," she said. "Bought 'em for a song when their careers were over. Them Mexican cattle are like Mexicans, real survivors, but there ain't much nourishment in this dry grass, and they need their mama to feed 'em."

Calling "Whooo-whooo-whooo! Come and get it or forget it!" she climbed out, dropped the tailgate, and with a nimbleness that amazed Castle, boosted herself into the bed, arthritic knees be damned. He jumped in after her, and they shoved the bales out and dragged them off the road.

"Christ, Sally, you do this by yourself?" asked Castle, sitting alongside her on the tailgate and watching the corrientes munching the green feed.

"Sure. Way I see it, I'm like a fella lost in a blizzard. If I don't keep moving, I'll freeze up and be dead in no time."

"Eighty and still going strong," he said cheerfully.

"Come from good stock both sides. Why, my ma had me when she was forty-two years old. She was born the year Billy the Kid got shot and lived on to see President Kennedy get shot."

Castle thought this an unusual way to describe a life span. "Good stock, all right, but . . . well, you never know . . . look, I don't want to keep any secrets from you. Blaine's been talking to me about—"

"What's gone to happen when I kick the bucket," she interrupted, sparing him the awkwardness of introducing the subject. "Reckon he told you about this trust idea."

"He did. And I think it's a good one."

"I don't."

"Why?"

"How Blaine explained it, I'd have to turn things over to a trustee. I will be damned if I'm gone to let some banker or lawyer I don't know, and who don't know no more about cows than I do about banking or the law, run things for me."

Her resistance, her stubbornness, were palpable, radiating from her like heat from a stove.

"You might listen to my advice," he said firmly. "I did this kind of thing for a living, and I made a good one."

"Thought you was a stockbroker."

"A financial consultant. A *senior* financial consultant. I managed money for clients who had a lot of it, and the ones who made more were the ones who listened. It wouldn't be fair to Blaine and Monica to leave them with a tax liability that—"

She tapped his knee and threw up her chin. "You think I'm being unfair?"

"Shortsighted," he answered. "A trust wouldn't cut you out of the picture. You can stipulate how your property is to be used, how you want your affairs to be run in the agreement. While you're alive and after you're gone."

She measured him with a long look. "That so? Blaine didn't say nothin' about that."

"You'd have to talk an expert about the details, but yeah, it is so."

Sally carefully lowered her feet to the ground, took a few steps forward, and stood looking at her steers, nuzzling the bales. Then she spun on her heels and marched back to plant herself in front of her nephew, her piercing blue eyes raised toward him. "Suppose I was to set up this agreement, and suppose I named you to be the trustee. What would you say to that, smarty-pants?"

Taken aback, Castle had nothing to say.

"If I was to go ahead, I'd want to keep it in the family. I'd rather it be you than some fella I don't know from Adam."

And, he thought, such an arrangement would make it easier for her to remain in the driver's seat. She could influence him in a way she could not her hypothetical banker or lawyer. He knew what he would have to do as a trustee—handle accounting, distribute Sally's income—and because her estate consisted of land and cattle, he would in practice manage her share of the ranch. Given his ignorance about raising livestock, that meant he would have to consult her on every major decision. He would be subject to her wishes, to her not-inconsiderable will. Did he want to entangle himself in all that? He foresaw many opportunities for pitfalls, for conflicts and arguments.

"I don't know anything about cows, either," he said, demurring.

"If you were smart enough to make yourself a Wall Street big shot, you're smart enough to learn, and I could teach you."

"I'd have to give it some thought."

"You do that, and I'll do the same. That's a fair trade."

Ben Erskine

There is a sequel to Tim Forbes's tale; to learn of it we must once again take imaginary flight from our time and place.

In Mexico, Quiroga's legend grows. More corridos about him are composed. The songs are sung in cantinas and around vaquero campfires. One ballad depicts George Ramsey as the true killer who swears to lies to save his own skin. Another sings of Quiroga's bold escape from custody and ends with him on the gallows, shouting defiance to the gringos: "Now spring the trap and slake your thirst for Mexican blood!"

Ben is aware of these sentiments. He knows the corridos have the power to rouse hearts to action. He expects retaliation. In April of 1923, when Ida is eight months gone with their second child, a courier arrives at the sheriff's office and delivers a typewritten note addressed to Ben. It is from the Tucson District Office of the U.S. Customs Service:

Dear Friend:

We have it from reliable informants that an American living in Mexico, one William Sykes, has been offered $500 to bump you off. Sykes has been reported to be in Cananea and is supposed to be dickering for more money. If we find out more, we will let you know. Forewarned is forearmed.

(Signed) Allen McDermott, Chief Customs Officer.

Ben has never heard of Sykes. He walks down to the Western Union office and wires T.J. Babcock, asking him to find out what he can. Then he starts for home in the new Model T pickup he has bought with six hundred dollars of the reward money.

The thirty-mile journey from Nogales to the IB-Bar takes an hour and a half. In twilight he pulls through the high wooden gateway in which the ranch's name and brand are carved. Australian heelers scamper across the yard to greet him. Martín Mendoza is shoeing a horse in the corral, smoke drifts from the kitchen stovepipe poking through the tin roof, kerosene lamps glow in the windows. All is well. He pauses to gaze with satisfaction at his homestead—the rock wall enclosing the yard, the house with its wraparound porch and the half-finished addition that will be a bedroom for his son, Frank, when the new baby comes along, the two spring-fed ponds, the windmill that rises like a giant steel flower. In one more year he will have proved up, and all this and the section of land will be his. He savors the prospect, but a troubling thought spoils his enjoyment: Ida is isolated out here, as isolated and vulnerable as Meg Palmer had been in her ghost-town post office. Martín is out on the range most of the day while Ben is at his job. He has taught Ida how to shoot, but he questions if she would pull a trigger in self-defense. There is an innocence about her, an invincible conviction that a little good lives in the worst of men, and that would cause her to hesitate, and hesitation could be fatal.

She comes to the door, her belly swollen under a floral print dress, her strong, square face cupped by her dark hair, which she has bobbed, flapper-style. Frank wriggles between her and the door frame and toddles toward Ben, small arms outstretched. "Fadda home!" he cries. Ben picks him up and rubs his head, and a fierce protectiveness balloons in his heart. There is nothing he would not do to keep this woman and this boy from harm. If Ida believes that some good is in the worst, he knows there is some evil in the best.

Over stew and biscuits he and Martín talk cattle—Martín has found a few cows with pink-eye—and then discuss another home improvement project; installing a gasoline pump to the windmill and laying pipe to the house to provide running water. Right now Ida must haul water for cooking, bathing, and washing clothes, and Ben is worried about the effect the heavy work will have on her, this late in her pregnancy. This concern, however, is at the moment superseded by another. He turns to her and says: "I'm thinking we ought to move to town. We could rent a house."

"What for?"

"It'll be easier on you."

"What about this place?"

"Martín could look after it. I'll be a gentleman rancher."

Ida rises to gather the dirty dishes. "I'm managing all right," she affirms, though a weariness in her voice suggests otherwise.

The dishes are placed in a metal basin; hot water is tapped from the water jacket attached to the stove. She washes, he dries, observing that her hands, though she is only twenty-four, are raw and cracked. Outside it is getting cold—the ranch is at 5,600 feet and nights are frigid even in the spring—but the stove coals make the kitchen almost uncomfortably warm. Martín goes out to the porch for a cigarette; Ida dislikes the smell of tobacco smoke. Ben stacks the dishes in a cabinet.

"It might be dangerous for you out here."

"That's nothing new."

He tells her about the warning from the customs officer.

She is shocked, holding onto her belly. "Somebody's out to get you?"

"It looks that way," he says.

That Sunday Ben and Martín are roofing the addition, setting rafters that extend outward more than a foot to make an eave and keep rain from eroding the adobe brick walls. The dogs start barking. Ben looks down and sees a figure standing by the ranch gate, a man in a suit. He calls that he's had car trouble. Before he can stop her, Ida comes out of the house and tells the stranger that the dogs won't bite. As he strides into the yard, Ben flies down the ladder, snatches his pistol from the bedroom, and jams it in his waistband, pulling his shirttails out to hide the gun. In the yard Ida tells him that the visitor's car has broken down. He is baby-faced, probably no older than she. His suit and shoes are worn, his shirt could use washing. Ben surmises that the stranger's youth and shabby appearance have beguiled his wife. He doesn't look like a hired killer.

"I'll take care of it. Go back in the house," Ben says.

He doesn't usually order her around, and she pauses.

"Go on, Ida," he says in the same peremptory tone; then, as she leaves, he asks the young man what is the matter with his car. He replies that he doesn't know, that it stalled on him at the bottom of the hill, and inquires if Ben could have a look at it. He shows no signs of nervousness; it's possible he's an honest traveler in distress.

Ben says, "I'll see what I can do."

He lags a half step behind the stranger as they walk down the road. At the top of the hill, he gazes at the car below, an old-model Ford with a canvas top, and notices something that doesn't look right.

"Expecting rain?"

"How's that?"

"Your bad-weather curtains are down."

The young man brushes his sleeve. "Keeps the dust out. Some."

Ben falls back another step, draws the pistol, and cracks the barrel over the stranger's skull, dropping him, then pulls him into the brush at the roadside. The man regains consciousness in a minute or two, blood trickling from his wound to paint a spiderweb across his face. Ben stands over him, the Luger pointed at his head.

"You never killed anybody in your life, Sykes," he says, and reads by the stranger's expression of mingled terror and surprise that he hasn't made a mistake in identification. "But whoever's in that car did. A Mexican, I'll guess. You got cut in for your looks. They figured I wouldn't be suspicious of a gringo with peach fuzz on his cheeks. You decoy me to your broke-down car, your partner takes care of the rest."

"Are you going to kill me?"

"If I wanted to kill you, you'd be dead already." He grabs Sykes by the lapels and pulls him to his feet. "You go tell your sidekick and whoever hired you that the next one doesn't get any conversation. He gets shot on sight."

He waits for Sykes to drive off before returning to the house. Ida is outside, feeding the chickens in the coop. "Get his car fixed?"

"I did," Ben says as he goes inside to return the pistol to its drawer.

"What was wrong with it?" she asks when he comes back out.

"Nothin' much."

She observes that he has tucked his shirt back into his trousers. She may be an innocent, but she is not an idiot. "Nothing wrong at all, I'll bet."

He doesn't reply and glances toward Martín, pounding nails into a rafter.

"I shouldn't have . . . ," Ida starts. "He looked so young and—"

"I know. Next time somebody comes calling, you let me answer the door."

"I don't want to move into town, but I will if you think it's best."

"I do. You'll have running water, electricity, a telephone, the works."

She pauses, standing there behind the chicken wire, a sack of ground corn in her hand. "It would make things easier on me if you quit."

"That wouldn't stop them from coming. Not now."

No, not now, for this is his fate, to pursue and be pursued. The law he had sworn to uphold, the law codified in books, lies lightly on the border, where the law of vengeance takes precedence. It has always been so; it will never be otherwise.

The couple rent a bungalow on Beck Street in Nogales, near the courthouse and a couple of blocks from the Southern Pacific tracks. There, aided by a Mexican midwife, Ida gives birth to a daughter, Grace, on May 21, 1923. The family occupy this address for almost seven years, spending frequent weekends at the ranch, the daily management of which is left in the Mendozas' capable hands.

As far as physical comforts go, Ida's life in town is much improved; in other respects, she continues to endure the peculiar hardships of being married to Benjamin Erskine. He is often gone for two or three days at a time, chasing criminals and bootleggers, for Prohibition is in effect, and the Mexican contrabandistas who used to smuggle liquor out of the United States are now earning a brisk livelihood smuggling it in, often with the connivance of American customs officers. Two or three of Ben's exploits are written up in pulp detective magazines, under such purple headlines as TWO-GUN LAW (although Ben carries only one, a .38 police special). One story recounts his arrest of a bank embezzler who fled into Mexico; another the capture of a burglar who'd almost beaten his victim, an elderly woman, to death. The publicity spreads his fame far beyond the confines of Santa Cruz County. He enjoys the spotlight as much as he relishes his perilous lawman's life; and having solved so many crimes, having survived so many dangers, he begins to think of himself as a favored of the gods, as bulletproof, so to speak. He comes to believe in his own legend.

Perhaps that explains why he takes risks beyond those inherent in his work. He again jumps into the treacherous mire of Mexican politics. Mystery men appear at his door at odd hours and in hurried whispers summon him to take part in some intrigue. He packs his valise and disappears, sometimes for hours, sometimes for a day or two, leaving his family to wonder if they will ever see him alive again. That Ida does not protest astonishes her friends, her sister, and her brother-in-law. It's possible that she believes he's been called away on official business or at any rate persuades herself that he has been, much as the wife of an unfaithful husband convinces herself that he really is working late.

How a full-time deputy sheriff manages to take periodic leaves of absence to play soldier of fortune must remain one of the unsolved mysteries of Ben's life. Likewise his activities in Mexico. There is no record of them, with one exception. In late 1929 an old bill comes due, the payment of which ends Ben's law enforcement career.

20

By early July unremitting heat forces those who dwell in the gated enclaves of Tucson and Phoenix into early morning tee-times and then to confinement in the air-conditioned insulation of their faux-adobe homes. But for those whose livelihoods are in thrall to the weather, that vanishing tribe of farmers and cattlemen, early July on the Sonoran Desert is the time when they begin to search for clouds—not the wan wisps of spring but fat cumulus sailing up from the south like fleets of fluffy blimps. These herald the black thunderheads pregnant with moisture from the Gulf of Mexico or the Sea of Cortez that build up over the mountains and break the yearly drought. People stare at the radar maps on television, watching for distant storms driving northward; they pay close attention to weather reports on the radio; they resort to more primitive methods of prediction, like sniffing the air for hints of dampness or testing the wind with their fingertips for a change in direction from west to south or east. The longer they wait, the more anxious they become. By now the grasses are as dry as strips of old newspaper, the oak leaves are brittle, the dust an inch thick on ranch roads. Cattle crowd the water trough; lean deer congregate on the banks of the few perennial streams; at night coyotes wail disconsolately under star-filled, niggardly skies. Every sentient being is on edge, anticipating the promised rains that will revive the world.

With that hope in mind, Blaine hired Tim McIntyre, the born-again cowboy, to help him and Gerardo gather the stock on the ranch's allotment and move them into the valley whose grass, God and meteorology willing, would soon look as green as Pennsylvania. The seven-mile drive took most of the day. When they reached the pasture, they found that the new fence, erected with so much effort, had again been cut in two places, and that more piles of migrant garbage has been strewn in the draw. They repaired the breaks and returned to the house well after dark. Blaine, Monica reported to Castle, fell into bed too tired to wash or eat and too angry to speak.

A worse calamity occurred three days later, when a range fire charred a thousand acres in another pasture on the San Ignacio's boundary with Mexico. The first sign of it, in the early morning, was a string of smoke dangling on the horizon; within half an hour flames whipped by a stiff breeze could be seen from ranch headquarters. This was an all-hands-on-deck emergency, for fifty cows and calves were grazing there. Blaine, Gerardo, Monica, and Castle raced to the fire, pulling four horses in a trailer, and found the cattle stampeding from the conflagration, some jumping fences, some crashing into them, mad-eyed and bawling. Mounting up, they galloped alongside the panicked herd, trying to direct it through a gate. When that proved futile, Blaine jumped from the saddle, cut a hole in the fence with wire cutters, and was nearly trampled when the animals broke for the opening. The fire leaped a dry wash and roared on under a pall black as oil. The riders could feel its heat on the backs of their necks as they turned away from it to push the herd for a mile, up over a shaggy ridge into a dirt tank, where at last they settled down.

Volunteer firefighters from Patagonia sped down the road west of the tank, sirens and Klaxons sending up an urban blare. A pumper truck from Nogales arrived, and a Forest Service helicopter dumped chemicals on the blaze; but it was finally doused by a massive thunderhead that had risen over the San Antonios, then leaned northward, like a falling tower. The sky darkened, and the first rains of the season fell, not in drops but in dense globules that stung the skin, that struck the parched earth almost with the force of hailstones. The storm was brief but intense, an orgasm of rain, and after it had passed, the tang of wet grass mingled with the odor of wet ashes. Drenched, the soot and sweat washed from his face, Castle trailed the others back toward the pasture, pulling up when they reached the ragged line where the fire's advance had been halted. Before them stretched a swath of smoldering earth that resembled an undulating parking lot newly paved with hot asphalt. Not all the cattle had escaped. The charred carcasses of two calves threw off a stench of singed meat and guts. Down the fence line a cow had apparently charged headlong into the barbed wire, become entangled, and in her frenzied attempts to get free, garrotted herself. Her rolling and thrashing had knocked the wires flat, allowing her calf to flee to safety. It stood not far off, a little bull, bawling for her. It was as if she had sacrificed herself.

"Y todavía más mala suerte," Gerardo mumbled, meaning Miguel, Miguel the Jonah.

In high boots turned down at the tops and a long fireman's coat, the Patagonia fire chief shambled up to Blaine. "It's out, but we'll stick around for a while case it gets to goin' again. Looks like some crossers started it. Found a campsite and a few of these." He held up in a gloved hand a blackened sterno can. "Probably left one or two burnin', and that was all it took."

Blaine touched his hat and looked at the dead calves, the strangled cow, and the motherless bull, and said nothing.

After the fire Castle settled back into his old routine of hiking with his dog, reading, and bird watching. Sometimes he pitched in with whatever chores Sally had assigned Miguel and practiced his Spanish while Miguel practiced his English. Two or three evenings a week he went over to Tessa's for dinner. They would dance to Ella Fitzgerald afterward, or go outside with her *Peterson's Field Guide to the Stars and Planets* and seek to identify constellations and star clusters. These were moments of deep joy to him, just the two of them beneath the great vault of the heavens; and yet a dissatisfaction had crept into him. He felt that he was merely passing time rather than living a life. He wanted to do something but couldn't think of what. He mulled his aunt's proposition. Serving as her trustee might give him some sense of purpose, but he procrastinated making a decision, chary of the complications. He had grown used to his autonomy, to the simplicity of his solitude.

One day after the water heater in his cabin sprang a leak, flooding his bathroom, he, Miguel, and Blaine traveled to the Ace Hardware in Sierra Vista to pick up a new one. Blaine's array of skills included plumbing, and he would know which kind of heater to buy, the right fittings and lengths of copper flex. He guided Castle on a shortcut down Forest Service roads that brought them through the back gate to Fort Huachuca and finally into Sierra Vista. It was a prosaic trip, a mundane errand, until, rounding a fishhook bend on their return, Castle nearly rear-ended a battered delivery van, disabled in the middle of the narrow road with a flat tire. A skinny Mexican stood off to the side, the spare propped against his legs, while another man, blond and powerfully built, loosened the lugs on the flat. Both jumped when Castle hit the brakes, his Suburban slewing to a halt barely two yards short of the van. He lowered the window and said they should have pulled off to change the tire.

"Nowhere to pull off," said the light-haired man, pointing the lug wrench at the manzanita and junipers choking both sides of the road. He looked like a tough character, an inch or two above six feet, with wide sloping shoulders, sinewy arms, and a mashed nose, but his voice had an adolescent timbre.

"Can't get around you for the same reason," Castle said irritably.

"If you wait a few minutes, we'll get this done."

He finished loosening the lugs, then wiggled the jack under the rear axle. When he bent over to pump the jack handle, the butt of a pistol popped out from a hip pocket of his jeans. That was not alarming in itself—a lot of people in southern Arizona carried guns; but when added to the other elements of the equation—two young men, a banged-up van on a lonely backcountry road—there were grounds to suspect criminal activity. Blaine pulled a ballpoint from his shirt pocket and wrote the van's license number on his palm.

"Señor Gil. Vámonos," Miguel said from the backseat.

Castle saw that he'd broken into a sweat, though the air-conditioning was on full power. The pistol must have spooked him. "No es posible. Espérate un momentito."

"Be interestin' to see what's inside that van," Blaine murmured.

Nothing was inside, as they saw when the blond opened the rear doors and tossed the jack and the flat tire into the cargo compartment. As he eased the van to the roadside, giving Castle just enough room to pass, his underfed, dark-complected companion sauntered up to the passenger side of the Suburban and motioned for a cigarette. Blaine gave him one; then, with more gestures, he begged a light.

"Next he'll ask me to smoke it for him."

The Mexican craned his head through the window to light the cigarette, his glance sliding toward Miguel, who made a jerky movement, as if he'd touched a live wire.

"Gracias," said the Mexican, and climbed into the van. With a wave, the other man signaled Castle to go around him. As he did, Blaine said, "Hold up a sec"; then to the van's driver: "Don't follow us. Quarter mile up, you'll come to a locked gate. Private property the other side. Mine. And no public access."

"Is that a fact?"

"Sure is. I've got your tag numbers, so if I find that lock busted, I'll know where to start lookin'."

"That's a helluva thing to say, bro," said the blond man, sounding injured.

"Only makin' things clear."

Before his cousin provoked another confrontation, Castle put the car in gear.

They had gone a mile or so when several loose thoughts lined up in his mind and tumbled into place, like the wheels in a slot machine. He stopped suddenly and turned to look at Miguel. "That was him, wasn't it?" he asked, tension in his voice.

Miguel, who was trying, with only partial success, not to appear frightened, shook his head. "No comprendo."

"El hombre con . . ." What the hell was the word for blond? *Amarillo*, yellow, would do. "El hombre con cabello amarillo . . . That was him?"

Miguel stammered that he still did not understand.

"Ask him if he recognized those guys back there," Castle said to Blaine. "Ask him if the blond guy was the one who killed his friends."

"Cuzzy, what the hell—"

"Miguel's been ready to piss his pants for the last fifteen minutes. Remember what he told us? That he and his friends were driven to the border by a skinny Mexican they nicknamed Pencil? That the guy who shot Héctor and Reynaldo was a big gringo with blond hair?"

"Yeah. Now you mention, yeah."

"Ask him."

This Blaine did, twice; and the second time, after a silence, Miguel answered softly, "Sí. Es el mismo."

LIEUTENANT SOTO, the detective responsible for the case, was a slender man with sleek black hair and skin the color of old ivory. At his desk in the sheriff's department, he showed Miguel several mug shots, none of which resembled the men they had seen. Miguel looked relieved.

"Let's talk to the boss, maybe he's got some ideas," Soto said, and brought them into Rodriguez's office.

The sheriff listened to the story, impatiently drumming his fingers on his desk. "You said the blond-haired guy had a broken nose," he asked Castle.

"I don't know if it was broken. Mashed—you know, askew."

"Askew? I like that. Askew. How was it *askew*?"

"Bent off to the side."

More drumming. Rodriguez's wedding ring clacked on the wood. Then he rolled his chair to a computer, tapped the keyboard, and spent two or three minutes scrolling through a list of some kind. When he found what he was looking for, he phoned a records clerk and requested an arrest file, reading the number from off the screen.

"It'll be a minute," he said, settling back, and gazed at Castle. "You sure do like playing cops and robbers."

Castle shrugged, unsure what to make of the remark. Blaine stood near a wall, an elbow propped on top of a file cabinet. Soto was seated next to Miguel, who stared at the floor, anxiously squeezing his baseball cap. He had to be thinking about the threat made to his wife months ago. At this point he probably wished he had been deported, sent home to Oaxaca, released from the manacles of his knowledge.

A female deputy appeared, deposited a file folder on the sheriff's desk, and left. Rodriguez pulled a photograph from the folder, glanced at it, and passed it to Miguel. Castle and Blaine moved to look over his shoulder and saw that it was the same man. Rodriguez covered the name on the mug shot and said, "No prompting. He's the witness."

Hunched over, frowning, chewing on his lip, Miguel studied the photo for what felt like a full minute before passing it back to the sheriff.

"¿Es este el hombre qúe vió matar a Héctor Valenzuela y Reynaldo Guzmán?" Rodriguez asked.

"Sí, es él," replied Miguel, who underwent a sudden transformation. His grimace faded, he stopped biting his lip, and he straightened his shoulders. "Yo lo vi dispararles con la pistola." Extending his arm, he pulled an imaginary trigger. "¡Boom! ¡Boom! Así. Primero Héctor y luego Reynaldo. ¡Boom! ¡Boom!"

"¿Estás seguro?"

"¡Sí! ¡Sí! Estoy seguero. El hombre en la foto es el que mató a mis amigos."

Castle was amazed by the change in Miguel. He seemed to have come to terms, to have resigned himself to his situation, and to have found in the resignation the resolve to see the thing through.

The sheriff questioned him some more—Castle could not follow the conversation—then gave the case file to Soto. "How about that, Mike? Looks like we've got a suspect. Miguel said he would identify him at a lineup. Let's get a warrant and issue a BOL. Anything on the license tags?"

"The van's registered to a guy in Phoenix," Soto replied. "Nothing on him, but I'll ask Phoenix to check."

Rodriguez turned to Blaine and Castle. "Did you get a look at the piece he was carrying?"

"Just the grips," answered Blaine. "A semiauto of some kind."

"Ballistics tests show the slugs came from a forty-caliber, probably a Ruger. Don't know for sure. Slugs were pretty damaged. If we pop this guy, I'd sure love to get my hands on his pistol. What we've got now in the way of forensic evidence is one step above pure shit."

Soto snickered. "And two steps above is eyewitness testimony. It's wrong fifty percent of the time."

"The suspense is killin' me," said Blaine. "Who are you lookin' for?"

"Name's William Cruz," the sheriff said. "The broken nose jogged my memory. I arrested him first time about ten years ago. Assault and battery. Cruz used to be a prizefighter and sometimes forgot when he was out of the ring. In 'ninety-seven we busted him again for dealing meth. Got four years in Florence. Did two and a half, the rest on probation."

Blaine traded glances with Castle. "He's called Billy Cruz?"

"Guess so," said Rodriguez. "Why?"

"Last month a guy I know in the Border Patrol told me this Cruz runs a wetback smuggling ring, that he's been crossin' illegals through our place."

"No shit. Wish they'd passed that on to us. Mike, make sure the BOL gets to the Border Patrol," he said to Soto, then returned his attentions to Blaine and Castle. "Don't go blabbing this around. It's a small county, and if Cruz hears there's a warrant out on him, he'll head south. And if you see him again, call me or Mike right away and leave him alone. This isn't somebody you want to mess with."

21

CURSED, thought The Professor, watching the endless miles of mesquite chaparral roll by. So far from God, so near the United States, a land cursed by geography—flat, dry, sun-bleached, promising nothing, yielding nothing—and by history, the "Route of the Missions" the guidebooks called this stretch of northern Sonora for the padres who trekked its wastes to build churches and save Yaqui and Pima souls so they would fly straight into the arms of God when they died, laboring in gold and silver mines to fill the treasuries of Spanish kings. Agave stalks stood like sentinels against the purpling sky, barbed paddles of prickly pear waited to afflict migrants trundling toward the border, and a moon halfway up the sky blanched the landscape, heightening its desolation. It looked like a vast plain whitened by a rain of salt and ash.

The Professor could smell that pallid light, and the color of the sky, for he was on a fine edge, a very fine edge, his senses commingling, the boundaries between them blurred. Ahead, the tour bus's tail-lights glowed in the darkness, and he smelled them, too, smelled their redness that is, while he saw the perfume of creosote the air-conditioning ducts sucked into the car—it was a shimmering blue trapezoid. His gift, multisensory awareness, perceiving reality in all its dimensions.

Félix, who was driving, made a visor with his hand against the glare of an oncoming car's brights, the first car they'd seen since leaving Magdalena, twenty minutes ago. Few motorists traveled these parts at night. Even the federal highway was almost as deserted as a country road.

The Professor looked at the cameraman, riding in the backseat, a video camera on his lap. "We'll pull them over in a minute. Stay in the car till I signal you."

He flipped a hand to acknowledge his instructions. Like Félix, he had been handpicked for tonight's operation. Both had served in the Special Air Mobile Battalion, and two of their former comrades had been featured victims in the Golden Roosters' hit DVD, which they had watched last week with The Professor, Comandante Zaragoza, and Joaquín Carrasco in the salon of Joaquín's fishing yacht in San Carlos harbor. If they had lacked motivation, the final sequence, the video showing the execution of their old captain, supplied more than enough. The Professor tried to look at matters dispassionately, analytically. Here was a new thing in the cartel wars. *Besos para mis enemigos.* The DVD was like those videos of beheadings and assassinations that al Qaeda threw out to the world to show what they were capable of, but far more sophisticated, even artful. Yvonne Menéndez had borrowed a page from the Islamist terrorists and improved on it, adding her own embellishments. Butchery set to music.

Joaquín had been dealt an insult he could not ignore. He had to retaliate. The Professor understood that; nonetheless, he'd argued against the means of reprisal that Joaquín chose, pointing out that the escalating violence had moved the U.S. State Department to issue travel warnings to its citizens to avoid the border. The tourist trade was suffering, Joaquín's legitimate enterprises were losing money. What he wanted done would probably worsen the situation. "You know, El Profesor," he'd said in a fatherly tone, "sometimes I think there is too much Anglo in your blood. You are too cold. You fail to understand that there are times when avenging one's honor is more important than money." A little slap on the wrist, but its meaning was plain enough: Joaquín wanted a massacre sufficiently spectacular to deter any more corridistas from lending their talents to Yvonne or any of his other rivals.

"¿Félix, listos?"

"Siempre," he replied, in an uninflected tone.

The Professor slapped the police light on the dash and turned it on. Félix swung out over the center line so the bus driver would see it flashing and pull off, but the bus kept going. Félix flicked the switch for the siren and gave it a couple of whoops, then switched it off as brakelights winked ahead and the bus—really a yacht-size recreational vehicle—rolled to a stop on the shoulder of the highway.

Félix pulled up several yards behind and left the light flashing to deter any Good Samaritans from stopping to assist what appeared to be a stranded vehicle. He and The Professor donned ski masks, in the unlikely event someone escaped. A car approached, eastbound. They waited till it passed, then jumped out, each armed with a silenced Tec-9 submachine gun, and hurried alongside the bus in a crouch. Slanting letters painted in sparkly gold spelled LOS GALLOS DE ORO—The Golden Roosters—on a side panel below the windows, in which subdued lights glowed.

The Professor banged on the forward door. "Judicial! Open up!"

"What is it? What is the trouble?" came a voice from inside.

"We are federal police! We have authorization to search this bus! Now open up, or there will be trouble!"

More voices. Then the driver opened the door. The Professor shot him twice, the reports sounding like popping champagne corks. He and Félix quickly stepped over the body, hopped up a step, and swung the submachine guns toward the rear lounge, where Víctor Castillo, his manager, his sidemen, and a couple of the band's girlfriends leaped from their seats, the flicker of a TV set attached to the roof playing across their stunned faces. One of the women screamed an instant before the two men opened fire in disciplined bursts, sweeping the muzzles back and forth. So much popping of champagne corks, it sounded like New Year's Eve. Bodies crashed to the floor and tumbled across the seats; bullets tore chunks out of the fake wood paneling, ripped holes in the vinyl seat cushions. Castillo, struck in the chest, was slammed against the bathroom door and slid to the floor. A sideman, a sleek gourd of a man, lunged for a window and died as he clawed at the glass. It was over in fifteen seconds. Félix jerked a pair of hospital slippers from his jacket pocket, covered his shoes, stepped into the pooling blood, and put a round into each head with his pistol. While he administered the coups de grâce, The Professor found the switch for the overhead lights on the instrument panel. The cameraman would need them for his cinematography.

"Which one is Castillo?" Félix called from the rear.

A little out of breath, The Professor pointed to the long, gaunt figure sprawled beneath the bathroom door. Castillo had a face that could have been painted by El Greco, a face whose lineaments, to The Professor, had texture—yes, he could feel its shape and the shape of the body on the tips of his fingers. At once smooth and rough, like a statue carved from wood. The statue of a saint, for Castillo looked like a martyred saint lying there full of holes, though writing a narco-corrido in honor of Yvonne Menéndez probably would disqualify him for canonization.

With a magician's flourish, Félix whipped out a sheet of printer paper bearing a message—"To Yvonne. From Your Enemies"—fixed it to an ice pick, and plunged the ice pick into Castillo's chest.

Breathless still—it had been years since he'd pulled a trigger; he was, so to speak, out of operational condition—The Professor went outside and waved to the videographer to come in and start filming.

"Five minutes, no more. Make sure you get closeups of each one, and the sign."

He and Félix, green eyes expressionless, stood back while the videographer panned and zoomed. The scene had a malignant beauty; the Golden Roosters' gold lamé shirts, drenched in red, were especially vivid. But this carnage wasn't art. Killing a dangerous adversary with one shot at close range was art. This was a typical Mexican festival of gore, the sort of mess The Professor abhorred. Extreme provocation, he supposed, called for an extreme response. Still, the violation of his aesthetics revolted him. He called Joaquín on his mobile.

"Hola. The concert has been canceled," he said.

Ben Erskine

Transcript 4—T.J. Babcock

One of the other times I talked to you, I told you that my wife had got religion to make up for the wrongs she done in the Revolution. Well, as time went on, she got more and more that way. Mass every day. Rosaries. In 1927 or about then I got a job as the foreman of a big ranch in the Altar Valley near to the town of Altar. I was paid good wages, but it still wasn't a whole lot when you've got five mouths to feed. Three girls, two boys. After number four I had told Ynez, "That's enough," but she would not hear of it. The Church said it was a mortal sin to stop babies from a-coming into the world, so right quick we had número cinco, another girl. Ynez had pretty much forgot about building a new Mexico and had got herself drunk on religion, and her bootlegger was the padre of the church over in Altar, Father Torres.

She got mixed up with the Cristeros. Maybe you heard of them. Folks who rebelled against the government on account of it had come down real hard on the Church, pretty much made outlaws out of padres and nuns. Things got right nasty, like they always do in Old Mexico. Federal soldiers arrested padres and a lot of times executed them right in front of their congregations. The padres fought back, a few of them even formed their own armies. You know how it is when folks decide they are fighting for the Lord Almighty. Some of these Cristero rebels raided public schools and hanged the teachers and pinned signs to them that said "Viva Cristo Rey."

Ynez didn't take no part in that kind of bloodiness, but she did go to secret meetings at Father Torres's church, and he got her to organize peons and vaqueros in and around town not to buy things at the store and not to send their kids to the public schools. Ynez and me had a couple knock-down drag-outs about this, but Ynez being Ynez, she wouldn't listen to my good sense for her to stop those activities.

So 1928 come along. Obregón was going to be made el presidente, but one of them crazy Cristeros assassinated him. The government really come down hard then, executing Cristeros and arresting the ones they didn't shoot, and Ynez was one that got arrested.

The prison was south of Altar and just as terrible and filthy as you would expect. First time I visited her there, I saw straw dummies against a wall for the firing squads to practice on, and a lot of bloodstains and bullet holes for when they wasn't practicing. They had another way of executing prisoners. They would starve them for days and not give them nothing to drink. Then when they were hungry enough to eat their shoes and thirsty enough to drink their own pee, they'd be fed all the tortillas and beans and water they could hold. The food would form a big glob in their bellies and bung them up, and they would die of a busted gut.

I didn't know where to turn. Ben and me had stayed in touch and I wrote him about my predicament. He wrote back and said, "We've got to get her out of there," and that he was going to contact our old colonel, Bracamonte, to find out if he could help. That man had done survived all the changes in government and now was a lieutenant general with some high-flown job in the Ministry of War. I didn't have much hope. You will remember that the colonel did not have a high opinion of the Church.

I didn't hear a thing for a long spell. There I was, trying to run a big ranch and raise up five niños and niñas all on my own and my wife in jail. Then a telegram come for me at the telegraph office in Altar. It was from the man himself, and it said I was to meet him at the prison on such and such a date. Near as I remember, it was middle of '29. We met in the warden's office, alone. It was a military prison and Bracamonte had told the warden to get lost for a spell. I hadn't seen the colonel in years, and he sure had changed, was getting on in years and going bald, and what he'd lost in hair he'd put on in flesh. He would have looked like a right prosperous businessman if it hadn't been for his uniform. He still had that big mustache, but it was gray now instead of black.

He didn't waste much time talking old times. Told me he'd heard from Ben, and sure, he could get Ynez out, but I had to do him a favor first, a big one. He laid it out. The new presidente, Calles, had done a few things that had not pleased some folks in the army, colonels and generals, and they had started a revolt. This bunch of officers had sent two men into the U.S. of A. to buy arms and ammunition and smuggle them into Mexico.

These two men were the colonels Hilario Pedroza and Nicolas López. They was operating in Nogales, the American side, and the government wanted them nabbed and turned over to the military authorities in Mexico. But on account of there wasn't an extradition treaty, the American government couldn't hand them over.

Then Bracamonte folded his hands on his considerable belly and said, "You, Babcock, will assist us in capturing these traitors." I about fell off my chair. How was I to do what the whole damn American government could not do? And he said, "Our friend, Don Benjamín, will apprehend them and turn them over to us. He is a sheriff. Certainly he can find a reason to arrest them." You mean, I asked him, that Ben's agreed to do this? And he said, "Don Benjamín is once more in my debt. Six years ago I helped him remove an American criminal from Mexico. Now he is to help me remove Mexican criminals from America. And you will help him."

I remembered all the fuss about Ben taking a murderer out of Nogales that some folks said was a Mexican citizen. I didn't know Bracamonte had had a hand in that. He said that Calles himself had authorized him to pay a reward for the job, a hundred thousand pesos to each one of us.

I come a little closer to falling off my chair, but I gave him a yes. He handed me a file with photos of López and Pedroza and some information about them, and said that Ben and me wasn't to worry about getting into trouble. Our names was to be kept secret, it was going to look like the two traitors had crossed into Mexico on their gun-running business and got nabbed by the Mexican army.

Ben couldn't ask a regular deputy to give him a hand. This here business was to be done on the sly in off-duty hours. He knew that using his badge to nab people for a foreign government was going over the line. But he had him a code—a man does you one, you do him one if he asks. And then there was me and Ynez—we were his old compas from the Revolution, and he couldn't let us down.

Me, I thought it was kinda peculiar. Years before, Bracamonte had paid us to smuggle guns into Mexico, now we was going to be paid to collar two fellas for doing the same thing. But that is the way of things in Mexico. The man who's your friend today could be your enemy tomorrow.

I got a room in the Montezuma Hotel on Grand. Ben set up a surveillance. López and Pedroza had a front, an import-export business, in a produce warehouse a ways up on Grand from my hotel. They was renting a house on Noon Hill with two gals I am right sure they were not married to. Ben and me would follow them sometimes in Ben's Model T, the two of us dressed to look like cowhands, which was easy for me, me being one. One night we tailed a truck from the warehouse way out into the desert—the Old Yaqui Trail that we knew like you do your own backyard—and saw an off-load of crates and Yaqui packing the crates onto burros. Like nothing had changed since 1915, except that now we was on the other side of the fence. Ben still had friends among the Yaqui, and later on got one of them to confirm that, sure, they were smuggling guns for López and Pedroza.

Another thing we found out—the colonels loved the picture show. Them and their whores went to the movie house downtown about every other night. We reckoned they'd seen the same double feature three times. Ben said, "That's where we'll nab them, when they're coming out of the movies." He set it up for a Wednesday night. Funny how I remember that, a Wednesday night.

We waited outside the movie house in a squad car, a big Pontiac I think it was. Ben was wearing his badge on his vest. He gave me a pair of handcuffs. I felt pretty nervous but kind of excited, too, like I was in a picture show myself. Another funny thing I remember is the movie that was playing that night—*The Wild Party,* with Clara Bow. The movie let out. López and Pedroza was easy to spot on account of they dressed like real dandies and had their whores with them. Pedroza was tall, maybe six foot, but López was a good three inches shorter than his girlfriend in her high heels.

We followed them to their car so as not to make a public fuss, me getting more nervous but Ben so cool I could have put a bottle of milk next to him and kept it fresh for a week. Just as they were getting into the car, Ben stepped up and said they was under arrest for entering the United States illegally. Pedroza drew back and pulled out a passport and said he had permission to be in the U.S. of A. López did the same thing. Ben looked at the permits or whatever they were and said they looked like forgeries to him and slapped the cuffs on Pedroza. I put mine on the little fella. The whores started in to making a fuss. They were Mexican gals and Ben told them to get lost or he'd arrest and deport them, too.

We hustled our prisoners into the squad car before a crowd could gather. The colonels were shouting that this was a big mistake, that they was going to call the Mexican consul and suchlike, and Ben told them to shut up—they weren't just illegal aliens, they were engaged in illegal activities, and we knew it.

It had been arranged ahead of time for Ben to call a number in Mexico when we had them in custody. It was all in a code. Sounds kind of silly to me now. Ben was supposed to say, "The tomatoes are ready for delivery," and then he would be told where to deliver them. I remember he made the call from his house on Beck Street. Don't know what his wife and kids must have thought, if they was awake. I stayed in the car, and truth to tell, I wasn't feeling real good about things. Hell, those colonels wasn't doing a thing worse than me and Ben had done back in 'fifteen. And I had a pretty good idea of what was going to happen to the tomatoes once they got delivered.

Ben come out, and we drove out of town, headed south down a road that didn't deserve to be called one. López said in this shaky voice, "Where are you taking us?" Ben answered that we was going to deport them. Pedroza got mad, said Ben was nothing but a regular cop and didn't have no authority to deport anybody. Ben stopped and took off his bandanna and gave me an extra one he had and said it would be best to gag them, and we did. "This is a hard thing we're doing," I said. "We have done a lot of hard things, T.J." said Ben. Then he was quiet for a spell. Then he said, "Think about Ynez. That will make it easier."

We come to the border fence. Ben cut it with his wire cutters, and we drove on through, down a two-track that was so rough we couldn't go no faster than a man can walk. After a time we saw lamps burning in a ranch house. Ben headed toward it. When we come to the gate, two sets of headlights flashed on and off, and somebody yelled, "¡Alto!" Next thing we knew, a whole squad of soldiers piled out of a truck and surrounded our car and opened the rear door and pulled out López and Pedroza. In spite of them being handcuffed, they put up quite a struggle. An officer shined a flashlight in their faces and said it was them. I recognized Bracamonte's voice. "You may get out," he said to Ben and me, and almost as soon as we did, a flashbulb went off and then again. Bracamonte said, "Please, step out of the way of the photographer. You do not want to be in these pictures." Of course, as I come to find out, we already was in one.

The photographer was a soldier, and he posed Bracamonte and the troopers with the prisoners and took some more pictures. When that got done, Bracamonte thanked us and said because of what we'd done, a lot of bloodshed would be halted in Mexico. I sure did want to believe that.

Bracamonte brought me and Ben to his car. A young officer climbed out with a satchel and opened it, and Bracamonte shined his flashlight on stacks of one-thousand-peso notes in bundles of fifty each. He gave two bundles to Ben and two to me and said, "You will come with me, Babcock. Your wife is to be released in the morning." I felt a whole lot better then, I surely did.

So Ben stuffed the bundles into his vest pockets and said "Hasta luego" and drove back to the U.S. of A. You know, money never did count a whole lot with him, and I partly expected him to turn down his share of the reward. Really, it was mordida, you know, a bribe. But when I look back on it, I think Ben took it as insurance. He had used his badge to capture two fellas for a foreign government and turned them over to be executed. He knew he would get fired if it ever got found out, so the money would come in handy just in case.

Next morning Ynez got released, and it was grand to hold her in my arms again. Bracamonte told me that López and Pedroza confessed to being traitors and gave him the names of other officers in on the rebellion. I reckon they was hoping to spare themselves the firing squad, but they got it anyway, right there in that same prison. Like Ben had said a long time before, long on justice, short on mercy.

A few months later the whole thing got found out.

First off, Bracamonte planted a phony story about the capture in the Mexican newspapers, and the Calles government rounded up the rebel officers that López and Pedroza had identified. But a few were not caught and somehow or another got hold of the truth and the photograph that was accidentally took of me and Ben. They gave what they had to a newspaper, *El Diario de Sonora.* It was a mouthpiece for the opposition that López and Pedroza had been part of. The funny thing was, my name was never mentioned in the article and the picture caption misidentified me as Ben! So if T.J. Babcock's name wasn't mud among certain parties in Old Mexico, his face surely was. Those certain parties started in to taking revenge. It was the end of the trail for Bracamonte—he got shot dead one morning in his driveway in Mexico City.

I felt bad for my old colonel, but now Ben and me had troubles of our own. That picture was like a wanted poster, and friends told me folks was out to get me and might even kidnap Ynez and my kids and that it would be a smart idea if we relocated north of the border—way north. I could take another hour to tell you how hard Ynez fought the notion of leaving her country, but it had to be done. I got work as a foreman on a ranch up to Prescott, and we headed there, me, Ynez, and the kids.

On our way we stopped off to pay a call on Ben at the sheriff's office. He knew he was in hot water. You see, a new government had taken over in 1930, first of the year, and the new presidente, fella the name of Ortiz Rubio, didn't want a scandal on his hands and to have it look like he'd anything to do with the kidnapping of López and Pedroza, so he wrote a letter of protest to the governor of Arizona demanding that some action be taken against Ben. You know the old rule, shit rolls downhill, if you'll pardon the expression. The governor passed the letter on to the Santa Cruz County Board of Supervisors.

A couple weeks later on, after we got settled on the new ranch, I telephoned Ben and found out that the board of supervisors had called the sheriff on the carpet, and then he called Ben on the carpet and asked him if he'd done what was said, and he told him that he did. Ben wasn't the kind to weasel out of things. This sheriff, I forgot his name, told Ben to turn in his badge. On account of Ben's fine record, he said he would keep the reason for it secret, something about Ben resigning for personal reasons. I remember I warned Ben that no matter what trouble he'd been in with his boss, he was in worse trouble with certain parties in Mexico. Friends of López and Pedroza probably knew where he lived and were going to come after him. He told me he had already figured that out and was prepared, and I did not doubt he was. Ben was always ready for trouble.

There you have it, except for one thing. My Ynez died in 1933, age of forty-one or so. The doc said it was a cancer of the breasts, but to my mind it was something else. There is a flower that blooms in the low desert at springtime, a white one that's called a dune primrose. Pulling Ynez out of Mexico up to Prescott was like tearing one of them primroses out of the sand and trying to make it live in those cold, piney mountains. So I'd saved her from the prison but lost her anyways. I brought her body down to Cananea and hired a band to play "La Adelita" when we laid her to rest in her native ground. There is no more to say.

22

MIGUEL WAITED for news that Cruz had been arrested and a summons to identify him at a lineup. After four days passed without a word, Castle phoned Soto and asked what was up. It seemed that Cruz had vanished. He had been traced to an address in an unincorporated area outside Nogales, where he was living with a brother of his late uncle; but when Soto and a detachment of deputy sheriffs got there to arrest him, he was gone. Enthusiastic questioning had persuaded the man to disclose that Cruz was in Mexico "on business," that is, assembling a group of illegals to smuggle into the United States. As far as Soto knew, Cruz was still there; someone—his relative or a friend—must have warned him that the police were looking for him. At any rate the Mexican authorities had been notified, a request for extradition issued. There was nothing more to be done except wait for the federales to pick him up and kick him back over the border. The detective did have some good news for Miguel—the "interests of justice" would be better served if he were to remain in the United States. The sheriff had asked Immigration to extend his temporary stay permit for another sixty days.

Hearing all this deflated Miguel. Identifying Cruz had been an act of moral courage; he could have pretended not to recognize the face in the photograph. He had been hoping that his bravery and honesty would be rewarded with an arrest, a trial, and a conclusive end to the nightmare he'd been living for more than six months. Now it was going to be prolonged, and the fact that he would get to be a legal resident for two more months did not cheer him.

Castle too felt let down. To keep Miguel, and himself, occupied, he decided to spruce up his cabin. Patch the stucco. Paint the place inside and out. Replace the junky furniture, which had neither the comforts of the modern nor the charm of the antique. Miguel proved expert at adobe plastering, troweling the stuff on so seamlessly, you couldn't tell the new stucco from the old once the walls were painted.

They were putting the finishing touches on the outside when Tessa dropped by. She jumped out of the car, waving what appeared to be a letter, and did not seem to notice the cabin's fresh exterior as she ran up to Castle and threw her arms around him. Beth was out of danger and coming home. Her unit had been withdrawn from Iraq and redeployed to Kuwait. From there it was to be sent back to its home base, Fort Bliss, Texas.

"I want to take you to lunch to celebrate, just like we did before." She smiled broadly. "I'll get blasted on margaritas and hold on to you to keep from falling."

They left in her car after he'd washed up and changed into clean Levi's and a polo shirt. The San Rafael, emerald green and speckled with gold and white flowers, could have been mistaken for a valley in Colorado in the springtime. Pillars of sunlight fell through the rain clouds gathering over the Patagonias, and as the clouds swept with the wind, the shafts moved with them, playing across the mountain slopes like hazy searchlights. In all this beauty Tessa saw the colors, the very forms of her happiness.

"Love it!" she exclaimed. "Love it here this time of year! Fort Bliss, is that perfect or what? It's only a day's drive from Tucson. I'm going to be there for the homecoming."

"Which is when?"

"She didn't say. I think that information is censored for now. I got the impression it won't be too long. I'd like it if you came with me. I want you to meet Beth."

"And I'd like to meet her—" He stopped as a picture composed itself in his mind: soldiers in desert camouflage marching past a crowd of spouses and parents, applauding and waving tiny American flags. He did not see himself in it. "Do you think that would be a good idea?" he asked.

"Why wouldn't it be?"

"Seeing us together . . ."

"Meeting the new man in her mother's life might be too much for her to deal with?" said Tessa, in a tone that scoffed at such a notion. "I've written her about you. Anyhow, she's been through a war. I would think she can deal with almost anything."

The reality was, Castle was more concerned with his own state of mind. Yes, he was in love with Tessa, but he wasn't sure what would come of their relationship. To meet Beth would signify a commitment he wasn't yet prepared to make, for he knew Amanda still had a claim on him. "Look, it might be better if you saw her first, by yourself. Get reacquainted. There'll be plenty of time for me later on."

"Fine," Tessa responded.

He was disappointing her. He was disappointed in himself and his tepid sensibleness. When they drove through a compact, violent thunderstorm, he changed the subject, to that ultimate of banalities, the weather. He mentioned that five inches had fallen on the San Ignacio so far. Tessa, his Miss Manners about local etiquette, chided him. Owing to the patchy, capricious nature of the monsoons, one ranch could get only a trace of rain while its neighbor was blessed with a deluge. To say that your place had received an abundance was bragging, and that was as tacky as bragging about how much money you made. He salaamed and begged her pardon. She forgave him because she could afford to. Her rain gauge had measured a little over four inches; if that kept up, her place would get twenty inches by the end of the season, and her grass-fed cattle would be as sleek as any fattened in feedlots.

"How is Blaine?" she asked. "He should be happy with this rain."

He was, Castle answered. But the migrant traffic was bedeviling him. The other day he found jerry cans of gasoline stashed in the brush—a smuggler's fuel cache. Instead of dumping the gas, he'd ridden horseback all the way back to the house for a bag of sugar and poured it into the jerry cans and left them there.

Tessa made a clicking sound with her tongue.

"He says it's a war between him and them," Castle said. "He's been talking about asking vigilantes to start patrolling the ranch. Sally and Monica have vetoed that. They don't want a bunch of strangers with guns wandering around the place."

"Don't blame them," Tessa said, peeling off the Duquesne road onto the Nogales highway. "And I don't blame him either. And I don't blame the Mexicans. Right over there, you've got people slaving away in maquiladoras for ten bucks a day." She pointed down the highway toward the houses cluttering the hillsides on the Sonoran side of Nogales. "And all they have to do is crawl under a fence or jump a wall, and they're making ten an hour sweeping floors at Wal-Mart. It's a no-brainer. I'd do the same thing. But I've had my fences cut. A couple of years ago McIntyre caught an illegal trying to steal my truck. I feel for those people, and at the same time they flat piss me off, and I think that I ought not to be of two minds about it."

"Life isn't talk radio," Castle said philosophically. "It's okay to be ambivalent."

They had lunch at La Roca. Tessa drank only one margarita and did not require support as they toured the shops on Avenida Obregón, looking for furniture for his redecoration project. Another storm accompanied them on the drive home. It was quick and sharp, a high wind shredded the clouds, and Tessa stopped at the pass beneath Mount Washington to gape at a double rainbow looped over the San Rafael and a full moon, distinct in the late afternoon sky, hovering between the shimmering arches.

"Sometimes it's so beautiful I almost feel guilty living here."

A pretty place where some ugly things happen. Castle decided to tell Tessa about his recent adventure. "Rodriguez wanted us to keep quiet about it, but now that Cruz has gone south, I guess it's all right."

"Like we didn't have enough going on around here. Oh Gil, you've done your bit. You will be careful from now on? Promise me you'll be careful."

He stroked the back of her neck, exposed by her upswept hair. It was an easy promise to make; he had everything, everything to live for.

"And all right," he added. "We'll go to Fort Bliss together."

Tessa punched him lightly in the arm. "You're getting better at this."

She turned up the San Ignacio road. An ambulance was coming toward them, its roof lights pulsing, its siren off. Tessa swung to the side to give it room to pass, and it flew by as fast as conditions would allow, its tires flinging clods of mud. When they got to the main house, they rushed in and found Monica in the living room with Gerardo and Elena, whose eyes glistened as she fingered a rosary.

"What is it?" Castle asked, alarmed. "What happened?"

Monica stood and placed her hands on his shoulders. "It's Sally. She went out to feed those steers of hers and ran off the road."

"Oh, Christ. How bad is it?"

"Don't know. Some sort of head injuries. She's unconscious. They're taking her to Holy Cross in Nogales. Blaine's with her. He's going to call when he knows something."

Castle and Tessa sat down and joined Monica in a vigil by the telephone. Sally had gone out after lunch, Monica related, ignoring her pleas to stay home because the roads were in bad shape, coated with mud slick as black ice. When she failed to return after three hours, Monica called Blaine on his cell.

"He and Gerardo were out on another fence-mending job," she went on. "It's a miracle I got through. They dropped what they were doing and went to look for her and found her truck, nose down in a ditch. It looked like she'd missed a turn. She was over the wheel, bleeding from the forehead. Blaine called nine-one-one, but he was in a dead zone, and so he drove back here and got them on a landline. He wanted a helicopter, but they couldn't get one up—it was raining like hell. So they sent the ambulance."

They waited an hour; then Elena warmed up leftovers, and they sat around the kitchen table, eating and telling stories about Sally. Monica spoke of the times her willfulness had worked to good effect. Years ago she led a campaign to force the power and phone companies to put their lines underground in the San Rafael. "That's why you don't see telephone poles and electrical towers up here. She didn't want them breaking up the view. And then she tried to talk our neighbors into taking down their fences, but she didn't win that one. She never was comfortable in the modern world. She wanted this valley to look like the place where she grew up."

"The Plains of Saint Augustine," said Castle.

"Yes, there. God, she could be pigheaded, but if it wasn't for her, this ranch wouldn't still be in the family. She kept it going after Jeff died, just her and two old cowboys who'd worked for the San Ignacio for years."

"Did she move here right after she lost her husband?" asked Tessa, shaking her head when Elena offered a second helping.

"Not long after. I don't know much about Frank. They were kind of an odd couple from what I heard. Frank had a degree in mine engineering, and Sally didn't get past eighth grade, if she got that far."

After a silence—there was something obituary in these reminiscences—Castle said, "She must have loved him a helluva lot, she never remarried." Then he glanced at Tessa, worried that she might think he was making an oblique reference to himself, which he wasn't.

Monica looked at him, pale eyes widening. "You didn't know?"

"What? She did?"

"When she was sixty. She'd robbed the cradle—he was fifty-five. He ran the feed store in Sonoita. Two months after the wedding she booted him out of the house and filed for divorce. Blaine and I couldn't figure it out. They seemed to get along. 'He couldn't do it no more, and he kept that from me,' Sally told us. We were floored. I asked her,

'You mean that makes a difference at your age?' and she said, 'Damn right it does. Don't expect it frequently, but I like to know it's possible, and he should of let me know anyway.' "

They all laughed. The phone rang then, and for the next few minutes Monica paced the kitchen, wrapping and unwrapping the cord around her fingers, saying little beyond an occasional "All right . . . Yes . . . I see . . ."

She hung up and slumped against the kitchen counter. "She's in a coma. They took CAT scans of her head. She's got a skull fracture and a brain hemorrhage, a subdural brain hemorrhage is what they told Blaine. They're going to evacuate her to Tucson tonight for an operation to relieve the pressure. Her chances aren't good."

She explained all this to Gerardo and Elena, who crossed herself. Monica was in tears. "I feel so responsible. I should have taken her car keys from her."

Castle told her not to blame herself; if he knew his obstinate aunt, she would have hot-wired her truck.

The operation was performed the next morning at the University of Arizona hospital. Sally did not regain consciousness and died two days later, at ten-thirty in the evening.

She was buried in Black Oak Pioneer Cemetery on a hot, still, overcast day in the middle of July. The cemetery was in the Canelo Hills, a short distance down a gravel road leading off a two-lane blacktop. At the entrance, a wrought-iron gate hung between massive stone pillars; her casket was transferred from the hearse to a wagon rented from a dude ranch, for Sally had asked in her will to be carried to her grave in that manner. The team pulled the wagon slowly through the gate, mourners shuffling behind. Many of Castle's maternal ancestors were tenanted in Black Oak, and as the funeral procession wended past their graves, he read names and dates and sometimes a one- or two-word biography etched into simple stone markers: a great-grandfather,

THOMAS ERSKINE—ARIZONA RANGER—1859-1901

a great-great-uncle whose wife must have died in childbirth, all three lying together,

JOSHUA PITTMAN 1861–1928

and his wife,

GABRIELA FLORES PITTMAN 1873–1894,

and

BABY PITTMAN June 2, 1894–June 2, 1894;

his grandparents,

BENJAMIN ERSKINE—Lawman-Rancher 1890–1956

and his wife,

IDA BARNES ERSKINE 1899–1951

and beside them,

JEFFREY ERSKINE—Cattleman 1888–1967

and beside him,

LILLY ERSKINE 1891–1969

Like the name and date he'd found scratched into the adobe brick, the terse, stark memorials gave him a sense of connection to this land, to the history his mother had hidden from him.

Sally's grave had been dug into a shady slope next to her husband's—

FRANK ERSKINE 1920–1952

—both facing east across the oak-studded hills toward the Huachuca Mountains, the vista uncluttered by power lines and telephone poles, and not a fence in sight. Castle thought this fitting. Open range.

She had been well known throughout Santa Cruz and Cochise counties, but with most of her friends gone before her or confined to beds and wheelchairs, the mourners were few, thirty or forty altogether, and nearly all of those were white-haired, craggy-faced cowboys and ranchmen and ranch women, people who belonged to a vanished time, the very last of their kind. Tessa and McIntyre and Rick Erskine, who'd broken off another tour to attend his grandmother's funeral, were the only ones there under fifty.

A country band played the old hymns and a minister spoke the old words as the casket was lowered into the raw hole in the ground. Blaine, wearing a suede sport jacket and a bolo tie over a starched white shirt, delivered a short eulogy, fighting to keep his composure.

"Thanks for comin'. All of you who knew my ma know she liked to give orders, and I reckon she's givin' 'em now, wherever she is. She followed the wagons in New Mexico when she was young, and I hope this one has brought her to a place where she's belly-deep in good green grass. She wouldn't of wanted me to say more, so I won't."

The band struck up "Shall We Gather by the River." Their singers, a man and a woman, harmonized on the lyrics, the crowd following their lead—

Shall we gather by the river,
The beautiful, beautiful river,
Gather with the saints by the river
That flows by the throne of God.

The voices and the high, breaking notes of a fiddle and mandolin rose into the quiet air, mingling with the thud of dirt falling on metal, as Blaine, Rick, and Castle took up shovels and covered Sally with the earth she loved.

23

The Internal Revenue Service, an agency not noted for sensitivity, left Blaine and Monica little time for grieving. They soon received an estate tax form by certified mail, and when they weren't busy planning for the summer roundup and branding, they were meeting with their lawyer in Tucson. Castle saw little of them; then Monica stopped by one day to tell him that they had received a lovely condolence letter from his sister, whom he'd phoned with the news.

The skin around Monica's eyes looked taut; worry creased her forehead. Castle invited her in for coffee, pouring from the blackened enamel pot. Holding her mug in both hands, Monica sank into one of the new leather armchairs Tessa had picked out for him in Tucson. "Well, they're all there now, Ben and Ida, Jeff and Lilly, Frank and Sally," Monica said. "She drove me nuts sometimes, but damn if I don't miss her."

Castle sat down and nodded. The absence that becomes a presence. Several times since the funeral, as he passed the main house, he looked at the corral, half expecting to see Sally in her bathrobe and rubber boots, calling "Come and get it or forget it" to the rickety longhorn, the swaybacked geldings with matted tails. Blaine had shipped the animals off the ranch but had kept the corrientes. "Ought to get rid of 'em but I can't," he'd said, and Castle knew what he meant. All those months he'd held on to Mandy's belongings, unable to move even a hairbrush from where she'd left it.

"You and Miguel have done quite a job on this place," Monica said, seeming to notice the new furniture, the freshly painted walls, and the varnished floors for the first time. "I don't think it's ever looked this good."

"Kitchen's next."

She sipped her coffee and stared thoughtfully at her feet. "Before you put any more into it, there's something you should know. It looks like we're facing a humongous tax bill. Our lawyer is going to try to work something out with the IRS, but"—she hesitated and raised her glance—"we're probably going to have to break up the ranch, sell Sally's half. We're putting it on the market, just in case."

Castle said nothing. Did he hear a note of reproof in that pronouncement? If he did, his own conscience had put it there. His aunt should have made provisions long ago, and he doubted a trust agreement could have been drawn up and been in force before she died, even if he'd said yes to her proposition right away. Still, he felt his delay was partly responsible for putting Blaine and Monica into this fix.

"This place would go with the sale," she went on. "So we wouldn't want you putting more of your time and money into it." He must have looked like an apartment dweller whose landlord has just told him his lease was not to be renewed, because she quickly added, "Don't worry. The chances that it would sell right away are pretty slim."

He pointed at her mug. "More coffee?"

She shook her head. He went to the kitchen and refilled his, thinking of the brick with the inscription—J. B. Erskine, 1912— that he and Miguel had recently plastered over. Sadness overtook him, a melancholy awareness of the impermanence of all things. "All the same, I'd better start looking for a place of my own. I should have done that months ago." He looked at Monica over the low partition dividing the kitchen from the living room. "It's strange. I've gotten attached—to you and Blaine, to this ranch, this valley, Tessa. I never thought I'd be attached to anyone or anything again in my life."

"For what it's worth, we've gotten attached to you. Blaine would never say so, but he feels it. It's like our families have been reunited after all these years." She rose, came over to him, and gave him a quick hug. "I've got to go. Our real estate agent is organizing a caravan. They'll be here tomorrow. Thought I'd warn you."

"I'll make sure there's no dirty dishes in the sink," he said.

A van arrived in the late morning, carrying eight land brokers led by a woman with short iron-gray hair. The cabin was their last stop after they'd driven around the property, taking pictures with their digital cameras. Castle stood outside as they trooped through the door, vinyl-covered notebooks in hand. Their inspection took only a few minutes. The gray-haired woman thanked him for his trouble and marched her colleagues back to the van. Watching it leave, he felt a little violated by these strangers who'd invaded his solitude. What was the San Ignacio to them? Another piece of dirt to be bought and sold. They could not hear its heartbeat.

A few days after it was put on the market, Monica invited him to dinner and a conference with their lawyer. Trusting in his financial experience, she said Blaine wanted his input. He parked in the yard, and, before going in, stood with his back against the car door, listening to the night music—a chorale of coyotes, the creak of the windmill, the rustle of cottonwoods. A drizzle had fallen in the afternoon, but the sky was clear now except for a few clouds drifting across the glittering stars. Craning his neck, he found Vega burning at the zenith, the Northern Cross, and the two other stars that formed the Summer Triangle, Deneb and Altair. In cosmological terms, these were next-door neighbors; and yet the distances between them and Earth were unimaginable. Such reflections of course humbled him—he was a transitory mote on the skin of a small blue planet in a minor solar system on an outer arm of a spiral galaxy that was itself a speck on the fabric of the universe—but he felt exalted at the same time. Thinking about his relationship to the heavens brought him to an awareness of his relationship to the Earth, specifically to the tiny piece of it he inhabited. Yesterday's talk with Monica had awakened him to a fact: he did not want to leave the San Ignacio, nor to see it split in two. His coming here had been more than a family reunion; it had restored his severed bonds to the land of his ancestors. Their hearts, stilled in their bodies, were in it, beating on in the grasses greened by the summer rains, in the everlasting miracle of the resurrected flowers, and so was his.

He went inside.

Castle had imagined the lawyer would be a gray eminence with a furrowed western face. The dark-haired man he was introduced to, Will Lovelace, looked as if he had just graduated high school. He was in fact in his early thirties. Castle had reached that stage in life when everyone between eighteen and thirty-five appears to be the same age.

They ate in the little-used dining room, which with its somber, heavy furniture and candles burning in wrought-iron holders looked like the dining hall of a Spanish monastery on the Day of the Dead. Felt like it, too. Monica was quiet, Blaine mourning his mother and also feeling an anticipatory sorrow for the San Ignacio's probable fate. Castle and Lovelace did most of the talking. The lawyer had recently discovered fly-fishing, and upon learning that Castle was accomplished in the art, probed him for tips. Built like an overtrained tennis pro, he ate as if he'd just come off a three-day fast, taking a second helping of steak and potatoes. After the apple pie and ice cream, which Lovelace polished off as thoroughly as he had the main course, scooping up pie crumbs with his fingers, Blaine pushed back in his chair and said, "All right, let's get this over with."

Monica snuffed the candle and turned on the lights, and the lawyer went to the guest room (he was staying the night) for his briefcase.

"I think I can make a pretty good case to the IRS," he declared, spreading papers on the table. "The ranch's net profits have averaged eighty thousand a year, round figures, for the last five years. A decent family income but not so impressive for a small business."

"Meaning what?" asked Monica, forefingers making a triangle under her chin.

"Meaning that the appraised value of Mrs. Erskine's estate is somewhat artificial. Her estate consists almost exclusively of land, and the land is good only for raising cattle. To get the real value, you have to factor in the income the land generated, which isn't all that much. So I'm confident I can convince the IRS that the estate is worth less than five million."

Blaine pushed his half-eaten pie around the plate. "How much less?"

"Realistically, they'd probably accept three to three and half million. Let's say three and half. Less the exemption, it's two and half taxable. That would knock your tax burden down to one and a quarter million."

"What I'd call a distinction without a difference," said Monica. "We haven't got one and a quarter any more than we've got two point five."

"We'd better keep it on the market," Blaine said, then studied the figures, twirling an unlit cigarette between his lips—Monica wouldn't allow smoking in the house. "But I can't tell you how much I hate the idea of sellin' half this place. To me, it's like cuttin' one part of your leg off to save the rest of it."

"Assuming we can sell it," Monica said with an undertone of desperation. "People aren't going to be lining up to buy part of a cattle ranch smack dab on the Mexican border."

"You forgot to say twenty dirt-road miles from the nearest town," Blaine added. He lit the cigarette, drawing a rebuking look from Monica, then pushed the paper with the table of figures toward Castle. "What do you think, Gil?"

Castle looked at Lovelace's proposal, noticing that he recommended paying off the taxes in five years rather than the fourteen allowed by the IRS—this to reduce the total interest payments. "That three and a half mil—how confident are you that you'll get the IRS to agree?" he asked in a voice neither Blaine nor Monica had heard before. It sounded a little unfamiliar to Castle himself, the voice his clients and partners had heard: firm, crisp, demanding.

The lawyer canted his head and affirmed that he was quite confident; he'd handled cases like this before.

Castle borrowed Lovelace's pen and scratch pad and, resting his head in one hand, made a few simple calculations. The result made no financial sense whatsoever, but the dollars and cents were only part of it. He knew, from all the families whose fortunes he'd managed, that when money and property intruded, the orbits of family relationships got knocked all to hell. Rivalries and conflicts arose, misunderstandings, friction. As he sat there multiplying and dividing and thinking, he was being his usual deliberate, temperate self, the same self that had demurred on his aunt's proposal, that had been reluctant to grant Tessa's simple wish to meet her daughter, a self he was getting tired of. After all, at the end of the five years, he would still have a lot of money in the bank, assuming a reasonable rate of growth in his investments. He could make it work. And after all this reflection and arithmetic, he came to a decision, or rather, his mind ratified a decision his heart had made earlier, when he was gazing at the stars.

"I'll pay the taxes," he said, looking up from the scratch pad.

The other three stared at him.

"You do whatever you can to get them knocked down," he said to Lovelace, "and I'll pay them."

Stretching an arm across the table, Blaine grasped his shoulder. "Me and Monica never borrowed a dime from a friend or a relative, and we never took charity, and we're too damn old to start now."

"It wouldn't be a loan or a gift. It would be an investment in the ranch. A partnership. We'd run the place together, like Ben and Jeff did."

"Cuzzy, we appreciate the offer, we surely do, but if you was to write out what you know about the cattle business, you couldn't fill up a postcard."

"But I do know something about the business part. As far as the cattle part goes, it isn't nuclear physics. I could learn."

No one spoke for half a minute. Blaine broke the hush. "Well, I'll be damned. Darlin', what do you think?" Looking at Monica.

"I'm not sure what to think at the moment," she said.

"What about you, counselor?"

"I don't see any problems," Lovelace answered. "You could reorganize into an S corporation, you and Monica as majority shareholders. But"—he turned to Castle—"forgive me for asking this, but could you . . . I assume you wouldn't have made the offer if . . . We are talking seven figures here."

Castle smiled into the earnest young face. "I'm good for the money. I used to be a Wall Street big shot."

24

TO BREAK THE BED *with Billy.* Yvonne liked the sound of it in English—the hard, alliterative consonants were more direct, punchier than the Spanish, desvencijar la cama con Billy. The bed, the king-size canopy bed, she loved the expanse of it, the coolness of the satin sheets she'd ordered from Mexico City, the privacy of it when the translucent curtains were drawn, as they were now. She felt that she and Billy were in a cocoon, a small world of their own, where in the act of love she could escape her cares for a while.

Privacy had become very rare in her life, what with a dozen bodyguards prowling the grounds outside, what with the foreman and his vaqueros coming and going. There always seemed to be some crisis to deal with, some client to meet with, a deal to be cut, an army officer coming to her with his hand out, local yokels begging her, their madrina, for plastic irrigation pipe or a generator or a tractor or any one of a thousand things the miserable government of this country should provide for them but could not or would not. And then there was the war and all the plotting and planning it required of her. Strike and counterstrike. Attack and reprisal. Carrasco's most recent stroke had been audacious, brilliant, she was forced to admit. The Golden Roosters would crow no more. Now she would have to go him one better. Such were the dynamics. Do unto me, and I shall do much worse unto you.

Sometimes she was plagued by doubts. Did she have the capacity to realize her aims? The demands on her time and energy were too much, and she had begun to violate her rule, *Never use product.* She wasn't using a lot, a few lines now and then to keep her going. The Gulf Cartel's coke was of the purest kind, as smooth in its way as a fine, well-aged tequila. No burn in her nostrils, and oh, the elevation it brought, the sense of well-being, the zip, the zing, the keen buzz.

She could use a long holiday, a month or two at her villa in Zihuatanejo. Or Cancún. Or Puerto Vallarta. How wonderful it would be to see the ocean again, to swim, to lie on hot white sands with . . . someone. With the Man of Her Dreams. Yvonne Menéndez did have a Man of Her Dreams. She didn't know what he looked like. She had never seen him. He was in fact invisible. He had first come to her when she was a girl on the ejido, one night after Dámaso had violated her. He lifted her off the bed in incredibly strong arms and carried her across the desert, away from that wretched hovel, away from her perverted stepfather. The fantasy was so powerful that she had felt herself levitating, then flying out of the dark room stinking of Dámaso's liquor-breath, his boozy sweat, and the marvelous thing was that she also felt secure in the powerful arms. She had nothing to fear, she would be safe for as long as they held her. He made many visits, rescuing her from her degradation, until she'd rescued herself. Sometimes she thought he might have been the father she'd never seen, not even in a photograph.

Billy Cruz was not he. Billy was strong, with his prizefighter's physique, and he was virile, as she'd known he would be from the start—three times last night and once more this morning!—but his powers were all in his body, while the Man of Her Dreams had a strength that transcended the physical. Billy was not capable of rescuing her, nor of making her safe and secure. As a matter of fact, it was she who had rescued him, offering him the sanctuary of her ranch until such time as his difficulties on the other side were resolved. Or until she had no further use for him. Or plain got sick of him.

Now she turned over on her side and passed her hand over his forehead, damp from their last lovemaking. Well no, it wasn't lovemaking, it was fucking. "I was just thinking," she said, "that it's lucky for you we met. By now you would be in a different bed than this one."

A grin formed under the wreckage of his nose. "I did my best to say thanks."

Thinks he's something, Yvonne thought. And that it's me, the vieja, who should be grateful. "I'm going to see my lawyer today, my American lawyer. He knows a lot of people. I'm going to ask him if he can fix your problem."

"Sure would be good if he can."

Yvonne wanted it fixed as well. She was disappointed in Billy for getting himself into such a bad pinch, and all over a couple of worthless toilet scrubbers. Running his operations from the Mexican side of the line was proving cumbersome. Not impossible, but more complicated, and she had enough complications on her plate.

"Murder is a big problem to take care of," she said. "Alex will need to know all the facts, so let me make sure I've got them straight. You shot those mojados because they didn't pay you. They were supposed to pay you when you picked them up, but they said they didn't have the money and then tried to run away. Is that right?"

Billy rolled off his back and lay looking at her, cradling his cheek in a hand. "That's right."

"Two of them. You don't know what happened to the third?"

"I figured he got separated, yeah."

"So for six months nothing happened, and then you are told the chotas want to question you about these killings. Did your friend tell you why it took them so long? Did they find some evidence? Why, all of a sudden, did they come looking for you?"

"Don't know. My friend is a Nogales cop. All he knew was that the third guy, some little verga, had ID'd me and the sheriff had issued a warrant for my arrest."

"And that's all?"

"That's it."

"There was a story in the newspapers that the mojados were carrying merca."

"That's bullshit. They didn't have a gram on them."

Yvonne believed she had a built-in lie detector in her sensory equipment, and though it wasn't registering a lie at the moment, it was telling her that there was something wrong in this sketchy story. "It's not much to go on, so I'll ask my lawyer to find out what he can. Then I think he'll want to speak to you. I need you en el otro lado, you know?"

"Sure. But I can run things okay from here for a while. All I need is a phone."

She nudged his shoulder, a gentle push, and when he lay again on his back, she swung her legs over to straddle him. "This is the only way you're ever going to fuck me, Billy."

He laughed and gave her ass a squeeze. "You're the type who likes to be on top."

"Yes, but you know what I mean."

"Sure."

"I want to trust you, chico, and I've learned that I trust people who know exactly what will happen if they"—she poked his crooked nose—"cheat me. If they"—another poke—"steal from me"—and another—"or snitch or "—and yet another—"lie to me."

DRESSED AS IF she were going to dinner in the capital, in a black skirt, a patterned cotton blouse, pantyhose, and sexy high heels with ankle straps, Yvonne met Alex Daoud for lunch at Las Palmeras in Agua Prieta's central plaza. Just before leaving the car, she removed a small glass vial from her purse and inhaled a couple of bumps of la puta blanca with a tiny gold spoon. The white witch sharpened her mind and curbed her appetite. With a younger lover, she didn't want to get fat. Alex and Julián were already seated when she entered, flanked by Heraclio and Marco and attended by a fawning maître d'. She'd bought the restaurant a year ago, or rather one of her companies had, and she'd spent a small fortune hiring a decorator to refurbish the place. The result was an unhappy marriage of styles, Roman villa wed to Spanish colonial, with Mexican fishing village thrown in—Las Palmeras served seafood, flown in fresh three times a week, snapper and grouper from the Gulf of Mexico, shrimp and tuna from the Sea of Cortez.

While her bodyguards went off to another table, from which they could keep an eye on the door, she sat down with her son and her lawyer and ordered camarones with a sauce made of prickly pear. Julián and Alex complimented her appearance—she looked ten years younger, Alex said—and indeed Yvonne felt younger, freshly fucked, a glow in her cheeks, Billy's ardent embraces had taken years off her.

She convened the meeting, speaking in English—despite years of practicing law on the border, Alex's Spanish was third-grade level, and anyway it was more prudent to conduct their affairs in English. The main item on the agenda was a problem at the Douglas border crossing, a few blocks from where they now sat. The U.S. Customs inspectors who were paid to give Menéndez family vehicles a less-than-thorough going-over had been removed from their posts.

"The word on the street is that they're under investigation," Alex said.

Because it was more concealable than mota, coke was crossed in cars through ports of entry. On the scale between an absolute necessity and a mere luxury, owning a badge or two in the customs service fell somewhere in the middle. If you knew when your man was on duty and in which lane, it made hauling merca so much easier and safer.

"You know their boss," Yvonne said. "What does he say?"

Alex spread his freakishly large hands. "If they are under investigation, he is, too. Or will be. And maybe I could be, too."

"You've been there before," she said, referring to the times in the past when he had been investigated by the FBI for money laundering. He'd survived without a dent. Not even disbarred.

"I'm not worried, but I'd advise you to use another crossing for the time being. And if you do use Douglas, you know—"

"Do a better job of modifying the vehicles," said Julián.

Alex tilted his head slyly. He was of Arab descent, Lebanese or Syrian, she didn't know which, and she disliked him, for his looks if for no other reason, goggle-eyes under a high, sloping forehead, thick lips, a fishhook of a nose. In a Mr. Ugly Universe contest, he would be a finalist. But he and Yvonne made a royal couple. She was the Queen of

Agua Prieta, he was the King of Douglas, having been at one time or another its mayor, its chief of police, and justice of the peace, besides serving two terms in the Arizona state legislature. He knew all sorts of people, the right kind of people. Few things happened in Douglas without his okay, and nothing happened without his knowing about it.

"It's too bad we don't have Vicente," she said as their meals arrived. "There was a genius with cars."

The two bumps had had the desired effect. She felt full after eating only three of the camarones. While Julián and Alex dived into their dishes, she sipped her wine, a Spanish red, and pondered this matter of the customs inspectors. It seemed to give new urgency to acquiring the San Ignacio. Her own port of entry twenty kilometers end to end, and no worries about investigations, mordida, and all the rest. Thinking of that transited her thoughts back to Billy's predicament. She gave Alex an abridged account, asking if there was anything he could do. Julián pouted. He disapproved of her mixing business with pleasure, of sleeping with "the help," as he put it. She did not regard Billy as "help"; more as her partner in an enterprise. Nor could she see what was so wrong with mixing business and pleasure. There was no point in having money and power if she couldn't have anything, or anyone, she wanted. What did her son know of a woman's needs anyway? Come to think of it, maybe the mariposa knew too much about a woman's needs.

"First thing I'll do is advise you to get Cruz off your ranch," Alex said of her request.

"I don't believe my mother would want to do that," Julián chimed in with a stupid leer.

The lawyer fluttered his bulging eyes at Julián, then at her. "For chrissake, Yvonne. You've got yourself a boy-toy?"

She blushed and was irritated with herself for blushing.

"Harboring an American fugitive can't do you any good," Alex went on.

Julián clinked his glass with his fork. "Exactly what I told her."

His voice chafed her nerves. "I am talking to Alex, all right? Escúchame, Alex, what can you do about this?"

"Do you want me to a recommend a good criminal lawyer?"

"No."

"You're asking if I can get a murder warrant quashed?" he said in an undertone.

"What is this 'quashed'?"

"Make it go away."

"Yes, that's what I'm asking. Make it go away."

"It wouldn't be easy. It would take time and money."

"But would it be impossible? Why should the gringos give a shit about a couple of fucking dead toilet scrubbers? All they talk about over there is how to stop the toilet scrubbers and strawberry pickers from coming in. So there's two less they don't have to worry about."

Alex made a pleading gesture. "I'll see what can be done. I can't promise more."

She needed to pee and have another snort. Pushing away from the table, she said, "And just so you know, I don't need him for *that.* For other reasons you don't have to know, I need him working for me on the other side."

She went to the ladies' room, her heels clattering on the clay-tile floors. Squatting in the stall, her knees shackled by her pantyhose and underwear, she took the vial from her purse, dipped the gold spoon, brought it to a nostril, cupped one hand under the spoon, and inhaled sharply. Then the other nostril. There. Dos y no más. She heard "El Degüello," the bugle call that Santa Anna had sounded at the Alamo to signal "No quarter," its Moorish notes chilling yet sad, as if to say, *We are sorry that we must slit your throats.* She removed her mobile from the purse and answered. It was Clemente Morales, her cousin, the real estate broker.

"Yvonne, where are you? I could not reach you at the ranch."

"At the moment, I am in the cuartito changing the canary's water."

Clemente laughed, then apologized for catching her in such an embarrassing position. He had good news for her. She said she could use some. What was it?

"That rancho you have your eye on, the San Ignacio, it's up for sale."

This was incredible. It was as if the desire in her heart had made this happen. "Where are you, Clemente?"

"In Douglas. At my office."

"I am across the street. At Las Palmeras. Get over here as soon as you can."

She exited the stall and at the mirror freshened her makeup and wiped her nose of residue.

Her cousin was a short, portly man, his face a smooth brown moon always beaming. A real estate agent had to project an air of cheerful optimism. He arrived after dessert and gave Yvonne a two-page printout of the listing.

DESERT DIAMOND LTD

Douglas, AZ • Agua Prieta, Son.

Specializing in large agricultural properties in southern Arizona and Sonora, Mexico

Designated Broker • Clemente Morales

SAN IGNACIO RANCH

SANTA CRUZ AND COCHISE COUNTY, ARIZONA

GENERAL DESCRIPTION: The San Ignacio Ranch was started in 1910 and is one of the oldest and largest continuously operated cattle ranches in southern Arizona . . .

Size and Land Tenure: The San Ignacio contains approximately 32,415 acres. The deeded land comprises four contiguous parcels totaling 19,850 acres. The ranch's grazing permit in the Coronado National Forest contains approximately 12,565 acres . . .

THIS RANCH IS TO BE SUBDIVIDED: *Two of the four parcels of deeded land are being offered for sale.* These parcels, 1 & 2, are in a single block totaling approximately 10,115 acres . . .

PRICE, TERMS, AND CONDITIONS: Parcels 1 & 2 of the San Ignacio Ranch are for sale for $5,000,000, cash.

Looking at the map on one page, she noticed that the two parcels for sale were not adjacent to the border. What the hell good would that do her? The photographs on the last page—broad rangelands with mountains in the background, a small house included in the sale—caught her attention, not because they were particularly striking but because they offered her the first glimpse of the land she coveted.

She looked at Clemente. "You said the ranch was for sale. This says only half of it is for sale."

"Yes. They are subdividing it."

"I don't want half of it. I want all of it."

"But all of it is not for sale."

"I see that, I just said that, you idiot," she snapped. She felt irritable again, jumpy. "Why are they selling only the half?"

"I am told they are having tax problems," answered Clemente, warily. He seemed afraid of saying something that would provoke her. "The old lady died. The old lady Erskine. She and her son owned the place. I am told she was killed in an automobile accident, so now the son has to pay the taxes on her estate, and he must sell the half to pay them. They have, you know, motivación. They are motivated sellers."

"They who? Who are you talking about now?"

"The son and his wife," said Clemente, thrusting his brown moon face forward. "They have motivation to sell."

Yvonne's curiosity was piqued. "You met them?"

"No."

"Then how do you know they are motivated?"

Clemente puffed his cheeks and sighed. "Because they must pay these taxes. Right now you could make them an offer for much less than what they are asking, and I think they would agree."

"What if you went to them and said you have a buyer who wants the whole place?" Julián interjected.

Clemente shrugged. "Everything is for sale, you know." He opened the folder containing the listing and took out a few snapshots. "They are having more problems than tax problems, I heard. There are a lot of mojados moving through that rancho, and a lot of it is a mess. It is possible they would want someone to take the place and the problems off their hands. I took these pictures when I was out there."

He dealt the photographs to Yvonne and Julián like playing cards. They showed holes cut into fences, a broken gate, garbage drifted across an arroyo. Billy's handiwork. Really her handiwork. But was it having the effect she intended? Guerrilla warfare. Attacking Erskine's state of mind. And what of her own state of mind? Her head was full of agitated thoughts, flitting and flashing like spots before her eyes. She rattled her fingernails on the table, then jumped up, went to the bathroom again, and sucked in two more bumps, so deeply that the powder seemed to blast right through her skull into her brain. Using product. Shit. Disgusted with herself, Yvonne ducked into the stall and went to dump the vial into the toilet, but just then the flickering mental spots vanished and euphoria surged through her. She put the bottle back in her purse and walked out, crossing the room with regal bearing, in full command of herself again, of the men at her table, the queen of dark waters.

"All right, what happens if they don't pay those taxes?" she asked her cousin.

It was Daoud who answered. "The government forecloses on the property. It goes up for auction, at a fire-sale price. They have nine months to start paying from the date of the deceased's death."

"They would be left with nothing."

"Pretty much, yeah."

She looked out the window at the plaza, awash in brilliant afternoon light, the bandstand and the trees beginning to cast shadows, the trees whose whitewashed trunks reminded her of the sycamores in the canyon, the ghost trees. Everything was very clear. The old lady Erskine had been struck down for her benefit, and for Rosario's benefit. *Those people did very well for themselves while we suffered.* Her mother's words coming back to her, she realized that as much as she wanted the ranch, she wanted more to see the Erskines ruined.

"Then I think I will wait them out. All of it, not half."

Clemente cleared his throat. "There is a risk. This is not my exclusive listing. There are other brokers involved. If the land sells between now and then, you will be out of luck."

"And how likely is that?"

"It takes a long time to sell a property like this."

"I'm used to taking risks."

"The Americans say, half a loaf is better than none," Julián said in a smirking singsong.

"Shut up!" she cried, and swatted her hand, accidentally knocking a glass to the floor, its shattering like a nail in her ears. Her outburst surprised her as much as it did her dining companions. "I am sick of all you telling me what cannot be done. Am I the only one at this table with balls?"

25

IT WAS A LONG RIDE from Carrasco's ranch to Bisbee, and The Professor thought he would amuse Nacho Gomez with a lecture on synesthesia. Nacho, however, was more bemused than amused. "You lost me with that limbic brain, cortex shit," he said.

"The limbic brain is right here," explained The Professor, tapping the base of his skull. "The old brain, the brain we knew with before we knew we knew. It's preconsciousness." The headlights flashed on a covey of Gambel's quail, scuttling across the road ahead. "You like to hunt those things, right? Your bird dog wouldn't point a roadrunner, would it? Or a hawk, a crow. It picks up a scent and knows it's quail. How? The dog sees the smell. It sees quail but not with its eyes."

"I'll have to ask my dog about that."

"You need to be more open-minded about this. You need to stop thinking I'm a little loco. Synesthetes have amazing memories for one thing, and that can be useful to people who do what we do."

Nacho took offense. "I don't think of what you do and what I do as the same thing."

"You're an undercover cop, and I'm an undercover criminal," said The Professor.

"You're more of a crooked cop."

"Amounts to the same thing. You and I, we're like spies for rival governments. We use the same techniques, the same deceptions, and every so often we find it expedient to join forces."

"Like now."

"Like now."

"So do you have an amazing memory?"

"I never forget a face or a name. Take when I was with DEA working the Juárez Cartel, for an example. I meet an El Paso city cop, half-Italian, half-Mexican guy who works narcotics undercover. It's just in passing, I don't talk to him more than five minutes. Weeks later I'm surveilling a stash house on the other side of the line. Who walks out, giving abrazos grandes to a couple of big-time traffickers? My cop. How do I recognize him? The sensory experience. When I met him, his face made a specific sound, something like wind chimes. I hear the chimes and say, 'I know that face,' and then the name comes back to me. Okay, is he working an investigation, or is he rogue? I need to know because I'm supposed to infiltrate the Juárez ring, and if he's in tight with them, I might have problems."

"Just in case he had an amazing memory, too," Nacho said.

"Exactly. Did some checking, found out he was kinked up, passed the word to El Paso Internal Investigations, they nailed him, and that cleared the way for me. See how useful this condition can be?"

"Always an education with El Profesor."

"I might start charging you tuition."

Nacho swung off the federal highway onto the local road to Naco, one hand on the wheel, the other massaging the back of his neck. He'd crossed into Mexico twelve hours ago on what was known as an Eewee—an EWI, Entry Without Inspection, that is, illegally through a gap in the boundary fence—then drove to Carrasco's ranch near Caborca for a strategy session with Carrasco, Zaragoza, and The Professor; and his day was far from over.

"I'd like to test your amazing powers," he said. "There's a photograph in my briefcase. Take a look at it."

The Professor withdrew the five-by-seven mug shot and held it under the map light. He laughed. "Are you having fun? His name's right on it."

"Yeah, but who is Billy Cruz?"

"The late Vicente's nephew. A pollero. He was drinking beers with his uncle the night Vicente got killed. He was sitting on Vicente's right."

"Pretty good. I'm not supposed to know you know that, but that's neither here nor there. All right, the test. Eight months ago, I showed you a newspaper clipping about an incident that took place on January twenty-first in the Huachucas. What did the story say?"

The Professor saw the story scroll through his mind, like a teleprompter, and summarized the salient facts, including the names of the victims and the surviving witness.

"Damn good. It seems Mr. Miguel Espinoza has identified Cruz as the shooter. The Santa Cruz County sheriff went to take him in, but somebody got word to Cruz, and he skipped. He's believed to be here in Mexico. A BOL was sent to the MexFeds. You're a MexFed, some of the time anyway. Have you seen it?"

"Not in my department."

"There are rumors he's hiding out on Yvonne's ranch. He's working for her."

"For her? The only people who hate pollos and polleros more than her are the Minutemen."

"La Roja may have diversified into the chicken business, and Cruz is her vice president in charge. Cruz is crossing illegals with her okay and cutting her in. So I've heard. Makes sense. A good alien smuggler can bring in fifty thousand a month."

"A gringo fugitive on the dodge in old Me-hee-co," The Professor quipped after absorbing this intelligence, which was new to him. "In an ever-changing world, it's comforting to know that some things never change."

"There's a point to all this," said Nacho, annoyed with the flippancy. "The sheriff is up for reelection in 'oh-four. He wants this guy. He wants to show the voters that he's doing something about violence on the border."

The Professor took it from there. "To continue the script, the sheriff's good friend, Agent Gomez, requests my assistance in locating and apprehending Mr. Cruz. A win-win. The Border Patrol busts the mero mero of an alien smuggling ring, the sheriff catches a killer."

"Not asking you to make a special effort, but you do owe me one."

"I'm paying you back. What's this? Interest?"

They drove on. La Roja—mixed up in alien smuggling? The Professor thought. He wouldn't have believed it. In fact, he didn't believe it.

Some distance away the lights of Naco glittered on the black face of the desert, a sparse clustering, sparse and faint compared with the klieg lights glaring across the border wall running east and west of the little town for five miles, the barrier constructed of steel landing mats, the kind used to build temporary military airfields, and where it ended, surveillance towers took over, picketing arroyos and shallow canyons. The Professor could not see the towers, but he knew they were there, tall steel poles with steel arms, at the ends of which cameras swiveled, transmitting greenish images to monitors in the Naco Border Patrol station. When one spied mules or mojados coming over, an agent grasped a joystick, took manual control of the camera, and tracking the scurrying figures on his screen, radioed mounted patrolmen wearing night-vision goggles under their cowboy hats—"Twelve walkers brushed up two hundred yards south of you"—to ride in and capture the crossers. Star Wars joining hands with the Old West, two myths linked by the gringo faith in technology to overcome, the Winchester repeating rifle that cleared the plains of buffalo and Indians ancestor to the electronic sensors and infrared cameras that kept the Mexicans out.

Or were supposed to keep them out. It was as strong and blind as any religious conviction, this faith, and it had turned America into a nation of lazy, superficial, Web-surfing fools playing video games, alienated from the beating heart of life. He, the synesthete, understood this better than most people. As he could see with his eyes and with more than his eyes, so could he know with his reason and with more than his reason, and what he knew was that the wetbacks got through in spite of the gadgets and gizmos because they lived at the depths the gringos had abandoned long ago; lived close to the bone and relied on wit and grit to overcome (in Juárez, he remembered, there had been a run on Phillips-head screwdrivers because the Mexicans pounded them into a barrier fence as pitons to climb out of the land of blood and memory into the land of machines and tomorrow); because they were driven by history—their destiny was manifest, too, in the North rather than in the West—and by emotion, the same lust for riches, or what to them were riches, that had pushed Coronado from Mexico City all the way into modern Kansas on his quest for the Seven Cities of Cibola. It was a kind of gold rush, this migration, bigger and more inexorable than the one in California a century and a half ago. The first gold rush could not have been stopped with high-tech towers and virtual barricades, had such marvels existed then; and this one would not be stopped, either. La reconquista would triumph in the end, and the Spanish tongue prevail in the lands where it had been silenced.

They entered Naco, where the atmosphere of an Old West border town lingered. Parts of it—dirt streets, quaint, mud-brick houses—looked like a set for a Clint Eastwood western. Some buildings would have to be blocked from the shot, like the cavernous disco hulking incongruously above the low-lying adobes, stores, and cantinas on the main drag. THE GALAXY, its neon sign said, one of Yvonne Menéndez's laundries. The Professor caught the scents of mesquite-burning stoves, of frying tacos and tortillas, and he saw the colors of the smells, violet, rose, pale yellow. A gang of burreros lurked on a street corner, all with the disheveled, worn-out look of grunts returned from a desert patrol.

"Dropped their loads, and now they're home for R and R," Nacho remarked. "You know, I kind of admire those guys. Tough dudes. Hump fifty pounds on your back for twenty-five miles, walk twenty-five back, and for five hundred bucks a trip."

"Two, three trips a month, you're talking real money to a Mexican kid," The Professor said. "New truck, new clothes, money to toss around in the clubs. Look at it this way. Every drug mule represents one wetback you don't have to deal with, and one more pissed-off, unemployed trabajador Mexico doesn't have to worry about starting a revolution. The social benefits are enormous."

"Yeah, right. Tough dudes all the same. Few years ago, when I was in the field, I busted a nineteen-year-old who got separated from the others way the fuck out in East Jesus. '¿Dónde está la mota?' I ask him, but he doesn't know squat about any dope, so I cuff him to a mesquite tree and ask him again. He still doesn't know. This goes on for fifteen minutes. Then I ask him for his mother's name and address. What do I want to know that for? 'Because,' I tell him, 'I'm a nice guy who wants your mamacita to know what happened to her son because he wouldn't tell me where the dope was.' He starts to shake, and I'm thinking, This is where I break him. Wrong. 'What dope?' he says. 'I don't carry no dope. I carry only the food and water.' They all say that. Finally I take out my piece, cock it, and stick it in the back of his head. 'One last time, you little pendejo, where is the fucking dope, or I'll blow your brains all over this tree.' Know what he says? 'Then I guess this is my time to die.' Holstered the pistol, let him go. He'd broken me."

"Another lesson learned," The Professor sighed. "Never make a threat you're not prepared to carry out."

"It was his first trip. He didn't know that."

"He does now."

In the single-lane port of entry, Nacho showed his badge to the inspector, and The Professor produced the Arizona driver's license identifying him by his American cryptonym, E. J. Carrington. Naco, Arizona, was smaller, darker, and less lively than Naco, Sonora. There was the mission-style border station, its handsome lines harking back to an era before the minimum-security prison became the default model for American municipal architecture, a bar where gringos on Social Security rubbed elbows with contrabandistas, and—not much else. Nacho proceeded up the Bisbee highway as a summer storm strafed the Mule Mountains. In a quarter of an hour he pulled into the San Jose Lodge, on Bisbee's outskirts, and he and The Professor went up to the second floor, where a U.S. Customs agent named Brent Pierce had rented a room.

"He's motivated," Nacho said as they climbed the stairs. "He was working the case that Yvonne fucked up with her snitch massacre."

"The Pond of Death. You're sure he's cool with this?"

"Won't be the first time he made a bargain with one devil to pop another."

Unlike the paunchy, clerkish Nacho, Pierce looked so much like an undercover cop, he might as well have been wearing a badge and uniform: shaggy hair, three-day growth of beard, the build of a steroid abuser. The set of clubs in a leather caddy standing beside the dresser did not go with his thuggish appearance; it was as if an outlaw biker had taken up golf.

Following the introductions, Pierce produced a bottle of Herradura from the minifridge and poured three generous shots into plastic cups.

"Too bad we don't have real glasses," he said apologetically, settling into a table chair turned backward. "Ruins the taste of a good tequila. Salud."

The Professor raised his cup and seated himself beside Nacho on the sofa. "Salud."

"Let's start by making sure we're on the same page," Pierce said. "Nacho tells me Carrasco wants what we want—Yvonne out of the picture. And that you've got some ideas about how we can get there. That's right?"

"It is."

"What does Carrasco need us for? He's got resources. Why doesn't he take care of her himself. Or sic the MexFeds on her?"

"You want me to count the ways?"

Pierce looked at him with dry, bright eyes, sniper's eyes. "Yeah, count the ways."

"One, Yvonne's got legal protection all the way up the food chain. Two, she's got the army on her side—that leaves the MexFeds out, unless you want Mexican cops shooting it out with Mexican troops. Three, she's franchised herself to the Gulf cartel, so she's got its gunman on call. Four, Joaquín wants the war over with. It's not doing anybody any good."

And, he thought, I'm sick of it, too. He'd been sick of it since the slaughter of the Golden Roosters.

Pierce wrapped his fence-post arms around the back of his chair. He looked capable of splintering the rungs with one good squeeze. "Violence up, profits down."

"In a phrase," The Professor said. "It will be a lot less messy if the U.S. takes care of Yvonne. Joaquín gets rid of her without any more bloodshed. Good for him, good for U.S. Customs."

"And exactly how is he going to cooperate with us, or us with him, however you want to put it?" asked Pierce.

"I'm on loan to you. Yvonne has never seen me—neither has her son, Julián. As far as I know, and that's pretty far, nobody in her organization knows what I look like. I'm going to infiltrate her Agua Prieta Cartel. I'm going to be your informant."

Pierce rose, refreshed the cups, then withdrew a club from his caddy and made a putt. "I'm all ears."

"I pose as an American coke dealer, make contact with Yvonne, and gain her confidence with a few buys. Once I've established myself as a reliable customer, I dangle temptation. I've got a big client who wants to do multikilo deals." Then, his glance switching between Nacho and Pierce: "You'll be the client. A heavy hitter but too suspicious to do deals in Mexico. You'll only do business in the U.S. That's how we lure her across the line with a load. The transaction goes down, you pop her, and no complications because she's a U.S. citizen. If we work it right, we net Julián, too. We decapitate the Menéndez organization."

Pierce replaced the putter. He was skeptical. The sting required a degree of recklessness in Yvonne that he didn't think she possessed. What made The Professor so confident he could win her trust to the point that she'd cross a load herself?

"Greed. She's the greediest bitch in the business. If the reward looks big enough to her, she'll take the risk."

Pierce squinted to indicate that he still wasn't persuaded.

"I've done this before," The Professor said, sounding like a salesman pitching himself.

"So Nacho informs me. A long time ago. You might be out of trim."

"You don't forget how. It's like riding a bike. If you're wondering what it would cost the U.S. government besides your salary, the answer is nothing. Carrasco will fund the buys."

The color of Pierce's eyes—they looked like aluminum disks—gave off a bitter smell. He turned them to Nacho. "You talked to the man himself?"

"This afternoon. It's The Professor's idea, but Joaquín is behind it, one hundred percent."

"All that Joaquín asks is that his role in it is kept under wraps," said The Professor. "We play it as a joint operation, U.S. Customs and the MexFeds join hands to take down a major drug dealer."

"Writing the headlines already?" asked Pierce. "There's the small problem of making Yvonne's acquaintance. How do you plan to do that?"

"I'm working on it. But I need to know before I go ahead that you're all in."

"You've got brass ones, I'll give you that much. If she makes you, the best you could hope for is that she takes less than three days to kill you."

Pierce swung off his chair and extended a hand that looked only a little smaller than a catcher's mitt.

The Professor shook it. "Actually," he said with a trace of British slur—*ekshulee*—"I'm looking forward to it. Should be fun."

26

SELDOM IN THE COURSE of his clandestine labors had The Professor resorted to Sherlock Holmes disguises; however, present circumstances dictated that he blend in with the scenery. His plan was to turn Billy Cruz, and that had brought him here, in what used to be Carrasco's territory but was now Yvonne's. He was behind enemy lines. Wearing a straw cowboy hat, jeans, and a dirty denim shirt, towing an empty two-horse trailer behind a Ford pickup that would have had a round-trip to the moon on its odometer if its odometer still worked—the dial had frozen at 300,000 kilometers at some point in the remote past—he was to all appearances a shabby vaquero in a shabby truck. Wide patches of rock and gravel scabbed the overgrazed hillsides, upon which scrawny cattle foraged or lazed under mesquite trees, branches bent and twisted, like arthritic fingers. No rain had fallen in a week—a break in the chubascos—and he hung well behind the convoy (three vans led by Billy Cruz in a white Dodge Ram) to keep from being choked and blinded by the dust. He had picked up the convoy at the Cananea motel where the mojados had been stashed overnight, then followed it down Mex-2 and onto the road to Santa Cruz, its destination. There, Billy would assemble his human cargo for a night run to the border, seven miles away.

Soldiers at the San Lazaro checkpoint flagged The Professor down, and as one, an Indian, listlessly searched the trailer, another peeked into the truck and asked where he was going. To a rancho to pick up some horses, he answered, and continued on. Approaching a cattle guard, a familiar stench assaulted his nostrils. Lying at the roadside was the bloated, fly-specked carcass of a horse, all four legs chopped off at the knee. The animal, blind or extremely stupid, must have attempted to cross the cattle guard and gotten trapped between the rails, blocking the road until someone shot it, amputated its lower legs, and towed it out of the way. The border. La linea. La frontera. Lovely part of the world.

Water was flowing in the Santa Cruz River, not much, maybe a foot. Beyond it was its namesake town, a compact, tidy settlement of flat-roofed houses and shops, ornate iron bars on the windows. Half a block ahead the convoy parked in front of a grocery. The Professor watched the drivers go into the store and come out ten minutes later, lugging supplies in plastic bags. Probably the standard pollo fare—cans of frijoles, sterno to heat them, bottled water, Electrolit. A boost to the local economy.

He reached under the seat for his Motorola handheld and radioed the federal police station. "I am in town and so is he. I will tell you to pick him up."

"Sí, mi capitán," a voice replied.

The small contingent of federales were his only allies here. They'd remained loyal to Joaquín after Yvonne's swift takeover, partly because she, calculating that her army patrons provided sufficient protection, had failed to cut them in.

He trailed the vehicles past the plaza to the Pemex station, where they gassed up. From there they proceeded up an unpaved side street, stopping at a mud-brick building with bedsheets curtaining its windows. A wetback hostel. A stash house. The migrants piled out of the vans, around forty of them clutching flight bags, backpacks, and small suitcases, and were hustled inside. Cruz went in with them, carrying an attaché case. The vans left, heading back to Cananea to pick up another load. Cruz emerged from the stash house after collecting his fees and drove back to the plaza, where a small clubfooted girl watched her playmates climbing on the water-tower girders and several young men idled on the benches, smoking, talking. Parked near the police station, on the opposite side of the plaza, The Professor observed Cruz summon the young men to his Dodge for a conference. These were the guides who would lead the migrants through the perils of serpents and scorpions and heat into El Norte, where dreams came true, though not always. Cruz looked quite relaxed, guzzling a beer as he gave instructions. Yvonne must have obtained the Sonoran license plates on his truck; there would be a forged Mexican registration in the glove compartment and a Mexican driver's license in his wallet, everything he needed to prove he was a citizen.

The streetlamps came on, the kids went home, the clubfooted girl hobbling behind, and the coyotes hurried off in the direction of the stash house. As Cruz pulled away, The Professor keyed his Motorola.

"He is leaving now, going south," he said, and gave the tag numbers and a description of the truck. "Remember, outside of town. Be sure no one sees the arrest."

"Sí, mi capitán."

He slouched behind the wheel, tipping the cowboy hat over his eyes, and waited. Twenty minutes later the radio crackled. They had picked him up, and no, there had been no trouble. Another twenty minutes passed. A federal police SUV pulled up in front of the whitewashed station, across from the courthouse. In handcuffs Cruz was led inside by two federales. The Professor bided his time, then walked up the street, past the church, and entered the station, so sparsely furnished it almost looked uninhabited. A cop sat at a desk, filling out the arrest report on a manual typewriter—the twenty-first century had not yet caught up to Santa Cruz and probably never would. The cop opened Cruz's attaché case, filled with bundles of hundred-dollar bills, maybe fifty thousand all together, a sight to tempt Saint Francis, and handed The Professor a plastic evidence bag containing Cruz's wallet and car keys. Inside the wallet were a thousand pesos and two hundred dollars in cash, a Mexican license issued to one Jaime Ortega, and tucked into a compartment, an Arizona license and credit cards in the name of William Cruz. Sloppy, he thought. Exceptionally sloppy. Cruz had flunked Fugitive 101.

He was in what passed for the lockup—a bare-walled room just big enough to accommodate a cot and a toilet. The room stank of urine, of every unwashed body that had spent any time there. Still cuffed, a disconsolate Cruz sat on the concrete floor, wedged into a corner. He couldn't sit on the cot, infested with fleas. The Professor motioned to the federale to take the handcuffs off.

"Buenas noches, Jaime. Quisiera tener unas palabritas con usted. ¿Está bien?"

Rubbing his wrists, his fingertips blackened by fingerprint ink, Cruz looked up warily from under his pale, scarred eyebrows. "¿Quién eres?"

"At the moment, the only friend you've got in the world."

Cruz blinked, hearing what appeared to be a vaquero address him in perfect English. "American?"

"That's not important, Jaime. I should say Billy. The only important thing is that I'm your friend."

"What—what are you . . . what do you want?"

"I want you to get up off the floor and sit on the toilet."

"Hey, bro—the floor's fine."

The Professor made a sound of dismay. "You're in trouble. You're an American citizen illegally in Mexico, with a phony driver's license under an assumed name. You've got a suitcase full of cash you can't account for. You're also wanted for questioning in Arizona about a double homicide. I'm sure the gentlemen who arrested you have gone over all that with you."

"What of it?"

"If you would like these troubles to go away, you'll do as I ask."

Cruz pulled himself to his feet and sat on the commode. Its acrid smell had a color and shape—a greenish blob—and Cruz's handsome but battered face made a distinctive sound, the sound of footsteps crunching on gravel.

"Who the hell are you?"

"Carrington. A few years ago you did time in the Arizona state penitentiary on drug charges. That's where you and I became friends."

"Never saw you in my life," said Cruz, after a silence.

"I know that. You know that. Yvonne Menéndez doesn't know that. You're going to introduce me to Yvonne, you're going to vouch for me. You're going to tell her that I'm your old cellmate from Florence, and that I want to do business with her. No mota, coke only, in quantity. That's what I want. I want to meet Yvonne Menéndez."

"Bro, I don't—"

The Professor signaled him to be quiet. "Let's make this conversation short and pleasant instead of long and unpleasant. Please don't tell me you don't know any Yvonne Menéndez. You're living on her ranch, you're running wets into the U.S. with her blessings, and you're fucking her."

Cruz stared at him for half a second before his glance skidded away. He muttered something.

"I'm not sure you appreciate your situation. If I leave here a disappointed man, the MexFeds are going to take you to the Nogales port of entry and hand you over to Sheriff Danny Rodriguez. He's got an eyewitness and evidence identifying you as the guy who killed a couple of Mexicans in January. They were carrying drugs, which you stole. Twenty-five years at least, maybe life, maybe, if the prosecutor does a bang-up job, a lethal injection. Now, I can understand why you might be willing to take that risk. A conviction is a possibility, the alternative is a certainty."

He was gaining Cruz's attention. "What alternative?"

"What Yvonne will do to you if she finds out that you and your deceased uncle were ripping her off."

"You're talking shit!" Cruz exclaimed.

"I'm a student of history, Billy, and I've done some research this past week or so into recent history. Vicente was a kleptomaniac, couldn't resist stealing from whoever he was working for, and he was stealing from Yvonne. Part of a load here, part of a load there. Sometimes he had problems crossing the stolen merca. That's when he'd call on his pollero nephew to rope a few mojados to mule it over. Then he'd split the proceeds with you. So one day last winter, you got three wets down on their luck to pack in about sixty, seventy kilos of mota. The plan was for them to move behind a vanload of illegals who were supposed to decoy the Border Patrol in case they were in the neighborhood. You were on the other side, waiting to pick up the load. But things went wrong. You didn't know what or why—I imagine you do now—all you knew was that your three mules didn't show. 'They're ripping me off!' is what you thought. You tracked them down and capped two. You couldn't find the third but figured you'd better snatch the load and get the hell out. That's exactly what you did."

Hands folded between his knees, Cruz did not respond.

"It's interesting when you think about it. It's, oh, ironic. You didn't know at the time that the woman you and your uncle had ripped off had ordered the illegals in the van to be massacred to teach a lesson. And she didn't know that right behind that van was another, with her merca in it. It scares *me* to think what she would do if she ever found out. And you being her fuck of the month would only make it worse. Hell hath no fury, et cetera. So here you are, between the rock—a murder trial—and the hard place—Yvonne Menéndez. No, you don't want me to leave here disappointed."

Cruz rubbed his face with both hands. "My best friend in the world."

"Best and only. All you have to do is make an introduction, and oh yeah, whenever you think of it, keep me informed about what your lover and patroness is up to."

"You didn't say nothing before about snitching."

"It must have slipped my mind."

"So what are you? DEA? ICE? FBI?"

"You've got a real command of the alphabet," The Professor said. "What I am doesn't matter. All that matters is for us to be friends."

27

"WANT YOU TO MEET my cousin and new partner," Blaine said to the bartender in the Wagon Wheel Saloon (PATAGONIA'S ORIGINAL COWBOY BAR—ESTABLISHED 1937 read the sign out front). "Signed the papers today."

The bartender, a tall and substantial man with a sweatband of brownish hair, thrust out his hand to Castle. "Word's all over town that you pulled Blaine's fat out of the fire. Don't know if I should congratulate you or feel sorry for you. What'll it be?"

It was Castle's first time in the Wagon Wheel. A vintage Hank Williams tune played on the jukebox, and two men circled the pool table chalking cues; a stuffed bobcat crouched on a fired-brick wall displaying antique firearms and frontier implements. Castle wanted a martini, but the saloon did not seem like a martini sort of place, so he ordered a Pacífico with a tequila chaser.

"And none of that well tequila that you can burn in a Coleman lantern," Blaine said. "My cuzzy has refined tastes."

"Will this do, sir?" asked the barkeep, holding up a bottle of Patrón Silver.

Blaine slapped two twenties on the bar and motioned with his finger that he was buying the house. A couple of women customers smiled at him discreetly, men in cowboy hats and baseball caps and work shirts, looking through shoals of cigarette smoke stirred by a hot August breeze blowing through the screen door, nodded or flipped two-finger salutes. Castle, garbed in the khakis, polo shirt, and loafers he'd worn to Lovelace's Tucson office, felt out of place, despite his new status as a working cattleman. He, Blaine, and Monica had signed the incorporation papers in the morning, and he had turned over a check made out to the Internal Revenue Service for the first payment on the estate taxes. Looking at the figure had brought on a wave of buyer's remorse—not the amount itself but the commitment it represented.

The bartender came back from attending another customer and poured himself a shot of the well tequila. "Need to light my inner Coleman lantern. Salud, you two."

"Salud," said Blaine, raising his beer.

"So the ranch is off the market? I can tell Ted Turner to forget it the next time he's in here?"

"As of too-day. And as of too-morrow, Gil gets to find out what he paid for. We're gone to—"

The sharp rap of an empty beer bottle on the bar interrupted Blaine. "Can a man get a drink around here?"

"Look who's here," drawled Blaine, glowering at the wasted figure standing between two seated patrons, holding a cue stick. "My offer don't apply to him," he said to the barkeep, who took the empty, pulled a fresh one from the cooler, and said, "Three-fifty."

"You oughta be careful who you let into this place," Blaine said in a loud voice.

Idaho Jim paid for his drink and threw a hard look at him. "I was just thinking the same thing."

He went to the pool table and, setting the beer on the floor, racked the balls. His partner, a Mexican with the dimensions of a retired nose tackle, broke the rack, the cue ball cracking like a starter's pistol, the balls exploding in all directions.

"You seem to have a problem with that guy," the bartender remarked to Blaine.

"More him with me. Who's the big Mexican?"

"Name is Linares. That's all I know."

Blaine fell into one of his brooding silences, then finished his beer. "Drink up, Gil. All of a sudden I don't feel like celebrating."

As they left, Idaho Jim crouched over the table to line up a shot. At the moment when he drew the cue stick, Blaine managed to bump into him on the way out the door. The tip made a splintering sound, and the cue ball dribbled off wide of its mark.

They had just got into Castle's Suburban when the Mexican giant appeared outside. Although his arms and hands spelled "blunt-force trauma," he wore an almost genial smile. "Hey, man, got to tell you something," he said, looking at Blaine. "You gotta lot of luck. You don't know how much. You shouldn't push it, you know?"

Blaine started to say something, but Castle backed out onto the street before he could say it.

DURING HIS EIGHT MONTHS at the San Ignacio, Castle had sampled the drudgery of the ranchman's life; the next morning, he got a chance to experience the romance of it: a gathering, which was the correct term for what tenderfeet called a roundup. Yesterday, after the near altercation at the Wagon Wheel, Blaine had given him a crash course in the terminologies of his newfound trade—the different parts of the stock saddle, the various kinds of bits and bridles—along with lectures on cattle breeds, species of grasses, the current cattle market, the San Ignacio's business plan (to sell yearling steers at 780 pounds). In delivering these tutorials, Blaine was determined to show that although the cattle business wasn't, in Castle's words, nuclear physics, it wasn't first grade, either.

Now, as the sky lightened to oyster gray, nine people rode out of ranch headquarters at an easy trot—Blaine, Monica, Gerardo, Castle, Tessa, McIntyre, and the manager of a neighboring ranch with his two young hands, an Anglo and a Mexican. There was no wind and no sound except for the hoofbeats. The Huachucas retarded the dawn, and Venus shone in the east, its brilliance fading as the sun rose behind the mountains, coloring a reef of clouds pale pink, then peach, and finally a fiery gold. The Mexican hand loped out ahead of the others. Blaine's neighbor rode after him, and after catching up, he smacked the young cowboy on the back with his hat and spoke to him sharply in Spanish. The cowboy pulled rein, then waited for the riders to pass before taking his place in the rear.

Castle asked what that was all about.

"A lesson in ett-ee-cut," answered his cousin. "You don't never ride out ahead of the cow boss. An old-time vaquero would of known that before he was out of diapers. These new ones don't know better."

They rode on for another mile, halting in a basin where Blaine gave out assignments: his neighbor and the two cowboys to take the right wing, gathering the pastures along the Mexican border; he, Monica, and Gerardo would take the middle; Tessa, McIntyre, and Castle the left. They were all to rendezvous in the basin, then drive the herd to the pastures near the shipping corrals for branding the next day.

"Tessa, you'll be in charge. Should be sixty head up in there. Show my cuzzy how it's done."

Tack creaked and jiggled, and the horses' legs swished in the tall grass, speckled by the mustard-colored flowers of camphor weed. In single file, Tessa leading and Castle behind on Comanche, they followed a ridgeline above a canyon a quarter mile wide at its mouth. Yellowhead crows perched on the fence wire flew off in clouds at the riders' approach. They eased their horses down to the canyon floor, split by an arroyo, through which a ribbon of water flowed, trickling over rock dams to form shining pools. A splendid buck antelope, hide like rubbed leather, burst from its bed, jumped the arroyo, and sprinted up the ridge without breaking stride. A dozen Angus cows with calves rested ahead, the cows with bright green tags dangling from their ears. Tessa advised Castle not to get too close or the calves would think he was part of the herd and follow him instead of their mothers. She was all business and looked it in a denim shirt, a sweat-stained hat, and scratched chaps. A flash of lust distracted Castle nonetheless, for she sat her horse like a show rider, her erect posture exaggerating the swell of her breasts, which needed no exaggerating, her hips, thighs, and bent knees forming a snaky curve.

She approached the herd at a slow walk, Castle on one side, McIntyre on the other. The cows heaved off their knees and immediately began to bawl for their calves, and each one seemed to know the sound of its mother's voice, though they all sounded alike to the human ear.

A short distance farther on, in an almost treeless meadow, another twenty head grazed. Leaving Castle to trail the first twelve, Tessa and McIntyre rode off, slapping their coiled lariats, and collected the animals. One cow bolted, her bull calf running after her. Tessa checked her, but the calf panicked and continued its flight. She shook out a loop and made a toss, the loop dropping over the little bull's neck as neatly as a ring over a stake. Tessa dallied; the calf flipped onto its side, then scrambled to its feet, shaken but unhurt. The chase, the throw, the capture had been all one fluid movement, and thrilling to see. Castle's heart swelled; it felt like a blossom, opening up.

They chased cows off ridges and out of gullies, through wooded side canyons and across hillside meadows. Delinquents attempted to escape, fleeing into tight defiles from which the Christian cowboy dislodged them with un-Christian epithets. On his own Castle ran down four miscreants, two with calves, two without, turned them, and brought them in, flushed from the exhilarating pursuit, pleased with himself for accomplishing the feat without supervision.

They pushed the herd at an easy pace to avoid overheating the calves—it was now past midmorning and well over ninety degrees—and stopped at the canyon mouth, riding in slow circles until the animals settled down, a milling mass, heads and backs haloed by flies. After making a count, they concluded they were short three head. McIntyre said he'd seen them in a side canyon. Tessa said she would hold herd while he looked for the strays. Castle volunteered to ride along.

"Thought you'd be a tad butt-sore by now," said McIntyre as they backtracked at a quick walk.

"I am, but this doesn't feel like work."

"Cowboying ain't work—it's a disease. Best job in the world, except when you're out here in a thunderstorm or it's twelve above with a norther slappin' your face." McIntyre ducked under a low branch. "There one of 'em is."

He motioned at a patch of black showing through the trees, where the side canyon met the main canyon. But the cow didn't move, and when they drew closer, they saw why: it was a black plastic tarp, partly camouflaged with cut tree branches, thrown over marijuana bales stacked like hay.

McIntyre looked around nervously, stood in the stirrups, and called out, "¡Buscamos ganado y nada más!" He hesitated a beat, then yelled again. "¡Buscamos ganado y nada más!"

"What's that?" asked Castle quietly.

"Tellin' 'em we're lookin for cattle and nothin' else. Don't want 'em to think we're law, or what'd be worse, bajadores lookin' to rip off their load."

"They're here? They're around?"

"Watchin' us right now, I'd bet, and make another bet at least one of 'em is carryin an assault rifle. Ain't gonna let a load this big get stole. Must be twenty bales, a thousand keys. Probably waitin' for a vehicle to make the pickup."

"Do we keep looking or get the hell out of here?"

McIntyre crossed his hands over the saddle horn. "The mules won't make no trouble for us, long as they know we ain't gonna make none for them."

They entered the side canyon, turning their heads back and forth, wary of surprising the drug runners. The landscape had changed; that is, Castle's view of it had, his imagination populating the underbrush and oak stands with smugglers watching his every move. Yet anger simmered under his uneasiness. Who the hell did these traffickers think they were to use his land—yes, it was his now—as a warehouse for their goods? He was not, as he might have been in the past, inclined to forgive those who had trespassed against him. He was beginning to think like Blaine.

They found the three strays and moved them to the herd by a different route, agreeing that the smugglers might not tolerate their passing by a second time. McIntyre asked, "Say, Gil, how many joints do you figure you could roll out of a thousand keys?"

Castle's skill wasn't at a level where he could herd cows, talk, and do arithmetic in his head at the same time, but he gave it a try. "Depends on how many grams to a joint. Say two. A thousand grams to a kilo, so that would make five hundred per kilo, times a thousand." He paused, picturing the zeroes. "Half a million."

The cowboy whistled through his teeth. "And that's just one load. I mean, *who* is smokin' all this shit?"

After rejoining Tessa, they pushed their sixty head to the basin and held there until the others came in. The neighboring rancher, recognizable at a distance by his flame-red bandanna, appeared first, riding point over the basin's southern rim. The cattle behind him appeared as a solid river of black, surging down the shallow slope; startled meadowlarks burst out of the grass in front of the herd. Blaine and Gerardo rode one flank, Monica and the Anglo hand the other, and the Mexican who didn't know his manners rode drag, a kerchief pulled over his mouth and nose. Castle thought it a grand sight.

Blaine rode over to Tessa and asked for a count. "They look good, don't they?" he said of the cattle, hemmed into the basin by the riders. "Gone to make some fine four-to-five-year-old cows."

Castle hated to spoil his mood with news of his discovery.

Blaine mopped his face. "Where?"

"Maybe a quarter mile up the canyon, on the north side."

The queer, oblique smile veered across his cousin's face. "Know what our grandpa would of done? Set fire to that stash, and when the dopers come out of the bushes to put it out, shot every one of the fuckin' bastards."

"That was then, and now is now," said Castle, a little irritated by the John Wayne theatrics. "And anyway, I didn't have a match."

"Yeah, and heck, Blaine," McIntyre said, "if you was to light up that much dope, everybody downwind for twenty miles would be stoned all day."

Castle laughed with Tessa. Blaine wasn't in a humorous frame of mind. "We've got to move this whole bunch through two gates, cuzzy. That can be easy sometimes, and sometimes it's like tryin' to shove a wet noodle up a bobcat's ass. Watch for a cow wants to bolt. Keep off to the side, so you can see how she turns her head. That way you'll know what she wants to do before she does."

The point rider seemed to tow the herd out of the basin single-handed. Mother cows again lowed to their young, and the calves squealed in response; the hands prodded stragglers with whistles and cries of "Yah! Yah!" The procession plodded across a muddy ciénaga, and then the pasture burned in the range fire and funneled into the first of the gates, bumping and jostling.

Following instructions, Castle kept his eyes on one young cow that showed signs of making a break for it. She was lagging behind, casting glances toward a creekbed. Before he could react, she took off at a dead run, her calf trotting after her on spindly legs. He spurred Comanche and chased her into the creek, where she veered abruptly. He went to turn the pinto, but inadvertently pulled back on the reins while jabbing with his spurs, leaving the horse totally confused.

Tessa rode up to him. "Give him his head," she said. "He knows better than you do."

Cow and calf were scampering down the creek. Castle slacked the reins and cued Comanche into a high lope. The cow spun to run away at a right angle to her original path, but Comanche, sensing her intent, quickly stopped her. When she whirled in the opposite direction, Tessa was there to cut her off. She was an obstinate, ill-tempered animal, for as they started to push her out of the creek, she jumped it and scrambled up the other side, almost trampling her calf.

Tessa flew at her, and leaning over in the saddle, she smacked her haunch with her coiled rope. "You dumb bitch! You almost stomped your kid!" Another smack. "You want to run, I'll run you! I'll run you till you drop!"

The lashing with rope and tongue tamed the obdurate cow. She fell into a docile walk.

Sweating, winded, Castle caught up. "That's a side to you I haven't seen, Tess."

Her face glowed from the exertion and the burst of temper. She drew a breath, about to speak, then thought better of it and looked at him, her lips parted.

They trailed the misbehaving cow and her calf back to the herd, which passed through the second gate without incident. Ahead, facing a road, were the steel rails and posts of the pens where the branding would take place. In the pasture the thirsty cattle ambled to a dirt tank, crowding it, like wild animals around a water hole. Plovers sprang from the grass-tufted banks, screeching alarms. Gerardo and McIntyre remained behind to watch the herd, while the others rode back to ranch headquarters by way of the old Spanish trace. Rain squalls drew across the face of the Huachucas and the light that tinged them had an almost unearthly glow.

"So did you learn anything, Mr. Nuclear Physicist?" Blaine asked, sitting his horse in a cowboy slouch, dried sweat rimming the armpits of his shirt.

"Think so."

"He learned that he isn't smarter than a good cow horse," Tessa said.

"Uh-huh. Well, you done all right for somebody who don't know his butt from a bucket."

Coming from Blaine, this was high praise, and Castle grinned. He'd had the time of his life.

THAT NIGHT he woke up in the house on Oenoke Ridge and gazed at Amanda as she slept. She was a beautiful sleeper, her extravagant auburn hair spread over the pillow, her face serene. He bent over to kiss her, and her eyes opened wide. It was actually a little frightening, the way her eyes snapped open, like doll's eyes, and then they were making love, Mandy's arms encircling him, her strong legs locked over the small of his back, tighter and tighter, and she began to crush the breath out of him. He tried to call her name but could make only a strangled, inarticulate cry. He felt himself to be in the embrace not of his Mandy but of some powerful being, coiled around him like a python. He clutched her limbs and with a superhuman effort broke their grip, the sudden release producing a triumphant relief as intense as the constriction had been. It was almost rapturous.

His alarm buzzed him into consciousness. He sat up, wrapped in the tangled bedsheets, and looked at Sam, white in the darkness of the room. The glowing numerals of his clock read four A.M. He was to be at the branding corrals at five. He was fully awake, yes, and yet the rapturous feeling did not dissipate as he swung out of bed, washed his face, dressed, and let Sam out to relieve herself; as he slugged down a cup of reheated coffee and stepped outside and stood under the paling sky to see Pegasus and Andromeda fading in the southwest. Driving to the corrals, he pondered the meaning of the dream. Three possibilities: in restless sleep, he'd become bound in the bedsheets and his subconscious created a dream of release. Or, the mystical explanation, it signified that Amanda had let him go. Or, the one he preferred, it was he who had let her go, in a final liberation from the clench of the past. A new love, a new happiness, a whole new life—he was free to embrace it all.

28

When Castle arrived at the corrals, the dawn looked like a forest fire blazing on the rim of the mountains. Blaine and Gerardo were with the herd, Tessa and Monica leaning against the rails, a regular pair of old-time cowgirls in their bandannas and high-peaked, dust-powdered hats. An array of branding irons lay atop a stove made from a rusty steel drum, with an acetylene tank and a pile of mesquite branches beside it. This wasn't the occasion to tell Tessa about his unusual dream, eager as he was to do it. She was all business, as she'd been yesterday, and so was Monica. They showed him the equipment: two sets of branding irons, one for heifers, the other for bull calves; a plierslike emasculator to make steers of the bulls; an ear notcher, which resembled a paper punch; and two syringe guns with graduated scales on the tubes, one to vaccinate the animals against bovine distemper, one against respiratory diseases. He was to do the inoculations, which required the least skill. Tessa would brand, and Monica would notch the ears and castrate, a task, she joked, that she tried not to enjoy too much.

She held a small bottle upside down and drew a milky liquid into one of the needles. It was to be injected into the fleshy flap at the top of a calf's foreleg. The second, filled with a clear fluid, was poked into the neck.

"Don't be shy, jab it right in," Monica instructed. "And don't mix them up. What I do"—she was speaking now as to one of her third graders—"is to hold the distemper in my right hand and the other one in my left and say to myself, 'right, leg, left, neck.' "

McIntyre drove in, pulling a horse trailer, followed by the neighbor and his cowhands. He and McIntyre mounted up and stationed themselves in a pen next to the corral. The cowboys, who would start the day as flankers, remained afoot. Monica tossed the mesquite into the brander and lit the acetylene torch under the wood. It made a low, compressed roaring, and then Tessa shoved the irons into the fire. Squinting against the new sun, Castle saw Blaine and Gerardo gathering the herd. Some minutes later they pushed the cattle into the holding pen, and the enchanting stillness of the morning was broken by a terrific din, punctuated by the yells of the mounted crew. They were cutting out half the cows to make it easier to rope, Tessa explained, raising her voice. "They keep half in so the calves don't completely freak out."

It began a little after six. Lariats twirled above the churning mass of beef, then flew from the riders' hands. Blaine and Gerardo pulled two calves into the corral while Blaine's neighbor and McIntyre blocked the mothers from chasing after their abducted young. The Anglo cowboy, who looked as though he didn't weigh much more than the heifer he wrestled to the ground, knelt on it as Gerardo nudged his horse forward to keep the rope taut. Monica leaped in to notch its ear; Castle, telling himself "right, leg, left, neck," jabbed the syringes. Tessa came in behind him, positioned the iron over the hindquarters, and pressed it into the hide, the stench of singed hair and flesh rising with the smoke. Gerardo slipped his loop, and the caterwauling animal ran back into the pen. Castle hopped over to the second heifer, flanked by the Mexican cowboy, and botched the first inoculation, squirting the vaccine down the foreleg. "Get another one, quick!" Monica yelled. He ran back, refilled the syringe, and was successful on his next try.

By that time two more had been dragged in, a heifer and a bull. Castle winced in sympathy as Monica, kneeling on one knee, cut around its testicle with a jackknife, then snipped the tube with the emasculator. Blood flecked her chaps. Blaine rode in, towing another bull. Just as Tessa branded it, its mother broke into the corral and charged around in a maternal fury, knocking the Anglo cowboy into the rails and almost doing the same to Castle before Gerardo drove her out.

The work went on for another hour. Castle fell into the rhythm of it, exulting in the speed, the coordination, the teamwork—branding was something of an athletic event. Dust and whirling ropes and a bedlam of bawling cattle. The sweet smell of flaming mesquite mixed in with the stink of manure and horseflesh and cowflesh and burned hide. Another hour. Ear notches and testicle cups piled up on a bench next to the brander. Cumulonimbus built mountains atop the mountains in the west, and lightning threaded the clouds. The air had weight, freighted with the humidity exported to the desert from the tropics, where the chubascos were born. The ground and roping crews traded places, Castle excepted. In furtherance of his education, Blaine promoted him to flanker, and he spent the third hour grappling with calves that writhed and kicked and thrashed. Before this experience he'd felt sorry for them, cute little Walt Disney creatures poked with needles, burned with irons, ears notched, balls cut off. After he got whacked in the knee and then knocked flat by a steer that twisted out of his arms, his sentiments were less benign.

They were finished by eleven o'clock, and all of them were lacquered in sweat and dust. The livestock were released from the pen to wander back to the pasture. Castle had begun the day stiff and sore from yesterday's gathering; now he felt as if he'd played a couple of quarters of football. Blaine's congratulatory slap on the back soothed the aches in his aging body.

They counted the triangular ear notches and the furry cups. Seventy-seven steers, eighty-nine heifers. One hundred eighty cows had calved in the spring, so the count of a hundred and sixty-six represented a 90 percent survival rate.

"Pretty good," Blaine declared. He sharpened a long mesquite stick, skewered a dozen testicles, and roasted them over the coals glowing in the brander. "We'll be havin' lunch at the house—these Rocky Mountain oysters are horsey-dervees."

Castle plucked one from the skewer, bit down, and gulped the gristly morsel. His cousin passed the kebab to Monica and Tessa, who abstained, then to the neighbor and his cowboys, who chomped them with relish. Gerardo and McIntyre, still in the saddle, were moving a few cows and calves that had drifted onto the road.

That was how Castle would remember the scene: the two mounted men, he and the others slouched against the corral, munching the oysters, the cattle on the road. He would remember that they all saw the van come flying over a rise in the road perhaps a hundred yards away. It sailed into the air like a stunt car, landed hard, blowing its front tires, and sped on, slewing on its rims. He would remember the pulsing lights of the pursuing Border Patrol wagon and everyone shouting to Gerardo and McIntyre to get out of the way and the two riders jabbing with their spurs and the horses leaping a culvert at the roadside and the cow and calf spinning around in panic to jump into the path of the oncoming van. It struck both almost at once. The calf, flipped into the air, crashed into the windshield; the cow was flung sideways, the lower half of a back leg severed at the joint. He would remember the shriek of shattering glass, the thud of metal on meat, and the van's side and rear doors busting open to spew bodies, bodies that turned acrobatic twists and midair somersaults, that flew with outspread arms like high divers. He would remember seizing Tessa by the waist and tossing her into the middle of the corral as the van tipped over and skidded toward them on its side before it careened into the rails with a sickening crunch.

His memories of the aftermath would forever be disjointed, a series of video clips out of sequence. A helicopter landing to evacuate the injured. Ambulances. A man staggering about, making spastic movements and uttering unintelligible sounds, a fist-size chunk missing from his skull, exposing part of his brain. A dead boy spread-eagled in the flooded culvert, his still eyes staring up through the water. Cries and moans. The horrible bellows of the injured cow. Gerardo limping, for his horse had bucked him off at the moment of the collision. A Border Patrolman reporting the statistics to the Sonoita station on his car radio—twenty-two migrants packed into the van, five killed, nine critically hurt. Blaine standing over the cow. The crack of his pistol.

29

WHILE YVONNE SAT in the grandstands waiting for the second race to begin, The Professor stood in line at the mutual windows. The instructions, passed to him through Billy Cruz, had been precise: he was to appear at the window marked "Large Teller" before the second race and place a certain advance bet. Someone would then tell him what to do next. He thought the Cochise County racetrack and fairgrounds a curious site for his introductory meeting with Yvonne, and he found the hugger-mugger arrangements a bit comic. The location was a favorable sign, however. She had almost as many cops and politicians on her payroll in Douglas as she did next door in Agua Prieta. She felt comfortable here, which suggested that luring her to the American side to do a deal, when the time came, would not be difficult.

He stepped up to the window and said, "Quinella on five and eight in the second."

As he took his ticket, a young man with sandy red hair, leaning against a post and reading a program, approached him. "Señor Carrington?" he asked, with a pronounced rolling of *r*'s.

The Professor nodded.

"Julián Menéndez," said the young man. "This way, please."

They were immediately joined by a black-haired primate wearing an embroidered shirt outside his pants. He and Julián guided The Professor to the stands, where Yvonne was seated on a vinyl pillow, across from the finish line and beside another pistolero, even heftier than the first. She wore fashionable sunglasses, a tight pair of midcalf canary yellow pants, and a black tank top exposing thin, fair, faintly freckled arms. She looked better than she did in photographs—the red hair not quite the worm's nest he'd seen in the pictures, and the taut body attractive enough to keep a thirty-five-year-old like Cruz interested, though Billy had other motivations in securing her affections—but her appearance was disappointing nonetheless. The Queen of Agua Prieta, author of massacres and of her husband's assassination, ought to be either stunningly glamorous or fascinatingly grotesque. Yvonne could have been almost any woman over fifty who'd kept her figure. Christ, she looked almost suburban in those yellow pants.

Except for the briefest glance, she did not acknowledge The Professor as he sat down. She studied the sheet for the second race, a thoroughbred maiden, three furlongs and seventy, half the track. On the far side the horses entered the starting gate. The announcer called, "And they're off!" Spectators rose from their seats, groaning or cheering. Yvonne followed the race through opera glasses, waving her curled-up program, shouting, "¡Ándale ocho!" A voice irritating to The Professor's ear yet pleasant to the touch—a feeling of smoothly sanded wood. "¡Ándale Sassy Prince!" Rounding the last turn, Sassy Prince had the rail and was leading the five horse, La Corona Blanca, with the rest of the field well behind. La Corona Blanca closed in the stretch but didn't have enough and finished second. "Bravo, Sassy Prince!" exclaimed Yvonne and sat down. "So I won the daily double." Her son and guardians offered sycophantic applause.

"And you?" she asked, turning to The Professor for the first time. She spoke in accentless English and addressed him as if they were old friends. "How did you do?"

"Five and eight were my quinella picks."

She looked at the tote board. "Then let us go collect."

They went downstairs to the windows and cashed their tickets. Sassy Prince paid off $980 on Yvonne's wager. She bet the entire amount on a horse called Cholla Tango to win the last race of the day.

"I own her. We'll have a look at her."

Passing a beer tent where a Norteño band was playing, they went to a roped-off holding pen, in which trainers were walking their horses before a crowd of onlookers—dark-skinned men in straw cowboy hats, light-skinned men in snappy Stetsons, several young women in sprayed-on Levi's, sexy in a trailer-trash sort of way. Yvonne herself was not without her erotic appeal—the allure of danger, he supposed. An excellent ass for a woman her age, shown off to best effect by the tight pants.

"That's her," said Yvonne, indicating a jet black thoroughbred filly. "I bought her a month ago. A three-year-old. She won her first race in Tucson, five and a half furlongs. This is her first run at six."

The Professor checked his program. "Its says here the owner is an Alex Daoud."

"The owner of record. Do you play the horses much, Carrington?"

"No."

"I have a system. I bet the colors of the jockey's silks. They give me a hunch, you know? I bet Sassy Prince to win because the colors said that was what would happen. My son calls that 'magical thinking,' but a lot of times, the magic works."

"Colors you can hear," he said. "Makes sense to me. I can smell colors."

"How interesting. Let us take a walk."

She slipped her arm into his, an intimacy that surprised him who was seldom surprised by anything. They strolled through the fairgrounds like a couple, Yvonne asking him cunning questions about his time in prison with Cruz. He'd anticipated that she would test him and had quizzed Cruz at length and was fairly sure that he knew more about her lover's incarceration than she did. He decided to chum the waters, saying that he was eager to make up for lost time in prison. A year ago Cruz's uncle Vicente had put him in touch with Carrasco, and he'd been buying from him, but—

"Carrasco?" she interrupted. "He's old and fat. A fat little old man and finished."

"That's why I'm here. I'm looking to line up a heavy hitter in Phoenix. He wants quantities Carrasco can't deliver."

She stopped walking in front of the mechanical bull concession, which presently had no riders, its operator lounging on a chair with a magazine. Yvonne didn't know what to make of Carrington. She approved of his appearance. So many of her customers looked like what they were, sleazy criminals, but the clean-shaven Carrington with his handsome if forgettable face could have passed for an insurance agent except for his blue eyes, which were very piercing, almost impossible to look into for more than a second. Her hunch, what Julián might have called "magical thinking," was that he could be a steady, reliable client. Yet there was something a little odd about him, a little off. She couldn't say what it was.

"You know, you don't sound like a gringo. The way you talk. Your accent."

A sharp ear, thought The Professor. He had learned that when manufacturing a tapestry of lies, it was often wise to weave in as many threads of truth as possible, so long as you remembered which was which. "My father was English, my mother Mexican, and I went to school in the States."

"So you speak Spanish?"

He made an open circle with thumb and forefinger. "Un poco. Enough to get by."

Just then a bugle call sounded, from inside her purse. She noticed his puzzled look and smiled. "My mobile's ring-tone."

" 'El Degüello,' " he said. "Santa Anna played it before he stormed the Alamo."

"Now, how did you know that?"

"I read a lot of history. Maybe you'll want to get that."

"The call can wait." She took his arm once more, moving away from the mechanical bull and its idle operator. "You're more important. What do you have in mind?"

"Bridal dresses," he answered, using a common metaphor. "Vestidas de novias. Sample material to start. A key."

Her mobile rang again. Aggravated, she answered. It was Clemente, her real estate cousin. Más tarde, she said. She was having a meeting.

"It is about the San Ignacio," Clemente replied.

Cupping the phone, she asked Carrington to excuse her a moment, and walked off a few steps, pressing a hand to her ear against the noise from the grandstands. The taxes had been paid; the property was no longer for sale, Clemente went on. The listing broker had told him herself. He then called the ranch to confirm and spoke to a woman, the daughter-in-law of the old woman. Yes, it was true. Off the market. He'd informed her that he had a buyer willing to make an offer on the whole place, but she said they weren't interested.

Yvonne was stunned. How, she asked, how could those people, those cowboys, come up with so much money in such a short time? Clemente had wondered that himself and had made discreet inquiries, discovering that someone, a friend or relative of the Erskines, some rich guy, had paid their tax liability. He could try to find out more if Yvonne wished . . . You do that! she commanded. He should find out all he could. She would speak to him later.

She snapped the mobile shut. That fucking family! The curse of her life. It was almost as if they'd known of her plans and desires and had deliberately thwarted them, merely to torment her more. Agitated thoughts collided in her mind, so filled with clarity only a few minutes ago.

"Please wait a few minutes," she said to Carrington, and went to the ladies' room, under the grandstands. Sitting in a stall, she took out her vial and miniature spoon and administered two bumps. She was now using an eighth a day to keep her mental scaffolding from collapsing. Julián had been nagging her—you're getting just like him, he'd chided, meaning Fermín. Like snorting powder was the same thing as smoking crack. That pest. If he would find a woman and get her pregnant, he'd have something to do besides monitor his mother's habits. What had she done to deserve an only son who would rather play the trumpet than screw a woman? But he was right. She should quit. She had, as a matter of fact, been planning to take a holiday in Zihuatanejo and get off the stuff, then maybe fly to New York to do some shopping. Not now, with Clemente's news. Now she would have to work harder, which would mean more of this shit. Two more snorts. No one could blame her if her addiction deepened. It would be the fault of those people. Her composure and self-assurance began to return, and she walked out with her most regal stride.

"Bad news?" Carrington asked.

She whisked the air. "A real estate deal. It fell through . . . never mind. You wanted a sample dress. All right. I can arrange delivery. Where? When?"

The Professor caught the pressured, too-rapid speech and noticed her swipe her nose with the back of her hand. How about that? Yvonne using product. Would that work to his advantage or disadvantage? "We haven't talked price," he said.

"Seventeen."

"Standard wholesale. Joaquín charges ten."

"Sure he does!" she said, an octave too loudly. "Shit product for a shit price! Let's get out of this fucking sun."

They retired to the bar tent and ordered two beers. It was nearly empty, the band was on a break, and he trusted Yvonne would keep her voice down.

"What happened with your real estate deal?" he asked. You never knew, in these things, what scrap of information might prove useful in the future.

"A ranch I want to buy . . . really, it's none of your business. Escúchame, Carrington. I don't like one-night stands. I'm interested only in long-term relationships."

"So am I." Why not? He thought. Why not a teaser? "The guy I'm trying to line up"—he flashed the spread fingers of both hands twice to signify twenty-kilo shipments—"on a steady basis, maybe once a week."

Yvonne's expression brightened—she fairly gleamed. He all but saw the numbers glowing on her mental calculator. A possible sixteen million a year wholesale. Hell, in a couple of years she could buy the Pyramid of the Sun.

"All right. Fifteen for the dress."

"That'll do."

The notes of "Call to Post" drifted from the track. Yvonne looked at her watch. "That should be the seventh. My filly runs in the next. Put a hundred on her to win, Carrington. I *know* she's going to win."

"The colors of the silks?"

"And other reasons."

Ben Erskine

Text of a letter submitted to the AHS by Grace Erskine Castle, daughter of Benjamin Erskine.

125 Scott's Cove Rd.
Darien, Conn.
November 14, 1966

Arizona Historical Society
929 E. 2nd St.
Tucson, Arizona

Gentlemen:

You asked in your letter of Nov. 3 for my reminiscences and observations about my father, specifically if I could add anything to the "scandal" involving his departure from the sheriff's department. I was only 7 going on 8 when it happened. I do remember our mother, Ida, telling my brother and me that we would be moving out to the ranch full-time because Father was no longer a deputy sheriff. The only explanation she gave was that he had quit over some undefined falling out with the then-sheriff, Edwin Cox. It wasn't until I was in college that I learned the truth, and even then accidentally. I was home on Christmas vacation, helping my mother clean out a closet, when I came across an article in a Mexican newspaper my parents had saved. I was fluent in Spanish and read it. This was probably the article you alluded to in your letter. I don't know what happened to it. Needless to say, I was pretty upset that my parents had lied to my brother Frank and me.

I confess that I have mixed feelings about my father. Not too long ago, as I was preparing a reading list for the senior English honors course I teach, I came across a comment D. H. Lawrence made about Fenimore Cooper's Leatherstocking Tales: *"The essential American soul is hard, isolate, stoic, and a killer." The first person I thought of was my father. Hard and stoical he was, and although he had a lot of friends, there was some part of him that was shut off to the world, even from his family. And I must admit he was a killer. (How painful it is to write that.) I heard one story that he had shot a Mexican horse thief when he was a teenager. I've also heard that he may have put as many as a dozen men in their graves. Some of these killings were justified, and some were, well, questionable.*

To cite one example, my father was mentioned prominently in a history of the U.S. Border Patrol that was published shortly after his death. To summarize, in 1938 he was serving as a county ranger in Santa Cruz County—a kind of part-time police officer. He was friends with a Border Patrol agent, Lee MacLeod. It seemed that he and my father had arrested a certain Mexican smuggler a number of times, but he was always released after a few days or weeks in jail. MacLeod and my father decided to get rid of this nuisance by ambushing him out in the Huachuca Mountains. They figured the body would never be found in that wild country, and that if it was, no one would know who shot him.

So what you have here are two law enforcement officers conspiring to murder a suspect. There is no other way I can put it. But the tables got turned. The smuggler ambushed MacLeod when he was alone on horse patrol. MacLeod crawled to a nearby ranch and lived long enough to identify his assailant. My father tracked the killer down and found him sitting at his campfire. Could have been a scene from a western. There was a modern wrinkle—he was smoking marijuana. The way the book described it, my father followed the smell like a bloodhound, sneaked up on the stoned smuggler, and shot him dead right there.

I have no idea how the author got this information. Nor can I verify its accuracy. Ben was, still is, a mythic figure, the subject of much lore, from which you can't always tease fact from fiction.

Assuming the story was true, I have a hard time reconciling that Ben Erskine with the father I knew. How clearly I recall him, after a tough day of branding or mending fences, planting a cactus garden in our front yard to make it more presentable, or caring for sick calves with almost maternal tenderness, or peeking into our rooms to make sure we were doing our homework. One memory that remains particularly vivid is of a stormy summer night after we'd moved out to the ranch permanently. I woke up crying to my parents that I needed to go to the toilet. A hard rain clattered against the tin roof, accompanied by loud peals of thunder and flashes of lightning. In his nightshirt, carrying an umbrella in one hand and holding my hand in the other, Father escorted me down the rickety boardwalk to the privy.

There came a deafening, terrifying crash as the whole yard lit up in a blaze of bluish white light. Lightning had struck the windmill. Father picked me up, he held me tight, and said, "It's all right, Grace." Then he set me down and opened the privy door. I don't know why this moment sticks in my mind. Possibly because, trembling though I was, I felt so secure in his arms.

I also have a hard time reconciling that Ben with the Ben in the Mexican newspaper. That he took money for turning those two men over to their executioners makes it all the more difficult to accept. It was something a common bounty hunter would have done.

Even during the Great Depression, we had our homestead free and clear and enough to eat. But the IB-Bar could barely sustain itself; cattle prices collapsed with the rest of the economy, and drought made things worse. My father told Martín Mendoza, our full-time cowboy, that he could no longer pay him a steady wage and suggested that he might be better off seeking other employment. Martín, however, figured that things were just as rough elsewhere and stayed on. We became one big family, the

Erskines and the Mendozas, struggling to make a go of it in the dry foothills of the Huachuca Mountains.

In the way of children, Frank and I were unaware of our parents' financial worries. We were, though, conscious of another sort of anxiety, the nature and origins of which were a mystery to us at the time. We didn't know that Pedroza and López's allies in Mexico wanted to even the score with my father. At night, whenever an automobile or wagon or horse was heard coming up the road, my parents would sit up alert as watchdogs. If we kids happened to be making noise, they would tell us, "Hush up. Listen." Then as the car or wagon or horse passed on by, "It's all right, it's nothing." Those words became a mantra in our household. "Hush up . . . Listen . . . It's all right, it's nothing."

The day came when it wasn't all right, when it was a lot more than nothing, and I will never forget it. It was a humid Sunday evening in 1931. Our family and the Mendozas were canning poblano peppers in the kitchen. Ida and Lourdes pan-roasted the peppers, then rinsed them in cold water, while the Mendozas' toddler played on the floor. Frank and I and the Mendozas' older child peeled the crisped skins, and Ben and Martín sterilized Mason jars in a pot of boiling water. It was a domestic scene that could have been a Depression-era magazine cover, except for one thing—both men were wearing pistols. They were never unarmed except when they were in bed.

The ranch dogs outside barked in alarm, the grown-ups stopped talking and listened briefly. A pack of coyotes yipped close by. Work and conversation resumed; we figured the coyotes had disturbed the dogs. My mother told my father that the rinse water needed changing, and he and Martín went outside to fill the buckets with fresh water.

I did not see all of what happened. I heard about it later from Martín. He saw someone leap up from behind the berm surrounding the pond next to the windmill, and he threw himself to the ground at the same moment a gun flashed twice. The bullets smacked into the back of the house. My father and Martín fired back. The gunman fell behind the berm. Martín yelled, "We got him!" and ran toward him to make sure. The gunman had only been slightly wounded. He sprang to his feet and grappled with Martín, trying to wrest Martín's gun, because he'd dropped his own. At that instant a second gunman, crouched behind the rock wall enclosing the yard, fired a rifle. My father whirled and shot back and saw him slump over the wall. Then the gunman wrestling with Martín broke free and sprinted for the house.

Inside, we were all lying on the kitchen floor, petrified. Lourdes was under the kitchen table, shielding her children with her ample body. Frank wailed, "Has Father been hurt?" From outside we heard my father holler, "Douse the lights! Lock the doors!" Lourdes scuttled out from under the table to snuff the lanterns as my mother ran to the door; but she was able to hook only the screen door before the gunman grabbed it and tried to tear it off the hinges. I can still see him, just before Lourdes put out the last lamp—a man with a huge, round, hairy face like a bearded melon and gold-crowned front teeth that made him look even more hideous. My mother seemed paralyzed by the sight. I was screaming. So were the Mendozas' kids. With her bare hands, Lourdes snatched the pot of boiling water from off the stove and flung it through the screen into the man's face. Scalded, howling like no creature I had ever heard, he staggered backward. That was when my father shot him through the temple from only two or three feet away. The way Martín described it, he raised his pistol and fired as calmly as if he were at a target range.

Inside, we heard the shot and the thud of a body falling onto the porch. For an awful moment I thought my father had been killed; then he called, "Is everybody all right?" My mother was transfixed, staring at the door like a blind woman. Ben appeared on the other side, and commanded us to stay inside and keep the doors locked till he and Martín made sure there weren't more attackers. Ida recovered from her paralysis and moved Frank and me into a corner, telling us in a shaky voice to stay put. After a while, we heard the Model T's motor kick over and the truck rattle off. Frank asked, "Where are they going?" Ida replied, "Never you mind!" They were, of course, carting the bodies away. She relit the lamps and thanked Lourdes for her courage and rubbed her blistered hands with butter. My brother wanted to know if the men were robbers, and our mother answered, yes, robbers, but that we were safe now.

I did not feel at all safe until Father and Martín returned. Uttering praises to God, Lourdes embraced her husband. But Ida, her head cocked to one side, looked at Ben the way you look at a stranger you think you know but can't quite place. Frank and I wanted to hug him, but something checked us, and we too stood staring at him. The mantle of the killer still clung to him, like the dirt and burrs clinging to his clothes. It was a kind of repulsive force that held us at a distance.

First he said, "It's taken care of." Our mother nodded. Then he said, "I'm sorry you and the kids had to . . . I am sorry this had to happen."

As I remember it, she was silent for a time. I can't speculate as to what she might have been thinking. But I did hear her say, finally, "It didn't have to happen."

I hope this account helps you in your project. If you need any further information, you know how to contact me.

Sincerely yours,

Grace Castle

30

THE MINUTEMEN ARRIVED at the San Ignacio at the beginning of September in a convoy of SUVs. They set up camp under the ramada in the ranch's alfalfa field and soon had it looking like a command post in Iraq: cots and sleeping bags lined up on one side, a mural-size relief map propped against a post, and a radio receiver on a makeshift table. Outside, an American flag flew above a yellow banner on which a rattlesnake coiled above the motto "Don't Tread on Me."

Blaine had summoned the vigilantes for a thirty-day "operation" over Castle's and Monica's objections. They did not want a crowd of armed strangers wandering around, but he had declared war on the coyotes and drug runners and illegal aliens. "Don't need no Iraq nor Afghanistan neither," he'd said. "Got us a fight right here." Castle was prepared to dislike the guest-guardians—the very word *vigilante* conjured images of gun-toting rednecks, gaunt night riders hot to hang a Mexican from the nearest tree. The only part of this picture that proved accurate was the gun-toting part—they all carried sidearms; otherwise, the thirteen men and two women were of Castle's age and older and in less than peak physical condition. A few probably had Medicare cards in their wallets: retirees bored with golf and gated communities, looking for adventure on the border. One or two spoke darkly of wetbacks and greasers and beaners, invaders polluting their America, but the rest played the role of earnest Concerned Citizen. By day they cleaned up the trash deposited by migrant bands or sat on lawn chairs, peering into Mexico through binoculars. By night they looked through night-vision goggles or patrolled in their SUVs. If they spotted border crossers, they did not rush in with blazing guns and hangman's nooses but called the Border Patrol. All in all they were a tolerable bunch, some even likable. And Castle was forced to admit that their presence made a difference; the traffic through the ranch dropped from a torrent to a trickle.

It wasn't the Minutemen who worried him; it was his cousin. None who'd seen those bodies flung from the van like rags from a basket would ever forget it, but Blaine was consumed by it. The plates of his inner geology had shifted, a crack had opened in his personality; its subterranean aspects, which had previously shown only glimpses of themselves, bulged to the surface. He dug his old combat uniform out of a trunk—tiger-stripe camouflage with a Special Forces patch sewn on one shoulder—and wore it on forays with the vigilantes, carrying his hunting rifle, a scoped .30-06, in addition to the Luger, his face darkened with shoe polish. He took a vacation from ranch work and spent hours at the vigilante headquarters, planning sorties, studying maps, joshing as he might have with his old A-team thirty-odd years ago. His speech grew peppered with martial jargon: avenues of approach; NDP (for night-defensive position); OP (for observation post); fields of fire. This metamorphosis disturbed Monica. "It's almost like he's back *there*," she'd said to Castle one day. "It's like he's enjoying this."

One afternoon Castle drove out to the ranch's alfalfa farm with Gerardo to learn how to operate the baler. After the lesson, he fell into a conversation with the Minutemen's leader, an intense, crew-cut man in his forties, easily the youngest of the whole crew.

"I had a talk with Blaine this morning, and maybe you should, too," the Minuteman said. "That guy is getting a little spooky. What happened was, he was out with two of my guys and they spotted some crossers hotfooting it on a ridgeline a couple hundred yards away. Couldn't tell if they were wets or mules. So one of my guys radios me to radio the Border Patrol, and while he's giving me the GPS coordinates, Blaine opens up with his rifle. Puts four, five rounds in front of them. I guess he's a pretty good shot, but at that range all it would've taken was a flinch, and we'd have a dead one to explain. We'd be in the shit. We're just trying to help you out. Don't want trouble like that. We don't want to get put in a bad light."

This cautious, public-relations-minded remark sounded odd coming from a vigilante, but then his band of paunchy senior citizens weren't really vigilantes. Castle related the episode to Monica, and that evening, in the living room of the main house, they pleaded with Blaine to settle down before somebody got hurt or worse. "Now, don't neither of you start givin' me advice I don't ask for," he said, the skewed smile bending his thin lips. Right then, sitting under the photograph of Ben Erskine wearing that same mirthless smirk as he raised his hat from the back of a rearing horse, Blaine looked like his grandfather's reincarnation.

Castle had heard from his daughters, having written them about his going into partnership on the ranch. Morgan, acting as spokeswoman for both, as usual, replied that she and Justine were sad to hear that his move to Arizona was now permanent, but they were also pleased that he was rebuilding his life. It appeared that he had at last achieved "closure." This whole notion of "closure," he thought, rose from a culture so marinated in television that it had come to see life as a miniseries, each episode resolved in an hour, and so on to the next.

As September 11 approached, fearing a relapse, he studiously avoided watching TV, listening to the radio, or looking at the newspapers. On the tenth he asked Monica if he could use her phone to order flowers. Was he making up for another quarrel with Tessa? she asked. No, he was sending them to Amanda's parents in Boston. "I want them to know I'm thinking of them," he said. It was only after he'd wired the flowers that he realized he'd spoken her name aloud for the first time in two years. The next day he treated himself with postoperative delicacy, testing his emotional pulse. It was more or less normal.

Toward the end of the month Sheriff Rodriguez called to say Miguel's visa extension had been approved. No, he'd added in answer to a question from Castle, there had been no further word on Cruz's whereabouts. The MexFeds had assured him that they were on the lookout, but he had his doubts. The Mexican cops were busy either fighting the drug cartels or working for them or both. Whatever the case, they were hunting big game, and Billy Cruz was a rabbit.

When Castle passed the news on to Miguel, he snorted and shrugged and said, "No le hace"—it makes no difference. His courage was not to be rewarded with a swift, conclusive end to his ordeal; he was to go on in a twilight of waiting, attended by the fear that Cruz or his cohorts would harm his wife and children. Soon it would be a year since he had left Oaxaca, and his luck was still bad. Castle grew impatient with him. His luck could have been a lot worse—he could have suffered Héctor and Reynaldo's fate. To console himself, Miguel began to scratch out a vegetable garden behind his Airstream trailer. This was not the time to plant; the summer rains had surrendered to the arid autumn. But he stayed at it with peasant doggedness, hoeing rows for corn, beans, and squash, planting seeds, hauling water by hand, spreading fertilizer. He said he wanted to see something grow.

BETH MCBRIDE came home toward the end of the month, and an excited Tessa drove to Fort Bliss to welcome her, but without Castle. It was Beth herself who had asked to see her mother alone, after learning that Tessa had planned to bring him. Mother and soldier-daughter stayed at a motel in El Paso, had dinner downtown, and went to a music festival.

"I organized the whole thing, like a tour director," Tessa told Castle the day after her return. They were dancing in her living room. There was an odd note in her voice, a forced gaiety, a brittleness. "On Sunday I planned for us to take one of those trolley tours to Juárez, and Beth said, 'Shit, no! I just want to sleep on a clean bed and not have to do one fucking thing.' Her language had gotten pretty rough, but what can you expect?"

They swayed to the bittersweet "But Not for Me." Castle was feeling a little ashamed of himself. He hadn't seen his girls for nine months and had no excuse for the separation beyond his self-imposed removal. Ashamed, too, that Morgan and Jussie had been able to live their lives and get on with their careers while Beth risked bombs and IEDs on the broken roads of Iraq.

"So she slept," Tessa went on. "Slept till noon, and . . . and . . ." Suddenly she stopped talking, stopped dancing, and began to sob.

"Tess, what is it? What's wrong?"

"Does something have to be wrong for me to cry?"

"You mean you're crying from happiness that she's back?"

"No! For chrissake, I want a drink."

She pulled away from him and went to a cupboard and poured two straight tequilas and handed one to him. She flopped onto the sofa, drank off half the glass, and then wiped her eyes with the back of her hand. It was trembling.

Castle sat beside her and held her. "What happened?"

"It's more what didn't happen," she said, regaining her composure. "All we did was hang around the motel pool, and we didn't talk much. It was like she had no idea what to say to me and I didn't know what to say to her. I wondered if she'd seen some things she never told me about. She seemed so far away, lying there right next to me. There's always been a certain space between us, but this time it felt like an ocean. So I took her to dinner again that night, to a lovely, elegant old hotel in downtown El Paso, and we sat through the whole meal like—like—you've seen them—old married couples who have learned to despise each other and sit there three feet from each other but it might as well be three miles. Beth drank like I'd never seen her drink, one glass of wine after another, till she'd polished off a bottle all by herself. Finally, I asked her, 'You wanted to see me alone. Is there was anything you need to talk about?' And she said, in this cold voice, 'Not a goddamn thing you'd ever understand.' And I shot back, 'Well, try me.' She just waved her hand and looked around the dining room, and then she said, loud enough to turn heads from the tables near us, 'Everybody in this fucking country sure is having a good time.' I got angry and reminded her that she wasn't in a mess hall, and she looked at me . . ." Tessa's voice broke. "Looked at me like she'd never seen me before. We went back to the motel and to bed without saying good night, and she was just as icy the next morning. That was yesterday. I almost couldn't make the drive home, I was so angry and so sad."

I'm glad I wasn't there, Castle thought, and then scolded himself for being selfish.

Tessa finished her drink. "I thought I'd got myself back together, but I guess not. I've got this horrible, horrible feeling that I'm losing her."

"You're not going to lose her," Castle assured her. "She needs time to decompress, a period of reentry." This sounded fatuous even to his own ears, as though Beth, like Justine, had just finished a tough year at law school.

The next number on the CD, "Lady Be Good," was too bouncy, too out of phase with the conversation. Tessa jumped up and shut the CD player off and sat down again, folding her legs under her. "The whole day today I've been seeing myself ten, twenty years from now, sitting in this room alone, my daughter estranged from me." She shivered at this bleak picture. "It's an irrational, maybe a hysterical thought, but . . ."

"But you're not going to be sitting here alone ten years from now," he interrupted. "Or twenty years from now. I'll be here. I'll always be here."

"Darling, please don't say that. You don't know what might happen."

"Then put it like this—as long as I've got a pulse, I'll be here. I know that. We can go to City Hall tomorrow and have the state of Arizona put an official seal on it."

The declaration stunned him as much as it did her. She clutched his arm and shook him gently. "My God. I don't need that. I don't need any seal. I need you."

"You've got me." He rose and turned the CD player on. Ella was singing "Someone from Somewhere." "One more dance?" he asked, clasping her hands and pulling her to her feet.

31

THEY WERE SHAMBLING UP both sides of the highway, pilgrim bands of ten or twenty, a few on horseback, most afoot in tennis shoes and rope sandals, for the October peregrinación to Magdalena de Kino could not be made by car or bus. One proved one's devotion by walking or riding a great distance. Village leaders held aloft banners bearing images of Father Kino and his patron saint, Francis Xavier, while the peregrinos carried in their rough brown hands tiny milagros to lay at the feet of the saint's effigy in hopes of a cure for whatever ailed them or a wife or child, that is, in the hopes of a miracle.

The Professor was moved by the medieval-looking processions; his chest swelled with pride for his Mexico. Where else in the world would you see hundreds of people trudge hundreds of kilometers because they believed in miracles? Certainly not in Gringoland, whose citizens talked the talk of faith but certainly did not *literally* walk the walk, did not indeed ever walk much farther than from their car to the front door of Wal-Mart. And they wondered how Mexicans could cross deserts and mountains to make beds in their motels and pluck Tyson's chickens for five dollars an hour! Here was why—they crossed deserts and mountains convinced that the hands of a seventeenth-century padre and a sixteenth-century saint would reach down from heaven to cure anything from a cleft lip to cancer.

Arriving early, as was his habit, he parked near the Palacio de Gobierno and strolled to the plaza. He'd bought his ranchito outside

Magdalena de Kino because its climate was salubrious, because it was the cleanest, prettiest town in all Sonora, its municipal buildings painted white as egret feathers, the tiled sidewalks under the porticos of the shops swept and washed daily, and barely a scrap of paper to be found in the shady parks. Because it was a town of miracles. In this digitized, globalized, capitalized, and in many ways anesthetized twenty-first century, there should be sanctuaries for the mysterious, like wildlife preserves. He passed a house with a sign on its door. ESTE HOGAR ES CATÓLICO. NO ACEPTAMOS PROPOGANDA PROTESTANTE NI DE OTRAS SECTAS. ¡VIVA CRISTO REY! ¡VIVA LA VIRGEN DE GUADALUPE, MADRE DE DIOS! Viva! he thought. Keep them out, the Baptists, the Pentecostalists, the Jehovah's Witnesses. In whatever form it was dished up, Protestantism was thin soup. Catholicism was—chicharrones! A street vendor was stirring a pot of them with a wooden paddle, succulent chunks of pork rind boiling in their own fat, and pilgrims starved from their treks lined up to buy the chicharrones and spread them on tortillas with shredded cheese.

Many more pilgrims jammed the plaza, filing past the tomb of Father Eusebio Kino, the good Jesuit who'd stood up for the Indians of the Pimería Alta. Lying in the dust several feet below street level, the skeleton could be viewed through a glass window, hands crossed over the pelvic bone. An old man who looked rather skeletal himself knelt by the rotunda, both knees on the paving stones, his arms outspread, his face, brown and seamed as a walnut, turned toward the sky. The Professor sat on a bench to watch him. Eyes shut, he was utterly still; only his lips moved in silent supplication. He had a truly tragic face, spare and gaunt, like Picasso's old guitarist. For what did the viejo pray? ¿Quién sabe? Here was another scene you wouldn't see in Gringoland. Imagine a scrubbed, blow-dried, well-dressed congregant in one of those air-conditioned, suburban auditoriums of religion kneeling on concrete for hours in the hot sun.

Glancing toward the Church of Santa María de Kino, he saw Billy Cruz waiting at the side door. Give that to Billy—he was punctual. Rising from the bench, a wave of dejection surged through The Professor. He was reluctant to leave the viejo and his magical devotions.

"¿Qué tal?" he said to Cruz, and then stepped into the side chapel, where peregrinos were passing by the life-size statue of Saint Francis, prone atop a pedestal, upon which they placed their milagros—small wood carvings of a hand or a foot or a leg or a heart or whatever body part was afflicted—then, murmuring prayers, raised and lowered the effigy's head.

"What the fuck is this?" asked Cruz.

"You're in a church, Billy," The Professor remonstrated. "They believe that if the feet of that statue go up when you lift the head, you'll be cured of all diseases. What this is, is magic. It's Mexico's secret weapon."

"Hey, bro, are we going to talk in a *church*?"

"I like doing business in churches. They're historical—and private. Just stick to English, and keep it to a whisper."

But this church was filled with pilgrims, not an empty pew to be found. There was a chance that someone who understood English might overhear. He led Cruz back outside and into the uncrowded rotunda, its dome splashed with murals of Padre Kino preaching to Pima converts, of cattle and goats and baskets and gourds and stacked ears of corn, all in bright colors, each shade filling The Professor's nostrils with its unique smell—a suite of odors as complicated as those in a French kitchen.

Cruz shook his head, bewildered. "I've got another one for—" He looked up, momentarily distracted by the figure of a Pima maiden on the dome. She was wearing a deerhide skirt and nothing else, and the muralist's thoughts must not have been on spiritual matters, for he'd given her a set of tits that would send the Playmate of the Month running to a surgeon for breast implants. "I've got another one for you," Cruz resumed, lowering his gaze. "Ten keys of white. They'll be packed into four cylinders of a pickup. It's going to cross at Campini Mesa at the end of the week."

Two hundred fifty thousand wholesale, street value two million, thought The Professor. "How sure is this?"

"I'm modifying the vehicle myself. I learned a few things from my uncle. And she wants me to cross a load of pollos down the line, to draw La Migra in case they're around. Said she'd cut me in."

"She usually moves white through Douglas. Campini Mesa is the dark side of the moon. Why there?"

"There's questions I don't ask, but I heard the Douglas crossing has gotten dicey."

Maybe, but The Professor suspected that Yvonne was pulling a fast one on her army protectors. They had spies on the border who kept them informed about drug movements to make sure they weren't getting cheated out of their just due. In his dealings with her, he'd heard her whine about the huge sums she had to pay her boys in uniform. One way to cut down on the mordida was to every now and then sneak a shipment down a remote back road. All the traffickers did it.

"I've gone out on a limb on this one," Cruz whispered. "She's getting flaky. Into the nose candy morning, noon, and night. Starting to suspect everybody, even her kid. He's pissed at her for keeping her nose in the bag so much, and she's pissed at him because he flushed a whole key of hers down the toilet."

"How do you stand?"

"Cool so far."

"She said anything about me?"

"You're cool, too. So far. I don't know what move you're planning to make, but if it was me, I'd make it sooner than later. Before she gets flakier."

The Professor ruminated on this assessment. Cruz's timely tips—in the past six weeks he'd snitched out two big loads of Yvonne's mota, duly intercepted by the federal police—were a sideshow, their purpose to provide proof that Comandante Zaragoza was fighting the drug trade. The trick was not to overdo it, provoking her into another take-no-prisoners snitch hunt, one that could lead to Billy. He wasn't ready to lose him, not yet, for there was the grand prize to consider. The Professor had made five controlled buys since August; he'd won Yvonne's confidence, even to the point that she'd brought him to her ranch twice and once to her airstrip, where he'd observed the off-loading of five hundred pounds of pristine Colombian cocaine. All in all, things were going as planned, but he was as aware as Cruz of her erratic behavior, the spells of gabby excitement alternating with spasms of paranoid belligerence. That night at the airstrip he'd watched her and her pair of watchdogs, Marco and Heraclio, testing the coke's quality by snorting lines off the magazine of an AK-47. Yvonne's way of showing she could outmacho the machos. She was laughing and joking, then abruptly turned on Marco, accusing him of taking one line more than she and threatening that she'd shoot him herself if he did that again. Pierce, the U.S. Customs operative, was content to play her for a while longer—he was used to lengthy investigations—but Joaquín was getting anxious. "When are you and your American chotas going to get this cunt out of the way?" It wasn't a question, it was a command.

"Let's both of us stay alert," The Professor said to Cruz. "That adjourns the meeting."

He started to rise from the pew. Cruz tugged his sleeve. "Not yet. I want out of this, Carrington. I want to get out from under her."

"Do you mean that literally?"

Cruz snickered. "Yeah, she won't let me do it to her no other way. That witness? I got word where he is. I figure you must know people. I figure you could help me out. I figure since I've done for you, you can do for me."

"That's a lot of figuring, Billy. What is it you figure I can do?"

"Set it up with the Border Patrol or Immigration to pop the pollo as an illegal alien. Get him deported. After he's on this side, I can take care of things on my own."

Here was an aspect to Cruz he hadn't seen yet—a capacity for subtle thought. "Leaving you free to go back home. I'll see what I can do, but no promises," he lied. For the time being he wanted Cruz right where he was. "And now the meeting is adjourned. You leave first."

Outside, he found an empty bench near the Kino rotunda, removed one of his mobiles from his pocket, and punched the country code for the United States, then Nacho's number. He'd decided to give this one to him rather than to Zaragoza, in the interest of maintaining good international relations.

"Haven't heard from you in a while," Nacho said.

"Busy. I'll get to the point. Our girl is shipping ten keys of white through Campini Mesa on Friday night in a pickup truck. Look in the engine block for the surprise. A load of wets will be crossed as a diversion. Any more details, you'll be the first to know. Now you owe me."

He broke the connection. He calculated that Yvonne's suspicions wouldn't fall on Cruz after the bust went down. After all, she'd cut him in—why would he snitch on the deal? On the bench kitty-corner from his, a young couple sat holding a plastic bag from a religious-icon store on their laps. Pilgrims streamed past him. He was to all appearances another gringo tourist, visiting Magdalena de Kino for the fiesta. He pulled out his second mobile and called Yvonne on hers, got no answer, and tried her landline at the ranch. Julián picked up. The Professor asked to speak to his mother.

"¡Hola, Carrington!" she said a minute later, sounding to be on one of her upswings. "¿Qué tal?"

"In inglés, por favor."

"All right. How's it going?"

"Good. I need to see you. The guy I told you about? From Phoenix?"

"What about him?"

"Got him lined up. He wants to do fifty as soon as you can get it."

A pause. "That is good news."

"Here's the thing. He'll only deal directly with you. Face-to-face. He's very mistrustful. And he won't do business in Mexico. He wants to meet on the U.S. side. That's what I need to see you about."

Another, longer pause. "Yes, you do. When can you get here?"

"Tomorrow morning."

"No good. I'm leaving for Zihuatanejo in the morning."

"This afternoon, then."

He signed off and walked across the plaza, feeling the old stirring, the hunter's quickness. The old man was still on his knees in front of Padre Kino's tomb. It had to be a big miracle he was praying for.

32

Castle was on his first cup of coffee when Blaine banged at his door. Work to do, cuzzy, he said after Castle let him in. Tessa had phoned him half an hour ago to report that the locked gate to her bull pasture had been knocked down and that three of her herd bulls had escaped onto San Ignacio land. She and McIntyre needed a hand to recapture the fugitives. This was a matter of some urgency for Blaine as well; the bulls had fled into a pasture where he grazed heifers that were too young to breed, their pelvic bones undeveloped. If the bulls got to them and impregnated them, they could die in calving.

Castle got his chaps and spurs and climbed into the truck beside Gerardo. The horses were already loaded in the trailer. Blaine's eyes were bloodshot, and he seemed on edge, more than usual. He'd been awake since three in the morning, when a Border Patrol helicopter had swooped over his house, the throbbing of rotor blades evoking old and unpleasant memories. Castle hadn't heard the helicopter, which his cousin thought remarkable. It had passed over twice, pretty low, and when he went outside to see what was going on, it was circling in the distance, sweeping spotlights across the Canelo Hills.

They learned the reason for the commotion when, nearing Tessa's Crown A Ranch, they were flagged down at a Border Patrol roadblock consisting of two trucks, one parked athwart the road with its roof strobes flashing, the other at the side, and four agents, all armed with assault rifles. The Border Patrol routinely set up roadblocks on main highways to discourage smugglers from using them. To come upon one in the back country was a rare thing, and a sign of real trouble. Blaine spotted Morales and asked what the hell was going on. Last night had been a busy one, answered the Navaho. First a convoy of crossers had been intercepted, and then there'd been a drug bust, an attempted drug bust, that is. Two men in a pickup truck, reported to be carrying cocaine, had opened fire on Border Patrol agents, led them on a high-speed chase, and got away.

"We think they made it back across the line, but we're still looking for them on this side," Morales said. "They were driving a silver GMC. If you see it, let us know right away. And stay clear of them," he warned. "These are serious people."

After they passed this information on to Tessa and McIntyre, Castle, concerned for her safety, urged her to stay home—the four men could find the bulls.

"They're my animals," she said. "And anyway, we're going to be off the roads."

IT HAD TO HAVE been the smugglers who'd crashed through her gate. It lay across a jeep trail, its crossbars bent, its padlocked chain wrapped around the gatepost that had been ripped from the ground by the impact. Fragments of glass and metal sparkled in the dust.

"Y aún más mala suerte," grumbled Gerardo as he and Castle dragged the gate off the jeep trail. The range fire. La Señora Sally. The terrible thing by the branding corrals—he ticked off the list like a court clerk reading an indictment on multiple charges. He didn't name the accused; he didn't need to.

"Must of hit that thing at sixty," McIntyre said. "Don't think the bulls got out too long ago."

Tessa buckled on her chaps and looked at the fresh hoofprints impressed over the tire tracks. "Let's hope they're not in a traveling mood."

"And not in no romantic mood neither," drawled Blaine, strapping on the Luger.

They unloaded the horses and followed the bulls' tracks into a sandy wash trenched by the monsoons, littered with brush piles deposited by flash floods. The land and the grass were dry once again and would stay dry until the winter snows and rains fell, if they fell. The third of October, the leaves in New England would be turning, Castle thought with a stab of nostalgia; but here green still clung to the sycamores, and the sun burned hot in an empty sky. Hooves plodding in sand, the strike of a horseshoe against a rock, wind and hawk glide, and from somewhere ahead a coyote's howl was followed by the cries of the pack, a demented yodeling that went suddenly silent, like a choir on a bandmaster's cue. It was unusual to hear them at this time of day. Found them something to eat, Blaine muttered. A dead calf, most likely. They rode on for another quarter mile, then caught a smell on the wind, a rank odor like roadkill after a day in the heat.

Blaine pulled rein. "Yup. Scavengin'. Got me a dead calf."

It was then that a coyote trotted toward them from out of the brush farther up the wash, with something hanging from its jaws, something dark and bloody and about a foot long. The riders were straight downwind, and the coyote was oblivious to their presence until Tessa said, "It's got a jackrabbit." It stopped at the sound of her voice and from thirty or forty yards away stared at the horses and humans, its bristling fur almost platinum in the bright light. Blaine cried out, "Jesus Christ!" and in the same instant he and Gerardo drew their pistols and fired, both shots missing, though one struck between the coyote's forelegs, spattering dirt into its face. It dropped its prey and fled, bushy tail low. The gunfire flushed the rest of the pack, a little distance beyond, five animals lined out and running fast as racehorses.

Blaine kicked his horse forward, calling over his shoulder, "Tess, you stay back here."

Castle, puzzled, rode after him and Gerardo to the creature that had fallen from the coyote's mouth. At first, Castle couldn't make it out. There was a lag of a few seconds between his first sight of the glistening blue thing wrapped in skeins of blood and his recognition of what it was; then another lag before his mind, denying the evidence of his senses, accepted the recognition. How Blaine and Gerardo had identified it at a distance astonished him. Now he too wanted to protect Tessa, out of some antiquated sense of male gallantry. Too late. She'd ignored Blaine's warning and ridden up, and when her eyes fell on it, she made a sound, a kind of wheeze, and pressed the back of her hand to her mouth. Castle nudged his horse next to hers and grasped her arm. He wasn't sure if he was afraid she would faint or he would.

"Lord amighty," McIntyre murmured.

"Tim, you stay here with her," said Blaine, then flicked his head. "Up there. The pack was up there."

He, Gerardo, and Castle found the body behind a mound of brush and sticks and dismounted, masking their mouths and noses with their bandannas. She was lying on her back, her face bloated and yellow green, and what they at first mistook for blood dripping from her nostrils were red ants filing into them, like miners into twin tunnels. Gerardo, who wasn't given to his wife's religious demonstrations, crossed himself. The slow, deliberate movement wasn't reverential; it was more of a wordless incantation. Castle felt it too, a presence to be warded off. *Something here that didn't used to be here.* He recalled Blaine's words from months ago, and the yelping of the coyotes from minutes ago, a demonic serenade, the devil's chorus. But they were really only coyotes that had come upon an easy meal. Meat. Protein. He could no longer hold the salty, sour lump in his gullet and pulled his bandanna down and went off to be sick.

"Reckon she couldn't keep up, the condition she was in," his cousin said when he was finished. "So she got left behind and most likely died of thirst."

"But why would she—"

"So her kid could get born in the States, that would be my guess. Jesus God, never saw nothin' like this, not even in 'Nam."

He went to his horse, took a spare shirt from his saddlebag, and walked back to where Tessa and McIntyre were waiting. They returned with him, Tessa steeling herself, Blaine carrying the—the baby, Castle said it to himself, the baby—swaddled in his shirt. He laid it next to its mother, and for the next half hour they piled rocks atop the bodies. McIntyre found two stout sticks, which he bound with a rawhide saddle string, and wedged the crucifix into the rocks. Blaine asked Castle if he had his GPS with him. He did.

"Then get the coordinates. I'll call the Border Patrol when we get home. They can come take her out of here. Maybe they got some way to find out who she was." He looked at the grave, then at McIntyre. "You got some words you can say?"

McIntyre removed his hat, and they all removed theirs and bowed their heads. After a short silence McIntyre looked up apologetically. "I can't think of nothin'. I can't think of a thing to say to this."

"Amen," said Blaine. "Done all we can. Now we got work to finish."

All color had drained from Tessa's face. Castle gave her an inquiring look—did she feel like carrying on?

"Let's go," she said.

They rode together but were no longer a team dedicated to a common task; they were five individuals, trapped within their private thoughts.

They found the bulls resting on a hillside above a meadow, so still they were like three big black boulders as, with heads lifted, they waited for a sign from the heifers congregated below. As the riders approached, they heaved off their knees and quick-trotted down the hill line abreast. Tessa and McIntyre rode out ahead and cut them off, while Blaine, Castle, and Gerardo hemmed them from the sides. Two were docile and quit their flight, but the third, the boss, bluff-charged Blaine, then pivoted and ran off again at top speed. Gerardo went after it and caught up in seconds. Leaning so far over it looked as though he would spill from the saddle, he snatched the bull's tail near the root and gave it a quick twist. The huge animal dropped as if it had been brain-shot, then rolled back onto its feet, chest heaving, snot flying from its flared nostrils. All bluster. The Mexican pushed it easily back up the hill.

"Vaquero!" Blaine said, clapping him on the shoulder. Gerardo acknowledged the compliment with a twitch of his head. Nothing more.

They herded the bulls back toward Tessa's ranch by way of a canyon shortcut through the Canelo Hills. Under other circumstances they would have been talking about Gerardo's feat of charro horsemanship, but the thing they had seen oppressed them and made them mute. The pleasure of finishing a hard job was absent. Castle wondered if his companions felt what he did—a mongrelized emotion bred of revulsion, pity, and shame. He had no reason to be ashamed, yet he was; it was as though he'd seen something forbidden, as though some dreadful secret had been revealed to him.

This day of troubles saved the worst for the last.

The canyon necked down into a ravine roughly as wide as a city street, cut banks rose ten feet high on both sides. The bulls plodded along single file, Tessa and McIntyre flanking them, Gerardo riding drag, Castle in front with his cousin. Rounding an oxbow bend, Blaine's Tequila stopped dead, bracing her rear legs like a roping horse. Scarcely ten yards away, near where a two-track plunged down into the ravine, a disabled truck faced them, its headlights shattered, its hood thrown open. His back to them, a thin man stood on the canted roof, calling in Spanish into a handheld radio. Calling out numbers he was reading from a GPS in his other hand. A second man was off to the side, digging a hole with a short-handled shovel, something like an army entrenching tool. He saw the riders first and called out to his companion, "¡Luis! ¡Ojo!" The man on the roof spun around, almost toppling from his perch.

People who have survived collisions or plane crashes often speak of seeing the event unfold in slow motion. That is how Castle's senses record the next several seconds, and the object that creates this illusion is a chrome-plated semiautomatic shoved in the man's belt, its ivory handles protruding over a shiny rodeo buckle. The radio and GPS drop from the man's hands and seem to float like falling leaves; his arm, as he catches his balance, appears to leisurely sweep across his midriff. Castle turns in the saddle and hollers to Tessa, a couple of yards behind him, "Tess! Watch out! Gun!" In the confined space, the pistol shot is nearly as loud as it would be in a room. Horses rear and shy, and the bulls stampede, one sideswiping the truck. Comanche lunges forward, and Castle half falls, half jumps from the saddle and glimpses the man tumbling from the roof—not, he realizes, because of the bull's collision with the truck but because he's been shot. He hits the ground and lies on his back, legs thrashing spastically, the pistol still in his belt, blood spreading across his shirt. Only when he stops kicking and lies still as a manikin do Castle's perceptions return to normal.

His first thought was for Tessa. Thrown by her frightened horse, she was sitting on the ground, shaking her head. He placed his hands under her arms and pulled her to her feet and held her, she him.

"What . . . what . . . ," she stammered.

"I don't know. I—," Castle began, then saw Blaine, the Luger at his side, kneel down and press a finger to the man's neck, just under one ear. He stood up, and they all five stared at the dead man and at one another for what felt like a much longer time than it was. It felt, to Castle, like forever. His heart beat erratically.

Finally Blaine spoke. "Thought you said he was goin' for the gun."

"No, I—"

"Looked to me like he was. Other one run off."

"Them bulls, too," McIntyre said. "Some day this has been."

"You and Gerardo go gather 'em. Couldn't of run far."

"It has been some day. That's all I've got to say. One *helluva* day."

As the two men rode away, Blaine stuck his head under the open hood of the pickup. "Come look at this."

The engine block had been partly disassembled, the valves, pistons, and connecting rods removed from four of the eight cylinders. Opening the pliers of his Leatherman, Blaine plucked a squashed sandwich bag from one of the cylinders. It was stoutly wrapped in tape, the kind used to repair radiator hose. He cut it open, and a fine white powder tinged faintly pink spilled to the ground, near the feet of the man he'd killed.

Blaine has killed a man. This fact now struck Castle in a delayed reaction. That the victim had been an armed drug smuggler seemed, for the moment irrelevant. *Thought you said he was goin' for the gun.* He'd said no such thing. If that's what Blaine had heard, it was because that's what he wanted to hear. Still, Castle felt somewhat complicit. His shout of that one word—*Gun!*—was all his cousin had needed to at last, at last strike back at these devils bedeviling him. And why had he, Castle, cried that alarm? Out of fear. To protect Tessa—and himself from suffering another loss.

Now Blaine was narrating a scenario: the drug runners, trying to elude the Border Patrol last night, had driven into the canyon, probably mistaking it for a road in the darkness. They'd bogged down and couldn't extricate the truck, not with half its cylinders out of operation. After a night in the wilds, they decided to abandon the vehicle and make their way back to Mexico on foot. The dead man had been radioing his boss with the GPS coordinates of where they'd buried the drugs.

Castle listened to this analysis, fascinated not by Blaine's reconstruction of events but by his matter-of-factness. He had just shot a man to death, and he was carrying on like some amateur crime solver, Miss Marple with a western drawl. "Who gives a shit about all that?" Castle said. "What do we do now?"

Blaine grabbed the shovel. "Follow the Three-S Rule. Shoot 'em, shovel 'em, shut up."

"You don't mean that."

He started digging. Castle picked up the bag of cocaine. "What do we do about this? Leave it here? Take it home and start selling it?"

"We bury him deep," said Blaine, grunting. "Then we call the Border Patrol, tell 'em we come across an abandoned truck and found the stuff in it." *Grunt.* "Tell 'em where it is, and if they do find this bastard"—*grunt*—"they'll think he was shot by another smuggler."

My God, Castle thought, he'd turn us all into conspirators. "That's not going to happen, Blaine."

Tessa stepped up, rubbing her back. "Gil's right."

Blaine kept digging.

She tugged at his arm. "There is no way we're going to pretend that what happened here didn't happen."

Castle went to snatch the shovel. "We're not going to lie for you, not about something like this."

Blaine planted the shovel and glanced at them. "Well, Jesus H. Christ. The Girl Scout and the Boy Scout. Just what would you do?"

"How does the truth sound?" said Castle. "I yelled 'Gun!,' you thought you heard me say he was reaching for it, you fired in what you thought was self-defense." He was aware that this was not entirely the truth, that he was weaving a kind of alibi, but it would have to do. "We'll back you up. I can't imagine there'd be any kind of investigation. It's not like this guy was an upstanding citizen."

Because a shooting and a corpse were involved, the matter fell under the sheriff's jurisdiction. Rodriguez was cooperative, and in the official report there was no question that the shooting of the Mexican, identified as one Luis Acevado, had been justifiable homicide. Castle pleaded with the sheriff to keep the episode quiet, which of course proved impossible. What with the border heating up in the fever swamps of the national consciousness, the story was too dramatic to ignore, too rich in clashing iconographies—the Old West versus the New West, Cowboys and Smugglers. **BORDER WARS. RANCHER SLAYS DRUG TRAFFICKER. $2M IN COCAINE CONFISCATED.** In some of the media accounts the truth underwent certain mutations. The smuggler drew his weapon before Blaine shot him, the smuggler actually fired, a falsehood to which the powder grains found in the Colt automatic's barrel lent credence. (These doubtlessly had come from the night before, when he'd shot at the pursuing Border Patrolmen.) Castle gave an interview to a Tucson TV station to correct the record, without much success. The reality was too ambiguous for a thirty-second segment or a fifteen-second radio spot or a four-hundred-word newspaper story.

The publicity made him uneasy, and not only because of its mutilation of the facts. Blaine, who had been prepared to conceal everything, now revealed everything. Everything and then some. He relished the spotlight, playing up the portrayal of himself as the straight-shooting cowboy, grandson of Arizona's last frontier lawman. Weird messages came from opposite ends of the political spectrum. An immigrant-rights group threatened to investigate if the killing had been justified and, if not, to bring suit against Blaine for violating Acevado's civil rights. Letters and e-mails of support arrived, some howls from the dank mole holes of the American soul—"Instead of shooting him, you should have done what those boys did to that nigger in Texas, chained him to your bumper and dragged him down the road till his head came off." Border bloggers, inhabiting the space occupied a generation ago by John Birchers and the Posse Comitatus, posted congratulations and offers of assistance. "Be happy to join you the next time out. I've got a smooth Ruger Mini-14 that kills nothing but Mexicans." Blaine encouraged this kind of response by failing to discourage it. In one interview he looked straight into the camera and said, "Anybody else wants to smuggle poison through my ranch is welcome to try."

33

LESS THAN TWENTY MILES AWAY, in the sala of her ranch house, Yvonne watched the interview on her satellite TV with Julián and Billy. It was her first glimpse of her enemy, and she did not find him physically appealing, though he wasn't as ugly as she wanted him to be. This man who was causing her so much trouble should look like the cucaracha that he was. Instead, with that narrow head and coxcomb of hair, he resembled an underfed gallo. He certainly was crowing.

Julián had phoned her in Zihuatanejo with the bad news, right after the story broke in the press. She'd immediately cut her holiday short and chartered a private plane to fly her and her security detail directly back to Los Tres Encinos. The loss of the load and her best runner was not catastrophic—Acevado was replaceable, and ten kilos of coke was a fraction of what she sold every week, representing no more to her than the spoilage of a few tomatoes would to a farmer who grew them by the hectare. It was the principle of the thing. To suffer such a loss not at the hands of La Migra or the DEA or the federales but at the hands of a stupid cowboy was a disgrace. The damage to her reputation, that was her concern. The Gulf Cartel and, more important, people within her own organization would think she was slipping. And then there was Billy's friend, Carrington. The day before she'd left for the seashore, he'd made her an extremely attractive proposition. Fifty kilos a week every week, his client wanted. She'd told him she would consider it while she was on vacation—she didn't like the demand to deal with her only on the U.S. side of the line. That didn't feel right. But if Carrington's customer was making a legitimate offer, he would go elsewhere if he thought she was incapable of guaranteeing safe delivery.

She hadn't had much time in Zihuatanejo, but even that little bit had been good for her. Not a line, not a bump. She'd eaten well, swum in the ocean, signed up for exercise classes at a resort. Her mind began to work as it used to. No nervous flitting from thought to thought—coke's illusion of mental quickness. A clear, straight, unwavering line, a laser beam. Flying back in the chartered Cessna, she'd seen that her methods of psychological warfare had been unsound. Really, she'd been too clever by half, thinking that she could harass and wear Erskine down. If anything, Erskine was wearing her down. He, whose family had ruined hers, had now made her look like an incompetent fool. But at least his killing of Acevado had clarified the situation. Direct, decisive action was required. The way was now open for her to realize her aims in a single stroke. By the time the plane landed at her airstrip, the rough outline of a plan had presented itself.

Before she could proceed, she had to demonstrate that she was in full control. She interrogated the runner who'd accompanied Acevado and who'd fled back to Mexico—had the load been snitched out, or had the two merely run into bad luck? Whatever the case, she was disappointed in Acevado's companion. A man of honor, a man with huevos, a *man*, would not have run away; he would have fought to the death. Everybody in her organization needed to be reminded that she would abide neither cowardice nor screwups. Marco and Heraclio took the cobarde to the airstrip, shot him in both legs, then drenched him in aviation fuel and burned him alive.

And then there was Billy, her Billy, who had given her so much pleasure, the field commander of her armies of toilet scrubbers and strawberry pickers. Billy's chickens were supposed to have decoyed La Migra but had failed. Why was that? she'd asked him on the night of her return as they lay naked on her bed. He couldn't explain it. "Shit happens" was all he'd said, a brilliant comment.

"It does, darling, but it usually happens for a reason."

He folded his hands on his belly and asked her meaning.

"That friend of yours, Carrington," she said. "He's got some client who wants to deal big, but I wonder if the client might be a chota. He says he won't do the deal except in the United States. I even wonder sometimes if Carrington is a chota." She turned onto her side and pulled Billy's ear to her breast. "Do you hear my little Chihuahua? He goes 'yip, yip' when something doesn't feel right. How did La Migra know where that load was going to cross?"

Billy lifted his head. "Hey, Yvonne, hey, c'mon—"

The unfortunate nose, the battered eyebrows, the thick blond hair. She'd grown fond of him, more than she'd thought she would, and it truly pained her to suspect that he might have betrayed her. Pained her more to think what she would have to do if he did.

She laughed. "I'm not thinking what you think I'm thinking," she lied. "My customer was going to pay me a quarter of a million wholesale for that load, and I promised you ten percent. Why would you snitch it out?"

"Snitch!" Billy protested, sitting up.

"I'm not accusing you, chico. Only thinking out loud. Why would you snitch and risk losing that kind of money?"

"That's right. That's exactly right."

And maybe it was, she thought, aware that she could be rationalizing. But not, she was pleased to say to her herself, entirely for emotional reasons. Billy would have a very constructive role to play in her plan. She'd refined it during the last couple of days but had so far kept it to herself. Now was the time to begin laying the groundwork, though she had no intention of revealing her entire scheme immediately. The people who were to carry it out would know only what they needed to know, no more.

Now, in the living room, she picked up the remote and turned the TV off. The interview with Erskine was over. "He seemed very proud of himself, that pendejo."

Julián and Billy agreed. She rose from between them and took a chair facing them. "He owes us two hundred and fifty thousand dollars, don't you think?"

Julián shrugged. Billy was likewise noncommittal.

"Well, he does, and we are going to collect." She turned to Julián. "I want that ranch put under surveillance. I want to know how many people are there. I want to know their comings and goings. I want to know when they wake up and when they go to bed and when they shit. I want to know everything about them."

Julián started to speak. She motioned to him to keep quiet and looked at Billy. "You know your way around pretty well. The human map. Would it be difficult for you to guide some people in there at night?"

He answered with a puzzled squint.

She said, "That seems like a simple question."

"In where, exactly?" he asked. "It's a big ranch."

"To the San Ignacio ranch house."

"No, it wouldn't be hard. But I don't think it's a good idea for me to be crossing the line right now, day or night."

"It would please me if you did. It wouldn't be for long. An hour or two at the most." He made a movement with his shoulders and gazed at her attentively. He was eager to please her. Of course he was, after their previous conversation, when she insinuated that he might have informed on her. Nevertheless, she thought to provide him with extra incentive. "I believe you have some business you need taken care of over there. Suppose I told you that this business will be taken care of if you do as I ask. Then you would be free to come and go just like you used to."

"That would be good, sure."

Julián crossed his legs in the way she hated and tilted his head backward, squeezing his eyes half shut. "Mother, I know what—"

"Shut up, mi hijo. You don't know anything."

Ben Erskine

In the archives of the Arizona Historical Society, photocopies of a trial transcript as thick as a blockbuster novel rest in a file box with an arrest report, an indictment, witness statements, depositions, and newspaper clippings. Reading through these documents, with some assistance from the imagination, powers us out of the present to a February morning in 1951.

We see a fog of sparkling dust hovering above a corral, where Brahma-crosses with pendulous dewlaps, massive shoulders, and obstreperous dispositions bawl and bang against the planks. Four riders circle the jostling mass of muscle and horn—Ben; two cowboys, Alberto Hernández and Jim Tierney; and Caroline Burton, a friend visiting from Scottsdale.

More than ten years have passed since Ben dissolved the IB-Bar and incorporated it into his brother's San Ignacio Ranch. This minor empire has done well, but last summer's monsoons were stingy, and the winter rains have been scarce. The dirt tanks are low, some are altogether dry, the range is in bad shape. Ben and Jeff have decided to lighten up by selling off some stock. The gathering began at dawn. Ben, Hernández, Tierney, and Caroline pushed the cattle out of the Huachucas and the Canelo Hills, then drove them down the road to the corral, with Ida riding drag in Ben's Chevrolet pickup. Now they are waiting for the two trucks contracted to haul the livestock to the shipping pens in Sonoita, a settlement clustered around a crossroads and a spur line of the Southern Pacific. Not very long ago they would have driven the herd to the pens, camping out overnight; but in recent years more and more fences have begun to snake across the land, and the roads have been improved to handle heavy-duty trucks. Transporting them this way prevents weight loss, and every pound counts; yet Ben misses the old drives, the open range.

A banged-up Dodge pickup towing a stock trailer arrives. It is driven by Rafael Quinn, a nearby rancher whom Ben has hired to haul any excess cattle. He turns off the road and stops by a wire gate and climbs out to open it. Hernández shouts above the lowing cows and steers, "Hey, Ben! He's at the wrong gate!" Ben eases his horse out of the corral and rides over to Rafe to point out his mistake and direct him to the right gate.

"You don't remember which one to go to?" Ben jokes. "Must be getting forgetful in your old age."

"Must be," Quinn laughs. He is close to Ben's age, a rawboned six-footer of mixed Irish and Mexican descent, more Mexican than Irish, though his reddish hair and blue green eyes and freckled complexion suggest it's the other way around. Glancing toward the corral, he motions at Caroline Burton. "Talking about old, I see you got an old lady workin' with you. Who's she?"

"Friend of Jeff's and Lilly's. And she ain't all that old."

Quinn flicks his eyebrows. His gaze swivels to Ida, standing beside the Chevy. "You got *two* old ladies. One old mare ain't enough for you, eh?"

Quinn is known for his vulgarities, and although Ben is accustomed to them, this one makes him bristle. "What kinda talk is that, Rafe?"

"I was makin' a joke."

"What would you think, I talked about your wife like that?"

"You couldn't," Quinn replies, cackling. "Mine ain't old." Meaning his second wife. He suffered a double loss during the war, his son killed in the South Pacific, his first wife dying shortly thereafter—of a broken heart, it was said. He did not remain a childless widower for long, marrying at age fifty-two a Mexican girl of nineteen. She has already borne two children and is pregnant with a third. "One young one is worth two old ones for sure," he says to Ben.

"All right, that's enough. We've got work to do."

"Just a joke, Ben."

"I do not see the humor in it."

The haulers have arrived, the trucks making a racket as they back up to the chutes.

"You can't take a joke? All I meant was"—Quinn spreads the palm of one hand and pounds its heel with the heel of the other—"how are your two old mares when it comes to that?"

"You garbage-mouth son of a bitch!" Ben swings out of the saddle, with as much speed and suppleness as his aging body will permit, and jabs a finger into Quinn's chest, jabs and jabs, like a woodpecker drilling a tree. "You're on my land, and you don't talk like that when you're on my land!"

"Reckon I can talk any way I damn well please anywhere," Quinn replies.

Although it is early afternoon, Ben can smell whiskey on Quinn's breath. "Not here you can't. I'll find somebody else to haul. Get the hell out of here."

The crust on the tempers of both men is thin, and now Quinn's cracks. "You can't take a little joke, you go to hell!"

"Clear out, goddamn you!"

"Chinga tu madre," Quinn curses, then gets into his pickup and backs out onto the road, the wheels spewing dirt as he speeds off.

Ben remounts and returns to the corral. Hernández asks, "What fire is he goin' to?" Ben doesn't answer, too angry to speak.

He remains angry all the while the cattle are loaded into the haulers' trucks and as he follows them in the pickup, Ida and Caroline sitting beside him, Ida in the middle. His Winchester 30-30 rattles in the gun rack behind him. He casts a quick look at Ida, dressed for ranch work in jeans, a barn coat, and her favorite hat, which with its stiff brim and high, indented peak resembles a scoutmaster's hat. She turned fifty-one in December. There is gray in her hair now, and though she's retained her trim figure, years of rough outdoor work have given her skin the texture of crumpled paper. The years have been hard on her. Ben knows he's been hard on her, with his frequent absences, the dangers to which he's exposed himself. Back in the thirties, after Ben lost his badge, she'd hoped he would devote himself to ranching full-time. She was dismayed when he joined the county rangers, without pay but with full powers to make arrests, for he could no more stay away from the life of pursuit, flight, and capture than a chain-smoker can stay away from cigarettes. He teamed up with customs agents to chase smugglers, one of whom got the drop on him in an unguarded moment and sent him to the hospital with a fractured skull. Ben had often said that no other woman could have stayed married to him for this long. The wife of his days for thirty-five years, he's been faithful to her, and the idea that he would pound her like an old mare disgusts him. He cannot erase Rafe's obscene gesture from his mind, nor the leer that accompanied it. His rage feeds on the image and on itself, a crown fire burning in his head that seems to suck the air from his lungs. He takes a washboard curve too fast and curses as the Chevy almost slews off the road.

"What's the matter?" Ida asks.

"Nothin'."

"Don't tell me 'nothin'.' "

"Me and Rafe had words is all."

"About what?"

"Nothin' I care to repeat."

At the stockyards, slatted red cattle cars are lined up behind an idling locomotive, its stack bleeding smoke into the air. The day is clear and chilly, and a sharp wind keens across the Sonoita grasslands, rising and falling toward the Mustang and Whetstone Mountains, miles away.

"This is gonna take a while," Otis Reed, the livestock inspector, says to Ida and Caroline. He motions at a small brick house a short distance beyond the tracks. "Why don't you ladies make yourselves comfortable? My wife will make you a cup of coffee."

The women accept the invitation and leave.

Ben now attends to the business of sale and shipment. While he leans over the hood of his pickup, doing the paperwork with Reed and the buyer, Hernández and Tierney unload the cattle and prod them into the chute and onto the weigh scales. Amid the noise—animals bellowing, hooves clattering on steel ramps, the idling locomotive's hisses and low rumble—Reed records the weight and description of each cow and steer, and Ben signs the forms for brand self-inspection. The tedious routine dampens the fire in his brain but does not extinguish it. Two old mares. That sly leer.

The work is almost done when, Rafe Quinn drives in hauling a few culls from another rancher's herd. As the culls are unloaded from Quinn's trailer, he spots Ben and walks toward him with quick, jerky strides. "Hey, where's your two old mares? Still with you, or did you ship 'em out?"

Ben knows he should let this go, but he doesn't; he can't. He goes up to the other man with the freckled face and taunting voice. "I don't want to hear one more goddamn word out of you."

"You'll hear plenty."

"Shut up!"

"I don't have to do nothing you tell me!"

He pushes Ben, who pushes back. It's a schoolboy shoving match between two old men and is almost comical until Ben takes a swing. The blow grazes Quinn's skull, knocking his hat off. Instantly Ben throws the opposite arm. It's more a swat than a punch, but it strikes Quinn's temple with enough force to stagger him.

"¡Cabrón! ¡Hijo de puta!" Quinn shouts, lapsing into Spanish in his fury. "I can't take care of you this way, but I'm goin' home for my gun, and I'll take care of you that way." He picks up his hat, smacks it against his thigh. "You wait right here."

And what does Ben say now? As the trial record will show, his exact words will be crucial to the prosecution's case.

Otis Reed will testify that he heard Ben say: "You go home and get your gun. I've got cattle to ship and I'll be right here."

Hernández will testify that he heard: "I've got these cattle to load and I'll be here till then. I don't want any more trouble with you."

Tierney will testify that he heard: "Go home and get your gun. I don't want any trouble with you. I've got cattle to ship and I'll be here till then."

As Quinn, still cursing, climbs into his truck, Reed squints at Ben. "What was that all about? Thought you and Rafe was friends."

"Just an argument. It's done with," Ben says.

"Said he's goin' to get a gun."

"Don't think nothin' of it. He won't be back."

Reed will quote that remark in his statement to the sheriff. He will repeat it in his testimony, and it will be crucial to the defense.

The two women return from their coffee break. Ben says nothing to them about the confrontation. They climb into the Chevy to get out of the wind while he, Reed, and the buyer finish the weighing and inspection. Tierney and Hernández begin to prod the cattle out of the pens into the railroad cars. Quinn's Dodge, without trailer, races into the stockyards and stops suddenly. Quinn flings the door open and jumps out, a rifle in his hands.

This sight douses Ben's anger, and an icy calm descends. In him, there is no lag between thought and action; the motions of mind and body occur simultaneously as he reaches into the pickup's cab to jerk his rifle from the rack, as he levers a round into the chamber while he sprints into the open to draw fire away from Ida and Caroline and other bystanders. His movements, supple, almost choreographed, are not those of a man approaching his sixty-first birthday. It's as though the years have fallen off him in this crisis. He raises a hand and yells, "Don't shoot, Rafe!"

Quinn fires and misses, the bullet passing so close to Ben's chest that he feels its shock wave. Falling to one knee to present a smaller target and steady his aim, he snaps off a shot that wings Quinn's left arm. The impact spins Quinn around; he drops the rifle and ducks behind his car. Hernández, who is closest to him, sees him reach inside and snatch a revolver from off the front seat. "He's got a pistol!" Hernández shouts. Ben's view is blocked by the car. He puts a bullet through the side window to flush Quinn into the open. The tactic succeeds. Quinn leaps up and fires over the hood, missing again.

Quinn dashes for the stock pens, which are made of stout planks spaced about a foot apart. Crouching behind the pens, he braces the pistol on a plank and fires a third time, the bullet striking the ground wide of its mark. Quinn is equatorial, all hot action and frantic movement; Ben is arctic, almost immobile, kneeling there in the dust. Now behold his wintry eye center the front sight post in the rear sight leaf, behold his finger quickly but smoothly pull the trigger.

The bullet chips the upper plank and bites into Quinn's chest, knocking him onto his back.

The entire action has taken less than half a minute, and Ida has watched it unfold through the windshield of the Chevrolet. All she knows is that Ben and Quinn have had words. How did that come to this? When she saw her husband drop to one knee after Quinn's first shot, she thought he'd been hit. She will later testify, "I was never so terrified in my life," and considering what she's been through in her life, that will be saying something.

She and Caroline get out and run to the men crowded around Quinn, lying with his face to the sky and a blood-rimmed hole below his right collarbone. Ben stands over him, the Winchester hanging at his side—almost sixty-one and still a dangerous man.

"I'm sorry this had to happen, Rafe," he says, as if they had been acting out parts scripted long ago.

Ida has heard those words like that before.

Quinn is breathing in short, shallow gasps, and with each breath a roseate bubble swells and pops in his mouth. He whispers, "Gimme another bullet."

"I'll do anything for you," says Ben, "but not that."

"All over a little joke."

Someone urges Quinn not to talk, an unnecessary exhortation. A bubble forms and breaks, his lips part and remain open, his eyes stop blinking.

Text of a letter submitted to the AHS by Grace Erskine Castle.

125 Scott's Cove Rd.
Darien, Conn.
January 9, 1967

Arizona Historical Society
929 E. 2nd St.
Tucson, Arizona

Gentlemen:

I'm writing in response to your most recent request for my impressions of, my reactions to, my father's trial on second-degree murder charges.

To tell you the truth, I feel peculiar writing to you, mostly because I'm telling you things about my father that I haven't even told my children. It's those mixed feelings I mentioned in my last letter. I've never been able to sort them out. And to be candid, I've been afraid that my son would end up hero-worshiping Ben, that he might see him as some kind of straight-shootin', hard-ridin' Old West swashbuckler and want to imitate him. That was the image a lot of young men had of him, like my nephew, Blaine Erskine.

My father did many brave and honorable things in his life. But he also did some things that make me cringe—to this day. His shooting of Mr. Quinn was one of those things. I hope I can explain why.

My mother had written and asked my brother and me to be at her side during the trial. It wasn't a problem for Frank—he was a mining engineer in Bisbee—but I was here in Connecticut, had a four-year-old boy to look after, and had just found out I was pregnant again. And it was a three-day train trip to Tucson. It goes without saying that I wasn't eager to see my father tried on a murder charge. And this, too: relations between us were very sour at that time.

I bring this up because it gives a glimpse into Ben's dark side. During the war my husband, Tony, and I eloped. He was a flight surgeon at the Army Air Corps base outside Tucson. We ran off when he got orders that he was being shipped overseas. Ben could not forgive me, he could not forgive Tony for failing to ask him for my hand. After our son was born in 1947, my mother took the train east to see her new grandson, and she came alone.

Whatever my feelings toward my father, I couldn't turn her down. My mother-in-law volunteered to look after our son. Pardon this aside, but I clearly recall her reaction to the newspaper stories Ida had mailed about the shooting, my father's arrest and indictment. My mother-in-law read them with a bemused expression, as if she were reading about the doings of some quirky tribe on the far side of the world. She assured me there was nothing to worry about—it looked like a clear-cut case of self-defense. Then she said, "Your father sounds like a colorful character, and a . . . how shall I put it? A bit of an anachronism?"

Those Arizona papers had had a field day with the color and the anachronisms. Headlines like "Gunfight at the Sonoita Corral!" and "Duel in the Sun!" Comparisons to Wyatt Earp and the OK Corral. That kind of thing.

The Sunset Limited pulled into Tucson at ten in the morning on May 7, 1951, the day before the trial. My aunt and uncle drove me to the San Ignacio. My parents were in Nogales, consulting with Ben's lawyer. They continued to live in their old house after the sale of the IB-Bar but had been staying with Jeff and Lilly for the past couple of weeks because it was closer to Nogales than the mountain place.

Frank and Sally, my sister-in-law, had arrived earlier with my nephew. Late in the afternoon my parents returned, and we all gathered in the living room of the main house. Ben, wearing Levi's, white shirt, bandanna, and green and black cowboy boots, lived up to the portrait painted of him in the newspapers as—I'm quoting almost directly—"the rangy, sunburned rancher, looking every inch the border lawman and frontiersman he'd once been."

My mother looked as if she'd aged ten years since I last saw her. And yet it was she who seemed in command, Ben who was subdued. After the preliminary greetings were over, she said, "Your father has something to say to you," then, with a sidelong look, cued him.

He expressed his thanks to me for coming so far in my condition, and then apologized for shutting my husband and me out of his life.

"I was damn mad at him and you," he said, "but you're right, I've been unreasonable. I ain't just saying that, Grace. I'm as sorry as a man can be. About a lot of things."

The first thing that comes to mind about the day the trial began is the Santa Cruz County courthouse. In case you haven't seen it, it's a square stone building painted desert tan and crowned by a bright tin dome topped by blindfolded Lady Justice with her sword and scales. It occupies a hilltop above Morley Avenue. From the street, three flights of steep stairs, flanked by cypress and orange trees, ascend to the front entrance. The builders' intention must have been to create the impression of a temple and to instill in all who made that climb, the innocent no less than guilty, appropriate feelings of reverence for the Anglo-Saxon system of justice.

All I felt, as I went up with Jeff and Lilly and an entourage of relations, were butterflies.

The courtroom was as crowded as a redneck bar on Saturday night or a Baptist church on Sunday morning. Overhead fans paddled against the May heat, to little effect. The county attorney sat beside an assistant at the prosecution's table, my father at the defense table with his lawyer. He looked rueful. He wasn't at all certain he was going to get off, and neither were we.

Our family sat on one side of the aisle, Quinn's on the other, like families at a wedding. I glanced over at Quinn's much-younger wife, Rosario, dressed in mourning. My memory of her hasn't dimmed. She had one of those classic Mexican faces—severe, dignified, tragic—and looked older than her years, what with her black dress, her black hair pulled into a bun, the matronly figure bestowed by bearing three children in five years. Three girls, I found out, the last one born only weeks earlier.

The clerk called the court to order, the jury—nine men, three women—filed in, the judge swooped to his lofty chair, and the ritual began.

The trial lasted four days, and when the prosecution rested, it was obvious that it did not have a strong case. Ida had not been allowed in the courtroom, as she was to appear as a witness for the defense. Midway through the third day she was called to the stand. I was rather proud of how composed she looked in her best suit, her only suit, in fact, a gray wool too warm for the season. Direct examination, cross-examination. I watched Rosario watching her, the woman of the man who had killed hers. Rosario's upright posture and impassive expression barely changed. Now and then she inclined her head to one side to listen to a man beside her whisper abridged translations of Ida's testimony.

The climax came on the fourth day, when Father spent two hours in the witness chair, testifying in his own defense. On cross-examination, he was unflappable, parrying the prosecutor's questions in his western drawl.

The judge called a recess before the attorneys made their closing arguments.

The prosecutor's was that Ben had not fired in self-defense, that the gun battle was actually a duel. Because he didn't leave after Quinn made his threat, he had, in effect, accepted a challenge. The county attorney contended that in a duel it makes no difference who fires first. I seem to recall him appealing to the jurors to act as social reformers—by returning a guilty verdict, they would demonstrate that Arizona was not going to tolerate a return to the days of rough frontier justice.

The defense attorney's argument was more succinct. He depicted Ben as the kind of man everyone would like to be, a man who'd exposed himself to fire and shot his assailant to protect his own life and the lives of his wife and innocent bystanders.

I rather doubted that the prosecutor's summation would sway the jury, but I confess that his comments stirred up some disloyal thoughts in me. As much as I wanted to support my father wholeheartedly, I couldn't help but wonder if the whole ghastly mess could have been avoided. Did he have to punch Quinn? Couldn't he have told my mother and the Burton woman, There's some trouble, let's go have some coffee till it blows over? My poor mother, after all she'd been through, had to witness that. But I knew my father's way. Never let an insult go unanswered; never back down; scour any stain to your honor with blood; if threatened, destroy the threat, even if the destruction breeds another threat in its turn. Quinn was no different—he too was a servant of pride and honor. Two old men who had outlived their time but didn't know it, two old men shooting at each other in a dusty shipping pen in the middle of the twentieth century, and over what? A dirty remark. Over nothing. Not that I believed my father was guilty of murder in any degree. To my mind, he was guilty of an unbending fealty to his own archaic code.

The jury deliberated less than an hour. We were summoned back into the courtroom. The jury foreman handed the verdict to the clerk of the court, who announced it: not guilty. My father showed no emotion.

We filed outside, into the copper light of late afternoon. Ida could not resist going up to Rosario. What she thought she could say to comfort the young woman I couldn't imagine. After she spoke her piece, Rosario looked up at her—she was barely over five feet tall—and answered in a venomous whisper. As she turned and walked off, my mother blanched. My Spanish had grown rusty, and it took me a moment to parse out Rosario's reply. I'll never forget it: "My hope, señora, is that you will suffer as I am, and if not you, your children, and if not them, their children."

A curse, as only a Mexican can deliver one when she really means it. We were shaken but collected ourselves and joined Father as he accepted the congratulations of friends and well-wishers. I felt a little embarrassed by my disloyal thoughts and kissed his cheek. He embraced me. As he held me, I was a little girl again, on the night the lightning struck the windmill. I felt that everything was going to be all right.

I should have known better. That summer Ida wrote that Father had received death threats, the acquittal having angered many Mexicans on both sides of the line. Some of their enmity had fallen on her. A week after the trial she'd gone shopping at a wholesale market on International Street, across from the border fence. As she parked, Mexican kids on a hill overlooking the fence bombarded her car with rocks. She'd begun to suffer spells of vertigo and sharp flashing headaches.

In September, when I was three months into a difficult pregnancy, the phone rang. It was my aunt Lilly, who said she had some very bad news. I knew what it was before she told me. That morning she, Ida, and my sister-in-law, who was visiting, had been stirring a chili for the ranch hands when my mother gave a short cry, clutched the back of her head, and said, "Oh, such a headache," and fell to the floor. She must have died immediately, for when my aunt and Sally went to her, they could feel the warmth passing out of her body. The doctor said it had been a massive cerebral hemorrhage. The funeral would be held day after tomorrow. Ida was only fifty-two.

There was no question of making another transcontinental journey in my condition. I supposed it was just as well. I could not have borne the sight of her lying in a coffin, nor of the coffin going down into a grave. I know some people thought that the strains of living with my father contributed to her early death. I'll admit it crossed my mind. It seemed to me that Father had been selfish, following the dictates of his nature and living as he chose, whatever the consequences to my mother or anyone else. Maybe Ben was too comfortable in his own skin; it made him literally hidebound, incapable of changing his ways.

A year after Ida's death, my brother was killed in an accident in the Phelps Dodge copper mine in Bisbee. They were blasting in the Lavender Pit, and he was crushed when tons of rock and debris fell on him. I traveled again to Arizona for his funeral. My father and I were devastated. In twelve months he'd lost his wife and son, I had lost a mother and a beloved brother. We buried Frank in Black Oak Cemetery. I consider myself a rational woman, so I say with some reluctance that I recalled Rosario's curse at the services and half believed it was responsible for their deaths.

For the next five years Ben lived alone at the mountain place, hiding out among those canyons and wooded draws like one of the solitary, unbranded bulls he'd pursued when he was young. Who knows what phantoms haunted him there on nights when the owls hooted and the coyotes sent up their dismal cries. Some in the family were worried he was going a little mad in his solitude. Uncle Jeff wrote that he and Ben were having a drink one night when they heard a car pull up. My father grabbed a flare gun (where had he got that? I wonder) and his pistol and ran outside, hiding behind his workshop. Then he fired the flare. It lit up the whole front yard, terrifying the people in the car. Turned out to be just a couple of tourists who had got lost and stopped to ask directions back to the highway.

To me, it sounded like the same old Ben, ever watchful for an attack by his enemies. It was lucky for him, Jeff, and especially the tourists that he didn't shoot first and ask questions later.

He did not isolate himself completely. My sister-in-law moved to the ranch with my nephew after Frank was killed. Sally wrote that Ben became a surrogate father to Blaine, teaching him riding, roping, shooting, tracking.

On a June morning in 1956 Blaine was sitting on a corral fence with two ranch hands watching Ben offer a lesson in horse breaking. The animal was a young stallion with an ugly temperament. Ben had settled him by forcing him to drag a railroad tie around the corral until he'd tired of it and stopped trying to escape. Now it was time for the next step—hazing, by waving a burlap sack in the horse's face to teach it not to rear and strike.

Ben entered the corral with the sack. When the horse went up on its back legs, pawing the air with its front hooves, he lunged forward, waving the sack. He was sixty-six years old, his reactions were slow, his body not as nimble as it once had been. The stallion struck him in the chest, knocking him down, and then rained blows on his head. The ranch hands grabbed lariats and roped the animal. Once it was subdued, they ran to Ben's aid and saw that there was nothing they could do. His skull had been crushed.

And so the man who had survived so many perils, who had evaded death at the hands of so many enemies, was killed as his father had been, by a rank horse.

And so did I, with my husband and two children, return to Arizona for yet another funeral, the last.

It was held in the community church in Patagonia, which could not hold all who'd come. The mourners flowed into the street, and I overheard the Mexicans among them whispering that it wasn't a horse that had killed Don Benjamín; it was a diablo, possessed by the wrathful soul of Rafael Quinn. Once more I thought of Rosario's curse and hoped she now was satisfied.

There is a strange postscript to this story. I learned a lesson: there are hazards to probing too deeply into one's family secrets; you may discover some best left undiscovered. After my father's funeral Sally and I sorted through the things in his house, while my husband cleaned out his workshop, a windowless tin shed where he'd taken up his former hobby, turning out horseshoes, bits, and belt buckles. Tony came in carrying a box and said something like, "Any idea what we should do with these?" He reached into the box and took out two human skulls. One had been embellished: antlers from a spikehorn buck protruded from holes drilled into the crown; the tusks of a javelina boar had been attached to the upper jaw, creating a fanglike effect. The companion skull had not been adorned, though it bore signs of botched attempts. There was a small hole in one temple and a larger one in the other, a jagged puncture slightly bigger than a fifty-cent piece. Its front teeth were missing. "Those might be here," said Tony, and dipped again into the box to pull out a kind of bracelet consisting of two thin, braided wires run through a set of gold teeth. All three of us were baffled and disturbed. Tony wondered aloud if my father had been robbing cemeteries. Sally replied, "This is the border. There's a lot of dead people around here ain't in cemeteries."

I learned later that day from one of the ranch hands that Ben sometimes placed the skulls in his window to ward off unwanted visitors. But where had *he found them? Then I remembered that terrible night in 1931 (described in my earlier letter) when the gunman with the gold teeth had tried to barge into our house.*

The next day I went to Patagonia to talk to Martín Mendoza. He was retired from cowboying, and he and Lourdes were living in a small trailer on Smelter Lane. When I brought up the incident, he said, "Los espectros y los huesos"—The ghosts and the bones. The way he said it gave me goose bumps. I asked what he was talking about. He then launched into a weird tale. In the early 1930s, after he'd quit the ranch and gone to work as a wrangler for the Civilian Conservation Corps, he overheard a work crew speaking excitedly about two skeletons they had come upon in a dry wash while they were clearing trails. From their description of the place, Martín realized they'd found the remains of the two gunmen he and Ben had buried after the fight. Flash floods must have unearthed the skeletons. The skulls on both were missing. The tale spread to other camps and ranches. One night a vaquero rode into the CCC camp on a sweat-lathered horse, reporting that he had fled from a pair of ghosts he'd seen wandering the hills. These phantoms were headless. When Martín heard that, he knew the cowboy had seen the spirits of the gunmen.

I didn't believe that ghosts were walking around, but I was very troubled by his revelation that the skeletons were missing their skulls. I asked Martín if he knew how they had come to be sin cabezas—without heads. He didn't know.

¿Quién sabe? Maybe the ghosts the vaquero sees are looking for their heads. I don't know."

I then asked if he remembered that one of the men had gold teeth, and he said he did. He'd seen them in the light of a flashlight when they were loading the bodies onto the truck. Then I asked—hesitantly, I might add—if he or my father had cut off the heads and taken the teeth. I recall that he was shocked, that he drew back, grimacing. "No, señora! I would be afraid to do such a thing! No, we do nothing but bury them."

I had one final question: "And you said it was in 1933 when the workmen found the skeletons?"

Martín wasn't sure. About then, he said.

So the skulls had been in Father's possession for more than twenty years, secreted away somewhere. He had gone out to that arroyo at some point between the gunfight and the time the remains were discovered and decapitated them. Why? A manhunter's trophies? Had he become so anesthetized that he saw nothing barbaric in this desecration? I assumed he had not taken his artifacts out of their hiding place until after my mother's death. I assumed further that that was when he did his creative work, extracted the teeth, affixed the horns, the tusks. The holes in the temples of the one had not been the result of bad workmanship; they'd been made by his bullet long, long before.

Ghosts and bones. Well, that's all Ben Erskine is now, his bones in the ground, his ghost stalking the corridors of my memory. I can only add that there were too many corners in my father's "hard and isolate" soul that I cannot penetrate and frankly don't wish to.

Sincerely yours,
Grace Castle

34

WAS SOMETHING OUTSIDE? Samantha's barking woke Castle at a postmidnight hour. He shook off his grogginess, got his spotlight and revolver from out of the bed-table drawer, and went outside. A full moon, so bright that the trees cast daylight shadows, almost made the spotlight unnecessary. As he swept it back and forth, a pair of eyes glittered in the beam like electrified emeralds; then he made out the squat, shaggy form of a javelina. He stepped off the porch and waved an arm. The animal fled.

"Only a pig," he said to Sam, returning inside. She padded after him into the bedroom, where he put the spotlight and the pistol away. Unable to get back to sleep, he read Seneca till his eyes grew heavy, then turned off the lamp.

The alarm buzzed at six. He and Blaine were going to truck a few culls to the Wilcox livestock auction today. These cows were, in Blaine's description, "nondoers," heifers that had failed to calve. Two weeks had passed since the shooting, the media hoopla was over, and Castle's life had reclaimed normality, or a decent facsimile of it. There were emotional aftershocks; the things he'd witnessed that day reeled in his mind, a kind of videotape that played and replayed. Blaine, to all appearances, was unaffected. It wasn't that Castle had grown tender-hearted about a drug smuggler. He simply thought that shooting someone at point-blank range, actually seeing him die, would change a man forever.

After dressing, he topped up a travel mug with coffee and walked over to Miguel's trailer, circling around the electric fence erected to keep deer and javelina out of his vegetable garden. Gerardo and Elena having gone to Chandler to visit one of their daughters for the weekend, Miguel was going to help load the culls and accompany Blaine and Castle to the auction. The Airstream door was ajar. Castle tapped on it, calling, "Hola, Miguel." Receiving no reply, he walked in and found it empty, the fold-down bed unmade. Miguel must have awakened early and gone to ranch headquarters on foot, which was odd; his experiences crossing the border had given him a distaste for walking anywhere when he could ride.

But when Castle arrived at the main house, no one answered his knock. Monica's car was in its usual spot alongside the house, but Blaine's truck was missing. Could they all have gone on to Wilcox without him? No, because the cows were in the corral, the stock trailer parked next to it. He tried the kitchen door. It was locked. He went around to the front door, which was open, and stepped inside. The hall light was on and Blaine's Luger lay on the floor. He charged into their bedroom, then ran out and searched the barn and toolshed. No one. He slumped against the corral boards, trying to think of what accounted for their disappearance. A logical reason. The windmill squealed, an unsettling sound, like a small animal caught in a trap. The dogs. Blaine's Australian heelers—why hadn't they barked when he pulled up? They always did. He left the corral and looked in the backyard. No dogs. Then, passing around to the side of the house, he noticed a paw sticking out from behind a front wheel of Monica's car. Bending down, he grabbed a hind leg, which was stiff as a pipe and cold to the touch, and when he dragged the dog out from under the car, he couldn't tell which one it was because half its head had been blown off.

Castle had not smoked a cigarette since his freshman year at Princeton, but he craved one now. His brain had shut down, a kind of mental power outage, and he imagined nicotine would light it up again. Wait. Blaine smoked. He burst into the house, going straight to the bedroom, where he began pulling drawers open like a burglar in a hurry. He found a fresh pack in the night table, tore it open, shook out a cigarette, and lighted it off the kitchen range. Sucking in the smoke, he nearly fainted. He sat down at the kitchen table and took a second, shallower drag. It did not have the dizzying effect of the first.

The fog of panic began to clear. Blaine, he remembered, never went anywhere without his cell. Castle dialed it from the kitchen phone and flinched when he heard its musical ring tone coming from inside the house. He ran toward the sound and found the cell phone on the desk in the office. Calling 911 seemed the only thing to do now. He was thinking of what to say to the dispatcher when his own cell phone rang. The caller ID flashed UNKNOWN CALLER. Maybe it was Blaine, phoning from another number. He answered.

"This is Mr. Castle?" asked a strange female voice.

"Yes," he answered in a shaky voice. "Who is this?"

"Don't be silly. Let me tell you something. We have Erskine and his wife in custody. They are in perfect health. If you want them to stay that way, you will do what we say."

He didn't respond. His throat felt as narrow as a straw.

"Do you want them to stay healthy or not?" the woman said. "Let me tell you something else. We have already killed one guy. It would be no problem to kill these two. Do you want that to happen?"

"Who is this?"

"Shut up and listen. Erskine owes us two hundred and fifty thousand dollars, but he doesn't have the money. You do. We know you do. You are a rich man. Right now, do you hear me? Right fucking now you are going to start getting this money. The banks close at five o'clock. You will have this money by that time, in cash. We will call you again and tell you what to do with it, so keep your mobile on. Is there anything you don't understand?"

"No . . . I . . ."

"Listen. Do not do anything stupid, like call the police. If you do something stupid, any stupid little thing, however insignificant, Erskine and his wife are dead. Maybe you don't believe me, so let me tell you one more thing. The guy we killed was Miguel Espinoza. Erskine is a tall, skinny man, his wife is named Monica, and she has blond hair and blue eyes. Do you believe what I'm saying to you, Mr. Castle?"

He croaked a yes.

"Five this afternoon," the caller said, and the connection went dead.

Castle stood in dazed immobility. He felt like a pedestrian who had looked both ways at an intersection and, seeing no traffic, stepped out into the street only to be struck by a bus. A quarter of a million dollars. How could he be expected to withdraw a quarter of a million dollars in a few hours? In cash. It made no sense. Why, if the kidnappers wanted money out of Blaine, would they have abducted Miguel? Could they really have murdered him? Could this be a hoax? No, of course not. They had his cell number. Blaine or Monica must have given it to them. *Sickness assails those leading the most sensible lives . . . retribution the utterly guiltless, violence the most secluded . . .* He'd read that passage only last night, once again, and once again had forgotten misfortune's power to impress itself on those who allowed themselves to forget it. He could not pardon himself this time. He had lived on the border long enough, had certainly seen enough to know that life on the line was precarious. Anything at any moment, all things were possible. He got into his car and returned to his—ha!—sanctuary, armed himself with the Smith and Wesson, kenneled Sam in the back, and drove off.

At first he intended to go to the San Ignacio's bank in Tucson and arrange for a wire transfer of $250,000 from his account in New York; but then he had second thoughts. A transaction like that would be a very red red flag. Questions would be asked, and answering them would take a lot more time than he had.

HE TURNED AROUND and drove to Tessa's ranch, checking in his rear and sideview mirrors to make sure that he wasn't being followed. He didn't want Tessa mixed up in this horror, but Blaine and Monica were her friends; she had to be told. Besides, and perhaps uppermost, he needed to talk things through, to figure out what to do.

At first she reacted as if she'd been struck, but then she heard him out calmly and poured two whiskeys and told him to sit down and go through everything again.

"Do you have it?" she asked, sitting beside him in her living room. "It's a dreadful question, but if it's not even possible to come up with the ransom, we have to think of what you'll say the next time they call."

"Sure I've got it, but I might as well not have it," he replied, and then explained why.

"What if you say that? That their demand is impossible to meet?"

"What do you suppose they'll say?" Castle scoffed. "Oh, all right, get as much as you can, any old amount will do? Those people must be crazy, thinking I can just withdraw a quarter of a million in cash in a few hours."

They sat without talking, staring into space, Then Tessa said, "You don't have any choice. You have got to call the police."

"That woman sounded like she meant what she said. No cops."

Tessa got up and grabbed her portable phone and placed it in his lap. "We have to assume the police will know what to do. You don't. I don't. We don't know who's got them or where they are. We're totally blind. You have to take the chance."

Castle could not believe his own words as he reported what had happened to Sheriff Rodriguez, whom he'd called out of a meeting. Afterward he heard only the sound of Rodriguez's breathing.

"Sheriff?"

"Yeah, I'm here. Where are you right now?"

Castle told him.

"Did you notice anyone following you?" Rodriguez asked.

"Not that I saw."

"Okay, stay where you are. It's possible they have the San Ignacio eyeballed. If they see people show up there, they'll probably carry out the threat."

"People?"

"Me, for one. The FBI, for another. Kidnapping is for the FBI. I'm going to contact their Tucson office as soon as I hang up. It's real, real important for you and Miss McBride to keep as calm as you can. Don't talk to anybody else about this till we get there. I mean absolutely nobody."

"But Rick, their son—"

"Let us handle that. Stay put, keep quiet."

BY LATE AFTERNOON a law enforcement convention had assembled in Tessa's living room: Rodriguez; a paunchy, bespectacled Border Patrol agent named Gomez (who reminded Castle that they had met before); and two FBI special agents, one lugging a case loaded with telephone recording devices and other electronic equipment. The sheriff and Gomez, wearing plain clothes, had arrived in an unmarked car, the FBI agents in what looked like a delivery van, which they parked in Tessa's hay barn.

One of the FBI men, with thorough formality, introduced himself as Ralph Inserra, senior resident agent of the Tucson Resident Agency. A lanky man with a widow's peak of black hair and a sallow complexion, he spoke in the flat tones of the Midwest. Straight away he assured Castle and Tessa that the FBI's first priority was to secure the safe release of the hostages.

Hostages. The word reverberated. Blaine and Monica were *hostages.*

"We'll do all we can to get them out," Inserra continued. "We've got every available agent assigned to this case, fifty of them."

"Fifty!" Castle's scalp prickled. "What if they're spotted?"

"I assure you, they won't be. The kidnappers won't know we've been called in." Inserra broke out a notebook. "I've got to get the background."

While the other agent plugged a voice-activated recorder into Castle's cell phone, installed a wiretap in Tessa's phone, and set up a small satellite dish, Inserra took a chair and quizzed Castle. Was the caller male or female? Female. Did she speak with an accent? No. Did he hear any other voices or sounds in the background? No. Were there any signs of forced entry or a struggle at the Erskines' house? No—except for Blaine's gun, it looked as if the kidnappers had been let in. How about the trailer? No signs there, either. Did Castle touch anything? Yes. Doorknobs, drawers. Did the caller say anything that might have given her location away, anything unusual?

Castle thought for a while. "She did say 'mobile.' To keep my mobile on, meaning my cell. Most people would say your cell phone."

Inserra and Gomez looked at each other. "Could be significant. An American would have said cell phone, a Mexican might call it a mobile. But you said you didn't hear an accent?"

"No."

"I know of one female who'd pull off a thing like this who doesn't talk with an accent," said Gomez, standing alongside Rodriguez by the fireplace.

"Let's not try to identify a suspect just yet. One thing at a time," Inserra said, somewhat annoyed. He turned to Castle. "We're going to try something. When they call, tell them you can't hear them on your cell and ask them to call back on the number here." He motioned at the technician. "It'll be easier to trace the call if they're calling from a landline. But my guess is that they're calling from a prepaid cell. We can try pinging the call. What I mean is, if the cell towers are within a reasonable range of here, we can at least get a general idea of where they're calling from. The important thing is for you to keep them on the line as long as you can, find out as much as you can."

Castle nodded dumbly as the agent produced from his briefcase a sheet of instructions on how to keep the kidnappers on the line and to pry as much information from them as possible. "Negotiating points," he called them. He asked Castle to study them, but the words blurred on the page, and reading glasses didn't help. The technical wizard, meanwhile, finished hooking up his equipment. Tessa went around serving coffee, as if she were the hostess at a neighborhood gathering. The veneer of normality made the situation feel all the more abnormal. She sat down next to Castle, taking his hand. Her palm was damp, and so was his. They waited.

Castle's watch read three minutes to five when his cell rang. The same woman's voice. He said he couldn't hear her and would she please call him back at another number? He gave it to her.

"You're a piece of shit, you know that?" she said. "You want something bad to happen?"

"If you want the money, you'll call me back," he replied, fighting to keep his voice steady. Then, his chest fluttering, he broke the connection. In a few moments the other phone jangled. Inserra donned a headset and jacked it into the recorder to monitor the call.

"You better not be fucking around, Castle," said the woman. "Have you got the money?"

PUT FORTH COOPERATIVE ATTITUDE, read one of the negotiating points, BUT INTRODUCE DELAY BY TELLING CALLER OF PROBLEMS OBTAINING FUNDS DEMANDED. "It's a lot of money to get in cash," he said stiffly. "I'll need time to get it, but I promise you that I will get it."

"You *are* a piece of shit. What are their lives worth to you?"

"I'm going to get the money, but it will take time." TELL KIDNAPPER/CALLER THAT NO RANSOM WILL BE PAID UNTIL PROOF OF LIFE IS FURNISHED. "But I need to know they're alive. I'm not going to pay you anything until I know they're alive. Put one of them on the phone, right now, please."

There were noises in the background, muffled voices, what sounded like a chair scraping against a floor. Then: "Gil . . . It's me . . . we're okay . . ."

That familiar drawl, all the swagger and strength gone out of it. Blaine sounded like he was eighty years old.

"Blaine!" Castle said. "Monica's all right?"

"Okay."

"But Miguel—did they—"

"That's enough," the woman cut in. "We will be generous. We will give you twenty-four hours to get the money. Exactly twenty-four hours. We will call you then and tell you where and when to bring it."

She disconnected. Castle put the phone down. The FBI agents, Rodriguez, and Gomez huddled around a laptop, pointing at a map on the screen and murmuring cryptically about "pings" and "triangulations."

"She was calling from a cell," Inserra announced, his naturally morose expression deepening. "We could trace a signal off just one tower, in this general area." He gestured vaguely at the computer screen. "Inside Mexico. That raises the stakes a lot. We can't operate in Mexico. We'll have to bring the MexFeds into this."

"Let's hear the recording," Gomez said.

The FBI agent reversed the disk and played back the conversation, and they all sat pitched forward in their seats, straining to hear every nuance, every inflection.

Gomez lit a cigarette, then as an afterthought politely asked Tessa if it was all right to smoke inside.

"For God's sake, yes," she said.

Gomez rose and again stood by the fireplace, allowing the smoke from his cigarette to drift up the chimney. "That's her. That's the lady herself, La Roja."

Tessa scowled. "*Who?* La Roja?"

"Yvonne Menéndez. La Roja because she's a redhead. She's la jefa of the Agua Prieta Cartel."

With a start, Castle recognized the name, recalling what Morales had told Blaine and him weeks and weeks ago. To know there was an identifiable person behind all this somehow made it less surreal, less menacing. It was like going to a doctor with mysterious symptoms and hearing his diagnosis; even if it turned out to be cancer, it was better to know than not to know.

"Yeah, I know about her and her partnership with Mr. Cruz," Gomez said to him after he'd related the conversation with Morales. "And the guy your cousin shot worked for her. This is payback, Mr. Castle. Yvonne is big on payback."

"Payback," Castle said under his breath. "But Miguel—what did he have to do with it?"

Rodriguez threaded his thick fingers together across his chest and gazed at the ceiling, as if in a moment of meditation. "Not a thing. We've heard that Cruz is hiding out on the Menéndez ranch, but so far the MexFeds haven't confirmed that. Cruz may have been mixed up in this kidnapping. Sure would be convenient for him to have Miguel out of the way. One other possibility is that they killed him—if they did—to show they mean business."

Castle said nothing, his heart at war with itself, sadness contending with a disgust of life, fear with anger. "We should have left him there, sheriff. We should have left him up there in Florence. We should have left well enough alone."

"People," said Inserra in the tone of a first sergeant, "people, we can spin theories later. We've got to get those hostages released, no matter what. Right now all we know is that they're on the other side, somewhere."

Gomez moved away from the fireplace and spread a hand across the map on the laptop's screen. "Yvonne's ranch is just south of the line, nine, ten miles. Odds are, that's where she's holding them." He faced the FBI agent. "I don't want to step on anybody's toes, but I know a MexFed captain who can help us out."

"And that would be who?" asked Inserra, his pitch and arching eyebrows suggesting that a Border Patrolman could not possibly have contacts superior to those of the FBI.

Gomez shrugged it off. "Gregorio Bonham. If anybody can find out where she's got them, he can."

"Any coordination with the MexFeds will be handled by our legal attaché in Mexico City."

"Bonham won't go for that, for a lot of reasons I won't mention," Gomez said. "But he's the guy we need to find them and get them out."

"Are you talking about a rescue operation?"

"I could be."

Inserra shook his head. "You know the MexFeds. They go charging in like Pancho Villa's cavalry, and we could have two dead hostages. It looks to me like paying the ransom may be the only way to get them out. Our office can help Mr. Castle put the money together tomorrow."

"I'm not sure the money is the big issue here. A quarter of a million is walking-around money to Yvonne. Anyway, isn't it our policy not to give in to terrorists?"

"These people are drug smugglers," Inserra said. "Thugs. They're not terrorists."

"Yeah, they are," Gomez shot back. "Just a different kind of terrorist. Go ahead, get the money. Meantime I can get in touch with Bonham. At least he might be able to find out where she's got them. Is that all right with you, Mr. Castle?"

His head was swimming again. He thought that if he stood up suddenly, he would black out. "It makes no sense. None of it makes any sense."

"If I were you, I wouldn't try making sense out of it. It is what it is, and we go from there."

35

THE PROFESSOR AND COMANDANTE ZARAGOZA SAT reading newspapers in the federal police comandancia in Cananea. The hour was late, and it was quiet, the sedate, men's-club rustling of the newsprint occasionally disturbed by cries issuing from the interrogation room in back.

Zaragoza, who'd arrived less than an hour ago, occupied the subcomandante's chair, his snakeskin cowboy boots up on the desk. The matter was urgent enough for him to have made a breakneck, all-lights-flashing, siren-wailing, 250-kilometer drive from his headquarters in Hermosillo. Now he had to wait for his boys to finish the prep work.

"I heard on the radio driving up that the Yankees took the second game of the series," he said, putting down his paper. He was an avid baseball fan, a great supporter of the Hermosillo Naranjaros. "Soriano hit in two, and that Japanese, how do you say? Maht-soo-ee, he hit a homer. First Jap to hit a homer in the series."

The Professor grunted. He preferred fútbol to beisbol and was reading about Monterey's coach in *El Sol de México.* Or pretending to read. It was hard to concentrate, his thoughts spinning.

He had often likened his line of work to night-flying a small plane without instruments. The margin for error being nearly zero, the clandestine operative never got a chance to become familiar with failure. He either succeeded, or he ended his career in a shallow grave. Which was why he'd found the failure of his mission to entrap Yvonne an experience as strange as it was distasteful. Not so long ago everything had been set up with Customs Agent Pierce. A motel room had been rented and bugged in Douglas, a hidden video camera installed, the money put together; but when The Professor phoned Yvonne in Zihuatanejo, saying that his clients were ready to deal and was she, she backed off. "They can meet me in Mexico, Carrington. It doesn't feel right."

She could not be persuaded to change her mind. Pierce was frustrated. The Professor traveled to Carrasco's ranch in Caborca and informed him that the sting wasn't going to come off. He was beside himself, offering half a million to kill the puta jodida down there, just shoot her while she was sunbathing. Pointing out that Yvonne traveled with a positively presidential security detail, The Professor said, "I'm not going to commit suicide for you, Joaquín," and advised patience while he developed a new approach.

Now it appeared that Yvonne had given him one. She'd pulled an incredible stunt, nabbing two gringos out of their home in the middle of the night, dragging them across the line, holding them for ransom. Gringos who were not mixed up in the trade. White, law-abiding gringos with a crisp Anglo name. Once this got into the press, as it was bound to, the patriots who wanted to build a wall from Brownsville to San Diego would be screaming for the National Guard to fix bayonets on the border. The effect on business would be disastrous. That was what had brought the comandante, summoned by The Professor's phone call, racing up from Hermosillo. Yvonne had at last overreached. She'd gotten away with so much for so long, she must have started to think she was a human flak jacket. But there was nothing in this abduction that would profit her patrons in the army and the government. Quite the contrary. In the outcry sure to come, questions would be asked. Who is this crazy woman, and why has Mexico not done something about her? Her protection would dissolve like adobe in a rainstorm.

"The Marlins are the underdogs," Zaragoza was saying. "But my money is on them."

"Why?" asked the Professor, indifferently.

"It's their pitching. Urbina, Beckett—"

A rap at the door interrupted the comandante's sports commentary. A federal policeman in a black uniform stuck his head inside. "He's ready."

"If you don't mind, I'll do the questioning, " The Professor said. "His Spanish isn't all that good."

They followed the policeman to the back room, where Cruz, stripped down to his underwear, was handcuffed to a cafeteria chair, a hood pulled over his head. Another cop stood behind him, holding an electric baton. The dense odors of sweat and urine hung in the air. The comandante motioned to remove the hood, and Cruz looked up startled into his lupine face and then into The Professor's. It was fortunate that he'd become familiar with Cruz's routines. Almost exactly five hours ago, following the call from Nacho, he'd ordered a squad of federales to stake out the casas ilegales where Cruz stashed his chickens. They found him, sometime later, at the El Mirador Motel and whisked him away.

"You know, I never thought I'd be talking to you like this again in a place like this," The Professor said. Then he sang merrily. " 'Oh, where have you been, Billy Boy, Billy Boy, oh, where have you been, charming Billy.' But we know, don't we? You were supposed to keep me abreast of Yvonne's activities. I'm extremely disappointed. Now's your chance to make amends. Sabes porque estoy aquí. Where is she hiding them?"

Cruz's head drooped. The cop behind him jerked it upright by the hair.

"This shouldn't take longer than five minutes. We're pressed for time."

"The ranch," Cruz answered, grimacing.

"Specifics."

"The almacén. The warehouse."

"What kind of shape are they are in?"

"I don't know."

The Professor took the prod and held the tip an inch from Cruz's groin. "If there are three words I hate to hear, it's *I don't know.*"

"I don't! They were okay last night. That was the last I saw of them. We didn't hurt them, I swear to God. We brought them to the warehouse and left them there, and they were okay then."

"Who is this we?"

"Me, Marco, Heraclio. I was the guide for them and three other guys Yvonne brought in. Pros from the Gulf Cartel. And the two girls."

"Girls?"

"That's how we got in. We paid them a thousand each to pretend to be wets who'd got lost and needed water and food. The ranch dogs were howling, and we shot them. We had silencers. Then the girls knocked at the door, and when Erskine answered, we moved in and took him down. Then we got his wife."

Clever, thought The Professor. The ruse had to have been Yvonne's idea. "Thought you said you didn't hurt him."

"We didn't. Just a tap on the head. He had a gun—"

"How about the mojado? You got to him the same way?"

Cruz was silent, but he yelped when The Professor gave him a little tap with the baton, on the inside of his thigh. A foretaste.

"We knew where his trailer was. Some of Yvonne's people had scoped the place out. The door didn't have a lock. Grabbed him."

"He's dead, right? Who killed him? I know you'll swear to God it wasn't you."

"It wasn't!" he cried out. "Heraclio shot him. After we crossed."

"How many people are guarding the warehouse? Don't say you don't know."

"Six, seven maybe."

"How are they armed?"

"AR-15s, pistols."

"Anything that might have slipped your mind?"

"The truck. She told us to take Erskine's truck. We drove them over in their truck."

"Why's that?"

"Can I say I don't know? Because I don't."

"Muchas gracias, Billy Boy. You have been a model of cooperation. You'll be staying with us for a while."

Retiring to the subcomandante's office, The Professor summarized the conversation for Zaragoza, who dropped into the desk chair and glanced at a wall map of the region, clicking his tongue. "If we can get those people out of there and capture her at the same time, if we can do that, it would make us look very good. We would be rid of her, Joaquín would be rid of her, and we would look very good."

Look very good in the eyes of the Americans, thought The Professor. We are always trying to please them even as we hate them. "And very bad if we mess it up," he said. "The problem is how. Her ranch, muy lejano, eh? There is no way to get onto it without her knowing about it."

"No way by road. And since we cannot come in by sea"—a grin—"that leaves the air. There are two helicopters I know of in Culiacán. I can contact the attorney general in the morning and have them flown to Hermosillo for refueling. Then . . ."

"She's got eyes and ears all over the place. I would say that before they crossed the highway"—The Professor poked a pencil at the Nogales-Hermosillo highway, Federal Route 15—"long before, her spies would spot them and warn her."

The comandante took out a pad of paper from a drawer and pushed it across the desk. "You have been on that ranch. Draw me a map of it. Show me where is her house, this warehouse, this airstrip. Show that to me."

After studying the sketch, he asked how far it was from the warehouse to the border.

"Más o menos, fifteen kilometers."

"Calderoni captured Pablo Acosta back in the eighties by flying helicopters in from the United States," said Zaragoza, referring to the legendary federale commander. "Flew right across the Río Bravo from the American side and hit him. So if we can do the same . . . we fly into the United States and refuel them there."

"Nogales," The Professor broke in, catching his line of thought.

"Nogales airport," Zaragoza said. "The helicopters take off from the American side of Nogales. They cross the line, *from a direction Yvonne does not expect.* Fifteen kilometers more, five minutes flying time, and we're on her"—forming talons with one hand, Zaragoza clutched the sketch and crumpled it—"como el halcón en la rata. We will need our best people for this one. We will need to talk to your American friends to get clearance."

The Professor expressed, without, he hoped, too much obsequiousness, admiration for Zaragoza's creative tactics; but he had to point out another difficulty. The hostages were in the warehouse *as of last night.* Yvonne may have moved them. Or she might move them between now and tomorrow. It would be wise to have somebody on the ground to report where they were, and where she was.

"I do not see how we can do that."

"I have an idea," The Professor said, and immediately picked up the phone and rousted Félix Cabrera out of bed. He lived in Cananea, which would save a great deal of travel time. He told Félix to meet him at the comandancia first thing in the morning. That done, he had one more person to wake up.

Nacho's wife answered, her voice thick with sleep. He apologized for phoning after midnight and asked to speak to Nacho, who, clearing his throat, said he'd been anxious to hear from him. The Professor briefed him on Cruz's revelations.

"*Cruz?* You've got Cruz?"

"In custody." Now was not the occasion to disclose that he'd known of Billy's whereabouts for a long time. "Remember a couple of weeks ago I said you owe me one? Here comes the bill. I want you to talk to your FBI compas and get clearance for two of our helicopters to land at Nogales airport tomorrow."

"Christ, you don't ask for much, do you?" said Nacho after a long silence.

"I'm asking for this."

"I'm getting the picture. Look, the FBI wants to avoid a rescue situation. They figure it's better to ransom them out, and I'm kind of leaning that way myself. I mean, you guys, the MexFeds, no offense, but you know—you guys are better with a meat cleaver than a scalpel."

"I don't make messes, Ignacio. Now you look. We think alike sometimes. Yvonne must have put a hell of a lot of planning into this, a lot of effort—"

"And, yeah," Nacho put in. "It couldn't be for the money. She wants something more."

"She always wants more."

"I'm thinking you're thinking she's going to kill them no matter what."

"Exactamente."

In the morning, he and Zaragoza having snatched four hours sleep at the Real del Cobre, The Professor rendezvoused with Félix at the federal police station, where Félix drew an assault rifle, a bulletproof vest, binoculars, and a portable radio. He instructed Félix on what he was to do, what to say, and how to conduct himself. He was an assassin and an enforcer, after all, unaccustomed to pretending to be anything else. This was a new thing he was being asked to do—play a role; but all The Professor needed was for him to make a convincing show for about half an hour. Félix was his usual self, listening intently, speaking hardly a word—the silent predator.

The Professor dialed Yvonne's mobile. Feigning ignorance of her present location and fishing for any signs that she suspected the police were on to her, he asked, "How is Zihuatanejo treating you?"

"Zihuatanejo was fine. I'm at the ranch now."

"All the better," he said.

"What can I do for you, Carrington?"

A little distant, a little cool, remarkably composed for someone who had just engineered a cross-border abduction.

"It's what we can do for each other. I talked with my friend. He's had a change of heart. He's willing to meet with you in Mexico, no problem."

"What are we talking about here?"

He cupped the mouthpiece and rose to shut the door; she might hear the comandante, who was in the next room, making arrangements for the helicopters. "A hundred," he replied. That should interest her. *More. I want more. Quiero más, siempre más.* "He has an airplane and a pilot lined up. What he would like to do is see what you've got, then check out your airstrip. It happens we're in Cananea right now and could be there soon."

"I am busy today, and what I do have is already spoken for."

"No business. A get-acquainted meeting. And a look at the landing strip."

"Busy, did you hear me?" she said sharply. "A couple of days maybe."

He was tired, there was a stale taste in his mouth, and despite a shower at the motel, he felt unwashed. He was also weary of dealing with this homicidal, sadistic bitch. Time to push things. "Maybe you should listen to me. Okay? You're making me look like a baboso. It's today or no. This isn't a guy you can jerk around. He can always walk with somebody else. A hundred keys, I said. You're not in the mood to make two million in one deal, okay, a la chingada."

She laughed her shrill laugh. "Carrington! You have a temper! Está bien. But you get here before noon. After that, I've got no time."

They made the drive in a Dodge 1500 confiscated from a freelancer who'd fallen behind in his mordida, the weapons and gear stowed in a false bottom. Past the great gray artificial mountains built from the tailings of the open-pit copper mines, up over the cerros, with open country spread below, tans and yellows embroidered by the green álamos bordering the Río Sonora. People died out here all the time, vanished as if they'd never been, and the danger enhanced the beauty of the landscape. Without it, it would only be scenery.

Back roads took them through Santa Cruz, then through the gate to Los Tres Encinos. Yvonne, accompanied by the two simians who clung to her side every waking moment except when she went to the bathroom and maybe even then, was already at the airstrip when they arrived. She was wearing her big straw hat, and her shirtsleeves were rolled down against the skin-shriveling sun.

"So that's her," Félix said as they pulled up. "Nice ass for an old lady."

"Don't call her a vieja where she can hear it."

They got out of the truck. One of the pistoleros—The Professor recognized him as the one called Marco—patted them down.

"Your boys at the gate already searched us," he said.

"They might have missed something."

"You're looking well, Yvonne. The rest was good for you. How is my friend Billy?"

"Fine, last time I saw him. I have no time for small talk, Carrington."

He introduced his client from Phoenix, Rubén Gutiérrez. She studied Félix as carefully as a portraitist, mistrust wrestling with greed. The latter won out. Capitalism with the muzzle off, The Professor thought. Greed and fear. She brought them to the ramada beside the airstrip. Marco and Heraclio lifted the steel mat covering the pit in which the coke was stored and opened a plastic fuel drum filled with kilo packages, each marked with the initials or symbols of its intended recipient.

Yvonne removed a bag of her personal stock—the vintner's reserve, so to speak—and passed it to Félix. "Straight from Colombia, no steps on it," she advertised, ever the saleswoman.

Félix dabbed a little on his tongue, then placed a little more on his fingernail and snorted it, pronouncing it "excelente, puro." If it was all this good, he would take a hundred kilos at the earliest possible date. Next week, Yvonne promised, and then they began to talk price. The Professor had encouraged Félix to drive a hard bargain, in the interest of distracting Yvonne. While they haggled, he sauntered onto the landing strip. Slipping a GPS from out of his pocket, he took a reading and marked a waypoint. The almacén stood about two hundred yards beyond the end of the runway and across an arroyo, a big white oblong building easily visible from the air. A few people were standing near it, but at this distance it was difficult to see how many and if they were guards or workers. As he moved for a closer look, Yvonne called from behind him, "Carrington! Where are you going?"

"Nowhere. Checking the condition of the airfield."

"You can land a jet on it. Come back here. Don't go wandering around."

That told him something: she didn't want anyone near the warehouse; the hostages were still in there. He walked back to the ramada, where Félix, playing his part well, insisted that for so large a quantity he would not pay more than fifteen thousand a kilo. Yvonne finally agreed, but only because she expected a long-term relationship.

A long-term relationship. They laughed about that as they drove out, tailed as far as the ranch gate by a carload of gunmen. About half a mile past the gate, The Professor shifted the Dodge into four-wheel and swung off into a wash, taking it around a bend to where it could not be seen from the road. If Yvonne had any lookouts posted nearby, the surrounding oak trees would hide the car from view. Félix quickly changed into a black jacket and black jeans, slid the truck bed open, and removed his rifle and gear and water jug. He left the bulletproof vest. Too heavy, he said. It would only slow him down. If he did his job right, no one would see him to shoot at him.

"You saw those low hills on the other side of the airfield," The Professor said, handing him the GPS. "A lot of mesquite, good cover. That's where you want to be, as close to the almacén as you can get. If you see anything, the hostages being moved, Yvonne going inside, anything, you let me know immediately. If your mobile doesn't work, use the radio."

Félix tossed a salute. "Sí, mi capitán. Es como en tiempos pasados."

"Claro. Like old times. You know, some people would say we are doing a good thing for bad reasons."

Félix snorted, then shouldered his assault rifle and backpack and slipped off into the brush. In ten seconds The Professor couldn't see him at all.

IT WAS PAST NOON by the time he returned to the comandancia in Cananea. There Zaragoza informed him that he'd secured two Bell 212s from the attorney general. They were now on their way to the Hermosillo airport to pick up the assault team—fifteen federales, his best boys, most of them with military experience. What he did not have was clearance from the Americans.

"United States Border Patrol. Agent Gomez speaking."

"Where are you?" asked The Professor.

"At a ranch. The Crown A. We're staying clear of the San Ignacio."

"The FBI guy is with you?"

"Yeah. Castle is in Tucson with some other FBI people, getting the ransom money."

"Guess where I just got back from? Yvonne's ranch. She's there, the hostages are there, and I've got my best man on the ground keeping an eye on things."

"Wait a minute. You've *seen* them? You've seen the Erskines?"

"No, but I know she's got them stashed in her warehouse. We've got two helicopters and fifteen agents waiting in Hermosillo for you people to give us the green light. What's the problem with the clearance?"

"I'll let you talk to the FBI."

After a silence he heard a voice that could have been an anchorman's in some midsize city in the American heartland. "Captain Bonham? This is Special Agent Ralph Inserra." He enunciated very slowly, assuming The Professor's English was poor, an assumption he corrected.

"Are you an American?" Inserra asked. "You sound like it."

"I am some of the time. We need that authorization. We're ready to go."

"And I want you to know we sure do appreciate your cooperation."

"I hear a *but* coming."

"Yeah. But we're asking you to hold off till we've got the victims released. The kidnappers are supposed to call at five and tell Castle where to drop the ransom. Then, we hope, they'll turn the hostages over."

"That might be a thin hope."

"Here's the thing, Captain. If this was only a matter of busting a drug boss, we'd say go ahead. Now. But we've got the lives of two U.S. citizens at stake. Getting them out, that's our number one concern."

The Professor assured him that that was likewise the concern of the Mexican Federal Judicial Police.

"Sure. *Sure.* If it does come to a rescue operation, we've got a top hostage rescue team in Quantico. They could give you all the support you need."

Yeah, The Professor thought. Top team. Like the bozos who fucked up that Waco operation in the 1990s. "Quantico, Virginia?" he said. "By the time they got here, I'm afraid it could be way too late."

"How long would it take for your helicopters to reach Nogales?" the FBI agent asked.

One hundred eighty miles, The Professor thought. A Bell 212 cruised at one twenty. "About an hour and a half."

"I've already called Washington. We should have clearance within the hour. If you put the birds in the air right now, they'll be authorized to land before they cross into our airspace. But your people are going to have sit tight at Nogales until the hostages are released."

The Professor did some more arithmetic. The ransom call at five. Give it at least another hour to make the exchange, if there was to be an exchange. Dusk at seven. He did not want to conduct the raid in darkness. It would be a close-run thing in daylight. He needed to educate this special agent in another mathematical reality. "This drug organization, the Agua Prieta Cartel," he began. "They've got eyes and ears on your side of the line, too. If the choppers take off now, they'll be in Nogales before three. I'll have two MexFed helicopters and fifteen MexFed agents hanging around the Nogales airport for three or four hours. We want them there just long enough to refuel and to brief the men. We can't risk losing the element of surprise. We can't risk flying in there at night. We want to move *now*."

"And we can't risk getting those people killed in a shoot-out between you and those thugs," replied Inserra following a pause. "Not till we've run out of other options."

"I think you will."

"Do you know something we don't?"

"I know her."

He hung up, the renegade in him prodding him to ignore Inserra's niggling cautions.

"We will do what they want," said Zaragoza after The Professor summarized the conversation with Inserra. The comandante did not want to risk losing the hostages, either. It would make the federales look inept, and the federales were supposed to come out looking good, looking glorious. Considering his close working relationship with them, Joaquín Carrasco would want that, too.

"Está bien," The Professor said. "But the helicopters must not leave right away. Three-thirty. That will get them to Nogales by five."

"I am going to lead the raid myself." Yes, of course. Then he would be legendary. Like Comandante Calderoni, captor of Pablo Acosta. "Vámonos, Profesor. Vámonos a Nogales."

36

IT WAS ODD, this anticipation, a queer excitement to it, as if he were waiting to be notified that he'd won the lottery rather than for a ransom demand. Tessa was in the kitchen, wiping counters, straightening cabinets, trying to draw a cloak of the ordinary over the extraordinary. When the phone rang—the kidnappers were prompt if nothing else—she leaped into the living room, where Castle waited with Gomez and the FBI agents. The Mexican police, Castle had been told, were going to rescue Blaine and Monica if that became necessary, take them out by helicopter. Like the Coast Guard plucking stranded sailors from the sea, a basket on a cable, and Blaine and Monica would be lifted up into safety—that was how he pictured it as he put the phone to his ear.

The woman again. "Have you got the money?"

"Yes."

"You will bring it to the crossing at Campini Mesa. You will leave now."

He glanced at cues Inserra had written out for him. DELAY IF POSSIBLE . . . DEMAND TO SEE VICTIMS . . .

"I don't know where that is," he said untruthfully.

"Then get a map and find it!" Her voice was piercing, like feedback.

"All right. I want to see my cousins. I won't turn the money over if I don't see them." He hesitated a beat. "Alive."

"You will see them. Alive. Come alone. Don't do anything stupid. We will be looking for your car. You drive a Chevrolet Suburban. Black with Connecticut license plates. Why haven't you changed your registration to Arizona?"

She laughed and hung up.

What felt like colonies of ants crawled up Castle's arms and across his shoulders to the back of his neck. They knew his car!

Inserra removed his headset and played back the voice recording. "What is this Campini Mesa? Where the hell is that?"

"It's in East Jesus," Gomez answered. "A kind of unofficial border crossing. Isolated as hell out there. I don't like it. I don't think he should go out there by himself."

"You heard what she said," Castle protested. "Alone."

Inserra tapped the headset on the array of the technician's electronic marvels. "I don't like it either. Is there any way we can follow him without being seen?"

"No. It's a mesa. It's wide open. Flat as Kansas." Gomez gazed up at Tessa's painting, hanging over the fireplace. "I can get some of our people to guide yours to set up a stationary in the hills overlooking Campini for ground surveillance. But if something goes wrong, they wouldn't be close enough to intervene."

Castle got off the sofa. "I'm going."

Inserra laid a hand on his wrist and gave him a stern lecture about the risks.

"Do you have the authority to stop me?"

"Short of handcuffing you to a chair, no."

"Then I'm going."

"All right. Can't stop you. But he"—he gestured to his partner—"is going to install an electronic tracking device on your car. A bumper-beeper. It won't take long, and no one will see it. And have your cell phone on. We might be able to keep tabs on where you are, same way we traced where the kidnappers' call came from." He turned to Tessa. "We'll do that from here, if that's not a problem."

She swallowed, bobbed her head in assent.

Gomez shook Castle's hand, wished him luck, and said he was going to Nogales to meet up with the Mexican police.

After he left, and while the technician attached the bumper-beeper, Tessa flew back into the kitchen to resume her busywork.

Castle went to her and put his arms around her waist. "This is going to turn out all right," he said with far more confidence than he felt.

She stood on tiptoe to pull a stack of dishes from a top shelf. "All right? How about Miguel? Is he all right? How can you say it'll be all right? It can only turn out to be less horrible than it is."

He turned her to face him. She pushed him away and folded her arms and rocked back and forth. "Why do you have to be the delivery boy? They don't know what you look like. One of those cops could pretend to be you."

"Tess, they know my car, my cell number. What else do they

know?" He was quiet for a time. "I've got to go anyway. If I hadn't yelled out 'gun,' maybe nothing would have happened, and—"

"Oh, bullshit! Blaine was spoiling for a fight, and you know it. Go on, go do it." She looked out the window at his car. "Just come back. Beth came back. You come back. Promise me that."

"In a couple of hours we're all going to be right here, all four of us," he said, and went into the other room for the satchel containing $250,000 in bundles of hundred-dollar bills. It had been quite a scene, collecting the money in the vault in downtown Tucson that morning, the bewildered bank officer looking on as the FBI people crammed the bills into the satchel.

As he drove off, his senses underwent a subtle alteration. He saw dark birds flitting in a tree behind Tessa's windmill, then realized they were shadows of the spinning blades. The crunching of his wheels on the dirt road sounded louder than it should have, like gravel pouring down a chute. Pulling out onto the San Rafael road, he noticed a man, beside a car pulled off to the roadside, setting a camera on a tripod. He was going to photograph a hawk clinging to a cottonwood branch stretched over the Santa Cruz River. Impossible. It was simply impossible that he, Castle, should be driving to the Mexican border with ransom money while someone else mere yards away took pictures of a hawk. The landscape through which he drove appeared familiar and strange at the same time. His distorted perceptions cast a threatening light, like the yellowing of a cloudy sky before a storm, on the trees, the grasslands, the hills. He felt himself to be in a foreign land where he didn't know the language or the customs or what to expect next.

He recognized this anxiety—it was the same that had descended on him when he'd visited Ground Zero nearly a year ago. Yet this was not an alien world, it was his own. *Just a different kind of terrorist*, Gomez had said yesterday. The same beast that had devoured Amanda had merely changed its outward shape, its name. Now it had materialized as someone called Yvonne Menéndez. Well, he wanted to look it in the eye without shrinking from it. Touch its flesh. Smell its breath. He wouldn't be truly free until he did.

A renewed sense of courage and resolve flowed into him as Campini Mesa came into view, wide and empty, the grass coppered by the sun dying over the Patagonias. Heat quivering off the land made the mountains look insubstantial, like mirages. He turned onto a jeep trail, and there, a quarter-mile away, was the crossing. A cattle guard and a gap in the boundary fence and Mexico beyond. He stopped the car and stood on the running board, looking southward. Then he saw a twirling dust cloud and the glint of a windshield.

THE NOGALES AIRPORT occupies a broad tableland called Palomas Mesa a few miles north of the city. It calls itself "Nogales International," as though it were a busy hub of global traffic, but it's a modest facility consisting of a small terminal, a tower, and a single runway, mostly for private planes.

Near the runway overrun, two black and white Bell helicopters, with their Mexican insignia taped over, were tethered to a refueling truck. Under the curious gazes of the truck driver and an airport worker, fifteen federal policemen, wearing civilian clothes but glaringly obvious nonetheless in bulletproof vests and with assault rifles slung over their shoulders, stood or squatted around The Professor and Comandante Zaragoza, between whom a hand-drawn map of Los Tres Encinos ranch was spread on the ground and pinned at the corners with rocks. As each agent was given his assignment, he snapped to attention and said, "Sí, mi capitán," or "Sí, mi comandante." The Professor was rather proud of them.

His biggest anxiety was not for the abilities of his men. It was five-thirty. At best only an hour of decent daylight remained, and now they had to wait for the hostages to be released. Twenty minutes ago Félix had sent a whispered radio message from his lookout post: the hostages had been taken out of the warehouse, put in a truck, and taken away. Where to, he couldn't say. Nacho answered that question when he pulled into the airport a short while later: Castle was delivering the ransom, and he'd demanded to see his relatives alive first. They were probably being driven to the rendezvous at Campini Mesa. As soon as he got word of their release, the federales would be free to strike and arrest Yvonne on kidnapping charges.

A GRAY AND RED VAN rolled to a stop on the Mexican side, about a hundred feet short of the crossing. Castle watched the driver scan the countryside with binoculars. Satisfied that Castle was alone, the driver, his face concealed by a ski mask, climbed out and called, in English, "Bring it over here."

He all but heard the fibrillations in his chest. *Brrrrit, brrrrit.* "Not till I see them," he shouted.

The driver opened the rear door. Another man, powerfully built and also masked, emerged, holding a pistol. He yanked Monica from the van, shoved her at the driver, then, waving the gun, summoned Blaine to step out. Blindfolded, handcuffed, and gagged with what appeared to be duct tape, they were dressed as they had been when they'd been seized nearly forty-eight hours ago, Monica in a long, blue nightgown, Blaine in boxer shorts. It was the joy of seeing them alive, it was anger at what had been done to them, it was their pathetic, hesitant, barefoot shuffling on the stony road as the gunman pushed them forward that caused Castle to run toward them, taking the satchel with him.

"Blaine! Monica! It's me. Gil!"

Blaine twitched his head, made a strangled sound. Castle let go of the satchel. "It's all there. Now let them go."

Kneeling on one knee, the driver unzipped the bag and fanned a stack of bills like a card player. "Has to be counted first, and the counting doesn't get done here." He stood, languorously, and gave Castle a pat down. "Wouldn't want you to try calling home," he said, confiscating the cell phone. He jerked a semiautomatic from his back pocket and pressed the muzzle behind Castle's ear. "Hands behind your back, asshole."

Though the mask muffled the voice, Castle recognized it. "You! You!"

Idaho Jim clasped a pair of plastic cuffs around his wrists and pushed him into the van. "Things got a way of coming around."

"GET OVER HERE!" Nacho hollered.

The Professor interrupted last-minute instructions to his men and walked over to Nacho's car.

"We've got a situation," Nacho said, waving his car radio's microphone. "The FBI put some of their people on a stationary to eyeball the drop site. Castle's been taken."

"How the fuck did that happen?"

"I don't know, but it sure does look like the money isn't all she wants. The FBI guy radioed me a second ago. They've got a GPS track on Castle's cell, and it's inside Mexico, and so I guess he is, too. And don't say 'I told you so.' "

"I'll say it anyway."

Without delay he radioed Félix. "They've got three hostages now," he said, pausing between each word because, at this long range, the signal was weak. "If . . . you . . . see . . . them . . . key . . . your . . . transmitter . . . three times. Key . . . it . . . once . . . now . . . to . . . acknowledge."

He heard the click. A cock-up, he thought, looking at the waning light. A bloody cock-up, that was how his father would have put it. At least the helicopters had spotlights.

37

YVONNE, IN THE LIBRARY, read over the documents that Clemente and Daoud had prepared for her last week. She'd told them that she'd contacted the Erskines and convinced them that they would be better off selling the San Ignacio, all of it. They'd accepted her offer. She instructed her lawyer and her cousin to draw up the contract, then she would close the deal herself. Clemente was disappointed that he would lose a substantial commission, but she'd promised to make it up to him.

"Have you looked at these?" she asked Julián, who was pulling leather-bound books out of a packing case and stacking them on the shelves. Julián often occupied himself with such domestic tasks when he was agitated. The interior decorator. "Are they in order?"

"They appear to be," he said, his back to her. He looked at the book he was holding. "This one is Ortega y Gasset. Should I put it under *O* or *G*?"

"Turn around and look at me."

She took in the narrow head, as if it had been squashed emerging from her womb, the bladelike nose, the mushy brown eyes, and experienced a wave of displeasure. "You need some liver pills, mi hijo. Pills to strengthen your liver. You have the brains for this business but not the liver."

"Which is why," he said, sneering, "we complement each other. With you, it is the other way around."

She refrained from slapping him. "What I have carried off required quite a lot of brains. The attention to every detail, nothing left to chance."

"The execution was sane, I will grant you that. It's the idea that is mad."

"I don't know if you are half the man I am or twice the woman. It has worked out, and all your forecasts of disaster have come to nothing."

He propped his slender body against the bookcase, holding the copy of the Ortega y Gasset over his crotch. "You know the old saying, 'Two can keep a secret if one is dead'? There are a lot of people who know this secret, including me."

Yvonne was more than shocked; she was hurt. "You are suggesting that I would—"

A woman who had commanded the death of her husband and a hundred other people—why not her son as well? thought Julián. The only thing he would not put past his mother was cannibalism. "Someone is bound to let a word slip."

Yvonne was so wounded by his insinuation that she in fact felt like killing him. "No, you're wrong. Everyone who knows about this has been involved in it, and that will keep their mouths shut. And if someone's tongue does slip, what of it? Nothing but loose talk. There will be no proof of anything."

That screech, lancing through him. "That's right. You've thought of every detail."

"Por supuesto." She stuffed the documents into her straw carryall, along with her purse gun, a Walther PK .32 caliber. "Come with me. You should feast your eyes on these people."

"My eyes are not hungry," Julián said.

Heraclio drove her to the almacén. Her nerves were strained. All the planning, the anxiety, the painstaking attention to those details had worn her out. Outside the warehouse, several of her boys were playing cards on an empty drum under the floodlight over the entrance.

"Bring those inside," she said, indicating their chairs.

Odors. Textures. Sounds. Castle was sitting on a smooth wooden floor, felt corrugated metal against his back, heard the muffled thump of a diesel generator outside. With his physical senses reduced by one, he concentrated on the others. They tethered him to reality, and if they slipped, he feared his mind would float off into some ghastly void. Smell. Smell, too. The place he was in reeked of a strong, vegetable odor. Cannabis.

A door opened. Footsteps on the plywood. Someone switched on a light, its glare filtering through his blindfold. But he was aware, too, through another kind of sense, of a change in the air, as if there had been a sudden drop in the barometric pressure. His ears actually popped as he heard the voice, keen as a nail, that had spoken to him on the phone. Four words in Spanish: "Allí. Delante del escritorio."

Strong hands gripped his upper arms, hauled him to his feet, and pushed him into a chair. The same was being done to Blaine and Monica. They were near him. He could smell them as he had in the van, the stench of their unwashed bodies, of urine and feces. They had been forced to lie in their own waste, a barbarity as incomprehensible as their abduction. Someone ripped the duct tape from his mouth, removed his handcuffs, and finally his blindfold. He blinked against the brightness of the fluorescent tubes crackling from a fixture hanging from a wooden beam. Monica, sitting between him and Blaine, looked at him furtively with bloodshot eyes, her lips forming a word that she did not utter, his name perhaps. Blaine, with a dazed stare into space, plucked at the tape residue sticking to the stubble on his jaws. Castle wasn't able to take in his surroundings all at once, only in segments. A small room in a larger structure, drywall partitions on three sides, a curving steel wall on the fourth. Two large armed men, bellies forming eaves over their belts, stood near the door. He, Blaine, and Monica sat in a row on folding chairs in front of a steel office desk. Behind it was the woman, the owner of the grating voice, the one called La Roja, Yvonne Menéndez. Tightly curled red hair above a high forehead, tiny pits cratering her cheekbones, thin, straight lips, like claw marks scratched beneath her small nose. Castle noticed incipient wattles under her chin, wrinkles crazing the V of her bosom, partly exposed by her open-neck shirt. The pockmarks lent a certain coarseness to her features; otherwise her appearance was ordinary, even banal, and this was somehow disconcerting. He'd expected the wicked queen in Snow White, with her flaring black brows, her vampiric mouth.

The woman did not say anything, only looked at them with a kind of curious expression, as if she weren't sure what they were doing there. He found the silence unbearable and said hoarsely, "I brought the money. What else do you want?"

Yvonne did not reply immediately. She was savoring her victory. Here they were, helpless before her, not the authors of her family's tragedies but heirs of the man who was, and that made them just as guilty. The man who'd killed her father when she was still in her mother's belly. Noticing the fine light hairs sprouting from Erskine's bare chest, she thought of what it would be like to pluck them out with her fingernails, one by one. She very nearly trembled as the cruelty inherent in her nature vied with the necessity to restrain it.

"It's being counted," she said at last. "But that's only a down payment for what you owe me." She let out a short, harsh laugh. "Believe it or not, this is a business meeting."

Monica sobbed. "For God's sake, let us go."

"I am going to. First you have to sign these." She withdrew a ballpoint and the documents from her carryall and placed them on the desk, the signature pages on top. "Sign these, all three of you, and then you'll be free to go. You first," she said to Erskine.

He looked at the papers, then looked at her, dumbfounded, his jaw slack.

"No? Then you."

She held the pen out to Castle.

He saw, in gothic letters at the top of one page, the words "Warranty Deed," and on the other, "Purchase Agreement." He read on in disbelief. "Agreement, made on this———day of———2003, by and between The San Ignacio Cattle Company, Blaine Erskine, Monica Erskine, and Gilespie Castle, sole owners, hereinafter referred to as the SELLERS, and LaMorita Enterprises, S.A., of Mexico City, Mexico, hereinafter referred to as the PURCHASER . . . The sellers agree to sell and convey and the purchaser agrees to purchase the real property described in Schedule A annexed hereto . . ."

An extortion! An elaborate, preposterous extortion. So preposterous, Castle chuckled hysterically. "My first name is misspelled. It has two *l*'s."

"That can be fixed."

"You must be insane. These aren't worth anything, with or without our signatures."

"Here is what they are worth," she said, withdrawing two cashier's checks, one made out to Castle for two and a half million dollars, the other to the Erskines for the same amount. "I know that is not a fair price, but your freedom is what I'm giving you in return. What is that worth to you?"

Castle looked at the checks and knew with awful certainty that they would never get the chance to cash them. INTRODUCE DELAY. Yes, delay until the police got here.

"Why . . . why . . . are you doing this?" Monica cried.

Yvonne sighed. "I knew someone would ask that. To make my mother happy in heaven."

To make her mother happy in heaven. What perfect nonsense. But Castle asked himself, Wasn't it an imperative to confront the nosenseness that led him to cross over an hour ago? All right, here it is, made flesh. Kidnapping. Murder. Extortion. All to make her mother happy in heaven.

Delay. Stall. Do anything. Sing a song. "You're not going to let us go," he said. "You can't. This agreement wouldn't be worth anything with us dead. It will be worth less than nothing with us alive."

Yvonne was getting fed up with these people. "Listen, you're going to sign it over, and I'm going to keep you here, all of you, till you do. A day, a month, I don't care." She looked at Erskine's wife and felt that she, Yvonne, deserved a reward for all her work, some amusement. Rising, she went round behind the wife's chair and pulled the straps of her nightgown down over her shoulders, her breasts spilling. The woman stank—she'd shit her pants when she was captured. She gasped, tugged at the straps, and began to cry harder. "I don't like boring guests," Yvonne said. "I like to be entertained. Your wife isn't young but not bad-looking, Erskine, and I've got a lot of men around here. You're going to watch. We're all going to watch."

Erskine jumped up. Marco and Heraclio rushed from the door, grabbed him, and wrestled him back in his chair.

"Goddamn you! Goddamn your soul!"

Yvonne was a little disappointed when, as she handed him the pen a second time, he signed the deed and agreement. She would have liked to see him forced to witness the defilement of his wife, yes, to watch her bent over a bale in the other room and the boys rutting her like goats. His balls would probably fall right off. But this was business, and business needed to be concluded.

After she'd obtained the other signatures, she stuffed the checks in Castle's pocket, then told Marco not to bother with the blindfolds and gags; the handcuffs would do for now. She flipped Erskine's car keys to Heraclio. Every detail. And the truck was one of those details. It would be found overturned and burned in a ditch on the Nogales highway, the bodies charred beyond recognition. A little mordida would be necessary to ensure a less-than-thorough accident investigation into the true cause of death. She knew that the victims would be identified eventually, that rumors of foul play would fly over the U.S. side; but there would be no evidence linking her to their deaths. In the end, all that would be said was that these three Americans had gone on a drive into Mexico and were killed in a fiery crash. Oddly, though, she didn't feel satisfied as they trooped outside. Erskine needed to know, and she needed him to know, that he and his kind had inherited a debt, not of the kind reckoned in numbers but in the accounting of the vengeful heart. Only then would her triumph be complete.

Outside, in the gathering dusk, a floodlight shone on Blaine's truck. Its presence here did not surprise Castle. He was past being surprised in this world of anything at any moment for any reason. Or for no reason. The three of them were shoved into the backseat. A peculiar serenity had come over him. He wondered how and where it was going to happen. A bullet to the backs of their heads? Here? Down the road? There was something strangely fated about all this. His only regret, and it was considerable, was that he would not keep his promise to Tessa.

The Menéndez woman stood by the rear door, facing Blaine through the open window. She said, "There is something I want to tell you, Erskine. Before I was married, my name was Quinn. Rafael was my father."

The name did not register in Castle's mind for four or five seconds, but when it did—*His name was Rafael Quinn but Rafe is what they called him*, Sally had told him—the no-senseness began to make sense, a terrible sense.

Then he heard the percussion of helicopter rotor blades.

POISED IN THE DOOR of the Bell, The Professor was shouting to the pilot through the helicopter's internal radio. "Get your lights on them! Drop us!"

The helicopter spun, as if caught in a vortex, then hovered. Its landing lights created a false noon in which he saw a white pickup truck and Yvonne, staring upward, stunned, as if a UFO were descending on her. The comandante's bird circled the almacén, muzzle flashes winking as his agents fired at her gunmen, who were scattering in panic. The doors of the truck burst open, and two men leaped out, one raising an assault rifle at The Professor's helicopter as it flared for a landing. He recognized Heraclio in the glare of the aircraft's light. Four or five federales opened up on him, bullets geysering dust. He crumpled. Another gunman, Marco, tore open the pickup's rear door and pulled out one of the hostages, the woman. He was about to drag her away, using her as a shield, when he fell hard. A split-second later Félix jumped out of the arroyo, from which he'd dropped the gunman with a single shot, ran toward the woman, and then was stopped before he could reach her by the maelstrom raised by the rotors.

"Don't shoot at the truck!" The Professor yelled as he stepped onto the skid and jumped to the ground.

The engines shut down, the air began to clear. He and his squad fanned out across the open space in front of the warehouse. The floodlight over its trolley door had been knocked out; a partial moon was all there was to see by. He sprinted over to the two male hostages, who were handcuffed and sprawled on their backs. A couple of agents helped them stand. One was clad only in his underwear—Erskine, he guessed. Not ten yards away Yvonne stood behind Erskine's wife, clutching her long hair, pressing a pistol to her temple. The Professor signaled his men to lower their weapons, then announced, with grand formality, that he was Capitán Bonham of the federal police, that her situation was hopeless, that she should let the woman go and surrender.

"Back away, or I'll kill this fucking bitch!"

Castle had never seen so feral a human being. He glanced sidelong at the policeman standing next to him, a light-haired, pale-complected Mexican who now spoke into his portable radio. A moment later another helicopter that had been circling overhead swooped in low, its landing lights stabbing the darkness, its blades churning up a miniature tornado. As the madwoman holding Monica threw up an arm to shield her face against the blast of dirt and gravel, Blaine let out a howl and, with his head down, rushed her.

"No!" Castle yelled and went to stop him, but felt a terrific blow to his ribs—had the cop struck him? He dropped to his knees, and then tumbled sideways and lay choking for breath.

Yvonne ran. She'd seen Erskine through the buffeting dust-cloud, charging her like a ram, his bound hands behind his back. At that moment, the woman broke free. Yvonne, half blinded by the dust and helicopter lights, emptied her Walther's clip at Erskine, but he slammed into her shoulder first, bowling her over and knocking the pistol from her hand. Without looking to see if she'd hit him, she got up and fled up the road toward the ranch house. Her one thought was to get to Julián's car and escape to Agua Prieta. She would be safe there. She was the queen of the city. Five kilometers. Could she run that far? She must. She was running so fast that when she tripped, she was flung forward. An instant later she heard the gunshot from behind her and knew she hadn't tripped. She clawed at the ground, but as she struggled to regain her footing, her right arm folded beneath her. There was a strange taste in her mouth, and blood pumped from her shoulder, streamed down her right arm, and dripped from her fingers. Her whole arm was numb; if she didn't see it, bleeding in the moonlight, she would not have known it was there. She was outraged. This was so undignified. Someone grabbed her under the opposite arm and yanked her upright and spun her around. She felt nauseous and, losing strength, sank to her knees.

"¡Chota!" she hissed when she saw Carrington standing over her with a drawn gun. "I knew you were a fucking chota!"

"Some of the time." The Professor took a step forward and, clutching her hair to hold her head steady, pressed his .40 caliber to her mouth. "Este beso es de tus enemigos," he said, and pulled the trigger.

He stood over Yvonne's corpse for a few moments. One bullet, one body. Those were his standards. He'd had to fire two, but then, he'd squeezed off the first one on the run, so failing to make a killing shot was excusable.

Right then he heard a shriek and ran back toward the almacén. When he got to the warehouse, he saw both helicopters parked side by side and the federales circled around several of Yvonne's pistoleros, who were facedown on the ground and handcuffed. Near the truck Erskine lay on his back, his arms locked beneath him, his wife kneeling over him, bowing up and down like a Muslim at prayer and screaming, screaming. The Professor went to her and gently stood her up and called to a policeman to take care of her. Erskine's eyes were open but did not see anything. Blood rimmed a hole in his chest. The Professor had seen him plow into Yvonne as her pistol went off, the reports muffled by the noise of the rotors, but he didn't know, till now, that she'd hit him. And a lucky shot it had been—in the heart.

As he picked up the handgun, Zarogosa shouted "¡Capitán! Over here."

The comandante was squatting over the other man, Castle. Yvonne had certainly gotten her licks in. He too had been shot, hit in the side, but he was still alive.

"We've got to get him out of here," Zaragoza said. "Yvonne?"

"Ella está muerta."

"Tanto mejor. She would only have run things from prison anyway."

The Professor bent down to have a look at the wounded man. Zaragoza had cut the plastic cuffs from his wrists and turned him onto his back. He was conscious, breathing in labored fashion. Lung shot. A good thing it was a .32 and not a nine; otherwise, he'd be dead, too. The bullet had entered below his right breast and exited through his ribs. The Professor jogged over to one of the 212s. Its radio was more powerful than the portable. He told the pilot which frequency to switch to, then keyed the transmitter and raised Nacho.

"Where are you now?"

"Nogales airport," Nacho radioed back. "What's the situation?"

Erskine's wife, supported by two cops, was still shrieking, loudly enough that The Professor had to plug an ear with a finger. "Erskine's dead, and so is Yvonne," he said. "We've got two live hostages, but one of them has been hit, Castle. Get a medical helicopter to the airport. We can fly him there in ten minutes."

"Something of a mess, Professor."

"Save that for later. Get a helicopter."

"Will do. How bad is Castle?"

"It's bad enough."

Castle did not know he'd been hurt until someone freed his hands and rolled him over and he grasped his side, feeling a warm, sticky dampness in his shirt. He'd pulled his hand away and saw it smeared with blood. *My God, I've been shot!* The words themselves struck him like a bullet. He had not heard a gun go off, nor had he felt any pain, only the impact. When Monica let out a nightmarish wail, he struggled to his hands and knees and caught sight of her, throwing herself at Blaine, prone on the ground, prone and motionless. Blaine, too? Blaine shot, too? No, no, no, he'd thought, and attempted to stand and go to Monica but fell backward, clutching his side again.

There was pain now, stabbing his ribs with each breath. He tried to gulp air but could manage only sips and wheezed when he exhaled. He closed his eyes. Someone shook him and said sternly, like a teacher reprimanding a pupil who'd nodded off in class, "Stay awake!" It was the Mexican cop, the fair-skinned one. Monica continued to wail, almost like a siren. "Blaine . . . ," Castle moaned. His lips stuck together. "Never mind that," the cop said in English. "He's going to be all right. Stay awake. Stay with us." Castle wanted to laugh, but it hurt too much. Where did the cop think he was going to go? He was beginning to feel drowsy and told himself, *Stay awake!* Then three men picked him up, one by his shoulders, two by the legs, and carried him into a helicopter. The light-skinned Mexican climbed in with him. The engine started, increased in pitch until he could hear nothing else. A sudden lurch, and the helicopter was airborne. Then he blacked out.

He woke up on a gurney, which was being rolled down a street or sidewalk. He heard the rattle of its wheels on pavement and saw faces above him, faces he did not recognize, and an IV drip bottle swaying from a stand above his head. Where was he? Facts. He was aware of a necessity to cling to every small, concrete fact he could. Stay awake! Some kind of device was wrapped around his chest. It squeezed and relaxed, gently squeezed and relaxed. A fact. A voice said, "Okay, lift." As he was raised off the gurney, he saw that he was on an airport runway. He was on a stretcher, and the stretcher was being placed inside another helicopter, smaller than the first. He noted that it was orange and white. More facts. EMTs slipped him into a snug Plexiglas pod, just big enough to accommodate him, and buckled safety belts, one over his waist, another over his ankles. Tubes and wires attached to his body snaked into the belly of the helicopter, where two EMTs, a woman and a man, sat behind the pilot's seat, their faces half lit by a soft infrared glow. The woman asked if he was in any pain, and he whispered, "Yes." There were mutterings about a dosage, something about his blood pressure and pulse rate, and then the female EMT rolled up his sleeve and gave him an injection.

The helicopter rose. Turning his head slightly, Castle observed city lights below and the headlights of a few cars, speeding down a highway. The aircraft made a tight turn, and they were soon racing over a vast darkness, with only scattered lights twinkling in it, like the lights of fishing boats on a midnight sea. He made out the silhouette of a mountain range, the Santa Ritas, he thought, but he wasn't sure. The morphine had taken effect, dulling the acute pain in his side. He actually felt euphoric. Turning his head again to look straight up through the

Plexiglas bubble, he beheld the most marvelous sight—the autumn stars, a million crystal rivets hammered into the sky. A big, square constellation sparkled directly overhead. Pegasus? Was it Pegasus? The woman said something to him. He couldn't make out what.

As the helicopter descended, he could see the glaze of lights that were Tucson in the distance, and he felt himself slipping back into unconsciousness. *Stay with us. Stay awake.* He pictured Tessa's long, strong body, the fall of her brown hair, the shy way she would raise her hand to her crooked teeth when she smiled. Once more she had summoned him back to life, with all its uncertainties, its dangers, its unforeseen calamities, its frustrated hopes and futile dreams, for all that *it was life.*

38

ROGER CLYNE and the Peacemakers played on The Professor's CD player: "Switchblade," a kind of American narco-corrido.

Pablo and Dan had a plan said
"We're gonna get rich,
Put the double-cross
on a double-crossin' narco-snitch . . .

A nasty beat, not like the epic but too-lyrical "Pancho and Lefty," but hard and low-down.

They said, "Amigo don'tcha worry
now we gonna disappear
Just for a couple of months," they said
Now it's been almost a year
Yeah if you want that kind of money,
Man you gotta stay brave
federales are pullin' bodies out of shallow graves.

Federales pullin' bodies out of shallow graves. He loved that line. Puttin' a few bodies in, too. He slapped and tapped the rhythm on the dashboard, the pitch of Clyne's gravelly voice all bright red spikes bouncing as The Professor's car bounced down the border road into Lochiel. La Noria had been its name before the Gadsden Purchase yanked it into the United States and some Scots cattleman had rechristened it after his ancestral town. It was a semi–ghost town now, the old border station, abandoned thirty years ago, decaying behind a chain-link fence, a few deserted houses, a whitewashed chapel atop a hill to serve the spiritual needs of its remaining inhabitants—a handful of vaqueros, desert hermits, border rats.

Later in the fall, I got a call, "Boy won'tcha come down,
Maybe put a name with a few unlucky faces we found."
Now no matter what I do, can't get my heart to mend
Somebody buried a switchblade in each of my friends.

Miguel Espinoza was one such unlucky face, found two days after the raid in an arroyo not far on the Mexican side. Billy had guided the police to his body, in the hopes his cooperativeness would win favor. It did not.

A dust devil conjured by a brisk winter wind pirouetted across the road, which turned northward through quivering cottonwoods. In a moment The Professor spotted Nacho's Jeep Cherokee and Nacho, huddled in a sheepskin jacket, sitting on a bench in front of the monument to Fray Marcos de Niza.

"Feliz Año Nuevo," he said, getting out of his car and blowing on his hands.

"New Year's was three weeks ago," Nacho replied. They hadn't seen each other since last November.

"Close enough," The Professor said. "What are you doing out here in the cold?"

"I was looking at that." He gestured at the commemorative plaque bolted into a slab marked by a tall concrete crucifix. The legend on the plaque briefly summarized the journey of Fray Marcos de Niza, who passed through this point in 1539—the first European to enter what would become, some 373 years later, the state of Arizona. "See, you've turned me into a student of history."

"Is that so? You could say that Fray Marcos was the first crosser."

"Except there wasn't a border in fifteen thirty-nine."

"And there won't be again one day."

"Please, no lectures about the reconquista and all that shit."

"I'll spare you. Ante todo, let's talk."

Pablo and Dan had a plan said, "We're gonna get rich, Put the double-cross on a double-crossin' narco-snitch . . ." The Professor could not get the lyrics out of his head. He sat down and snitched on an expendable load, four hundred pounds to cross Montezuma Pass day after tomorrow. Nacho snitched in his fashion, providing generalities about forthcoming Border Patrol operations but nothing too specific, nothing that would compromise his integrity. Scrap of information for scrap of information, their stock in trade, for it was in their mutual interest to maintain some sort of order, now that Yvonne and her disruptions were over. Organized crime was better than disorganized crime. They went from there to another matter of mutual interest—the gangs of bajadores who were preying on drug runners. Scavengers, hyenas.

In twenty minutes they were done, and The Professor brought his associate up to date on other matters. There was a possibility that he would testify at Cruz's forthcoming trial on federal kidnapping and conspiracy charges.

Nacho laughed. "That should get him off. I can't think of a more impeachable witness than you."

"Right. His lawyer will say he was tortured into making his confession, and to a foreign law-enforcement agency. But I'm not so sure there'll be a trial. Cruz might plead out. You see, there's Miguel's body. We can charge Cruz as an accessory to murder in Mexico. Where would you rather do time—a federal prison here or in one of ours?"

"Miguel. That poor son of a bitch. I was talking to Castle the other day. He's a bleeding heart. He's been sending Miguel's salary to his wife every week. Said it's the least he can do."

The Professor looked again at the narrative of Fray Marcos's adventures. "Miguel got caught in the crossfire of a family feud," he said.

"Yeah. Castle mentioned something like that to me. That his grandfather had shot La Roja's father way back when, and that's what she was paying them back for."

"There was more to it," said The Professor. "Castle and his lady friend took me and Zaragoza to dinner at La Roca after he got out of the hospital. They wanted to thank us."

"Don't imagine Erskine's wife was there," Nacho said sourly. "She hasn't got much to thank you for."

"She'd be dead, too, if we hadn't moved. And Erskine himself would be alive if he hadn't played hero of the hour."

"It was still a mess."

"Less of a mess than it would have been," said The Professor, piqued by Nacho's criticism.

"You were saying that there was more to it."

"There was some point in the evening when I was thinking out loud, wondering why Yvonne would go so far just to get her hands on a ranch. With her money, she could have bought ten ranches. That's when Castle told me about the grandfather. He said he was going to do some research into the old man's life. You know how I like that kind of thing, so I gave him a hand whenever I had some free time. Dug up quite a bit at the Arizona Historical Society, and it explained a lot of things."

"Like what?"

"Yvonne's father wasn't the only one the old man killed. He spilled a lot of blood, and some of it didn't need to be spilled, and maybe Castle and Erskine had to pay for it."

Nacho turned up his collar and shoved his hands into the sheepskin's pockets. "That sounds a little, you know, far-out."

"The past is never dead, Nacho. It's always with us. The sins of the father. Grandfather in this case. Not that I think what he did was sinning. But then, my standards are pretty low."

"Well, Erskine sure paid for them," Nacho said. "And his wife, too."

"Did you know Castle lost his wife in nine-eleven?"

Nacho nodded.

"It's the whole reason he came out here, he told me," The Professor went on. "You could say he was trying to escape history. Kind of fascinating when you think about it. His family history and the big history of what's happening here coming together."

"He couldn't escape it, that's what you're saying?"

"Exactamente."

A Note About the Author

Philip Caputo worked for nine years for the *Chicago Tribune* and shared a Pulitzer Prize in 1972 for his reporting on election fraud in Chicago. He is the author of seven other works of fiction, four works of nonfiction, and two memoirs, including *A Rumor of War*, about his service in Vietnam. He divides his time between Connecticut and Arizona.

A Note on the Type

The Ben Erskine segments were set in Bodoni, a typeface named after Giambattista Bodoni (1740–1813), the celebrated printer and type designer of Parma.

The balance of this book was set in Janson, a typeface long thought to have been made by the Dutchman Anton Janson, who was a practicing typefounder in Leipzig during the years 1668–1687. However, it has been conclusively demonstrated that these types are actually the work of Nicholas Kis (1650–1702), a Hungarian, who most probably learned his trade from the master Dutch typefounder Dirk Voskens.

Composed by Creative Graphics, Allentown, Pennsylvania
Printed and bound by Berryville Graphics, Berryville, Virginia
Designed by Virginia Tan